WILLA CATHER'S
COLLECTED SHORT FICTION
1892–1912

WILLA CATHER'S

Collected

UNIVERSITY OF NEBRASKA PRESS • LINCOLN AND LONDON

1892-1912

Short

Fiction

Volume I · THE BOHEMIAN GIRL
Volume II · THE TROLL GARDEN
Volume III · ON THE DIVIDE

Edited by
VIRGINIA FAULKNER

Introduction by
MILDRED R. BENNETT

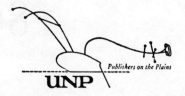

Publishers on the Plains

UNP

First printing: September 1965
First Revised Edition: November 1970

Most recent printing indicated by the first digit below:
  4   5   6   7   8   9   10

Manufactured in the United States of America

Dedicated to the memory of

ELSIE M. CATHER

January 13, 1890—May 24, 1964

Publisher's Preface

✣ ✣ ✣

"Success is never so interesting as struggle—not even to the successful," Willa Cather declared in the preface to the 1932 edition of *The Song of the Lark*; and in "Old Mrs. Harris," another work with strong auto-biographical overtones, she chose Michelet's aphorism, "The end is nothing; the road is all," as a motto for Vickie Templeton, the character who is her young self.

These dicta from her own writings might be invoked if one were called upon to defend the propriety of a publishing project which runs counter to the author's express wishes. For Willa Cather's attitude toward the stories that preceded her 1913 novel, *O Pioneers!*, is well known: she had put them behind her and she hoped that they would be forgotten—not merely her undergraduate efforts and the potboilers of her newspaper days, but even the stories written when, as managing editor of *McClure's* and the author of two books, she already was something of a mogul in the literary world. E. K. Brown, in *Willa Cather: A Critical Biography*, tells us that Miss Cather "disliked to be reminded of [these] stories ...; she was glad that she had the copyright and could prevent the republication of any among them. She compared her attitude to that of an apple-grower careful of his reputation: the fruit that was below standard must be left forgotten on the ground; only the sound apples should be collected." Of the forty-five stories collected here, only three—and those in revised form—were found worthy of inclusion in the "Library Edition," which represents Willa Cather's final judgment on her work. Thus, by Miss Cather's absolute standards there are no "sound apples" in this book.

While we know of no critic who agrees with Miss Cather's wholesale condemnation of her early writings, certainly none would dispute her right to supervise the body of her work during her lifetime, her right to suppress those stories which she considered substandard and whose publication not only would be personally embarrassing but would strike her as dishonest merchandising—trading on her reputation to vend an inferior product. Further, none would dispute her right—in fact, her obligation—to indicate which of her writings are those by which she wished to be measured. Such value judgments are of the first importance in studying an author's work.

Willa Cather's judgment has been recorded, and it will not be overlooked or slighted. But it can hardly be fully understood without reference to those productions which she considered inferior. The study of an author—any author—cannot be limited to the work of his artistic maturity or to such works as he or any other individual shall prescribe. If we are to arrive at a just estimate of Willa Cather's achievement, we must know the beginning as well as the middle and the end of the road she traveled.

Since her death in 1947, the passing years have served only to burnish Willa Cather's reputation; viewed in the lengthening perspective of time her artistic stature has consistently increased. We are convinced that this collection of the stories written from 1892 through 1912, crude and flawed though some of them undeniably are, far from detracting from Miss Cather's later work, will add another dimension to our appreciation of it. As Bernice Slote has pointed out in her discussion of the relationship between Willa Cather's poetry and the whole of her writing: "Perhaps more than most artists she worked a single, intricate design in which elements changed names and language and form but always remained a part of the body. Nothing in Cather's work is unrelated to the whole. In the poems (as in the first stories, some of which she also rejected), we find the early sketches, the first motifs, the suggested design of her major work."* The present volume confirms this insight into the organic character of the Cather canon: Here are the first glimpses of a whole galaxy of Cather heroines—Alexandra Bergson and Marie Shabata, "My Ántonia" and Lena Lingard, Cressida Garnett, Thea Kronborg, Lucy Gayheart; here the first expression of characteristic themes and attitudes, the first outlines of landscapes, incidents, and episodes which will reappear again and again in the later writings.

If it is true that not more than ten or twelve of the stories collected here will finally be classed as "sound apples," even by critics less emotionally involved than their author, nonetheless throughout this volume the world evoked is the magical Catherian world of the pioneer and the artist, and the voice that speaks in it is the authentic voice of Willa Cather,

* Willa Cather, *April Twilights* (1903), edited with an introduction by Bernice Slote (rev. ed.; Lincoln: University of Nebraska Press, 1968), p. ix.

inimitable even in the morning of her genius. Moreover, the stories are rich in the special virtues of youth, and in them we find a full-bloodedness, an abounding vitality and *joie de vivre*, that is not present in the later, more perfect narratives. Viewed collectively, the stories afford a graphic picture of the process by which an ardent, headstrong, immensely gifted young creature, eager, ambitious, profligate of her energy and talents, constitutionally unable to do things by halves, ready to tackle anything and take on the world in the bargain, is transformed into the dedicated artist whose work, more than that of any other modern master, is touched with the serene radiance we associate with the poets of classical antiquity. We have long known the dedicated artist; here we come to know the aspiring young woman.

We are profoundly grateful to Willa Cather's literary trustees, Miss Edith Lewis and Mr. Alfred A. Knopf, for sanctioning the publication of this volume.

❈   ❈   ❈

The revised edition of WILLA CATHER'S COLLECTED SHORT FICTION, 1892–1912, includes a recently proved, unsigned story dating from 1893, "The Elopement of Allen Poole." It is a story of particular interest and importance both because it is the first known published work in which Miss Cather drew on her childhood memories of Virginia and because of its connections with her last published novel, *Sapphira and the Slave Girl* (1940). The Chronology, the Bibliography of Short Fiction, 1892–1912, the Checklist of Short Fiction, 1915–1948, and the Bibliography of Selected Biographical and Critical Writings have been corrected and expanded in the light of recent research. We also have corrected factual and formal errors in the notes and Introduction and emended misprints in the text.

The Arrangement of the Text

✻ ✻ ✻

The stories in this collection, with the exceptions noted below, are presented in reverse chronology according to date of first publication. Thus, the first story in the book is the most recent—" The Bohemian Girl," which appeared in August, 1912—and the last is "Peter," first published in May, 1892. This plan has been adopted in an attempt to reconcile the claims of the general reader, interested in the stories for their own sake, and the scholar who may wish, for example, to study the development of Willa Cather's style. For the scholar's purposes a chronological arrangement is the most convenient; however, to begin the book with the earliest work would mean that the reader is immediately confronted with the stories of least intrinsic merit. If, on the other hand, we follow a reverse chronology, the book opens with rich, accomplished stories, enjoyable in their own right, and closes with the apprentice work, which gains appreciably in interest when approached with an eye for its connections with the later stories.

The three volumes of the collection correspond to different phases of the author's professional career. The Volume I stories belong to the years (1906–1912) Willa Cather was on the editorial staff of McClure's, in New York; those in Volume II to the 1901–1906 period when she was a Pittsburgh high school teacher. Her years as a journalist in the east (1896–1901) and, before that, in Nebraska are covered by the two groups of stories in Volume III. Reverse chronology is strictly maintained in Volumes I and III, but not in Volume II, which is comprised of the seven stories collected by the author in The Troll Garden. Since a chronological arrangement would have destroyed the interweaving pattern Willa Cather intended, these stories are presented here in the same sequence as in her 1905 collection.

A note at the end of each story gives the place and date of first publication; additional bibliographical data and biographical information appear opposite the first text page of each volume and on page 481, between the two groups of stories in Volume III.

Contents

✤ ✤ ✤

Introduction

Mildred R. Bennett

❋ ❋ ❋

In speaking of her early fiction Willa Cather more than once made the point that like other young writers she had thought books and stories should be made out of "interesting material" and like them had found the new more exciting than the familiar. She believed that "usually the young writer must have his affair with the external material he covets; must imitate and strive to follow the masters he most admires, until he finds he is starving for reality . . ."; only then would he begin to work with his own material, write from his deepest experience.[1]

True enough, a number of the stories in this collection (and also Willa Cather's first novel, *Alexander's Bridge*, written in 1911) are the sort of "literary excursions" to which she was referring, but in her own case she began with her own material—her first published story, "Peter," reappears as an episode in *My Ántonia*—and returned to it at intervals during the twenty years that passed before she came back to it for good. Moreover, myriad connections, sometimes overt and obvious, sometimes subtle and shadowy, interweave between the 1892–1912 stories and the body of writing that follows them. Like the later works, these early stories often incorporate directly or indirectly Willa Cather's day-to-day experiences and her memories of the past, her current enthusiasms and aversions and notions about things, and they illuminate best if seen in a biographical context as well as in relation to the entire Cather canon. It may be useful, therefore, to begin with a brief scrutiny of Willa Cather's life from her birth up through her thirty-ninth year—when, with the writing of *O Pioneers!*, the time came that she could say: "In this one I hit the home pasture . . . ."[2]

1. "My First Novels [There Were Two]," in *Willa Cather on Writing* (New York: Alfred A. Knopf, 1949), pp. 91–97; Preface to the 1922 edition of *Alexander's Bridge* (Boston: Houghton Mifflin Co., 1922), pp. v–ix.
2. Inscribed by Willa Cather in the copy of *O Pioneers!* belonging to her friend Carrie Miner Sherwood.

I

Born in Virginia on December 7, 1873, Willa Cather lived her first nine years in a post-Civil War community where her grandfather was sheriff, her father his reluctant deputy, and her mother a loyal Confederate. From this region rich in tradition and lush with moisture, Willa was brought to the empty prairie of Webster County, in south-central Nebraska, where only the dry, wind-swept land could claim a past. But history was being made there before her eyes, and the traditions of a world older than the Old Dominion lived on in the "colonies of European people, Slavonic, Germanic, Scandinavian, Latin spread across our bronze prairies like the daubs of color on a painter's palette."[3]

After a year on the Divide—the tableland between the Little Blue and Republican rivers—the family moved to the county seat, Red Cloud, a division point on the Burlington Railroad. On Willa's visits to the immigrant settlers in their soddies and dugouts, they had told her of their home countries; now in Red Cloud she heard tales of that breed of men who had dreamed a railroad across half a continent. She came to know founding fathers such as former Governor Silas Garber, Red Cloud's first citizen in a double sense; misfits and drifters like her music teacher, Professor Schindelmeisser, who came from nowhere and disappeared into nowhere; artists like Peoriana Sill, who once had painted the Bay of Naples from the boudoir window of the Queen of Italy.

Some Cather critics and biographers have insisted upon the cultural impoverishment of life in what they invariably describe as a raw (or crude) little frontier town, but Willa Cather's reiterated emphasis on the crucial importance to the artist of his first fifteen years does not refer only to the impression made upon her by "the wild land" and the Bohemian and Scandinavian settlers. The Cathers were cultivated people: the nineteenth-century English and American classics, the Bible, and Shakespeare, were staples in the family reading, and Willa was not yet in her teens when she began studying Latin and Greek with William Ducker, a retired British scholar with a passion for the classics. Next door to the Cathers lived the Charles Wieners, of cosmopolitan background, who spoke French and German and introduced Willa to French literature. Through another neighbor, Mrs. James Miner, an accomplished pianist, she became acquainted with operatic themes and arias; touring theatrical companies opened the door into still another world. Her tastes bore the

3. Willa Cather, "Nebraska: The End of the First Cycle," *The Nation*, CXVII (September 5, 1923), 236.

indelible imprint of these early cultural experiences, and in 1890, when she left the "clean, well-planted little prairie town, with white fences and good green yards"[4] for Lincoln and the University of Nebraska preparatory school, Willa was by no means the untutored roughneck run in off the prairie that she later implied she had been.

During her university years (one year in prep, four in the university), as James R. Shively has recorded, Willa lived in an atmosphere of "intense intellectual competition and stimulation." The student body, which numbered less than a thousand when she matriculated in the fall of 1891,

> included many who were later to achieve distinction—four as state governors, one as a United States Senator, two as members of Congress, and two as chancellors of state universities. Classmates of Miss Cather who would later distinguish themselves in scholarship included William L. Westermann, an authority on Greek and Egyptian history; Hartley B. Alexander, poet, philosopher, and literary scholar; and Louise Pound, famous for her research in folklore, balladry, linguistics, and literary history.[5]

To this list should be added the names of Louise Pound's brother, Roscoe, future Dean of the Harvard Law School, then studying for his Ph.D. in botany; Alvin S. Johnson, editor of the *New Republic* and one of the founders of the New School for Social Research; and Harvey E. Newbranch, editor of the *Omaha Evening World-Herald*, who received the Pulitzer Prize for editorial writing in 1920.

Thrust into this new milieu the seventeen-year-old Willa not only felt quite at ease, but unhesitatingly went her unconventional way in everything from her style of dress (severely tailored) and hair-do (an early version of the Eton crop) to her opinions on how Shakespeare should be taught. (Recalling her days as a "shave-headed prep," Willa admitted to her friend Mariel Gere that her self-confidence must have

---

4. Willa Cather, *My Ántonia* (Sentry Edition; Boston: Houghton Mifflin, 1961), p. 145.

5. James R. Shively, *Willa Cather's Campus Years* (Lincoln: University of Nebraska Press, 1950), pp. 19–20. Among faculty notables were the chancellor, James H. Canfield, subsequently president of Ohio State University and Librarian of Columbia University; Charles E. Bessey, famed botanist and one-time president of the American Association for the Advancement of Science; August Hjalmar Edgren, philologist and member of the first Nobel Prize Committee; and General John J. Pershing, then a lieutenant, the commandant of the cadet corps, and instructor in mathematics.

been odious.[6]) In her sophomore year she let her hair grow to play Lady Macbeth in a student production and her style of dress became more conventional, but she remained as opinionated and argumentative as ever.

Mariel's father, Charles H. Gere, founder and publisher of the leading Lincoln newspaper, the *Nebraska State Journal*, published on March 1, 1891, an essay by Willa on Thomas Carlyle; written for her English class, it had been sent to the paper by her instructor. In retrospect, according to E. K. Brown, its publication "seemed to Willa Cather to have been a decisive event. She had come to Lincoln intending to take a chiefly scientific course, and later to specialize in medicine. The sight of her work in print . . . had an effect upon her which she could only describe as 'hypnotic.' Henceforth it was clear that her aim must be to write."[7] She began to contribute stories, poems, and miscellaneous pieces to the student literary magazine, the *Hesperian*, and served on its staff in her sophomore and junior years.

If the sight of her work in print determined her to become an author, events of 1893—national, local, and personal—compelled her to begin writing for money. Eighteen ninety-three was a panic year: banks failed throughout the United States and depression settled over the land; locally, no rain fell, crops withered, and taxes went unpaid. In Willa's immediate circle, death took her maternal grandmother, Rachel Boak, her mentor, William Ducker, and her neighbor, Mrs. Wiener. Furthermore, Willa's father, Charles F. Cather, was among the many suffering financial damage. The Cathers owned tracts of land, but the parched fields brought in no tax money. Willa had six younger brothers and sisters, and though Roscoe, the eldest son, taught school to help out, Mr. Cather found it difficult to pay his bills. Confronted with these depressing realities, Willa accepted with enthusiasm an invitation to become a regular contributor to the *State Journal*.[8] She began writing a

6. Willa Cather to Mariel Gere, May 2, 1896. The letters cited in this introduction, including those to Mr. and Mrs. Charles H. Gere, to Frances Gere, and to Will Owen Jones, editor of the *State Journal*, are in the Nebraska State Historical Society Collections. Because of restrictions in Willa Cather's will, her letters may not be quoted.

7. E. K. Brown, *Willa Cather: A Critical Biography* (New York: Alfred A. Knopf, 1953), pp. 51–52.

8. Later statements made by Willa Cather are responsible for the erroneous impression that while attending university she had to work to keep from starving. Unquestionably she found plenty of uses for the extra money she earned—including loaning it to her actress friends—but her father provided the necessary funds for her education, even though he went into debt to do so. See Mildred R. Bennett, *The World of Willa Cather* (Lincoln: University of Nebraska Press, 1961), p. 233, and pp. 216 and 257.

Sunday column and play reviews in the fall of 1893; from that time on, while she continued to attend classes and participate in university activities, the focus of her interest gradually shifted from the campus to the downtown scene, with special emphasis on local theatrical offerings. Those were the great days of the Road, and most of the reigning stage stars and actor-managers brought their companies to Lincoln—where, like as not, they would be cut down to size by the razor-sharp and uninhibited comments of the *Journal*'s young lady drama critic. In her Sunday columns, along with her own observations Willa relayed theatrical gossip gleaned from out-of-town papers; she also kept her readers informed of doings in the musical world—including the latest eccentricities and caprices of operatic prima donnas.

An impressive, even startling, feature of Willa Cather's journalistic writings is their quantity.[9] As an undergraduate she managed to turn out an astonishing number of Sunday columns, reviews, and articles; and during her five most active years as a newspaperwoman she must have averaged well over a quarter of a million words annually. In comparison with the economy of the later, canonical writings—such distillations as *A Lost Lady*, *My Mortal Enemy*, and *Sapphira*—this torrent of words points up a major difference between Willa Cather in the first decade of her career and Willa Cather in the years of her artistic maturity.

In at least one other respect the young Willa Cather seems to be almost the diametric opposite of the formidable, reclusive artist whom the world knew (or rather, was not permitted to know) during the last quarter century of her life. Far from being withdrawn and stand-offish, the young Willa was outgoing and gregarious: she wanted to be in the thick of things, to see for herself and have her say. Back in Red Cloud after her graduation she bewailed her "bitter exile," referred to the town as "Siberia," and urgently appealed to Lincoln friends to help her secure a teaching post at the university.[10] Even though one of her stories, "On the Divide," had just appeared in the *Overland Monthly*, and she harbored a painful conviction that her friends expected great things of her as a writer, her first concern was not writing but escape from stagnation into life: the world of music, drama, art. In seeking a job away from home she had the excuse of economic necessity—the financial burden on her father had

---

9. Two collections—*The Kingdom of Art* and *The World and the Parish*—have been published by the University of Nebraska Press. See Selected Bibliography.

10. Willa Cather to Mariel Gere, January 2, March 12, 1896; Willa Cather to Charles H. Gere, March 14, 1896.

not lessened—but if writing had really assumed the most important place in her life, she could have stayed in Red Cloud, with pen and paper, time, and a roof over her head.

Willa did not receive the teaching appointment, but through the instrumentality of Charles Gere, late in June, 1896, she went east to assume the managing editorship of a newly reorganized Pittsburgh magazine, the *Home Monthly*. Overjoyed at her deliverance, she described to Mariel Gere how intoxicating it was, after the train got east of Chicago, to see hills and streams and woods; in fact, her high spirits were so apparent that the conductor had asked if she was getting home. And, wrote Willa, this was just how she felt.[11] She did not then suspect that she had been forever branded by the prairie, and that her life was to be a tug of war between East and West.

❖   ❖   ❖

In exuberant letters to Mariel and Mrs. Gere, Willa told of her first crowded days on the *Home Monthly*. Since it was an infant magazine, contributors were scarce and Willa herself wrote half the first issue under a variety of pseudonyms. In addition to doing all the manuscript reading, proofing, planning of future issues, and corresponding with authors, she had to help her inexperienced foreman in the composing room. But everyone cooperated, and she had a stenographer who knew how to spell (Willa's own spelling was distinctly substandard, though not without a certain addled charm). The magazine featured articles on care of the teeth and gardening, fashions, and homey advice: trash in Willa's view, but apparently trash that people wanted to read. In any case she was determined to stick at her job and prove herself to the people back in Nebraska; her serious writing would have to keep until she had time for it.[12] By December, she had organized her work to the point that she could start sending a weekly column, "The Passing Show," back to the *State Journal*.

We owe a delightful portrait of Willa at this period to George Seibel, one of the earliest of her Pittsburgh friends, then a freelance newspaperman, later director of the Carnegie Free Library at Allegheny, Pennsylvania. In a 1949 article he told of his first meeting with the editor of the *Home Monthly*—she "looked about eighteen; she was plump and

11. Willa Cather to Mariel Gere, n.d. Headed: "Pittsburgh, Friday."
12. Willa Cather to Mrs. Charles H. Gere, July 13, 1896; Willa Cather to Mariel Gere, August 4, 1896.

dimpled, with dreamy eyes and an eager mind." Through this encounter "was established an understanding by which Willa Cather came to the Seibel home once or twice a week to read French. Our reading covered a vast territory."[13] In an earlier article he had gone into detail:

> We started in on Alphonse Daudet's "Femme d' Artistes"; we finished with Edmond Rostand's "Cyrano de Bergerac." . . . It was the wildest rodeo of French literature ever put on between Paris, France, and Paris, Texas. We ranged from De Musset and Verlaine, with their tears and absinthe, to Victor Hugo and Theophile Gautier, in purple waistcoats and alexandrian armor . . . but our most arduous adventure was the siege of Carthage in Flaubert's "Salammbo."
>
> Flaubert was our chief delight, and Willa's impeccable style was achieved by a sedulous study of this merciless master. . . . All these prodigies were achieved upon a simple home dietary of noodle soup and potato salad, with copious draughts of Balzacian coffee. But on Christmas Eves she would munch the needles of spruce or fir, which she accounted an epicurean delicacy. Sometimes she would voice regret that she was not a boa constrictor, who could feed full of Christmas evergreens and then curl up luxuriously under the tree to purr in rivalry with our cat. . . . To one of these Christmas Eves, Willa brought a young friend, wide eyed and sweet voiced. Her name was Dorothy Canfield, and she too has achieved an honored place in American Literature as Dorothy Canfield Fisher.[14]

In a letter to Seibel which appeared with his recollections, Mrs. Fisher said that of course she remembered perfectly well "that Christmas Eve when Willa Cather and I went to help trim your Christmas tree. . . ." The girls had known each other in Lincoln when Dorothy's father, James H. Canfield, had been chancellor of the university; in 1895 (the year Willa graduated) he had accepted the presidency of Ohio State University and the Canfields had moved to Columbus. In 1896 Dorothy spent Christmas in Pittsburgh with Willa.

By that time, Mrs. Fisher wrote in a subsequent article,

> [Willa] had more prestige than ever for me, because she was earning her own living, was getting (as I remember it) the munificent salary of a hundred dollars a month (this really was munificent in the 1890's),

13. George Seibel, "Miss Willa Cather from Nebraska," *New Colophon*, II, Pt. 7 (1949), 195–208.
14. George Seibel, "The Quiet Observer," *Musical Forecast*, June, 1947, pp. 5, 11.

was living on her own, in a boarding house, free to do whatever she wanted, out of her office hours.

This kind of success and independence for a young woman was not in the least taken for granted in the '90's. . . . It cast a glamor over Willa which enhanced the admiration we had felt for her during the college years, because of her gift for writing. I was immensely grateful for Willa's invitation to me . . . .[15]

In the same article Mrs. Fisher spoke of that evening as "a deep draught of the most concentrated essence of Christmas I've ever had." She recalled that there was "wonderful, cosmopolitan talk. . . . Willa had studied both French and German in her college classes, and of course there had been professors at the University who spoke these languages. But this was the first household where she had come and gone familiarly where cultivated Germans used their mother tongue freely, as naturally as English. With her passionate appreciation of every opportunity for enlarging the horizon of her culture, she drank in admiringly the atmosphere of this pleasant, friendly home . . . ."

In June, 1897, Willa visited the Canfields in Columbus en route to Nebraska. In July she wrote the Seibels from Red Cloud that the *Home Monthly* had been sold and that she had severed connections with it but would return to Pittsburgh before September. She was planning to go into regular newspaper work, and asked Mr. Seibel's advice.[16] In the interim she settled down to write. Her work was going well when a wire came offering her a job on the *Pittsburgh Daily Leader* at $75.00 a month. Willa made immediate arrangements to leave, although with some regret, for she had been writing better stories. Probably she went out too much in Pittsburgh for the good of her work—but then, after all, one couldn't be a hermit. She would have next summer and many other summers for her writing, and in Pittsburgh there would be Calvé and Bernhardt and all the rest of her idols.[17]

Hardly a week after her return to Pittsburgh, however, Willa wrote Mariel Gere a long, homesick letter. Everyone seemed glad to see her— five men had met her at the train—but already she was tired of the gay

15. The late Dorothy Canfield Fisher kindly permitted the author to make use of the original manuscript of the article, published in part as a feature story, "Novelist Recalls Christmas in Blue-and-Gold Pittsburgh," *Chicago Tribune Magazine of Books*, December 21, 1947.

16. Willa Cather to George Seibel, July 23, 1897.

17. Willa Cather to Will Owen Jones, n.d. Headed: "Red Cloud, Tuesday."

Bohemian life. A west wind was blowing and it made her ache to be home; she missed her brothers Roscoe and Douglas, she longed for the baby of the family, Jack. Whatever made her suppose she would be happy so far away from Nebraska? One shouldn't be an exile. (At this point, apparently, Pittsburgh, not Red Cloud, was "Siberia.") In her new job on the day telegraph desk she edited and wrote headlines for all the telegraph news that came in from eight A.M. to three P.M.; the rest of the day and all her evenings were free except Saturday when she worked until midnight. She was continuing to do drama criticism, for which she would be paid extra.[18] All in all, these duties would seem enough to keep anyone occupied, but Willa found time to write "The Passing Show," which she now sent to the Lincoln *Courier*, a weekly paper edited by her friend Sarah B. Harris, and to conduct a book column (under the pseudonym "Helen Delay") for the *Home Monthly*.

This rigorous and demanding life, whose compensations were chiefly music and the theater and the opportunities to meet celebrities of the day, continued until Willa's resignation from the *Leader* in the spring of 1900. In 1898 the routine grind was alleviated by a vacation in Red Cloud and a hunting trip in the Black Hills and Wyoming with her brothers. Earlier in the year there had been a week in New York (memorable for a lunch with one of Willa's favorite actresses, Mme Modjeska) and a fortnight in Washington, D.C. Here she visited her father's cousin, Howard Gore, a professor of geodesy at Columbian University, who was about to leave on the Wellman Polar Expedition. Dr. Gore's friends offered a change from the composers, singers, writers, and stage people whom Willa had been meeting in Pittsburgh; a letter to Frances Gere mentions such dinner companions as the Turkish chargé d'affaires, the Norwegian ambassador, and the secretary of the German legation, to say nothing of one Herr Otto Schenfeldt who, Willa confided, was so pro-Spanish that the government screened his mail (the United States had declared war on Spain just the week before). Most of her letter, however, was devoted to rhapsodic praise of her cousin's wife, Lillian Thekla Brandthall, daughter of a former Norwegian ambassador and kin of King Oscar II of Sweden; this glamorous creature could sing Grieg's songs and read Ibsen like no one else—exactly Willa's idea of "l'étoile du Nord."[19]

Nineteen hundred opened on an auspicious note with the appearance

18. Willa Cather to Mariel Gere, n.d. [September 19, 1897].
19. Willa Cather to Frances Gere, June 23, 1898.

in the January *Cosmopolitan* of her story, "Eric Hermannson's Soul."
Perhaps its acceptance contributed to her decision to leave the *Leader*;
also, and more important, a new Pittsburgh magazine, *The Library*,
opened its pages to her for the twenty-six numbers that it lasted. During
the summer she visited her cousins in Washington, and secured a part-
time job there editing translations. In November the *Ladies' Home
Journal* published her article about the composer Ethelbert Nevin. Of the
celebrities she had met in Pittsburgh, Nevin was perhaps the one Willa
knew the best: she had praised him in the highest terms in letters to the
Geres, saying she was prouder of his friendship than of anything that had
happened to her.[20] In December she began contributing a Washington
column to Pittsburgh and Lincoln papers. But supporting herself as a
freelance was a precarious business at best, and in March, 1901, when the
opportunity presented itself she was glad to accept a teaching post in
Pittsburgh's Central High School.

Earlier—probably on a visit to Pittsburgh at Christmas—she had
talked with George Seibel about obtaining a teaching position. She felt
that her journalistic writing was leading nowhere; she needed time for her
serious work, and teachers had their summer months free. Thanks to
loyal friends, the job had been secured, but Willa did not find teaching
easy. During the spring term she taught Latin, and by the end of the
semester had lost twenty pounds.[21] Subsequently, to her relief, she was
transferred to the English department, and in 1903 went on to a better
paying position in the American Literature department at Allegheny
High School.

By then, however, her circumstances had been radically altered for
the better. Sometime during 1899 she met Isabelle McClung, the daughter
of a prominent Pittsburgh judge, and as a result of their meeting Willa's
days of batching it in a boarding house were over. Large of mind and
heart, Isabelle "became for Willa Cather what every writer needs most,
the helping friend."[22] Willa was invited to make her home with the
McClung family, and from this time on until she left Pittsburgh in 1906
lived in the McClung mansion on Murray Hill Avenue.

20. Willa Cather to Mariel Gere, January 10, 1898; Willa Cather to Mariel Gere,
n.d. The opening and closing pages are missing, but it is apparent from the text that the
letter was written in late November or early December, 1898.

21. Willa Cather to George and Helen Seibel, July 17, 1901.

22. Elizabeth Moorhead, *These Too Were Here: Louise Homer and Willa Cather*
(Pittsburgh: University of Pittsburgh Press, 1950), p. 50.

Living in the McClung house with its solidity and comfort, its well-trained servants and ordered routine, made a great change in Willa Cather's life. . . . Although she still had to get up at six in the morning and take a long, and, in winter, a very cold streetcar ride to and from her work; and although she taught, as she did anything she undertook, with a great expenditure of vital energy, she enjoyed a tranquillity and physical comfort in the McClung house she had probably never before experienced. Isabelle McClung fitted up a sewing-room at the top of the house as a study for her, and she wrote here on week-ends and holidays, and during school vacations; . . .[23]

Except for a few scattered articles and a series of travel letters written on her first trip abroad in 1902, Willa now devoted herself wholly to poetry and fiction. Her first book, a volume of verse titled *April Twilights*, appeared in 1903, and a collection of short stories, *The Troll Garden*, in 1905. Her work had attracted the attention of that dynamic publishing genius, S. S. McClure, and after meetings with him in Pittsburgh and New York, Willa was offered an associate editorship on the staff of *McClure's Magazine*. She had grave reservations;[24] McClure was known to be a man difficult to work for—in fact, virtually the entire staff resigned in a body in March, 1906—but in the end Willa accepted his offer. In June she moved to New York and took an apartment on Washington Square.

❋   ❋   ❋

Despite her misgivings, Willa Cather and McClure understood each other from the start, and throughout her years on the magazine remained in perfect accord. Her first major assignment—to reorganize, verify, and rewrite a series of articles on the founder of Christian Science, Mary Baker Eddy—kept Willa in Boston for most of 1907 and part of 1908. Early in the latter year she met Sarah Orne Jewett, whose friendship and counsel meant so much to her; indeed, Miss Jewett's letter of advice, written in December, 1908, was, in E. K. Brown's judgment "the most

23. Edith Lewis, *Willa Cather Living: A Personal Record* (New York: Alfred A. Knopf, 1953), pp. 53–54.
24. Willa Cather's friend and biographer, the late Elizabeth Shepley Sergeant wrote that the move to New York "was a hard decision to make (she used to tell me) because of Willa's now established Pittsburgh roots and affections and, above all, because of her love of teaching the young" (*Willa Cather: A Memoir* [Lincoln: University of Nebraska Press, 1963], p. 28).

important letter, beyond a question, that Willa Cather ever received."[25]
The letter warned Willa that it was impossible for her to work so hard
and yet have her gifts mature as they should; "... if you don't keep and
guard and mature your force, and above all, have time and quiet to
perfect your work, you will be writing things not much better than you
did five years ago. ... Your vivid, exciting companionship in the office
must not be your audience, you must find your own quiet centre of life,
and write from that to the world that holds offices, and all society, all
Bohemia; the city, the country—in short, you must write to the human
heart. ..." By anyone's standards Willa was a success on *McClure's*—
she had been promoted to the managing editorship in April, 1908—
but the stories she was writing dissatisfied her and she realized that she
could never find her own "quiet centre of life" in the supercharged
atmosphere of the magazine office.

Still she could not yet afford to give up her job, and exhausting
though it was, Willa Cather's editorial tenure on *McClure's* proved in
many ways an enriching experience. Edith Lewis, who was on the staff
at this time, has written that "Mr. McClure's confidence in Willa Cather,
and his belief in her talent, her growing success both as a writer and an
editor, and the greater freedom and breadth and colour of her life after
she left Pittsburgh had, I think, given her a sense of sureness, a happiness
of expectation she had not felt before."[26] On trips to England in 1909 and
1911, prospecting for manuscripts and authors, she had the entrée to the
London literary circle and met H. G. Wells, Yeats, Lady Gregory, and
many others. She made numerous trips, too, to visit her friends in
Pittsburgh and Boston, and summertime visits to her family in Red Cloud.

Somehow or other, in the intervals of work and travel, she managed
to complete a novel, *Alexander's Bridge*, derived in part from some of her
London encounters. It was accepted for publication by Houghton
Mifflin, and, having arranged for it to run as a serial in *McClure's*, Willa
took a long leave of absence. With Isabelle McClung as her companion,
she rented a house in Cherry Valley, New York; in this "quiet centre,"
toward the end of 1911 she wrote a long short story, "The Bohemian
Girl," which appeared in *McClure's* in August, 1912. By then she was no
longer on the magazine staff.

25. Brown, *Willa Cather*, p. 140.   The letter, dated December 13, 1908, will be found
in *Letters of Sarah Orne Jewett*, ed. Annie Fields (Boston: Houghton Mifflin, 1911), pp. 247–
250.
26. Lewis, *Willa Cather Living*, p. 69.

It is uncertain at exactly what date Willa Cather left *McClure's*. According to E. K. Brown, she resigned prior to a trip in the spring of 1912 to visit her brother Douglas in Winslow, Arizona; but this is contradicted by a letter to Mariel Gere, written from Winslow, which mentions that Mr. McClure had let her come west after an illness in February and that she is planning to stay as long as he can spare her.[27] At any rate, we have Willa Cather's word for it that during her months in the Southwest—"a country I really did care about, and among people who were part of the country"—books like *Alexander's Bridge* which followed a conventional pattern came to seem to her unnecessary and superficial; "I did no writing down there, but I recovered from the conventional editorial point of view."[28] She determined that the next book she wrote would be entirely for herself, and on her return to the east set to work on *O Pioneers!*.

At last she had found the road she was destined to travel. From that time on, prepared and disciplined by twenty years of trial and discovery, Willa Cather moved steadily forward on her great journey.

II

Anything approaching a full-dress critical appraisal of the forty-four stories in the present collection cannot be attempted in this introduction. In the discussion which follows the aim is less to evaluate the stories than to stimulate the reader's interest in them: to suggest, by noting a few typical examples, the manifold connections between the 1892–1912 stories and the later writings; to point out some instances of the genesis and development of characters, incidents, settings, and thematic elements; and to draw attention to one or two of the fascinating Catherian "recurrences"—the repeated use of certain objects, images, or attributes in a variety of contexts. Pervasive relationships, transmutations, and reprises characterize Willa Cather's art from first to last, and the recognition of their presence adds an extra dimension both to the world her writing creates and to the reader's enjoyment of it.

❋   ❋   ❋

27. Brown, *Willa Cather*, p. 169. The letter from Willa Cather to Mariel Gere is dated April 24, 1912. Edith Lewis, in *Willa Cather Living*, pp. 79–80, writes: "Whether, on her return to New York [from Cherry Valley], she definitely resigned from *McClure's*, or whether she merely renewed her leave of absence, I do not remember; but she did not afterward go back to regular work on the magazine."

28. Willa Cather, "My First Novels [There Were Two]," (See note 1, above), pp. 91–92.

Although in her later years Willa Cather closed the door firmly on all but a fraction of the work that had preceded *O Pioneers!* and did her best to discourage inquiry concerning it, in interviews before she achieved world-wide fame as a novelist she made some illuminating statements concerning her literary beginnings. Her initial impulse to write, she told Latrobe Carroll in 1921, came from "an enthusiasm for a kind of country and a kind of people, rather than ambition." She spoke of the Divide and the immigrant families—Danes, Swedes, Norwegians, and Bohemians—of whom she had grown fond, "particularly the old women, who used to tell me of their home country. I used to think them underrated, and wanted to explain them to their neighbors. Their stories used to go round and round in my head at night." She had a good memory for mannerisms and turns of speech, she said, and

> the phraseology of those people stuck in my mind. If I had made notes, or should make them now, the material collected would be dead. No, it's memory—the memory that goes with the vocation. When I sit down to write, turns of phrase I've forgotten for years come back like white ink before fire. I think that most of the basic material a writer works with is acquired before he is fifteen. . . .
>
> Back in the files of the college magazine [The *Hesperian*], there were once several of my perfectly honest but very clumsy attempts to give the story of some of the Scandinavian and Bohemian settlers who lived not far from my father's farm. In those sketches, I simply tried to tell about the people without much regard for style. These early stories were bald, clumsy, and emotional. As I got toward my senior year, I began to admire, for the first time, writing for writing's sake. In those days, no one seemed so wonderful as Henry James; for me, he was the perfect writer.[29]

Willa Cather's remarks about the sketches of settlers clearly refer to four of the eight signed stories which appeared before she left Nebraska in June, 1896: "Peter," "Lou, the Prophet," "The Clemency of the Court," and "On the Divide." Dealing respectively with a Bohemian, a Dane, a Russian, and a Norwegian, each story is concerned with some aspect of the immigrant's attempt to adjust to life in a new and harsh environment—the master theme of so many of the later canonical writings.

29. Latrobe Carroll, "Willa Sibert Cather," *The Bookman*, LIII (May, 1921), 212–216.

Moreover, as has been noted, Cather's first story, "Peter," reappeared twenty-five years later as an episode (the suicide of Mr. Shimerda) in *My Ántonia*, and the title character in her second story, "Lou, the Prophet," anticipates Crazy Ivar in *O Pioneers!*. A mention of Lou occurs in "On the Divide," which has characters and place names in common with "Eric Hermannson's Soul," published in 1900, and with *My Ántonia*.[30] While the picture of plains life which emerges from this first group of Nebraska stories is one of almost unalleviated grimness, Cather's "enthusiasm for a kind of country" does gleam through in occasional descriptive passages, as when the dying Serge, in "The Clemency of the Court," thinks "how lovely the plains would look in the morning when the sun was up; how the sunflowers would shake themselves in the wind, how the corn leaves would shine and how the cobwebs would sparkle all over the grass and the air would be clear and blue...."[31]

Three of the other 1892–1896 stories—"A Son of the Celestial," "A Night at Greenway Court," and "A Tale of the White Pyramid"— take place in locales far removed from Nebraska, and the two latter are remote in time as well as in space. Yet in these stories too the central figures are aliens or immigrants—Yung the Chinese in San Francisco, the colonists in Virginia, the nameless hero-stranger in ancient Egypt. One might almost add that the fourth story, "'The Fear That Walks by Noonday,'" partakes of the immigrant theme, for it deals with the supernatural —and surely ghosts, avenging spirits, and their ilk must be thought of as coming from another land.

In the six-year span from July, 1896, to the fall of 1902, beyond a doubt a good many more stories came from Willa Cather's pen than the twenty which can be safely attributed to her. This period included her

30. In a letter of December 31, 1938, to Edward Wagenknecht, Willa Cather stated that "On the Divide" (1896) and "El Dorado: A Kansas Recessional" (1901) were retouched by one of her college professors and published without her consent. It is true that her first story, "Peter" (1892), published in her freshman year at university, was touched up by her English instructor, Herbert Bates, and submitted to *The Mahogany Tree* without her knowledge. But it is a little difficult to credit the Bates connection with "On the Divide," which appeared six months after Willa Cather's graduation from the university, and even more difficult with respect to "El Dorado," which came out when Willa Cather had been living in the east for more than six years and was an established journalist. In the same letter to Professor Wagenknecht, Willa Cather also disclaimed sole authorship of several other stories published in the 1900–1902 period (see note 47, below).

31. See page 521. Hereafter all page references given in the text refer to the present book.

most active years as a journalist when she was writing under a half-dozen pseudonyms—a practice which seems to have begun during her first hectic weeks as editor of the *Home Monthly* when she was pouring out fiction, nonfiction, and poetry in a desperate effort to fill the magazine's pages. Of five 1896 stories in the *Home Monthly* definitely identified as Cather's, two appeared under pseudonyms: a hastily concocted potboiler, "The Burglar's Christmas," and a children's story, "The Princess Baladina —Her Adventure," which has both charm and humor. Perhaps it already had been written, or at least existed as an oral narrative, before she came east; we know from her youngest sister, the late Elsie Cather, that another 1896 children's story, "The Strategy of the Were-Wolf Dog," was one of a series invented by Willa Cather and her brothers Roscoe and Douglas for the entertainment of the younger children.[32]

The other 1896 stories are "Tommy, the Unsentimental"—which E. K. Brown considered the equal of any work Willa Cather was to do until she wrote "The Sculptor's Funeral" nine years later[33]—and a two-part serial, "The Count of Crow's Nest." In "Tommy," whose setting, Southdown, is the first of many fictional projections of Red Cloud, the author betrays her loneliness for the great high wind of the prairie and her own kind of people; like Tommy, her heroine, she was a favorite with the town's elder statesmen (two of whom would sit for a memorable portrait in "Two Friends" [1932]), and she had frequently preferred their company to that of her contemporaries. Although "The Count of Crow's Nest" owes more to Anthony Hope (whose romance, *The Prisoner of Zenda*, Cather admired) than to her own experience, she could write of boarding-house life from firsthand knowledge, and a touch of autobiography appears in one character's reflections on his personal situation:

> Buchanan was just out of college, an honor man of whom great things were expected, and was waiting about Chicago to find a drive wheel to which to apply his undisputed genius. He found this waiting to see what one is good for one of the most trying tasks allotted to the sons of men. . . . He knew that he was gifted in more ways than one, but he knew equally well that he was painfully immature, and that between him and success of any kind lay an indefinable, intangible something which only time could dispose of. (p. 449)

32. Elsie M. Cather to Mildred R. Bennett, January 23, no year, probably 1956.
33. Brown, *Willa Cather*, p. 80.

In one episode of the story Cather draws on her knowledge of singers and the musical world, and one must admit that she writes with more assurance about a second-rate soprano than about an impoverished nobleman "with no duty but to keep an escutcheon that is only a name and a sword that the world no longer needs" (p. 457).

Although in 1897, after her resignation from the *Home Monthly*, Cather gave as a paramount reason for her return to Pittsburgh the presence there of opera stars and great actresses like Calvé and Bernhardt, the performing arts figure in only three of the fifteen stories belonging to the 1897–1902 years. But Cather's fiction, considered apart from her journalistic writing, is not a reliable index to her interests at this time: as reporter and critic, she was constantly writing about opera singers and actors and actresses and composers and authors. The reader will find her earliest fictional treatments of the prima donna temperament appearing in "Nanette: An Aside" (1897) and "A Singer's Romance," a 1900 reworking of "Nanette." In these stories Cather sets down some of her esthetic principles and expresses her conviction that artistic fulfillment is achieved at the expense of human relationships. Thea Kronborg, in *The Song of the Lark* (1915), was speaking for all of Cather's artist heroines when she said: "Your work becomes your personal life. . . . It takes you up, and uses you, and spins you out; and that is your life. Not much else can happen to you."[34] Compared to Cather's later renderings of opera singers, Traduttori and Selma Schumann appear florid and overdrawn, but they are akin to Thea, Kitty Ayrshire, and all the others in their essential characteristics—their imperious vitality and their matter-of-fact, almost sardonic acceptance of the emotionally deprived life which (so Cather insists again and again) their art demands. The idea that the sacrifice art requires is greater for a woman than for a man comes into "The Prodigies" (1897), a Jamesian tale of the exploitation of two gifted children by their relentlessly ambitious mother. An envious friend of the family, whose musical career ended with her marriage, has dreamed that she herself would be blessed with a boy and girl who were just such prodigies, "and the boy would do all the great things that she had not done. She knew well enough that if the cruelly exacting life of art is not wholly denied to a woman, it is offered to her at a terrible price" (p. 413).

The setting of "A Resurrection," the first of nine stories with a western background to appear in the 1897–1902 years, is Brownville, a

34. Willa Cather, *The Song of the Lark* (rev. ed.; Boston: Houghton Mifflin, 1937), p. 546.

Missouri River town which Willa Cather had visited in 1894 to gather material for a *Journal* article commemorating the fortieth anniversary of its settlement. In the days of the steamboat trade Brownville had flourished mightily; the first newspaper in Nebraska Territory had been printed there and "in an upstairs room of Senator Tipton's big house on the hill was stretched the first telegraph wire that linked Nebraska with the civilization of the east and made it a part of the big world."[35] But "when the steamboat trade went under it carried Brownville with it," and in 1894 even though "all the old ruins about the town suggest that it once reached a high state of civilization," nothing remained but "the trees and the quiet and . . . the dilapidation" and a dwindling population "composed mostly of 'river folks' and a nondescript people who have come up the river from nowhere." Among the inhabitants only one seemed to Willa Cather above the dead level: "a young girl who even dared to laugh and make jokes at the old town. But when I noticed an unusually large diamond on her third finger . . . I understood her elation and reckless indifference. I suppose one could be desperately in love, even in Brownville." Perhaps "A Resurrection" had its inception in that encounter.

Another kind of boom-and-bust frontier town—the kind that existed almost entirely on paper or in the mind of the promoter—is the scene of "El Dorado: A Kansas Recessional" (1901). Paper towns were a common enough phenomenon during all phases of western expansion. As Everett Dick has written: "In pamphlets, brochures, and planted newspaper stories, the various interests—legitimate and illegitimate— propagandized the rich endowments and natural advantages of the particular localities to which they wished to attract settlers. Only too often, however, the glowing pictures that were painted were more closely akin to pipe dreams than to sober fact, and in some cases promotional schemes amounted to outright fraud."[36] Describing one such scheme in "El Dorado," Cather again dramatizes the plight of an individual from an older culture—in this case, that of the southern United States—who is unable to adapt himself to the unfamiliar and harsh conditions of pioneer life on the plains.

35. Willa Cather, "An Old River Metropolis," *Nebraska State Journal*, August 12, 1894, p. 13. Another version of this article signed with the pseudonym George Overing and retitled "The Hottest Day I Ever Spent" appeared in *The Library*, I (July 7, 1900), 3–4. Apparently the new title did not exaggerate; fifty-one years after her visit the author referred again to the terrible heat (Willa Cather to Mariel Gere, May 1, 1945).

36. Everett Dick, *Tales of the Frontier: From Lewis and Clark to the Last Roundup* (Lincoln: University of Nebraska Press, 1963), p. 119.

"The Sentimentality of William Tavener" (1900) is unique in all of Cather's writings in that it combines Virginia and Nebraska settings. The Back Creek country from which the Tavener family has migrated to McPherson County, Nebraska, provides the background for Willa Cather's last novel, *Sapphira and the Slave Girl* (1940), and one of the characters in the novel, the boy Tap, is mentioned in the story. But quite apart from this connection, "William Tavener" commands our interest, and its economical, low-keyed narrative style distinctly suggests the author's later manner.

Two other 1900 stories, "Eric Hermannson's Soul" and "The Dance at Chevalier's" (the latter signed with the pseudonym Henry Nicklemann), return to the terrain, the people, and something of the mood of "On the Divide." "Eric," the better of the two, is one of the most important of the early stories. In confronting Margaret Elliot, product of an "ultra-refined civilization which tries to cheat nature," with the primitive Eric, "the wildest lad on all the Divide," Cather for the first time opposes East and West, and makes explicit the struggle that was pulling her in two—the conflict between her yearning for the cultural richness and precious traditions of the urban East and her love of the wild land. Here, too, one senses Cather's feeling for the earth, the sky, and physical perfection in man or woman.

Linking "Eric" with both earlier and later work is the character originally introduced in "On the Divide" as Lena Yensen, the pretty, giggly, flirtatious, and—ultimately—complaisant object of Canute's brutal wooing. In "Eric Hermannson's Soul" she has become Lena Hanson—"whose name was a reproach through all the Divide country," who received Eric "attired in a pink wrapper and silk stockings and tiny pink slippers, . . . had lived in big cities and knew the ways of townfolk, who had never worked in the fields and had kept her hands white and soft, her throat fair and tender, who had heard great singers in Denver and Salt Lake, and who knew the strange language of flattery and idleness and mirth" (pp. 360–361). Restored to respectability as Olena Yenson, daughter of a Norwegian settler, in "The Bohemian Girl" (1912), she is one of the guests at Olaf Ericson's barn-raising—"rather inconveniently plump, handsome in a smooth, heavy way, with a fine color and good-natured, sleepy eyes. She was redolent of violet sachet powder, and had warm, soft, white hands, but she danced divinely, moving as smoothly as the tide coming in" (p. 31). And finally, in *My Ántonia* appears the beguiling Lena Lingard in whom one recognizes attributes of all three of her predecessors. She has worked in the fields but "her legs and arms, curiously enough, . . . kept a miraculous whiteness"; she is respectable but because of her effect on the menfolk, the ladies of the Norwegian colony frown on her. On the dance floor

> Lena moved without exertion, rather indolently, and her hand often accented the rhythm softly on her partner's shoulder. . . . The music seemed to put her into a soft, waking dream, and her violet-coloured eyes looked sleepily and confidingly at one from under her long lashes. When she sighed she exhaled a heavy perfume of sachet powder. To dance 'Home, Sweet Home,' with Lena was like coming in with the tide. She danced every dance like a waltz, and it was always the same waltz—the waltz of coming home to something, of inevitable, fated return.[37]

From the juxtaposition of the four Lenas, one may gain some idea of how Cather developed a one-dimensional character, nonexistent apart from the printed page, into an autonomous being, more real than many "real" people, who persists in the reader's memory even when he has forgotten the precise context in which she figured. If there were no girls like Lena Lingard in the world, says the narrator in *My Ántonia*, there would be no poetry. Such a statement about Lena Yensen would sound like high-flown nonsense; that it seems right and true of Lena Lingard measures one aspect of Cather's accomplishment.

A related but more complex kind of alchemy is at work in Cather's use of the memories associated with the "dearest possession" of her childhood—the sandbar island in the Republican River, where she and her brothers and their friends fished and camped, were in turn Long John Silver and Huck Finn and mighty Caesar, read and spun tales and dreamed, and "in the light of the driftwood fire . . . planned the conquest of the world" (p. 273). The emotional charge emanating from this cluster of memories infuses not only the Nebraska stories but also the novels whose setting is the Southwest—another kind of country for which Willa Cather had an enthusiasm. "The Way of the World" (1898), which may be thought of as a kind of prologue to the cycle of scenes and episodes linked by the island associations, introduces a band of children— Speckle Burnham, Jimmy Templeton, Reinholt Birkner, and others— who will reappear under these and other names as adolescents and adults in nearly a dozen novels and stories. Here they are seen as citizens of

37. Cather, *My Ántonia*, pp. 222–223. The paraphrased sentence which follows appears on p. 270.

Speckleville, the fictional counterpart of the play town, Sandy Point, with its packing-case stores and post office and piano-box hotel, which grew up along the south fence of the Cather back yard. (Sandy Point's founder and duly elected mayor was Willa Cather; her only political rival ran a store which kept tablets, pencils, and whistles, and was content to be alderman.[38]) Our first view of the island comes in the opening paragraph of "The Treasure of Far Island" (1902): lying "about two miles up from Empire City [Red Cloud] in a turbid little Nebraska river," it is overgrown with "thousands of yellow-green creek willows and cottonwood seedlings, brilliantly green, even when the hottest winds blow," and along its east coast lies a long, irregular beach, "dazzling white, ripple marked, and full of possibilities for the imagination" (p. 265). Revisiting the island on his first trip home in twelve years, Douglass Burnham (Speckle), now a successful playwright, remembers the days of his boyhood when all was "exultation and romance—sea fights and splendid galleys and Roman triumphs and brilliant caravans winding through the desert" (p. 280). The essence of the story is distilled in a 1903 poem which Willa Cather dedicated to her brothers Roscoe and Douglas; it recalls their "vanished kingdom" and fixes the image of the children

> who lay and planned at moonrise,
> On an island in a western river,
> Of the conquest of the world together.[39]

A little masterpiece, "The Enchanted Bluff" (1909), transports the reader back to that time—to a night when "six sworn to the spirit of the stream" sat around their watch fire, and, as the moon rose "like a galleon in full sail," speculated about the enthralling possibility that Coronado and his men had passed that way on their quest for the fabled seven cities of gold. One of the boys tells of the Mesa Encantada—"down in New Mexico somewheres . . . a big red rock there that goes right up out of the sand for about nine hundred feet. . . . They call it the Enchanted Bluff down there, because no white man has even been on top of it" (p. 74). Climbing the Enchanted Bluff now takes its place among the boys' projects for the unlimited future.

Fleetingly reprised in *Alexander's Bridge* (1912)—through a train window Alexander sees a group of boys sitting around a little fire, and

38. Bennett, *The World of Willa Cather*, pp. 172–173, 250.

39. Willa Cather, *April Twilights (1903)*, edited with an introduction by Bernice Slote (rev. ed.; Lincoln: University of Nebraska Press, 1968), p. 3. See also the discussion of incremental repetition as a creative process, pp. xxxv ff.

"his mind [goes] back a long way, to a campfire on a sandbar in a Western river"⁴⁰—the island gathering, in transmuted form, becomes one of *My Ántonia's* most beautiful and evocative chapters. Here one sees the river throughout a long, lazy summer day from the morning when the dew glittered on the grasses until late afternoon when there was "a shimmer of gold on the brown river" and "the light trembled in the willow thickets."⁴¹ At Ántonia's request, Jim Burden tells of the Spaniards' search for the golden cities and of his strong belief that Coronado had been along this very river, for a farmer "in the county north of ours, when he was breaking sod, . . . turned up a metal stirrup of fine workmanship, and a sword with a Spanish inscription on the blade." Similarly, in *Death Comes for the Archbishop* (1927), a Spanish sword hilt is found in the earth near a water-head, "a spring overhung by the sharp-leafed variety of cottonwood called water willow," outside the Mexican settlement of Agua Secreta.⁴² But the climactic episode connected with these memories is reached in an earlier novel, *The Professor's House* (1925), when Tom Outland discovers the little city of stone in the side of his enchanted bluff, the Blue Mesa.⁴³ The boys sworn to the spirit of the stream also appear in *A Lost Lady* (1923); the island, locked in winter, is a key setting in *Lucy Gayheart* (1935); and a 1932 story, "Old Mrs. Harris," provides one more glimpse of the back yard strewn with packing cases first seen in "The Way of the World."⁴⁴

The train whistle, "that cold, vibrant scream, the world-wide call for men,"⁴⁵ stirring as a trumpet note to youngsters growing up in Willa Cather's west, echoes through many of her pages. No fewer than six of the stories in this collection open with scenes aboard a train or at a railroad station, and some of her most admirable characters—as well as some of the most contemptible—are railroad men. Although it was preceded by "The Westbound Train" (1899), a sketch in play form, "The Affair at Grover Station" (1900) is the first story in which Cather

40. Willa Cather, *Alexander's Bridge* (Boston: Houghton Mifflin, 1912), p. 146.
41. Cather, *My Ántonia*, p. 244. The quotation immediately following appears on p. 243.
42. Willa Cather, *Death Comes for the Archbishop* (New York: Alfred A. Knopf, 1927), pp. 31–32.
43. Willa Cather, *The Professor's House* (New York: Alfred A. Knopf, 1925), pp. 199 ff.
44. Willa Cather, *A Lost Lady* (New York: Alfred A. Knopf, 1923), pp. 14 ff.; *Lucy Gayheart* (New York: Alfred A. Knopf, 1935), pp. 7 ff.; and "Old Mrs. Harris," in *Obscure Destinies* (New York: Alfred A. Knopf, 1932), p. 113.
45. "The Sculptor's Funeral," p. 174. Cf. "The whistle seemed to call us to dare the world of men" in "The Night Express," *April Twilights (1903)*, p. 36.

makes serious use of a railroad background. In the summer of 1898 she visited her brother Douglas, then cashier for the Burlington line in Cheyenne, Wyoming, and the following summer they met again in Red Cloud. No doubt the story dates from that time, for it was worked out with Douglas's help.[46] There is a curious link between Freymark, the villain of "Grover Station," and Yung, the title character in one of the *Hesperian* stories, "A Son of the Celestial." Freymark, who is half-Chinese, belongs to "a race that was in its mort cloth before Europe's swaddling clothes were made" (p. 343). The same figure describes Yung (p. 527), but is omitted in a 1900 reworking of the story, "The Conversion of Sum Loo."

Roscoe and Douglas, the brothers nearest to her in age, were Willa Cather's close companions, but she had a special love for her youngest brother, Jack; the creation of the little lad in "Jack-a-Boy" (1901) gives expression to her feeling for him. The boarding-house background in this story recalls that in "The Count of Crow's Nest," and one of the boarders, the old professor, has a good deal in common with the central character in "The Professor's Commencement."[47] The latter story and "The Treasure of Far Island" were the last to appear under Willa Cather's byline before those which she ultimately collected in *The Troll Garden*.

❊   ❊   ❊

During the final phase of her life in Pittsburgh, Willa Cather devoted herself almost exclusively to poetry and fiction. Thanks to her teaching position, the necessity to make her writing pay was no longer an over-riding concern; she could afford to work slowly and carefully. Moreover,

46. Elsie M. Cather to Mildred R. Bennett, February 3, no year, probably 1956.

47. In the December 31, 1938, letter to Professor Wagenknecht (see note 30, above), Willa Cather also disclaimed sole authorship of two other stories published in the *New England Magazine*, "The Professor's Commencement" and "The Treasure of Far Island"; also of "Jack-a-Boy" and "Eric Hermannson's Soul," which appeared respectively in the *Saturday Evening Post* and *Cosmopolitan*. However, E. K. Brown in his authorized biography refers to Cather's placing her work in the *New England Magazine* (p. 113) and comments at some length on "The Treasure of Far Island" (pp. 40, 110). Nowhere does he state or imply that these stories or any other Cather story except "Peter" are the work of any hand but her own. It should also be noted that Willa Cather, in a July 17, 1901, letter to George and Helen Seibel, mentions that her mother is sending to elderly relatives copies of the *New England Magazine*, with her current story, "The Professor's Commencement"; she does not suggest credit for authorship should be shared. Further, the central situation in "Jack-a-Boy" has a direct parallel in Willa Cather's own experience: she nursed her little brother Jack through a serious illness in the summer of 1893. For a discussion of Cather's motives in dissociating herself from her early stories, see Curtis Bradford, "Willa Cather's Uncollected Short Stories," *American Literature*, XXVI (January, 1955), 547–550.

she was beginning to receive recognition as a writer of unusual promise: her 1903 poetry collection, *April Twilights*, was reviewed favorably for the most part, as was her first book of prose, *The Troll Garden* (1905).[48]

Since the stories in the latter volume are extensively treated in existing Cather criticism, they call for little comment here. Four of the seven— "'A Death in the Desert,'" "A Wagner Matinee," "The Sculptor's Funeral," and "Paul's Case"—appeared in magazines as well as in the book, and in the light of hindsight one can see that in these stories Cather was working with her own material, whereas the three tales specially written for the collection are the kind of "literary excursion" she later deplored. Stories from the two groups, as E. K. Brown has pointed out, are presented alternately throughout *The Troll Garden*: the first, third, and fifth stories (those previously unpublished) concern "artists in relation with persons of great wealth"; the second, fourth, and sixth portray "an artist or a person of artistic temperament from the prairies return[ing] to them in defeat," while the seventh story, "Paul's Case," functions as a sort of coda.[49] One could also say that the first six stories are about two kinds of women: those who inflict suffering and those who suffer. Flavia in "Flavia and Her Artists," Harvey Merrick's mother in "The Sculptor's Funeral," and Lady Treffinger in "The Marriage of Phaedra" belong to the first group; Katharine in "'A Death in the Desert,'" Caroline in "The Garden Lodge," and Aunt Georgiana in "A Wagner Matinee" to the second. The conclusion Cather draws, stated in "Paul's Case," seems to be that life will betray the sensitive person, artist or no.

In these stories written deliberately and with conscious art, no less than in the outpourings of her journalistic years, one finds memories, anticipations, and reprises: Aunt Georgiana and her husband, for example, measure off their quarter-section homestead "by driving across the prairie in a wagon, to the wheel of which they had tied a red cotton handkerchief, and counting off its revolutions" (p. 236), just as the author's own Aunt Franc and Uncle George Cather had done, and "the jolt of the tied wheel" will recur in a 1923 poem, "Macon Prairie."[50] As an instance of a

48. For a discussion of the *April Twilight* reviews, see the introduction in *April Twilights* (*1903*), pp. xvi ff. The *New York Times*, the *Dial*, the *Reader*, the *Critic*, and the *Independent* all had good things to say about *The Troll Garden*, but the *Bookman* called it "a collection of freak stories that are either lurid, hysterical, or unwholesome" (*Bookman*, XXI [August, 1905], 612).

49. Brown, *Willa Cather*, pp. 113–123.

50. Willa Cather, "Macon Prairie" in *April Twilights and Other Poems* (New York: Alfred A. Knopf, 1923), p. 58. See also Bennett, *The World of Willa Cather*, p. 12.

connection between stories wholly dissimilar in tone and subject matter, note that the last line of "Flavia and Her Artists," spoken by Miss Broadwood—"if you meet any of our artists, tell them you have left Caius Marius among the ruins of Carthage" (p. 172)—echoes the ending of "The Way of the World"—Speckle "sat down with his empty pails in his deserted town, as Caius Marius once sat among the ruins of Carthage" (p. 404). Whether the repetition was an oversight or intentional, there is more than one ironic parallel to be drawn.

When she put together her 1920 collection, *Youth and the Bright Medusa,* Cather rejected the three "literary excursions" and retained the other four stories in revised form. "'A Death in the Desert'" and "A Wagner Matinee" already had been thoroughly pruned and polished in 1905 for inclusion in *The Troll Garden,* and Cather's additional revisions in 1920 were of the same general kind—directed toward cutting away superfluous detail and substituting simpler, more specific language—changes which tended to make the stories less personal, less sentimental. But even after "'A Death in the Desert'" had undergone two reworkings it apparently failed to meet her standards, for it was omitted from the collected works (1937–1941).

❈   ❈   ❈

Despite Willa Cather's dissatisfaction with the fiction she wrote during her six years on *McClure's,* and even when—as in "The Willing Muse" and "Eleanor's House"—she bows too humbly at the shrine of Henry James, the work of this period has an ease and an authority that reflect her increasing technical skill. In the best sense of the word, Willa Cather was a professional: she knew that there is no such thing as an artist who is not also a craftsman, and her choice of such craftsmen *par excellence* as James and Flaubert as literary models had, in the long run, a salutary effect on her style, if only as a needed corrective to her youthful fondness for "purple patches" and to a kind of mechanical glibness, a dependence on stock phrases and a tendency to run on—to saturate rather than to pinpoint, which had developed when she had columns to fill and deadlines to meet.

In addition to the two stories mentioned above, "The Namesake" and "The Profile" also appeared in 1907. Elizabeth Sergeant has pointed out that the latter story reveals a characteristic temperamental twist—"the author's strange abhorrence for physical defect."[51] One of the

51. Sergeant, *Willa Cather: A Memoir,* p. 71.

characters speaks of the human body as sanctified by Nature's purpose, decent or comely in any natural function or attitude, "but lop away so much as a finger, and you have wounded the creature beyond reparation" (p. 125). And indeed it does seem that Cather is preoccupied almost to an obsessional degree with mutilation—particularly of the hand. As examples among the stories in this collection, Eric, in "The Bohemian Girl," tears his hand on a cornsheller (p. 40); in "The Namesake," Lyon's hand and forearm are torn away by exploding shrapnel (p. 144); and in "Behind the Singer Tower," an opera tenor jumping from the burning hotel flings out his arm as he falls and his hand, "snapped off at the wrist as cleanly as if it had been taken off by a cutlass," is found on a window ledge (p. 45). Among later works, in the 1931 novel *Shadows on the Rock*, when a missionary is feasting with a party of Huron converts, "they pulled a human hand out of the kettle to show him that he had eaten of an Iroquois prisoner";[52] and in *Sapphira and the Slave Girl* the old Negro woman, Aunt Jezebel, on being told that she must eat to keep up her strength, replies that she "'cain't think of nothin' [she] could relish, lessen maybe it was a li'l pickaninny's hand.'"[53] This particular "recurrence" runs through Cather's work literally from first to last: Serge, in the 1893 story "The Clemency of the Court," is tied up by his arms until "they were paralyzed from the shoulder down so that the guard had to feed him like a baby" (p. 521) and in the unfinished novel of fourteenth-century Avignon, *Hard Punishments*, which Willa Cather worked on in her last years, one of the two central characters, a peasant boy named Pierre, was punished for thievery by being strung up by his thumbs, with the result that "his hands are now useless."[54] While it is always dangerous to look for a clinical explanation of "temperamental twists" as they are revealed in an artist's work, there may be a connection between this particular recurrence and a traumatic incident of the author's childhood: according to Edith Lewis, when Willa Cather was five years old, a half-witted Negro boy, armed with a clasp knife, threatened to cut off her hand.[55]

Like "The Profile," "The Namesake" is set in Paris and has an artist for the central character, but the setting simply provides a framework for the story, which probably sprang from the same root as the 1902

52. Willa Cather, *Shadows on the Rock* (New York: Alfred A. Knopf, 1931), p. 152.

53. Willa Cather, *Sapphira and the Slave Girl* (New York: Alfred A. Knopf, 1940), p. 89.

54. Willa Cather, *Five Stories* (Vintage Books; New York: Alfred A. Knopf, 1957), p. 200.

55. Lewis, *Willa Cather Living*, p. 10.

poem, "The Namesake," dedicated to an uncle killed in the Civil War, William Sibert Boak, whose middle name Willa Cather appropriated.[56] The imagery in one deeply emotional passage—in which the narrator speaks of the "feeling that artists know when we, rarely, achieve truth in our work; the feeling of union with some great force, of purpose and security" (p. 146)—is akin to Jim Burden's feeling in *My Ántonia*—"that is happiness; to be dissolved into something complete and great."[57] Another line from the same passage in "The Namesake"—"my life seemed to be pouring out of me and running into the ground"—is echoed in *O Pioneers!* when Emil, "wild with joy," is racing to his rendezvous with Marie—"his life poured itself out along the road before him."[58]

"On the Gulls' Road," the only story to appear in 1908, earned a letter of praise from Sarah Orne Jewett—she had read the story with "deep happiness and recognition," and went on to say: "It made me feel very near to the writer's young and loving heart. You have drawn your two figures of the wife and her husband with unerring touches and wonderful tenderness for her. It makes me the more sure that you are far on your road toward a fine and long story of a very high class." Miss Jewett felt that it was perhaps a mistake for a woman to write in a man's character, "but oh, how close—how tender—how true the feeling is! the sea air blows through the very letters on the page."[59] Another Catherian "recurrence" perhaps had its beginning in this story: the turquoise in the ring worn by Lars Ebbling (p. 81) will reappear as an object symbolizing love and death in three novels. In a scene between the ill-fated lovers of *O Pioneers!*, Emil drops into Marie's lap "a handful of uncut turquoises, as big as marbles" and Marie "gaz[es] in rapture at the soft blue color of the stones."[60] In *The Song of the Lark*, Ray Kennedy, the brakeman who is selflessly devoted to Thea and who is killed in a trainwreck, displays to her a keepsake he has brought back from the Cliff-Dwellers' burial mounds: "a stone, soft and blue as a robin's egg, lay in the hard palm of

56. The name on Willa Cather's birth certificate is Wilella and was originally inscribed thus in the family Bible; she herself emended it to Willa. During her childhood for a time she called herself Willa Love Cather after Dr. Love who attended at her birth; later she exchanged the Love for Sibert averring that she had been named for the uncle memorialized in the poem. Although she eventually dropped Sibert from her byline, she continued to use the initial on her stationery and her will is signed Willa Sibert Cather. See Bennett, *The World of Willa Cather*, pp. 234–235.

57. Cather, *My Ántonia*, p. 18.

58. Cather, *O Pioneers!*, p. 258.

59. *Letters of Sarah Orne Jewett*, pp. 246–247.

60. Cather, *O Pioneers!*, p. 224.

his hand. It was a turquoise, rubbed smooth in the Indian finish. . . ."[61]
Similarly, in *The Professor's House*, Tom Outland, who is destined to be
killed in World War I, makes a gift to his love, Rosamund, and her
sister: "two lumps of soft blue stone, the colour of robins' eggs, or of the
sea on halcyon days of summer."[62] A turquoise also figures as a fateful
object in the tale of ancient Mexico related by Don Hedger to Eden Bower
in "Coming, Aphrodite!": The Queen of the Aztecs "had a jewel of
great value, a turquoise that had fallen from the sun, and had the image of
the sun upon it." When she desired a young man she sent a slave to him
with the jewel "for a sign that he should come to her"; in each case,
the rendezvous ends in death for the young man.[63]

Nineteen nine was the year of "The Enchanted Bluff," a high point,
perhaps the highest, of Cather's accomplishment up to that time; in 1910
she began work on *Alexander's Bridge* and no stories or poems appeared
during that year. But 1911 brought "The Joy of Nelly Deane," whose
vivid heroine has some characteristics in common with Marie Tovesky
and Lucy Gayheart, and whose tragic yet joyful story is a sketch in
miniature of Lucy's. Comparing the description of so small a detail as
the eyes of these three heroines, the reader again gains some notion of the
developing and refining processes of Cather's art. Nelly has "yellow-
brown eyes, which dilated so easily and sparkled with a kind of golden
effervescence" (p. 56). Marie also has yellow-brown eyes: "Everyone
noticed [them]; the brown iris had golden glints that made them look like
gold-stone, or, in softer lights, like that Colorado mineral called tiger-
eye."[64] As for Lucy, "There was something in her nature that was like
her movements, something direct and unhesitating and joyous, and in
her golden-brown eyes. They were not gentle brown eyes, but flashed
with gold sparks like that Colorado stone we call the tiger-eye."[65]

"Behind the Singer Tower," which appeared in the spring of 1912
when Willa Cather was in New Mexico recovering, as she said, from the
conventional editorial point of view, is in some respects the most surprising
story in the collection. Among her other writings it is most closely related
to *Alexander's Bridge*, and since it dates from the same period it perhaps
may be thought of as a by-product of that novel. The central character,

61. Cather, *The Song of the Lark*, p. 148.

62. Cather, *The Professor's House*, p. 120.

63. Willa Cather, *Youth and the Bright Medusa* (new ed.; New York: Alfred A. Knopf, 1945), p. 44.

64. Cather, *O Pioneers!*, p. 11.

65. Cather, *Lucy Gayheart*, p. 4.

Fred Hallet, is an engineer as was Bartley Alexander; and just as the crisis in *Alexander's Bridge* parallels an actual event—the collapse of the Quebec bridge on August 29, 1907—so does the disastrous hotel fire in the story appear to have been suggested by the Windsor Hotel fire of March 17, 1899. "Behind the Singer Tower," as Curtis Bradford has noted, is Willa Cather's one attempt at direct social criticism: "Its rejection of the American metropolis is told in terms of the aspiring skyscraper, its most characteristic symbol," and the story

> seems to indicate that Miss Cather had taken in more of the muck-raking attitude that maintained at *McClure's* than is generally supposed. There was much of the social critic in Willa Cather, but save in a few instances she was critical by implication rather than by direct statement. . . . If we can judge from a single story, "Behind the Singer Tower" indicates that she would have succeeded as a social critic had she wished to.[66]

But when Willa Cather left the metropolis for a "quiet centre," following the completion of *Alexander's Bridge* and "Behind the Singer Tower," what she chose to write about—or found herself writing about—was "a kind of country and a kind of people" for which she had an enthusiasm. "The Bohemian Girl" was both a departure and a return, an end and a beginning. Once it was written, whether Willa Cather knew it or not, the home pasture lay just ahead.

66. Bradford, "Willa Cather's Uncollected Short Stories," pp. 546–547.

Volume I

THE
BOHEMIAN
GIRL

✼ ✼ ✼

The nine stories collected in Volume I were written by Willa Cather between the summer of 1906, when she came to New York to join the editorial staff of McClure's, and January of 1912, the year that she resigned from the magazine to devote herself entirely to writing. Apart from assignments undertaken for McClure's, these stories, the short novel Alexander's Bridge, and a half-dozen poems comprise the body of Willa Cather's work during this phase of her career. Four of the stories came out in 1907; one in 1908; one in 1909; none in 1910 (the year that she began work on Alexander's Bridge); one in 1911; and two (including "The Bohemian Girl," published after her resignation) in 1912.

The noticeable slacking-off of Willa Cather's productivity in 1908 coincides with her promotion to the managing editorship of McClure's. Not only were her responsibilities heavier but the range of her editorial duties was wider—she made two trips to England in quest of new authors and manuscripts—with the result that the undisturbed intervals for her own work became progressively fewer and farther between. Although the magazine flourished under her direction, in the words of her biographer, E. K. Brown, "the price of Willa Cather's success was nervous exhaustion."

After completing Alexander's Bridge in the fall of 1911, Willa Cather took a protracted leave of absence, and toward the end of the year finished a story in a vein quite different from any she had written in the past decade; called "The Bohemian Girl," it had a Nebraska setting. Before she left on a trip to the Southwest she finished a second Nebraska story, "Alexandra," and she was still absorbed in it when she visited her family in Red Cloud, Nebraska, in June, 1912. According to her friend Edith Lewis, "It was a long time since [Willa Cather] had been back in that country with so free a mind. That summer she lived with it as she had done in the days before she became an editor. . . . She began to think about another story, in the same key as 'Alexandra,' which she planned to call 'The White Mulberry Tree.' Eventually . . . the two stories came together in her mind and became O Pioneers!"—the first of the classic novels on which Willa Cather's fame rests. Writing it she had "the feeling that at last she knew the path she wanted to travel."

Volume I begins with the immediate precursor of O Pioneers!, "The Bohemian Girl," published in August, 1912, and retraces the route Willa Cather had followed back to the first of the 1907 stories, "The Namesake." Except for "The Enchanted Bluff," which was included in the posthumous Five Stories (1956), none of the stories has previously been reprinted.

The Bohemian Girl

✤ ✤ ✤

The transcontinental express swung along the windings of the Sand River Valley, and in the rear seat of the observation car a young man sat greatly at his ease, not in the least discomfited by the fierce sunlight which beat in upon his brown face and neck and strong back. There was a look of relaxation and of great passivity about his broad shoulders, which seemed almost too heavy until he stood up and squared them. He wore a pale flannel shirt and a blue silk necktie with loose ends. His trousers were wide and belted at the waist, and his short sack coat hung open. His heavy shoes had seen good service. His reddish-brown hair, like his clothes, had a foreign cut. He had deep-set, dark blue eyes under heavy reddish eyebrows. His face was kept clean only by close shaving, and even the sharpest razor left a glint of yellow in the smooth brown of his skin. His teeth and the palms of his hands were very white. His head, which looked hard and stubborn, lay indolently in the green cushion of the wicker chair, and as he looked out at the ripe summer country a teasing, not unkindly smile played over his lips. Once, as he basked thus comfortably, a quick light flashed in his eyes, curiously dilating the pupils, and his mouth became a hard, straight line, gradually relaxing into its former smile of rather kindly mockery. He told himself, apparently, that there was no point in getting excited; and he seemed a master hand at taking his ease when he could. Neither the sharp whistle of the locomotive nor the brakeman's call disturbed him. It was not until after the train had stopped that he rose, put on a Panama hat, took from the rack a small valise and a flute case, and stepped deliberately to the station platform. The baggage was already unloaded, and the stranger presented a check for a battered sole-leather steamer trunk.

"Can you keep it here for a day or two?" he asked the agent. "I may send for it, and I may not."

"Depends on whether you like the country, I suppose?" demanded the agent in a challenging tone.

"Just so."

The agent shrugged his shoulders, looked scornfully at the small trunk, which was marked "N. E.," and handed out a claim check without further comment. The stranger watched him as he caught one end of the trunk and dragged it into the express room. The agent's manner seemed to remind him of something amusing. "Doesn't seem to be a very big place," he remarked, looking about.

"It's big enough for us," snapped the agent, as he banged the trunk into a corner.

That remark, apparently, was what Nils Ericson had wanted. He chuckled quietly as he took a leather strap from his pocket and swung his valise around his shoulder. Then he settled his Panama securely on his head, turned up his trousers, tucked the flute case under his arm, and started off across the fields. He gave the town, as he would have said, a wide berth, and cut through a great fenced pasture, emerging, when he rolled under the barbed wire at the farther corner, upon a white dusty road which ran straight up from the river valley to the high prairies, where the ripe wheat stood yellow and the tin roofs and weathercocks were twinkling in the fierce sunlight. By the time Nils had done three miles, the sun was sinking and the farm wagons on their way home from town came rattling by, covering him with dust and making him sneeze. When one of the farmers pulled up and offered to give him a lift, he clambered in willingly. The driver was a thin, grizzled old man with a long lean neck and a foolish sort of beard, like a goat's. "How fur ye goin'?" he asked, as he clucked to his horses and started off.

"Do you go by the Ericson place?"

"Which Ericson?" The old man drew in his reins as if he expected to stop again.

"Preacher Ericson's."

"Oh, the Old Lady Ericson's!" He turned and looked at Nils. "La, me! If you're goin' out there you might 'a' rid out in the automobile. That's a pity, now. The Old Lady Ericson was in town with her auto. You might 'a' heard it snortin' anywhere about the post office er the butcher shop."

"Has she a motor?" asked the stranger absently.

"'Deed an' she has! She runs into town every night about this time for her mail and meat for supper. Some folks say she's afraid her auto won't get exercise enough, but I say that's jealousy."

[4]

"Aren't there any other motors about here?"

"Oh, yes! we have fourteen in all. But nobody else gets around like the Old Lady Ericson. She's out, rain er shine, over the whole county, chargin' into town and out amongst her farms, an' up to her sons' places. Sure you ain't goin' to the wrong place?" He craned his neck and looked at Nils' flute case with eager curiosity. "The old woman ain't got any piany that I knows on. Olaf, he has a grand. His wife's musical; took lessons in Chicago."

"I'm going up there tomorrow," said Nils imperturbably. He saw that the driver took him for a piano tuner.

"Oh, I see!" The old man screwed up his eyes mysteriously. He was a little dashed by the stranger's noncommunicativeness, but he soon broke out again.

"I'm one o' Mis' Ericson's tenants. Look after one of her places. I did own the place myself oncet, but I lost it a while back, in the bad years just after the World's Fair. Just as well, too, I say. Lets you out o' payin' taxes. The Ericsons do own most of the county now. I remember the old preacher's fav'rite text used to be, 'To them that hath shall be given.' They've spread something wonderful—run over this here country like bindweed. But I ain't one that begretches it to 'em. Folks is entitled to what they kin git; and they're hustlers. Olaf, he's in the Legislature now, and a likely man fur Congress. Listen, if that ain't the old woman comin' now. Want I should stop her?"

Nils shook his head. He heard the deep chug-chug of a motor vibrating steadily in the clear twilight behind them. The pale lights of the car swam over the hill, and the old man slapped his reins and turned clear out of the road, ducking his head at the first of three angry snorts from behind. The motor was running at a hot, even speed, and passed without turning an inch from its course. The driver was a stalwart woman who sat at ease in the front seat and drove her car bareheaded. She left a cloud of dust and a trail of gasoline behind her. Her tenant threw back his head and sneezed.

"Whew! I sometimes say I'd as lief be *before* Mrs. Ericson as behind her. She does beat all! Nearly seventy, and never lets another soul touch that car. Puts it into commission herself every morning, and keeps it tuned up by the hitch-bar all day. I never stop work for a drink o' water that I don't hear her a-churnin' up the road. I reckon her darter-in-laws never sets down easy nowadays. Never know when she'll pop in. Mis' Otto, she says to me: 'We're so afraid that thing'll blow up and do Ma some injury yet, she's so turrible venturesome.' Says I: 'I wouldn't stew, Mis'

Otto; the old lady'll drive that car to the funeral of every darter-in-law she's got.' That was after the old woman had jumped a turrible bad culvert."

The stranger heard vaguely what the old man was saying. Just now he was experiencing something very much like homesickness, and he was wondering what had brought it about. The mention of a name or two, perhaps; the rattle of a wagon along a dusty road; the rank, resinous smell of sunflowers and ironweed, which the night damp brought up from the draws and low places; perhaps, more than all, the dancing lights of the motor that had plunged by. He squared his shoulders with a comfortable sense of strength.

The wagon, as it jolted westward, climbed a pretty steady upgrade. The country, receding from the rough river valley, swelled more and more gently, as if it had been smoothed out by the wind. On one of the last of the rugged ridges, at the end of a branch road, stood a grim square house with a tin roof and double porches. Behind the house stretched a row of broken, wind-racked poplars, and down the hill slope to the left straggled the sheds and stables. The old man stopped his horses where the Ericsons' road branched across a dry sand creek that wound about the foot of the hill.

"That's the old lady's place. Want I should drive in?"

"No, thank you. I'll roll out here. Much obliged to you. Good night."

His passenger stepped down over the front wheel, and the old man drove on reluctantly, looking back as if he would like to see how the stranger would be received.

As Nils was crossing the dry creek he heard the restive tramp of a horse coming toward him down the hill. Instantly he flashed out of the road and stood behind a thicket of wild plum bushes that grew in the sandy bed. Peering through the dusk, he saw a light horse, under tight rein, descending the hill at a sharp walk. The rider was a slender woman— barely visible against the dark hillside—wearing an old-fashioned derby hat and a long riding skirt. She sat lightly in the saddle, with her chin high, and seemed to be looking into the distance. As she passed the plum thicket her horse snuffed the air and shied. She struck him, pulling him in sharply, with an angry exclamation, *"Blázne!"* in Bohemian. Once in the main road, she let him out into a lope, and they soon emerged upon the crest of high land, where they moved along the skyline, silhouetted against the band of faint color that lingered in the west. This horse and rider, with their free, rhythmical gallop, were the only moving things to be seen on the face of the flat country. They seemed, in the last sad light of evening, not to be there accidentally, but as an inevitable detail of the landscape.

Nils watched them until they had shrunk to a mere moving speck against the sky, then he crossed the sand creek and climbed the hill. When he reached the gate the front of the house was dark, but a light was shining from the side windows. The pigs were squealing in the hog corral, and Nils could see a tall boy, who carried two big wooden buckets, moving about among them. Halfway between the barn and the house, the windmill wheezed lazily. Following the path that ran around to the back porch, Nils stopped to look through the screen door into the lamplit kitchen. The kitchen was the largest room in the house; Nils remembered that his older brothers used to give dances there when he was a boy. Beside the stove stood a little girl with two light yellow braids and a broad, flushed face, peering anxiously into a frying pan. In the dining room beyond, a large, broad-shouldered woman was moving about the table. She walked with an active, springy step. Her face was heavy and florid, almost without wrinkles, and her hair was black at seventy. Nils felt proud of her as he watched her deliberate activity; never a momentary hesitation, or a movement that did not tell. He waited until she came out into the kitchen and, brushing the child aside, took her place at the stove. Then he tapped on the screen door and entered.

"It's nobody but Nils, Mother. I expect you weren't looking for me."

Mrs. Ericson turned away from the stove and stood staring at him. "Bring the lamp, Hilda, and let me look."

Nils laughed and unslung his valise. "What's the matter, Mother? Don't you know me?"

Mrs. Ericson put down the lamp. "You must be Nils. You don't look very different, anyway."

"Nor you, Mother. You hold your own. Don't you wear glasses yet?"

"Only to read by. Where's your trunk, Nils?"

"Oh, I left that in town. I thought it might not be convenient for you to have company so near threshing-time."

"Don't be foolish, Nils." Mrs. Ericson turned back to the stove. "I don't thresh now. I hitched the wheat land onto the next farm and have a tenant. Hilda, take some hot water up to the company room, and go call little Eric."

[7]

The tow-haired child, who had been standing in mute amazement, took up the tea kettle and withdrew, giving Nils a long, admiring look from the door of the kitchen stairs.

"Who's the youngster?" Nils asked, dropping down on the bench behind the kitchen stove.

"One of your Cousin Henrik's."

"How long has Cousin Henrik been dead?"

"Six years. There are two boys. One stays with Peter and one with Anders. Olaf is their guardeen."

There was a clatter of pails on the porch, and a tall, lanky boy peered wonderingly in through the screen door. He had a fair, gentle face and big gray eyes, and wisps of soft yellow hair hung down under his cap. Nils sprang up and pulled him into the kitchen, hugging him and slapping him on the shoulders. "Well, if it isn't my kid! Look at the size of him! Don't you know me, Eric?"

The boy reddened under his sunburn and freckles, and hung his head. "I guess it's Nils," he said shyly.

"You're a good guesser," laughed Nils giving the lad's hand a swing. To himself he was thinking: "That's why the little girl looked so friendly. He's taught her to like me. He was only six when I went away, and he's remembered for twelve years."

Eric stood fumbling with his cap and smiling. "You look just like I thought you would," he ventured.

"Go wash your hands, Eric," called Mrs. Ericson. "I've got cob corn for supper, Nils. You used to like it. I guess you don't get much of that in the old country. Here's Hilda; she'll take you up to your room. You'll want to get the dust off you before you eat."

Mrs. Ericson went into the dining room to lay another plate, and the little girl came up and nodded to Nils as if to let him know that his room was ready. He put out his hand and she took it, with a startled glance up at his face. Little Eric dropped his towel, threw an arm about Nils and one about Hilda, gave them a clumsy squeeze, and then stumbled out to the porch.

During supper Nils heard exactly how much land each of his eight grown brothers farmed, how their crops were coming on, and how much live stock they were feeding. His mother watched him narrowly as she talked. "You've got better looking, Nils," she remarked abruptly, whereupon he grinned and the children giggled. Eric, although he was eighteen and as tall as Nils, was always accounted a child, being the last of so many sons. His face seemed childlike, too, Nils thought, and he had the open, wandering eyes of a little boy. All the others had been men at his age.

After supper Nils went out to the front porch and sat down on the step to smoke a pipe. Mrs. Ericson drew a rocking chair up near him and began to knit busily. It was one of the few Old World customs she had kept up, for she could not bear to sit with idle hands.

"Where's little Eric, Mother?"

"He's helping Hilda with the dishes. He does it of his own will; I don't like a boy to be too handy about the house."

"He seems like a nice kid."

"He's very obedient."

Nils smiled a little in the dark. It was just as well to shift the line of conversation. "What are you knitting there, Mother?"

"Baby stockings. The boys keep me busy." Mrs. Ericson chuckled and clicked her needles.

"How many grandchildren have you?"

"Only thirty-one now. Olaf lost his three. They were sickly, like their mother."

"I supposed he had a second crop by this time!"

"His second wife has no children. She's too proud. She tears about on horseback all the time. But she'll get caught up with, yet. She sets herself very high, though nobody knows what for. They were low enough Bohemians she came of. I never thought much of Bohemians; always drinking."

Nils puffed away at his pipe in silence, and Mrs. Ericson knitted on. In a few moments she added grimly: "She was down here tonight, just before you came. She'd like to quarrel with me and come between me and Olaf, but I don't give her the chance. I suppose you'll be bringing a wife home some day."

"I don't know. I've never thought much about it."

"Well, perhaps it's best as it is," suggested Mrs. Ericson hopefully. "You'd never be contented tied down to the land. There was roving blood in your father's family, and it's come out in you. I expect your own way of life suits you best." Mrs. Ericson had dropped into a blandly agreeable tone which Nils well remembered. It seemed to amuse him a good deal and his white teeth flashed behind his pipe. His mother's strategies had always diverted him, even when he was a boy—they were so flimsy and patent, so illy proportioned to her vigor and force. "They've been waiting to see which way I'd jump," he reflected. He felt that Mrs. Ericson was pondering his case deeply as she sat clicking her needles.

"I don't suppose you've ever got used to steady work," she went on presently. "Men ain't apt to if they roam around too long. It's a pity you didn't come back the year after the World's Fair. Your father picked up a good bit of land cheap then, in the hard times, and I expect maybe he'd have give you a farm. It's too bad you put off comin' back so long, for I always thought he meant to do something by you."

Nils laughed and shook the ashes out of his pipe. "I'd have missed a lot if I had come back then. But I'm sorry I didn't get back to see father."

"Well, I suppose we have to miss things at one end or the other. Perhaps you are as well satisfied with your own doings, now, as you'd have been with a farm," said Mrs. Ericson reassuringly.

"Land's a good thing to have," Nils commented, as he lit another match and sheltered it with his hand.

His mother looked sharply at his face until the match burned out. "Only when you stay on it!" she hastened to say.

Eric came round the house by the path just then, and Nils rose, with a yawn. "Mother, if you don't mind, Eric and I will take a little tramp before bedtime. It will make me sleep."

"Very well; only don't stay long. I'll sit up and wait for you. I like to lock up myself."

Nils put his hand on Eric's shoulder, and the two tramped down the hill and across the sand creek into the dusty highroad beyond. Neither spoke. They swung along at an even gait, Nils puffing at his pipe. There was no moon, and the white road and the wide fields lay faint in the starlight. Over everything was darkness and thick silence, and the smell of dust and sunflowers. The brothers followed the road for a mile or more without finding a place to sit down. Finally, Nils perched on a stile over the wire fence, and Eric sat on the lower step.

"I began to think you never would come back, Nils," said the boy softly.

"Didn't I promise you I would?"

"Yes; but people don't bother about promises they make to babies. Did you really know you were going away for good when you went to Chicago with the cattle that time?"

"I thought it very likely, if I could make my way."

"I don't see how you did it, Nils. Not many fellows could." Eric rubbed his shoulder against his brother's knee.

"The hard thing was leaving home—you and father. It was easy enough, once I got beyond Chicago. Of course I got awful homesick; used to cry myself to sleep. But I'd burned my bridges."

"You had always wanted to go, hadn't you?"

"Always. Do you still sleep in our little room? Is that cottonwood still by the window?"

Eric nodded eagerly and smiled up at his brother in the gray darkness.

"You remember how we always said the leaves were whispering when they rustled at night? Well, they always whispered to me about the sea. Sometimes they said names out of the geography books. In a high wind they had a desperate sound, like something trying to tear loose."

"How funny, Nils," said Eric dreamily, resting his chin on his hand. "That tree still talks like that, and 'most always it talks to me about you."

They sat a while longer, watching the stars. At last Eric whispered anxiously: "Hadn't we better go back now? Mother will get tired waiting for us." They rose and took a short cut home, through the pasture.

II

The next morning Nils woke with the first flood of light that came with dawn. The white-plastered walls of his room reflected the glare that shone through the thin window shades, and he found it impossible to sleep. He dressed hurriedly and slipped down the hall and up the back stairs to the half-story room which he used to share with his little brother. Eric, in a skimpy nightshirt, was sitting on the edge of the bed, rubbing his eyes, his pale yellow hair standing up in tufts all over his head. When he saw Nils, he murmured something confusedly and hustled his long legs into his trousers. "I didn't expect you'd be up so early, Nils," he said, as his head emerged from his blue shirt.

"Oh, you thought I was a dude, did you?" Nils gave him a playful tap which bent the tall boy up like a clasp knife. "See here; I must teach you to box." Nils thrust his hands into his pockets and walked about. "You haven't changed things much up here. Got most of my old traps, haven't you?"

He took down a bent, withered piece of sapling that hung over the dresser. "If this isn't the stick Lou Sandberg killed himself with!"

The boy looked up from his shoe-lacing.

"Yes; you never used to let me play with that. Just how did he do it, Nils? You were with father when he found Lou, weren't you?"

"Yes. Father was going off to preach somewhere, and, as we drove along, Lou's place looked sort of forlorn, and we thought we'd stop and cheer him up. When we found him father said he'd been dead a couple days. He'd tied a piece of binding twine round his neck, made a noose in each end, fixed the nooses over the ends of a bent stick, and let the stick spring straight; strangled himself."·

"What made him kill himself such a silly way?"

The simplicity of the boy's question set Nils laughing. He clapped little Eric on the shoulder. "What made him such a silly as to kill himself at all, I should say!"

"Oh, well! But his hogs had the cholera, and all up and died on him, didn't they?"

"Sure they did; but he didn't have cholera; and there were plenty of hogs left in the world, weren't there?"

"Well, but, if they weren't his, how could they do him any good?" Eric asked, in astonishment.

"Oh, scat! He could have had lots of fun with other people's hogs. He was a chump, Lou Sandberg. To kill yourself for a pig—think of that, now!" Nils laughed all the way downstairs, and quite embarrassed little Eric, who fell to scrubbing his face and hands at the tin basin. While he was parting his wet hair at the kitchen looking glass, a heavy tread sounded on the stairs. The boy dropped his comb. "Gracious, there's Mother. We must have talked too long." He hurried out to the shed, slipped on his overalls, and disappeared with the milking pails.

Mrs. Ericson came in, wearing a clean white apron, her black hair shining from the application of a wet brush.

"Good morning, Mother. Can't I make the fire for you?"

"No, thank you, Nils. It's no trouble to make a cob fire, and I like to manage the kitchen stove myself." Mrs. Ericson paused with a shovel full of ashes in her hand. "I expect you will be wanting to see your brothers as soon as possible. I'll take you up to Anders' place this morning. He's threshing, and most of our boys are over there."

"Will Olaf be there?"

Mrs. Ericson went on taking out the ashes, and spoke between shovels. "No; Olaf's wheat is all in, put away in his new barn. He got six thousand bushel this year. He's going to town today to get men to finish roofing his barn."

"So Olaf is building a new barn?" Nils asked absently.

"Biggest one in the county, and almost done. You'll likely be here for the barn-raising. He's going to have a supper and a dance as soon as everybody's done threshing. Says it keeps the voters in a good humor. I tell him that's all nonsense; but Olaf has a long head for politics."

"Does Olaf farm all Cousin Henrik's land?"

Mrs. Ericson frowned as she blew into the faint smoke curling up about the cobs. "Yes; he holds it in trust for the children, Hilda and her brothers. He keeps strict account of everything he raises on it, and puts the proceeds out at compound interest for them."

Nils smiled as he watched the little flames shoot up. The door of the back stairs opened, and Hilda emerged, her arms behind her, buttoning up her long gingham apron as she came. He nodded to her gaily, and she twinkled at him out of her little blue eyes, set far apart over her wide cheekbones.

"There, Hilda, you grind the coffee—and just put in an extra handful; I expect your Cousin Nils likes his strong," said Mrs. Ericson, as she went out to the shed.

Nils turned to look at the little girl, who gripped the coffee grinder between her knees and ground so hard that her two braids bobbed and her face flushed under its broad spattering of freckles. He noticed on her middle finger something that had not been there last night, and that had evidently been put on for company: a tiny gold ring with a clumsily set garnet stone. As her hand went round and round he touched the ring with the tip of his finger, smiling.

Hilda glanced toward the shed door through which Mrs. Ericson had disappeared. "My Cousin Clara gave me that," she whispered bashfully. "She's Cousin Olaf's wife."

III

Mrs. Olaf Ericson—Clara Vavrika, as many people still called her—was moving restlessly about her big bare house that morning. Her husband had left for the county town before his wife was out of bed—her lateness in rising was one of the many things the Ericson family had against her. Clara seldom came downstairs before eight o'clock, and this morning she was even later, for she had dressed with unusual care. She put on, however, only a tight-fitting black dress, which people thereabouts thought very plain. She was a tall, dark woman of thirty, with a rather sallow complexion and a touch of dull salmon red in her cheeks, where the blood seemed to burn under her brown skin. Her hair, parted evenly above her low forehead, was so black that there were distinctly blue lights in it. Her black eyebrows were delicate half-moons and her lashes were long and heavy. Her eyes slanted a little, as if she had a strain of Tartar or gypsy blood, and were sometimes full of fiery determination and sometimes dull and opaque. Her expression was never altogether amiable; was often, indeed, distinctly sullen, or, when she was animated, sarcastic. She was most attractive in profile, for then one saw to advantage her small, well-shaped head and delicate ears, and felt at once that here was a very positive, if not an altogether pleasing, personality.

The entire management of Mrs. Olaf's household devolved upon her aunt, Johanna Vavrika, a superstitious, doting woman of fifty. When Clara was a little girl her mother died, and Johanna's life had been spent in ungrudging service to her niece. Clara, like many self-willed and discontented persons, was really very apt, without knowing it, to do as other people told her, and to let her destiny be decided for her by intelligences much below her own. It was her Aunt Johanna who had humored and spoiled her in her girlhood, who had got her off to Chicago to study piano, and who had finally persuaded her to marry Olaf Ericson as the best match she would be likely to make in that part of the country. Johanna Vavrika had been deeply scarred by smallpox in the old country. She was short and fat, homely and jolly and sentimental. She was so broad, and took such short steps when she walked, that her brother, Joe Vavrika, always called her his duck. She adored her niece because of her talent, because of her good looks and masterful ways, but most of all because of her selfishness.

Clara's marriage with Olaf Ericson was Johanna's particular triumph. She was inordinately proud of Olaf's position, and she found a sufficiently exciting career in managing Clara's house, in keeping it above the criticism of the Ericsons, in pampering Olaf to keep him from finding fault with his wife, and in concealing from every one Clara's domestic infelicities. While Clara slept of a morning, Johanna Vavrika was bustling about, seeing that Olaf and the men had their breakfast, and that the cleaning or the butter-making or the washing was properly begun by the two girls in the kitchen. Then, at about eight o'clock, she would take Clara's coffee up to her, and chat with her while she drank it, telling her what was going on in the house. Old Mrs. Ericson frequently said that her daughter-in-law would not know what day of the week it was if Johanna did not tell her every morning. Mrs. Ericson despised and pitied Johanna, but did not wholly dislike her. The one thing she hated in her daughter-in-law above everything else was the way in which Clara could come it over people. It enraged her that the affairs of her son's big, barnlike house went on as well as they did, and she used to feel that in this world we have to wait overlong to see the guilty punished. "Suppose Johanna Vavrika died or got sick?" the old lady used to say to Olaf. "Your wife wouldn't know where to look for her own dishcloth." Olaf only shrugged his shoulders. The fact remained that Johanna did not die, and, although Mrs. Ericson often told her she was looking poorly, she was never ill. She seldom left the house, and she slept in a little room off the kitchen. No Ericson, by night or day, could come prying about there to find fault without her knowing it. Her one weakness was that she was an incurable talker, and she sometimes made trouble without meaning to.

This morning Clara was tying a wine-colored ribbon about her throat when Johanna appeared with her coffee. After putting the tray on a sewing table, she began to make Clara's bed, chattering the while in Bohemian.

"Well, Olaf got off early, and the girls are baking. I'm going down presently to make some poppy-seed bread for Olaf. He asked for prune preserves at breakfast, and I told him I was out of them, and to bring some prunes and honey and cloves from town."

Clara poured her coffee. "Ugh! I don't see how men can eat so much sweet stuff. In the morning, too!"

Her aunt chuckled knowingly. "Bait a bear with honey, as we say in the old country."

"Was he cross?" her niece asked indifferently.

"Olaf? Oh, no! He was in fine spirits. He's never cross if you know how to take him. I never knew a man to make so little fuss about bills. I gave him a list of things to get a yard long, and he didn't say a word; just folded it up and put it in his pocket."

"I can well believe he didn't say a word," Clara remarked with a shrug. "Some day he'll forget how to talk."

"Oh, but they say he's a grand speaker in the Legislature. He knows when to keep quiet. That's why he's got such influence in politics. The people have confidence in him." Johanna beat up a pillow and held it under her fat chin while she slipped on the case. Her niece laughed.

"Maybe we could make people believe we were wise, Aunty, if we held our tongues. Why did you tell Mrs. Ericson that Norman threw me again last Saturday and turned my foot? She's been talking to Olaf."

[15]

Johanna fell into great confusion. "Oh, but, my precious, the old lady asked for you, and she's always so angry if I can't give an excuse. Anyhow, she needn't talk; she's always tearing up something with that motor of hers."

When her aunt clattered down to the kitchen, Clara went to dust the parlor. Since there was not much there to dust, this did not take very long. Olaf had built the house new for her before their marriage, but her interest in furnishing it had been short-lived. It went, indeed, little beyond a bathtub and her piano. They had disagreed about almost every other article of furniture, and Clara had said she would rather have her house empty than full of things she didn't want. The house was set in a hillside, and the west windows of the parlor looked out above the kitchen yard thirty feet below. The east windows opened directly into the front yard. At one of the latter, Clara, while she was dusting, heard a low whistle. She did not turn at once, but listened intently as she drew her cloth slowly along the round of a chair. Yes, there it was:

I dreamt that I dwelt in ma-a-arble halls.

She turned and saw Nils Ericson laughing in the sunlight, his hat in his hand, just outside the window. As she crossed the room he leaned against the wire screen. "Aren't you at all surprised to see me, Clara Vavrika?"

"No; I was expecting to see you. Mother Ericson telephoned Olaf last night that you were here."

Nils squinted and gave a long whistle. "Telephoned? That must have been while Eric and I were out walking. Isn't she enterprising? Lift this screen, won't you?"

Clara lifted the screen, and Nils swung his leg across the window sill. As he stepped into the room she said: "You didn't think you were going to get ahead of your mother, did you?"

He threw his hat on the piano. "Oh, I do sometimes. You see, I'm ahead of her now. I'm supposed to be in Anders' wheat field. But, as we were leaving, Mother ran her car into a soft place beside the road and sank up to the hubs. While they were going for horses to pull her out, I cut away behind the stacks and escaped." Nils chuckled. Clara's dull eyes lit up as she looked at him admiringly.

"You've got them guessing already. I don't know what your mother said to Olaf over the telephone, but he came back looking as if he'd seen a ghost, and he didn't go to bed until a dreadful hour—ten o'clock, I should think. He sat out on the porch in the dark like a graven image.

It had been one of his talkative days, too." They both laughed, easily and lightly, like people who have laughed a great deal together; but they remained standing.

"Anders and Otto and Peter looked as if they had seen ghosts, too, over in the threshing field. What's the matter with them all?"

Clara gave him a quick, searching look. "Well, for one thing, they've always been afraid you have the other will."

Nils looked interested. "The other will?"

"Yes. A later one. They knew your father made another, but they never knew what he did with it. They almost tore the old house to pieces looking for it. They always suspected that he carried on a clandestine correspondence with you, for the one thing he would do was to get his own mail himself. So they thought he might have sent the new will to you for safekeeping. The old one, leaving everything to your mother, was made long before you went away, and it's understood among them that it cuts you out—that she will leave all the property to the others. Your father made the second will to prevent that. I've been hoping you had it. It would be such fun to spring it on them." Clara laughed mirthfully, a thing she did not often do now.

Nils shook his head reprovingly. "Come, now, you're malicious."

"No, I'm not. But I'd like something to happen to stir them all up, just for once. There never was such a family for having nothing ever happen to them but dinner and threshing. I'd almost be willing to die, just to have a funeral. *You* wouldn't stand it for three weeks."

Nils bent over the piano and began pecking at the keys with the finger of one hand. "I wouldn't? My dear young lady, how do you know what I can stand? *You* wouldn't wait to find out."

Clara flushed darkly and frowned. "I didn't believe you would ever come back—" she said defiantly.

"Eric believed I would, and he was only a baby when I went away. However, all's well that ends well, and I haven't come back to be a skeleton at the feast. We mustn't quarrel. Mother will be here with a search warrant pretty soon." He swung round and faced her, thrusting his hands into his coat pockets. "Come, you ought to be glad to see me, if you want something to happen. I'm something, even without a will. We can have a little fun, can't we? I think we can!"

She echoed him, "I think we can!" They both laughed and their eyes sparkled. Clara Vavrika looked ten years younger than when she had put the velvet ribbon about her throat that morning.

[17]

"You know, I'm so tickled to see mother," Nils went on. "I didn't know I was so proud of her. A regular pile driver. How about little pigtails, down at the house? Is Olaf doing the square thing by those children?"

Clara frowned pensively. "Olaf has to do something that looks like the square thing, now that he's a public man!" She glanced drolly at Nils. "But he makes a good commission out of it. On Sundays they all get together here and figure. He lets Peter and Anders put in big bills for the keep of the two boys, and he pays them out of the estate. They are always having what they call accountings. Olaf gets something out of it, too. I don't know just how they do it, but it's entirely a family matter, as they say. And when the Ericsons say that—" Clara lifted her eyebrows.

Just then the angry *honk-honk* of an approaching motor sounded from down the road. Their eyes met and they began to laugh. They laughed as children do when they can not contain themselves, and can not explain the cause of their mirth to grown people, but share it perfectly together. When Clara Vavrika sat down at the piano after he was gone, she felt that she had laughed away a dozen years. She practised as if the house were burning over her head.

When Nils greeted his mother and climbed into the front seat of the motor beside her, Mrs. Ericson looked grim, but she made no comment upon his truancy until she had turned her car and was retracing her revolutions along the road that ran by Olaf's big pasture. Then she remarked dryly:

"If I were you I wouldn't see too much of Olaf's wife while you are here. She's the kind of woman who can't see much of men without getting herself talked about. She was a good deal talked about before he married her."

"Hasn't Olaf tamed her?" Nils asked indifferently.

Mrs. Ericson shrugged her massive shoulders. "Olaf don't seem to have much luck, when it comes to wives. The first one was meek enough, but she was always ailing. And this one has her own way. He says if he quarreled with her she'd go back to her father, and then he'd lose the Bohemian vote. There are a great many Bohunks in this district. But when you find a man under his wife's thumb you can always be sure there's a soft spot in him somewhere."

Nils thought of his own father, and smiled. "She brought him a good deal of money, didn't she, besides the Bohemian vote?"

Mrs. Ericson sniffed. "Well, she has a fair half section in her own name, but I can't see as that does Olaf much good. She will have a good deal of property some day, if old Vavrika don't marry again. But I don't consider a saloonkeeper's money as good as other people's money."

Nils laughed outright. "Come, Mother, don't let your prejudices carry you that far. Money's money. Old Vavrika's a mighty decent sort of saloonkeeper. Nothing rowdy about him."

Mrs. Ericson spoke up angrily: "Oh, I know you always stood up for them! But hanging around there when you were a boy never did you any good, Nils, nor any of the other boys who went there. There weren't so many after her when she married Olaf, let me tell you. She knew enough to grab her chance."

Nils settled back in his seat. "Of course I liked to go there, Mother, and you were always cross about it. You never took the trouble to find out that it was the one jolly house in this country for a boy to go to. All the rest of you were working yourselves to death, and the houses were mostly a mess, full of babies and washing and flies. Oh, it was all right—I understand that; but you are young only once, and I happened to be young then. Now, Vavrika's was always jolly. He played the violin, and I used to take my flute, and Clara played the piano, and Johanna used to sing Bohemian songs. She always had a big supper for us—herrings and pickles and poppy-seed bread, and lots of cake and preserves. Old Joe had been in the army in the old country, and he could tell lots of good stories. I can see him cutting bread, at the head of the table, now. I don't know what I'd have done when I was a kid if it hadn't been for the Vavrikas, really."

"And all the time he was taking money that other people had worked hard in the fields for," Mrs. Ericson observed.

"So do the circuses, Mother, and they're a good thing. People ought to get fun for some of their money. Even father liked old Joe."

"Your father," Mrs. Ericson said grimly, "liked everybody."

As they crossed the sand creek and turned into her own place, Mrs. Ericson observed, "There's Olaf's buggy. He's stopped on his way from town." Nils shook himself and prepared to greet his brother, who was waiting on the porch.

Olaf was a big, heavy Norwegian, slow of speech and movement. His head was large and square, like a block of wood. When Nils, at a distance, tried to remember what his brother looked like, he could recall only his heavy head, high forehead, large nostrils, and pale blue eyes, set far apart. Olaf's features were rudimentary: the thing one noticed was the face itself, wide and flat and pale, devoid of any expression, betraying his fifty years as little as it betrayed anything else, and powerful by reason of its very stolidness. When Olaf shook hands with Nils he looked at him from under his light eyebrows, but Nils felt that no one could ever say what that pale look might mean. The one thing he had always felt in Olaf was a heavy stubbornness, like the unyielding stickiness of wet loam against the plow. He had always found Olaf the most difficult of his brothers.

"How do you do, Nils? Expect to stay with us long?"

"Oh, I may stay forever," Nils answered gaily. "I like this country better than I used to."

"There's been some work put into it since you left," Olaf remarked.

"Exactly. I think it's about ready to live in now—and I'm about ready to settle down." Nils saw his brother lower his big head. ("Exactly like a bull," he thought.) "Mother's been persuading me to slow down now, and go in for farming," he went on lightly.

Olaf made a deep sound in his throat. "Farming ain't learned in a day," he brought out, still looking at the ground.

"Oh, I know! But I pick things up quickly." Nils had not meant to antagonize his brother, and he did not know now why he was doing it. "Of course," he went on, "I shouldn't expect to make a big success, as you fellows have done. But then, I'm not ambitious. I won't want much. A little land, and some cattle, maybe."

Olaf still stared at the ground, his head down. He wanted to ask Nils what he had been doing all these years, that he didn't have a business somewhere he couldn't afford to leave; why he hadn't more pride than to come back with only a little sole-leather trunk to show for himself, and to present himself as the only failure in the family. He did not ask one of these questions, but he made them all felt distinctly.

"Humph!" Nils thought. "No wonder the man never talks, when he can butt his ideas into you like that without ever saying a word. I suppose he uses that kind of smokeless powder on his wife all the time. But I guess she has her innings." He chuckled, and Olaf looked up. "Never mind me, Olaf. I laugh without knowing why, like little Eric. He's another cheerful dog."

"Eric," said Olaf slowly, "is a spoiled kid. He's just let his mother's best cow go dry because he don't milk her right. I was hoping you'd take him away somewhere and put him into business. If he don't do any good among strangers, he never will." This was a long speech for Olaf, and as he finished it he climbed into his buggy.

Nils shrugged his shoulders. "Same old tricks," he thought. "Hits from behind you every time. What a whale of a man!" He turned and went round to the kitchen, where his mother was scolding little Eric for letting the gasoline get low.

IV

Joe Vavrika's saloon was not in the county seat, where Olaf and Mrs. Ericson did their trading, but in a cheerfuller place, a little Bohemian settlement which lay at the other end of the county, ten level miles north of Olaf's farm. Clara rode up to see her father almost every day. Vavrika's house was, so to speak, in the back yard of his saloon. The garden between the two buildings was inclosed by a high board fence as tight as a partition, and in summer Joe kept beer tables and wooden benches among the gooseberry bushes under his little cherry tree. At one of these tables Nils Ericson was seated in the late afternoon, three days after his return home. Joe had gone in to serve a customer, and Nils was lounging on his elbows, looking rather mournfully into his half-emptied pitcher, when he heard a laugh across the little garden. Clara, in her riding habit, was standing at the back door of the house, under the grapevine trellis that old Joe had grown there long ago. Nils rose.

"Come out and keep your father and me company. We've been gossiping all afternoon. Nobody to bother us but the flies."

She shook her head. "No, I never come out here any more. Olaf doesn't like it. I must live up to my position, you know."

"You mean to tell me you never come out and chat with the boys, as you used to? He *has* tamed you! Who keeps up these flower beds?"

"I come out on Sundays, when father is alone, and read the Bohemian papers to him. But I am never here when the bar is open. What have you two been doing?"

"Talking, as I told you. I've been telling him about my travels. I find I can't talk much at home, not even to Eric."

Clara reached up and poked with her riding-whip at a white moth that was fluttering in the sunlight among the vine leaves. "I suppose you will never tell me about all those things."

"Where can I tell them? Not in Olaf's house, certainly. What's the matter with our talking here?" He pointed persuasively with his hat to the bushes and the green table, where the flies were singing lazily above the empty beer glasses.

Clara shook her head weakly. "No, it wouldn't do. Besides, I am going now."

"I'm on Eric's mare. Would you be angry if I overtook you?"

Clara looked back and laughed. "You might try and see. I can leave you if I don't want you. Eric's mare can't keep up with Norman."

Nils went into the bar and attempted to pay his score. Big Joe, six feet four, with curly yellow hair and mustache, clapped him on the shoulder. "Not a God-damn a your money go in my drawer, you hear? Only next time you bring your flute, te-te-te-te-te-ty." Joe wagged his fingers in imitation of the flute player's position. "My Clara, she come all-a-time Sundays an' play for me. She not like to play at Ericson's place." He shook his yellow curls and laughed. "Not a God-damn a fun at Ericson's. You come a Sunday. You like-a fun. No forget de flute." Joe talked very rapidly and always tumbled over his English. He seldom spoke it to his customers, and had never learned much.

Nils swung himself into the saddle and trotted to the west end of the village, where the houses and gardens scattered into prairie land and the road turned south. Far ahead of him, in the declining light, he saw Clara Vavrika's slender figure, loitering on horseback. He touched his mare with the whip, and shot along the white, level road, under the reddening sky. When he overtook Olaf's wife he saw that she had been crying. "What's the matter, Clara Vavrika?" he asked kindly.

"Oh, I get blue sometimes. It was awfully jolly living there with father. I wonder why I ever went away."

Nils spoke in a low, kind tone that he sometimes used with women: "That's what I've been wondering these many years. You were the last girl in the country I'd have picked for a wife for Olaf. What made you do it, Clara?"

"I suppose I really did it to oblige the neighbors"—Clara tossed her head. "People were beginning to wonder."

"To wonder?"

"Yes—why I didn't get married. I suppose I didn't like to keep them in suspense. I've discovered that most girls marry out of consideration for the neighborhood."

Nils bent his head toward her and his white teeth flashed. "I'd have gambled that one girl I knew would say, 'Let the neighborhood be damned.'"

Clara shook her head mournfully. "You see, they have it on you, Nils; that is, if you're a woman. They say you're beginning to go off. That's what makes us get married: we can't stand the laugh."

Nils looked sidewise at her. He had never seen her head droop before. Resignation was the last thing he would have expected of her. "In your case, there wasn't something else?"

"Something else?"

"I mean, you didn't do it to spite somebody? Somebody who didn't come back?"

Clara drew herself up. "Oh, I never thought you'd come back. Not after I stopped writing to you, at least. *That* was all over, long before I married Olaf."

"It never occurred to you, then, that the meanest thing you could do to me was to marry Olaf?"

Clara laughed. "No; I didn't know you were so fond of Olaf."

Nils smoothed his horse's mane with his glove. "You know, Clara Vavrika, you are never going to stick it out. You'll cut away some day, and I've been thinking you might as well cut away with me."

Clara threw up her chin. "Oh, you don't know me as well as you think. I won't cut away. Sometimes, when I'm with father, I feel like it. But I can hold out as long as the Ericsons can. They've never got the best of me yet, and one can live, so long as one isn't beaten. If I go back to father, it's all up with Olaf in politics. He knows that, and he never goes much beyond sulking. I've as much wit as the Ericsons. I'll never leave them unless I can show them a thing or two."

"You mean unless you can come it over them?"

"Yes—unless I go away with a man who is cleverer than they are, and who has more money."

Nils whistled. "Dear me, you are demanding a good deal. The Ericsons, take the lot of them, are a bunch to beat. But I should think the excitement of tormenting them would have worn off by this time."

"It has, I'm afraid," Clara admitted mournfully.

"Then why don't you cut away? There are more amusing games than this in the world. When I came home I thought it might amuse me to bully a few quarter sections out of the Ericsons; but I've almost decided I can get more fun for my money somewhere else."

Clara took in her breath sharply. "Ah, you have got the other will! That was why you came home!"

"No, it wasn't. I came home to see how you were getting on with Olaf."

Clara struck her horse with the whip, and in a bound she was far ahead of him. Nils dropped one word, "Damn!" and whipped after her; but she leaned forward in her saddle and fairly cut the wind. Her long riding skirt rippled in the still air behind her. The sun was just sinking behind the stubble in a vast, clear sky, and the shadows drew across the fields so rapidly that Nils could scarcely keep in sight the dark figure on the road. When he overtook her he caught her horse by the bridle. Norman reared, and Nils was frightened for her; but Clara kept her seat.

"Let me go, Nils Ericson!" she cried. "I hate you more than any of them. You were created to torture me, the whole tribe of you—to make me suffer in every possible way."

She struck her horse again and galloped away from him. Nils set his teeth and looked thoughtful. He rode slowly home along the deserted road, watching the stars come out in the clear violet sky. They flashed softly into the limpid heavens, like jewels let fall into clear water. They were a reproach, he felt, to a sordid world. As he turned across the sand creek, he looked up at the North Star and smiled, as if there were an understanding between them. His mother scolded him for being late for supper.

V

On Sunday afternoon Joe Vavrika, in his shirtsleeves and carpet slippers, was sitting in his garden, smoking a long-tasseled porcelain pipe with a hunting scene painted on the bowl. Clara sat under the cherry tree, reading aloud to him from the weekly Bohemian papers. She had worn a white muslin dress under her riding habit, and the leaves of the cherry tree threw a pattern of sharp shadows over her skirt. The black cat was dozing in the sunlight at her feet, and Joe's dachshund was scratching a hole under the scarlet geraniums and dreaming of badgers. Joe was filling his pipe for the third time since dinner, when he heard a knocking on the fence. He broke into a loud guffaw and unlatched the little door that led into the street. He did not call Nils by name, but caught him by the hand and dragged him in. Clara stiffened and the color deepened under her dark skin. Nils, too, felt a little awkward. He had not seen her since the night when she rode away from him and left him alone on the level road between the fields. Joe dragged him to the wooden bench beside the green table.

"You bring de flute," he cried, tapping the leather case under Nils' arm. "Ah, das-a good! Now we have some liddle fun like old times. I got somet'ing good for you." Joe shook his finger at Nils and winked his blue eye, a bright clear eye, full of fire, though the tiny bloodvessels on the ball were always a little distended. "I got somet'ing for you from"—he paused and waved his hand— "Hongarie. You know Hongarie? You wait!" He pushed Nils down on the bench, and went through the back door of his saloon.

Nils looked at Clara, who sat frigidly with her white skirts drawn tight about her. "He didn't tell you he had asked me to come, did he? He wanted a party and proceeded to arrange it. Isn't he fun? Don't be cross; let's give him a good time."

Clara smiled and shook out her skirt. "Isn't that like father? And he has sat here so meekly all day. Well, I won't pout. I'm glad you came. He doesn't have very many good times now any more. There are so few of his kind left. The second generation are a tame lot."

Joe came back with a flask in one hand and three wine glasses caught by the stems between the fingers of the other. These he placed on the table with an air of ceremony, and, going behind Nils, held the flask between him and the sun, squinting into it admiringly. "You know dis, Tokai? A great friend of mine, he bring dis to me, a present out of Hongarie. You know how much it cost, dis wine? Chust so much what it weigh in gold. Nobody but de nobles drink him in Bohemie. Many, many years I save him up, dis Tokai." Joe whipped out his official corkscrew and delicately removed the cork. "De old man die what bring him to me, an' dis wine he lay on his belly in my cellar an' sleep. An' now," carefully pouring out the heavy yellow wine, "an' now he wake up; and maybe he wake us up, too!" He carried one of the glasses to his daughter and presented it with great gallantry.

Clara shook her head, but, seeing her father's disappointment, relented. "You taste it first. I don't want so much."

Joe sampled it with a beatific expression, and turned to Nils. "You drink him slow, dis wine. He very soft, but he go down hot. You see!"

After a second glass Nils declared that he couldn't take any more without getting sleepy. "Now get your fiddle, Vavrika," he said as he opened his flute case.

But Joe settled back in his wooden rocker and wagged his big carpet slipper. "No-no-no-no-no-no-no! No play fiddle now any more: too much ache in de finger," waving them, "all-a-time rheumatiz. You play de flute, te-tety-te-tety-te. Bohemie songs."

"I've forgotten all the Bohemian songs I used to play with you and Johanna. But here's one that will make Clara pout. You remember how her eyes used to snap when we called her the Bohemian Girl?" Nils lifted his flute and began "When Other Lips and Other Hearts," and Joe hummed the air in a husky baritone, waving his carpet slipper. "Oh-h-h, das-a fine music," he cried, clapping his hands as Nils finished. "Now 'Marble Halls, Marble Halls'! Clara, you sing him."

Clara smiled and leaned back in her chair, beginning softly:

> "I dreamt that I dwelt in ma-a-arble halls,
>   With vassals and serfs at my knee,"

and Joe hummed like a big bumblebee.

"There's one more you always played," Clara said quietly; "I remember that best." She locked her hands over her knee and began "The Heart Bowed Down," and sang it through without groping for the words. She was singing with a good deal of warmth when she came to the end of the old song:

> For memory is the only friend
>   That grief can call its own.

Joe flashed out his red silk handkerchief and blew his nose, shaking his head. "No-no-no-no-no-no-no! Too sad, too sad! I not like-a dat. Play quick somet'ing gay now."

Nils put his lips to the instrument, and Joe lay back in his chair, laughing and singing, "Oh, Evelina, Sweet Evelina!" Clara laughed, too. Long ago, when she and Nils went to high school, the model student of their class was a very homely girl in thick spectacles. Her name was Evelina Oleson; she had a long, swinging walk which somehow suggested the measure of that song, and they used mercilessly to sing it at her.

"Dat ugly Oleson girl, she teach in de school," Joe gasped, "an' she still walk chust like dat, yup-a, yup-a, yup-a, chust like a camel she go! Now, Nils, we have some more li'l drink. Oh, yes-yes-yes-yes-yes-yes-yes! Dis time you haf to drink, and Clara she haf to, so she show she not jealous. So, we all drink to your girl. You not tell her name, eh? No-no-no, I no make you tell. She pretty, eh? She make good sweetheart? I bet!" Joe winked and lifted his glass. "How soon you get married?"

Nils screwed up his eyes. "That I don't know. When she says."

Joe threw out his chest. "Das-a way boys talks. No way for mans. Mans say, 'You come to de church, an' get a hurry on you.' Das-a way mans talks."

"Maybe Nils hasn't got enough to keep a wife," put in Clara ironically. "How about that, Nils?" she asked him frankly, as if she wanted to know.

Nils looked at her coolly, raising one eyebrow. "Oh, I can keep her, all right."

"The way she wants to be kept?"

"With my wife, I'll decide that," replied Nils calmly. "I'll give her what's good for her."

Clara made a wry face. "You'll give her the strap, I expect, like old Peter Oleson gave his wife."

"When she needs it," said Nils lazily, locking his hands behind his head and squinting up through the leaves of the cherry tree. "Do you remember the time I squeezed the cherries all over your clean dress, and Aunt Johanna boxed my ears for me? My gracious, weren't you mad! You had both hands full of cherries, and I squeezed 'em and made the juice fly all over you. I liked to have fun with you; you'd get so mad."

"We *did* have fun, didn't we? None of the other kids ever had so much fun. We knew how to play."

Nils dropped his elbows on the table and looked steadily across at her. "I've played with lots of girls since, but I haven't found one who was such good fun."

Clara laughed. The late afternoon sun was shining full in her face, and deep in the back of her eyes there shone something fiery, like the yellow drops of Tokai in the brown glass bottle. "Can you still play, or are you only pretending?"

"I can play better than I used to, and harder."

"Don't you ever work, then?" She had not intended to say it. It slipped out because she was confused enough to say just the wrong thing.

"I work between times." Nils' steady gaze still beat upon her. "Don't you worry about my working, Mrs. Ericson. You're getting like all the rest of them." He reached his brown, warm hand across the table and dropped it on Clara's, which was cold as an icicle. "Last call for play, Mrs. Ericson!" Clara shivered, and suddenly her hands and cheeks grew warm. Her fingers lingered in his a moment, and they looked at each other earnestly. Joe Vavrika had put the mouth of the bottle to his lips and was swallowing the last drops of the Tokai, standing. The sun, just about to sink behind his shop, glistened on the bright glass, on his flushed face and curly yellow hair. "Look," Clara whispered; "that's the way I want to grow old."

VI

On the day of Olaf Ericson's barn-raising, his wife, for once in a way, rose early. Johanna Vavrika had been baking cakes and frying and boiling and spicing meats for a week beforehand, but it was not until the day before the party was to take place that Clara showed any interest in it. Then she was seized with one of her fitful spasms of energy, and took the wagon and little Eric and spent the day on Plum Creek, gathering vines and swamp goldenrod to decorate the barn.

By four o'clock in the afternoon buggies and wagons began to arrive at the big unpainted building in front of Olaf's house. When Nils and his mother came at five, there were more than fifty people in the barn, and a great drove of children. On the ground floor stood six long tables, set with the crockery of seven flourishing Ericson families, lent for the occasion. In the middle of each table was a big yellow pumpkin, hollowed out and filled with woodbine. In one corner of the barn, behind a pile of green-and-white-striped watermelons, was a circle of chairs for the old people; the younger guests sat on bushel measures or barbed-wire spools, and the children tumbled about in the haymow. The box stalls Clara had converted into booths. The framework was hidden by goldenrod and sheaves of wheat, and the partitions were covered with wild grapevines full of fruit. At one of these Johanna Vavrika watched over her cooked meats, enough to provision an army; and at the next her kitchen girls had ranged the ice-cream freezers, and Clara was already cutting pies and cakes against the hour of serving. At the third stall, little Hilda, in a bright pink lawn dress, dispensed lemonade throughout the afternoon. Olaf, as a public man, had thought it inadvisable to serve beer in his barn; but Joe Vavrika had come over with two demijohns concealed in his buggy, and after his arrival the wagon shed was much frequented by the men.

"Hasn't Cousin Clara fixed things lovely?" little Hilda whispered, when Nils went up to her stall and asked for lemonade.

Nils leaned against the booth, talking to the excited little girl and watching the people. The barn faced the west, and the sun, pouring in at the big doors, filled the whole interior with a golden light, through which filtered fine particles of dust from the haymow, where the children were romping. There was a great chattering from the stall where Johanna Vavrika exhibited to the admiring women her platters heaped with fried chicken, her roasts of beef, boiled tongues, and baked hams with cloves stuck in the crisp brown fat and garnished with tansy and parsley. The

older women, having assured themselves that there were twenty kinds of
cake, not counting cookies, and three dozen fat pies, repaired to the corner
behind the pile of watermelons, put on their white aprons, and fell to their
knitting and fancywork. They were a fine company of old women, and a
Dutch painter would have loved to find them there together, where the
sun made bright patches on the floor and sent long, quivering shafts of
gold through the dusky shade up among the rafters. There were fat, rosy
old women who looked hot in their best black dresses; spare, alert old
women with brown, dark-veined hands; and several of almost heroic
frame, not less massive than old Mrs. Ericson herself. Few of them wore
glasses, and old Mrs. Svendsen, a Danish woman, who was quite bald,
wore the only cap among them. Mrs. Oleson, who had twelve big grandchildren, could still show two braids of yellow hair as thick as her own
wrists. Among all these grandmothers there were more brown heads than
white. They all had a pleased, prosperous air, as if they were more than
satisfied with themselves and with life. Nils, leaning against Hilda's
lemonade stand, watched them as they sat chattering in four languages,
their fingers never lagging behind their tongues.

"Look at them over there," he whispered, detaining Clara as she
passed him. "Aren't they the Old Guard? I've just counted thirty hands.
I guess they've wrung many a chicken's neck and warmed many a boy's
jacket for him in their time."

In reality he fell into amazement when he thought of the Herculean
labors those fifteen pairs of hands had performed: of the cows they had
milked, the butter they had made, the gardens they had planted, the
children and grandchildren they had tended, the brooms they had worn
out, the mountains of food they had cooked. It made him dizzy. Clara
Vavrika smiled a hard, enigmatical smile at him and walked rapidly away.
Nils' eyes followed her white figure as she went toward the house. He
watched her walking alone in the sunlight, looked at her slender, defiant
shoulders and her little hard-set head with its coils of blue-black hair.
"No," he reflected; "she'd never be like them, not if she lived here a
hundred years. She'd only grow more bitter. You can't tame a wild thing;
you can only chain it. People aren't all alike. I mustn't lose my nerve."
He gave Hilda's pigtail a parting tweak and set out after Clara. "Where
to?" he asked, as he came upon her in the kitchen.

"I'm going to the cellar for preserves."

"Let me go with you. I never get a moment alone with you. Why
do you keep out of my way?"

Clara laughed. "I don't usually get in anybody's way."

Nils followed her down the stairs and to the far corner of the cellar, where a basement window let in a stream of light. From a swinging shelf Clara selected several glass jars, each labeled in Johanna's careful hand. Nils took up a brown flask. "What's this? It looks good."

"It is. It's some French brandy father gave me when I was married. Would you like some? Have you a corkscrew? I'll get glasses."

When she brought them, Nils took them from her and put them down on the window sill. "Clara Vavrika, do you remember how crazy I used to be about you?"

Clara shrugged her shoulders. "Boys are always crazy about somebody or other. I dare say some silly has been crazy about Evelina Oleson. You got over it in a hurry."

"Because I didn't come back, you mean? I had to get on, you know, and it was hard sledding at first. Then I heard you'd married Olaf."

"And then you stayed away from a broken heart," Clara laughed.

"And then I began to think about you more than I had since I first went away. I began to wonder if you were really as you had seemed to me when I was a boy. I thought I'd like to see. I've had lots of girls, but no one ever pulled me the same way. The more I thought about you, the more I remembered how it used to be—like hearing a wild tune you can't resist, calling you out at night. It had been a long while since anything had pulled me out of my boots, and I wondered whether anything ever could again." Nils thrust his hands into his coat pockets and squared his shoulders, as his mother sometimes squared hers, as Olaf, in a clumsier manner, squared his. "So I thought I'd come back and see. Of course the family have tried to do me, and I rather thought I'd bring out father's will and make a fuss. But they can have their old land; they've put enough sweat into it." He took the flask and filled the two glasses carefully to the brim. "I've found out what I want from the Ericsons. Drink *skoal*, Clara." He lifted his glass, and Clara took hers with downcast eyes. "Look at me, Clara Vavrika. *Skoal!*"

She raised her burning eyes and answered fiercely: "*Skoal!*"

The barn supper began at six o'clock and lasted for two hilarious hours. Yense Nelson had made a wager that he could eat two whole fried chickens, and he did. Eli Swanson stowed away two whole custard pies, and Nick Hermanson ate a chocolate layer cake to the last crumb. There was even a cooky contest among the children, and one thin, slablike

Bohemian boy consumed sixteen and won the prize, a gingerbread pig which Johanna Vavrika had carefully decorated with red candies and burnt sugar. Fritz Sweiheart, the German carpenter, won in the pickle contest, but he disappeared soon after supper and was not seen for the rest of the evening. Joe Vavrika said that Fritz could have managed the pickles all right, but he had sampled the demijohn in his buggy too often before sitting down to the table.

While the supper was being cleared away the two fiddlers began to tune up for the dance. Clara was to accompany them on her old upright piano, which had been brought down from her father's. By this time Nils had renewed old acquaintances. Since his interview with Clara in the cellar, he had been busy telling all the old women how young they looked, and all the young ones how pretty they were, and assuring the men that they had here the best farmland in the world. He had made himself so agreeable that old Mrs. Ericson's friends began to come up to her and tell how lucky she was to get her smart son back again, and please to get him to play his flute. Joe Vavrika, who could still play very well when he forgot that he had rheumatism, caught up a fiddle from Johnny Oleson and played a crazy Bohemian dance tune that set the wheels going. When he dropped the bow every one was ready to dance.

Olaf, in a frock coat and a solemn made-up necktie, led the grand march with his mother. Clara had kept well out of *that* by sticking to the piano. She played the march with a pompous solemnity which greatly amused the prodigal son, who went over and stood behind her.

"Oh, aren't you rubbing it into them, Clara Vavrika? And aren't you lucky to have me here, or all your wit would be thrown away."

"I'm used to being witty for myself. It saves my life."

The fiddles struck up a polka, and Nils convulsed Joe Vavrika by leading out Evelina Oleson, the homely schoolteacher. His next partner was a very fat Swedish girl, who, although she was an heiress, had not been asked for the first dance, but had stood against the wall in her tight, high-heeled shoes, nervously fingering a lace handkerchief. She was soon out of breath, so Nils led her, pleased and panting, to her seat, and went over to the piano, from which Clara had been watching his gallantry. "Ask Olena Yenson," she whispered. "She waltzes beautifully."

Olena, too, was rather inconveniently plump, handsome in a smooth, heavy way, with a fine color and good-natured, sleepy eyes. She was redolent of violet sachet powder, and had warm, soft, white hands, but she danced divinely, moving as smoothly as the tide coming in. "There, that's something like," Nils said as he released her. "You'll give me the next waltz, won't you? Now I must go and dance with my little cousin."

Hilda was greatly excited when Nils went up to her stall and held out his arm. Her little eyes sparkled, but she declared that she could not leave her lemonade. Old Mrs. Ericson, who happened along at this moment, said she would attend to that, and Hilda came out, as pink as her pink dress. The dance was a schottische, and in a moment her yellow braids were fairly standing on end. "Bravo!" Nils cried encouragingly. "Where did you learn to dance so nicely?"

"My Cousin Clara taught me," the little girl panted.

Nils found Eric sitting with a group of boys who were too awkward or too shy to dance, and told him that he must dance the next waltz with Hilda.

The boy screwed up his shoulders. "Aw, Nils, I can't dance. My feet are too big; I look silly."

"Don't be thinking about yourself. It doesn't matter how boys look."

Nils had never spoken to him so sharply before, and Eric made haste to scramble out of his corner and brush the straw from his coat.

Clara nodded approvingly. "Good for you, Nils. I've been trying to get hold of him. They dance very nicely together; I sometimes play for them."

"I'm obliged to you for teaching him. There's no reason why he should grow up to be a lout."

"He'll never be that. He's more like you than any of them. Only he hasn't your courage." From her slanting eyes Clara shot forth one of those keen glances, admiring and at the same time challenging, which she seldom bestowed on any one, and which seemed to say, "Yes, I admire you, but I am your equal."

Clara was proving a much better host than Olaf, who, once the supper was over, seemed to feel no interest in anything but the lanterns. He had brought a locomotive headlight from town to light the revels, and he kept skulking about it as if he feared the mere light from it might set his new barn on fire. His wife, on the contrary, was cordial to every one, was animated and even gay. The deep salmon color in her cheeks burned vividly, and her eyes were full of life. She gave the piano over to the fat Swedish heiress, pulled her father away from the corner where he sat gossiping with his cronies, and made him dance a Bohemian dance with her. In his youth Joe had been a famous dancer, and his daughter got him so limbered up that every one sat round and applauded them. The old ladies were particularly delighted, and made them go through the dance again. From their corner where they watched and commented, the old women kept time with their feet and hands, and whenever the fiddles struck up a new air old Mrs. Svendsen's white cap would begin to bob.

Clara was waltzing with little Eric when Nils came up to them, brushed his brother aside, and swung her out among the dancers. "Remember how we used to waltz on rollers at the old skating rink in town? I suppose people don't do that any more. We used to keep it up for hours. You know, we never did moon around as other boys and girls did. It was dead serious with us from the beginning. When we were most in love with each other, we used to fight. You were always pinching people; your fingers were like little nippers. A regular snapping turtle, you were. Lord, how you'd like Stockholm! Sit out in the streets in front of cafés and talk all night in summer. Just like a reception—officers and ladies and funny English people. Jolliest people in the world, the Swedes, once you get them going. Always drinking things—champagne and stout mixed, half-and-half; serve it out of big pitchers, and serve plenty. Slow pulse, you know; they can stand a lot. Once they light up, they're glowworms, I can tell you."

"All the same, you don't really like gay people."

"*I* don't?"

"No; I could see that when you were looking at the old women there this afternoon. They're the kind you really admire, after all; women like your mother. And that's the kind you'll marry."

"Is it, Miss Wisdom? You'll see who I'll marry, and she won't have a domestic virtue to bless herself with. She'll be a snapping turtle, and she'll be a match for me. All the same, they're a fine bunch of old dames over there. You admire them yourself."

"No, I don't; I detest them."

"You won't, when you look back on them from Stockholm or Budapest. Freedom settles all that. Oh, but you're the real Bohemian Girl, Clara Vavrika!" Nils laughed down at her sullen frown and began mockingly to sing:

> "Oh, how could a poor gypsy maiden like me
> Expect the proud bride of a baron to be?"

Clara clutched his shoulder. "Hush, Nils; every one is looking at you."

"I don't care. They can't gossip. It's all in the family, as the Ericsons say when they divide up little Hilda's patrimony amongst them. Besides, we'll give them something to talk about when we hit the trail. Lord, it will be a godsend to them! They haven't had anything so interesting to chatter about since the grasshopper year. It'll give them a new lease of life. And Olaf won't lose the Bohemian vote, either. They'll have the laugh on him so that they'll vote two apiece. They'll send him to Congress. They'll never forget his barn party, or us. They'll always remember us as we're dancing together now. We're making a legend. Where's my waltz, boys?" he called as they whirled past the fiddlers.

The musicians grinned, looked at each other, hesitated, and began a new air; and Nils sang with them, as the couples fell from a quick waltz to a long, slow glide:

> "When other lips and other hearts
> Their tale of love shall tell,
> In language whose excess imparts
> The power they feel so well."

The old women applauded vigorously. "What a gay one he is, that Nils!" And old Mrs. Svendsen's cap lurched dreamily from side to side to the flowing measure of the dance.

> Of days that have as ha-a-p-py been,
> And you'll remember me.

VII

The moonlight flooded that great, silent land. The reaped fields lay yellow in it. The straw stacks and poplar windbreaks threw sharp black shadows. The roads were white rivers of dust. The sky was a deep, crystalline blue, and the stars were few and faint. Everything seemed to have succumbed, to have sunk to sleep, under the great, golden, tender, midsummer moon. The splendor of it seemed to transcend human life and human fate. The senses were too feeble to take it in, and every time one looked up at the sky one felt unequal to it, as if one were sitting deaf under the waves of a great river of melody. Near the road, Nils Ericson was lying against a straw stack in Olaf's wheat field. His own life seemed strange and unfamiliar to him, as if it were something he had read about, or dreamed, and forgotten. He lay very still, watching the white road that ran in front of him, lost itself among the fields, and then, at a distance, reappeared over a little hill. At last, against this white band he saw something moving rapidly, and he got up and walked to the edge of the field. "She is passing the row of poplars now," he thought. He heard the padded beat of hoofs along the dusty road, and as she came into sight he stepped out and waved his arms. Then, for fear of frightening the horse, he drew back and waited. Clara had seen him, and she came up at a walk. Nils took the horse by the bit and stroked his neck.

"What are you doing out so late, Clara Vavrika? I went to the house, but Johanna told me you had gone to your father's."

"Who can stay in the house on a night like this? Aren't you out yourself?"

"Ah, but that's another matter."

Nils turned the horse into the field.

"What are you doing? Where are you taking Norman?"

"Not far, but I want to talk to you tonight; I have something to say to you. I can't talk to you at the house, with Olaf sitting there on the porch, weighing a thousand tons."

Clara laughed. "He won't be sitting there now. He's in bed by this time, and asleep—weighing a thousand tons."

Nils plodded on across the stubble. "Are you really going to spend the rest of your life like this, night after night, summer after summer? Haven't you anything better to do on a night like this than to wear yourself and Norman out tearing across the country to your father's and back? Besides, your father won't live forever, you know. His little place will be shut up or sold, and then you'll have nobody but the Ericsons. You'll have to fasten down the hatches for the winter then."

Clara moved her head restlessly. "Don't talk about that. I try never to think of it. If I lost father I'd lose everything, even my hold over the Ericsons."

"Bah! You'd lose a good deal more than that. You'd lose your race, everything that makes you yourself. You've lost a good deal of it now."

"Of what?"

"Of your love of life, your capacity for delight."

Clara put her hands up to her face. "I haven't, Nils Ericson, I haven't! Say anything to me but that. I won't have it!" she declared vehemently.

Nils led the horse up to a straw stack, and turned to Clara, looking at her intently, as he had looked at her that Sunday afternoon at Vavrika's. "But why do you fight for that so? What good is the power to enjoy, if you never enjoy? Your hands are cold again; what are you afraid of all the time? Ah, you're afraid of losing it; that's what's the matter with you! And you will, Clara Vavrika, you will! When I used to know you—listen; you've caught a wild bird in your hand, haven't you, and felt its heart beat so hard that you were afraid it would shatter its little body to pieces? Well, you used to be just like that, a slender, eager thing with a wild delight inside you. That is how I remembered you. And I come back and find you—a bitter woman. This is a perfect ferret fight here; you live by biting and being bitten. Can't you remember what life used to be? Can't you remember that old delight? I've never forgotten it, or known its like, on land or sea."

He drew the horse under the shadow of the straw stack. Clara felt him take her foot out of the stirrup, and she slid softly down into his arms. He kissed her slowly. He was a deliberate man, but his nerves were steel when he wanted anything. Something flashed out from him like a knife out of a sheath. Clara felt everything slipping away from her; she was flooded by the summer night. He thrust his hand into his pocket, and then held it out at arm's length. "Look," he said. The shadow of the straw stack fell sharp across his wrist, and in the palm of his hand she saw a silver dollar shining. "That's my pile," he muttered; "will you go with me?"

Clara nodded, and dropped her forehead on his shoulder.

Nils took a deep breath. "Will you go with me tonight?"

"Where?" she whispered softly.

"To town, to catch the midnight flyer."

Clara lifted her head and pulled herself together. "Are you crazy, Nils? We couldn't go away like that."

"That's the only way we ever will go. You can't sit on the bank and think about it. You have to plunge. That's the way I've always done, and it's the right way for people like you and me. There's nothing so dangerous as sitting still. You've only got one life, one youth, and you can let it slip through your fingers if you want to; nothing easier. Most people do that. You'd be better off tramping the roads with me than you are here." Nils held back her head and looked into her eyes. "But I'm not that kind of a tramp, Clara. You won't have to take in sewing. I'm with a Norwegian shipping line; came over on business with the New York offices, but now I'm going straight back to Bergen. I expect I've got as much money as the Ericsons. Father sent me a little to get started. They never knew about that. There, I hadn't meant to tell you; I wanted you to come on your own nerve."

Clara looked off across the fields. "It isn't that, Nils, but something seems to hold me. I'm afraid to pull against it. It comes out of the ground, I think."

"I know all about that. One has to tear loose. You're not needed here. Your father will understand; he's made like us. As for Olaf, Johanna will take better care of him than ever you could. It's now or never, Clara Vavrika. My bag's at the station; I smuggled it there yesterday."

Clara clung to him and hid her face against his shoulder. "Not tonight," she whispered. "Sit here and talk to me tonight. I don't want to go anywhere tonight. I may never love you like this again."

Nils laughed through his teeth. "You can't come that on me. That's not my way, Clara Vavrika. Eric's mare is over there behind the stacks, and I'm off on the midnight. It's goodbye, or off across the world with me. My carriage won't wait. I've written a letter to Olaf; I'll mail it in town. When he reads it he won't bother us—not if I know him. He'd rather have the land. Besides, I could demand an investigation of his administration of Cousin Henrik's estate, and that would be bad for a public man. You've no clothes, I know; but you can sit up tonight, and we can get everything on the way. Where's your old dash, Clara Vavrika? What's become of your Bohemian blood? I used to think you had courage enough for anything. Where's your nerve—what are you waiting for?"

Clara drew back her head, and he saw the slumberous fire in her eyes. "For you to say one thing, Nils Ericson."

"I never say that thing to any woman, Clara Vavrika." He leaned back, lifted her gently from the ground, and whispered through his teeth: "But I'll never, never let you go, not to any man on earth but me! Do you understand me? Now, wait here."

Clara sank down on a sheaf of wheat and covered her face with her hands. She did not know what she was going to do—whether she would go or stay. The great, silent country seemed to lay a spell upon her. The ground seemed to hold her as if by roots. Her knees were soft under her. She felt as if she could not bear separation from her old sorrows, from her old discontent. They were dear to her, they had kept her alive, they were a part of her. There would be nothing left of her if she were wrenched away from them. Never could she pass beyond that skyline against which her restlessness had beat so many times. She felt as if her soul had built itself a nest there on that horizon at which she looked every morning and every evening, and it was dear to her, inexpressibly dear. She pressed her fingers against her eyeballs to shut it out. Beside her she heard the tramping of horses in the soft earth. Nils said nothing to her. He put his hands under her arms and lifted her lightly to her saddle. Then he swung himself into his own.

"We shall have to ride fast to catch the midnight train. A last gallop, Clara Vavrika. Forward!"

There was a start, a thud of hoofs along the moonlit road, two dark shadows going over the hill; and then the great, still land stretched untroubled under the azure night. Two shadows had passed.

VIII

A year after the flight of Olaf Ericson's wife, the night train was steaming across the plains of Iowa. The conductor was hurrying through one of the day coaches, his lantern on his arm, when a lank, fair-haired boy sat up in one of the plush seats and tweaked him by the coat.

"What is the next stop, please, sir?"

"Red Oak, Iowa. But you go through to Chicago, don't you?" He looked down, and noticed that the boy's eyes were red and his face was drawn, as if he were in trouble.

"Yes. But I was wondering whether I could get off at the next place and get a train back to Omaha."

"Well, I suppose you could. Live in Omaha?"

"No. In the western part of the State. How soon do we get to Red Oak?"

"Forty minutes. You'd better make up your mind, so I can tell the baggageman to put your trunk off."

"Oh, never mind about that! I mean, I haven't got any," the boy added, blushing.

"Run away," the conductor thought, as he slammed the coach door behind him.

Eric Ericson crumpled down in his seat and put his brown hand to his forehead. He had been crying, and he had had no supper, and his head was aching violently. "Oh, what shall I do?" he thought, as he looked dully down at his big shoes. "Nils will be ashamed of me; I haven't got any spunk."

Ever since Nils had run away with his brother's wife, life at home had been hard for little Eric. His mother and Olaf both suspected him of complicity. Mrs. Ericson was harsh and faultfinding, constantly wounding the boy's pride; and Olaf was always setting her against him.

Joe Vavrika heard often from his daughter. Clara had always been fond of her father, and happiness made her kinder. She wrote him long accounts of the voyage to Bergen, and of the trip she and Nils took through Bohemia to the little town where her father had grown up and where she herself was born. She visited all her kinsmen there, and sent her father news of his brother, who was a priest; of his sister, who had married a horse-breeder—of their big farm and their many children. These letters Joe always managed to read to little Eric. They contained messages for Eric and Hilda. Clara sent presents, too, which Eric never dared to take home and which poor little Hilda never even saw, though she loved to hear Eric tell about them when they were out getting the eggs together. But Olaf once saw Eric coming out of Vavrika's house—the old man had never asked the boy to come into his saloon—and Olaf went straight to his mother and told her. That night Mrs. Ericson came to Eric's room after he was in bed and made a terrible scene. She could be very terrifying when she was really angry. She forbade him ever to speak to Vavrika again, and after that night she would not allow him to go to town alone. So it was a long while before Eric got any more news of his brother. But old Joe suspected what was going on, and he carried Clara's letters about in his pocket. One Sunday he drove out to see a German friend of his, and chanced to catch sight of Eric, sitting by the cattle pond in the big pasture. They went together into Fritz Oberlies' barn, and read the letters and talked things over. Eric admitted that things were getting hard for him at home. That very night old Joe sat down and laboriously penned a statement of the case to his daughter.

Things got no better for Eric. His mother and Olaf felt that, how-ever closely he was watched, he still, as they said, "heard." Mrs. Ericson could not admit neutrality. She had sent Johanna Vavrika packing back to her brother's, though Olaf would much rather have kept her than Anders' eldest daughter, whom Mrs. Ericson installed in her place. He was not so highhanded as his mother, and he once sulkily told her that she might better have taught her granddaughter to cook before she sent Johanna away. Olaf could have borne a good deal for the sake of prunes spiced in honey, the secret of which Johanna had taken away with her.

At last two letters came to Joe Vavrika: one from Nils, inclosing a postal order for money to pay Eric's passage to Bergen, and one from Clara, saying that Nils had a place for Eric in the offices of his company, that he was to live with them, and that they were only waiting for him to come. He was to leave New York on one of the boats of Nils' own line; the captain was one of their friends, and Eric was to make himself known at once.

Nils' directions were so explicit that a baby could have followed them, Eric felt. And here he was, nearing Red Oak, Iowa, and rocking backward and forward in despair. Never had he loved his brother so much, and never had the big world called to him so hard. But there was a lump in his throat which would not go down. Ever since nightfall he had been tormented by the thought of his mother, alone in that big house that had sent forth so many men. Her unkindness now seemed so little, and her loneliness so great. He remembered everything she had ever done for him: how frightened she had been when he tore his hand in the corn-sheller, and how she wouldn't let Olaf scold him. When Nils went away he didn't leave his mother all alone, or he would never have gone. Eric felt sure of that.

The train whistled. The conductor came in, smiling not unkindly. "Well, young man, what are you going to do? We stop at Red Oak in three minutes."

"Yes, thank you. I'll let you know." The conductor went out, and the boy doubled up with misery. He couldn't let his one chance go like this. He felt for his breast pocket and crackled Nils' kind letter to give him courage. He didn't want Nils to be ashamed of him. The train stopped. Suddenly he remembered his brother's kind, twinkling eyes, that always looked at you as if from far away. The lump in his throat softened. "Ah, but Nils, Nils would *understand*!" he thought. "That's just it about Nils; he always understands."

A lank, pale boy with a canvas telescope stumbled off the train to the Red Oak siding, just as the conductor called, "All aboard!"

The next night Mrs. Ericson was sitting alone in her wooden rocking chair on the front porch. Little Hilda had been sent to bed and had cried herself to sleep. The old woman's knitting was in her lap, but her hands lay motionless on top of it. For more than an hour she had not moved a muscle. She simply sat, as only the Ericsons and the mountains can sit. The house was dark, and there was no sound but the croaking of the frogs down in the pond of the little pasture.

Eric did not come home by the road, but across the fields, where no one could see him. He set his telescope down softly in the kitchen shed, and slipped noiselessly along the path to the front porch. He sat down on the step without saying anything. Mrs. Ericson made no sign, and the frogs croaked on. At last the boy spoke timidly.

"I've come back, Mother."

"Very well," said Mrs. Ericson.

Eric leaned over and picked up a little stick out of the grass.

"How about the milking?" he faltered.

"That's been done, hours ago."

"Who did you get?"

"Get? I did it myself. I can milk as good as any of you."

Eric slid along the step nearer to her. "Oh, Mother, why did you?" he asked sorrowfully. "Why didn't you get one of Otto's boys?"

"I didn't want anybody to know I was in need of a boy," said Mrs. Ericson bitterly. She looked straight in front of her and her mouth tightened. "I always meant to give you the home farm," she added.

The boy started and slid closer. "Oh, Mother," he faltered, "I don't care about the farm. I came back because I thought you might be needing me, maybe." He hung his head and got no further.

"Very well," said Mrs. Ericson. Her hand went out from her suddenly and rested on his head. Her fingers twined themselves in his soft, pale hair. His tears splashed down on the boards; happiness filled his heart.

First published in *McClure's*, XXXIX (August, 1912), 420–424, 426–427, 430, 432–443.

Behind the Singer Tower

✤ ✤ ✤

It was a hot, close night in May, the night after the burning of the Mont Blanc Hotel, and some half dozen of us who had been thrown together, more or less, during that terrible day, accepted Fred Hallet's invitation to go for a turn in his launch, which was tied up in the North River. We were all tired and unstrung and heartsick, and the quiet of the night and the coolness on the water relaxed our tense nerves a little. None of us talked much as we slid down the river and out into the bay. We were in a kind of stupor. When the launch ran out into the harbor, we saw an Atlantic liner come steaming up the big sea road. She passed so near to us that we could see her crowded steerage decks.

"It's the *Re di Napoli*," said Johnson of the *Herald*. "She's going to land her first cabin passengers tonight, evidently. Those people are terribly proud of their new docks in the North River; feel they've come up in the world."

We ruffled easily along through the bay, looking behind us at the wide circle of lights that rim the horizon from east to west and from west to east, all the way round except for that narrow, much-traveled highway, the road to the open sea. Running a launch about the harbor at night is a good deal like bicycling among the motors on Fifth Avenue. That night there was probably no less activity than usual; the turtle-backed ferry boats swung to and fro, the tugs screamed and panted beside the freight cars they were towing on barges, the Coney Island boats threw out their streams of light and faded away. Boats of every shape and purpose went about their business and made noise enough as they did it, doubtless. But to us, after what we had been seeing and hearing all day long, the place seemed unnaturally quiet and the night unnaturally black. There was a brooding mournfulness over the harbor, as if the ghost of helplessness and terror were abroad in the darkness. One felt a solemnity in the misty spring sky where only a few stars shone, pale and far apart, and in the sighs of the heavy black water that rolled up into the light. The city itself, as we looked back at it, seemed enveloped in a tragic self-consciousness. Those incredible towers of stone and steel seemed, in the mist, to be grouped confusedly together, as if they were confronting each other with a question. They looked positively lonely, like the great trees left after a forest is cut away. One might fancy that the city was protesting, was asserting its helplessness, its irresponsibility for its physical conformation, for the direction it had taken. It was an irregular parallelogram pressed between two hemispheres, and, like any other solid squeezed in a vise, it shot upward.

There were six of us in the launch: two newspapermen—Johnson and myself; Fred Hallet, the engineer, and one of his draftsmen; a lawyer from the District Attorney's office; and Zablowski, a young Jewish doctor from the Rockefeller Institute. We did not talk; there was only one thing to talk about, and we had had enough of that. Before we left town the death list of the Mont Blanc had gone above three hundred.

The Mont Blanc was the complete expression of the New York idea in architecture; a thirty-five story hotel which made the Plaza look modest. Its prices, like its proportions, as the newspapers had so often asseverated, outscaled everything in the known world. And it was still standing there, massive and brutally unconcerned, only a little blackened about its thousand windows and with the foolish fire escapes in its court melted down. About the fire itself nobody knew much. It had begun on the twelfth story, broken out through the windows, shot up long streamers that had gone in at the windows above, and so on up to the top. A high wind and much upholstery and oiled wood had given it incredible speed.

On the night of the fire the hotel was full of people from everywhere, and by morning half a dozen trusts had lost their presidents, two states had lost their governors, and one of the great European powers had lost its ambassador. So many businesses had been disorganized that Wall Street had shut down for the day. They had been snuffed out, these important men, as lightly as the casual guests who had come to town to spend money, or as the pampered opera singers who had returned from an overland tour and were waiting to sail on Saturday. The lists were still vague, for whether the victims had jumped or not, identification was difficult, and, in either case, they had met with obliteration, absolute effacement, as when a drop of water falls into the sea.

Out of all I had seen that day, one thing kept recurring to me; perhaps because it was so little in the face of a destruction so vast. In the afternoon, when I was going over the building with the firemen, I found, on the ledge of a window on the fifteenth floor, a man's hand snapped off at the wrist as cleanly as if it had been taken off by a cutlass—he had thrown out his arm in falling.

It had belonged to Graziani, the tenor, who had occupied a suite on the thirty-second floor. We identified it by a little-finger ring, which had been given to him by the German Emperor. Yes, it was the same hand. I had seen it often enough when he placed it so confidently over his chest as he began his "Celeste Aida," or when he lifted—much too often, alas! —his little glasses of white arrack at Martin's. When he toured the world he must have whatever was most costly and most characteristic in every city; in New York he had the thirty-second floor, poor fellow! He had plunged from there toward the cobwebby life nets stretched five hundred feet below on the asphalt. Well, at any rate, he would never drag out an obese old age in the English country house he had built near Naples.

Heretofore fires in fireproof buildings of many stories had occurred only in factory lofts, and the people who perished in them, fur workers and garment workers, were obscure for more reasons than one; most of them bore names unpronounceable to the American tongue; many of them had no kinsmen, no history, no record anywhere.

But we realized that, after the burning of the Mont Blanc, the New York idea would be called to account by every state in the Union, by all the great capitals of the world. Never before, in a single day, had so many of the names that feed and furnish the newspapers appeared in their columns all together, and for the last time.

In New York the matter of height was spoken of jocularly and triumphantly. The very window cleaners always joked about it as they buckled themselves fast outside your office in the forty-fifth story of the Wertheimer tower, though the average for window cleaners, who, for one reason or another, dropped to the pavement was something over one a day. In a city with so many millions of windows that was not perhaps an unreasonable percentage. But we felt that the Mont Blanc disaster would bring our particular type of building into unpleasant prominence, as the cholera used to make Naples and the conditions of life there too much a matter of discussion, or as the earthquake of 1906 gave such undesirable notoriety to the affairs of San Francisco.

For once we were actually afraid of being too much in the public eye, of being overadvertised. As I looked at the great incandescent signs along the Jersey shore, blazing across the night the names of beer and perfumes and corsets, it occurred to me that, after all, that kind of thing could be overdone; a single name, a single question, could be blazed too far. Our whole scheme of life and progress and profit was perpendicular.

There was nothing for us but height. We were whipped up the ladder. We depended upon the ever-growing possibilities of girders and rivets as Holland depends on her dikes.

"Did you ever notice," Johnson remarked when we were about halfway across to Staten Island, "what a Jewy-looking thing the Singer Tower is when it's lit up? The fellow who placed those incandescents must have had a sense of humor. It's exactly like the Jewish high priest in the old Bible dictionaries."

He pointed back, outlining with his forefinger the jeweled miter, the high, sloping shoulders, and the hands pressed together in the traditional posture of prayer.

Zablowski, the young Jewish doctor, smiled and shook his head. He was a very handsome fellow, with sad, thoughtful eyes, and we were all fond of him, especially Hallet, who was always teasing him. "No, it's not Semitic, Johnson," he said. "That high-peaked turban is more apt to be Persian. He's a Magi or a fire-worshiper of some sort, your high priest. When you get nearer he looks like a Buddha, with two bright rings in his ears."

Zablowski pointed with his cigar toward the blurred Babylonian heights crowding each other on the narrow tip of the island. Among them rose the colossal figure of the Singer Tower, watching over the city and the harbor like a presiding Genius. He had come out of Asia quietly in the night, no one knew just when or how, and the Statue of Liberty, holding her feeble taper in the gloom off to our left, was but an archeological survival.

"Who could have foreseen that she, in her high-mindedness, would ever spawn a great heathen idol like that?" Hallet exclaimed. "But that's what idealism comes to in the end, Zablowski."

Zablowski laughed mournfully. "What did you expect, Hallet? You've used us for your ends—waste for your machine, and now you talk about infection. Of course we brought germs from over there," he nodded toward the northeast.

"Well, you're all here at any rate, and I won't argue with you about all that tonight," said Hallet wearily. "The fact is," he went on as he lit a cigar and settled deeper into his chair, "when we met the *Re di Napoli* back there, she set me thinking. She recalled something that happened when I was a boy just out of Tech; when I was working under Merryweather on the Mont Blanc foundation."

We all looked up. Stanley Merryweather was the most successful manipulator of structural steel in New York, and Hallet was the most intelligent; the enmity between them was one of the legends of the Engineers' Society.

Hallet saw our interest and smiled. "I suppose you've heard yarns about why Merryweather and I don't even pretend to get on. People say we went to school together and then had a terrible row of some sort. The fact is, we never did get on, and back there in the foundation work of the Mont Blanc our ways definitely parted. You know how Merryweather happened to get going? He was the only nephew of old Hughie Macfarlane, and Macfarlane was the pioneer in steel construction. He dreamed the dream. When he was a lad working for the Pennsylvania Bridge Company, he saw Manhattan just as it towers there tonight. Well, Macfarlane was aging and he had no children, so he took his sister's son to make an engineer of him. Macfarlane was a thoroughgoing Scotch Presbyterian, sound Pittsburgh stock, but his sister had committed an indiscretion. She had married a professor of languages in a theological seminary out there; a professor who knew too much about some Oriental tongues I needn't name to be altogether safe. It didn't show much in the old professor, who looked like a Baptist preacher except for his short, thick hands, and of course it is very much veiled in Stanley. When he came up to the Massachusetts Tech he was a big, handsome boy, but there was something in his moist, bright blue eye—well, something that you would recognize, Zablowski."

Zablowski chuckled and inclined his head delicately forward.

Hallet continued: "Yes, in Stanley Merryweather there were racial characteristics. He was handsome and jolly and glitteringly frank and almost insultingly cordial, and yet he was never really popular. He was quick and superficial, built for high speed and a light load. He liked to come it over people, but when you had him, he always crawled. Didn't seem to hurt him one bit to back down. If you made a fool of him tonight —well, 'Tomorrow's another day,' he'd say lightly, and tomorrow he'd blossom out in a new suit of clothes and a necktie of some unusual weave and haunting color. He had the feeling for color and texture. The worst of it was that, as truly as I'm sitting here, he never bore a grudge toward the fellow who'd called his bluff and shown him up for a lush growth; no ill feeling at all, Zablowski. He simply didn't know what that meant—"

Hallet's sentence trailed and hung wistfully in the air, while Zablowski put his hand penitently to his forehead.

"Well, Merryweather was quick and he had plenty of spurt and a taking manner, and he didn't know there had ever been such a thing as modesty or reverence in the world. He got all round the old man, and old Mac was perfectly foolish about him. It was always: 'Is it well with the young man Absalom?' Stanley was a year ahead of me in school, and when he came out of Tech the old man took him right into the business. He married a burgeoning Jewish beauty, Fanny Reizenstein, the daughter of the importer, and he hung her with the jewels of the East until she looked like the Song of Solomon done into motion pictures. I will say for Stanley that he never pretended that anything stronger than Botticelli hurt his eyes. He opened like a lotus flower to the sun and made a streak of color, even in New York. Stanley always felt that Boston hadn't done well by him, and he enjoyed throwing jobs to old Tech men. 'Largess, largess, Lord Marmion, all as he lighted down.' When they began breaking ground for the Mont Blanc I applied for a job because I wanted experience in deep foundation work. Stanley beamed at me across his mirror-finish mahogany and offered me something better, but it was foundation work I wanted, so early in the spring I went into the hole with a gang of twenty dagos.

"It was an awful summer, the worst New York can do in the way of heat, and I guess that's the worst in the world, excepting India maybe. We sweated away, I and my twenty dagos, and I learned a good deal—more than I ever meant to. Now there was one of those men I liked, and it's about him I must tell you. His name was Caesaro, but he was so little that the other dagos in the hole called him Caesarino, Little Caesar. He was from the island of Ischia, and I had been there when a young lad with my sister who was ill. I knew the particular goat track Caesarino hailed from, and maybe I had seen him there among all the swarms of eager, panting little animals that roll around in the dust and somehow worry through famine and fever and earthquake, with such a curiously hot spark of life in them and such delight in being allowed to live at all.

"Caesarino's father was dead and his older brother was married and had a little swarm of his own to look out for. Caesarino and the next two boys were coral divers and went out with the fleet twice a year; when they were at home they worked about by the day in the vineyards. He couldn't remember ever having had any clothes on in summer until he was ten; spent all his time swimming and diving and sprawling about among the nets on the beach. I've seen 'em, those wild little water dogs; look like little seals with their round eyes and their hair always dripping. Caesarino thought he could make more money in New York than he made diving for coral, and he was the mainstay of the family. There were ever so many little water dogs after him; his father had done the best he could to insure the perpetuity of his breed before he went under the lava to begin all over again by helping to make the vines grow in that marvelously fruitful volcanic soil. Little Caesar came to New York, and that is where we begin.

"He was one of the twenty crumpled, broken little men who worked with me down in that big hole. I first noticed him because he was so young, and so eager to please, and because he was so especially frightened. Wouldn't you be at all this terrifying, complicated machinery, after sun and happy nakedness and a goat track on a volcanic island? Haven't you ever noticed how, when a dago is hurt on the railroad and they trundle him into the station on a truck, another dago always runs alongside him, holding his hand and looking the more scared of the two? Little Caesar ran about the hole looking like that. He was afraid of everything he touched. He never knew what might go off. Suppose we went to work for some great and powerful nation in Asia that had a civilization built on sciences we knew nothing of, as ours is built on physics and chemistry and higher mathematics; and suppose we knew that to these people we were absolutely meaningless as social beings, were waste to clean their engines, as Zablowski says; that we were there to do the dangerous work, to be poisoned in caissons under rivers, blown up by blasts, drowned in coal mines, and that these masters of ours were as indifferent to us individually as the Carthaginians were to their mercenaries? I'll tell you we'd guard the precious little spark of life with trembling hands."

"But I say—" sputtered the lawyer from the District Attorney's office.

"I know, I know, Chambers." Hallet put out a soothing hand. "*We* don't want 'em, God knows. They come. But why do they come? It's the pressure of their time and ours. It's not rich pickings they've got where I've worked with them, let me tell you. Well, Caesarino, with the others, came. The first morning I went on my job he was there, more scared of a new boss than any of the others; literally quaking. He was only twenty-three and lighter than the other men, and he was afraid I'd notice that. I thought he would pull his shoulder blades loose. After one big heave I stopped beside him and dropped a word: 'Buono soldato.' In a moment he was grinning with all his teeth, and he squeaked out: 'Buono soldato, da boss he talka dago!' That was the beginning of our acquaintance."

Hallet paused a moment and smoked thoughtfully. He was a soft man for the iron age, I reflected, and it was easy enough to see why Stanley Merryweather had beaten him in the race. There is a string to every big contract in New York, and Hallet was always tripping over the string.

"From that time on we were friends. I knew just six words of Italian, but that summer I got so I could understand his fool dialect pretty well. I used to feel ashamed of the way he'd look at me, like a girl in love. You see, I was the only thing he wasn't afraid of. On Sundays we used to poke off to a beach somewhere, and he'd lie in the water all day and tell me about the coral divers and the bottom of the Mediterranean. I got very fond of him. It was my first summer in New York and I was lonesome, too. The game down here looked pretty ugly to me. There were plenty of disagreeable things to think about, and it was better fun to see how much soda water Caesarino could drink. He never drank wine. He used to say: 'At home—oh, yes-a! At New York,' making that wise little gesture with the forefinger between his eyes, 'niente. Sav'-a da mon'.' But even his economy had its weak spots. He was very fond of candy, and he was always buying 'pop-a corn off-a da push-a cart.'

"However, he had sent home a good deal of money, and his mother was ailing and he was so frightened about her and so generally homesick that I urged him to go back to Ischia for the winter. There was a poor prospect for steady work, and if he went home he wouldn't be out much more than if he stayed in New York working on half time. He backed and filled and agonized a good deal, but when I at last got him to the point of engaging his passage he was the happiest dago on Manhattan Island. He told me about it all a hundred times.

"His mother, from the piccola casa on the cliff, could see all the boats go by to Naples. She always watched for them. Possibly he would be able to see her from the steamer, or at least the casa, or certainly the place where the casa stood.

"All this time we were making things move in the hole. Old Macfarlane wasn't around much in those days. He passed on the results, but Stanley had a free hand as to ways and means. He made amazing mistakes, harrowing blunders. His path was strewn with hairbreadth escapes, but they never dampened his courage or took the spurt out of him. After a close shave he'd simply duck his head and smile brightly and say: 'Well, I got *that* across, old Persimmons!' I'm not underestimating the value of dash and intrepidity. He made the wheels go round. One of his maxims was that men are cheaper than machinery. He smashed up a lot of hands, but he always got out under the fellow-servant act. 'Never been caught yet, huh?' he used to say with his pleasant, confiding wink. I'd been complaining to him for a long while about the cabling, but he always put me off; sometimes with a surly insinuation that I was nervous about my own head, but oftener with fine good humor. At last something did happen in the hole.

"It happened one night late in August, after a stretch of heat that broke the thermometers. For a week there hadn't been a dry human being in New York. Your linen went down three minutes after you put it on. We moved about insulated in moisture, like the fishes in the sea. That night I couldn't go down into the hole right away. When you once got down there the heat from the boilers and the steam from the diamond drills made a temperature that was beyond anything the human frame was meant to endure. I stood looking down for a long while, I remember. It was a hole nearly three acres square, and on one side the Savoyard rose up twenty stories, a straight blank, brick wall. You know what a mess such a hole is; great boulders of rock and deep pits of sand and gulleys of water, with drills puffing everywhere and little crumpled men crawling about like tumblebugs under the stream from the searchlight. When you got down into the hole, the wall of the Savoyard seemed to go clear up the sky; that pale blue enamel sky of a midsummer New York night. Six of my men were moving a diamond drill and settling it into a new place, when one of the big clamshells that swung back and forth over the hole fell with its load of sand—the worn cabling, of course. It was directly over my men when it fell. They couldn't hear anything for the noise of the drill; didn't know anything had happened until it struck them. They were bending over, huddled together, and the thing came down on them like a brick dropped on an ant hill. They were all buried, Caesarino among them. When we got them out, two were dead and the others were dying. My boy was the first we reached. The edge of the clamshell had struck him, and he was all broken to pieces. The moment we got his head out he began chattering like a monkey. I put my ear down to his lips—the other drills were still going—and he was talking about what I had forgotten, that his steamer ticket was in his pocket and that he was to sail next Saturday. '*È necessario, signore, è necessario,*' he kept repeating. He had written his family what boat he was coming on, and his mother would be at the door, watching it when it went by to Naples. '*È necessario, signore, è necessario.*'

"When the ambulances got there the orderlies lifted two of the men and had them carried up to the street, but when they turned to Caesarino they dismissed him with a shrug, glancing at him with the contemptuous expression that ambulance orderlies come to have when they see that a man is too much shattered to pick up. He saw the look, and a boy who doesn't know the language learns to read looks. He broke into sobs and began to beat the rock with his hands. 'Curs-a da hole, curs-a da hole, curs-a da build'!' he screamed, bruising his fists on the shale. I caught his hands and leaned over him. '*Buono soldato, buono soldato,*' I said in his ear. His shrieks stopped, and his sobs quivered down. He looked at me— '*Buono soldato,*' he whispered, '*ma, perchè?*' Then the hemorrhage from his mouth shut him off, and he began to choke. In a few minutes it was all over with Little Caesar.

"About that time Merryweather showed up. Some one had telephoned him, and he had come down in his car. He was a little frightened and pleasurably excited. He has the truly journalistic mind—saving your presence, gentlemen—and he likes anything that bites on the tongue. He looked things over and ducked his head and grinned good-naturedly. 'Well, I guess you've got your new cabling out of me now, huh, Freddy?' he said to me. I went up to the car with him. His hand shook a little as he shielded a match to light his cigarette. 'Don't get shaky, Freddy. That wasn't so worse,' he said, as he stepped into his car.

"For the next few days I was busy seeing that the boy didn't get buried in a trench with a brass tag around his neck. On Saturday night I got his pay envelope, and he was paid for only half of the night he was killed; the accident happened about eleven o'clock. I didn't fool with any paymaster. On Monday morning I went straight to Merryweather's office, stormed his bower of rose and gold, and put that envelope on the mahogany between us. 'Merryweather,' said I, 'this is going to cost you something. I hear the relatives of the other fellows have all signed off for a few hundred, but this little dago hadn't any relatives here, and he's going to have the best lawyers in New York to prosecute his claim for him.'

"Stanley flew into one of his quick tempers. 'What business is it of yours, and what are you out to do us for?'

"'I'm out to get every cent that's coming to this boy's family.'

"'How in hell is that any concern of yours?'

"'Never mind that. But we've got one awfully good case, Stanley. I happen to be the man who reported to you on that cabling again and again. I have a copy of the letter I wrote you about it when you were at Mount Desert, and I have your reply.'

"Stanley whirled around in his swivel chair and reached for his checkbook. 'How much are you gouging for?' he asked with his baronial pout.

"'Just all the courts will give me. I want it settled there,' I said, and I got up to go.

"'Well, you've chosen your class, sir,' he broke out, ruffling up red. 'You can stay in a hole with the guineas till the end of time for all of me. That's where you've put yourself.'

"I got my money out of that concern and sent it off to the old woman in Ischia, and that's the end of the story. You all know Merryweather. He's the first man in my business since his uncle died, but we manage to keep clear of each other. The Mont Blanc was a milestone for me; one road ended there and another began. It was only a little accident, such as happens in New York every day in the year, but that one happened near me. There's a lot of waste about building a city. Usually the destruction all goes on in the cellar; it's only when it hits high, as it did last night, that it sets us thinking. Wherever there is the greatest output of energy, wherever the blind human race is exerting itself most furiously, there's bound to be tumult and disaster. Here we are, six men, with our pitiful few years to live and our one little chance for happiness, throwing everything we have into that conflagration on Manhattan Island, helping, with every nerve in us, with everything our brain cells can generate, with our very creature heat, to swell its glare, its noise, its luxury, and its power. Why do we do it? And why, in heaven's name, do *they* do it? *Ma, perchè*? as Caesarino said that night in the hole. Why did he, from that lazy volcanic island, so tiny, so forgotten, where life is simple and pellucid and tranquil, shaping itself to tradition and ancestral manners as water shapes itself to the jar, why did he come so far to cast his little spark in the bonfire? And the thousands like him, from islands even smaller and more remote, why do they come, like iron dust to the magnet, like moths to the flame? There must be something wonderful coming. When the frenzy is over, when the furnace has cooled, what marvel will be left on Manhattan Island?"

"What has been left often enough before," said Zablowski dreamily. "What was left in India, only not half so much."

Hallet disregarded him. "What it will be is a new idea of some sort. That's all that ever comes, really. That's what we are all the slaves of, though we don't know it. It's the whip that cracks over us till we drop. Even Merryweather—and that's where the gods have the laugh on him— every firm he crushes to the wall, every deal he puts through, every cocktail he pours down his throat, he does it in the service of this unborn Idea, that he will never know anything about. Some day it will dawn, serene and clear, and your Moloch on the Singer Tower over there will get down and do it Asian obeisance."

We reflected on this while the launch, returning toward the city, ruffled through the dark furrows of water that kept rolling up into the light. Johnson looked back at the black sea road and said quietly:

"Well, anyhow, we are the people who are doing it, and whatever it is, it will be ours."

Hallet laughed. "Don't call anything ours, Johnson, while Zablowski is around."

"Zablowski," Johnson said irritably, "why don't you *ever* hit back?"

First published in *Collier's*, XLIX (May 18, 1912), 16–17, 41.

The Joy of Nelly Deane

✳ ✳ ✳

Nell and I were almost ready to go on for the last act of *Queen Esther*, and we had for the moment got rid of our three patient dressers, Mrs. Dow, Mrs. Freeze, and Mrs. Spinny. Nell was peering over my shoulder into the little cracked looking glass that Mrs. Dow had taken from its nail on her kitchen wall and brought down to the church under her shawl that morning. When she realized that we were alone, Nell whispered to me in the quick, fierce way she had:

"Say, Peggy, won't you go up and stay with me tonight? Scott Spinny's asked to take me home, and I don't want to walk up with him alone."

"I guess so, if you'll ask my mother."

"Oh, I'll fix her!" Nell laughed, with a toss of her head which meant that she usually got what she wanted, even from people much less tractable than my mother.

In a moment our tiring-women were back again. The three old ladies—at least they seemed old to us—fluttered about us, more agitated than we were ourselves. It seemed as though they would never leave off patting Nell and touching her up. They kept trying things this way and that, never able in the end to decide which way was best. They wouldn't hear to her using rouge, and as they powdered her neck and arms, Mrs. Freeze murmured that she hoped we wouldn't get into the habit of using such things. Mrs. Spinny divided her time between pulling up and tucking down the "illusion" that filled in the square neck of Nelly's dress. She didn't like things much low, she said; but after she had pulled it up, she stood back and looked at Nell thoughtfully through her glasses. While the excited girl was reaching for this and that, buttoning a slipper, pinning down a curl, Mrs. Spinny's smile softened more and more until, just

[55]

before Esther made her entrance, the old lady tiptoed up to her and softly tucked the illusion down as far as it would go.

"She's so pink; it seems a pity not," she whispered apologetically to Mrs. Dow.

Every one admitted that Nelly was the prettiest girl in Riverbend, and the gayest—oh, the gayest! When she was not singing, she was laughing. When she was not laid up with a broken arm, the outcome of a foolhardy coasting feat, or suspended from school because she ran away at recess to go buggy-riding with Guy Franklin, she was sure to be up to mischief of some sort. Twice she broke through the ice and got soused in the river because she never looked where she skated or cared what happened so long as she went fast enough. After the second of these duckings our three dressers declared that she was trying to be a Baptist despite herself.

Mrs. Spinny and Mrs. Freeze and Mrs. Dow, who were always hovering about Nelly, often whispered to me their hope that she would eventually come into our church and not "go with the Methodists"; her family were Wesleyans. But to me these artless plans of theirs never wholly explained their watchful affection. They had good daughters themselves—except Mrs. Spinny, who had only the sullen Scott—and they loved their plain girls and thanked God for them. But they loved Nelly differently. They were proud of her pretty figure and yellow-brown eyes, which dilated so easily and sparkled with a kind of golden effervescence. They were always making pretty things for her, always coaxing her to come to the sewing circle, where she knotted her thread, and put in the wrong sleeve, and laughed and chattered and said a great many things that she should not have said, and somehow always warmed their hearts. I think they loved her for her unquenchable joy.

All the Baptist ladies liked Nell, even those who criticized her most severely, but the three who were first in fighting the battles of our little church, who held it together by their prayers and the labor of their hands, watched over her as they did over Mrs. Dow's century plant before it blossomed. They looked for her on Sunday morning and smiled at her as she hurried, always a little late, up to the choir. When she rose and stood behind the organ and sang "There Is a Green Hill," one could see Mrs. Dow and Mrs. Freeze settle back in their accustomed seats and look up at her as if she had just come from that hill and had brought them glad tidings.

It was because I sang contralto, or, as we said, alto, in the Baptist choir that Nell and I became friends. She was so gay and grown up, so busy with parties and dances and picnics, that I would scarcely have seen much of her had we not sung together. She liked me better than she did any of the older girls, who tried clumsily to be like her, and I felt almost as solicitous and admiring as did Mrs. Dow and Mrs. Spinny. I think even then I must have loved to see her bloom and glow, and I loved to hear her sing, in "The Ninety and Nine,"

But one was out on the hills away

in her sweet, strong voice. Nell had never had a singing lesson, but she had sung from the time she could talk, and Mrs. Dow used fondly to say that it was singing so much that made her figure so pretty.

After I went into the choir it was found to be easier to get Nelly to choir practice. If I stopped outside her gate on my way to church and coaxed her, she usually laughed, ran in for her hat and jacket, and went along with me. The three old ladies fostered our friendship, and because I was "quiet," they esteemed me a good influence for Nelly. This view was propounded in a sewing-circle discussion and, leaking down to us through our mothers, greatly amused us. Dear old ladies! It was so manifestly for what Nell was that they loved her, and yet they were always looking for "influences" to change her.

The *Queen Esther* performance had cost us three months of hard practice, and it was not easy to keep Nell up to attending the tedious rehearsals. Some of the boys we knew were in the chorus of Assyrian youths, but the solo cast was made up of older people, and Nell found them very poky. We gave the cantata in the Baptist church on Christmas Eve, "to a crowded house," as the Riverbend *Messenger* truly chronicled. The country folk for miles about had come in through a deep snow, and their teams and wagons stood in a long row at the hitch-bars on each side of the church door. It was certainly Nelly's night, for however much the tenor—he was her schoolmaster, and naturally thought poorly of her—might try to eclipse her in his dolorous solos about the rivers of Babylon, there could be no doubt as to whom the people had come to hear—and to see.

After the performance was over, our fathers and mothers came back to the dressing rooms—the little rooms behind the baptistry where the candidates for baptism were robed—to congratulate us, and Nell persuaded my mother to let me go home with her. This arrangement may not have been wholly agreeable to Scott Spinny, who stood glumly waiting at the baptistry door; though I used to think he dogged Nell's steps not so much for any pleasure he got from being with her as for the pleasure of keeping other people away. Dear little Mrs. Spinny was perpetually in a state of humiliation on account of his bad manners, and she tried by a very special tenderness to make up to Nelly for the remissness of her ungracious son.

Scott was a spare, muscular fellow, good-looking, but with a face so set and dark that I used to think it very like the castings he sold. He was taciturn and domineering, and Nell rather liked to provoke him. Her father was so easy with her that she seemed to enjoy being ordered about now and then. That night, when every one was praising her and telling her how well she sang and how pretty she looked, Scott only said, as we came out of the dressing room:

"Have you got your high shoes on?"

"No; but I've got rubbers on over my low ones. Mother doesn't care."

"Well, you just go back and put 'em on as fast as you can."

Nell made a face at him and ran back, laughing. Her mother, fat, comfortable Mrs. Deane, was immensely amused at this.

"That's right, Scott," she chuckled. "You can do enough more with her than I can. She walks right over me an' Jud."

Scott grinned. If he was proud of Nelly, the last thing he wished to do was to show it. When she came back he began to nag again. "What are you going to do with all those flowers? They'll freeze stiff as pokers."

"Well, there won't none of *your* flowers freeze, Scott Spinny, so there!" Nell snapped. She had the best of him that time, and the Assyrian youths rejoiced. They were most of them high-school boys, and the poorest of them had "chipped in" and sent all the way to Denver for Queen Esther's flowers. There were bouquets from half a dozen townspeople, too, but none from Scott. Scott was a prosperous hardware merchant and notoriously penurious, though he saved his face, as the boys said, by giving liberally to the church.

"There's no use freezing the fool things, anyhow. You get me some newspapers, and I'll wrap 'em up." Scott took from his pocket a folded copy of the Riverbend *Messenger* and began laboriously to wrap up one of the bouquets. When we left the church door he bore three large newspaper bundles, carrying them as carefully as if they had been so many newly frosted wedding cakes, and left Nell and me to shift for ourselves as we floundered along the snow-burdened sidewalk.

Although it was after midnight, lights were shining from many of the little wooden houses, and the roofs and shrubbery were so deep in snow that Riverbend looked as if it had been tucked down into a warm bed. The companies of people, all coming from church, tramping this way and that toward their homes and calling "Good night" and "Merry Christmas" as they parted company, all seemed to us very unusual and exciting.

When we got home, Mrs. Deane had a cold supper ready, and Jud Deane had already taken off his shoes and fallen to on his fried chicken and pie. He was so proud of his pretty daughter that he must give her her Christmas presents then and there, and he went into the sleeping chamber behind the dining room and from the depths of his wife's closet brought out a short sealskin jacket and a round cap and made Nelly put them on.

Mrs. Deane, who sat busy between a plate of spice cake and a tray piled with her famous whipped cream tarts, laughed inordinately at his behavior.

"Ain't he worse than any kid you ever see? He's been running to that closet like a cat shut away from her kittens. I wonder Nell ain't caught on before this. I did think he'd make out now to keep 'em till Christmas morning; but he's never made out to keep anything yet."

That was true enough, and fortunately Jud's inability to keep anything seemed always to present a highly humorous aspect to his wife. Mrs. Deane put her heart into her cooking, and said that so long as a man was a good provider she had no cause to complain. Other people were not so charitable toward Jud's failing. I remember how many strictures were passed upon that little sealskin and how he was censured for his extravagance. But what a public-spirited thing, after all, it was for him to do! How, the winter through, we all enjoyed seeing Nell skating on the river or running about the town with the brown collar turned up about her bright cheeks and her hair blowing out from under the round cap! "No seal," Mrs. Dow said, "would have begrudged it to her. Why should we?" This was at the sewing circle, when the new coat was under grave discussion.

At last Nelly and I got upstairs and undressed, and the pad of Jud's slippered feet about the kitchen premises—where he was carrying up from the cellar things that might freeze—ceased. He called "Good night, daughter," from the foot of the stairs, and the house grew quiet. But one is not a prima donna the first time for nothing, and it seemed as if we could not go to bed. Our light must have burned long after every other

in Riverbend was out. The muslin curtains of Nell's bed were drawn back;
Mrs. Deane had turned down the white counterpane and taken off the
shams and smoothed the pillows for us. But their fair plumpness offered
no temptation to two such hot young heads. We could not let go of life
even for a little while. We sat and talked in Nell's cozy room, where
there was a tiny, white fur rug—the only one in Riverbend—before the
bed; and there were white sash curtains, and the prettiest little desk and
dressing table I had ever seen. It was a warm, gay little room, flooded all
day long with sunlight from east and south windows that had climbing
roses all about them in summer. About the dresser were photographs of
adoring high school boys; and one of Guy Franklin, much groomed and
barbered, in a dress coat and a boutonnière. I never liked to see that
photograph there. The home boys looked properly modest and bashful
on the dresser, but he seemed to be staring impudently all the time.

I knew nothing definite against Guy, but in Riverbend all "traveling
men" were considered worldly and wicked. He traveled for a Chicago
dry-goods firm, and our fathers didn't like him because he put extravagant
ideas into our mothers' heads. He had very smooth and flattering ways,
and he introduced into our simple community a great variety of perfumes
and scented soaps, and he always reminded me of the merchants in Caesar,
who brought into Gaul "those things which effeminate the mind," as we
translated that delightfully easy passage.

Nell was sitting before the dressing table in her nightgown, holding
the new fur coat and rubbing her cheek against it, when I saw a sudden
gleam of tears in her eyes. "You know, Peggy," she said in her quick, impetuous way, "this makes me feel bad. I've got a secret from my daddy."

I can see her now, so pink and eager, her brown hair in two springy
braids down her back, and her eyes shining with tears and with something
even softer and more tremulous.

"I'm engaged, Peggy," she whispered, "really and truly."

She leaned forward, unbuttoning her nightgown, and there on her
breast, hung by a little gold chain about her neck, was a diamond ring—
Guy Franklin's solitaire; every one in Riverbend knew it well.

"I'm going to live in Chicago, and take singing lessons, and go to
operas, and do all those nice things—oh, everything! I know you don't
like him, Peggy, but you know you *are* a kid. You'll see how it is yourself
when you grow up. He's so *different* from our boys, and he's just terribly
in love with me. And then, Peggy,"—flushing all down over her soft
shoulders,—"I'm awfully fond of him, too. Awfully."

"Are you, Nell, truly?" I whispered. She seemed so changed to me by the warm light in her eyes and that delicate suffusion of color. I felt as I did when I got up early on picnic mornings in summer, and saw the dawn come up in the breathless sky above the river meadows and make all the corn fields golden.

"Sure I do, Peggy; don't look so solemn. It's nothing to look that way about, kid. It's nice." She threw her arms about me suddenly and hugged me.

"I hate to think about your going so far away from us all, Nell."

"Oh, you'll love to come and visit me. Just you wait."

She began breathlessly to go over things Guy Franklin had told her about Chicago, until I seemed to see it all looming up out there under the stars that kept watch over our little sleeping town. We had neither of us ever been to a city, but we knew what it would be like. We heard it throbbing like great engines, and calling to us, that faraway world. Even after we had opened the windows and scurried into bed, we seemed to feel a pulsation across all the miles of snow. The winter silence trembled with it, and the air was full of something new that seemed to break over us in soft waves. In that snug, warm little bed I had a sense of imminent change and danger. I was somehow afraid for Nelly when I heard her breathing so quickly beside me, and I put my arm about her protectingly as we drifted toward sleep.

In the following spring we were both graduated from the Riverbend high school, and I went away to college. My family moved to Denver, and during the next four years I heard very little of Nelly Deane. My life was crowded with new people and new experiences, and I am afraid I held her little in mind. I heard indirectly that Jud Deane had lost what little property he owned in a luckless venture in Cripple Creek, and that he had been able to keep his house in Riverbend only through the clemency of his creditors. Guy Franklin had his route changed and did not go to Riverbend any more. He married the daughter of a rich cattleman out near Long Pine, and ran a dry-goods store of his own. Mrs. Dow wrote me a long letter about once a year, and in one of these she told me that Nelly was teaching in the sixth grade in the Riverbend school.

Dear Nelly does not like teaching very well. The children try her, and she is so pretty it seems a pity for her to be tied down to uncongenial employment. Scott is still very attentive, and I have noticed him look up at the window of Nelly's room in a very determined way as he goes home to dinner. Scott continues prosperous; he has made money during these hard times and now owns both our hardware stores. He is close, but a very honorable fellow. Nelly seems to hold off, but I think Mrs. Spinny has hopes. Nothing would please her more. If Scott were more careful about his appearance, it would help. He of course gets black about his business, and Nelly, you know, is very dainty. People do say his mother does his courting for him, she is so eager. If only Scott does not turn out hard and penurious like his father! We must all have our schooling in this life, but I don't want Nelly's to be too severe. She is a dear girl, and keeps her color.

Mrs. Dow's own schooling had been none too easy. Her husband had long been crippled with rheumatism, and was bitter and faultfinding. Her daughters had married poorly, and one of her sons had fallen into evil ways. But her letters were always cheerful, and in one of them she gently remonstrated with me because I "seemed inclined to take a sad view of life."

In the winter vacation of my senior year I stopped on my way home to visit Mrs. Dow. The first thing she told me when I got into her old buckboard at the station was that "Scott had at last prevailed," and that Nelly was to marry him in the spring. As a preliminary step, Nelly was about to join the Baptist church. "Just think, you will be here for her baptizing! How that will please Nelly! She is to be immersed tomorrow night."

I met Scott Spinny in the post office that morning and he gave me a hard grip with one black hand. There was something grim and saturnine about his powerful body and bearded face and his strong, cold hands. I wondered what perverse fate had driven him for eight years to dog the footsteps of a girl whose charm was due to qualities naturally distasteful to him. It still seems strange to me that in easygoing Riverbend, where there were so many boys who could have lived contentedly enough with my little grasshopper, it was the pushing ant who must have her and all her careless ways.

By a kind of unformulated etiquette one did not call upon candidates for baptism on the day of the ceremony, so I had my first glimpse of Nelly that evening. The baptistry was a cemented pit directly under the pulpit rostrum, over which we had our stage when we sang *Queen Esther*. I sat through the sermon somewhat nervously. After the minister, in his long, black gown, had gone down into the water and the choir had finished singing, the door from the dressing room opened, and, led by one of the deacons, Nelly came down the steps into the pool. Oh, she looked so little and meek and chastened! Her white cashmere robe clung about her, and her brown hair was brushed straight back and hung in two soft braids from a little head bent humbly. As she stepped down into the water I shivered with the cold of it, and I remembered sharply how much I had loved her. She went down until the water was well above her waist, and stood white and small, with her hands crossed on her breast, while the minister said the words about being buried with Christ in baptism. Then, lying in his arm, she disappeared under the dark water. "It will be like that when she dies," I thought, and a quick pain caught my heart. The choir began to sing "Washed in the Blood of the Lamb" as she rose again, the door behind the baptistry opened, revealing those three dear guardians, Mrs. Dow, Mrs. Freeze, and Mrs. Spinny, and she went up into their arms.

I went to see Nell next day, up in the little room of many memories. Such a sad, sad visit! She seemed changed—a little embarrassed and quietly despairing. We talked of many of the old Riverbend girls and boys, but she did not mention Guy Franklin or Scott Spinny, except to say that her father had got work in Scott's hardware store. She begged me, putting her hands on my shoulders with something of her old impulsiveness, to come and stay a few days with her. But I was afraid—afraid of what she might tell me and of what I might say. When I sat in that room with all her trinkets, the foolish harvest of her girlhood, lying about, and the white curtains and the little white rug, I thought of Scott Spinny with positive terror and could feel his hard grip on my hand again. I made the best excuse I could about having to hurry on to Denver; but she gave me one quick look, and her eyes ceased to plead. I saw that she understood me perfectly. We had known each other so well. Just once, when I got up to go and had trouble with my veil, she laughed her old merry laugh and told me there were some things I would never learn, for all my schooling.

The next day, when Mrs. Dow drove me down to the station to catch the morning train for Denver, I saw Nelly hurrying to school with several books under her arm. She had been working up her lessons at home, I thought. She was never quick at her books, dear Nell.

It was ten years before I again visited Riverbend. I had been in Rome for a long time, and had fallen into bitter homesickness. One morning, sitting among the dahlias and asters that bloom so bravely upon those gigantic heaps of earth-red ruins that were once the palaces of the Caesars, I broke the seal of one of Mrs. Dow's long yearly letters. It brought so much sad news that I resolved then and there to go home to Riverbend, the only place that had ever really been home to me. Mrs. Dow wrote me that her husband, after years of illness, had died in the cold spell last March. "So good and patient toward the last," she wrote, "and so afraid of giving extra trouble." There was another thing she saved until the last. She wrote on and on, dear woman, about new babies and village improvements, as if she could not bear to tell me; and then it came:

> You will be sad to hear that two months ago our dear Nelly left us. It was a terrible blow to us all. I cannot write about it yet, I fear. I wake up every morning feeling that I ought to go to her. She went three days after her little boy was born. The baby is a fine child and will live, I think, in spite of everything. He and her little girl, now eight years old, whom she named Margaret, after you, have gone to Mrs. Spinny's. She loves them more than if they were her own. It seems as if already they had made her quite young again. I wish you could see Nelly's children.

Ah, that was what I wanted, to see Nelly's children! The wish came aching from my heart along with the bitter homesick tears; along with a quick, torturing recollection that flashed upon me, as I looked about and tried to collect myself, of how we two had sat in our sunny seat in the corner of the old bare schoolroom one September afternoon and learned the names of the seven hills together. In that place, at that moment, after so many years, how it all came back to me—the warm sun on my back, the chattering girl beside me, the curly hair, the laughing yellow eyes, the stubby little finger on the page! I felt as if even then, when we sat in the sun with our heads together, it was all arranged, written out like a story, that at this moment I should be sitting among the crumbling bricks and drying grass, and she should be lying in the place I knew so well, on that green hill far away.

Mrs. Dow sat with her Christmas sewing in the familiar sitting room, where the carpet and the wallpaper and the tablecover had all faded into soft, dull colors, and even the chromo of Hagar and Ishmael had been toned to the sobriety of age. In the bay window the tall wire flowerstand still bore its little terraces of potted plants, and the big fuchsia and the

Martha Washington geranium had blossomed for Christmastide. Mrs. Dow herself did not look greatly changed to me. Her hair, thin ever since I could remember it, was now quite white, but her spare, wiry little person had all its old activity, and her eyes gleamed with the old friendliness behind her silver-bowed glasses. Her gray house dress seemed just like those she used to wear when I ran in after school to take her angelfood cake down to the church supper.

The house sat on a hill, and from behind the geraniums I could see pretty much all of Riverbend, tucked down in the soft snow, and the air above was full of big, loose flakes, falling from a gray sky which betokened settled weather. Indoors the hard-coal burner made a tropical temperature, and glowed a warm orange from its isinglass sides. We sat and visited, the two of us, with a great sense of comfort and completeness. I had reached Riverbend only that morning, and Mrs. Dow, who had been haunted by thoughts of shipwreck and suffering upon wintry seas, kept urging me to draw nearer to the fire and suggesting incidental refreshment. We had chattered all through the winter morning and most of the afternoon, taking up one after another of the Riverbend girls and boys, and agreeing that we had reason to be well satisfied with most of them. Finally, after a long pause in which I had listened to the contented ticking of the clock and the crackle of the coal, I put the question I had until then held back:

"And now, Mrs. Dow, tell me about the one we loved best of all. Since I got your letter I've thought of her every day. Tell me all about Scott and Nelly."

The tears flashed behind her glasses, and she smoothed the little pink bag on her knee.

"Well, dear, I'm afraid Scott proved to be a hard man, like his father. But we must remember that Nelly always had Mrs. Spinny. I never saw anything like the love there was between those two. After Nelly lost her own father and mother, she looked to Mrs. Spinny for everything. When Scott was too unreasonable, his mother could 'most always prevail upon him. She never lifted a hand to fight her own battles with Scott's father, but she was never afraid to speak up for Nelly. And then Nelly took great comfort of her little girl. Such a lovely child!"

"Had she been very ill before the little baby came?"

"No, Margaret; I'm afraid 't was all because they had the wrong doctor. I feel confident that either Doctor Tom or Doctor Jones could have brought her through. But, you see, Scott had offended them both, and they'd stopped trading at his store, so he would have young Doctor

Fox, a boy just out of college and a stranger. He got scared and didn't know what to do. Mrs. Spinny felt he wasn't doing right, so she sent for Mrs. Freeze and me. It seemed like Nelly had got discouraged. Scott would move into their big new house before the plastering was dry, and though 't was summer, she had taken a terrible cold that seemed to have drained her, and she took no interest in fixing the place up. Mrs. Spinny had been down with her back again and wasn't able to help, and things was just anyway. We won't talk about that, Margaret; I think 't would hurt Mrs. Spinny to have you know. She nearly died of mortification when she sent for us, and blamed her poor back. We did get Nelly fixed up nicely before she died. I prevailed upon Doctor Tom to come in at the last, and it 'most broke his heart. 'Why, Mis' Dow,' he said, 'if you'd only have come and told me how 't was, I'd have come and carried her right off in my arms.'"

"Oh, Mrs. Dow," I cried, "then it needn't have been?"

Mrs. Dow dropped her needle and clasped her hands quickly. "We mustn't look at it that way, dear," she said tremulously and a little sternly; "we mustn't let ourselves. We must just feel that our Lord wanted her *then*, and took her to Himself. When it was all over, she did look so like a child of God, young and trusting, like she did on her baptizing night, you remember?"

I felt that Mrs. Dow did not want to talk any more about Nelly then, and, indeed, I had little heart to listen; so I told her I would go for a walk, and suggested that I might stop at Mrs. Spinny's to see the children.

Mrs. Dow looked up thoughtfully at the clock. "I doubt if you'll find little Margaret there now. It's half-past four, and she'll have been out of school an hour and more. She'll be most likely coasting on Lupton's Hill. She usually makes for it with her sled the minute she is out of the schoolhouse door. You know, it's the old hill where you all used to slide. If you stop in at the church about six o'clock, you'll likely find Mrs. Spinny there with the baby. I promised to go down and help Mrs. Freeze finish up the tree, and Mrs. Spinny said she'd run in with the baby, if 't wasn't too bitter. She won't leave him alone with the Swede girl. She's like a young woman with her first."

Lupton's Hill was at the other end of town, and when I got there the dusk was thickening, drawing blue shadows over the snowy fields. There were perhaps twenty children creeping up the hill or whizzing down the packed sled track. When I had been watching them for some minutes, I heard a lusty shout, and a little red sled shot past me into the deep snow-drift beyond. The child was quite buried for a moment, then she struggled out and stood dusting the snow from her short coat and red woolen comforter. She wore a brown fur cap, which was too big for her and of an old-fashioned shape, such as girls wore long ago, but I would have known her without the cap. Mrs. Dow had said a beautiful child, and there would not be two like this in Riverbend. She was off before I had time to speak to her, going up the hill at a trot, her sturdy little legs plowing through the trampled snow. When she reached the top she never paused to take breath, but threw herself upon her sled and came down with a whoop that was quenched only by the deep drift at the end.

"Are you Margaret Spinny?" I asked as she struggled out in a cloud of snow.

"Yes, 'm." She approached me with frank curiosity, pulling her little sled behind her. "Are you the strange lady staying at Mrs. Dow's?" I nodded, and she began to look my clothes over with respectful interest.

"Your grandmother is to be at the church at six o'clock, isn't she?"

"Yes, 'm."

"Well, suppose we walk up there now. It's nearly six, and all the other children are going home." She hesitated, and looked up at the faintly gleaming track on the hill slope. "Do you want another slide? Is that it?" I asked.

"Do you mind?" she asked shyly.

"No. I'll wait for you. Take your time; don't run."

Two little boys were still hanging about the slide, and they cheered her as she came down, her comforter streaming in the wind.

"Now," she announced, getting up out of the drift, "I'll show you where the church is."

"Shall I tie your comforter again?"

"No, 'm, thanks. I'm plenty warm." She put her mittened hand confidingly in mine and trudged along beside me.

Mrs. Dow must have heard us tramping up the snowy steps of the church, for she met us at the door. Every one had gone except the old ladies. A kerosene lamp flickered over the Sunday school chart, with the lesson-picture of the Wise Men, and the little barrel stove threw out a deep glow over the three white heads that bent above the baby. There the three friends sat, patting him, and smoothing his dress, and playing with his hands, which made theirs look so brown.

"You ain't seen nothing finer in all your travels," said Mrs. Spinny, and they all laughed.

They showed me his full chest and how strong his back was; had me feel the golden fuzz on his head, and made him look at me with his round, bright eyes. He laughed and reared himself in my arms as I took him up and held him close to me. He was so warm and tingling with life, and he had the flush of new beginnings, of the new morning and the new rose. He seemed to have come so lately from his mother's heart! It was as if I held her youth and all her young joy. As I put my cheek down against his, he spied a pink flower in my hat, and making a gleeful sound, he lunged at it with both fists.

"Don't let him spoil it," murmured Mrs. Spinny. "He loves color so—like Nelly."

First published in *Century*, LXXXII (October, 1911), 859–867.

The Enchanted Bluff

We had our swim before sundown, and while we were cooking our supper the oblique rays of light made a dazzling glare on the white sand about us. The translucent red ball itself sank behind the brown stretches of corn field as we sat down to eat, and the warm layer of air that had rested over the water and our clean sand bar grew fresher and smelled of the rank ironweed and sunflowers growing on the flatter shore. The river was brown and sluggish, like any other of the half-dozen streams that water the Nebraska corn lands. On one shore was an irregular line of bald clay bluffs where a few scrub oaks with thick trunks and flat, twisted tops threw light shadows on the long grass. The western shore was low and level, with corn fields that stretched to the skyline, and all along the water's edge were little sandy coves and beaches where slim cottonwoods and willow saplings flickered.

The turbulence of the river in springtime discouraged milling, and, beyond keeping the old red bridge in repair, the busy farmers did not concern themselves with the stream; so the Sandtown boys were left in undisputed possession. In the autumn we hunted quail through the miles of stubble and fodder land along the flat shore, and, after the winter skating season was over and the ice had gone out, the spring freshets and flooded bottoms gave us our great excitement of the year. The channel was never the same for two successive seasons. Every spring the swollen stream undermined a bluff to the east, or bit out a few acres of corn field to the west and whirled the soil away to deposit it in spumy mud banks somewhere else. When the water fell low in midsummer, new sand bars were thus exposed to dry and whiten in the August sun. Sometimes these were banked so firmly that the fury of the next freshet failed to unseat them; the little willow seedlings emerged triumphantly from the yellow froth, broke into spring leaf, shot up into summer growth, and with their mesh of roots bound together the moist sand beneath them against the batterings of another April. Here and there a cottonwood soon glittered among them, quivering in the low current of air that, even on breathless days when the dust hung like smoke above the wagon road, trembled along the face of the water.

It was on such an island, in the third summer of its yellow green, that we built our watch fire; not in the thicket of dancing willow wands, but on the level terrace of fine sand which had been added that spring; a little new bit of world, beautifully ridged with ripple marks, and strewn with the tiny skeletons of turtles and fish, all as white and dry as if they had been expertly cured. We had been careful not to mar the freshness of the place, although we often swam to it on summer evenings and lay on the sand to rest.

This was our last watch fire of the year, and there were reasons why I should remember it better than any of the others. Next week the other boys were to file back to their old places in the Sandtown High School, but I was to go up to the Divide to teach my first country school in the Norwegian district. I was already homesick at the thought of quitting the boys with whom I had always played; of leaving the river, and going up into a windy plain that was all windmills and corn fields and big pastures; where there was nothing wilful or unmanageable in the landscape, no new islands, and no chance of unfamiliar birds—such as often followed the watercourses.

Other boys came and went and used the river for fishing or skating, but we six were sworn to the spirit of the stream, and we were friends mainly because of the river. There were the two Hassler boys, Fritz and Otto, sons of the little German tailor. They were the youngest of us; ragged boys of ten and twelve, with sunburned hair, weather-stained faces, and pale blue eyes. Otto, the elder, was the best mathematician in school, and clever at his books, but he always dropped out in the spring term as if the river could not get on without him. He and Fritz caught the fat, horned catfish and sold them about the town, and they lived so much in the water that they were as brown and sandy as the river itself.

There was Percy Pound, a fat, freckled boy with chubby cheeks, who took half a dozen boys' story-papers and was always being kept in for reading detective stories behind his desk. There was Tip Smith, destined by his freckles and red hair to be the buffoon in all our games, though he walked like a timid little old man and had a funny, cracked laugh. Tip worked hard in his father's grocery store every afternoon, and swept it out before school in the morning. Even his recreations were laborious. He collected cigarette cards and tin tobacco-tags indefatigably, and would sit for hours humped up over a snarling little scroll-saw which he kept in his attic. His dearest possessions were some little pill bottles that purported to contain grains of wheat from the Holy Land, water from the Jordan and the Dead Sea, and earth from the Mount of Olives. His father had bought these dull things from a Baptist missionary who peddled them, and Tip seemed to derive great satisfaction from their remote origin.

The tall boy was Arthur Adams. He had fine hazel eyes that were almost too reflective and sympathetic for a boy, and such a pleasant voice that we all loved to hear him read aloud. Even when he had to read poetry aloud at school, no one ever thought of laughing. To be sure, he was not at school very much of the time. He was seventeen and should have finished the High School the year before, but he was always off somewhere with his gun. Arthur's mother was dead, and his father, who was feverishly absorbed in promoting schemes, wanted to send the boy away to school and get him off his hands; but Arthur always begged off for another year and promised to study. I remember him as a tall, brown boy with an intelligent face, always lounging among a lot of us little fellows, laughing at us oftener than with us, but such a soft, satisfied laugh that we felt rather flattered when we provoked it. In after-years people said that Arthur had been given to evil ways even as a lad, and it is true that we often saw him with the gambler's sons and with old Spanish Fanny's boy, but if he learned anything ugly in their company he never betrayed it to us. We would have followed Arthur anywhere, and I am bound to say that he led us into no worse places than the cattail marshes and the stubble fields. These, then, were the boys who camped with me that summer night upon the sand bar.

After we finished our supper we beat the willow thicket for driftwood. By the time we had collected enough, night had fallen, and the pungent, weedy smell from the shore increased with the coolness. We threw ourselves down about the fire and made another futile effort to show Percy Pound the Little Dipper. We had tried it often before, but he could never be got past the big one.

"You see those three big stars just below the handle, with the bright one in the middle?" said Otto Hassler; "that's Orion's belt, and the bright one is the clasp." I crawled behind Otto's shoulder and sighted up

his arm to the star that seemed perched upon the tip of his steady forefinger. The Hassler boys did seine-fishing at night, and they knew a
good many stars.

Percy gave up the Little Dipper and lay back on the sand, his hands
clasped under his head. "I can see the North Star," he announced, contentedly, pointing toward it with his big toe. "Anyone might get lost
and need to know that."

We all looked up at it.

"How do you suppose Columbus felt when his compass didn't
point north any more?" Tip asked.

Otto shook his head. "My father says that there was another North
Star once, and that maybe this one won't last always. I wonder what
would happen to us down here if anything went wrong with it?"

Arthur chuckled. "I wouldn't worry, Ott. Nothing's apt to happen
to it in your time. Look at the Milky Way! There must be lots of good
dead Indians."

We lay back and looked, meditating, at the dark cover of the
world. The gurgle of the water had become heavier. We had often
noticed a mutinous, complaining note in it at night, quite different
from its cheerful daytime chuckle, and seeming like the voice of a much
deeper and more powerful stream. Our water had always these two
moods: the one of sunny complaisance, the other of inconsolable, passionate regret.

"Queer how the stars are all in sort of diagrams," remarked Otto.
"You could do most any proposition in geometry with 'em. They always
look as if they meant something. Some folks say everybody's fortune is
all written out in the stars, don't they?"

"They believe so in the old country," Fritz affirmed.

But Arthur only laughed at him. "You're thinking of Napoleon,
Fritzey. He had a star that went out when he began to lose battles. I guess
the stars don't keep any close tally on Sandtown folks."

We were speculating on how many times we could count a hundred
before the evening star went down behind the corn fields, when someone
cried, "There comes the moon, and it's as big as a cart wheel!"

We all jumped up to greet it as it swam over the bluffs behind us.
It came up like a galleon in full sail; an enormous, barbaric thing, red as
an angry heathen god.

"When the moon came up red like that, the Aztecs used to sacrifice
their prisoners on the temple top," Percy announced.

"Go on, Perce. You got that out of *Golden Days*. Do you believe that, Arthur?" I appealed.

Arthur answered, quite seriously: "Like as not. The moon was one of their gods. When my father was in Mexico City he saw the stone where they used to sacrifice their prisoners."

As we dropped down by the fire again some one asked whether the Mound-Builders were older than the Aztecs. When we once got upon the Mound-Builders we never willingly got away from them, and we were still conjecturing when we heard a loud splash in the water.

"Must have been a big cat jumping," said Fritz. "They do sometimes. They must see bugs in the dark. Look what a track the moon makes!"

There was a long, silvery streak on the water, and where the current fretted over a big log it boiled up like gold pieces.

"Suppose there ever *was* any gold hid away in this old river?" Fritz asked. He lay like a little brown Indian, close to the fire, his chin on his hand and his bare feet in the air. His brother laughed at him, but Arthur took his suggestion seriously.

"Some of the Spaniards thought there was gold up here somewhere. Seven cities chuck full of gold, they had it, and Coronado and his men came up to hunt it. The Spaniards were all over this country once."

Percy looked interested. "Was that before the Mormons went through?"

We all laughed at this.

"Long enough before. Before the Pilgrim Fathers, Perce. Maybe they came along this very river. They always followed the watercourses."

"I wonder where this river really does begin?" Tip mused. That was an old and a favorite mystery which the map did not clearly explain. On the map the little black line stopped somewhere in western Kansas; but since rivers generally rose in mountains, it was only reasonable to suppose that ours came from the Rockies. Its destination, we knew, was the Missouri, and the Hassler boys always maintained that we could embark at Sandtown in floodtime, follow our noses, and eventually arrive at New Orleans. Now they took up their old argument. "If us boys had grit enough to try it, it wouldn't take no time to get to Kansas City and St. Joe."

We began to talk about the places we wanted to go to. The Hassler boys wanted to see the stockyards in Kansas City, and Percy wanted to see a big store in Chicago. Arthur was interlocutor and did not betray himself.

"Now it's your turn, Tip."

Tip rolled over on his elbow and poked the fire, and his eyes looked shyly out of his queer, tight little face. "My place is awful far away. My Uncle Bill told me about it."

Tip's Uncle Bill was a wanderer, bitten with mining fever, who had drifted into Sandtown with a broken arm, and when it was well had drifted out again.

"Where is it?"

"Aw, it's down in New Mexico somewheres. There aren't no railroads or anything. You have to go on mules, and you run out of water before you get there and have to drink canned tomatoes."

"Well, go on, kid. What's it like when you do get there?"

Tip sat up and excitedly began his story.

"There's a big red rock there that goes right up out of the sand for about nine hundred feet. The country's flat all around it, and this here rock goes up all by itself, like a monument. They call it the Enchanted Bluff down there, because no white man has ever been on top if it. The sides are smooth rock, and straight up, like a wall. The Indians say that hundreds of years ago, before the Spaniards came, there was a village away up there in the air. The tribe that lived there had some sort of steps, made out of wood and bark, hung down over the face of the bluff, and the braves went down to hunt and carried water up in big jars swung on their backs. They kept a big supply of water and dried meat up there, and never went down except to hunt. They were a peaceful tribe that made cloth and pottery, and they went up there to get out of the wars. You see, they could pick off any war party that tried to get up their little steps. The Indians say they were a handsome people, and they had some sort of queer religion. Uncle Bill thinks they were Cliff-Dwellers who had got into trouble and left home. They weren't fighters, anyhow.

"One time the braves were down hunting and an awful storm came up—a kind of waterspout—and when they got back to their rock they found their little staircase had been all broken to pieces, and only a few steps were left hanging away up in the air. While they were camped at the foot of the rock, wondering what to do, a war party from the north came along and massacred 'em to a man, with all the old folks and women looking on from the rock. Then the war party went on south and left the village to get down the best way they could. Of course they never got down. They starved to death up there, and when the war party came back on their way north, they could hear the children crying from the edge of the bluff where they had crawled out, but they didn't see a sign of a grown Indian, and nobody has ever been up there since."

We exclaimed at this dolorous legend and sat up.

"There couldn't have been many people up there," Percy demurred. "How big is the top, Tip?"

"Oh, pretty big. Big enough so that the rock doesn't look nearly as tall as it is. The top's bigger than the base. The bluff is sort of worn away for several hundred feet up. That's one reason it's so hard to climb."

I asked how the Indians got up, in the first place.

"Nobody knows how they got up or when. A hunting party came along once and saw that there was a town up there, and that was all."

Otto rubbed his chin and looked thoughtful. "Of course there must be some way to get up there. Couldn't people get a rope over someway and pull a ladder up?"

Tip's little eyes were shining with excitement. "I know a way. Me and Uncle Bill talked it all over. There's a kind of rocket that would take a rope over—life-savers use 'em—and then you could hoist a rope ladder and peg it down at the bottom and make it tight with guy ropes on the other side. I'm going to climb that there bluff, and I've got it all planned out."

Fritz asked what he expected to find when he got up there.

"Bones, maybe, or the ruins of their town, or pottery, or some of their idols. There might be 'most anything up there. Anyhow, I want to see."

"Sure nobody else has been up there, Tip?" Arthur asked.

"Dead sure. Hardly anybody ever goes down there. Some hunters tried to cut steps in the rock once, but they didn't get higher than a man can reach. The Bluff's all red granite, and Uncle Bill thinks it's a boulder the glaciers left. It's a queer place, anyhow. Nothing but cactus and desert for hundreds of miles, and yet right under the Bluff there's good water and plenty of grass. That's why the bison used to go down there."

Suddenly we heard a scream above our fire, and jumped up to see a dark, slim bird floating southward far above us—a whooping crane, we knew by her cry and her long neck. We ran to the edge of the island, hoping we might see her alight, but she wavered southward along the rivercourse until we lost her. The Hassler boys declared that by the look of the heavens it must be after midnight, so we threw more wood on our fire, put on our jackets, and curled down in the warm sand. Several of us pretended to doze, but I fancy we were really thinking about Tip's Bluff and the extinct people. Over in the wood the ring doves were calling mournfully to one another, and once we heard a dog bark, far away. "Somebody getting into old Tommy's melon patch," Fritz murmured sleepily, but nobody answered him. By and by Percy spoke out of the shadows.

"Say, Tip, when you go down there will you take me with you?"

"Maybe."

"Suppose one of us beats you down there, Tip?"

"Whoever gets to the Bluff first has got to promise to tell the rest of us exactly what he finds," remarked one of the Hassler boys, and to this we all readily assented.

Somewhat reassured, I dropped off to sleep. I must have dreamed about a race for the Bluff, for I awoke in a kind of fear that other people were getting ahead of me and that I was losing my chance. I sat up in my damp clothes and looked at the other boys, who lay tumbled in uneasy attitudes about the dead fire. It was still dark, but the sky was blue with the last wonderful azure of night. The stars glistened like crystal globes, and trembled as if they shone through a depth of clear water. Even as I watched, they began to pale and the sky brightened. Day came suddenly, almost instantaneously. I turned for another look at the blue night, and it was gone. Everywhere the birds began to call, and all manner of little insects began to chirp and hop about in the willows. A breeze sprang up from the west and brought the heavy smell of ripened corn. The boys rolled over and shook themselves. We stripped and plunged into the river just as the sun came up over the windy bluffs.

When I came home to Sandtown at Christmas time, we skated out to our island and talked over the whole project of the Enchanted Bluff, renewing our resolution to find it.

Although that was twenty years ago, none of us have ever climbed the Enchanted Bluff. Percy Pound is a stockbroker in Kansas City and will go nowhere that his red touring car cannot carry him. Otto Hassler went on the railroad and lost his foot braking; after which he and Fritz succeeded their father as the town tailors.

Arthur sat about the sleepy little town all his life—he died before he was twenty-five. The last time I saw him, when I was home on one of my college vacations, he was sitting in a steamer chair under a cottonwood tree in the little yard behind one of the two Sandtown saloons. He was very untidy and his hand was not steady, but when he rose, unabashed, to greet me, his eyes were as clear and warm as ever. When I had talked with him for an hour and heard him laugh again, I wondered how it was that when Nature had taken such pains with a man, from his hands to the arch of his long foot, she had ever lost him in Sandtown. He joked about Tip Smith's Bluff, and declared he was going down there just as soon as the weather got cooler; he thought the Grand Canyon might be worth while, too.

I was perfectly sure when I left him that he would never get beyond the high plank fence and the comfortable shade of the cottonwood. And, indeed, it was under that very tree that he died one summer morning.

Tip Smith still talks about going to New Mexico. He married a slatternly, unthrifty country girl, has been much tied to a perambulator, and has grown stooped and gray from irregular meals and broken sleep. But the worst of his difficulties are now over, and he has, as he says, come into easy water. When I was last in Sandtown I walked home with him late one moonlight night, after he had balanced his cash and shut up his store. We took the long way around and sat down on the schoolhouse steps, and between us we quite revived the romance of the lone red rock and the extinct people. Tip insists that he still means to go down there, but he thinks now he will wait until his boy Bert is old enough to go with him. Bert has been let into the story, and thinks of nothing but the Enchanted Bluff.

First published in *Harper's*, CXVIII (April, 1909), 774–778, 780–781.

On the Gulls' Road

The Ambassador's Story

✳ ✳ ✳

It often happens that one or another of my friends stops before a red chalk
drawing in my study and asks me where I ever found so lovely a creature.
I have never told the story of that picture to any one, and the beautiful
woman on the wall, until yesterday, in all these twenty years has spoken
to no one but me. Yesterday a young painter, a countryman of mine,
came to consult me on a matter of business, and upon seeing my drawing
of Alexandra Ebbling, straightway forgot his errand. He examined the
date upon the sketch and asked me, very earnestly, if I could tell him
whether the lady were still living. When I answered him, he stepped back
from the picture and said slowly:

"So long ago? She must have been very young. She was happy?"

"As to that, who can say—about any one of us?" I replied. "Out of
all that is supposed to make for happiness, she had very little."

He shrugged his shoulders and turned away to the window, saying
as he did so: "Well, there is very little use in troubling about anything,
when we can stand here and look at her, and you can tell me that she has
been dead all these years, and that she had very little."

We returned to the object of his visit, but when he bade me goodbye
at the door his troubled gaze again went back to the drawing, and it was
only by turning sharply about that he took his eyes away from her.

I went back to my study fire, and as the rain kept away less impetuous
visitors, I had a long time in which to think of Mrs. Ebbling. I even got
out the little box she gave me, which I had not opened for years, and
when Mrs. Hemway brought my tea I had barely time to close the lid
and defeat her disapproving gaze.

My young countryman's perplexity, as he looked at Mrs. Ebbling,
had recalled to me the delight and pain she gave me when I was of his

years. I sat looking at her face and trying to see it through his eyes—
freshly, as I saw it first upon the deck of the *Germania*, twenty years ago.
Was it her loveliness, I often ask myself, or her loneliness, or her simplicity,
or was it merely my own youth? Was her mystery only that of the mysterious North out of which she came? I still feel that she was very different
from all the beautiful and brilliant women I have known; as the night is
different from the day, or as the sea is different from the land. But this is
our story, as it comes back to me.

For two years I had been studying Italian and working in the capacity
of clerk to the American legation at Rome, and I was going home to
secure my first consular appointment. Upon boarding my steamer at
Genoa, I saw my luggage into my cabin and then started for a rapid circuit
of the deck. Everything promised well. The boat was thinly peopled,
even for a July crossing; the decks were roomy; the day was fine; the sea
was blue; I was sure of my appointment, and, best of all, I was coming
back to Italy. All these things were in my mind when I stopped sharply
before a *chaise longue* placed sidewise near the stern. Its occupant was a
woman, apparently ill, who lay with her eyes closed, and in her open
arm was a chubby little red-haired girl, asleep. I can still remember that
first glance at Mrs. Ebbling, and how I stopped as a wheel does when the
band slips. Her splendid, vigorous body lay still and relaxed under the
loose folds of her clothing, her white throat and arms and red-gold hair
were drenched with sunlight. Such hair as it was: wayward as some kind
of gleaming seaweed that curls and undulates with the tide. A moment
gave me her face; the high cheekbones, the thin cheeks, the gentle chin,
arching back to a girlish throat, and singular loveliness of the mouth.
Even then it flashed through me that the mouth gave the whole face its
peculiar beauty and distinction. It was proud and sad and tender, and
strangely calm. The curve of the lips could not have been cut more cleanly
with the most delicate instrument, and whatever shade of feeling passed
over them seemed to partake of their exquisiteness.

But I am anticipating. While I stood stupidly staring (as if, at twenty-
five, I had never before beheld a beautiful woman) the whistles broke into
a hoarse scream, and the deck under us began to vibrate. The woman
opened her eyes, and the little girl struggled into a sitting position, rolled
out of her mother's arm, and ran to the deck rail. After putting my chair
near the stern, I went forward to see the gangplank up and did not return
until we were dragging out to sea at the end of a long towline.

The woman in the *chaise longue* was still alone. She lay there all day, looking at the sea. The little girl, Carin, played noisily about the deck. Occasionally she returned and struggled up into the chair, plunged her head, round and red as a little pumpkin, against her mother's shoulder in an impetuous embrace, and then struggled down again with a lively flourishing of arms and legs. Her mother took such opportunities to pull up the child's socks or to smooth the fiery little braids; her beautiful hands, rather large and very white, played about the riotous little girl with a quieting tenderness. Carin chattered away in Italian and kept asking for her father, only to be told that he was busy.

When any of the ship's officers passed, they stopped for a word with my neighbor, and I heard the first mate address her as Mrs. Ebbling. When they spoke to her, she smiled appreciatively and answered in low, faltering Italian, but I fancied that she was glad when they passed on and left her to her fixed contemplation of the sea. Her eyes seemed to drink the color of it all day long, and after every interruption they went back to it. There was a kind of pleasure in watching her satisfaction, a kind of excitement in wondering what the water made her remember or forget. She seemed not to wish to talk to any one, but I knew I should like to hear whatever she might be thinking. One could catch some hint of her thoughts, I imagined, from the shadows that came and went across her lips, like the reflection of light clouds. She had a pile of books beside her, but she did not read, and neither could I. I gave up trying at last, and watched the sea, very conscious of her presence, almost of her thoughts. When the sun dropped low and shone in her face, I rose and asked if she would like me to move her chair. She smiled and thanked me, but said the sun was good for her. Her yellow-hazel eyes followed me for a moment and then went back to the sea.

After the first bugle sounded for dinner, a heavy man in uniform came up the deck and stood beside the *chaise longue*, looking down at its two occupants with a smile of satisfied possession. The breast of his trim coat was hidden by waves of soft blond beard, as long and heavy as a woman's hair, which blew about his face in glittering profusion. He wore a large turquoise ring upon the thick hand that he rubbed good-humoredly over the little girl's head. To her he spoke Italian, but he and his wife conversed in some Scandinavian tongue. He stood stroking his fine beard until the second bugle blew, then bent stiffly from his hips, like a soldier, and patted his wife's hand as it lay on the arm of her chair. He hurried down the deck, taking stock of the passengers as he went, and stopped before a thin girl with frizzed hair and a lace coat, asking her a facetious question in thick English. They began to talk about Chicago and went below. Later I saw him at the head of his table in the dining room, the befrizzed Chicago lady on his left. They must have got a famous start at luncheon, for by the end of the dinner Ebbling was peeling figs for her and presenting them on the end of a fork.

The Doctor confided to me that Ebbling was the chief engineer and the dandy of the boat; but this time he would have to behave himself, for he had brought his sick wife along for the voyage. She had a bad heart valve, he added, and was in a serious way.

After dinner Ebbling disappeared, presumably to his engines, and at ten o'clock, when the stewardess came to put Mrs. Ebbling to bed, I helped her to rise from her chair, and the second mate ran up and supported her down to her cabin. About midnight I found the engineer in the card room, playing with the Doctor, an Italian naval officer, and the commodore of a Long Island yacht club. His face was even pinker than it had been at dinner, and his fine beard was full of smoke. I thought a long while about Ebbling and his wife before I went to sleep.

The next morning we tied up at Naples to take on our cargo, and I went on shore for the day. I did not, however, entirely escape the ubiquitous engineer, whom I saw lunching with the Long Island commodore at a hotel in the Santa Lucia. When I returned to the boat in the early evening, the passengers had gone down to dinner, and I found Mrs. Ebbling quite alone upon the deserted deck. I approached her and asked whether she had had a dull day. She looked up smiling and shook her head, as if her Italian had quite failed her. I saw that she was flushed with excitement, and her yellow eyes were shining like two clear topazes.

"Dull? Oh, no! I love to watch Naples from the sea, in this white heat. She has just lain there on her hillside among the vines and laughed for me all day long. I have been able to pick out many of the places I like best."

I felt that she was really going to talk to me at last. She had turned to me frankly, as to an old acquaintance, and seemed not to be hiding from me anything of what she felt. I sat down in a glow of pleasure and excitement and asked her if she knew Naples well.

"Oh, yes! I lived there for a year after I was first married. My husband has a great many friends in Naples. But he was at sea most of the time, so I went about alone. Nothing helps one to know a city like that. I came first by sea, like this. Directly to Naples from Finmark, and I had never been South before." Mrs. Ebbling stopped and looked over my shoulder. Then, with a quick, eager glance at me, she said abruptly: "It was like a baptism of fire. Nothing has ever been quite the same since. Imagine how this bay looked to a Finmark girl. It seemed like the overture to Italy."

I laughed. "And then one goes up the country—song by song and wine by wine."

Mrs. Ebbling sighed. "Ah, yes. It must be fine to follow it. I have never been away from the seaports myself. We live now in Genoa."

The deck steward brought her tray, and I moved forward a little and stood by the rail. When I looked back, she smiled and nodded to let me know that she was not missing anything. I could feel her intentness as keenly as if she were standing beside me.

The sun had disappeared over the high ridge behind the city, and the stone pines stood black and flat against the fires of the afterglow. The lilac haze that hung over the long, lazy slopes of Vesuvius warmed with golden light, and films of blue vapor began to float down toward Baiæ. The sky, the sea, and the city between them turned a shimmering violet, fading grayer as the lights began to glow like luminous pearls along the water-front—the necklace of an irreclaimable queen. Behind me I heard a low exclamation; a slight, stifled sound, but it seemed the perfect vocalization of that weariness with which we at last let go of beauty, after we have held it until the senses are darkened. When I turned to her again, she seemed to have fallen asleep.

That night, as we were moving out to sea and the tail lights of Naples were winking across the widening stretch of black water, I helped Mrs. Ebbling to the foot of the stairway. She drew herself up from her chair with effort and leaned on me wearily. I could have carried her all night without fatigue.

"May I come and talk to you tomorrow?" I asked. She did not reply at once. "Like an old friend?" I added. She gave me her languid hand, and her mouth, set with the exertion of walking, softened altogether. "*Grazia,*" she murmured.

I returned to the deck and joined a group of my countrywomen, who, primed with inexhaustible information, were discussing the baseness of Renaissance art. They were intelligent and alert, and as they leaned forward in their deck chairs under the circle of light, their faces recalled to me Rembrandt's picture of a clinical lecture. I heard them through, against my will, and then went to the stern to smoke and to see the last of the island lights. The sky had clouded over, and a soft, melancholy wind was rushing over the sea. I could not help thinking how disappointed I would be if rain should keep Mrs. Ebbling in her cabin tomorrow. My mind played constantly with her image. At one moment she was very clear and directly in front of me; the next she was far away. Whatever else I thought about, some part of my consciousness was busy with Mrs. Ebbling; hunting for her, finding her, losing her, then groping again. How was it that I was so conscious of whatever she might be feeling? that when she sat still behind me and watched the evening sky, I had had a sense of speed and change, almost of danger; and when she was tired and sighed, I had wished for night and loneliness.

II

Though when we are young we seldom think much about it, there is now and again a golden day when we feel a sudden, arrogant pride in our youth; in the lightness of our feet and the strength of our arms, in the warm fluid that courses so surely within us; when we are conscious of something powerful and mercurial in our breasts, which comes up wave after wave and leaves us irresponsible and free. All the next morning I felt this flow of life, which continually impelled me toward Mrs. Ebbling. After the merest greeting, however, I kept away. I found it pleasant to thwart myself, to measure myself against a current that was sure to carry me with it in the end. I was content to let her watch the sea —the sea that seemed now to have come into me, warm and soft, still and strong. I played shuffleboard with the Commodore, who was anxious to keep down his figure, and ran about the deck with the stout legs of the little pumpkin-colored Carin about my neck. It was not until the child was having her afternoon nap below that I at last came up and stood beside her mother.

"You are better today," I exclaimed, looking down at her white gown. She colored unreasonably, and I laughed with a familiarity which she must have accepted as the mere foolish noise of happiness, or it would have seemed impertinent.

We talked at first of a hundred trivial things, and we watched the sea. The coast of Sardinia had lain to our port for some hours and would lie there for hours to come, now advancing in rocky promontories, now retreating behind blue bays. It was the naked south coast of the island, and though our course held very near the shore, not a village or habitation was visible; there was not even a goatherd's hut hidden away among the low pinkish sand hills. Pinkish sand hills and yellow headlands; with dull-colored scrubby bushes massed about their bases and following the dried watercourses. A narrow strip of beach glistened like white paint between the purple sea and the umber rocks, and the whole island lay gleaming in the yellow sunshine and translucent air. Not a wave broke on that fringe of white sand, not the shadow of a cloud played across the bare hills. In the air about us there was no sound but that of a vessel moving rapidly through absolutely still water. She seemed like some great sea-animal, swimming silently, her head well up. The sea before us was so rich and heavy and opaque that it might have been lapis lazuli. It was the blue of legend, simply; the color that satisfies the soul like sleep.

And it was of the sea we talked, for it was the substance of Mrs. Ebbling's story. She seemed always to have been swept along by ocean streams, warm or cold, and to have hovered about the edge of great waters. She was born and had grown up in a little fishing town on the Arctic Ocean. Her father was a doctor, a widower, who lived with his daughter and who divided his time between his books and his fishing rod. Her uncle was skipper on a coasting vessel, and with him she had made many trips along the Norwegian coast. But she was always reading and thinking about the blue seas of the South.

"There was a curious old woman in our village, Dame Ericson, who had been in Italy in her youth. She had gone to Rome to study art, and had copied a great many pictures there. She was well connected, but had little money, and as she grew older and poorer she sold her pictures one by one, until there was scarcely a well-to-do family in our district that did not own one of Dame Ericson's paintings. But she brought home many other strange things; a little orange tree which she cherished until the day of her death, and bits of colored marble, and sea shells and pieces of coral, and a thin flask full of water from the Mediterranean. When I was a little girl she used to show me her things and tell me about the South; about the coral fishers, and the pink islands, and the smoking mountains, and the old, underground Naples. I suppose the water in her flask was like any other, but it never seemed so to me. It looked so elastic and alive, that I used to think if one unsealed the bottle something penetrating and fruitful might leap out and work an enchantment over Finmark."

Lars Ebbling, I learned, was one of her father's friends. She could remember him from the time when she was a little girl and he a dashing young man who used to come home from the sea and make a stir in the village. After he got his promotion to an Atlantic liner and went South, she did not see him until the summer she was twenty, when he came home to marry her. That was five years ago. The little girl, Carin, was three. From her talk, one might have supposed that Ebbling was proprietor of the Mediterranean and its adjacent lands, and could have kept her away at his pleasure. Her own rights in him she seemed not to consider.

But we wasted very little time on Lars Ebbling. We talked, like two very young persons, of arms and men, of the sea beneath us and the shores it washed. We were carried a little beyond ourselves, for we were in the presence of the things of youth that never change; fleeing past them. Tomorrow they would be gone, and no effort of will or memory could bring them back again. All about us was the sea of great adventure, and below us, caught somewhere in its gleaming meshes, were the bones of nations and navies . . . nations and navies that gave youth its hope and made life something more than a hunger of the bowels. The unpeopled Sardinian coast unfolded gently before us, like something left over out of a world that was gone; a place that might well have had no later news since the corn ships brought the tidings of Actium.

"I shall never go to Sardinia," said Mrs. Ebbling. "It could not possibly be as beautiful as this."

"Neither shall I," I replied.

As I was going down to dinner that evening, I was stopped by Lars Ebbling, freshly brushed and scented, wearing a white uniform, and polished and glistening as one of his own engines. He smiled at me with his own kind of geniality. "You have been very kind to talk to my wife," he explained. "It is very bad for her this trip that she speaks no English. I am indebted to you."

I told him curtly that he was mistaken, but my acrimony made no impression upon his blandness. I felt that I should certainly strike the fellow if he stood there much longer, running his blue ring up and down his beard. I should probably have hated any man who was Mrs. Ebbling's husband, but Ebbling made me sick.

III

The next day I began my drawing of Mrs. Ebbling. She seemed pleased and a little puzzled when I asked her to sit for me. It occurred to me that she had always been among dull people who took her looks as a matter of course, and that she was not at all sure that she was really beautiful. I can see now her quick, confused look of pleasure. I thought very little about the drawing then, except that the making of it gave me an opportunity to study her face; to look as long as I pleased into her yellow eyes, at the noble lines of her mouth, at her splendid, vigorous hair.

"We have a yellow vine at home," I told her, "that is very like your hair. It seems to be growing while one looks at it, and it twines and tangles about itself and throws out little tendrils in the wind."

"Has it any name?"

"We call it love vine."

How little a thing could disconcert her!

As for me, nothing disconcerted me. I awoke every morning with a sense of speed and joy. At night I loved to hear the swish of the water rushing by. As fast as the pistons could carry us, as fast as the water could bear us, we were going forward to something delightful; to something together. When Mrs. Ebbling told me that she and her husband would be five days in the docks in New York and then return to Genoa, I was not disturbed, for I did not believe her. I came and went, and she sat still all day, watching the water. I heard an American lady say that she watched it like one who is going to die, but even that did not frighten me: I somehow felt that she had promised me to live.

All those long blue days when I sat beside her talking about Finmark and the sea, she must have known that I loved her. I sat with my hands idle on my knees and let the tide come up in me. It carried me so swiftly that, across the narrow space of deck between us, it must have swayed her, too, a little. I had no wish to disturb or distress her. If a little, a very little of it reached her, I was satisfied. If it drew her softly, but drew her, I wanted no more. Sometimes I could see that even the light pressure of my thoughts made her paler. One still evening, after a long talk, she whispered to me, "You must go and walk now, and—don't think about me." She had been held too long and too closely in my thoughts, and she begged me to release her for a little while. I went out into the bow and put her far away, at the skyline, with the faintest star, and thought of her gently across the water. When I went back to her, she was asleep.

But even in those first days I had my hours of misery. Why, for instance, should she have been born in Finmark, and why should Lars Ebbling have been her only door of escape? Why should she be silently taking leave of the world at the age when I was just beginning it, having had nothing, nothing of whatever is worth while?

She never talked about taking leave of things, and yet I sometimes felt that she was counting the sunsets. One yellow afternoon, when we were gliding between the shores of Spain and Africa, she spoke of her illness for the first time. I had got some magnolias at Gibraltar, and she wore a bunch of them in her girdle and the rest lay on her lap. She held the cool leaves against her cheek and fingered the white petals. "I can never," she remarked, "get enough of the flowers of the South. They make me breathless, just as they did at first. Because of them I should like to live a long while—almost forever."

I leaned forward and looked at her. "We could live almost forever if we had enough courage. It's of our lives that we die. If we had the courage to change it all, to run away to some blue coast like that over there, we could live on and on, until we were tired."

She smiled tolerantly and looked southward through half-shut eyes. "I am afraid I should never have courage enough to go behind that mountain, at least. Look at it, it looks as if it hid horrible things."

A sea mist, blown in from the Atlantic, began to mask the impassive African coast, and above the fog, the gray mountain peak took on the angry red of the sunset. It burned sullen and threatening until the dark land drew the night about her and settled back into the sea. We watched it sink, while under us, slowly but ever increasing, we felt the throb of the Atlantic come and go, the thrill of the vast, untamed waters of that lugubrious and passionate sea. I drew Mrs. Ebbling's wraps about her and shut the magnolias under her cloak. When I left her, she slipped me one warm, white flower.

IV

From the Straits of Gibraltar we dropped into the abyss, and by morning we were rolling in the trough of a sea that drew us down and held us deep, shaking us gently back and forth until the timbers creaked, and then shooting us out on the crest of a swelling mountain. The water was bright and blue, but so cold that the breath of it penetrated one's bones, as if the chill of the deep under-fathoms of the sea were being loosed upon us. There were not more than a dozen people upon the deck that morning, and Mrs. Ebbling was sheltered behind the stern, muffled in a sea jacket, with drops of moisture upon her long lashes and on her hair. When a shower of icy spray beat back over the deck rail, she took it gleefully.

"After all," she insisted, "this is my own kind of water; the kind I was born in. This is first cousin to the Pole waters, and the sea we have left is only a kind of fairy tale. It's like the burnt-out volcanoes; its day is over. This is the real sea now, where the doings of the world go on."

"It is not our reality, at any rate," I answered.

"Oh, yes, it is! These are the waters that carry men to their work, and they will carry you to yours."

I sat down and watched her hair grow more alive and iridescent in the moisture. "You are pleased to take an attitude," I complained.

"No, I don't love realities any more than another, but I admit them, all the same."

"And who are you and I to define the realities?"

"Our minds define them clearly enough, yours and mine, every-body's. Those are the lines we never cross, though we flee from the equator to the Pole. I have never really got out of Finmark, of course. I shall live and die in a fishing town on the Arctic Ocean, and the blue seas and the pink islands are as much a dream as they ever were. All the same, I shall continue to dream them."

The Gulf Stream gave us warm blue days again, but pale, like sad memories. The water had faded, and the thin, tepid sunshine made something tighten about one's heart. The stars watched us coldly, and seemed always to be asking me what I was going to do. The advancing line on the chart, which at first had been mere foolishness, began to mean something, and the wind from the west brought disturbing fears and forebodings. I slept lightly, and all day I was restless and uncertain except when I was with Mrs. Ebbling. She quieted me as she did little Carin, and soothed me without saying anything, as she had done that evening at Naples when we watched the sunset. It seemed to me that every day her eyes grew more tender and her lips more calm. A kind of fortitude seemed to be gathering about her mouth, and I dreaded it. Yet when, in an involuntary glance, I put to her the question that tortured me, her eyes always met mine steadily, deep and gentle and full of reassurance. That I had my word at last, happened almost by accident.

On the second night out from shore there was the concert for the Sailors' Orphanage, and Mrs. Ebbling dressed and went down to dinner for the first time, and sat on her husband's right. I was not the only one who was glad to see her. Even the women were pleased. She wore a pale green gown, and she came up out of it regally white and gold. I was so proud that I blushed when any one spoke of her. After dinner she was standing by her deck chair talking to her husband when people began to go below for the concert. She took up a long cloak and attempted to put it on. The wind blew the light thing about, and Ebbling chatted and smiled his public smile while she struggled with it. Suddenly his roving eye caught sight of the Chicago girl, who was having a similar difficulty with her draperies, and he pranced half the length of the deck to assist her. I had been watching from the rail, and when she was left alone I threw my cigar away and wrapped Mrs. Ebbling up roughly.

"Don't go down," I begged. "Stay up here. I want to talk to you."

She hesitated a moment and looked at me thoughtfully. Then, with a sigh, she sat down. Every one hurried down to the saloon, and we were absolutely alone at last, behind the shelter of the stern, with the thick darkness all about us and a warm east wind rushing over the sea. I was too sore and angry to think. I leaned toward her, holding the arm of her chair with both hands, and began anywhere.

"You remember those two blue coasts out of Gibraltar? It shall be either one you choose, if you will come with me. I have not much money, but we shall get on somehow. There has got to be an end of this. We are neither one of us cowards, and this is humiliating, intolerable."

She sat looking down at her hands, and I pulled her chair impatiently toward me.

"I felt," she said at last, "that you were going to say something like this. You are sorry for me, and I don't wish to be pitied. You think Ebbling neglects me, but you are mistaken. He has had his disappointments, too. He wants children and a gay, hospitable house, and he is tied to a sick woman who cannot get on with people. He has more to complain of than I have, and yet he bears with me. I am grateful to him, and there is no more to be said."

"Oh, isn't there?" I cried, "and I?"

She laid her hand entreatingly upon my arm. "Ah, you! you! Don't ask me to talk about that. *You*——" Her fingers slipped down my coat sleeve to my hand and pressed it. I caught her two hands and held them, telling her I would never let them go.

"And you meant to leave me day after tomorrow, to say goodbye to me as you will to the other people on this boat? You meant to cut me adrift like this, with my heart on fire and all my life unspent in me?"

She sighed despondently. "I am willing to suffer—whatever I must suffer—to have had you," she answered simply. "I was ill—and so lonely—and it came so quickly and quietly. Ah, don't begrudge it to me!

Do not leave me in bitterness. If I have been wrong, forgive me." She bowed her head and pressed my fingers entreatingly. A warm tear splashed on my hand. It occurred to me that she bore my anger as she bore little Carin's importunities, as she bore Ebbling. What a circle of pettiness she had about her! I fell back in my chair and my hands dropped at my side. I felt like a creature with its back broken. I asked her what she wished me to do.

"Don't ask me," she whispered. "There is nothing that we can do. I thought you knew that. You forget that—that I am too ill to begin my life over. Even if there were nothing else in the way, that would be enough. And that is what has made it all possible, our loving each other, I mean. If I were well, we couldn't have had even this much. Don't reproach me. Hasn't it been at all pleasant to you to find me waiting for you every morning, to feel me thinking of you when you went to sleep? Every night I have watched the sea for you, as if it were mine and I had made it, and I have listened to the water rushing by you, full of sleep and youth and hope. And everything you had done or said during the day came back to me, and when I went to sleep it was only to feel you more. You see there was never any one else; I have never thought of any one in the dark but you." She spoke pleadingly, and her voice had sunk so low that I could scarcely hear her.

"And yet you will do nothing," I groaned. "You will dare nothing. You will give me nothing."

"Don't say that. When I leave you day after tomorrow, I shall have given you all my life. I can't tell you how, but it is true. There is something in each of us that does not belong to the family or to society, not even to ourselves. Sometimes it is given in marriage, and sometimes it is given in love, but oftener it is never given at all. We have nothing to do with giving or withholding it. It is a wild thing that sings in us once and flies away and never comes back, and mine has flown to you. When one loves like that, it is enough, somehow. The other things can go if they must. That is why I can live without you, and die without you."

I caught her hands and looked into her eyes that shone warm in the darkness. She shivered and whispered in a tone so different from any I ever heard from her before or afterward: "Do you grudge it to me? You are so young and strong, and you have everything before you. I shall have only a little while to want you in—and I could want you forever and not weary." I kissed her hair, her cheeks, her lips, until her head fell forward on my shoulder and she put my face away with her soft, trembling fingers. She took my hand and held it close to her, in both her own. We sat silent, and the moments came and went, bringing us closer and closer, and the wind and water rushed by us, obliterating our tomorrows and all our yesterdays.

The next day Mrs. Ebbling kept her cabin, and I sat stupidly by her chair until dark, with the rugged little girl to keep me company, and an occasional nod from the engineer.

I saw Mrs. Ebbling again only for a few moments, when we were coming into the New York harbor. She wore a street dress and a hat, and these alone would have made her seem far away from me. She was very pale, and looked down when she spoke to me, as if she had been guilty of a wrong toward me. I have never been able to remember that interview without heartache and shame, but then I was too desperate to care about anything. I stood like a wooden post and let her approach me, let her speak to me, let her leave me. She came up to me as if it were a hard thing to do, and held out a little package, timidly, and her gloved hand shook as if she were afraid of me.

"I want to give you something," she said. "You will not want it now, so I shall ask you to keep it until you hear from me. You gave me your address a long time ago, when you were making that drawing. Some day I shall write to you and ask you to open this. You must not come to tell me goodbye this morning, but I shall be watching you when you go ashore. Please don't forget that."

I took the little box mechanically and thanked her. I think my eyes must have filled, for she uttered an exclamation of pity, touched my sleeve quickly, and left me. It was one of those strange, low, musical exclamations which meant everything and nothing, like the one that had thrilled me that night at Naples, and it was the last sound I ever heard from her lips.

An hour later I went on shore, one of those who crowded over the gangplank the moment it was lowered. But the next afternoon I wandered back to the docks and went on board the *Germania*. I asked for the engineer, and he came up in his shirt sleeves from the engine room. He was red and dishevelled, angry and voluble; his bright eye had a hard glint, and I did not once see his masterful smile. When he heard my inquiry he became profane. Mrs. Ebbling had sailed for Bremen on the *Hohenstauffen* that morning at eleven o'clock. She had decided to return by the northern route and pay a visit to her father in Finmark. She was in no condition to travel alone, he said. He evidently smarted under her extravagance. But who, he asked, with a blow of his fist on the rail, could stand between a woman and her whim? She had always been a wilful girl, and she had a doting father behind her. When she set her head with the wind, there was no holding her; she ought to have married the Arctic Ocean. I think Ebbling was still talking when I walked away.

I spent that winter in New York. My consular appointment hung fire (indeed, I did not pursue it with much enthusiasm), and I had a good many idle hours in which to think of Mrs. Ebbling. She had never mentioned the name of her father's village, and somehow I could never quite bring myself to go to the docks when Ebbling's boat was in and ask for news of her. More than once I made up my mind definitely to go to Finmark and take my chance at finding her; the shipping people would know where Ebbling came from. But I never went. I have often wondered why. When my resolve was made and my courage high, when I could almost feel myself approaching her, suddenly everything crumbled under me, and I fell back as I had done that night when I dropped her hands, after telling her, only a moment before, that I would never let them go.

In the twilight of a wet March day, when the gutters were running black outside and the Square was liquefying under crusts of dirty snow, the housekeeper brought me a damp letter which bore a blurred foreign postmark. It was from Niels Nannestad, who wrote that it was his sad duty to inform me that his daughter, Alexandra Ebbling, had died on the second day of February, in the twenty-sixth year of her age. Complying with her request, he inclosed a letter which she had written some days before her death.

I at last brought myself to break the seal of the second letter. It read thus:

My Friend:—You may open now the little package I gave you. May I ask you to keep it? I gave it to you because there is no one else who would care about it in just that way. Ever since I left you I have been thinking what it would be like to live a lifetime caring and being cared for like that. It was not the life I was meant to live, and yet, in a way, I have been living it ever since I first knew you.

Of course you understand now why I could not go with you. I would have spoiled your life for you. Besides that, I was ill—and I was too proud to give you the shadow of myself. I had much to give you, if you had come earlier. As it was, I was ashamed. Vanity sometimes saves us when nothing else will, and mine saved you. Thank you for everything. I hold this to my heart, where I once held your hand.

Alexandra

The dusk had thickened into night long before I got up from my chair and took the little box from its place in my desk drawer. I opened it and lifted out a thick coil, cut from where her hair grew thickest and brightest. It was tied firmly at one end, and when it fell over my arm it curled and clung about my sleeve like a living thing set free. How it gleamed, how it still gleams in the firelight! It was warm and softly scented under my lips, and stirred under my breath like seaweed in the tide. This, and a withered magnolia flower, and two pink sea shells; nothing more. And it was all twenty years ago!

First published in *McClure's*, XXXII (December, 1908), 145–152.

Eleanor's House

❊ ❊ ❊

"Shall you, then," Harriet ventured, "go to Fortuney?" The girl threw a startled glance toward the corner of the garden where Westfield and Harold were examining a leak in the basin of the little fountain, and Harriet was sorry that she had put the question so directly. Ethel's reply, when it came, seemed a mere emission of breath rather than articulation.

"I think we shall go later. It's very trying for him there, of course. He hasn't been there since." She relapsed into silence—indeed, she had never come very far out of it—and Harriet called to Westfield. She found that she couldn't help resenting Ethel's singular inadeptness at keeping herself in hand.

"Come, Robert. Harold is tired after his journey, and he and Ethel must have much to say to each other."

Both Harold and his wife, however, broke into hurried random remarks with an eagerness which seemed like a protest.

"It is delightful to be near you here at Arques, with only a wall between our gardens," Ethel spurred herself to say. "It will mean so much to Harold. He has so many old associations with you, Mrs. Westfield."

The two men had come back to the tea table, and as the younger one overheard his wife's last remark, his handsome brown face took on the blackness of disapproval.

Ethel glanced at him furtively, but Harriet was unable to detect whether she realized just why or to what extent her remark had been unfortunate. She certainly looked as if she might not be particularly acute, drooping about in her big garden hat and her limp white frock, which had not been very well put on. However, some sense of maladroitness certainly penetrated her vagueness, for she shrank behind the tea table, gathering her scarf about her shoulders as if she were mysteriously blown upon by a chilling current.

The Westfields drew together to take their leave. Harold stepped to his wife's side as they went toward the gate with their guests, and put his hand lightly on her shoulder, at which she waveringly emerged from her eclipse and smiled.

Harriet could not help looking back at them from under her sunshade as they stood there in the gateway; the man with his tense brown face and abstracted smile, the girl drooping, positively swaying in her softness and uncertainty.

When they reached the sunny square of their own garden, Harriet sank into a wicker chair in the deep shadow of the stucco wall and addressed her husband with conviction:

"I know now, my dear, why he wished so much to come. I sensed it yesterday, when I first met her. But now that I've seen them together, it's perfectly clear. He brought her here to keep her away from Fortuney, and he's counting on us to help him."

Westfield, who was carefully examining his rose trees, looked at his wife with interest and frank bewilderment, a form of interrogation with which she was perfectly familiar.

"If there is one thing that's plainer even than his misery," Harriet continued, "it is that she is headed toward Fortuney. They've been married over two years, and he couldn't, I suppose, keep her across the Channel any longer. So he has simply deflected her course, and we are the pretext."

"Certainly," Westfield admitted, as he looked up from his pruning, "one feels something not altogether comfortable with them, but why should it be Fortuney any more than a hundred other things? There are opportunities enough for people who wish to play at cross-purposes."

"Ah! But Fortuney," sighed his wife, "Fortuney's the summing up of all his past. It's Eleanor herself. How could he, Robert, take this poor girl there? It would be cruelty. The figure she'd cut in a place of such distinction!"

"I should think that if he could marry her, he could take her to Fortuney," Westfield maintained bluntly.

"Oh, as to his marrying her! But I suppose we are all to blame for that—all his and Eleanor's old friends. We certainly failed him. We fled at the poor fellow's approach. We simply couldn't face the extent of his bereavement. He seemed a mere fragment of a man dragged out from under the wreckage. They had so grown together that when she died there was nothing in him left whole. We dreaded him, and were glad enough to get him off to India. I even hoped he would marry out there.

When the news came that he had, I supposed that would end it; that he would become merely a chapter in natural history. But, you see, he hasn't; he's more widowed than before. He can't do anything well without her. You see, he couldn't even do this."

"This?" repeated Westfield, quitting his gardening abruptly. "Am I to understand that she would have been of assistance in selecting another wife for him?"

Harriet preferred to ignore that his tone implied an enormity. "She would certainly have kept him from getting into such a box as he's in now. She could at least have found him some one who wouldn't lacerate him by her every movement. Oh, that poor, limp, tactless, terrified girl! Have you noticed the exasperating way in which she walks, even? It's as if she were treading pain, forbearing and forgiving, when she but steps to the tea table. There was never a person so haunted by the notion of her own untidy picturesqueness. It wears her thin and consumes her, like her unhappy passion. I know how he feels; he hates the way she likes what she likes, and he hates the way she dislikes what she doesn't like. And, mark my words, she is bent upon Fortuney. That, at least, Robert, he certainly can't permit. At Fortuney, Eleanor is living still. The place is so intensely, so rarely personal. The girl has fixed her eye, made up her mind. It's symbolic to her, too, and she's circling about it; she can't endure to be kept out. Yesterday, when I went to see her, she couldn't wait to begin explaining her husband to me. She seemed to be afraid I might think she hadn't poked into everything."

While his wife grew more and more vehement, Westfield lay back in a garden chair, half succumbing to the drowsy warmth of the afternoon.

"It seems to me," he remarked, with a discreet yawn, "that the poor child is only putting up a good fight against the tormenting suspicion that she hasn't got into anything. She may be just decently trying to conceal her uncertainty."

Harriet looked at him intently for a moment, watching the shadows of the sycamore leaves play across his face, and then laughed indulgently. "The idea of her decently trying to conceal anything amuses me. So that's how much you know of her!" she sighed. "She's taken you in just as she took him. He doubtless thought she wouldn't poke; that she would go on keeping the door of the chamber, breathing faint benedictions and smiling her moonbeam smile as he came and went. But, under all her meekness and air of poetically foregoing, she has a forthcomingness and an outputtingness which all the brutality he's driven to can't discourage.

[97]

I've known her kind before! You may clip their tendrils every day of your life only to find them renewed and sweetly taking hold the next morning. She'd find the crevices in polished alabaster. Can't you see what she wants?" Mrs. Westfield sat up with flashing eyes. "She wants to be to him what Eleanor was; she sees no reason why she shouldn't be!"

Westfield rubbed the stiff blond hair above his ear in perplexity. "Well, why, in Heaven's name, shouldn't she be? He married her. What less can she expect?"

"Oh, Robert!" cried Harriet, as if he had uttered something impious. "But then, you never knew them. Why, Eleanor made him. He is the work of her hands. She saved him from being something terrible."

Westfield smiled ironically.

"Was he, then, in his natural state, so—so very much worse?"

"Oh, he was better than he is now, even then. But he was somehow terribly off the key. He was the most immature thing ever born into the world. Youth was a disease with him; he almost died of it. He was so absorbed in his own waking up, and he so overestimated its importance. He made such a clamor about it and so thrust it upon one that I used to wonder whether he would ever get past the stage of opening packages under the Christmas tree and shouting. I suppose he did know that his experiences were not unique, but I'm sure he felt that the degree of them was peculiarly his.

"When he met Eleanor he lost himself, and that was what he needed. She happened to be born tempered and poised. There never was a time when she wasn't discriminating. She could enjoy all kinds of things and people, but she was never, never mistaken in the kind. The beauty of it was that her distinctions had nothing to do with reason; they were purely shades of feeling.

"Well, you can conjecture what followed. She gave him the one thing which made everything else he had pertinent and dignified. He simply had better fiber than any of us realized, and she saw it. She was infallible in detecting quality.

"Two years after their marriage, I spent six weeks with them at Fortuney, and even then I saw their possibilities, what they would do for each other. And they went on and on. They had all there is—except children. I suppose they were selfish. As Eleanor once said to me, they needed only eternity and each other. But, whatever it was, it was Olympian."

II

Harriet was walking one morning on the green hill that rises, topped by its sprawling feudal ruin, behind Arques-la-Bataille. The sunlight still had the magical golden hue of early day, and the dew shone on the smooth, grassy folds and clefts that mark the outlines of the old fortifications. Below lay the delicately colored town—seen through a grove of glistening white birches—the shining, sinuous curves of the little river, and the green, open stretches of the pleasant Norman country.

As she skirted the base of one of the thick towers on the inner edge of the moat, her sunshade over her shoulder and her white shoes gray with dew, she all but stepped upon a man who lay in a shaded corner within the elbow of the wall and the tower, his straw hat tilted over his eyes.

"Why, Harold Forscythe!" she exclaimed breathlessly.

He sprang to his feet, baring his head in the sun.

"Sit down, do," he urged. "It's quite dry there—the masonry crops out—and the view's delightful."

"You didn't seem to be doing much with the view as I came up." Harriet put down her sunshade and stood looking at him, taking in his careless morning dress, his gray, unshaven face and heavy eyes. "But I shall sit down," she affectionately assured him, "to look at you, since I have so few opportunities. Why haven't you been to see me?"

Forscythe gazed attentively at her canvas shoes, hesitating and thrusting out his lower lip, an impetuous mannerism she had liked in him as a boy. "Perhaps—perhaps I haven't quite dared," he suggested.

"Which means," commented Harriet reproachfully, "that you accredit me with a very disagreeable kind of stupidity."

"You? Oh, dear, no! I didn't—I don't. How could you suppose it?" He helped her to her seat on the slant of gray rock, moving about her solicitously, but avoiding her eyes.

"Then why do you stand there, hesitating?"

"I was just thinking"—he shot her a nervous glance from under a frown—"whether I ought not to cut away now, on your account. I'm in the devil of a way in the early morning sometimes."

Mrs. Westfield looked at him compassionately as he stood poking the turf with his stick. She wondered how he could have reached eight-and-thirty without growing at all older than he had been in his twenties. And yet, that was just what their happiness had done for them. If it had kept them young, gloriously and resplendently young, it had also kept them from arriving anywhere. It had prolonged his flowering time, but it hadn't mellowed him. Growing older would have meant making concessions. He had never made any; had not even learned how, and was still striking back like a boy.

Harriet pointed to the turf beside her, and he dropped down suddenly.

"I'm really not fit to see any one this morning. These first hours—" He shrugged his shoulders and began to pull the grass blades swiftly, one at a time.

"Are hard for you?"

He nodded.

"Because they used to be your happiest?" Harriet continued, feeling her way.

"It's queer," he said quietly, "but in the morning I often feel such an absurd certainty of finding her. I suppose one has more vitality at this time of day, a keener sense of things."

"My poor boy! Is it still as hard as that?"

"Did you for a moment suppose that it would ever be any—easier?" he asked, with a short laugh.

"I hoped so. Oh, I hoped so."

Forscythe shook his head. "You know why I haven't been to see you," he brought out abruptly.

Harriet touched his arm. "You ought not to be afraid with me. If I didn't love her as much as you did, at least I never loved anything else so well."

"I know. That's one reason I came here. You were always together when I first knew her, and it's easy to see her beside you. Sometimes I think the image of her—coming down the stairs, crossing the garden, holding out her hand—is growing dimmer, and that terrifies me. Some people and some places give me the feeling of her." He stopped with a jerk, and threw a pebble across the moat, where the sloping bank, softened and made shallower by the slow centuries, was yellow with buttercups.

"But that feeling, Harold, must be more in you than anywhere. There's where she willed it and breathed it and stored it for years."

Harold was looking fixedly at the bare spot under his hand and pulling the grass blades out delicately. When he spoke, his voice fairly startled her with its sound of water working underground.

"It was like that once, but now I lose it sometimes—for weeks together. It's like trying to hold some delicate scent in your nostrils, and heavier odors come in and blur it."

"My poor boy, what can I say to you?" Harriet's eyes were so dim that she could only put out a hand to be sure that he was there. He pressed it and held it a moment.

"You don't have to say anything. Your thinking reaches me. It's extraordinary how we can be trained down, how little we can do with. If she could only have written to me—if there could have been a sign, a shadow on the grass or in the sky, to show that she went on with me, it would have been enough. And now—I wouldn't ask anything but to be left alone with my hurt. It's all that's left me. It's the most precious thing in the world."

"Oh, but that, my dear Harold, is too terrible! She couldn't have endured your doing it," murmured Harriet, overcome.

"Yes, she could. She'd have done it. She'd have kept me alive in her anguish, in her incompleteness."

Mrs. Westfield put out her hand entreatingly to stop him. He had lain beside her on the grass so often in the days of his courtship, of his first tempestuous happiness. It was incredible that he should have changed so little. He hadn't grown older, or wiser, or, in himself, better. He had simply grown more and more to be Eleanor. The misery of his entanglement touched her afresh, and she put her hands to her eyes and murmured, "Oh, that poor little Ethel! How could you do it?"

She heard him bound up, and when she lifted her face he was half the length of the wall away. She called to him, but he waved his hat meaninglessly, and she watched him hurry across the smooth green swell of the hill. Harriet leaned back into the warm angle of masonry and tried to settle into the deep peace of the place, where so many follies and passions had spent themselves and ebbed back into the stillness of the grass. But a sense of pain kept throbbing about her. It seemed to come from the spot where poor Forscythe had lain, and to rise like a miasma between her and the farms and orchards and the gray-green windings of the river. When at last she rose with a sigh, she murmured to herself, "Oh, my poor Eleanor! If you know, I pity you. Wherever you are, I pity you."

III

The silence once broken, Forscythe came often to Mrs. Westfield's garden. He spent whole mornings there, watching her embroider, or walked with her about the ruins on the hilltop, or along the streams that wound through the fertile farm country. Though he said little himself, he made it supremely easy for her to talk. He followed her about in grateful silence while she told him, freely and almost lightly, of her girlhood with Eleanor Sanford; of their life at a convent-school in Paris; of the copy of *Manon Lescault* which they kept sewed up in the little pine pillow they had brought from Schenectady; of the adroit machinations by which, on her fête-day, under the guardianship of an innocent aunt from Albany, Eleanor had managed to convey all her birthday roses out to Père-la-Chaise and arrange them under de Musset's willow.

Harriet even found a quiet happiness in being with him. She felt that he was making amends; that she could trust him not to renew the terrible experience which had crushed her at their first meeting on the hill. When he spoke of Eleanor at all, it was only to recall the beauty of their companionship, a thing she loved to reflect upon. For if they had been selfish, at least their selfishness had never taken the form of comfortable indolence. They had kept the edge of their zest for action; their affection had never grown stocky and middle-aged. How, Harriet often asked herself, could two people have crowded so much into ten circumscribed mortal years? And, of course, the best of it was that all the things they did and the places they went to and the people they knew didn't in the least matter, were only the incidental music of their drama.

The end, when it came, had, by the mercy of Heaven, come suddenly. An illness of three days at Fortuney, their own place on the Oise, and it was over. He was flung out into space to find his way alone; to keep fighting about in his circle, forever yearning toward the center.

One morning, when Harold asked her to go for a long walk into the country, Harriet felt from the moment they left the town behind them that he had something serious to say to her. They were having their déjeuner in the garden of a little auberge, sitting at a table beside a yellow clay wall overgrown with wall peaches, when he told her that he was going away.

"I don't know for just how long. Perhaps a week; perhaps two. I'd hate to have you misunderstand. I don't want you to underestimate the good you've done me these last weeks. But, you see, this is a sort of—a sort of tryst," he explained, smiling faintly. "We got stranded once in an absurd little town down on the Mediterranean, not far from Hyères. We liked it and stayed for days, and when we left, Eleanor said we'd go back every year when the grapes were ripe. We never did go back, for that was the last year. But I've been there that same week every autumn. The people there all remember her. It's a little bit of a place."

Harriet looked at him, holding her breath. The black kitten came up and brushed against him, tapping his arm with its paw and mewing to be fed.

"Is that why you go away so much? Ethel has told me. She said there was some business, but I doubted that."

"I'm sorry it has to be so. Of course, I feel despicable—do all the time, for that matter." He wiped his face and hands miserably with his napkin and pushed back his chair. "You see," he went on, beginning to make geometrical figures in the sand with his walking stick, "you see, I can't settle down to anything, and I'm so driven. There are times when places pull me—places where things happened, you know. Not big things, but just our own things." He stopped, and then added thoughtfully, "Going to miss her is almost what going to meet her used to be. I get in such a state of impatience."

Harriet couldn't, she simply couldn't, altogether despise him, and it was because, as he said, she did know. They sat in the quiet, sunny little garden, full of dahlias and sunflowers and the hum of bees, and she remembered what Eleanor had told her about this fishing village where they had lived on figs and goat's milk and watched the meager vintage being gathered; how, when they had to leave it, got into their compartment and flashed away along the panoramic Mediterranean shore, she had cried—she who never wept for pain or weariness, Harriet put in fondly. It was not the blue bay and the lavender and the pine hills they were leaving, but some peculiar shade of being together. Yet they were always leaving that. Every day brought colors in the sky, on the sea, in the heart, which could not possibly come just so again. That tomorrow's would be just as beautiful never quite satisfied them. They wanted it all. Yes, whatever they were, those two, they were Olympian.

As they were nearing home in the late afternoon, Forscythe turned suddenly to Harriet. "I shall have to count on you for something while I am away, you know."

"About the business? Oh, yes, I'll understand."

"And you'll do what you can for her, won't you?" he asked shakily. "It's such a hellish existence for her. I'd do anything if I could undo what I've done—anything."

Harriet paused a moment. "It simply can't, you know, go on like this."

"Yes, yes, I know that," he replied abstractedly. "But that's not the worst of it. The worst is that sometimes I feel as if Eleanor wants me to give her up; that she can't stand it any longer and is begging me to let her rest."

Harriet tried to look at him, but he had turned away his face.

IV

Forscythe's absence stretched beyond a fortnight, and no one seemed very definitely informed as to when he might return. Meanwhile, Mrs. Westfield had his wife considerably upon her hands. She could not, indeed, account for the degree to which she seemed responsible. It was always there, groping for her and pulling at her, as she told Westfield. The garden wall was not high enough to shut out entirely the other side; the girl pacing the gravel paths with the meek, bent step which poor Harriet found so exasperating, her wistful eyes peering from under her garden hat, her preposterous skirts trailing behind her like the brier-torn gown of some wandering Griselda.

During the long, dull hours in which they had their tea together, Harriet realized more and more the justice of the girl's position—of her claim, since she apparently had no position that one could well define. The reasonableness of it was all the more trying since Harriet felt so compelled to deny it. They read and walked and talked, and the subject to which they never alluded was always in the air. It was in the girl's long, silent, entreating looks; in her thin hands, nervously clasping and unclasping; in her ceaseless pacing about. Harriet distinctly felt that she was working herself up to something, and she declared to Westfield every morning that, whatever it was, she wouldn't be a party to it.

"I can understand perfectly," she insisted to her husband, "how he did it. He married her to talk to her about Eleanor. Eleanor had been the theme of their courtship. The rest of the world went on attending to its own business and shaking him off, and she stopped and sympathized and let him pour himself out. He didn't see, I suppose, why he shouldn't have just a wife like other men, for it didn't occur to him that he couldn't be just a husband. He thought she'd be content to console; he never dreamed she'd try to heal."

As for Ethel, Harriet had to admit that she, too, could be perfectly accounted for. She had gone into it, doubtless, in the spirit of self-sacrifice, a mood she was romantically fond of permitting herself and humanly

ELEANOR'S HOUSE

unable to live up to. She had married him in one stage of feeling, and had inevitably arrived at another—had come, indeed, to the place where she must be just one thing to him. What she was, or was not, hung on the throw of the dice in a way that savored of trembling captives and barbarous manners, and Harriet had to acknowledge that almost anything might be expected of a woman who had let herself go to such lengths and had yet got nowhere worth mentioning.

"She is certainly going to do something," Harriet declared. "But whatever can she hope to do now? What weapon has she left? How is she, after she's poured herself out so, ever to gather herself up again? What she'll do is the horror. It's sure to be ineffectual, and it's equally sure to have distinctly dramatic aspects."

Harriet was not, however, quite prepared for the issue which confronted her one morning. She sat down shaken and aghast when Ethel, pale and wraith-like, glided somnambulantly into her garden and asked whether Mrs. Westfield would accompany her to Fortuney on the following day.

"But, my dear girl, ought you to go there alone?"

"Without Harold, you mean?" the other inaudibly suggested. "Yes, I think I ought. He has such a dread of going back there, and yet I feel that he'll never be satisfied until he gets among his own things. He would be happier if he took the shock and had done with it. And my going there first might make it easier for him."

Harriet stared. "Don't you think he should be left to decide that for himself?" she reasoned mildly. "He may wish to forget the place in so far as he can."

"He doesn't forget," Ethel replied simply. "He thinks about it all the time. He ought to live there; it's his home. He ought not," she brought out, with a fierce little burst, "to be kept away."

"I don't know that he or any one else can do much in regard to that," commented Harriet dryly.

"He ought to live there," Ethel repeated automatically; "and it might make it easier for him if I went first."

"How?" gasped Mrs. Westfield.

"It might," she insisted childishly, twisting her handkerchief around her fingers. "We can take an early train and get there in the afternoon. It's but a short drive from the station. I am sure"—she looked pleadingly at Harriet—"I'm sure he'd like it better if you went with me."

[105]

Harriet made a clutch at herself and looked pointedly at the ground. "I really don't see how I could, Ethel. It doesn't seem to me a proper thing to do."

Ethel sat straight and still. Her liquid eyes brimmed over and the tears rolled mildly down her cheeks. "I'm sorry it seems wrong to you. Of course you can't go if it does. I shall go alone, then, tomorrow." She rose and stood poised in uncertainty, her hand on the back of the chair.

Harriet moved quickly toward her. The girl's infatuate obstinacy carried a power with it.

"But why, dear child, do you wish me to go with you? What good could that possibly do?"

There was a long silence, trembling and gentle tears. At last Ethel murmured: "I thought, because you were her friend, that would make it better. If you were with me, it couldn't seem quite so—indelicate." Her shoulders shook with a sudden wrench of feeling and she pressed her hands over her face. "You see," she faltered, "I'm so at a loss. I haven't— any one."

Harriet put an arm firmly about her drooping slenderness. "Well, for this venture, at least, you shall have me. I can't see it, but I'm willing to go; more willing than I am that you should go alone. I must tell Robert and ask him to look up the trains for us."

The girl drew gently away from her and stood in an attitude of deep dejection. "It's difficult for you, too, our being here. We ought never to have come. And I must not take advantage of you. Before letting you go with me, I must tell you the real reason why I am going to Fortuney."

"The real reason?" echoed Harriet.

"Yes. I think he's there now."

"Harold? At Fortuney?"

"Yes. I haven't heard from him for five days. Then it was only a telegram, dated from Pontoise. That's very near Fortuney. Since then I haven't had a word."

"You poor child, how dreadful! Come here and tell me about it." Harriet drew her to a chair, into which she sank limply.

"There's nothing to tell, except what one fears. I've lost sleep until I imagine all sorts of horrible things. If he has been alone there for days, shut up with all those memories, who knows what may have happened to him? I shouldn't, you know, feel like this if he were with—any one. But this—oh, you are all against me! You none of you understand. You think I am trying to make him—inconstant" (for the first time her voice broke into passionate scorn). "But there's no other way to save him. It's simply killing him. He's been frightfully ill twice, once in London and once before we left India. The London doctors told me that unless he was got out of this state he might do almost anything. They even wanted me to leave him. So, you see, I must do something."

Harriet sat down on the stool beside her and took her hand.

"Why don't you, then, my dear, do it—leave him?"

The girl looked wildly toward the garden wall. "I can't—not now. I might have once, perhaps. Oh!" with a burst of trembling, "don't, please don't talk about it. Just help me to save him if you can."

"Had you rather, Ethel, that I went to Fortuney alone?" Harriet suggested hopefully.

The girl shook her head. "No; he'd know I sent you, and he'd think I was afraid. I am, of course, but not in the way he thinks. I've never crossed him in anything, but we can't go on like this any longer. I'll go, and he'll just have to—choose."

Having seen Ethel safely to her own door, Harriet went to her husband, who was at work in the library, and told him to what she had committed herself. Westfield received the intelligence with marked discouragement. He disliked her being drawn more and more into the Forscythes' affairs, which he found very depressing and disconcerting, and he flatly declared that he wanted nothing so much as to get away from all that hysteria next door and finish the summer in Switzerland.

"It's an obsession with her to get to Fortuney," Harriet explained. "To her it somehow means getting into everything she's out of. I really can't have her thinking I'm against her in that definite, petty sort of way. So I've promised to go. Besides, if she is going down there, where all Eleanor's things are—"

"Ah, so it's to keep her out, and not to help her in, that you're going," Westfield deduced.

"I declare to you, I don't know which it is. I'm going for both of them—for her and for Eleanor."

V

Fortuney stood in its cluster of cool green, halfway up the hillside and overlooking the green loop of the river. Harriet remembered, as she approached it, how Eleanor used to say that after the South, it was good to come back and rest her eyes there. Nowhere were skies so gray, streams so clear, or fields so pleasantly interspersed with woodland. The hill on which the house stood overlooked an island where the haymakers were busy cutting a second crop, swinging their bright scythes in the long grass and stopping to hail the heavy lumber barges as they passed slowly up the glassy river.

Ethel insisted upon leaving the carriage by the roadside, so the two women alighted and walked up the long driveway that wound under the linden trees. An old man who was clipping the hedge looked curiously at them as they passed. Except for the snipping of his big shears and occasional halloos from the island, a pale, sunny quiet lay over the place, and their approach, Harriet reflected, certainly savored all too much of a reluctance to break it. She looked at Ethel with all the exasperation of fatigue, and felt that there was something positively stealthy about her soft, driven tread.

The front door was open, but, as they approached, a bent old woman ran out from the garden behind the house, her apron full of gourds, calling to them as she ran. Ethel addressed her without embarrassment: "I am Madame Forscythe. Monsieur is awaiting me. Yes, I know that he is ill. You need not announce me."

The old woman tried to detain her by salutations and questions, tried to explain that she would immediately get rooms ready for Madame and her friend. Why had she not been told?

But Ethel brushed past her, seeming to float over the threshold and up the staircase, while Harriet followed her, protesting. They went through the salon, the library, into Harold's study, straight toward the room which had been Eleanor's.

"Let us wait for him here in his study, please, Ethel," Harriet whispered. "We've no right to steal upon any one like this."

But Ethel seemed drawn like the victim of mesmerism. The door opening from the study into Eleanor's room was hung with a heavy curtain. She lifted it, and there they paused, noiselessly. It was just as Harriet remembered it; the tapestries, the prie-Dieu, the Louis Seize furniture—absolutely unchanged, except that her own portrait, by Constant, hung where Harold's used to be. Across the foot of the bed, in a tennis shirt and trousers, lay Harold himself, asleep. He was lying on his side, his face turned toward the door and one arm thrown over his head. The habit of being on his guard must have sharpened his senses, for as they looked at him he awoke and sprang up, flushed and disordered.

"Ethel, what on earth—?" he cried hotly.

She was frightened enough now. She trembled from head to foot and pressed her hands tightly over her breast. "You never told me not to come," she panted. "You only said," with a wild burst of reproach, "that you couldn't."

Harold gripped the foot of the bed with both hands and his voice shook with anger. "Please go downstairs and wait in the reception room, while I ask Mrs. Westfield to enlighten me."

Something leaped into Ethel's eyes as she took another step forward into the room and let the curtain fall behind her. "I won't go, Harold, until you go with me," she cried. Drawing up her frail shoulders, she glanced desperately about her—at the room, at her husband, at Harriet, and finally at her, the handsome, disdainful face which glowed out of the canvas. "You have no right to come here secretly," she broke out. "It's shameful to her as well as to me. I'm not afraid of her. She couldn't but loathe you for what you do to me. She couldn't have been so contemptible as you all make her—so jealous!"

Forscythe swung round on his heel, his clenched hands hanging at his side, and, throwing back his head, faced the picture.

"Jealous? Of whom—my God!"

"Harold!" cried Mrs. Westfield entreatingly.

But she was too late. The girl had slipped to the floor as if she had been cut down.

VI

One rainy night, four weeks after her visit to Fortuney, Forscythe stood at Mrs. Westfield's door, his hat in his hand, bidding her good night. Harriet looked worn and troubled, but Forscythe himself was calm.

"I'm so glad you gave me a chance at Fortuney, Harold. I couldn't bear to see it go to strangers. I'll keep it just as it is—as it was; you may be sure of that, and if ever you wish to come back—"

Forscythe spoke up quickly: "I don't think I shall be coming back again, Mrs. Westfield. And please don't hesitate to make any changes. As I've tried to tell you, I don't feel the need of it any longer. She has come back to me as much as she ever can."

"In another person?"

Harold smiled a little and shook his head. "In another way. She lived and died, dear Harriet, and I'm all there is to show for it. That's pitiful enough, but I must do what I can. I shall die very far short of the mark—but she was always generous."

He held out his hand to Mrs. Westfield and took hers resolutely, though she hesitated as if to detain him.

"Tell Ethel I shall go over to see her in the morning before you leave, and thank her for her message," Harriet murmured.

"Please come. She has been seeing to the packing in spite of me, and is quite worn out. She'll be herself again, once I get her back to Surrey, and she's very keen about going to America. Good night, dear lady," he called after him as he crossed the veranda.

Harriet heard him splash down the gravel walk to the gate and then closed the door. She went slowly through the hall and into her husband's study, where she sat quietly down by the wood fire.

Westfield rose from his work and looked at her with concern.

"Why didn't you send that madman home long ago, Harriet? It's past midnight, and you're completely done out. You look like a ghost." He opened a cabinet and poured her a glass of wine.

"I feel like one, dear. I'm beginning to feel my age. I've no spirit to hold it off any longer. I'm going to buy Fortuney and give up to it. It will be pleasant to grow old there in that atmosphere of lovely things past and forgotten."

Westfield sat down on the arm of her chair and drew her head to him. "He is really going to sell it, then? He has come round sure enough, hasn't he?"

"Oh, he melts the heart in me, Robert. He makes me feel so old and lonely; that he and I are left over from another age—a lovely time that's gone. He's giving up everything. He's going to take her home to America after her child is born."

"Her child?"

"Yes. He didn't know until after that dreadful day at Fortuney. She had never told any one. He says he's so glad—that it will make up to her for everything. Oh, Robert! if only Eleanor had left him children all this wouldn't have been."

"Do you think," Westfield asked after a long silence, "that he is glad?"

"I know it. He's been so gentle and comprehending with her." Harriet stopped to dry the tears on her cheek, and put her head down on her husband's shoulder. "And oh, Robert, I never would have believed that he could be so splendid about it. It's as if he had come up to his possibilities for the first time, through this silly, infatuated girl, while Eleanor, who gave him kingdoms—"

She cried softly on his shoulder for a long while, and then he felt that she was thinking. When at last she looked up, she smiled gratefully into his eyes.

"Well, we'll have Fortuney, dearest. We'll have all that's left of them. He'll never turn back; I feel such a strength in him now. He'll go on doing it and being finer and finer. And do you know, Robert," her lips trembled again, but she still smiled from her misty eyes, "if Eleanor knows, I believe she'll be glad; for—oh, my Eleanor!—she loved him beyond anything, beyond even his love."

First published in *McClure's*, XXIX (October, 1907), 623–630.

The Willing Muse

❖ ❖ ❖

Various opinions were held among Kenneth Gray's friends regarding his approaching marriage, but on the whole it was considered a hopeful venture, and, what was with some of us much more to the point, a hopeful indication. From the hour his engagement was an assured relation, he had seemed to gain. There was now a certain intention in his step, an eager, almost confident flash behind his thick glasses, which cheered his friends like indications of recovery after long illness. Even his shoulders seemed to droop less despondently and his head to sit upon them more securely. Those of us who knew him best drew a long sigh of relief that Kenneth had at last managed to get right with the current.

If, on the insecurity of a meager income and a career at its belated dawn, he was to marry at all, we felt that a special indulgence of destiny had allowed him to fix his choice upon Bertha Torrence. If there was anywhere a woman who seemed able to give him what he needed, to play upon him a continual stream of inspiriting confidence, to order the very simple affairs which he had so besottedly bungled, surely Bertha was the woman.

There were certain of his friends in Olympia who held out that it was a mistake for him to marry a woman who followed his own profession; who was, indeed, already much more within the public consciousness than Kenneth himself. To refute such arguments, one had only to ask what was possible between that and a housekeeper. Could any one conceive of Kenneth's living in daily intercourse with a woman who had no immediate and personal interest in letters, bitten to the bone as he was by his slow, consuming passion?

Perhaps, in so far as I was concerned, my personal satisfaction at Kenneth's projected marriage was not without its alloy of selfishness, and I think more than one of us counted upon carrying lighter hearts to his wedding than we had known in his company for some time. It was not that we did not believe in him. Hadn't it become a fixed habit to believe? But we, perhaps, felt slightly aggrieved that our faith had not wrought for him the miracles we could have hoped. We were, we found, willing enough to place the direct administration, the first responsibility, upon Bertha's firm young shoulders.

With Harrison, the musical critic, and me, Kenneth was an old issue. We had been college classmates of his, out in Olympia, Ohio, and even then no one had questioned his calling and election, unless it was Kenneth himself. But he had taxed us all sorely, the town and the college, and he had continued to tax us long afterward. As Harrison put it, he had kept us all holding our breath for years. There was never such a man for getting people into a fever of interest and determination for him, for making people (even people who had very vague surmises as to the particular eminence toward which he might be headed) fervidly desire to push him and for refusing, on any terms, to be pushed. There was nothing more individual about Kenneth than his inability to be exploited. Coercion and encouragement spent themselves upon him like summer rain.

He was thirty-five when his first book, *Charles de Montpensier*, was published, and the work was, to those who knew its author intimately, a kind of record of his inverse development. It was first conceived and written as a prose drama, then amplified into an historical novel, and had finally been compressed into a psychological study of two hundred pages, in which the action was hushed to a whisper and the teeming pageantry of his background, which he had spent years in developing and which had cost him several laborious summers in France and Italy, was reduced to a shadowy atmosphere, suggestive enough, doubtless, but presenting very little that was appreciable to the eyes of the flesh. The majority of Kenneth's readers, even those baptized into his faith, must have recalled the fable of the mouse and the mountain. As for those of us who had travailed with him, confident as we were of the high order of the ultimate production, we had a baffled feeling that there had been a distressing leakage of power. However, when this study of the High Constable of Bourbon was followed by an exquisite prose idyl, *The Wood of Ronsard*, we began to take heart, and when we learned that a stimulus so reassuring as a determination to marry had hurried this charming bit of romance into the world, we felt that Kenneth had at last entered upon the future that had seemed for so long only a step before him.

Since Gray's arrival in New York, Harrison and I had had more than ever the feeling of having him on our hands. He had been so long accustomed to the respectful calm of Olympia that he was unable to find his way about in a new environment. He was incapable of falling in with any of the prevailing attitudes, and even of civilly tolerating them in other people. Commercialism wounded him, flippancy put him out of countenance, and he clung stubbornly to certain fond, Olympian superstitions regarding his profession. One by one his new acquaintances chilled, offended by his arrogant reception of their genial efforts to put him in the way of things. Even those of us who had known him at his best, and who remembered the summer evenings in his garden at Olympia, found his seriousness and punctilious reservations tedious in the broad glare of short, noisy working days.

Some weeks before the day set for Kenneth's marriage, I learned that it might be necessary for me to go to Paris for a time to take the place of our correspondent there, who had fallen into precarious health, and I called at Bertha's apartment for a serious talk with her. I found her in the high tide of work; but she made a point of accepting interruptions agreeably, just as she made a point of looking astonishingly well, of being indispensable in an appalling number of "circles," and of generally nullifying the traditional reproach attaching to clever women.

"In all loyalty to you both," I remarked, "I feel that I ought to remind you that you are accepting a responsibility."

"His uncertainty, you mean?"

"Oh, I mean all of them—the barriers which are so intangible he cannot climb them and so terrifying he can't jump them, which lie between him and everything."

Bertha looked at me thoughtfully out of her candid blue eyes. "But what he needs is, after all, so little compared with what he has."

"What he has," I admitted, "is inestimably precious; but the problem is to keep it from going back into the ground with him."

She shot a glance of alarm at me from under her blond lashes. "But certainly he is endlessly more capable of doing than any of us. With such depth to draw from, how can he possibly fail?"

"Perhaps it's his succeeding that I fear more than anything. I think the fair way to measure Kenneth is by what he simply can't do."

"The cheap, you mean?" she asked reflectively. "Oh, that he will never do. We may just eliminate that from our discussion. The problem is simply to make him mine his vein, even if, from his fanciful angle of vision, it's at first a losing business."

"Ah, my dear young lady, but it's just his fanciful angle, as you so happily term it, that puts a stop to everything, and I've never quite dared to urge him past his scruples, though I'm not saying I could if I would. If there is anything at all in the whole business, any element of chosenness, of a special call, any such value in individual tone as he fancies, then, the question is, dare one urge him?"

"Nonsense!" snapped Bertha, drawing up her slender shoulders with decision—I had purposely set out to exhaust her patience—"you have all put a halo about him until he daren't move for fear of putting it out. What he needs is simply to keep at it. How much satisfaction do you suppose he gets out of hanging back?"

"The point, it seems to me, my dear Bertha, is not that, but the remarkableness of any one's having the conviction, the moral force, just now and under the circumstances, to hang back at all. There must be either very much or very little in a man when he refuses to make the most of his vogue and sell out on a rising market. If he would rather bring up a little water out of the well than turn the river across his lands, has one a right to coerce him?" I put my shaft home steadily, and Bertha caught fire with proper spirit.

"All I can say is, that it's a miracle he's as adaptable as he is. I simply can't understand what you meant, you and Harrison, by keeping him out there in Ohio so long."

"But we didn't," I expostulated. "We didn't keep him there. We only did not succeed in getting him away. We, too, had our scruples. He had his old house there, and his garden, his friends, and the peace of God. And then, Olympia isn't a bad sort of place. It kept his feeling fresh, at least, and in fifteen years or so you'll begin to know the value of that. There everything centers about the college, and every one reads, just as every one goes to church. It's a part of the decent, comely life of the place. In Olympia there is a deep-seated, old-fashioned respect for the printed page, and Kenneth naturally found himself in the place of official sanctity. The townswomen reverently attended his college lectures, along with their sons and daughters, and, had he been corruptible, he might have established a walled supremacy of personal devotion behind which he could have sheltered himself to the end of his days."

"But he didn't, you see," said Bertha, triumphantly; "which is proof that he was meant for the open waters. Oh, we shall do fine things, I promise you! I can just fancy the hushed breath of the place for wonder at him. And his rose garden! Will people never have done with his rose garden! I remember you and Harrison told me of it, with an air, before I had met Kenneth at all. I wonder that you didn't keep him down there forever from a pure sense of the picturesque. What sort of days and nights do you imagine he passed in his garden, in his miserably uncertain state? I suppose we should all like well enough to grow roses, if we had nothing else to do."

I felt that Bertha was considerately keeping her eyes from the clock, and I rose to go.

"Well, Bertha, I suppose the only reason we haven't brought him to a worse pass than we have, is just the fact that he happens to have been born an anachronism, and such a stubborn one that we leave him pretty much where we found him."

II

After Kenneth's wedding, I left immediately for Paris, and during the next four years I knew of the Grays only what I could sense from Kenneth's labored letters, ever more astonishing in their aridity, and from the parcels I received twice a year by book-post, containing Bertha's latest work. I never picked up an American periodical that Bertha's name was not the first to greet my eye on the advertising pages. She surpassed all legendary accounts of phenomenal productiveness, and I could feel no anxiety for the fortunes of the pair while Bertha's publishers thought her worth such a display of heavy type. There was scarcely a phase of colonial life left untouched by her, and her last, *The Maid of Domremy*, showed that she had fairly crowded herself out of her own field.

The real wonder was, that, making so many, she could make them so well—should make them, indeed, rather better and better. Even were one so unreasonable as to consider her gain a loss, there was no denying it. I read her latest, one after another, as they arrived, with growing interest and amazement, wholly unable to justify my first suspicion. There was every evidence that she had absorbed from Kenneth like a water plant, but none that she had used him more violently than a clever woman may properly use her husband. Knowing him as I did, I could never accredit him with having any hand in Bertha's intrepid, wholehearted, unimpeachable conventionality. One could not exactly call her unscrupulous; one could observe only that no predicament embarrassed her; that she went ahead and pulled it off.

When I returned to New York, I found a curious state of feeling prevalent concerning the Grays. Bertha was *la fille du régiment* more than ever. Every one championed her, every one went to her teas, every one was smilingly and conspicuously present in her triumph. Even those who had formerly stood somewhat aloof, now found no courage to dissent. With Bertha herself so gracious, so eager to please, the charge of pettiness, of jealousy, even, could be too easily incurred. She quite floated the sourest and heaviest upon her rising tide.

There was, however, the undertow. I felt it even before I had actually made sure of it—in the peculiar warmth with which people spoke of Kenneth. In him they saw their own grievances magnified until he became symbolic. Publicly every one talked of Bertha; but behind closed doors it was of Kenneth they spoke—*sotto voce* and with a shake of the head. As he had published nothing since his marriage, this smothered feeling had resulted in a new and sumptuous edition of *Montpensier* and *The Wood of Ronsard*; one of those final, votive editions, suggestive of the bust and the catafalque.

I called upon the Grays at the first opportunity. They had moved from their downtown flat into a new apartment house on Eighty-fifth street. The servant who took my card did not return, but Kenneth himself stumbled into the reception hall, overturning a gilt chair in his haste, and gripped my hands as if he would never let them go. He held on to my arm as he took me to his study, telling me again and again that I couldn't possibly know what pleasure it gave him to see me. When he dropped limply into his desk chair, he seemed really quite overcome with excitement. It was not until I asked him about his wife that he collected himself and began to talk coherently.

"I'm sorry I can't speak to her now," he explained, rapidly twirling a paper cutter between his long fingers. "She won't be free until four o'clock. She will be so pleased that I'm almost tempted to call her at once. But she's so overworked, poor girl, and she will go out so much."

"My dear Kenneth, how does she ever manage it all? She must have nerves of iron."

"Oh, she's wonderful, wonderful!" he exclaimed, brushing his limp hair back from his forehead with a perplexed gesture. "As to how she does it, I really don't know much more than you. It all gets done, somehow." He glanced quickly toward the partition, through which we heard the steady clicking of a typewriter. "I scarcely know what she is up to until her proofs come in. I usually go at those with her." He darted a piercing look at me, and I wondered whether he had got a hint of the malicious stories which found their way about concerning his varied usefulness to Bertha.

"If you'll excuse me for a moment, Philip," he went on, "I'll finish a letter that must go out this afternoon, and then I shall be quite free."

He turned in his revolving chair to a desk littered deep with papers, and began writing hurriedly. I could see that the simplest kind of composition still perplexed and disconcerted him. He stopped, hesitated, bit his nails, then scratched desperately ahead, darting an annoyed glance at the partition as if the sharp, regular click of the machine bewildered him.

He had grown older, I noticed, but it was good to see him again—his limp, straight hair, which always hung down in a triangle over his high forehead; his lean cheek, loose under lip, and long whimsical chin; his faded, serious eyes, which were always peering inquiringly from behind his thick glasses; his long, tremulous fingers, which handled a pen as uncertainly as ever. There was a general looseness of articulation about his gaunt frame that made his every movement seem more or less haphazard.

On the desk lay a heap of letters, the envelopes marked "answered" in Kenneth's small, irregular hand, and all of them, I noticed, addressed to Bertha. In the open drawer at his left were half a dozen manuscript envelopes, addressed to her in as many different hands.

"What on earth!" I gasped. "Does Bertha conduct a literary agency as well?"

Kenneth swung round in his chair, and made a wry face as he glanced at the contents of the drawer. "It's almost as bad as that. Really, it's the most abominable nuisance. But we're the victims of success, as Bertha says. Sometimes a dozen manuscripts come in to her for criticism in one week. She dislikes to hurt any one's feelings, so one of us usually takes a look at them."

"Bertha's correspondence must be something of a responsibility in itself," I ventured.

"Oh, it is, I assure you. People are most inconsiderate. I'm rather glad, though, when it piles up like this and I can take a hand at it. It gives me an excuse for putting off my own work, and you know how I welcome any pretext," he added, with a flushed, embarrassed smile.

"What are you doing, anyhow? I don't know where you'll ever learn industry if Bertha can't teach you."

"I'm working, I'm working," he insisted, hurriedly crossing out the last sentence of his letter and blotting it carefully. "You know how reprehensibly slow I am. It seems to grow on me. I'm finishing up some studies in the French Renaissance. They'll be ready by next fall, I think." As he spoke, he again glanced hurriedly over the closely written page before him; then, stopping abruptly, he tore the sheet across the middle. "Really, you've quite upset me. Tell me about yourself, Philip. Are you going out to Olympia?"

"That depends upon whether I remain here or decamp immediately for China, which prospect is in the cards. Olympia is greatly changed, Harrison tells me."

Kenneth sighed and sank deeper into his chair, reaching again for the paper cutter. "Ruined completely. Capital and enterprise have broken in even there. They've all sorts of new industries, and the place is black with smoke and thick with noise from sunrise to sunset. I still own my house there, but I seldom go back. I don't know where we're bound for, I'm sure. There must be places, somewhere in the world, where a man can take a book or two and drop behind the procession for an hour; but they seem impossibly far from here."

I could not help smiling at the deeply despondent gaze which he fixed upon the paper cutter. "But the procession itself is the thing we've got to enjoy," I suggested, "the mere sense of speed."

"I suppose so, I suppose so," he reiterated, wiping his forehead with his handkerchief. "The six-day bicycle race seems to be what we've all come to, and doubtless one form of it's as much worth while as another. We don't get anywhere, but we go. We certainly go; and that's what we're after. You'll be lucky if you are sent to China. There must be calm there as yet, I imagine."

Our conversation went on fitfully, with interruptions, irrelevant remarks, and much laughter, as talk goes between two persons who have once been frank with each other, and who find that frankness has become impossible. My coming had clearly upset him, and his agitation of manner visibly increased when he spoke of his wife. He wiped his forehead and hands repeatedly, and finally opened a window. He fairly wrested the conversation out of my hands and was continually interrupting and forestalling me, as if he were apprehensive that I might say something he did not wish to hear. He started and leaned forward in his chair whenever I approached a question.

At last we were aware of a sudden slack in the tension; the typewriter had stopped. Kenneth looked at his watch, and disappeared through a door into his wife's study. When he returned, Bertha was beside him, her hand on his shoulder, taller, straighter, younger than I had left her—positively childlike in her freshness and candor.

"Didn't I tell you," she cried, "that we should do fine things?"

III

A few weeks later I was sent to Hong Kong, where I remained for two years. Before my return to America, I was ordered into the interior for eight months, during which time my mail was to be held for me at the consul's office in Canton, the port where I was to take ship for home. Once in the Sze Chuen province, floods and bad roads delayed me to such an extent that I barely reached Canton on the day my vessel sailed. I hurried on board with all my letters unread, having had barely time to examine the instructions from my paper.

We were well out at sea when I opened a letter from Harrison in which he gave an account of Kenneth Gray's disappearance. He had, Harrison stated, gone out to Olympia to dispose of his property there which, since the development of the town, had greatly increased in value. He completed his business after a week's stay, and left for New York by the night train, several of his friends accompanying him to the station. Since that night he had not been seen or heard of. Detectives had been at work; hospitals and morgues had been searched without result.

The date of this communication put me beside myself. It had awaited me in Canton for nearly seven months, and Gray had last been seen on the tenth of November, four months before the date of Harrison's letter, which was written as soon as the matter was made public. It was eleven months, then, since Kenneth Gray had been seen in America. During my long voyage I went through an accumulated bulk of American newspapers, but found nothing more reassuring than occasional items to the effect that the mystery surrounding Gray's disappearance remained unsolved. In a "literary supplement" of comparatively recent date, I came upon a notice to the effect that the new novel by Bertha Torrence Gray, announced for spring publication, would, owing to the excruciating experience through which the young authoress had lately passed, be delayed until the autumn.

I bore my suspense as best I could across ocean and continent. When I arrived in New York, I went from the ferry to the *Messenger* office, and, once there, directly to Harrison's room.

"What's all this," I cried, "about Kenneth Gray? I tell you I saw Gray in Canton ten months ago."

Harrison sprang to his feet and put his finger to his lip.

"Hush! Don't say another word! There are leaky walls about here. Go and attend to your business, and then come back and go to lunch with me. In the meantime, be careful not to discuss Gray with any one."

Four hours later, when we were sitting in a quiet corner of a café, Harrison dismissed the waiter and turned to me. "Now," he said, leaning across the table, "if you can be sufficiently guarded, you may tell me what you know about our friend."

"Well," I replied, "it would have been, under ordinary circumstances, a commonplace thing enough. On the day before I started for the interior, I was in Canton, making some last purchases to complete my outfit. I stepped out of a shop on one of the crooked streets in the old part of the city, and I saw him as plainly as I see you, being trundled by in a jinrikisha, got up in a helmet and white duck, a fat white umbrella across his knees, peering hopefully out through his glasses. He was so like himself, his look and attitude, his curious chin poked forward, that I simply stood and stared until he had passed me and turned a corner, vanishing like a stereopticon picture traveling across the screen. I hurried to the banks, the big hotels, to the consul's, getting no word of him, but leaving letters for him everywhere. My party started the next day, and I was compelled to leave for an eight-months' nightmare in the interior. I got back to Canton barely in time to catch my steamer, and did not open your letter until we were down the river and losing sight of land. Either I saw Kenneth, or I am a subject for the Society for Psychical Research."

"Just so," said Harrison, peering mysteriously above his coffee cup. "And now forget it. Simply disabuse yourself of any notion that you've seen him since we crossed the ferry with you three years ago. It's your last service to him, probably."

"Speak up," I cried, exasperated. "I've had about all of this I can stand. I came near wiring the story in from San Francisco. I don't know why I didn't."

"Well, here's to whatever withheld you! When a man comes to the pass where he wants to wipe himself off the face of the earth, when it's the last play he can make for his self-respect, the only decent thing is to let him do it. You know the yielding stuff he's made of well enough to appreciate the amount of pressure it must have taken to harden him to such an exit. I'm sure I never supposed he had it in him."

"But what, short of insanity—"

"Insanity? Nonsense! I wonder that people don't do it oftener. The pressure simply got past the bearing-point. His life was going, and going for nothing—worse than nothing. His future was chalked out for him, and whichever way he turned he was confronted by his unescapable destiny. In the light of Bertha's splendid success, he couldn't be churlish or ungracious; he had to play his little part along with the rest of us. And Bertha, you know, has passed all the limits of nature, not to speak of decorum. They come as certainly as the seasons, her new ones, each cleverer and more damnable than the last. And yet there is nothing that one can actually put one's finger on—not, at least, without saying the word that would lay us open to a charge which as her friends we are none of us willing to incur, and which no one would listen to if it were said.

"I tell you," Harrison continued, "the whole thing sickened him. He had dried up like a stockfish. His brain was beaten into torpidity by the mere hammer of her machine, as by so many tiny mallets. He had lived to help lessen the value of all that he held precious, to disprove all that he wanted to believe. Having ridden to victory under the banners of what he most despised, there was nothing for him but to live in the blaze of her conquest, and that was the very measure of his fall. His usefulness to the world was over when he had done what he did for Bertha. I don't believe he even knew where he stood; the thing had gone so, seemed to answer the purpose so wonderfully well, and there was never anything that one could really put one's finger on—except all of it. It was a trial of faith, and Bertha had won out so beautifully. He had proved the fallacy of his own position. There was nothing left for him to say. I'm sure I don't know whether he had anything left to think."

"Do you remember," I said slowly, "I used to hold that, in the end, Kenneth would be measured by what he didn't do, by what he couldn't do? What a wonder he was at not being able to do it. Surely, if Bertha couldn't convince him, fire and faggots couldn't."

"For, after all," sighed Harrison, as we rose to go, "Bertha is a wonderful woman—a woman of her time and people; and she has managed, in spite of her fatal facility, to be enough sight better than most of us."

First published in *Century*, LXXIV (August, 1907), 550–551, 553–557.

The Profile

✳ ✳ ✳

The subject of discussion at the Impressionists' Club was a picture, *Circe's Swine*, by a young German painter; a grotesque study showing the enchantress among a herd of bestial things, variously diverging from the human type—furry-eared fauns, shaggy-hipped satyrs, apes with pink palms, snuffing jackals, and thick-jowled swine, all with more or less of human intelligence protesting mutely from their hideous lineaments.

"They are all errors, these freakish excesses," declared an old painter of the Second Empire. "Triboulet, Quasimodo, Gwynplaine, have no proper place in art. Such art belongs to the Huns and Iroquois, who could only be stirred by laceration and dismemberment. The only effects of horror properly within the province of the artist are psychological. Everything else is a mere matter of the abattoir. The body, as Nature has evolved it, is sanctified by her purpose; in any natural function or attitude decent and comely. But lop away so much as a finger, and you have wounded the creature beyond reparation."

Once launched upon this subject, there was no stopping the old lion, and several of his confrères were relieved when Aaron Dunlap quietly rose and left the room. They felt that this was a subject which might well be distasteful to him.

I

Dunlap was a portrait painter—preferably a painter of women. He had the faculty of transferring personalities to his canvas, rather than of putting conceptions there. He was finely sensitive to the merest prettiness, was tender and indulgent of it, careful never to deflower a pretty woman of her little charm, however commonplace.

Nicer critics always discerned, even in his most radiant portraits, a certain quiet element of sympathy, almost of pity, in the treatment. The sharp, flexible profile of Madame R—— of the Française; the worn,

[125]

but subtle and all-capricious physiognomy of her great Semitic rival;* the plump contours of a shopkeeper's pretty wife—Dunlap treated them with equal respect and fidelity. He accepted each as she was, and could touch even obvious prettiness with dignity. Behind the delicate pleasure manifested in his treatment of a beautiful face, one could divine the sadness of knowledge, and one felt that the painter had yearned to arrest what was so fleeting and to hold it back from the cruelty of the years. At an exhibition of Dunlap's pictures, the old painter of the Second Empire had said, with a sigh, that he ought to get together all his portraits of young women and call them "Les Fiançées," so abloom were they with the confidence of their beautiful secret. Then, with that sensitiveness to style, which comes from long and passionate study of form, the old painter had added reflectively, "And, after all, how sad a thing it is to be young."

Dunlap had come from a country where women are hardly used. He had grown up on a farm in the remote mountains of West Virginia, and his mother had died of pneumonia contracted from taking her place at the washtub too soon after the birth of a child. When a boy, he had been apprenticed to his grandfather, a country cobbler, who, in his drunken rages, used to beat his wife with odd strips of shoe leather. The painter's hands still bore the mark of that apprenticeship, and the suffering of the mountain women he had seen about him in his childhood had left him almost morbidly sensitive.

Just how or why Dunlap had come to Paris, none of his fellow-painters had ever learned. When he ran away from his grandfather, he had been sent by a missionary fund to some sectarian college in his own state, after which he had taught a country school for three winters and saved money enough for his passage. He arrived in Paris with something less than a hundred dollars, wholly ignorant of the language, without friends, and, apparently, without especial qualifications for study there.

Perhaps the real reason that he never succumbed to want was, that he was never afraid of it. He felt that he could never be really hungry so long as the poplars flickered along the gray quay behind the Louvre; never friendless while the gay busses rolled home across the bridges through the violet twilight, and the barge lights winked above the water.

Little by little his stripes were healed, his agony of ignorance alleviated. The city herself taught him whatever was needful for him to know. She repeated with him that fanciful romance which she has played at with

* Rachel (1820–1858) and Sarah Bernhardt (1844–1923).

youth for centuries, in which her spontaneity is ever young. She gave him of her best, quickened in him a sense of the more slight and feminine fairness in things; trained his hand and eye to the subtleties of the thousand types of subtle beauty in which she abounds; made him, after a delicate and chivalrous fashion, the expiator of his mountain race. He lived in a bright atmosphere of clear vision and happy associations, delighted at having to do with what was fair and exquisitely brief.

Life went on so during the first ten years of his residence in Paris—a happiness which, despite its almost timorous modesty, tempted fate. It was after Dunlap's name had become somewhat the fashion, that he chanced one day, in a café on the Boulevard St. Michel, to be of some service to an American who was having trouble about his order. After assisting him, Dunlap had some conversation with the man, a Californian, whose wheatlands comprised acres enough for a principality, and whose enthusiasm was as fresh as a boy's. Several days later, at the Luxembourg, he met him again, standing in a state of abject bewilderment before Manet's *Olympe*. Dunlap again came to his rescue and took him off to lunch, after which they went to the painter's studio. The acquaintance warmed on both sides, and, before they separated, Dunlap was engaged to paint the old gentleman's daughter, agreeing that the sittings should be at the house on the Boulevard de Courcelles, which the family had taken for the winter.

When Dunlap called at the house, he went through one of the most excruciating experiences of his life. He found Mrs. Gilbert and her daughter waiting to receive him. The shock of the introduction over, the strain of desultory conversation began. The only thing that made conversation tolerable—though it added a new element of perplexity— was the girl's seeming unconsciousness, her utter openness and unabashed- ness. She laughed and spoke, almost with coquetry, of the honor of sitting to him, of having heard that he was fastidious as to his subjects. Dunlap felt that he wanted to rush from the house and escape the situation which confronted him. The conviction kept recurring that it had just happened, had come upon her since last she had passed a mirror; that she would suddenly become conscious of it, and be suffocated with shame. He felt as if some one ought to tell her and lead her away.

"Shall we get to work?" she asked presently, apparently curious and eager to begin. "How do you wish me to sit to you?"

Dunlap murmured something about usually asking his sitters to decide that for themselves.

"Suppose we try a profile, then?" she suggested carelessly, sitting down in a carved wooden chair.

For the first time since he had entered the room, Dunlap felt the pressure about his throat relax. For the first time it was entirely turned from him, and he could not see it at all. What he did see was a girlish profile, unusually firm for a thing so softly colored; oval, flower-tinted, and shadowed by soft, blonde hair that wound about her head and curled and clung about her brow and neck and ears.

Dunlap began setting up his easel, recovering from his first discomfort and grateful to the girl for having solved his difficulty so gracefully. But no sooner was it turned from him than he felt a strong desire to see it again. Perhaps it had been only a delusion, after all; the clear profile before him so absolutely contradicted it. He went behind her chair to experiment with the window shades, and there, as he drew them up and down, he could look unseen. He gazed long and hard, to blunt his curiosity once and for all, and prevent a further temptation to covert glances. It had evidently been caused by a deep burn, as if from a splash of molten metal. It drew the left eye and the corner of the mouth; made of her smile a grinning distortion, like the shameful conception of some despairing medieval imagination. It was as if some grotesque mask, worn for disport, were just slipping sidewise from her face.

When Dunlap crossed to the right again, he found the same clear profile awaiting him, the same curves of twining, silken hair. "What courage," he thought, "what magnificent courage!" His heart ached at the injustice of it; that her very beauty, the alert, girlish figure, the firm, smooth throat and chin, even her delicate hands, should, through an inch or two of seared flesh, seem tainted and false. He felt that in a plain woman it would have been so much less horrible.

Dunlap left the house overcast by a haunting sense of tragedy, and for the rest of the day he was a prey to distressing memories. All that he had tried to forget seemed no longer dim and faraway—like the cruelties of vanished civilizations—but present and painfully near. He thought of his mother and grandmother, of his little sister, who had died from the bite of a copperhead snake, as if they were creatures yet unreleased from suffering.

II

From the first, Virginia's interest in the portrait never wavered; yet, as the sittings progressed, it became evident to Dunlap that her enthusiasm for the picture was but accessory to her interest in him. By her every look and action she asserted her feeling, as a woman, young and handsome and independent, may sometimes do.

As time went on, he was drawn to her by what had once repelled him. Her courageous candor appealed to his chivalry, and he came to love her, not despite the scar, but, in a manner, for its very sake. He had some indefinite feeling that love might heal her; that in time her hurt might disappear, like the deformities imposed by enchantment to test the hardihood of lovers.

He gathered from her attitude, as well as from that of her family, that the thing had never been mentioned to her, never alluded to by word or look. Both her father and mother had made it their first care to shield her. Had she ever, in the streets of some foreign city, heard a brutal allusion to it? He shuddered to think of such a possibility. Was she not living for the moment when she could throw down the mask and point to it and weep, to be comforted for all time? He looked forward to the hour when there would be no lie of unconsciousness between them. The moment must come when she would give him her confidence; perhaps it would be only a whisper, a gesture, a guiding of his hand in the dark; but, however it might come, it was the pledge he awaited.

During the last few weeks before his marriage, the scar, through the mere strength of his anticipation, had ceased to exist for him. He had already entered to the perfect creature which he felt must dwell behind it; the soul of tragic serenity and twofold loveliness.

They went to the South for their honeymoon, through the Midi and along the coast to Italy. Never, by word or sign, did Virginia reveal any consciousness of what he felt must be said once, and only once, between them. She was spirited, adventurous, impassioned; she exacted much, but she gave magnificently. Her interests in the material world were absorbing, and she demanded continual excitement and continual novelty. Granted these, her good spirits were unfailing.

It was during their wedding journey that he discovered her two all-absorbing interests, which were to become intensified as years went on: her passion for dress and her feverish admiration of physical beauty, whether in men or women or children. This touched Dunlap deeply, as it seemed in a manner an admission of a thing she could not speak.

Before their return to Paris Dunlap had, for the time, quite renounced his hope of completely winning her confidence. He tried to believe his exclusion just; he told himself that it was only a part of her splendid self-respect. He thought of how, from her very childhood, she had been fashioning, day by day, that armor of unconsciousness in which she sheathed her scar. After all, so deep a hurt could, perhaps, be bared to any one rather than the man she loved.

Yet, he felt that their life was enmeshed in falsehood; that he could not live year after year with a woman who shut so deep a part of her nature from him; that since he had married a woman outwardly different from others, he must have that within her which other women did not possess. Until this was granted him, he felt there would be a sacredness lacking in their relation which it peculiarly ought to have. He counted upon the birth of her child to bring this about. It would touch deeper than he could hope to do, and with fingers that could not wound. That would be a tenderness more penetrating, more softening than passion; without pride or caprice; a feeling that would dwell most in the one part of her he had failed to reach. The child, certainly, she could not shut out; whatever hardness or defiant shame it was that held him away from her, her maternity would bring enlightenment; would bring that sad wisdom, that admission of the necessity and destiny to suffer, which is, somehow, so essential in a woman.

Virginia's child was a girl, a sickly baby which cried miserably from the day it was born. The listless, wailing, almost unwilling battle for life that daily went on before his eyes saddened Dunlap profoundly. All his painter's sophistries fell away from him, and more than ever his early destiny seemed closing about him. There was, then, no escaping from the cruelty of physical things—no matter how high and bright the sunshine, how gray and poplar-clad the ways of one's life. The more willing the child seemed to relinquish its feeble hold, the more tenderly he loved it, and the more determinedly he fought to save it.

Virginia, on the contrary, had almost from the first exhibited a marked indifference toward her daughter. She showed plainly that the sight of its wan, aged little face was unpleasant to her; she disliked being clutched by its skeleton fingers, and said its wailing made her head ache. She was always taking Madame de Montebello and her handsome children to drive in the Bois, but she was never to be seen with little Eleanor. If her friends asked to see the child, she usually put them off, saying that she was asleep or in her bath.

When Dunlap once impatiently asked her whether she never intended to permit any one to see her daughter, she replied coldly: "Certainly, when she has filled out and begins to look like something."

Little Eleanor grew into a shy, awkward child, who slipped about the house like an unwelcome dependent. She was four years old when a cousin of Virginia's came from California to spend a winter in Paris. Virginia had know her only slightly at home, but, as she proved to be a charming girl, and as she was ill-equipped to bear the hardships of a winter in a *pension*, the Dunlaps insisted upon her staying with them. The cousin's name was also Eleanor—she had been called so after Virginia's mother—and, from the first, the two Eleanors seemed drawn to each other. Miss Vane was studying, and went out to her lectures every day, but whenever she was at home, little Eleanor was with her. The child would sit quietly in her room while she wrote, playing with anything her cousin happened to give her; or would lie for hours on the hearth rug, whispering to her woolly dog. Dunlap felt a weight lifted from his mind. Whenever Eleanor was at home, he knew that the child was happy.

He had long ceased to expect any solicitude for her from Virginia. That had gone with everything else. It was one of so many disappointments that he took it rather as a matter of course, and it seldom occurred to him that it might have been otherwise. For two years he had been living like a man who knows that some reptile has housed itself and hatched its young in his cellar, and who never cautiously puts his foot out of his bed without the dread of touching its coils. The change in his feeling toward his wife kept him in perpetual apprehension; it seemed to threaten everything he held dear, even his self-respect. His life was a continual effort of self-control, and he found it necessary to make frequent trips to London or sketching tours into Brittany to escape from the strain of the repression he put upon himself. Under this state of things, Dunlap aged perceptibly, and his friends made various and usual conjectures. Whether Virginia was conscious of the change in him, he never knew. Her feeling for him had, in its very nature, been as temporary as it was violent; it had abated naturally, and she probably took for granted that the same readjustment had taken place in him. Perhaps she was too much engrossed in other things to notice it at all.

In Dunlap the change seemed never to be finally established, but forever painfully working. Whereas he had once seen the scar on his wife's face not at all, he now saw it continually. Inch by inch it had crept over her whole countenance. Yet the scar itself seemed now a trivial thing; he had known for a long time that the burn had gone deeper than the flesh.

Virginia's extravagant fondness for gaiety seemed to increase, and her mania for lavish display, doubtless common enough in the Californian wheat empire, was a discordant note in Paris. Dunlap found himself condemned to an existence which daily did violence to his sense of propriety. His wife gave fêtes, the cost of which was noised abroad by the Associated Press and flaunted in American newspapers. Her vanity, the pageantries of her toilet, made them both ridiculous, he felt. She was a woman now, with a husband and child; she had no longer a pretext for keeping up the pitiful bravado under which she had hidden the smarting pride of her girlhood.

He became more and more convinced that she had been shielded from a realization of her disfigurement only to the end of a shocking perversity. Her costumes, her very jewels, blazed defiance. Her confidence became almost insolent, and her laugh was nothing but a frantic denial of a thing so cruelly obvious. The unconsciousness he had once reverenced now continually tempted his brutality, and when he felt himself reduced to the point of actual vituperation, he fled to Normandy or Languedoc to save himself. He had begun, indeed, to feel strangely out of place in Paris. The ancient comfort of the city, never lacking in the days when he had known cold and hunger, failed him now. A certain sordidness had spread itself over ways and places once singularly perfect and pure.

III

One evening when Virginia refused to allow little Eleanor to go down to the music room to see some pantomine performers who were to entertain their guests, Dunlap, to conceal his displeasure, stepped quickly out upon the balcony and closed the window behind him. He stood for some moments in the cold, clear night air.

"God help me," he groaned. "Some day I shall tell her. I shall hold her and tell her."

When he entered the house again, it was by another window, and his anger had cooled. As he stepped into the hallway, he met Eleanor the elder, going upstairs with the little girl in her arms. For the life of him he could not refrain from appealing for sympathy to her kind, grave eyes. He was so hurt, so sick, that he could have put his face down beside the child's and wept.

"Give her to me, little cousin. She is too heavy for you," he said gently, as they went upstairs together.

He remembered with resentment his wife's perfectly candid and care-less jests about his fondness for her cousin. After he had put the little girl down in Eleanor's room, as they leaned together above the child's head in the firelight, he became, for the first time, really aware. A sudden tender-ness weakened him. He put out his hand and took hers, which was holding the child's, and murmured: "Thank you, thank you, little cousin."

She started violently and caught her hand away from him, trembling all over. Dunlap left the room, thrice more miserable than he had entered it.

After that evening he noticed that Eleanor avoided meeting him alone. Virginia also noticed it, but upon this point she was consistently silent. One morning, as Dunlap was leaving his wife's dressing room, having been to consult her as to whether she intended going to the ball at the Russian Embassy, she called him back. She was carefully arranging her beautiful hair, which she always dressed herself, and said carelessly, without looking up at him:

"Eleanor has a foolish notion of returning home in March. I wish you would speak to her about it. Her family expect her to stay until June, and her going now would be commented upon."

"I scarcely see how I can interfere," he replied coolly. "She doubtless has her reasons."

"Her reasons are not far to seek, I should say," remarked Virginia, carefully slipping the pins into the yellow coils of her hair. "She is pathetically ingenuous about it. I should think you might improve upon the present state of affairs if you were to treat it—well, say a trifle more lightly. That would put her more at ease, at least."

"What nonsense, Virginia," he exclaimed, laughing unnaturally and closing the door behind him with guarded gentleness.

That evening Dunlap joined his wife in her dressing room, his coat on his arm and his hat in his hand. The maid had gone upstairs to hunt for Virginia's last year's fur shoes, as the pair warming before the grate would not fit over her new dancing slippers. Virginia was standing before the mirror, carefully surveying the effect of a new gown, which struck her husband as more than usually conspicuous and defiant. He watched her arranging a pink-and-gold butterfly in her hair and held his peace, but when she put on a pink chiffon collar, with a flaring bow which came directly under her left cheek, in spite of himself he shuddered.

"For heaven's sake, Virginia, take that thing off," he cried. "You ought really to be more careful about such extremes. They only emphasize the scar." He was frightened at the brittleness of his own voice; it seemed to whistle dryly in the air like his grandfather's thong.

She caught her breath and wheeled suddenly about, her face crimson and then gray. She opened her lips twice, but no sound escaped them. He saw the muscles of her throat stiffen, and she began to shudder convulsively, like one who has been plunged into icy water. He started toward her, sick with pity; at last, perhaps—but she pointed him steadily to the door, her eyes as hard as shell, and bright and small, like the sleepless eyes of reptiles.

He went to bed with the sick feeling of a man who has tortured an animal, yet with a certain sense of relief and finality which he had not known in years.

When he came down to breakfast in the morning, the butler told him that Madame and her maid had left for Nice by the early train. Mademoiselle Vane had gone out to her lectures. Madame requested that Monsieur take Mademoiselle to the opera in the evening, where the widowed sister of Madame de Montebello would join them; she would come home with them to remain until Madame's return. Dunlap accepted these instructions as a matter of course, and announced that he would not dine at home.

When he entered the hall upon his return that evening, he heard little Eleanor sobbing, and she flew to meet him, with her dress burned, and her hands black. Dunlap smelled the sickening odor of ointments. The nurse followed with explanations. The doctor was upstairs. Mademoiselle Vane always used a little alcohol lamp in making her toilet; tonight, when she touched a match to it, it exploded. Little Eleanor was leaning against her dressing table at the time, and her dress caught fire; Mademoiselle Vane had wrapped the rug about her and extinguished it. When the nurse arrived, Mademoiselle Vane was standing in the middle of the floor, plucking at her scorched hair, her face and arms badly burned. She had bent over the lamp in lighting it, and had received the full force of the explosion in her face. The doctor was unable to discover what the explosive had been, as it was entirely consumed. Mademoiselle always filled the little lamp herself; all the servants knew about it, for Madame had sent the nurse to borrow it on several occasions, when little Eleanor had the earache.

The next morning Dunlap received a telegram from his wife, stating that she would go to St. Petersburg for the remainder of the winter. In May he heard that she had sailed for America, and a year later her attorneys wrote that she had begun action for divorce. Immediately after the decree was granted, Dunlap married Eleanor Vane. He never met or directly heard from Virginia again, though when she returned to Russia and took up her residence in St. Petersburg, the fame of her toilets spread even to Paris.

Society, always prone to crude antitheses, knew of Dunlap only that he had painted many of the most beautiful women of his time, that he had been twice married, and that each of his wives had been disfigured by a scar on the face.

First published in *McClure's*, XXIX (June, 1907), 135–140.

The Namesake

❋ ❋ ❋

Seven of us, students, sat one evening in Hartwell's studio on the Boulevard St. Michel. We were all fellow-countrymen, one from New
Hampshire, one from Colorado, another from Nevada, several from the
farmlands of the Middle West, and I myself from California. Lyon
Hartwell, though born abroad, was simply, as every one knew, "from
America." He seemed, almost more than any other one living man, to
mean all of it—from ocean to ocean. When he was in Paris, his studio
was always open to the seven of us who were there that evening, and we
intruded upon his leisure as often as we thought permissible.

Although we were within the terms of the easiest of all intimacies,
and although the great sculptor, even when he was more than usually
silent, was at all times the most gravely cordial of hosts, yet, on that long
remembered evening, as the sunlight died on the burnished brown of the
horse chestnuts below the windows, a perceptible dullness yawned through
our conversation.

We were, indeed, somewhat low in spirit, for one of our number,
Charley Bentley, was leaving us indefinitely, in response to an imperative
summons from home. Tomorrow his studio, just across the hall from
Hartwell's, was to pass into other hands, and Bentley's luggage was even
now piled in discouraged resignation before his door. The various bales
and boxes seemed literally to weigh upon us as we sat in his neighbor's
hospitable rooms, drearily putting in the time until he should leave us to
catch the ten o'clock express for Dieppe.

The day we had got through very comfortably, for Bentley made it
the occasion of a somewhat pretentious luncheon at Maxim's. There had
been twelve of us at table, and the two young Poles were so thirsty, the
Gascon so fabulously entertaining, that it was near upon five o'clock when
we put down our liqueur glasses for the last time, and the red, perspiring
waiter, having pocketed the reward of his arduous and protracted services,
bowed us affably to the door, flourishing his napkin and brushing back
the streaks of wet, black hair from his rosy forehead. Our guests having

betaken themselves belated to their respective engagements, the rest of us returned with Bentley—only to be confronted by the depressing array before his door. A glance about his denuded rooms had sufficed to chill the glow of the afternoon, and we fled across the hall in a body and begged Lyon Hartwell to take us in.

Bentley had said very little about it, but we all knew what it meant to him to be called home. Each of us knew what it would mean to himself, and each had felt something of that quickened sense of opportunity which comes at seeing another man in any way counted out of the race. Never had the game seemed so enchanting, the chance to play it such a piece of unmerited, unbelievable good fortune.

It must have been, I think, about the middle of October, for I remember that the sycamores were almost bare in the Luxembourg Gardens that morning, and the terraces about the queens of France were strewn with crackling brown leaves. The fat red roses, out the summer long on the stand of the old flower woman at the corner, had given place to dahlias and purple asters. First glimpses of autumn toilettes flashed from the carriages; wonderful little bonnes nodded at one along the Champs Élysées; and in the Quarter an occasional feather boa, red or black or white, brushed one's coat sleeve in the gay twilight of the early evening. The crisp, sunny autumn air was all day full of the stir of people and carriages and of the cheer of salutations; greetings of the students, returned brown and bearded from their holiday, gossip of people come back from Trouville, from St. Valery, from Dieppe, from all over Brittany and the Norman coast. Everywhere was the joyousness of return, the taking up again of life and work and play.

I had felt ever since early morning that this was the saddest of all possible seasons for saying goodbye to that old, old city of youth, and to that little corner of it on the south shore which since the Dark Ages themselves—yes, and before—has been so peculiarly the land of the young.

I can recall our very postures as we lounged about Hartwell's rooms that evening, with Bentley making occasional hurried trips to his desolated workrooms across the hall—as if haunted by a feeling of having forgotten something—or stopping to poke nervously at his *perroquets*, which he had bequeathed to Hartwell, gilt cage and all. Our host himself sat on the couch, his big, bronze-like shoulders backed up against the window, his shaggy head, beaked nose, and long chin cut clean against the gray light.

Our drowsing interest, in so far as it could be said to be fixed upon anything, was centered upon Hartwell's new figure, which stood on the block ready to be cast in bronze, intended as a monument for some American battlefield. He called it *The Color Sergeant*. It was the figure of a young soldier running, clutching the folds of a flag, the staff of which had been shot away. We had known it in all the stages of its growth, and the splendid action and feeling of the thing had come to have a kind of special significance for the half dozen of us who often gathered at Hartwell's rooms—though, in truth, there was as much to dishearten one as to inflame, in the case of a man who had done so much in a field so amazingly difficult; who had thrown up in bronze all the restless, teeming force of that adventurous wave still climbing westward in our own land across the waters. We recalled his *Scout*, his *Pioneer*, his *Gold Seekers*, and those monuments in which he had invested one and another of the heroes of the Civil War with such convincing dignity and power.

"Where in the world does he get the heat to make an idea like that carry?" Bentley remarked morosely, scowling at the clay figure. "Hang me, Hartwell, if I don't think it's just because you're not really an American at all, that you can look at it like that."

The big man shifted uneasily against the window. "Yes," he replied smiling, "perhaps there is something in that. My citizenship was somewhat belated and emotional in its flowering. I've half a mind to tell you about it, Bentley," He rose uncertainly, and, after hesitating a moment, went back into his workroom, where he began fumbling among the litter in the corners.

At the prospect of any sort of personal expression from Hartwell, we glanced questioningly at one another; for although he made us feel that he liked to have us about, we were always held at a distance by a certain diffidence of his. There were rare occasions—when he was in the heat of work or of ideas—when he forgot to be shy, but they were so exceptional that no flattery was quite so seductive as being taken for a moment into Hartwell's confidence. Even in the matter of opinions— the commonest of currency in our circle—he was niggardly and prone to qualify. No man ever guarded his mystery more effectually. There was a singular, intense spell, therefore, about those few evenings when he had broken through this excessive modesty, or shyness, or melancholy, and had, as it were, committed himself.

When Hartwell returned from the back room, he brought with him an unframed canvas which he put on an easel near his clay figure. We drew close about it, for the darkness was rapidly coming on. Despite the dullness of the light, we instantly recognized the boy of Hartwell's *Color Sergeant*. It was the portrait of a very handsome lad in uniform, standing beside a charger impossibly rearing. Not only in his radiant countenance and flashing eyes, but in every line of his young body there was an energy, a gallantry, a joy of life, that arrested and challenged one.

"Yes, that's where I got the notion," Hartwell remarked, wandering back to his seat in the window. "I've wanted to do it for years, but I've never felt quite sure of myself. I was afraid of missing it. He was an uncle of mine, my father's half brother, and I was named for him. He was killed in one of the big battles of Sixty-four, when I was a child. I never saw him—never knew him until he had been dead for twenty years. And then, one night, I came to know him as we sometimes do living persons intimately, in a single moment."

He paused to knock the ashes out of his short pipe, refilled it, and puffed at it thoughtfully for a few moments with his hands on his knees. Then, settling back heavily among the cushions and looking absently out of the window, he began his story. As he proceeded further and further into the experience which he was trying to convey to us, his voice sank so low and was sometimes so charged with feeling, that I almost thought he had forgotten our presence and was remembering aloud. Even Bentley forgot his nervousness in astonishment and sat breathless under the spell of the man's thus breathing his memories out into the dusk.

"It was just fifteen years ago this last spring that I first went home, and Bentley's having to cut away like this brings it all back to me.

"I was born, you know, in Italy. My father was a sculptor, though I dare say you've not heard of him. He was one of those first fellows who went over after Story and Powers—went to Italy for 'Art,' quite simply; to lift from its native bough the willing, iridescent bird. Their story is told, informingly enough, by some of those ingenuous marble things at the Metropolitan. My father came over some time before the outbreak of the Civil War, and was regarded as a renegade by his family because he did not go home to enter the army. His half brother, the only child of my grandfather's second marriage, enlisted at fifteen and was killed the next year. I was ten years old when the news of his death reached us. My mother died the following winter, and I was sent away to a Jesuit school, while my father, already ill himself, stayed on at Rome, chipping away at his Indian maidens and marble goddesses, still gloomily seeking the thing for which he had made himself the most unhappy of exiles.

"He died when I was fourteen, but even before that I had been put to work under an Italian sculptor. He had an almost morbid desire that I should carry on his work, under, as he often pointed out to me, conditions so much more auspicious. He left me in the charge of his one intimate friend, an American gentleman in the consulate at Rome, and his instructions were that I was to be educated there and to live there until I was twenty-one. After I was of age, I came to Paris and studied under one master after another until I was nearly thirty. Then, almost for the first time, I was confronted by a duty which was not my pleasure.

"My grandfather's death, at an advanced age, left an invalid maiden sister of my father's quite alone in the world. She had suffered for years from a cerebral disease, a slow decay of the faculties which rendered her almost helpless. I decided to go to America and, if possible, bring her back to Paris, where I seemed on my way toward what my poor father had wished for me.

"On my arrival at my father's birthplace, however, I found that this was not to be thought of. To tear this timid, feeble, shrinking creature, doubly aged by years and illness, from the spot where she had been rooted for a lifetime, would have been little short of brutality. To leave her to the care of strangers seemed equally heartless. There was clearly nothing for me to do but to remain and wait for that slow and painless malady to run its course. I was there something over two years.

"My grandfather's home, his father's homestead before him, lay on the high banks of a river in western Pennsylvania. The little town twelve miles down the stream, whither my great-grandfather used to drive his ox-wagon on market days, had become, in two generations, one of the largest manufacturing cities in the world. For hundreds of miles about us the gentle hill slopes were honeycombed with gas wells and coal shafts; oil derricks creaked in every valley and meadow; the brooks were sluggish and discolored with crude petroleum, and the air was impregnated by its searching odor. The great glass and iron manufactories had come up and up the river almost to our very door; their smoky exhalations brooded over us, and their crashing was always in our ears. I was plunged into the very incandescence of human energy. But, though my nerves tingled with the feverish, passionate endeavor which snapped in the very air about me, none of these great arteries seemed to feed me; this tumultuous life did not warm me. On every side were the great muddy rivers, the ragged mountains from which the timber was being ruthlessly torn away, the vast tracts of wild country, and the gulches that were like wounds in the earth; everywhere the glare of that relentless energy which followed me like a searchlight and seemed to scorch and consume me. I could only hide my self in the tangled garden, where the dropping of a leaf or the whistle of a bird was the only incident.

"The Hartwell homestead had been sold away little by little, until all that remained of it was garden and orchard. The house, a square brick structure, stood in the midst of a great garden which sloped toward the river, ending in a grassy bank which fell some forty feet to the water's edge. The garden was now little more than a tangle of neglected shrubbery; damp, rank, and of that intense blue-green peculiar to vegetation in smoky places where the sun shines but rarely, and the mists form early in the evening and hang late in the morning.

"I shall never forget it as I saw it first, when I arrived there in the chill of a backward June. The long, rank grass, thick and soft and falling in billows, was always wet until midday. The gravel walks were bordered with great lilac bushes, mock orange, and bridal wreath. Back of the house was a neglected rose garden, surrounded by a low stone wall over which the long suckers trailed and matted. They had wound their pink, thorny tentacles, layer upon layer, about the lock and the hinges of the rusty iron gate. Even the porches of the house, and the very windows, were damp and heavy with growth: wistaria, clematis, honeysuckle, and trumpet vine. The garden was grown up with trees, especially that part of it which lay above the river. The bark of the old locusts was blackened by the smoke that crept continually up the valley, and their feathery foliage, so merry in its color, seemed peculiarly precious under that somber sky. There were sycamores and copper beeches; gnarled apple trees, too old to bear; and fall pear trees, hung with a sharp, hard fruit in October; all with a leafage singularly rich and luxuriant, and peculiarly vivid in color. The oaks about the house had been old trees when my great-grandfather built his cabin there, more than a century before, and this garden was almost the only spot for miles along the river where any of the original forest growth still survived. The smoke from the mills was fatal to trees of the larger sort, and even these had the look of doomed things—bent a little toward the town and seemed to wait with head inclined before that oncoming, shrieking force.

"About the river, too, there was a strange hush, a tragic submission —it was so leaden and sullen in its color, and it flowed so soundlessly forever past our door.

"I sat there every evening, on the high veranda overlooking it, watching the dim outlines of the steep hills on the other shore, the flicker of the lights on the island, where there was a boathouse, and listening to the call of the boatmen through the mist. The mist came as certainly as night, whitened by moonshine or starshine. The tin water pipes went splash,

splash, with it all evening, and the wind, when it rose at all, was little more than a sighing in the heavy grasses.

"At first it was to think of my distant friends and my old life that I used to sit there; but after awhile it was simply to watch the days and weeks go by, like the river which seemed to carry them away.

"Within the house I was never at home. Month followed month, and yet I could feel no sense of kinship with anything there. Under the roof where my father and grandfather were born, I remained utterly detached. The somber rooms never spoke to me, the old furniture never seemed tinctured with race. This portrait of my boy uncle was the only thing to which I could draw near, the only link with anything I had ever known before.

"There is a good deal of my father in the face, but it is my father transformed and glorified; his hesitating discontent drowned in a kind of triumph. From my first day in that house, I continually turned to this handsome kinsman of mine, wondering in what terms he had lived and had his hope; what he had found there to look like that, to bound at one, after all those years, so joyously out of the canvas.

"From the timid, clouded old woman over whose life I had come to watch, I learned that in the back yard, near the old rose garden, there was a locust tree which my uncle had planted. After his death, while it was still a slender sapling, his mother had a seat built round it, and she used to sit there on summer evenings. His grave was under the apple trees in the old orchard.

"My aunt could tell me little more than this. There were days when she seemed not to remember him at all.

"It was from an old soldier in the village that I learned the boy's story. Lyon was, the old man told me, but fourteen when the first enlistment occurred, but was even then eager to go. He was in the court-house square every evening to watch the recruits at their drill, and when the home company was ordered off he rode into the city on his pony to see the men board the train and to wave them goodbye. The next year he spent at home with a tutor, but when he was fifteen he held his parents to their promise and went into the army. He was color sergeant of his regiment and fell in a charge upon the breastworks of a fort about a year after his enlistment.

"The veteran showed me an account of this charge which had been written for the village paper by one of my uncle's comrades who had seen his part in the engagement. It seems that as his company were running at full speed across the bottom lands toward the fortified hill, a shell burst over them. This comrade, running beside my uncle, saw the colors waver and sink as if falling, and looked to see that the boy's hand and forearm had been torn away by the exploding shrapnel. The boy, he thought, did not realize the extent of his injury, for he laughed, shouted something which his comrade did not catch, caught the flag in his left hand, and ran on up the hill. They went splendidly up over the breastworks, but just as my uncle, his colors flying, reached the top of the embankment, a second shell carried away his left arm at the armpit, and he fell over the wall with the flag settling about him.

"It was because this story was ever present with me, because I was unable to shake it off, that I began to read such books as my grandfather had collected upon the Civil War. I found that this war was fought largely by boys, that more men enlisted at eighteen than at any other age. When I thought of those battlefields—and I thought of them much in those days—there was always that glory of youth above them, that impetuous, generous passion stirring the long lines on the march, the blue battalions in the plain. The bugle, whenever I have heard it since, has always seemed to me the very golden throat of that boyhood which spent itself so gaily, so incredibly.

"I used often to wonder how it was that this uncle of mine, who seemed to have possessed all the charm and brilliancy allotted to his family and to have lived up its vitality in one splendid hour, had left so little trace in the house where he was born and where he had awaited his destiny. Look as I would, I could find no letters from him, no clothing or books that might have been his. He had been dead but twenty years, and yet nothing seemed to have survived except the tree he had planted. It seemed incredible and cruel that no physical memory of him should linger to be cherished among his kindred—nothing but the dull image in the brain of that aged sister. I used to pace the garden walks in the evening, wondering that no breath of his, no echo of his laugh, of his call to his pony or his whistle to his dogs, should linger about those shaded paths where the pale roses exhaled their dewy, country smell. Sometimes, in the dim starlight, I have thought that I heard on the grasses beside me the stir of a footfall lighter than my own, and under the black arch of the lilacs I have fancied that he bore me company.

"There was, I found, one day in the year for which my old aunt waited, and which stood out from the months that were all of a sameness to her. On the thirtieth of May she insisted that I should bring down the big flag from the attic and run it up upon the tall flagstaff beside Lyon's tree in the garden. Later in the morning she went with me to carry some of the garden flowers to the grave in the orchard—a grave scarcely larger than a child's.

"I had noticed, when I was hunting for the flag in the attic, a leather trunk with my own name stamped upon it, but was unable to find the key. My aunt was all day less apathetic than usual; she seemed to realize more clearly who I was, and to wish me to be with her. I did not have an opportunity to return to the attic until after dinner that evening, when I carried a lamp upstairs and easily forced the lock of the trunk. I found all the things that I had looked for; put away, doubtless, by his mother, and still smelling faintly of lavender and rose leaves; his clothes, his exercise books, his letters from the army, his first boots, his riding whip, some of his toys, even. I took them out and replaced them gently. As I was about to shut the lid, I picked up a copy of the Æneid, on the flyleaf of which was written in a slanting, boyish hand,

Lyon Hartwell, January, 1862.

He had gone to the wars in Sixty-three, I remembered.

"My uncle, I gathered, was none too apt at his Latin, for the pages were dog-eared and rubbed and interlined, the margins mottled with pencil sketches—bugles, stacked bayonets, and artillery carriages. In the act of putting the book down, I happened to run over the pages to the end, and on the flyleaf at the back I saw his name again, and a drawing—with his initials and a date—of the Federal flag; above it, written in a kind of arch and in the same unformed hand:

> Oh, say, can you see by the dawn's early light
> What so proudly we hailed at the twilight's last gleaming?

It was a stiff, wooden sketch, not unlike a detail from some Egyptian inscription, but, the moment I saw it, wind and color seemed to touch it. I caught up the book, blew out the lamp, and rushed down into the garden.

"I seemed, somehow, at last to have known him; to have been with him in that careless, unconscious moment and to have known him as he was then.

"As I sat there in the rush of this realization, the wind began to rise, stirring the light foliage of the locust over my head and bringing, fresher than before, the woody odor of the pale roses that overran the little neglected garden. Then, as it grew stronger, it brought the sound of something sighing and stirring over my head in the perfumed darkness.

"I thought of that sad one of the Destinies who, as the Greeks believed, watched from birth over those marked for a violent or untimely death. Oh, I could see him, there in the shine of the morning, his book idly on his knee, his flashing eyes looking straight before him, and at his side that grave figure, hidden in her draperies, her eyes following his, but seeing so much farther—seeing what he never saw, that great moment at the end, when he swayed above his comrades on the earthen wall.

"All the while, the bunting I had run up in the morning flapped fold against fold, heaving and tossing softly in the dark—against a sky so black with rain clouds that I could see above me only the blur of something in soft, troubled motion.

"The experience of that night, coming so overwhelmingly to a man so dead, almost rent me in pieces. It was the same feeling that artists know when we, rarely, achieve truth in our work; the feeling of union with some great force, of purpose and security, of being glad that we have lived. For the first time I felt the pull of race and blood and kindred, and felt beating within me things that had not begun with me. It was as if the earth under my feet had grasped and rooted me, and were pouring its essence into me. I sat there until the dawn of morning, and all night long my life seemed to be pouring out of me and running into the ground."

Hartwell drew a long breath that lifted his heavy shoulders, and then let them fall again. He shifted a little and faced more squarely the scattered, silent company before him. The darkness had made us almost invisible to each other, and, except for the occasional red circuit of a cigarette end traveling upward from the arm of a chair, he might have supposed us all asleep.

"And so," Hartwell added thoughtfully, "I naturally feel an interest in fellows who are going home. It's always an experience."

No one said anything, and in a moment there was a loud rap at the door—the concierge, come to take down Bentley's luggage and to announce that the cab was below. Bentley got his hat and coat, enjoined Hartwell to take good care of his *perroquets*, gave each of us a grip of the hand, and went briskly down the long flights of stairs. We followed him into the street, calling our good wishes, and saw him start on his drive across the lighted city to the Gare St. Lazare.

First published in *McClure's*, XXVIII (March, 1907), 492–497.

Volume II

THE
TROLL
GARDEN

✳ ✳ ✳

The Troll Garden, *Willa Cather's first published volume of prose, came out in March, 1905. The seven stories comprising it were probably written between October, 1902, and the fall of 1904, when Willa Cather was a teacher of English in Pittsburgh high schools and lived at the home of Judge and Mrs. Samuel A. McClung as the guest of their daughter Isabelle. Three of the stories— "Flavia and Her Artists," "The Garden Lodge," and "The Marriage of Phaedra"—were first published in* The Troll Garden; *they were never reprinted during Willa Cather's lifetime. "'A Death in the Desert'" (1903) and "A Wagner Matinee" (1904) first appeared in* Scribner's *and* Everybody's Magazine, *respectively, and were extensively reworked before being collected. "The Sculptor's Funeral" and "Paul's Case" both ran in* McClure's, *one in January, 1905, the other in April. Subsequently these four stories were revised by the author and included in her 1920 collection,* Youth and the Bright Medusa. *With the exception of "'A Death in the Desert'" they also were included in* The Novels and Stories of Willa Cather (1937–1941).

The volume was dedicated to Isabelle McClung, and carried two epigraphs. The first, a stanza from The Goblin Market *by Christina Rossetti, was placed opposite the title page:*

> We must not look at Goblin men,
> We must not buy their fruits;
> Who knows upon what soil they fed
> Their hungry thirsty roots?

The second, on the title page itself, is a quotation from Charles Kingsley's The Roman and the Teuton: *"A fairy palace, with a fairy garden; ... inside the trolls dwell, ... working at their magic forges, making and making always things rare and strange."*

The stories are presented here in the order in which they appeared in The Troll Garden, *without regard to date of first publication. Except for the emendations listed on pages 580–581, the text follows exactly that of the 1905 edition.*

Flavia and Her Artists

❖ ❖ ❖

As the train neared Tarrytown, Imogen Willard began to wonder why she had consented to be one of Flavia's house party at all. She had not felt enthusiastic about it since leaving the city, and was experiencing a prolonged ebb of purpose, a current of chilling indecision, under which she vainly sought for the motive which had induced her to accept Flavia's invitation.

Perhaps it was a vague curiosity to see Flavia's husband, who had been the magician of her childhood and the hero of innumerable Arabian fairy tales. Perhaps it was a desire to see M. Roux, whom Flavia had announced as the especial attraction of the occasion. Perhaps it was a wish to study that remarkable woman in her own setting.

Imogen admitted a mild curiosity concerning Flavia. She was in the habit of taking people rather seriously, but somehow found it impossible to take Flavia so, because of the very vehemence and insistence with which Flavia demanded it. Submerged in her studies, Imogen had, of late years, seen very little of Flavia; but Flavia, in her hurried visits to New York, between her excursions from studio to studio—her luncheons with this lady who had to play at a matinée, and her dinners with that singer who had an evening concert—had seen enough of her friend's handsome daughter to conceive for her an inclination of such violence and assurance as only Flavia could afford. The fact that Imogen had shown rather marked capacity in certain esoteric lines of scholarship, and had decided to specialize in a well-sounding branch of philology at the Ecole des Chartes, had fairly placed her in that category of "interesting people" whom Flavia considered her natural affinities, and lawful prey.

When Imogen stepped upon the station platform she was immediately appropriated by her hostess, whose commanding figure and assurance of attire she had recognized from a distance. She was hurried into a high tilbury and Flavia, taking the driver's cushion beside her, gathered up the reins with an experienced hand.

"My dear girl," she remarked, as she turned the horses up the street, "I was afraid the train might be late. M. Roux insisted upon coming up by boat and did not arrive until after seven."

"To think of M. Roux's being in this part of the world at all, and subject to the vicissitudes of river boats! Why in the world did he come over?" queried Imogen with lively interest. "He is the sort of man who must dissolve and become a shadow outside of Paris."

"Oh, we have a houseful of the most interesting people," said Flavia, professionally. "We have actually managed to get Ivan Schemetzkin. He was ill in California at the close of his concert tour, you know, and he is recuperating with us, after his wearing journey from the coast. Then there is Jules Martel, the painter; Signor Donati, the tenor; Professor Schotte, who has dug up Assyria, you know; Restzhoff, the Russian chemist; Alcée Buisson, the philologist; Frank Wellington, the novelist; and Will Maidenwood, the editor of *Woman*. Then there is my second cousin, Jemima Broadwood, who made such a hit in Pinero's comedy last winter, and Frau Lichtenfeld. *Have* you read her?"

Imogen confessed her utter ignorance of Frau Lichtenfeld, and Flavia went on.

"Well, she is a most remarkable person; one of those advanced German women, a militant iconoclast, and this drive will not be long enough to permit of my telling you her history. Such a story! Her novels were the talk of all Germany when I was there last, and several of them have been suppressed—an honour in Germany, I understand. 'At Whose Door' has been translated. I am so unfortunate as not to read German."

"I'm all excitement at the prospect of meeting Miss Broadwood," said Imogen. "I've seen her in nearly everything she does. Her stage personality is delightful. She always reminds me of a nice, clean, pink-and-white boy who has just had his cold bath, and come down all aglow for a run before breakfast."

"Yes, but isn't it unfortunate that she will limit herself to those minor comedy parts that are so little appreciated in this country? One ought to be satisfied with nothing less than the best, ought one?" The peculiar, breathy tone in which Flavia always uttered that word "best," the most worn in her vocabulary, always jarred on Imogen and always made her obdurate.

"I don't at all agree with you," she said reservedly. "I thought everyone admitted that the most remarkable thing about Miss Broadwood is her admirable sense of fitness, which is rare enough in her profession."

Flavia could not endure being contradicted; she always seemed to regard it in the light of a defeat, and usually coloured unbecomingly. Now she changed the subject.

"Look, my dear," she cried, "there is Frau Lichtenfeld now, coming to meet us. Doesn't she look as if she had just escaped out of Walhalla? She is actually over six feet."

Imogen saw a woman of immense stature, in a very short skirt and a broad, flapping sun hat, striding down the hillside at a long, swinging gait. The refugee from Walhalla approached, panting. Her heavy, Teutonic features were scarlet from the rigour of her exercise, and her hair, under her flapping sun hat, was tightly befrizzled about her brow. She fixed her sharp little eyes upon Imogen and extended both her hands.

"So this is the little friend?" she cried, in a rolling baritone.

Imogen was quite as tall as her hostess; but everything, she reflected, is comparative. After the introduction Flavia apologized.

"I wish I could ask you to drive up with us, Frau Lichtenfeld."

"Ah, no!" cried the giantess, drooping her head in humorous caricature of a time-honoured pose of the heroines of sentimental romances. "It has never been my fate to be fitted into corners. I have never known the sweet privileges of the tiny."

Laughing, Flavia started the ponies, and the colossal woman, standing in the middle of the dusty road, took off her wide hat and waved them a farewell which, in scope of gesture, recalled the salute of a plumed cavalier.

When they arrived at the house, Imogen looked about her with keen curiosity, for this was veritably the work of Flavia's hands, the materialization of hopes long deferred. They passed directly into a large, square hall with a gallery on three sides, studio fashion. This opened at one end into a Dutch breakfast-room, beyond which was the large dining-room. At the other end of the hall was the music-room. There was a smoking-room, which one entered through the library behind the staircase. On the second floor there was the same general arrangement; a square hall, and, opening from it, the guest chambers, or, as Miss Broadwood termed them, the "cages."

When Imogen went to her room, the guests had begun to return from their various afternoon excursions. Boys were gliding through the halls with ice-water, covered trays, and flowers, colliding with maids and valets who carried shoes and other articles of wearing apparel. Yet, all this was done in response to inaudible bells, on felt soles, and in hushed voices, so that there was very little confusion about it.

Flavia had at last builded her house and hewn out her seven pillars; there could be no doubt, now, that the asylum for talent, the sanatorium of the arts, so long projected, was an accomplished fact. Her ambition had long ago outgrown the dimensions of her house on Prairie Avenue; besides, she had bitterly complained that in Chicago traditions were against her. Her project had been delayed by Arthur's doggedly standing out for the Michigan woods, but Flavia knew well enough that certain of the *aves rares*—"the best"—could not be lured so far away from the seaport, so she declared herself for the historic Hudson and knew no retreat. The establishing of a New York office had at length overthrown Arthur's last valid objection to quitting the lake country for three months of the year; and Arthur could be wearied into anything, as those who knew him knew.

Flavia's house was the mirror of her exultation; it was a temple to the gods of Victory, a sort of triumphal arch. In her earlier days she had swallowed experiences that would have unmanned one of less torrential enthusiasm or blind pertinacity. But, of late years, her determination had told; she saw less and less of those mysterious persons with mysterious obstacles in their path and mysterious grievances against the world, who had once frequented her house on Prairie Avenue. In the stead of this multitude of the unarrived, she had now the few, the select, "the best." Of all that band of indigent retainers who had once fed at her board like the suitors in the halls of Penelope, only Alcée Buisson still retained his right of entrée. He alone had remembered that ambition hath a knapsack at his back, wherein he puts alms to oblivion, and he alone had been considerate enough to do what Flavia had expected of him, and give his name a current value in the world. Then, as Miss Broadwood put it, "he was her first real one,"—and Flavia, like Mahomet, could remember her first believer.

The "House of Song," as Miss Broadwood had called it, was the outcome of Flavia's more exalted strategies. A woman who made less a point of sympathizing with their delicate organisms, might have sought to plunge these phosphorescent pieces into the tepid bath of domestic life; but Flavia's discernment was deeper. This must be a refuge where the shrinking soul, the sensitive brain, should be unconstrained; where the caprice of fancy should outweigh the civil code, if necessary. She considered that this much Arthur owed her; for she, in her turn, had made concessions. Flavia, had, indeed, quite an equipment of epigrams to the effect that our century creates the iron genii which evolve its fairy tales:

but the fact that her husband's name was annually painted upon some ten thousand threshing machines, in reality contributed very little to her happiness.

Arthur Hamilton was born, and had spent his boyhood in the West Indies, and physically he had never lost the brand of the tropics. His father, after inventing the machine which bore his name, had returned to the States to patent and manufacture it. After leaving college, Arthur had spent five years ranching in the West and travelling abroad. Upon his father's death he had returned to Chicago and, to the astonishment of all his friends, had taken up the business,—without any demonstration of enthusiasm, but with quiet perseverance, marked ability, and amazing industry. Why or how a self-sufficient, rather ascetic man of thirty, indifferent in manner, wholly negative in all other personal relations, should have doggedly wooed and finally married Flavia Malcolm, was a problem that had vexed older heads than Imogen's.

While Imogen was dressing she heard a knock at her door, and a young woman entered whom she at once recognized as Jemima Broadwood—"Jimmy" Broadwood, she was called by people in her own profession. While there was something unmistakably professional in her frank *savoir-faire*, "Jimmy's" was one of those faces to which the rouge never seems to stick. Her eyes were keen and grey as a windy April sky, and so far from having been seared by calcium lights, you might have fancied they had never looked on anything less bucolic than growing fields and country fairs. She wore her thick, brown hair short and parted at the side; and, rather than hinting at freakishness, this seemed admirably in keeping with her fresh, boyish countenance. She extended to Imogen a large, well-shaped hand which it was a pleasure to clasp.

"Ah! you are Miss Willard, and I see I need not introduce myself. Flavia said you were kind enough to express a wish to meet me, and I preferred to meet you alone. Do you mind if I smoke?"

"Why, certainly not," said Imogen, somewhat disconcerted and looking hurriedly about for matches.

"There, be calm, I'm always prepared," said Miss Broadwood, checking Imogen's flurry with a soothing gesture, and producing an oddly-fashioned silver match-case from some mysterious recess in her dinner-gown. She sat down in a deep chair, crossed her patent-leather Oxfords, and lit her cigarette. "This match-box," she went on meditatively, "once belonged to a Prussian officer. He shot himself in his bath-tub, and I bought it at the sale of his effects."

Imogen had not yet found any suitable reply to make to this rather irrelevant confidence, when Miss Broadwood turned to her cordially: "I'm awfully glad you've come, Miss Willard, though I've not quite decided why you did it. I wanted very much to meet you. Flavia gave me your thesis to read."

"Why, how funny!" ejaculated Imogen.

"On the contrary," remarked Miss Broadwood. "I thought it decidedly lacked humour."

"I meant," stammered Imogen, beginning to feel very much like Alice in Wonderland, "I meant that I thought it rather strange Mrs. Hamilton should fancy you would be interested."

Miss Broadwood laughed heartily. "Now, don't let my rudeness frighten you. Really, I found it very interesting, and no end impressive. You see, most people in my profession are good for absolutely nothing else, and, therefore, they have a deep and abiding conviction that in some other line they might have shone. Strange to say, scholarship is the object of our envious and particular admiration. Anything in type impresses us greatly; that's why so many of us marry authors or newspapermen and lead miserable lives." Miss Broadwood saw that she had rather disconcerted Imogen, and blithely tacked in another direction. "You see," she went on, tossing aside her half-consumed cigarette, "some years ago Flavia would not have deemed me worthy to open the pages of your thesis—nor to be one of her house party of the chosen, for that matter. I've Pinero to thank for both pleasures. It all depends on the class of business I'm playing whether I'm in favour or not. Flavia is my second cousin, you know, so I can say whatever disagreeable things I choose with perfect good grace. I'm quite desperate for someone to laugh with, so I'm going to fasten myself upon you—for, of course, one can't expect any of these gypsy-dago people to see anything funny. I don't intend you shall lose the humour of the situation. What do you think of Flavia's infirmary for the arts, anyway?"

"Well, it's rather too soon for me to have any opinion at all," said Imogen, as she again turned to her dressing. "So far, you are the only one of the artists I've met."

"One of them?" echoed Miss Broadwood. "One of the *artists*? My offence may be rank, my dear, but I really don't deserve that. Come, now, whatever badges of my tribe I may bear upon me, just let me divest you of any notion that I take myself seriously."

Imogen turned from the mirror in blank astonishment, and sat down on the arm of a chair, facing her visitor. "I can't fathom you at all, Miss Broadwood," she said frankly. "Why shouldn't you take yourself seriously? What's the use of beating about the bush? Surely you know that you are one of the few players on this side of the water who have at all the spirit of natural or ingenuous comedy?"

"Thank you, my dear. Now we are quite even about the thesis, aren't we? Oh! did you mean it? Well, you *are* a clever girl. But you see it doesn't do to permit oneself to look at it in that light. If we do, we always go to pieces, and waste our substance a-starring as the unhappy daughter of the Capulets. But there, I hear Flavia coming to take you down; and just remember I'm not one of them; the artists, I mean."

Flavia conducted Imogen and Miss Broadwood downstairs. As they reached the lower hall they heard voices from the music-room, and dim figures were lurking in the shadows under the gallery, but their hostess led straight to the smoking-room. The June evening was chilly, and a fire had been lighted in the fireplace. Through the deepening dusk the firelight flickered upon the pipes and curious weapons on the wall, and threw an orange glow over the Turkish hangings. One side of the smoking-room was entirely of glass, separating it from the conservatory, which was flooded with white light from the electric bulbs. There was about the darkened room some suggestion of certain chambers in the Arabian Nights, opening on a court of palms. Perhaps it was partially this memory-evoking suggestion that caused Imogen to start so violently when she saw dimly, in a blur of shadow, the figure of a man, who sat smoking in a low, deep chair before the fire. He was long, and thin, and brown. His long, nerveless hands drooped from the arms of his chair. A brown mustache shaded his mouth, and his eyes were sleepy and apathetic. When Imogen entered, he rose indolently and gave her his hand, his manner barely courteous.

"I am glad you arrived promptly, Miss Willard," he said with an indifferent drawl. "Flavia was afraid you might be late. You had a pleasant ride up, I hope?"

"O, very, thank you, Mr. Hamilton," she replied, feeling that he did not particularly care whether she replied at all.

Flavia explained that she had not yet had time to dress for dinner, as she had been attending to Mr. Will Maidenwood, who had become faint after hurting his finger in an obdurate window, and immediately excused herself. As she left, Hamilton turned to Miss Broadwood with a rather spiritless smile.

"Well, Jimmy," he remarked, "I brought up a piano box full of fireworks for the boys. How do you suppose we'll manage to keep them until the Fourth?"

"We can't, unless we steel ourselves to deny there are any on the premises," said Miss Broadwood, seating herself on a low stool by Hamilton's chair, and leaning back against the mantel. "Have you seen Helen, and has she told you the tragedy of the tooth?"

"She met me at the station, with her tooth wrapped up in tissue paper. I had tea with her an hour ago. Better sit down, Miss Willard"; he rose and pushed a chair toward Imogen, who was standing peering into the conservatory. "We are scheduled to dine at seven, but they seldom get around before eight."

By this time Imogen had made out that here the plural pronoun, third person, always referred to the artists. As Hamilton's manner did not spur one to cordial intercourse, and as his attention seemed directed to Miss Broadwood, in so far as it could be said to be directed to any one, she sat down facing the conservatory and watched him, unable to decide in how far he was identical with the man who had first met Flavia Malcolm in her mother's house, twelve years ago. Did he at all remember having known her as a little girl, and why did his indifference hurt her so, after all these years? Had some remnant of her childish affection for him gone on living, somewhere down in the sealed caves of her consciousness, and had she really expected to find it possible to be fond of him again? Suddenly she saw a light in the man's sleepy eyes, an unmistakable expression of interest and pleasure that fairly startled her. She turned quickly in the direction of his glance, and saw Flavia, just entering, dressed for dinner and lit by the effulgence of her most radiant manner. Most people considered Flavia handsome, and there was no gainsaying that she carried her five-and-thirty years splendidly. Her figure had never grown matronly, and her face was of the sort that does not show wear. Its blond tints were as fresh and enduring as enamel,—and quite as hard. Its usual expression was one of tense, often strained, animation, which compressed her lips nervously. A perfect scream of animation, Miss Broadwood had called it—created and maintained by sheer, indomitable force of will. Flavia's appearance on any scene whatever made a ripple, caused a certain agitation and recognition, and, among impressionable people, a certain uneasiness. For all her sparkling assurance of manner, Flavia was certainly always ill at ease, and even more certainly anxious. She seemed not convinced of the established order of material things, seemed always trying to conceal her feeling that walls might crumble, chasms open, or the fabric of her life fly to the winds in irretrievable entanglement. At least this was the impression Imogen got from that note in Flavia which was so manifestly false.

Hamilton's keen, quick, satisfied glance at his wife had recalled to Imogen all her inventory of speculations about them. She looked at him with compassionate surprise. As a child she had never permitted herself to believe that Hamilton cared at all for the woman who had taken him away from her; and since she had begun to think about them again, it had never occurred to her that any one could become attached to Flavia in that deeply personal and exclusive sense. It seemed quite as irrational as trying to possess oneself of Broadway at noon.

When they went out to dinner, Imogen realized the completeness of Flavia's triumph. They were people of one name, mostly, like kings; people whose names stirred the imagination like a romance or a melody. With the notable exception of M. Roux, Imogen had seen most of them before, either in concert halls or lecture rooms; but they looked noticeably older and dimmer than she remembered them.

Opposite her sat Schemetzkin, the Russian pianist, a short, corpulent man, with an apoplectic face and purplish skin, his thick, iron-grey hair tossed back from his forehead. Next the German giantess sat the Italian tenor—the tiniest of men—pale, with soft, light hair, much in disorder, very red lips, and fingers yellowed by cigarettes. Frau Lichtenfeld shone in a gown of emerald green, fitting so closely as to enhance her natural floridness. However, to do the good lady justice, let her attire be never so modest, it gave an effect of barbaric splendour. At her left sat Herr Schotte, the Assyriologist, whose features were effectually concealed by the convergence of his hair and beard, and whose glasses were continually falling into his plate. This gentleman had removed more tons of earth in the course of his explorations than had any of his confrères, and his vigorous attack upon his food seemed to suggest the strenuous nature of his accustomed toil. His eyes were small and deeply set, and his forehead bulged fiercely above his eyes in a bony ridge. His heavy brows completed the leonine suggestion of his face. Even to Imogen, who knew something of his work and greatly respected it, he was entirely too reminiscent of the stone age to be altogether an agreeable dinner companion. He seemed, indeed, to have absorbed something of the savagery of those early types of life which he continually studied.

Frank Wellington, the young Kansas man who had been two years out of Harvard and had published three historical novels, sat next Mr.

Will Maidenwood, who was still pale from his recent sufferings, and carried his hand bandaged. They took little part in the general conversation, but, like the lion and the unicorn, were always at it; discussing, every time they met, whether there were or were not passages in Mr. Wellington's works which should be eliminated, out of consideration for the Young Person. Wellington had fallen into the hands of a great American syndicate which most effectually befriended struggling authors whose struggles were in the right direction, and which had guaranteed to make him famous before he was thirty. Feeling the security of his position, he stoutly defended those passages which jarred upon the sensitive nerves of the young editor of *Woman*. Maidenwood, in the smoothest of voices, urged the necessity of the author's recognizing certain restrictions at the outset, and Miss Broadwood, who joined the argument quite without invitation or encouragement, seconded him with pointed and malicious remarks which caused the young editor manifest discomfort. Restzhoff, the chemist, demanded the attention of the entire company for his exposition of his devices for manufacturing ice-cream from vegetable oils, and for administering drugs in bonbons.

Flavia, always noticeably restless at dinner, was somewhat apathetic toward the advocate of peptonized chocolate, and was plainly concerned about the sudden departure of M. Roux, who had announced that it would be necessary for him to leave to-morrow. M. Emile Roux, who sat at Flavia's right, was a man in middle life and quite bald, clearly without personal vanity, though his publishers preferred to circulate only those of his portraits taken in his ambrosial youth. Imogen was considerably shocked at his unlikeness to the slender, black-stocked Rolla he had looked at twenty. He had declined into the florid, settled heaviness of indifference and approaching age. There was, however, a certain look of durability and solidity about him; the look of a man who has earned the right to be fat and bald, and even silent at dinner if he chooses.

Throughout the discussion between Wellington and Will Maidenwood, though they invited his participation, he remained silent, betraying no sign either of interest or contempt. Since his arrival he had directed most of his conversation to Hamilton, who had never read one of his twelve great novels. This perplexed and troubled Flavia. On the night of his arrival, Jules Martel had enthusiastically declared, "There are schools and schools, manners and manners; but Roux is Roux, and Paris sets its watches by his clock." Flavia had already repeated this remark to Imogen. It haunted her, and each time she quoted it she was impressed anew.

Flavia shifted the conversation uneasily, evidently exasperated and excited by her repeated failures to draw the novelist out. "Monsieur Roux," she began abruptly, with her most animated smile, "I remember so well a statement I read some years ago in your 'Mes Études des Femmes,' to the effect that you had never met a really intellectual woman. May I ask, without being impertinent, whether that assertion still represents your experience?"

"I meant, madam," said the novelist conservatively, "intellectual in a sense very special, as we say of men in whom the purely intellectual functions seem almost independent."

"And you still think a woman so constituted a mythical personage?" persisted Flavia, nodding her head encouragingly.

"*Une Méduse*, madam, who, if she were discovered, would transmute us all into stone," said the novelist, bowing gravely. "If she existed at all," he added deliberately, "it was my business to find her, and she has cost me many a vain pilgrimage. Like Rudel of Tripoli, I have crossed seas and penetrated deserts to seek her out. I have, indeed, encountered women of learning whose industry I have been compelled to respect; many who have possessed beauty and charm and perplexing cleverness; a few with remarkable information, and a sort of fatal facility."

"And Mrs. Browning, George Eliot, and your own Mme. Dudevant?" queried Flavia with that fervid enthusiasm with which she could, on occasion, utter things simply incomprehensible for their banality—at her feats of this sort Miss Broadwood was wont to sit breathless with admiration.

"Madam, while the intellect was undeniably present in the performances of those women, it was only the stick of the rocket. Although this woman has eluded me, I have studied her conditions and perturbations as astronomers conjecture the orbits of planets they have never seen. If she exists, she is probably neither an artist nor a woman with a mission, but an obscure personage, with imperative intellectual needs, who absorbs rather than produces."

Flavia, still nodding nervously, fixed a strained glance of interrogation upon M. Roux. "Then you think she would be a woman whose first necessity would be to know, whose instincts would be satisfied only with the best, who could draw from others; appreciative, merely?"

The novelist lifted his dull eyes to his interlocutress with an untranslatable smile, and a slight inclination of his shoulders. "Exactly so; you are really remarkable, madam," he added, in a tone of cold astonishment.

After dinner the guests took their coffee in the music-room, where Schemetzkin sat down at the piano to drum rag-time, and give his celebrated imitation of the boarding-school girl's execution of Chopin. He flatly refused to play anything more serious, and would practise only in the morning, when he had the music-room to himself. Hamilton and M. Roux repaired to the smoking-room to discuss the necessity of extending the tax on manufactured articles in France,—one of those conversations which particularly exasperated Flavia.

After Schemetzkin had grimaced and tortured the keyboard with malicious vulgarities for half an hour, Signor Donati, to put an end to his torture, consented to sing, and Flavia and Imogen went to fetch Arthur to play his accompaniments. Hamilton rose with an annoyed look, and placed his cigarette on the mantel. "Why yes, Flavia, I'll accompany him, provided he sings something with a melody, Italian arias or ballads, and provided the recital is not interminable."

"You will join us, M. Roux?"

"Thank you, but I have some letters to write," replied the novelist bowing.

As Flavia had remarked to Imogen, "Arthur really played accompaniments remarkably well." To hear him recalled vividly the days of her childhood, when he always used to spend his business vacations at her mother's home in Maine. He had possessed for her that almost hypnotic influence which young men sometimes exert upon little girls. It was a sort of phantom love affair, subjective and fanciful, a precocity of instinct, like that tender and maternal concern which some little girls feel for their dolls. Yet this childish infatuation is capable of all the depressions and exaltations of love itself; it has its bitter jealousies, cruel disappointments, its exacting caprices.

Summer after summer she had awaited his coming and wept at his departure, indifferent to the gayer young men who had called her their sweetheart, and laughed at everything she said. Although Hamilton never said so, she had been always quite sure that he was fond of her. When he pulled her up the river to hunt for fairy knolls shut about by low, hanging willows, he was often silent for an hour at a time, yet she never felt that he was bored or was neglecting her. He would lie in the sand smoking, his eyes half closed, watching her play, and she was always conscious that she was entertaining him. Sometimes he would take a copy of "Alice in Wonderland" in his pocket, and no one could read it as he could, laughing at her with his dark eyes, when anything amused him.

No one else could laugh so, with just their eyes, and without moving a muscle of their face. Though he usually smiled at passages that seemed not at all funny to the child, she always laughed gleefully, because he was so seldom moved to mirth that any such demonstration delighted her and she took the credit of it entirely to herself. Her own inclination had been for serious stories, with sad endings, like the Little Mermaid, which he had once told her in an unguarded moment when she had a cold, and was put to bed early on her birthday night and cried because she could not have her party. But he highly disapproved of this preference, and had called it a morbid taste, and always shook his finger at her when she asked for the story. When she had been particularly good, or particularly neglected by other people, then he would sometimes melt and tell her the story, and never laugh at her if she enjoyed the "sad ending" even to tears. When Flavia had taken him away and he came no more, she wept inconsolably for the space of two weeks, and refused to learn her lessons. Then she found the story of the Little Mermaid herself, and forgot him.

Imogen had discovered at dinner that he could still smile at one secretly, out of his eyes, and that he had the old manner of outwardly seeming bored, but letting you know that he was not. She was intensely curious about his exact state of feeling toward his wife, and more curious still to catch a sense of his final adjustment to the conditions of life in general. This, she could not help feeling, she might get again—if she could have him alone for an hour, in some place where there was a little river and a sandy cove bordered by drooping willows, and a blue sky seen through white sycamore boughs.

That evening, before retiring, Flavia entered her husband's room, where he sat in his smoking-jacket, in one of his favourite low chairs.

"I suppose it's a grave responsibility to bring an ardent, serious young thing like Imogen here among all these fascinating personages," she remarked reflectively. "But, after all, one can never tell. These grave, silent girls have their own charm, even for facile people."

"O, so that is your plan?" queried her husband dryly. "I was wondering why you got her up here. She doesn't seem to mix well with the faciles. At least, so it struck me."

Flavia paid no heed to this jeering remark, but repeated, "No, after all, it may not be a bad thing."

"Then do consign her to that shaken reed, the tenor," said her husband yawning. "I remember she used to have a taste for the pathetic."

"And then," remarked Flavia coquettishly, "after all, I owe her mother a return in kind. She was not afraid to trifle with destiny."

But Hamilton was asleep in his chair.

Next morning Imogen found only Miss Broadwood in the breakfast-room.

"Good-morning, my dear girl, whatever are you doing up so early? They never breakfast before eleven. Most of them take their coffee in their room. Take this place by me."

Miss Broadwood looked particularly fresh and encouraging in her blue serge walking-skirt, her open jacket displaying an expanse of stiff, white, shirt bosom, dotted with some almost imperceptible figure, and a dark blue-and-white necktie, neatly knotted under her wide, rolling collar. She wore a white rosebud in the lapel of her coat, and decidedly she seemed more than ever like a nice, clean boy on his holiday. Imogen was just hoping that they would breakfast alone when Miss Broadwood exclaimed, "Ah, there comes Arthur with the children. That's the reward of early rising in this house; you never get to see the youngsters at any other time."

Hamilton entered, followed by two dark, handsome little boys. The girl, who was very tiny, blonde like her mother, and exceedingly frail, he carried in his arms. The boys came up and said good-morning with an ease and cheerfulness uncommon, even in well-bred children, but the little girl hid her face on her father's shoulder.

"She's a shy little lady," he explained, as he put her gently down in her chair. "I'm afraid she's like her father; she can't seem to get used to meeting people. And you, Miss Willard, did you dream of the White Rabbit or the little mermaid?"

"O, I dreamed of them all! All the personages of that buried civilization," cried Imogen, delighted that his estranged manner of the night before had entirely vanished, and feeling that, somehow, the old confidential relations had been restored during the night.

"Come, William," said Miss Broadwood, turning to the younger of the two boys, "and what did you dream about?"

"We dreamed," said William gravely—he was the more assertive of the two and always spoke for both—"we dreamed that there were fireworks hidden in the basement of the carriage-house; lots and lots of fireworks."

His elder brother looked up at him with apprehensive astonishment, while Miss Broadwood hastily put her napkin to her lips, and Hamilton dropped his eyes. "If little boys dream things, they are so apt not to come true," he reflected sadly. This shook even the redoubtable William, and he glanced nervously at his brother. "But do things vanish just because they have been dreamed?" he objected.

"Generally that is the very best reason for their vanishing," said Arthur gravely.

"But, father, people can't help what they dream," remonstrated Edward gently.

"Oh, come! You're making these children talk like a Maeterlinck dialogue," laughed Miss Broadwood.

Flavia presently entered, a book in her hand, and bade them all good-morning. "Come, little people, which story shall it be this morning?" she asked winningly. Greatly excited, the children followed her into the garden. "She does then, sometimes," murmured Imogen as they left the breakfast-room.

"Oh, yes, to be sure," said Miss Broadwood cheerfully. "She reads a story to them every morning in the most picturesque part of the garden. The mother of the Gracchi, you know. She does so long, she says, for the time when they will be intellectual companions for her. What do you say to a walk over the hills?"

As they left the house they met Frau Lichtenfeld and the bushy Herr Schotte—the professor cut an astonishing figure in golf stockings—returning from a walk and engaged in an animated conversation on the tendencies of German fiction.

"Aren't they the most attractive little children," exclaimed Imogen as they wound down the road toward the river.

"Yes, and you must not fail to tell Flavia that you think so. She will look at you in a sort of startled way and say, 'Yes, aren't they?' and maybe she will go off and hunt them up and have tea with them, to fully appreciate them. She is awfully afraid of missing anything good, is Flavia. The way those youngsters manage to conceal their guilty presence in the House of Song is a wonder."

"But don't any of the artist-folk fancy children?" asked Imogen.

"Yes, they just fancy them and no more. The chemist remarked the other day that children are like certain salts which need not be actualized because the formulae are quite sufficient for practical purposes. I don't see how even Flavia can endure to have that man about."

"I have always been rather curious to know what Arthur thinks of it all," remarked Imogen cautiously.

"Thinks of it!" ejaculated Miss Broadwood. "Why, my dear, what would any man think of having his house turned into an hotel, habited by freaks who discharge his servants, borrow his money, and insult his neighbours? This place is shunned like a lazaretto!"

"Well, then, why does he—why does he——" persisted Imogen.

"Bah!" interrupted Miss Broadwood impatiently, "why did he in the first place? That's the question."

"Marry her, you mean?" said Imogen colouring.

"Exactly so," said Miss Broadwood sharply, as she snapped the lid of her match-box.

"I suppose that is a question rather beyond us, and certainly one which we cannot discuss," said Imogen. "But his toleration on this one point puzzles me, quite apart from other complications."

"Toleration? Why this point, as you call it, simply *is* Flavia. Who could conceive of her without it? I don't know where it's all going to end, I'm sure, and I'm equally sure that, if it were not for Arthur, I shouldn't care," declared Miss Broadwood, drawing her shoulders together.

"But will it end at all, now?"

"Such an absurd state of things can't go on indefinitely. A man isn't going to see his wife make a guy of herself forever, is he? Chaos has already begun in the servants' quarters. There are six different languages spoken there now. You see, it's all on an entirely false basis. Flavia hasn't the slightest notion of what these people are really like, their good and their bad alike escape her. They, on the other hand, can't imagine what she is driving at. Now, Arthur is worse off than either faction; he is not in the fairy story in that he sees these people exactly as they are, *but* he is utterly unable to see Flavia as they see her. There you have the situation. Why can't he see her as we do? My dear, that has kept me awake o' nights. This man who has thought so much and lived so much, who is naturally a critic, really takes Flavia at very nearly her own estimate. But now I am entering upon a wilderness. From a brief acquaintance with her, you can know nothing of the icy fastnesses of Flavia's self-esteem. It's like St. Peter's; you can't realize its magnitude at once. You have to grow into a sense of it by living under its shadow. It has perplexed even Emile Roux, that merciless dissector of egoism. She has puzzled him the more because he saw at a glance what some of them do not perceive at once, and what will be mercifully concealed from Arthur until the trump sounds; namely, that all Flavia's artists have done or ever will do means exactly as much to her as a symphony means to an oyster; that there is no bridge by which the significance of any work of art could be conveyed to her."

"Then, in the name of goodness, why does she bother?" gasped Imogen. "She is pretty, wealthy, well-established; why should she bother?"

"That's what M. Roux has kept asking himself. I can't pretend to analyse it. She reads papers on the Literary Landmarks of Paris, and the Loves of the Poets, and that sort of thing, to clubs out in Chicago. To Flavia it is more necessary to be called clever than to breathe. I would give a good deal to know that glum Frenchman's diagnosis. He has been watching her out of those fishy eyes of his as a biologist watches a hemisphereless frog."

For several days after M. Roux's departure, Flavia gave an embarrassing share of her attention to Imogen. Embarrassing, because Imogen had the feeling of being energetically and futilely explored, she knew not for what. She felt herself under the globe of an air pump, expected to yield up something. When she confined the conversation to matters of general interest, Flavia conveyed to her with some pique that her one endeavour in life had been to fit herself to converse with her friends upon those things which vitally interested them. "One has no right to accept their best from people unless one gives, isn't it so? I want to be able to give——!" she declared vaguely. Yet whenever Imogen strove to pay her tithes and plunged bravely into her plans for study next winter, Flavia grew absent-minded and interrupted her by amazing generalizations or by such embarrassing questions as, "And these grim studies really have charm for you; you are quite buried in them; they make other things seem light and ephemeral?"

"I rather feel as though I had got in here under false pretences," Imogen confided to Miss Broadwood, "I'm sure I don't know what it is that she wants of me."

"Ah," chuckled Jemima, "you are not equal to these heart to heart talks with Flavia. You utterly fail to communicate to her the atmosphere of that untroubled joy in which you dwell. You must remember that she gets no feeling out of things herself, and she demands that you impart yours to her by some process of psychic transmission. I once met a blind girl, blind from birth, who could discuss the peculiarities of the Barbizon school with just Flavia's glibness and enthusiasm. Ordinarily Flavia knows how to get what she wants from people, and her memory is wonderful. One evening I heard her giving Frau Lichtenfeld some random impressions about Hedda Gabler which she extracted from me five years ago; giving them with an impassioned conviction of which I was never guilty. But I have known other people who could appropriate your stories and opinions; Flavia is infinitely more subtle than that; she can soak up the very thrash and drift of your day dreams, and take the very thrills off your back, as it were."

After some days of unsuccessful effort, Flavia withdrew herself, and Imogen found Hamilton ready to catch her when she was tossed a-field. He seemed only to have been awaiting this crisis, and at once their old intimacy re-established itself as a thing inevitable and beautifully prepared for. She convinced herself that she had not been mistaken in him, despite all the doubts that had come up in later years, and this renewal of faith set more than one question thumping in her brain. "How did he, how can he?" she kept repeating with a tinge of her childish resentment, "what right had he to waste anything so fine?"

When Imogen and Arthur were returning from a walk before luncheon one morning about a week after M. Roux's departure, they noticed an absorbed group before one of the hall windows. Herr Schotte and Restzhoff sat on the window seat with a newspaper between them, while Wellington, Schemetzkin, and Will Maidenwood looked over their shoulders. They seemed intensely interested, Herr Schotte occasionally pounding his knees with his fists in ebullitions of barbaric glee. When Imogen entered the hall, however, the men were all sauntering toward the breakfast-room and the paper was lying innocently on the divan. During luncheon the personnel of that window group were unwontedly animated and agreeable,—all save Schemetzkin, whose stare was blanker than ever, as though Roux's mantle of insulting indifference had fallen upon him, in addition to his own oblivious self absorption. Will Maidenwood seemed embarrassed and annoyed; the chemist employed himself with making polite speeches to Hamilton.—Flavia did not come down to lunch—and there was a malicious gleam under Herr Schotte's eyebrows. Frank Wellington announced nervously that an imperative letter from his protecting syndicate summoned him to the city.

After luncheon the men went to the golf links, and Imogen, at the first opportunity, possessed herself of the newspaper which had been left on the divan. One of the first things that caught her eye was an article headed "Roux on Tuft Hunters; The Advanced American Woman as He Sees Her; Aggressive, Superficial and Insincere." The entire interview was nothing more nor less than a satiric characterization of Flavia, a-quiver with irritation and vitriolic malice. No one could mistake it; it was done with all his deftness of portraiture. Imogen had not finished the article when she heard a footstep, and clutching the paper she started precipitately toward the stairway as Arthur entered. He put out his hand, looking critically at her distressed face.

"Wait a moment, Miss Willard," he said peremptorily, "I want to see whether we can find what it was that so interested our friends this morning. Give me the paper, please."

Imogen grew quite white as he opened the journal. She reached forward and crumpled it with her hands. "Please don't, please don't," she pleaded, "it's something I don't want you to see. Oh! why will you? It's just something low and despicable that you can't notice."

Arthur had gently loosed her hands, and he pointed her to a chair. He lit a cigar and read the article through without comment. When he had finished it, he walked to the fireplace, struck a match, and tossed the flaming journal between the brass andirons.

"You are right," he remarked as he came back, dusting his hands with his handkerchief. "It's quite impossible to comment. There are extremes of blackguardism for which we have no name. The only thing necessary is to see that Flavia gets no wind of this. This seems to be my cue to act; poor girl."

Imogen looked at him tearfully; she could only murmur, "Oh, why did you read it!"

Hamilton laughed spiritlessly. "Come, don't you worry about it. You always took other people's troubles too seriously. When you were little and all the world was gay and everybody happy, you must needs get the Little Mermaid's troubles to grieve over. Come with me into the music-room. You remember the musical setting I once made you for the Lay of the Jabberwock? I was trying it over the other night, long after you were in bed, and I decided it was quite as fine as the Erl-King music. How I wish I could give you some of the cake that Alice ate and make you a little girl again. Then, when you had got through the glass door into the little garden, you could call to me, perhaps, and tell me all the fine things that were going on there. What a pity it is that you ever grew up!" he added, laughing, and Imogen, too, was thinking just that.

At dinner that evening, Flavia, with fatal persistence, insisted upon turning the conversation to M. Roux. She had been reading one of his novels and had remembered anew that Paris set its watches by his clock.

Imogen surmised that she was tortured by a feeling that she had not sufficiently appreciated him while she had had him. When she first mentioned his name, she was answered only by the pall of silence that fell over the company. Then everyone began to talk at once, as though to correct a false position. They spoke of him with a fervid, defiant admiration, with the sort of hot praise that covers a double purpose. Imogen fancied she could see that they felt a kind of relief at what the man had done, even those who despised him for doing it; that they felt a spiteful hate against Flavia, as though she had tricked them, and a certain contempt for themselves that they had been beguiled. She was reminded of the fury of the crowd in the fairy tale, when once the child had called out that the king was in his night-clothes. Surely these people knew no more about Flavia than they had known before, but the mere fact that the thing had been said, altered the situation. Flavia, meanwhile, sat chattering amiably, pathetically unconscious of her nakedness.

Hamilton lounged, fingering the stem of his wine glass, gazing down the table at one face after another and studying the various degrees of self-consciousness they exhibited. Imogen's eyes followed his, fearfully. When a lull came in the spasmodic flow of conversation, Arthur, leaning back in his chair, remarked deliberately, "As for M. Roux, his very profession places him in that class of men whom society has never been able to accept unconditionally because it has never been able to assume that they have any ordered notion of taste. He and his ilk remain, with the mountebanks and snake charmers, people indispensable to our civilization, but wholly unreclaimed by it; people whom we receive, but whose invitations we do not accept."

Fortunately for Flavia, this mine was not exploded until just before the coffee was brought. Her laughter was pitiful to hear; it echoed through the silent room as in a vault, while she made some tremulously light remark about her husband's drollery, grim as a jest from the dying. No one responded and she sat nodding her head like a mechanical toy and smiling her white, set smile through her teeth, until Alcée Buisson and Frau Lichtenfeld came to her support.

After dinner the guests retired immediately to their rooms, and Imogen went upstairs on tiptoe, feeling the echo of breakage and the dust of crumbling in the air. She wondered whether Flavia's habitual note of uneasiness were not, in a manner, prophetic, and a sort of unconscious premonition, after all. She sat down to write a letter, but she found herself so nervous, her head so hot and her hands so cold, that she soon abandoned the effort. Just as she was about to seek Miss Broadwood, Flavia entered and embraced her hysterically.

"My dearest girl," she began, "was there ever such an unfortunate and incomprehensible speech made before? Of course it is scarcely necessary to explain to you poor Arthur's lack of tact, and that he meant nothing. But they! Can they be expected to understand? He will feel wretchedly about it when he realizes what he has done, but in the meantime? And M. Roux, of all men! When we were so fortunate as to get him, and he made himself so unreservedly agreeable, and I fancied that, in his way, Arthur quite admired him. My dear, you have no idea what that speech has done. Schemetzkin and Herr Schotte have already sent me word that they must leave us to-morrow. Such a thing from a host!" Flavia paused, choked by tears of vexation and despair.

Imogen was thoroughly disconcerted; this was the first time she had ever seen Flavia betray any personal emotion which was indubitably genuine. She replied with what consolation she could. "Need they take it personally at all? It was a mere observation upon a class of people——"

"Which he knows nothing whatever about, and with whom he has no sympathy," interrupted Flavia. "Ah, my dear, you could not be *expected* to understand. You can't realize, knowing Arthur as you do, his entire lack of any aesthetic sense whatever. He is absolutely *nil*, stone deaf and stark blind, on that side. He doesn't mean to be brutal, it is just the brutality of utter ignorance. They always feel it—they are so sensitive to unsympathetic influences, you know; they know it the moment they come into the house. I have spent my life apologizing for him and struggling to conceal it; but in spite of me, he wounds them; his very attitude, even in silence, offends them. Heavens! do I not know, is it not perpetually and forever wounding me? But there has never been anything so dreadful as this, never! If I could conceive of any possible motive, even!"

"But, surely, Mrs. Hamilton, it was, after all, a mere expression of opinion, such as we are any of us likely to venture upon any subject whatever. It was neither more personal nor more extravagant than many of M. Roux's remarks."

"But, Imogen, certainly M. Roux has the right. It is a part of his art, and that is altogether another matter. Oh, this is not the only instance!" continued Flavia passionately, "I've always had that narrow, bigoted prejudice to contend with. It has always held me back. But this——!"

"I think you mistake his attitude," replied Imogen, feeling a flush that made her ears tingle, "that is, I fancy he is more appreciative than he seems. A man can't be very demonstrative about those things—not if he is a real man. I should not think you would care much about saving the feelings of people who are too narrow to admit of any other point of view than their own." She stopped, finding herself in the impossible position of attempting to explain Hamilton to his wife; a task which, if once begun, would necessitate an entire course of enlightenment which she doubted Flavia's ability to receive, and which she could offer only with very poor grace.

"That's just where it stings most," here Flavia began pacing the floor, "it is just because they have all shown such tolerance, and have treated Arthur with such unfailing consideration, that I can find no reasonable pretext for his rancour. How can he fail to see the value of such friendships on the children's account, if for nothing else! What an advantage for them to grow up among such associations! Even though he cares nothing about these things himself he might realize that. Is there nothing I could say by way of explanation? To them, I mean? If some one were to explain to them how unfortunately limited he is in these things——"

"I'm afraid I cannot advise you," said Imogen decidedly, "but that, at least, seems to me impossible."

Flavia took her hand and glanced at her affectionately, nodding nervously. "Of course, dear girl, I can't ask you to be quite frank with me. Poor child, you are trembling and your hands are icy. Poor Arthur! But you must not judge him by this altogether; think how much he misses in life. What a cruel shock you've had. I'll send you some sherry. Good-night, my dear."

When Flavia shut the door, Imogen burst into a fit of nervous weeping.

Next morning she awoke after a troubled and restless night. At eight o'clock Miss Broadwood entered in a red and white striped bath-robe.

"Up, up, and see the great doom's image!" she cried, her eyes sparkling with excitement. "The hall is full of trunks, they are packing. What bolt has fallen? It's you, *ma chérie*, you've brought Ulysses home again and the slaughter has begun!" she blew a cloud of smoke triumphantly from her lips and threw herself into a chair beside the bed.

Imogen, rising on her elbow, plunged excitedly into the story of the Roux interview, which Miss Broadwood heard with the keenest interest, frequently interrupting her by exclamations of delight. When Imogen reached the dramatic scene which terminated in the destruction of the newspaper, Miss Broadwood rose and took a turn about the room, violently switching the tasselled cords of her bath-robe.

"Stop a moment," she cried, "you mean to tell me that he had such a heaven-sent means to bring her to her senses and didn't use it, that he held such a weapon and threw it away?"

"Use it?" cried Imogen unsteadily, "of course he didn't! He bared his back to the tormentor, signed himself over to punishment in that speech he made at dinner, which every one understands but Flavia. She was here for an hour last night and disregarded every limit of taste in her maledictions."

"My dear!" cried Miss Broadwood, catching her hand in inordinate delight at the situation, "do you see what he has done? There'll be no end to it. Why he has sacrificed himself to spare the very vanity that devours him, put rancours in the vessels of his peace, and his eternal jewel given to the common enemy of man, to make them kings, the seed of Banquo kings! He is magnificent!"

"Isn't he always that?" cried Imogen hotly. "He's like a pillar of sanity and law in this house of shams and swollen vanities, where people stalk about with a sort of mad-house dignity, each one fancying himself a king or a pope. If you could have heard that woman talk of him! Why she thinks him stupid, bigoted, blinded by middle-class prejudices. She talked about his having no aesthetic sense, and insisted that her artists had always shown him tolerance. I don't know why it should get on my nerves so, I'm sure, but her stupidity and assurance are enough to drive one to the brink of collapse."

"Yes, as opposed to his singular fineness, they are calculated to do just that," said Miss Broadwood gravely, wisely ignoring Imogen's tears. "But what has been is nothing to what will be. Just wait until Flavia's black swans have flown! You ought not to try to stick it out; that would only make it harder for every one. Suppose you let me telephone your mother to wire you to come home by the evening train?"

"Anything, rather than have her come at me like that again. It puts me in a perfectly impossible position, and he *is* so fine!"

"Of course it does," said Miss Broadwood sympathetically, "and there is no good to be got from facing it. I will stay, because such things interest me, and Frau Lichtenfeld will stay because she has no money to get away, and Buisson will stay because he feels somewhat responsible. These complications are interesting enough to cold-blooded folk like myself who have an eye for the dramatic element, but they are distracting and demoralizing to young people with any serious purpose in life."

Miss Broadwood's counsel was all the more generous seeing that, for her, the most interesting element of this dénouement would be eliminated by Imogen's departure. "If she goes now, she'll get over it," soliloquized Miss Broadwood, "if she stays she'll be wrung for him, and the hurt may go deep enough to last. I haven't the heart to see her spoiling things for herself." She telephoned Mrs. Willard, and helped Imogen to pack. She even took it upon herself to break the news of Imogen's going to Arthur, who remarked, as he rolled a cigarette in his nerveless fingers:

"Right enough, too. What should she do here with old cynics like you and me, Jimmy? Seeing that she is brim full of dates and formulae and other positivisms, and is so girt about with illusions that she still casts a shadow in the sun. You've been very tender of her, haven't you? I've watched you. And to think it may all be gone when we see her next. 'The common fate of all things rare,' you know. What a good fellow you are, anyway, Jimmy," he added, putting his hands affectionately on her shoulders.

Arthur went with them to the station. Flavia was so prostrated by the concerted action of her guests that she was able to see Imogen only for a moment in her darkened sleeping chamber, where she kissed her hysterically, without lifting her head, bandaged in aromatic vinegar. On the way to the station both Arthur and Imogen threw the burden of keeping up appearances entirely upon Miss Broadwood, who blithely rose to the occasion. When Hamilton carried Imogen's bag into the car, Miss Broadwood detained her for a moment, whispering as she gave her a large, warm handclasp, "I'll come to see you when I get back to town; and, in the meantime, if you meet any of our artists, tell them you have left Caius Marius among the ruins of Carthage."

First published in *The Troll Garden* (New York: McClure, Phillips & Co., 1905), pp. 1–54.

The Sculptor's Funeral

❄ ❄ ❄

A group of the townspeople stood on the station siding of a little Kansas town, awaiting the coming of the night train, which was already twenty minutes overdue. The snow had fallen thick over everything; in the pale starlight the line of bluffs across the wide, white meadows south of the town made soft, smoke-coloured curves against the clear sky. The men on the siding stood first on one foot and then on the other, their hands thrust deep into their trousers pockets, their overcoats open, their shoulders screwed up with the cold; and they glanced from time to time toward the southeast, where the railroad track wound along the river shore. They conversed in low tones and moved about restlessly, seeming uncertain as to what was expected of them. There was but one of the company who looked as though he knew exactly why he was there; and he kept conspicuously apart; walking to the far end of the platform, returning to the station door, then pacing up the track again, his chin sunk in the high collar of his overcoat, his burly shoulders drooping forward, his gait heavy and dogged. Presently he was approached by a tall, spare, grizzled man clad in a faded Grand Army suit, who shuffled out from the group and advanced with a certain deference, craning his neck forward until his back made the angle of a jack-knife three-quarters open.

"I reckon she's a-goin' to be pretty late agin to-night, Jim," he remarked in a squeaky falsetto. "S'pose it's the snow?"

"I don't know," responded the other man with a shade of annoyance, speaking from out an astonishing cataract of red beard that grew fiercely and thickly in all directions.

The spare man shifted the quill toothpick he was chewing to the other side of his mouth. "It ain't likely that anybody from the East will come with the corpse, I s'pose," he went on reflectively.

"I don't know," responded the other, more curtly than before.

"It's too bad he didn't belong to some lodge or other. I like an order funeral myself. They seem more appropriate for people of some repytation," the spare man continued, with an ingratiating concession in his shrill voice, as he carefully placed his toothpick in his vest pocket. He always carried the flag at the G.A.R. funerals in the town.

The heavy man turned on his heel, without replying, and walked up the siding. The spare man shuffled back to the uneasy group. "Jim's ez full ez a tick, ez ushel," he commented commiseratingly.

Just then a distant whistle sounded, and there was a shuffling of feet on the platform. A number of lanky boys of all ages appeared as suddenly and slimily as eels wakened by the crack of thunder; some came from the waiting-room, where they had been warming themselves by the red stove, or half asleep on the slat benches; others uncoiled themselves from baggage trucks or slid out of express wagons. Two clambered down from the driver's seat of a hearse that stood backed up against the siding. They straightened their stooping shoulders and lifted their heads, and a flash of momentary animation kindled their dull eyes at that cold, vibrant scream, the world-wide call for men. It stirred them like the note of a trumpet; just as it had often stirred the man who was coming home to-night, in his boyhood.

The night express shot, red as a rocket, from out the eastward marsh lands and wound along the river shore under the long lines of shivering poplars that sentinelled the meadows, the escaping steam hanging in grey masses against the pale sky and blotting out the Milky Way. In a moment the red glare from the headlight streamed up the snow-covered track before the siding and glittered on the wet, black rails. The burly man with the dishevelled red beard walked swiftly up the platform toward the approaching train, uncovering his head as he went. The group of men behind him hesitated, glanced questioningly at one another, and awkwardly followed his example. The train stopped, and the crowd shuffled up to the express car just as the door was thrown open, the spare man in the G.A.R. suit thrusting his head forward with curiosity. The express messenger appeared in the doorway, accompanied by a young man in a long ulster and travelling cap.

"Are Mr. Merrick's friends here?" inquired the young man.

The group on the platform swayed and shuffled uneasily. Philip Phelps, the banker, responded with dignity: "We have come to take charge of the body. Mr. Merrick's father is very feeble and can't be about."

"Send the agent out here," growled the express messenger, "and tell the operator to lend a hand."

The coffin was got out of its rough box and down on the snowy platform. The townspeople drew back enough to make room for it and then formed a close semicircle about it, looking curiously at the palm leaf which lay across the black cover. No one said anything. The baggage man stood by his truck, waiting to get at the trunks. The engine panted heavily, and the fireman dodged in and out among the wheels with his yellow torch and long oil-can, snapping the spindle boxes. The young Bostonian, one of the dead sculptor's pupils who had come with the body, looked about him helplessly. He turned to the banker, the only one of that black, uneasy, stoop-shouldered group who seemed enough of an individual to be addressed.

"None of Mr. Merrick's brothers are here?" he asked uncertainly.

The man with the red beard for the first time stepped up and joined the group. "No, they have not come yet; the family is scattered. The body will be taken directly to the house." He stooped and took hold of one of the handles of the coffin.

"Take the long hill road up, Thompson, it will be easier on the horses," called the liveryman as the undertaker snapped the door of the hearse and prepared to mount to the driver's seat.

Laird, the red-bearded lawyer, turned again to the stranger: "We didn't know whether there would be any one with him or not," he explained. "It's a long walk, so you'd better go up in the hack." He pointed to a single battered conveyance, but the young man replied stiffly: "Thank you, but I think I will go up with the hearse. If you don't object," turning to the undertaker, "I'll ride with you."

They clambered up over the wheels and drove off in the starlight up the long, white hill toward the town. The lamps in the still village were shining from under the low, snow-burdened roofs; and beyond, on every side, the plains reached out into emptiness, peaceful and wide as the soft sky itself, and wrapped in a tangible, white silence.

When the hearse backed up to a wooden sidewalk before a naked, weather-beaten frame house, the same composite, ill-defined group that had stood upon the station siding was huddled about the gate. The front yard was an icy swamp, and a couple of warped planks, extending from the sidewalk to the door, made a sort of rickety footbridge. The gate hung on one hinge, and was opened wide with difficulty. Steavens, the young stranger, noticed that something black was tied to the knob of the front door.

The grating sound made by the casket, at it was drawn from the hearse, was answered by a scream from the house; the front door was wrenched open, and a tall, corpulent woman rushed out bareheaded into the snow and flung herself upon the coffin, shrieking: "My boy, my boy! And this is how you've come home to me!"

As Steavens turned away and closed his eyes with a shudder of unutterable repulsion, another woman, also tall, but flat and angular, dressed entirely in black, darted out of the house and caught Mrs. Merrick by the shoulders, crying sharply: "Come, come, mother; you musn't go on like this!" Her tone changed to one of obsequious solemnity as she turned to the banker: "The parlour is ready, Mr. Phelps."

The bearers carried the coffin along the narrow boards, while the undertaker ran ahead with the coffin-rests. They bore it into a large, unheated room that smelled of dampness and disuse and furniture polish, and set it down under a hanging lamp ornamented with jingling glass prisms and before a "Rogers group" of John Alden and Priscilla, wreathed with smilax. Henry Steavens stared about him with the sickening conviction that there had been some horrible mistake, and that he had somehow arrived at the wrong destination. He looked painfully about over the clover-green Brussels, the fat plush upholstery; among the hand-painted china plaques and panels, and vases, for some mark of identification, for something that might once conceivably have belonged to Harvey Merrick. It was not until he recognized his friend in the crayon portrait of a little boy in kilts and curls hanging above the piano, that he felt willing to let any of these people approach the coffin.

"Take the lid off, Mr. Thompson; let me see my boy's face," wailed the elder woman between her sobs. This time Steavens looked fearfully, almost beseechingly into her face, red and swollen under its masses of strong, black, shiny hair. He flushed, dropped his eyes, and then, almost incredulously, looked again. There was a kind of power about her face— a kind of brutal handsomeness, even, but it was scarred and furrowed by violence, and so coloured and coarsened by fiercer passions that grief seemed never to have laid a gentle finger there. The long nose was distended and knobbed at the end, and there were deep lines on either side of it; her heavy, black brows almost met across her forehead, her teeth were large and square, and set far apart—teeth that could tear. She filled the room; the men were obliterated, seemed tossed about like twigs in an angry water, and even Steavens felt himself being drawn into the whirlpool.

The daughter—the tall, raw-boned woman in crêpe, with a mourning comb in her hair which curiously lengthened her long face—sat stiffly upon the sofa, her hands, conspicuous for their large knuckles, folded in her lap, her mouth and eyes drawn down, solemnly awaiting the opening of the coffin. Near the door stood a mulatto woman, evidently a servant in the house, with a timid bearing and an emaciated face pitifully sad and gentle. She was weeping silently, the corner of her calico apron lifted to her eyes, occasionally suppressing a long, quivering sob. Steavens walked over and stood beside her.

Feeble steps were heard on the stairs, and an old man, tall and frail, odorous of pipe smoke, with shaggy, unkept grey hair and a dingy beard, tobacco stained about the mouth, entered uncertainly. He went slowly up to the coffin and stood rolling a blue cotton handkerchief between his hands, seeming so pained and embarrassed by his wife's orgy of grief that he had no consciousness of anything else.

"There, there, Annie, dear, don't take on so," he quavered timidly, putting out a shaking hand and awkwardly patting her elbow. She turned with a cry, and sank upon his shoulder with such violence that he tottered a little. He did not even glance toward the coffin, but continued to look at her with a dull, frightened, appealing expression, as a spaniel looks at the whip. His sunken cheeks slowly reddened and burned with miserable shame. When his wife rushed from the room, her daughter strode after her with set lips. The servant stole up to the coffin, bent over it for a moment, and then slipped away to the kitchen, leaving Steavens, the lawyer and the father to themselves. The old man stood trembling and looking down at his dead son's face. The sculptor's splendid head seemed even more noble in its rigid stillness than in life. The dark hair had crept down upon the wide forehead; the face seemed strangely long, but in it there was not that beautiful and chaste repose which we expect to find in the faces of the dead. The brows were so drawn that there were two deep lines above the beaked nose, and the chin was thrust forward defiantly. It was as though the strain of life had been so sharp and bitter that death could not at once wholly relax the tension and smooth the countenance into perfect peace—as though he were still guarding something precious and holy, which might even yet be wrested from him.

The old man's lips were working under his stained beard. He turned to the lawyer with timid deference: "Phelps and the rest are comin' back to set up with Harve, ain't they?" he asked. "Thank 'ee, Jim, thank 'ee." He brushed the hair back gently from his son's forehead. "He was a good boy, Jim; always a good boy. He was ez gentle ez a child and the kindest of 'em all—only we didn't none of us ever onderstand him." The tears trickled slowly down his beard and dropped upon the sculptor's coat.

"Martin, Martin. Oh, Martin! come here," his wife wailed from the top of the stairs. The old man started timorously: "Yes, Annie, I'm coming." He turned away, hesitated, stood for a moment in miserable indecision; then reached back and patted the dead man's hair softly, and stumbled from the room.

"Poor old man, I didn't think he had any tears left. Seems as if his eyes would have gone dry long ago. At his age nothing cuts very deep," remarked the lawyer.

Something in his tone made Steavens glance up. While the mother had been in the room, the young man had scarcely seen anyone else; but now, from the moment he first glanced into Jim Laird's florid face and blood-shot eyes, he knew that he had found what he had been heartsick at not finding before—the feeling, the understanding, that must exist in some one, even here.

The man was red as his beard, with features swollen and blurred by dissipation, and a hot, blazing blue eye. His face was strained—that of a man who is controlling himself with difficulty—and he kept plucking at his beard with a sort of fierce resentment. Steavens, sitting by the window, watched him turn down the glaring lamp, still its jangling pendants with an angry gesture, and then stand with his hands locked behind him, staring down into the master's face. He could not help wondering what link there could have been between the porcelain vessel and so sooty a lump of potter's clay.

From the kitchen an uproar was sounding; when the dining-room door opened, the import of it was clear. The mother was abusing the maid for having forgotten to make the dressing for the chicken salad which had been prepared for the watchers. Steavens had never heard anything in the least like it; it was injured, emotional, dramatic abuse, unique and masterly in its excruciating cruelty, as violent and unrestrained as had been her grief of twenty minutes before. With a shudder of disgust the lawyer went into the dining-room and closed the door into the kitchen.

"Poor Roxy's getting it now," he remarked when he came back. "The Merricks took her out of the poor-house years ago; and if her loyalty would let her, I guess the poor old thing could tell tales that would curdle your blood. She's the mulatto woman who was standing in here a while ago, with her apron to her eyes. The old woman is a fury; there never was anybody like her for demonstrative piety and ingenious cruelty. She made Harvey's life a hell for him when he lived at home; he was so sick ashamed of it. I never could see how he kept himself so sweet."

"He was wonderful," said Steavens slowly, "wonderful; but until to-night I have never known how wonderful."

"That is the true and eternal wonder of it, anyway; that it can come even from such a dung heap as this," the lawyer cried, with a sweeping gesture which seemed to indicate much more than the four walls within which they stood.

"I think I'll see whether I can get a little air. The room is so close I am beginning to feel rather faint," murmured Steavens, struggling with one of the windows. The sash was stuck, however, and would not yield, so he sat down dejectedly and began pulling at his collar. The lawyer came over, loosened the sash with one blow of his red fist and sent the window up a few inches. Steavens thanked him, but the nausea which had been gradually climbing into his throat for the last half hour left him with but one desire—a desperate feeling that he must get away from this place with what was left of Harvey Merrick. Oh, he comprehended well enough now the quiet bitterness of the smile that he had seen so often on his master's lips!

He remembered that once, when Merrick returned from a visit home, he brought with him a singularly feeling and suggestive bas-relief of a thin, faded old woman, sitting and sewing something pinned to her knee; while a full-lipped, full-blooded little urchin, his trousers held up by a single gallus, stood beside her, impatiently twitching her gown to call her attention to a butterfly he had caught. Steavens, impressed by the tender and delicate modelling of the thin, tired face, had asked him if it were his mother. He remembered the dull flush that had burned up in the sculptor's face.

The lawyer was sitting in a rocking-chair beside the coffin, his head thrown back and his eyes closed. Steavens looked at him earnestly, puzzled at the line of the chin, and wondering why a man should conceal a feature of such distinction under that disfiguring shock of beard. Suddenly, as though he felt the young sculptor's keen glance, he opened his eyes.

"Was he always a good deal of an oyster?" he asked abruptly. "He was terribly shy as a boy."

"Yes, he was an oyster, since you put it so," rejoined Steavens. "Although he could be very fond of people, he always gave one the impression of being detached. He disliked violent emotion; he was reflective, and rather distrustful of himself—except, of course, as regarded his work. He was sure-footed enough there. He distrusted men pretty thoroughly and women even more, yet somehow without believing ill of them. He was determined, indeed, to believe the best, but he seemed afraid to investigate."

"A burnt dog dreads the fire," said the lawyer grimly, and closed his eyes.

Steavens went on and on, reconstructing that whole miserable boyhood. All this raw, biting ugliness had been the portion of the man whose tastes were refined beyond the limits of the reasonable—whose mind was an exhaustless gallery of beautiful impressions, and so sensitive that the mere shadow of a poplar leaf flickering against a sunny wall would be etched and held there forever. Surely, if ever a man had the magic word in his finger tips, it was Merrick. Whatever he touched, he revealed its holiest secret; liberated it from enchantment and restored it to its pristine loveliness, like the Arabian prince who fought the enchantress spell for spell. Upon whatever he had come in contact with, he had left a beautiful record of the experience—a sort of ethereal signature; a scent, a sound, a colour that was his own.

Steavens understood now the real tragedy of his master's life; neither love nor wine, as many had conjectured; but a blow which had fallen earlier and cut deeper than these could have done—a shame not his, and yet so unescapably his, to hide in his heart from his very boyhood. And without—the frontier warfare; the yearning of a boy, cast ashore upon a desert of newness and ugliness and sordidness, for all that is chastened and old, and noble with traditions.

At eleven o'clock the tall, flat woman in black crêpe entered and announced that the watchers were arriving, and asked them "to step into the dining-room." As Steavens rose, the lawyer said dryly: "You go on— it'll be a good experience for you, doubtless; as for me, I'm not equal to that crowd to-night; I've had twenty years of them."

As Steavens closed the door after him he glanced back at the lawyer, sitting by the coffin in the dim light, with his chin resting on his hand.

The same misty group that had stood before the door of the express car shuffled into the dining-room. In the light of the kerosene lamp they separated and became individuals. The minister, a pale, feeble-looking man with white hair and blond chin-whiskers, took his seat beside a small side table and placed his Bible upon it. The Grand Army man sat down behind the stove and tilted his chair back comfortably against the wall, fishing his quill toothpick from his waistcoat pocket. The two bankers, Phelps and Elder, sat off in a corner behind the dinner-table, where they could finish their discussion of the new usury law and its effect on chattel security loans. The real estate agent, an old man with a smiling, hypocritical face, soon joined them. The coal and lumber dealer and the cattle shipper sat on opposite sides of the hard coal-burner, their feet on the nickel-work. Steavens took a book from his pocket and began to read. The talk around him ranged through various topics of local interest while the house was quieting down. When it was clear that the members of the family were in bed, the Grand Army man hitched his shoulders and, untangling his long legs, caught his heels on the rounds of his chair.

"S'pose there'll be a will, Phelps?" he queried in his weak falsetto.

The banker laughed disagreeably and began trimming his nails with a pearl-handled pocket-knife.

"There'll scarcely be any need for one, will there?" he queried in his turn.

The restless Grand Army man shifted his position again, getting his knees still nearer his chin. "Why, the ole man says Harve's done right well lately," he chirped.

The other banker spoke up. "I reckon he means by that Harve ain't asked him to mortgage any more farms lately, so as he could go on with his education."

"Seems like my mind don't reach back to a time when Harve wasn't bein' edycated," tittered the Grand Army man.

There was a general chuckle. The minister took out his handkerchief and blew his nose sonorously. Banker Phelps closed his knife with a snap. "It's too bad the old man's sons didn't turn out better," he remarked with reflective authority. "They never hung together. He spent money enough on Harve to stock a dozen cattle-farms and he might as well have poured it into Sand Creek. If Harve had stayed at home and helped nurse what little they had, and gone into stock on the old man's bottom farm, they might all have been well fixed. But the old man had to trust everything to tenants and was cheated right and left."

"Harve never could have handled stock none," interposed the cattleman. "He hadn't it in him to be sharp. Do you remember when he bought Sander's mules for eight-year-olds, when everybody in town knew that Sander's father-in-law give 'em to his wife for a wedding present eighteen years before, an' they was full-grown mules then."

Everyone chuckled, and the Grand Army man rubbed his knees with a spasm of childish delight.

"Harve never was much account for anything practical, and he shore was never fond of work," began the coal and lumber dealer. "I mind the last time he was home; the day he left, when the old man was out to the barn helpin' his hand hitch up to take Harve to the train, and Cal Moots was patchin' up the fence, Harve, he come out on the step and sings out, in his lady-like voice: 'Cal Moots, Cal Moots! please come cord my trunk.'"

"That's Harve for you," approved the Grand Army man gleefully. "I kin hear him howlin' yet when he was a big feller in long pants and his mother used to whale him with a rawhide in the barn for lettin' the cows git foundered in the cornfield when he was drivin' 'em home from pasture. He killed a cow of mine that a-way onct—a pure Jersey and the best milker I had, an' the ole man had to put up for her. Harve, he was watchin' the sun set acrost the marshes when the anamile got away; he argued that sunset was oncommon fine."

"Where the old man made his mistake was in sending the boy East to school," said Phelps, stroking his goatee and speaking in a deliberate, judicial tone. "There was where he got his head full of trapesing to Paris and all such folly. What Harve needed, of all people, was a course in some first-class Kansas City business college."

The letters were swimming before Steavens's eyes. Was it possible that these men did not understand, that the palm on the coffin meant nothing to them? The very name of their town would have remained forever buried in the postal guide had it not been now and again mentioned in the world in connection with Harvey Merrick's. He remembered what his master had said to him on the day of his death, after the congestion of both lungs had shut off any probability of recovery, and the sculptor had asked his pupil to send his body home. "It's not a pleasant place to be lying while the world is moving and doing and bettering," he had said with a feeble smile, "but it rather seems as though we ought to go back to the place we came from in the end. The townspeople will come in for a look at me; and after they have had their say I shan't have much to fear from the judgment of God. The wings of the Victory, in there"—with a weak gesture toward his studio—"will not shelter me."

The cattleman took up the comment. "Forty's young for a Merrick to cash in; they usually hang on pretty well. Probably he helped it along with whisky."

"His mother's people were not long lived, and Harvey never had a robust constitution," said the minister mildly. He would have liked to say more. He had been the boy's Sunday-school teacher, and had been fond of him; but he felt that he was not in a position to speak. His own sons had turned out badly, and it was not a year since one of them had made his last trip home in the express car, shot in a gambling-house in the Black Hills.

"Nevertheless, there is no disputin' that Harve frequently looked upon the wine when it was red, also variegated, and it shore made an oncommon fool of him," moralized the cattleman.

Just then the door leading into the parlour rattled loudly, and everyone started involuntarily, looking relieved when only Jim Laird came out. His red face was convulsed with anger, and the Grand Army man ducked his head when he saw the spark in his blue, blood-shot eye. They were all afraid of Jim; he was a drunkard, but he could twist the law to suit his client's needs as no other man in all western Kansas could do; and there were many who tried. The lawyer closed the door gently behind him, leaned back against it and folded his arms, cocking his head a little to one side. When he assumed this attitude in the court-room, ears were always pricked up, as it usually foretold a flood of withering sarcasm.

"I've been with you gentlemen before," he began in a dry, even tone, "when you've sat by the coffins of boys born and raised in this town; and, if I remember rightly, you were never any too well satisfied when you checked them up. What's the matter, anyhow? Why is it that reputable young men are as scarce as millionaires in Sand City? It might almost seem to a stranger that there was some way something the matter with your progressive town. Why did Ruben Sayer, the brightest young lawyer you ever turned out, after he had come home from the university as straight as a die, take to drinking and forge a check and shoot himself? Why did Bill Merrit's son die of the shakes in a saloon in Omaha? Why was Mr. Thomas's son, here, shot in a gambling-house? Why did young Adams burn his mill to beat the insurance companies and go to the pen?"

The lawyer paused and unfolded his arms, laying one clenched fist quietly on the table. "I'll tell you why. Because you drummed nothing but money and knavery into their ears from the time they wore knicker-bockers; because you carped away at them as you've been carping here to-night, holding our friends Phelps and Elder up to them for their models, as our grandfathers held up George Washington and John Adams. But the boys, worse luck, were young, and raw at the business you put them to; and how could they match coppers with such artists as Phelps and Elder? You wanted them to be successful rascals; they were only unsuccessful ones—that's all the difference. There was only one boy ever raised in this borderland between ruffianism and civilization, who didn't come to grief, and you hated Harvey Merrick more for winning out than you hated all the other boys who got under the wheels. Lord, Lord, how you did hate him! Phelps, here, is fond of saying that he could buy and sell us all out any time he's a mind to; but he knew Harve wouldn't have given a tinker's damn for his bank and all his cattle-farms put together; and a lack of appreciation, that way, goes hard with Phelps.

"Old Nimrod, here, thinks Harve drank too much; and this from such as Nimrod and me!

"Brother Elder says Harve was too free with the old man's money—fell short in filial consideration, maybe. Well, we can all remember the very tone in which brother Elder swore his own father was a liar, in the county court; and we all know that the old man came out of that partner-ship with his son as bare as a sheared lamb. But maybe I'm getting personal, and I'd better be driving ahead at what I want to say."

The lawyer paused a moment, squared his heavy shoulders, and went on: "Harvey Merrick and I went to school together, back East. We were dead in earnest, and we wanted you all to be proud of us some day. We meant to be great men. Even I, and I haven't lost my sense of humour, gentlemen, I meant to be a great man. I came back here to practise, and I found you didn't in the least want me to be a great man. You wanted me to be a shrewd lawyer—oh, yes! Our veteran here wanted me to get him an increase of pension, because he had dyspepsia; Phelps wanted a new county survey that would put the widow Wilson's little bottom farm inside his south line; Elder wanted to lend money at 5 per cent a month, and get it collected; old Stark here wanted to wheedle old women up in Vermont into investing their annuities in real estate mortgages that are not worth the paper they are written on. Oh, you needed me hard enough, and you'll go on needing me; and that's why I'm not afraid to plug the truth home to you this once.

"Well, I came back here and became the damned shyster you wanted me to be. You pretend to have some sort of respect for me; and yet you'll stand up and throw mud at Harvey Merrick, whose soul you couldn't dirty and whose hands you couldn't tie. Oh, you're a discriminating lot of Christians! There have been times when the sight of Harvey's name in some Eastern paper has made me hang my head like a whipped dog; and, again, times when I liked to think of him off there in the world, away from all this hog-wallow, doing his great work and climbing the big, clean up-grade he'd set for himself.

"And we? Now that we've fought and lied and sweated and stolen, and hated as only the disappointed strugglers in a bitter, dead little Western town know how to do, what have we got to show for it? Harvey Merrick wouldn't have given one sunset over your marshes for all you've got put together, and you know it. It's not for me to say why, in the inscrutable wisdom of God, a genius should ever have been called from this place of hatred and bitter waters; but I want this Boston man to know that the drivel he's been hearing here to-night is the only tribute any truly great man could ever have from such a lot of sick, side-tracked, burnt-dog, land-poor sharks as the here-present financiers of Sand City—upon which town may God have mercy!"

The lawyer thrust out his hand to Steavens as he passed him, caught up his overcoat in the hall, and had left the house before the Grand Army man had had time to lift his ducked head and crane his long neck about at his fellows.

Next day Jim Laird was drunk and unable to attend the funeral services. Steavens called twice at his office, but was compelled to start East without seeing him. He had a presentiment that he would hear from him again, and left his address on the lawyer's table; but if Laird found it, he never acknowledged it. The thing in him that Harvey Merrick had loved must have gone underground with Harvey Merrick's coffin; for it never spoke again, and Jim got the cold he died of driving across the Colorado mountains to defend one of Phelps's sons who had got into trouble out there by cutting government timber.

First published in *McClure's*, XXIV (January, 1905), 329–336.

The Garden Lodge

✴ ✴ ✴

When Caroline Noble's friends learned that Raymond d'Esquerré was to spend a month at her place on the Sound before he sailed to fill his engagement for the London opera season, they considered it another striking instance of the perversity of things. That the month was May, and the most mild and florescent of all the blue-and-white Mays the middle coast had known in years, but added to their sense of wrong. D'Esquerré, they learned, was ensconced in the lodge in the apple orchard, just beyond Caroline's glorious garden, and report went that at almost any hour the sound of the tenor's voice and of Caroline's crashing accompaniment could be heard floating through the open windows, out among the snowy apple boughs. The Sound, steel-blue and dotted with white sails, was splendidly seen from the windows of the lodge. The garden to the left and the orchard to the right had never been so riotous with spring, and had burst into impassioned bloom, as if to accommodate Caroline, though she was certainly the last woman to whom the witchery of Freya could be attributed; the last woman, as her friends affirmed, to at all adequately appreciate and make the most of such a setting for the great tenor.

Of course, they admitted, Caroline was musical—well, she ought to be!—but in that as in everything she was paramountly cool-headed, slow of impulse, and disgustingly practical; in that, as in everything else, she had herself so provokingly well in hand. Of course it would be she, always mistress of herself in any situation, she who would never be lifted one inch from the ground by it, and who would go on superintending her gardeners and workmen as usual, it would be she who got him. Perhaps some of them suspected that this was exactly why she did get him, and it but nettled them the more.

Caroline's coolness, her capableness, her general success, especially exasperated people because they felt that, for the most part, she had made herself what she was; that she had cold-bloodedly set about complying with the demands of life and making her position comfortable and master-ful. That was why, everyone said, she had married Howard Noble. Women who did not get through life so well as Caroline, who could not make such good terms either with fortune or their husbands, who did not find their health so unfailingly good, or hold their looks so well, or manage their children so easily, or give such distinction to all they did, were fond of stamping Caroline as a materialist and called her hard.

The impression of cold calculation, of having a definite policy, which Caroline gave, was far from a false one; but there was this to be said for her, that there were extenuating circumstances which her friends could not know.

If Caroline held determinedly to the middle course, if she was apt to regard with distrust everything which inclined toward extravagance, it was not because she was unacquainted with other standards than her own, or had never seen another side of life. She had grown up in Brooklyn, in a shabby little house under the vacillating administration of her father, a music teacher who usually neglected his duties to write orchestral com-positions for which the world seemed to have no especial need. His spirit was warped by bitter vindictiveness and puerile self-commiseration, and he spent his days in scorn of the labour that brought him bread and in pitiful devotion to the labour that brought him only disappointment, writing interminable scores which demanded of the orchestra everything under heaven except melody.

It was not a cheerful home for a girl to grow up in. The mother, who idolized her husband as the music lord of the future, was left to a life-long battle with broom and dust-pan, to never ending conciliatory overtures to the butcher and grocer, to the making of her own gowns and of Caroline's, and to the delicate task of mollifying Auguste's neglected pupils.

The son, Heinrich, a painter, Caroline's only brother, had inherited all his father's vindictive sensitiveness without his capacity for slavish application. His little studio on the third floor had been much frequented by young men as unsuccessful as himself, who met there to give them-selves over to contemptuous derision of this or that artist whose industry and stupidity had won him recognition. Heinrich, when he worked at all, did newspaper sketches at twenty-five dollars a week. He was too indolent and vacillating to set himself seriously to his art, too irascible and poig-nantly self-conscious to make a living, too much addicted to lying late in bed, to the incontinent reading of poetry and to the use of chloral, to be anything very positive except painful. At twenty-six he shot himself in a frenzy, and the whole wretched affair had effectually shattered his mother's health and brought on the decline of which she died. Caroline had been fond of him, but she felt a certain relief when he no longer wandered about the little house, commenting ironically upon its shabbiness, a Turkish cap on his head and a cigarette hanging from between his long, tremulous fingers.

After her mother's death Caroline assumed the management of that bankrupt establishment. The funeral expenses were unpaid, and Auguste's pupils had been frightened away by the shock of successive disasters and the general atmosphere of wretchedness that pervaded the house. Auguste himself was writing a symphonic poem, Icarus, dedicated to the memory of his son. Caroline was barely twenty when she was called upon to face this tangle of difficulties, but she reviewed the situation candidly. The house had served its time at the shrine of idealism; vague, distressing, unsatisfied yearnings had brought it low enough. Her mother, thirty years before, had eloped and left Germany with her music teacher, to give herself over to life-long, drudging bondage at the kitchen range. Ever since Caroline could remember, the law in the house had been a sort of mystic worship of things distant, intangible and unattainable. The family had lived in successive ebullitions of generous enthusiasm, in talk of masters and masterpieces, only to come down to the cold facts in the case; to boiled mutton and to the necessity of turning the dining-room carpet. All these emotional pyrotechnics had ended in petty jealousies, in neglected duties and in cowardly fear of the little grocer on the corner.

From her childhood she had hated it, that humiliating and uncertain existence, with its glib tongue and empty pockets, its poetic ideals and sordid realities, its indolence and poverty tricked out in paper roses. Even as a little girl, when vague dreams beset her, when she wanted to lie late in bed and commune with visions, or to leap and sing because the sooty little trees along the street were putting out their first pale leaves in the sunshine, she would clench her hands and go to help her mother sponge the spots from her father's waistcoat or press Heinrich's trousers. Her mother never permitted the slightest question concerning anything Auguste or Heinrich saw fit to do, but from the time Caroline could reason at all she could not help thinking that many things went wrong at home. She knew, for example, that her father's pupils ought not to be kept waiting half an hour while he discussed Schopenhauer with some bearded socialist over a dish of herrings and a spotted tablecloth. She knew that Heinrich ought not to give a dinner on Heine's birthday, when the laundress had not been paid for a month and when he frequently had to ask his mother for carfare. Certainly Caroline had served her apprenticeship to idealism and to all the embarrassing inconsistencies which it sometimes entails, and she decided to deny herself this diffuse, ineffectual answer to the sharp questions of life.

When she came into the control of herself and the house, she refused to proceed any further with her musical education. Her father, who had intended to make a concert pianist of her, set this down as another item in his long list of disappointments and his grievances against the world. She was young and pretty, and she had worn turned gowns and soiled gloves and improvised hats all her life. She wanted the luxury of being like other people, of being honest from her hat to her boots, of having nothing to hide, not even in the matter of stockings, and she was willing to work for it. She rented a little studio away from that house of misfortune, and began to give lessons. She managed well and was the sort of girl people liked to help. The bills were paid and Auguste went on composing, growing indignant only when she refused to insist that her pupils should study his compositions for the piano. She began to get engagements in New York to play accompaniments at song recitals. She dressed well, made herself agreeable, and gave herself a chance. She never permitted herself to look further than a step ahead, and set herself with all the strength of her will to see things as they are and meet them squarely in the broad day. There were two things she feared even more than poverty; the part of one that sets up an idol and the part of one that bows down and worships it.

When Caroline was twenty-four she married Howard Noble, then a widower of forty, who had been for ten years a power in Wall Street. Then, for the first time, she had paused to take breath. It took a substantialness as unquestionable as his; his money, his position, his energy, the big vigour of his robust person, to satisfy her that she was entirely safe. Then she relaxed a little, feeling that there was a barrier to be counted upon between her and that world of visions and quagmires and failure.

Caroline had been married for six years when Raymond d'Esquerré came to stay with them. He came chiefly because Caroline was what she was; because he, too, felt occasionally the need of getting out of Klingsor's garden, of dropping down somewhere for a time near a quiet nature, a cool head, a strong hand. The hours he had spent in the garden lodge were hours of such concentrated study as, in his fevered life, he seldom got in anywhere. She had, as he told Noble, a fine appreciation of the seriousness of work.

One evening two weeks after d'Esquerré had sailed, Caroline was in the library giving her husband an account of the work she had laid out for the gardeners. She superintended the care of the grounds herself. Her garden, indeed, had become quite a part of her; a sort of beautiful adjunct, like gowns or jewels. It was a famous spot, and Noble was very proud of it.

"What do you think, Caroline, of having the garden lodge torn down and putting a new summer-house there at the end of the arbour; a big rustic affair where you could have tea served in mid-summer?" he asked.

"The lodge?" repeated Caroline looking at him quickly. "Why, that seems almost a shame, doesn't it, after d'Esquerré has used it?"

Noble put down his book with a smile of amusement.

"Are you going to be sentimental about it? Why, I'd sacrifice the whole place to see that come to pass. But I don't believe you could do it for an hour together."

"I don't believe so, either," said his wife, smiling.

Noble took up his book again and Caroline went into the music-room to practise. She was not ready to have the lodge torn down. She had gone there for a quiet hour every day during the two weeks since d'Esquerré had left them. It was the sheerest sentiment she had ever permitted herself. She was ashamed of it, but she was childishly unwilling to let it go.

Caroline went to bed soon after her husband, but she was not able to sleep. The night was close and warm, presaging storm. The wind had fallen and the water slept, fixed and motionless as the sand. She rose and thrust her feet into slippers and putting a dressing-gown over her shoulders opened the door of her husband's room; he was sleeping soundly. She went into the hall and down the stairs; then, leaving the house through a side door, stepped into the vine covered arbour that led to the garden lodge. The scent of the June roses was heavy in the still air, and the stones that paved the path felt pleasantly cool through the thin soles of her slippers. Heat-lightning flashed continuously from the bank of clouds that had gathered over the sea, but the shore was flooded with moonlight and, beyond, the rim of the Sound lay smooth and shining. Caroline had the key of the lodge, and the door creaked as she opened it. She stepped into the long, low room radiant with the moonlight which streamed through the bow window and lay in a silvery pool along the waxed floor. Even that part of the room which lay in the shadow was vaguely illuminated; the piano, the tall candlesticks, the picture frames and white casts standing out as clearly in the half-light as did the sycamores and black poplars of the garden against the still, expectant night sky. Caroline sat down to think it all over. She had come here to do just that every day of the two weeks since d'Esquerré's departure, but, far from ever having reached a conclusion, she had succeeded only in losing her way in a maze of memories—sometimes bewilderingly confused, sometimes too acutely distinct—where there was neither path, nor clue, nor any hope of finality. She had, she realized, defeated a life-long regimen; completely confounded herself by falling unaware and incontinently into that luxury of revery which, even as a little girl, she had so determinedly denied herself; she had been developing with alarming celerity that part of one which sets up an idol and that part of one which bows down and worships it.

It was a mistake, she felt, ever to have asked d'Esquerré to come at all. She had an angry feeling that she had done it rather in self-defiance, to rid herself finally of that instinctive fear of him which had always troubled and perplexed her. She knew that she had reckoned with herself before he came; but she had been equal to so much that she had never really doubted she would be equal to this. She had come to believe, indeed, almost arrogantly in her own mallcability and endurance; she had done so much with herself that she had come to think that there was nothing which she could not do; like swimmers, overbold, who reckon upon their strength and their power to hoard it, forgetting the ever changing moods of their adversary, the sea.

And d'Esquerré was a man to reckon with. Caroline did not deceive herself now upon that score. She admitted it humbly enough, and since she had said good-bye to him she had not been free for a moment from the sense of his formidable power. It formed the undercurrent of her consciousness; whatever she might be doing or thinking, it went on, involuntarily, like her breathing; sometimes welling up until suddenly she found herself suffocating. There was a moment of this to-night, and Caroline rose and stood shuddering, looking about her in the blue duskiness of the silent room. She had not been here at night before, and the spirit of the place seemed more troubled and insistent than ever it had been in the quiet of the afternoons. Caroline brushed her hair back from her damp forehead and went over to the bow window. After raising it she sat down upon the low seat. Leaning her head against the sill, and loosening her night-gown at the throat, she half closed her eyes and looked off into the troubled night, watching the play of the sheet-lightning upon the massing clouds between the pointed tops of the poplars.

Yes, she knew, she knew well enough, of what absurdities this spell was woven; she mocked, even while she winced. His power, she knew, lay not so much in anything that he actually had—though he had so much—or in anything that he actually was; but in what he suggested, in what he seemed picturesque enough to have or be—and that was just anything that one chose to believe or to desire. His appeal was all the more persuasive and alluring that it was to the imagination alone, that it was as indefinite and impersonal as those cults of idealism which so have their way with women. What he had was that, in his mere personality, he quickened and in a measure gratified that something without which—to women—life is no better than sawdust, and to the desire for which most of their mistakes and tragedies and astonishingly poor bargains are due.

D'Esquerré had become the centre of a movement, and the Metropolitan had become the temple of a cult. When he could be induced to cross the Atlantic, the opera season in New York was successful; when he could not, the management lost money; so much everyone knew. It was understood, too, that his superb art had disproportionately little to do with his peculiar position. Women swayed the balance this way or that; the opera, the orchestra, even his own glorious art, achieved at such a cost, were but the accessories of himself; like the scenery and costumes and even the soprano, they all went to produce atmosphere, were the mere mechanics of the beautiful illusion.

Caroline understood all this; to-night was not the first time that she had put it to herself so. She had seen the same feeling in other people; watched for it in her friends, studied it in the house night after night when he sang, candidly putting herself among a thousand others.

D'Esquerré's arrival in the early winter was the signal for a feminine hegira toward New York. On the nights when he sang, women flocked to the Metropolitan from mansions and hotels, from typewriter desks, school-rooms, shops and fitting-rooms. They were of all conditions and complexions. Women of the world who accepted him knowingly, as they sometimes took champagne for its agreeable effect; sisters of charity and overworked shop-girls, who received him devoutly; withered women who had taken doctorate degrees and who worshipped furtively through prism spectacles; business women and women of affairs, the Amazons who dwelt afar from men in the stony fastnesses of apartment houses. They all entered into the same romance; dreamed, in terms as various as the hues of phantasy, the same dream; drew the same quick breath when he stepped upon the stage, and, at his exit, felt the same dull pain of shouldering the pack again.

There were the maimed, even; those who came on crutches, who were pitted by smallpox or grotesquely painted by cruel birth stains. These, too, entered with him into enchantment. Stout matrons became slender girls again; worn spinsters felt their cheeks flush with the tenderness of their lost youth. Young and old, however hideous, however fair, they yielded up their heat—whether quick or latent—sat hungering for the mystic bread wherewith he fed them at this eucharist of sentiment.

Sometimes when the house was crowded from the orchestra to the last row of the gallery, when the air was charged with this ecstasy of fancy, he himself was the victim of the burning reflection of his power. They acted upon him in turn; he felt their fervent and despairing appeal to him; it stirred him as the spring drives the sap up into an old tree; he, too, burst into bloom. For the moment he, too, believed again, desired again, he knew not what, but something.

But it was not in these exalted moments that Caroline had learned to fear him most. It was in the quiet, tired reserve, the dullness, even, that kept him company between these outbursts that she found that exhausting drain upon her sympathies which was the very pith and substance of their alliance. It was the tacit admission of disappointment under all this glamour of success—the helplessness of the enchanter to at all enchant himself—that awoke in her an illogical, womanish desire to in some way compensate, to make it up to him.

She had observed drastically to herself that it was her eighteenth year he awoke in her—those hard years she had spent in turning gowns and placating tradesmen, and which she had never had time to live. After all, she reflected, it was better to allow one's self a little youth; to dance a little at the carnival and to live these things when they are natural and lovely, not to have them coming back on one and demanding arrears when they are humiliating and impossible. She went over to-night all the catalogue of her self-deprivations; recalled how, in the light of her father's example, she had even refused to humour her innocent taste for improvising at the piano; how, when she began to teach, after her mother's death, she had struck out one little indulgence after another, reducing her life to a relentless routine, unvarying as clockwork. It seemed to her that ever since d'Esquerré first came into the house she had been haunted by an imploring little girlish ghost that followed her about, wringing its hands and entreating for an hour of life.

The storm had held off unconscionably long; the air within the lodge was stifling, and without the garden waited, breathless. Everything seemed pervaded by a poignant distress; the hush of feverish, intolerable expectation. The still earth, the heavy flowers, even the growing darkness, breathed the exhaustion of protracted waiting. Caroline felt that she ought to go; that it was wrong to stay; that the hour and the place were as treacherous as her own reflections. She rose and began to pace the floor, stepping softly, as though in fear of awakening some one, her figure, in its thin drapery, diaphanously vague and white. Still unable to shake off the obsession of the intense stillness, she sat down at the piano and began to run over the first act of the *Walküre*, the last of his rôles they had practised together; playing listlessly and absently at first, but with gradually increasing seriousness. Perhaps it was the still heat of the summer night, perhaps it was the heavy odours from the garden that came in through the open windows; but as she played there grew and grew the feeling that he was there, beside her, standing in his accustomed place. In the duet at the end of the first act she heard him clearly: "*Thou art the Spring for which I sighed in Winter's cold embraces.*" Once as he sang it, he had put his arm about her, his one hand under her heart, while with the other he took her right from the keyboard, holding her as he always held *Sieglinde* when he drew her toward the window. She had been wonderfully the mistress of herself at the time; neither repellent nor acquiescent. She remembered that she had rather exulted, then, in her self-control—which he had seemed to take for granted, though there was perhaps the whisper of a question from the hand under her heart. "*Thou art the Spring for which I sighed in Winter's cold embraces.*" Caroline lifted her hands quickly from the keyboard, and she bowed her head in them, sobbing.

The storm broke and the rain beat in, spattering her night-dress until she rose and lowered the windows. She dropped upon the couch and began fighting over again the battles of other days, while the ghosts of the slain rose as from a sowing of dragon's teeth. The shadows of things, always so scorned and flouted, bore down upon her merciless and triumphant. It was not enough; this happy, useful, well-ordered life was not enough. It did not satisfy, it was not even real. No, the other things, the shadows—they were the realities. Her father, poor Heinrich, even her mother, who had been able to sustain her poor romance and keep her little illusions amid the tasks of a scullion, were nearer happiness than she. Her sure foundation was but made ground, after all, and the people in Klingsor's garden were more fortunate, however barren the sands from which they conjured their paradise.

The lodge was still and silent; her fit of weeping over, Caroline made no sound, and within the room, as without in the garden, was the blackness of storm. Only now and then a flash of lightning showed a woman's slender figure rigid on the couch, her face buried in her hands.

Toward morning, when the occasional rumbling of thunder was heard no more and the beat of the raindrops upon the orchard leaves was steadier, she fell asleep and did not waken until the first red streaks of dawn shone through the twisted boughs of the apple trees. There was a moment between world and world, when, neither asleep nor awake, she felt her dream grow thin, melting away from her, felt the warmth under her heart growing cold. Something seemed to slip from the clinging hold of her arms, and she groaned protestingly through her parted lips, following it a little way with fluttering hands. Then her eyes opened wide and she sprang up and sat holding dizzily to the cushions of the couch, staring down at her bare, cold feet, at her labouring breast, rising and falling under her open night-dress.

The dream was gone, but the feverish reality of it still pervaded her and she held it as the vibrating string holds a tone. In the last hour the shadows had had their way with Caroline. They had shown her the nothingness of time and space, of system and discipline, of closed doors and broad waters. Shuddering, she thought of the Arabian fairy tale in which the Genii brought the princess of China to the sleeping prince of Damascus, and carried her through the air back to her palace at dawn. Caroline closed her eyes and dropped her elbows weakly upon her knees, her shoulders sinking together. The horror was that it had not come from without, but from within. The dream was no blind chance; it was the expression of something she had kept so close a prisoner that she had never seen it herself; it was the wail from the donjon deeps when the watch slept. Only as the outcome of such a night of sorcery could the thing have been loosed to straighten its limbs and measure itself with her; so heavy were the chains upon it, so many a fathom deep it was crushed down into darkness. The fact that d'Esquerré happened to be on the other side of the world meant nothing; had he been here, beside her, it could scarcely have hurt her self-respect so much. As it was, she was without even the extenuation of an outer impulse, and she could scarcely have despised herself more had she come to him here in the night three weeks ago and thrown herself down upon the stone slab at the door there.

Caroline rose unsteadily and crept guiltily from the lodge and along the path under the arbour, terrified lest the servants should be stirring, trembling with the chill air, while the wet shrubbery, brushing against her, drenched her night-dress until it clung about her limbs.

At breakfast her husband looked across the table at her with concern. "It seems to me that you are looking rather fagged, Caroline. It was a beastly night to sleep. Why don't you go up to the mountains until this hot weather is over? By the way, were you in earnest about letting the lodge stand?"

Caroline laughed quietly. "No, I find I was not very serious. I haven't sentiment enough to forego a summer-house. Will you tell Baker to come to-morrow to talk it over with me? If we are to have a house party, I should like to put him to work on it at once."

Noble gave her a glance, half humorous, half vexed. "Do you know I am rather disappointed?" he said. "I had almost hoped that, just for once, you know, you would be a little bit foolish."

"Not now that I've slept over it," replied Caroline, and they both rose from the table, laughing.

First published in *The Troll Garden* (New York: McClure, Phillips & Co., 1905), pp. 85–110.

"A Death in the Desert"

❉ ❉ ❉

Everett Hilgarde was conscious that the man in the seat across the aisle was looking at him intently. He was a large, florid man, wore a conspicuous diamond solitaire upon his third finger, and Everett judged him to be a travelling salesman of some sort. He had the air of an adaptable fellow who had been about the world and who could keep cool and clean under almost any circumstances.

The "High Line Flyer," as this train was derisively called among railroad men, was jerking along through the hot afternoon over the monotonous country between Holdrege and Cheyenne. Besides the blond man and himself the only occupants of the car were two dusty, bedraggled-looking girls who had been to the Exposition at Chicago, and who were earnestly discussing the cost of their first trip out of Colorado. The four uncomfortable passengers were covered with a sediment of fine, yellow dust which clung to their hair and eyebrows like gold powder. It blew up in clouds from the bleak, lifeless country through which they passed, until they were one colour with the sage-brush and sand-hills. The grey and yellow desert was varied only by occasional ruins of deserted towns, and the little red boxes of station-houses, where the spindling trees and sickly vines in the blue-grass yards made little green reserves fenced off in that confusing wilderness of sand.

As the slanting rays of the sun beat in stronger and stronger through the car-windows, the blond gentleman asked the ladies' permission to remove his coat, and sat in his lavender striped shirt-sleeves, with a black silk handkerchief tucked carefully about his collar. He had seemed interested in Everett since they had boarded the train at Holdrege, and kept glancing at him curiously and then looking reflectively out of the window, as though he were trying to recall something. But wherever Everett went someone was almost sure to look at him with that curious interest, and it had ceased to embarrass or annoy him. Presently the stranger, seeming satisfied with his observation, leaned back in his seat, half closed his eyes, and began softly to whistle the Spring Song from *Proserpine*, the cantata that a dozen years before had made its young composer famous in a night. Everett had heard that air on guitars in Old Mexico, on mandolins at college glees, on cottage organs in New England hamlets, and only two weeks ago he had heard it played on sleighbells at a variety theatre in Denver. There was literally no way of escaping his brother's precocity. Adriance could live on the other side of the Atlantic, where his youthful indiscretions were forgotten in his mature achievements, but his brother had never been able to outrun *Proserpine*, and here he found it again in the Colorado sand-hills. Not that Everett was exactly ashamed of *Proserpine*; only a man of genius could have written it, but it was the sort of thing that a man of genius outgrows as soon as he can.

Everett unbent a trifle and smiled at his neighbour across the aisle. Immediately the large man rose and coming over dropped into the seat facing Hilgarde, extending his card.

"Dusty ride, isn't it? I don't mind it myself; I'm used to it. Born and bred in de briar patch, like Br'er Rabbit. I've been trying to place you for a long time; I think I must have met you before."

"Thank you," said Everett, taking the card; "my name is Hilgarde. You've probably met my brother, Adriance; people often mistake me for him."

The travelling-man brought his hand down upon his knee with such vehemence that the solitaire blazed.

"So I was right after all, and if you're not Adriance Hilgarde you're his double. I thought I couldn't be mistaken. Seen him? Well, I guess! I never missed one of his recitals at the Auditorium, and he played the piano score of *Proserpine* through to us once at the Chicago Press Club. I used to be on the *Commercial* there before I began to travel for the publishing department of the concern. So you're Hilgarde's brother, and here I've run into you at the jumping-off place. Sounds like a newspaper yarn, doesn't it?"

The travelling-man laughed and offered Everett a cigar and plied him with questions on the only subject that people ever seemed to care to talk to Everett about. At length the salesman and the two girls alighted at a Colorado way station, and Everett went on to Cheyenne alone.

The train pulled into Cheyenne at nine o'clock, late by a matter of four hours or so; but no one seemed particularly concerned at its tardiness except the station agent, who grumbled at being kept in the office over

time on a summer night. When Everett alighted from the train he walked
down the platform and stopped at the track crossing, uncertain as to
what direction he should take to reach a hotel. A phaeton stood near the
crossing and a woman held the reins. She was dressed in white, and her
figure was clearly silhouetted against the cushions, though it was too dark
to see her face. Everett had scarcely noticed her, when the switch-engine
came puffing up from the opposite direction, and the headlight threw a
strong glare of light on his face. Suddenly the woman in the phaeton
uttered a low cry and dropped the reins. Everett started forward and
caught the horse's head, but the animal only lifted its ears and whisked
its tail in impatient surprise. The woman sat perfectly still, her head sunk
between her shoulders and her handkerchief pressed to her face. Another
woman came out of the depot and hurried toward the phaeton, crying,
"Katharine, dear, what is the matter?"

Everett hesitated a moment in painful embarrassment, then lifted
his hat and passed on. He was accustomed to sudden recognitions in the
most impossible places, especially by women, but this cry out of the
night had shaken him.

While Everett was breakfasting the next morning, the head waiter
leaned over his chair to murmur that there was a gentleman waiting to
see him in the parlour. Everett finished his coffee, and went in the direction
indicated, where he found his visitor restlessly pacing the floor. His whole
manner betrayed a high degree of agitation, though his physique was not
that of a man whose nerves lie near the surface. He was something below
medium height, square-shouldered and solidly built. His thick, closely cut
hair was beginning to show grey about the ears, and his bronzed face was
heavily lined. His square brown hands were locked behind him, and he
held his shoulders like a man conscious of responsibilities, yet, as he turned
to greet Everett, there was an incongruous diffidence in his address.

"Good-morning, Mr. Hilgarde," he said, extending his hand; "I
found your name on the hotel register. My name is Gaylord. I'm afraid
my sister startled you at the station last night, Mr. Hilgarde, and I've come
around to apologize."

"Ah! the young lady in the phaeton? I'm sure I didn't know whether
I had anything to do with her alarm or not. If I did, it is I who owe the
apology."

The man coloured a little under the dark brown of his face.

"Oh, it's nothing you could help, sir, I fully understand that. You
see, my sister used to be a pupil of your brother's, and it seems you favour

him; and when the switch-engine threw a light on your face it startled her."

Everett wheeled about in his chair. "Oh! *Katharine* Gaylord! Is it possible! Now it's you who have given me a turn. Why, I used to know her when I was a boy. What on earth——"

"Is she doing here?" said Gaylord, grimly filling out the pause. "You've got at the heart of the matter. You knew my sister had been in bad health for a long time?"

"No, I had never heard a word of that. The last I knew of her she was singing in London. My brother and I correspond infrequently, and seldom get beyond family matters. I am deeply sorry to hear this. There are many reasons why I am [more] concerned than I can tell you."

The lines in Charley Gaylord's brow relaxed a little.

"What I'm trying to say, Mr. Hilgarde, is that she wants to see you. I hate to ask you, but she's so set on it. We live several miles out of town, but my rig's below, and I can take you out any time you can go."

"I can go now, and it will give me real pleasure to do so," said Everett, quickly. "I'll get my hat and be with you in a moment."

When he came downstairs Everett found a cart at the door, and Charley Gaylord drew a long sigh of relief as he gathered up the reins and settled back into his own element.

"You see, I think I'd better tell you something about my sister before you see her, and I don't know just where to begin. She travelled in Europe with your brother and his wife, and sang at a lot of his concerts; but I don't know just how much you know about her."

"Very little, except that my brother always thought her the most gifted of his pupils, and that when I knew her she was very young and very beautiful and turned my head sadly for a while."

Everett saw that Gaylord's mind was quite engrossed by his grief. He was wrought up to the point where his reserve and sense of proportion had quite left him, and his trouble was the one vital thing in the world. "That's the whole thing," he went on, flecking his horses with the whip.

"She was a great woman, as you say, and she didn't come of a great family. She had to fight her own way from the first. She got to Chicago, and then to New York, and then to Europe, where she went up like lightning, and got a taste for it all; and now she's dying here like a rat in a hole, out of her own world, and she can't fall back into ours. We've grown apart, some way—miles and miles apart—and I'm afraid she's fearfully unhappy."

"It's a very tragic story that you are telling me, Gaylord," said Everett. They were well out into the country now, spinning along over the dusty plains of red grass, with the ragged blue outline of the mountains before them.

"Tragic!" cried Gaylord, starting up in his seat, "my God, man, nobody will ever know how tragic. It's a tragedy I live with and eat with and sleep with, until I've lost my grip on everything. You see she had made a good bit of money, but she spent it all going to health resorts. It's her lungs, you know. I've got money enough to send her anywhere, but the doctors all say it's no use. She hasn't the ghost of a chance. It's just getting through the days now. I had no notion she was half so bad before she came to me. She just wrote that she was all run down. Now that she's here, I think she'd be happier anywhere under the sun, but she won't leave. She says it's easier to let go of life here, and that to go East would be dying twice. There was a time when I was a brakeman with a run out of Bird City, Iowa, and she was a little thing I could carry on my shoulder, when I could get her everything on earth she wanted, and she hadn't a wish my $80 a month didn't cover; and now, when I've got a little property together, I can't buy her a night's sleep!"

Everett saw that, whatever Charley Gaylord's present status in the world might be, he had brought the brakeman's heart up the ladder with him, and the brakeman's frank avowal of sentiment. Presently Gaylord went on:

"You can understand how she has outgrown her family. We're all a pretty common sort, railroaders from away back. My father was a conductor. He died when we were kids. Maggie, my other sister, who lives with me, was a telegraph operator here while I was getting my grip on things. We had no education to speak of. I have to hire a stenographer because I can't spell straight—the Almighty couldn't teach me to spell. The things that make up life to Kate are all Greek to me, and there's scarcely a point where we touch any more, except in our recollections of the old times when we were all young and happy together, and Kate sang in a church choir in Bird City. But I believe, Mr. Hilgarde, that if she can see just one person like you, who knows about the things and people she's interested in, it will give her about the only comfort she can have now."

The reins slackened in Charley Gaylord's hand as they drew up before a showily painted house with many gables and a round tower.

"Here we are," he said, turning to Everett, "and I guess we understand each other."

They were met at the door by a thin, colourless woman, whom Gaylord introduced as "My sister, Maggie." She asked her brother to show Mr. Hilgarde into the music-room, where Katharine wished to see him alone.

When Everett entered the music-room he gave a little start of surprise, feeling that he had stepped from the glaring Wyoming sunlight into some New York studio that he had always known. He wondered which it was of those countless studios, high up under the roofs, over banks and shops and wholesale houses, that this room resembled, and he looked incredulously out of the window at the grey plain that ended in the great upheaval of the Rockies.

The haunting air of familiarity about the room perplexed him. Was it a copy of some particular studio he knew, or was it merely the studio atmosphere that seemed so individual and poignantly reminiscent here in Wyoming? He sat down in a reading-chair and looked keenly about him. Suddenly his eye fell upon a large photograph of his brother above the piano. Then it all became clear to him: this was veritably his brother's room. If it were not an exact copy of one of the many studios that Adriance had fitted up in various parts of the world, wearying of them and leaving almost before the renovator's varnish had dried, it was at least in the same tone. In every detail Adriance's taste was so manifest that the room seemed to exhale his personality.

Among the photographs on the wall there was one of Katharine Gaylord, taken in the days when Everett had known her, and when the flash of her eye or the flutter of her skirt was enough to set his boyish heart in a tumult. Even now, he stood before the portrait with a certain degree of embarrassment. It was the face of a woman already old in her first youth, thoroughly sophisticated and a trifle hard, and it told of what her brother had called her fight. The *camaraderie* of her frank, confident eyes was qualified by the deep lines about her mouth and the curve of the lips, which was both sad and cynical. Certainly she had more good-will than confidence toward the world, and the bravado of her smile could not conceal the shadow of an unrest that was almost discontent. The chief charm of the woman, as Everett had known her, lay in her superb figure and in her eyes, which possessed a warm, life-giving quality like the sunlight; eyes which glowed with a sort of perpetual *salutat* to the world. Her head, Everett remembered as peculiarly well shaped and proudly poised. There had been always a little of the imperatrix about her, and her pose in the photograph revived all his old impressions of her unattachedness, of how absolutely and valiantly she stood alone.

Everett was still standing before the picture, his hands behind him and his head inclined, when he heard the door open. A very tall woman advanced toward him, holding out her hand. As she started to speak she coughed slightly, then, laughing, said, in a low, rich voice, a trifle husky: "You see I make the traditional Camille entrance—with the cough. How good of you to come, Mr. Hilgarde."

Everett was acutely conscious that while addressing him she was not looking at him at all, and, as he assured her of his pleasure in coming, he was glad to have an opportunity to collect himself. He had not reckoned upon the ravages of a long illness. The long, loose folds of her white gown had been especially designed to conceal the sharp outlines of her emaciated body, but the stamp of her disease was there; simple and ugly and obtrusive, a pitiless fact that could not be disguised or evaded. The splendid shoulders were stooped, there was a swaying unevenness in her gait, her arms seemed disproportionately long, and her hands were transparently white, and cold to the touch. The changes in her face were less obvious; the proud carriage of the head, the warm, clear eyes, even the delicate flush of colour in her cheeks, all defiantly remained, though they were all in a lower key—older, sadder, softer.

She sat down upon the divan and began nervously to arrange the pillows. "I know I'm not an inspiring object to look upon, but you must be quite frank and sensible about that and get used to it at once, for we've no time to lose. And if I'm a trifle irritable you won't mind?—for I'm more than usually nervous."

"Don't bother with me this morning, if you are tired," urged Everett. "I can come quite as well to-morrow."

"Gracious, no!" she protested, with a flash of that quick, keen humour that he remembered as a part of her. "It's solitude that I'm tired to death of—solitude and the wrong kind of people. You see, the minister, not content with reading the prayers for the sick, called on me this morning. He happened to be riding by on his bicycle and felt it his duty to stop. Of course, he disapproves of my profession, and I think he takes it for granted that I have a dark past. The funniest feature of his conversation is that he is always excusing my own vocation to me—condoning it, you know—and trying to patch up my peace with my conscience by suggesting possible noble uses for what he kindly calls my talent."

Everett laughed. "Oh! I'm afraid I'm not the person to call after such a serious gentleman—I can't sustain the situation. At my best I don't reach higher than low comedy. Have you decided to which one of the noble uses you will devote yourself?"

Katharine lifted her hands in a gesture of renunciation and exclaimed: "I'm not equal to any of them, not even the least noble. I didn't study that method."

She laughed and went on nervously: "The parson's not so bad. His English never offends me, and he has read Gibbon's 'Decline and Fall,' all five volumes, and that's something. Then, he has been to New York, and that's a great deal. But how we are losing time! Do tell me about New York; Charley says you're just on from there. How does it look and taste and smell just now? I think a whiff of the Jersey ferry would be as flagons of cod-liver oil to me. Who conspicuously walks the Rialto now, and what does he or she wear? Are the trees still green in Madison Square, or have they grown brown and dusty? Does the chaste Diana on the Garden Theatre still keep her vestal vows through all the exasperating changes of weather? Who has your brother's old studio now, and what misguided aspirants practise their scales in the rookeries about Carnegie Hall? What do people go to see at the theatres, and what do they eat and drink there in the world nowadays? You see, I'm homesick for it all, from the Battery to Riverside. Oh, let me die in Harlem!" she was interrupted by a violent attack of coughing, and Everett, embarrassed by her discomfort, plunged into gossip about the professional people he had met in town during the summer, and the musical outlook for the winter. He was diagraming with his pencil, on the back of an old envelope he found in his pocket, some new mechanical device to be used at the Metropolitan in the production of the *Rheingold*, when he became conscious that she was looking at him intently, and that he was talking to the four walls.

Katharine was lying back among the pillows, watching him through half-closed eyes, as a painter looks at a picture. He finished his explanation vaguely enough and put the envelope back in his pocket. As he did so, she said, quietly: "How wonderfully like Adriance you are!" and he felt as though a crisis of some sort had been met and tided over.

He laughed, looking up at her with a touch of pride in his eyes that made them seem quite boyish. "Yes, isn't it absurd? It's almost as awkward as looking like Napoleon—But, after all, there are some advantages. It has made some of his friends like me, and I hope it will make you."

Katharine smiled and gave him a quick, meaning glance from under her lashes. "Oh, it did that long ago. What a haughty, reserved youth you were then, and how you used to stare at people, and then blush and look cross if they paid you back in your own coin. Do you remember that night when you took me home from a rehearsal, and scarcely spoke a word to me?"

"It was the silence of admiration," protested Everett, "very crude and boyish, but very sincere and not a little painful. Perhaps you suspected something of the sort? I remember you saw fit to be very grown up and worldly."

"I believe I suspected a pose; the one that college boys usually affect with singers—'an earthen vessel in love with a star,' you know. But it rather surprised me in you, for you must have seen a good deal of your brother's pupils. Or had you an omnivorous capacity, and elasticity that always met the occasion?"

"Don't ask a man to confess the follies of his youth," said Everett, smiling a little sadly; "I am sensitive about some of them even now. But I was not so sophisticated as you imagined. I saw my brother's pupils come and go, but that was about all. Sometimes I was called on to play accompaniments, or to fill out a vacancy at a rehearsal, or to order a carriage for an infuriated soprano who had thrown up her part. But they never spent any time on me, unless it was to notice the resemblance you speak of."

"Yes," observed Katharine, thoughtfully, "I noticed it then, too; but it has grown as you have grown older. That is rather strange, when you have lived such different lives. It's not merely an ordinary family likeness of feature, you know, but a sort of interchangeable individuality; the suggestion of the other man's personality in your face—like an air transposed to another key. But I'm not attempting to define it; it's beyond me; something altogether unusual and a trifle—well, uncanny," she finished, laughing.

"I remember," Everett said, seriously, twirling the pencil between his fingers and looking, as he sat with his head thrown back, out under the red window-blind which was raised just a little, and as it swung back and forth in the wind revealed the glaring panorama of the desert—a blinding stretch of yellow, flat as the sea in dead calm, splotched here and there with deep purple shadows; and, beyond, the ragged blue outline of the mountains and the peaks of snow, white as the white clouds—"I remember, when I was a little fellow I used to be very sensitive about it. I don't think it exactly displeased me, or that I would have had it otherwise if I could, but it seemed to me like a birthmark, or something not to be lightly spoken of. People were naturally always fonder of Ad than of me, and I used to feel the chill of reflected light pretty often. It came into even my relations with my mother. Ad went abroad to study when he was absurdly young, you know, and mother was all broken up over it. She did her whole duty by each of us, but it was sort of generally understood among us that she'd have made burnt-offerings of us all for Ad any day. I was a little fellow then, and when she sat alone on the porch in the summer dusk, she used sometimes to call me to her and turn my face up in the light that streamed out through the shutters and kiss me, and then I always knew she was thinking of Adriance."

"Poor little chap," said Katharine, and her tone was a trifle huskier than usual. "How fond people have always been of Adriance! Now tell me the latest news of him. I haven't heard, except through the press, for a year or more. He was in Algiers then, in the valley of the Chelif, riding horseback night and day in an Arabian costume, and in his usual enthusiastic fashion he had quite made up his mind to adopt the Mahometan faith and become as nearly an Arab as possible. How many countries and faiths has he adopted, I wonder? Probably he was playing Arab to himself all the time. I remember he was a sixteenth-century duke in Florence once for weeks together."

"Oh, that's Adriance," chuckled Everett. "He is himself barely long enough to write checks and be measured for his clothes. I didn't hear from him while he was an Arab; I missed that."

"He was writing an Algerian *suite* for the piano then; it must be in the publisher's hands by this time. I have been too ill to answer his letter, and have lost touch with him."

Everett drew a letter from his pocket. "This came about a month ago. It's chiefly about his new opera, which is to be brought out in London next winter. Read it at your leisure."

"I think I shall keep it as a hostage, so that I may be sure you will come again. Now I want you to play for me. Whatever you like; but if there is anything new in the world, in mercy lét me hear it. For nine months I have heard nothing but 'The Baggage Coach Ahead' and 'She is My Baby's Mother.'"

He sat down at the piano, and Katharine sat near him, absorbed in his remarkable physical likeness to his brother, and trying to discover in just what it consisted. She told herself that it was very much as though a sculptor's finished work had been rudely copied in wood. He was of a larger build than Adriance, and his shoulders were broad and heavy, while those of his brother were slender and rather girlish. His face was of the same oval mould, but it was grey, and darkened about the mouth by continual shaving. His eyes were of the same inconstant April colour, but they were reflective and rather dull; while Adriance's were always points of high light, and always meaning another thing than the thing they meant yesterday. But it was hard to see why this earnest man should so continually suggest that lyric, youthful face that was as gay as his was grave. For Adriance, though he was ten years the elder, and though his hair was streaked with silver, had the face of a boy of twenty, so mobile that it told his thoughts before he could put them into words. A contralto, famous for the extravagance of her vocal methods and of her affections had once said of him that the shepherd-boys who sang in the Vale of Tempe must certainly have looked like young Hilgarde; and the comparison had been appropriated by a hundred shyer women who preferred to quote.

As Everett sat smoking on the veranda of the Inter-Ocean House that night, he was a victim to random recollections. His infatuation for Katharine Gaylord, visionary as it was, had been the most serious of his boyish love-affairs, and had long disturbed his bachelor dreams. He was painfully timid in everything relating to the emotions, and his hurt had withdrawn him from the society of women. The fact that it was all so done and dead and far behind him, and that the woman had lived her life out since then, gave him an oppressive sense of age and loss. He bethought himself of something he had read about "sitting by the hearth and remembering the faces of women without desire," and felt himself an octogenarian.

He remembered how bitter and morose he had grown during his stay at his brother's studio when Katharine Gaylord was working there, and how he had wounded Adriance on the night of his last concert in New York. He had sat there in the box while his brother and Katharine were called back again and again after the last number, watching the roses go up over the footlights until they were stacked half as high as the piano, brooding, in his sullen boy's heart, upon the pride those two felt in each other's work—spurring each other to their best and beautifully contending in song. The footlights had seemed a hard, glittering line drawn sharply between their life and his; a circle of flame set about those splendid children of genius. He walked back to his hotel alone, and sat in his

window staring out on Madison Square until long after midnight, re-
solving to beat no more at doors that he could never enter, and realizing
more keenly than ever before how far this glorious world of beautiful
creations lay from the paths of men like himself. He told himself that he
had in common with this woman only the baser uses of life.

Everett's week in Cheyenne stretched to three, and he saw no
prospect of release except through the thing he dreaded. The bright,
windy days of the Wyoming autumn passed swiftly. Letters and telegrams
came urging him to hasten his trip to the coast, but he resolutely post-
poned his business engagements. The mornings he spent on one of Charley
Gaylord's ponies, or fishing in the mountains, and in the evenings he sat
in his room writing letters or reading. In the afternoon he was usually at
his post of duty. Destiny, he reflected, seems to have very positive notions
about the sort of parts we are fitted to play. The scene changes and the
compensation varies, but in the end we usually find that we have played
the same class of business from first to last. Everett had been a stop-gap all
his life. He remembered going through a looking-glass labyrinth when he
was a boy, and trying gallery after gallery, only at every turn to bump his
nose against his own face—which, indeed, was not his own, but his
brother's. No matter what his mission, east or west, by land or sea, he
was sure to find himself employed in his brother's business, one of the
tributary lives which helped to swell the shining current of Adriance
Hilgarde's. It was not the first time that his duty had been to comfort, as
best he could, one of the broken things his brother's imperious speed had
cast aside and forgotten. He made no attempt to analyse the situation or to
state it in exact terms; but he felt Katharine Gaylord's need for him, and
he accepted it as a commission from his brother to help this woman to die.
Day by day he felt her demands on him grow more imperious, her need
for him grow more acute and positive; and day by day he felt that in his
peculiar relation to her, his own individuality played a smaller and smaller
part. His power to minister to her comfort, he saw, lay solely in his link
with his brother's life. He understood all that his physical resemblance
meant to her. He knew that she sat by him always watching for some
common trick of gesture, some familiar play of expression, some illusion
of light and shadow, in which he should seem wholly Adriance. He
knew that she lived upon this and that her disease fed upon it; that it sent
shudders of remembrance through her and that in the exhaustion which
followed this turmoil of her dying senses, she slept deep and sweet, and

dreamed of youth and art and days in a certain old Florentine garden, and not of bitterness and death.

The question which most perplexed him was, "How much shall I know? How much does she wish me to know?" A few days after his first meeting with Katharine Gaylord, he had cabled his brother to write her. He had merely said that she was mortally ill; he could depend on Adriance to say the right thing—that was a part of his gift. Adriance always said not only the right thing, but the opportune, graceful, exquisite thing. His phrases took the colour of the moment and the then present condition, so that they never savoured of perfunctory compliment or frequent usage. He always caught the lyric essence of the moment, the poetic suggestion of every situation. Moreover, he usually did the right thing, the opportune, graceful, exquisite thing—except, when he did very cruel things—bent upon making people happy when their existence touched his, just as he insisted that his material environment should be beautiful; lavishing upon those near him all the warmth and radiance of his rich nature, all the homage of the poet and troubadour, and, when they were no longer near, forgetting—for that also was a part of Adriance's gift.

Three weeks after Everett had sent his cable, when he made his daily call at the gaily painted ranch-house, he found Katharine laughing like a school-girl. "Have you ever thought," she said, as he entered the music-room, "how much these séances of ours are like Heine's 'Florentine Nights,' except that I don't give you an opportunity to monopolize the conversation as Heine did?" She held his hand longer than usual as she greeted him, and looked searchingly up into his face. "You are the kindest man living, the kindest," she added, softly.

Everett's grey face coloured faintly as he drew his hand away, for he felt that this time she was looking at him and not at a whimsical caricature of his brother. "Why, what have I done now?" he asked, lamely. "I can't remember having sent you any stale candy or champagne since yesterday."

She drew a letter with a foreign postmark from between the leaves of a book and held it out, smiling. "You got him to write it. Don't say you didn't, for it came direct, you see, and the last address I gave him was a place in Florida. This deed shall be remembered of you when I am with the just in Paradise. But one thing you did not ask him to do, for you didn't know about it. He has sent me his latest work, the new sonata, the most ambitious thing he has ever done, and you are to play it for me directly, though it looks horribly intricate. But first for the letter; I think you would better read it aloud to me."

Everett sat down in a low chair facing the window-seat in which she reclined with a barricade of pillows behind her. He opened the letter, his lashes half-veiling his kind eyes, and saw to his satisfaction that it was a long one; wonderfully tactful and tender, even for Adriance, who was tender with his valet and his stable-boy, with his old gondolier and the beggar-women who prayed to the saints for him.

The letter was from Granada, written in the Alhambra, as he sat by the fountain of the Patio di Lindaraxa. The air was heavy with the warm fragrance of the South and full of the sound of splashing, running water, as it had been in a certain old garden in Florence, long ago. The sky was one great turquoise, heated until it glowed. The wonderful Moorish arches threw graceful blue shadows all about him. He had sketched an outline of them on the margin of his notepaper. The subtleties of Arabic decoration had cast an unholy spell over him, and the brutal exaggerations of Gothic art were a bad dream, easily forgotten. The Alhambra itself had, from the first, seemed perfectly familiar to him, and he knew that he must have trod that court, sleek and brown and obsequious, centuries before Ferdinand rode into Andalusia. The letter was full of confidences about his work, and delicate allusions to their old happy days of study and comradeship, and of her own work, still so warmly remembered and appreciatively discussed everywhere he went.

As Everett folded the letter he felt that Adriance had divined the thing needed and had risen to it in his own wonderful way. The letter was consistently egotistical, and seemed to him even a trifle patronizing, yet it was just what she had wanted. A strong realization of his brother's charm and intensity and power came over him; he felt the breath of that whirlwind of flame in which Adriance passed, consuming all in his path, and himself even more resolutely than he consumed others. Then he looked down at this white, burnt-out brand that lay before him. "Like him, isn't it?" she said, quietly.

"I think I can scarcely answer his letter, but when you see him next you can do that for me. I want you to tell him many things for me, yet they can all be summed up in this: I want him to grow wholly into his best and greatest self, even at the cost of the dear boyishness that is half his charm to you and me. Do you understand me?"

"I know perfectly well what you mean," answered Everett, thoughtfully. "I have often felt so about him myself. And yet it's difficult to prescribe for those fellows; so little makes, so little mars."

Katharine raised herself upon her elbow, and her face flushed with feverish earnestness. "Ah, but it is the waste of himself that I mean; his lashing himself out on stupid and uncomprehending people until they take him at their own estimate. He can kindle marble, strike fire from putty, but is it worth what it costs him?"

"Come, come," expostulated Everett, alarmed at her excitement. "Where is the new sonata? Let him speak for himself."

He sat down at the piano and began playing the first movement which was indeed the voice of Adriance, his proper speech. The sonata was the most ambitious work he had done up to that time, and marked the transition from his purely lyric vein to a deeper and nobler style. Everett played intelligently and with that sympathetic comprehension which seems peculiar to a certain lovable class of men who never accomplish anything in particular. When he had finished he turned to Katharine.

"How he has grown!" she cried. "What the three last years have done for him! He used to write only the tragedies of passion; but this is the tragedy of the soul, the shadow coexistent with the soul. This is the tragedy of effort and failure, the thing Keats called hell. This is my tragedy, as I lie here spent by the race-course, listening to the feet of the runners as they pass me—ah, God! the swift feet of the runners!"

She turned her face away and covered it with her straining hands. Everett crossed over to her quickly and knelt beside her. In all the days he had known her she had never before, beyond an occasional ironical jest, given voice to the bitterness of her own defeat. Her courage had become a point of pride with him, and to see it going sickened him.

"Don't do it," he gasped. "I can't stand it, I really can't, I feel it too much. We mustn't speak of that; it's too tragic and too vast."

When she turned her face back to him there was a ghost of the old, brave, cynical smile on it, more bitter than the tears she could not shed. "No, I won't be so ungenerous; I will save that for the watches of the night when I have no better company. Now you may mix me another drink of some sort. Formerly, when it was not *if* I should ever sing Brunhilda, but quite simply when I *should* sing Brunhilda, I was always starving myself, and thinking what I might drink and what I might not. But broken music-boxes may drink whatsoever they list, and no one cares whether they lose their figure. Run over that theme at the beginning again. That, at least, is not new. It was running in his head when we were in Venice years ago, and he used to drum it on his glass at the dinner-table. He had just begun to work it out when the late autumn came on, and the paleness of the Adriatic oppressed him, and he decided to go to

Florence for the winter, and lost touch with the theme during his illness. Do you remember those frightful days? All the people who have loved him are not strong enough to save him from himself! When I got word from Florence that he had been ill, I was in Nice filling a concert engagement. His wife was hurrying to him from Paris, but I reached him first. I arrived at dusk, in a terrific storm. They had taken an old palace there for the winter, and I found him in the library—a long, dark room full of old Latin books and heavy furniture and bronzes. He was sitting by a wood fire at one end of the room, looking, oh, so worn and pale!—as he always does when he is ill, you know. Ah, it is so good that you *do* know! Even his red smoking-jacket lent no colour to his face. His first words were not to tell me how ill he had been, but that that morning he had been well enough to put the last strokes to the score of his '*Souvenirs d'Automne*,' and he was, as I most like to remember him; so calm and happy and tired; not gay, as he usually is, but just contented and tired with that heavenly tiredness that comes after a good work done at last. Outside, the rain poured down in torrents, and the wind moaned for the pain of all the world and sobbed in the branches of the shivering olives and about the walls of that desolated old palace. How that night comes back to me! There were no lights in the room, only the wood fire which glowed upon the hard features of the bronze Dante like the reflection of purgatorial flames, and threw long black shadows about us; beyond us it scarcely penetrated the gloom at all. Adriance sat staring at the fire with the weariness of all his life in his eyes, and of all the other lives that must aspire and suffer to make up one such life as his. Somehow the wind with all its world-pain had got into the room, and the cold rain was in our eyes, and the wave came up in both of us at once—that awful vague, universal pain, that cold fear of life and death and God and hope—and we were like two clinging together on a spar in mid-ocean after the shipwreck of everything. Then we heard the front door open with a great gust of wind that shook even the walls, and the servants came running with lights, announcing that Madame had returned, '*and in the book we read no more that night.*'"

She gave the old line with a certain bitter humour, and with the hard, bright smile in which of old she had wrapped her weakness as in a glittering garment. That ironical smile, worn like a mask through so many years, had gradually changed even the lines of her face completely, and when she looked in the mirror she saw not herself, but the scathing critic, the amused observer and satirist of herself. Everett dropped his head upon his hand and sat looking at the rug. "How much you have cared!" he said.

"Ah, yes, I cared," she replied, closing her eyes with a long-drawn sigh of relief; and lying perfectly still, she went on: "You can't imagine what a comfort it is to have you know how I cared, what a relief it is to be able to tell it to some one. I used to want to shriek it out to the world in the long nights when I could not sleep. It seemed to me that I could not die with it. It demanded some sort of expression. And now that you know, you would scarcely believe how much less sharp the anguish of it is."

Everett continued to look helplessly at the floor. "I was not sure how much you wanted me to know," he said.

"Oh, I intended you should know from the first time I looked into your face, when you came that day with Charley. I flatter myself that I have been able to conceal it when I chose, though I suppose women always think that. The more observing ones may have seen, but discerning people are usually discreet and often kind, for we usually bleed a little before we begin to discern. But I wanted you to know; you are so like him that it is almost like telling him himself. At least, I feel now that he will know some day, and then I will be quite sacred from his compassion, for we none of us dare pity the dead. Since it was what my life has chiefly meant, I should like him to know. On the whole, I am not ashamed of it. I have fought a good fight."

"And has he never known at all?" asked Everett, in a thick voice.

"Oh! never at all in the way that you mean. Of course, he is accustomed to looking into the eyes of women and finding love there; when he doesn't find it there he thinks he must have been guilty of some discourtesy and is miserable about it. He has a genuine fondness for every one who is not stupid or gloomy, or old or preternaturally ugly. Granted youth and cheerfulness, and a moderate amount of wit and some tact, and Adriance will always be glad to see you coming around the corner. I shared with the rest; shared the smiles and the gallantries and the droll little sermons. It was quite like a Sunday-school picnic; we wore our best clothes and a smile and took our turns. It was his kindness that was hardest. I have pretty well used my life up at standing punishment."

"Don't; you'll make me hate him," groaned Everett.

Katharine laughed and began to play nervously with her fan. "It wasn't in the slightest degree his fault; that is the most grotesque part of it. Why, it had really begun before I ever met him. I fought my way to him, and I drank my doom greedily enough."

Everett rose and stood hesitating. "I think I must go. You ought to be quiet, and I don't think I can hear any more just now."

She put out her hand and took his playfully. "You've put in three weeks at this sort of thing, haven't you? Well, it may never be to your glory in this world, perhaps, but it's been the mercy of heaven to me, and it ought to square accounts for a much worse life than yours will ever be."

Everett knelt beside her, saying, brokenly: "I stayed because I wanted to be with you, that's all. I have never cared about other women since I met you in New York when I was a lad. You are a part of my destiny, and I could not leave you if I would."

She put her hands on his shoulders and shook her head. "No, no; don't tell me that. I have seen enough of tragedy, God knows: don't show me any more just as the curtain is going down. No, no, it was only a boy's fancy, and your divine pity and my utter pitiableness have recalled it for a moment. One does not love the dying, dear friend. If some fancy of that sort had been left over from boyhood, this would rid you of it, and that were well. Now go, and you will come again to-morrow, as long as there are to-morrows, will you not?" She took his hand with a smile that lifted the mask from her soul, that was both courage and despair, and full of infinite loyalty and tenderness, as she said softly:

"*For ever and for ever, farewell, Cassius;*
If we do meet again, why, we shall smile;
If not, why then, this parting was well made."

The courage in her eyes was like the clear light of a star to him as he went out.

On the night of Adriance Hilgarde's opening concert in Paris, Everett sat by the bed in the ranch-house in Wyoming, watching over the last battle that we have with the flesh before we are done with it and free of it forever. At times it seemed that the serene soul of her must have left already and found some refuge from the storm, and only the tenacious animal life were left to do battle with death. She laboured under a delusion at once pitiful and merciful, thinking that she was in the Pullman on her way to New York, going back to her life and her work. When she aroused from her stupor, it was only to ask the porter to waken her half an hour out of Jersey City, or to remonstrate with him about the delays and the roughness of the road. At midnight Everett and the nurse were left alone with her. Poor Charley Gaylord had lain down on a couch outside the door. Everett sat looking at the sputtering night-lamp until it made his eyes ache. His head dropped forward on the foot of the bed, and he sank into a heavy, distressful slumber. He was dreaming of Adriance's concert in Paris, and of Adriance, the troubadour, smiling and debonair, with his boyish face and the touch of silver grey in his hair. He heard the applause and he saw the roses going up over the footlights until they were stacked half as high as the piano, and the petals fell and scattered, making crimson splotches on the floor. Down this crimson pathway came Adriance with his youthful step, leading his prima donna by the hand; a dark woman this time, with Spanish eyes.

The nurse touched him on the shoulder, he started and awoke. She screened the lamp with her hand. Everett saw that Katharine was awake and conscious, and struggling a little. He lifted her gently on his arm and began to fan her. She laid her hands lightly on his hair and looked into his face with eyes that seemed never to have wept or doubted. "Ah, dear Adriance, dear, dear," she whispered.

Everett went to call her brother, but when they came back the madness of art was over for Katharine.

Two days later Everett was pacing the station siding, waiting for the west-bound train. Charley Gaylord walked beside him, but the two men had nothing to say to each other. Everett's bags were piled on the truck, and his step was hurried and his eyes were full of impatience, as he gazed again and again up the track, watching for the train. Gaylord's impatience was not less than his own; these two, who had grown so close, had now become painful and impossible to each other, and longed for the wrench of farewell.

As the train pulled in, Everett wrung Gaylord's hand among the crowd of alighting passengers. The people of a German opera company, *en route* for the coast, rushed by them in frantic haste to snatch their breakfast during the stop. Everett heard an exclamation in a broad German dialect, and a massive woman whose figure persistently escaped from her stays in the most improbable places rushed up to him, her blond hair disordered by the wind, and glowing with joyful surprise she caught his coat-sleeve with her tightly gloved hands.

"*Herr Gott*, Adriance, *lieber Freund*," she cried, emotionally.

Everett quickly withdrew his arm, and lifted his hat, blushing. "Pardon me, madame, but I see that you have mistaken me for Adriance Hilgarde. I am his brother," he said, quietly, and turning from the crestfallen singer he hurried into the car.

First published in *Scribner's*, XXXIII (January, 1903), 109–121.

The Marriage of Phaedra

✳ ✳ ✳

The sequence of events was such that MacMaster did not make his pilgrimage to Hugh Treffinger's studio until three years after that painter's death. MacMaster was himself a painter, an American of the Gallicized type, who spent his winters in New York, his summers in Paris, and no inconsiderable amount of time on the broad waters between. He had often contemplated stopping in London on one of his return trips in the late autumn, but he had always deferred leaving Paris until the prick of necessity drove him home by the quickest and shortest route.

Treffinger was a comparatively young man at the time of his death, and there had seemed no occasion for haste until haste was of no avail. Then, possibly, though there had been some correspondence between them, MacMaster felt certain qualms about meeting in the flesh a man who in the flesh was so diversely reported. His intercourse with Treffinger's work had been so deep and satisfying, so apart from other appreciations, that he rather dreaded a critical juncture of any sort. He had always felt himself singularly inadept in personal relations, and in this case he had avoided the issue until it was no longer to be feared or hoped for. There still remained, however, Treffinger's great unfinished picture, the *Marriage of Phaedra*, which had never left his studio, and of which MacMaster's friends had now and again brought report that it was the painter's most characteristic production.

The young man arrived in London in the evening, and the next morning went out to Kensington to find Treffinger's studio. It lay in one of the perplexing by-streets off Holland Road, and the number he found on a door set in a high garden wall, the top of which was covered with broken green glass and over which a budding lilac-bush nodded. Treffinger's plate was still there, and a card requesting visitors to ring for the attendant. In response to MacMaster's ring, the door was opened by a cleanly built little man, clad in a shooting jacket and trousers that had been made for an ampler figure. He had a fresh complexion, eyes of that

common uncertain shade of grey, and was closely shaven except for the
incipient mutton-chops on his ruddy cheeks. He bore himself in a manner
strikingly capable, and there was a sort of trimness and alertness about him,
despite the too-generous shoulders of his coat. In one hand he held a
bulldog pipe, and in the other a copy of *Sporting Life*. While MacMaster
was explaining the purpose of his call, he noticed that the man surveyed
him critically, though not impertinently. He was admitted into a little
tank of a lodge made of white-washed stone, the back door and windows
opening upon a garden. A visitor's book and a pile of catalogues lay on a
deal table, together with a bottle of ink and some rusty pens. The wall
was ornamented with photographs and coloured prints of racing
favourites.

"The studio is h'only open to the public on Saturdays and Sundays,"
explained the man—he referred to himself as "Jymes"—"but of course
we make exceptions in the case of pynters. Lydy Elling Treffinger 'erself
is on the Continent, but Sir 'Ugh's orders was that pynters was to 'ave the
run of the place." He selected a key from his pocket and threw open the
door into the studio which, like the lodge, was built against the wall of
the garden.

MacMaster entered a long, narrow room, built of smoothed planks,
painted a light green; cold and damp even on that fine May morning.
The room was utterly bare of furniture—unless a step-ladder, a model
throne, and a rack laden with large leather portfolios could be accounted
such—and was windowless, without other openings than the door and
the skylight, under which hung the unfinished picture itself. MacMaster
had never seen so many of Treffinger's paintings together. He knew the
painter had married a woman with money and had been able to keep such
of his pictures as he wished. These, with all of his replicas and studies, he
had left as a sort of common legacy to the younger men of the school
he had originated.

As soon as he was left alone, MacMaster sat down on the edge of the
model throne before the unfinished picture. Here indeed was what he
had come for; it rather paralysed his receptivity for the moment, but
gradually the thing found its way to him.

At one o'clock he was standing before the collection of studies done
for *Boccaccio's Garden* when he heard a voice at his elbow.

"Pardon, sir, but I was just about to lock up and go to lunch. Are
you lookin' for the figure study of Boccaccio 'imself?" James queried
respectfully. "Lydy Elling Treffinger give it to Mr. Rossiter to take down
to Oxford for some lectures he's been a-giving there."

"Did he never paint out his studies, then?" asked MacMaster with perplexity. "Here are two completed ones for this picture. Why did he keep them?"

"I don't know as I could say as to that, sir," replied James, smiling indulgently, "but that was 'is way. That is to say, 'e pynted out very frequent, but 'e always made two studies to stand; one in water colours and one in oils, before 'e went at the final picture,—to say nothink of all the pose studies 'e made in pencil before he begun on the composition proper at all. He was that particular. You see 'e wasn't so keen for the final effect as for the proper pyntin' of 'is pictures. 'E used to say they ought to be well made, the same as any other h'article of trade. I can lay my 'and on the pose studies for you, sir." He rummaged in one of the portfolios and produced half a dozen drawings. "These three," he continued, "was discarded: these two was the pose he finally accepted; this one without alteration, as it were."

"That's in Paris, as I remember," James continued reflectively. "It went with the *Saint Cecilia* into the Baron H—'s collection. Could you tell me, sir, 'as 'e it still? I don't like to lose account of them, but some 'as changed 'ands since Sir 'Ugh's death."

"H—'s collection is still intact, I believe," replied MacMaster. "You were with Treffinger long?"

"From my boyhood, sir," replied James with gravity. "I was a stable boy when 'e took me."

"You were his man, then?"

"That's it, sir. Nobody else ever done anything around the studio. I always mixed 'is colours and 'e taught me to do a share of the varnishin'; 'e said as 'ow there wasn't a 'ouse in England as could do it proper. You aynt looked at the *Marriage* yet, sir?" he asked abruptly, glancing doubtfully at MacMaster, and indicating with his thumb the picture under the north light.

"Not very closely. I prefer to begin with something simpler; that's rather appalling, at first glance," replied MacMaster.

"Well may you say that, sir," said James warmly. "That one regular killed Sir 'Ugh; it regular broke 'im up, and nothink will ever convince me as 'ow it didn't bring on 'is second stroke."

When MacMaster walked back to High Street to take his bus, his mind was divided between two exultant convictions. He felt that he had not only found Treffinger's greatest picture, but that, in James, he had discovered a kind of cryptic index to the painter's personality—a clue which, if tactfully followed, might lead to much.

Several days after his first visit to the studio, MacMaster wrote to Lady Mary Percy, telling her that he would be in London for some time and asking her if he might call. Lady Mary was an only sister of Lady Ellen Treffinger, the painter's widow, and MacMaster had known her during one winter he spent at Nice. He had known her, indeed, very well, and Lady Mary, who was astonishingly frank and communicative upon all subjects, had been no less so upon the matter of her sister's unfortunate marriage.

In her reply to his note, Lady Mary named an afternoon when she would be alone. She was as good as her word, and when MacMaster arrived he found the drawing-room empty. Lady Mary entered shortly after he was announced. She was a tall woman, thin and stiffly jointed; and her body stood out under the folds of her gown with the rigour of cast-iron. This rather metallic suggestion was further carried out in her heavily knuckled hands, her stiff grey hair and long, bold-featured face, which was saved from freakishness only by her alert eyes.

"Really," said Lady Mary, taking a seat beside him and giving him a sort of military inspection through her nose-glasses, "Really, I had begun to fear that I had lost you altogether. It's four years since I saw you at Nice, isn't it? I was in Paris last winter, but I heard nothing from you."

"I was in New York then."

"It occurred to me that you might be. And why are you in London?"

"Can you ask?" replied MacMaster gallantly.

Lady Mary smiled ironically. "But for what else, incidentally?"

"Well, incidentally, I came to see Treffinger's studio and his unfinished picture. Since I've been here, I've decided to stay the summer. I'm even thinking of attempting to do a biography of him."

"So that is what brought you to London?"

"Not exactly. I had really no intention of anything so serious when I came. It's his last picture, I fancy, that has rather thrust it upon me. The notion has settled down on me like a thing destined."

"You'll not be offended if I question the clemency of such a destiny," remarked Lady Mary dryly. "Isn't there rather a surplus of books on that subject already?"

"Such as they are. Oh, I've read them all," here MacMaster faced Lady Mary triumphantly. "He has quite escaped your amiable critics," he added, smiling.

"I know well enough what you think, and I daresay we are not much on art," said Lady Mary with tolerant good humour. "We leave that to peoples who have no physique. Treffinger made a stir for a time, but it seems that we are not capable of a sustained appreciation of such extraordinary methods. In the end we go back to the pictures we find agreeable and unperplexing. He was regarded as an experiment, I fancy; and now it seems that he was rather an unsuccessful one. If you've come to us in a missionary spirit, we'll tolerate you politely, but we'll laugh in our sleeve, I warn you."

"That really doesn't daunt me, Lady Mary," declared MacMaster blandly. "As I told you, I'm a man with a mission."

Lady Mary laughed her hoarse baritone laugh. "Bravo! and you've come to me for inspiration for your panegyric?"

MacMaster smiled with some embarrassment. "Not altogether for that purpose. But I want to consult you, Lady Mary, about the advisability of troubling Lady Ellen Treffinger in the matter. It seems scarcely legitimate to go on without asking her to give some sort of grace to my proceedings, yet I feared the whole subject might be painful to her. I shall rely wholly upon your discretion."

"I think she would prefer to be consulted," replied Lady Mary judicially. "I can't understand how she endures to have the wretched affair continually raked up, but she does. She seems to feel a sort of moral responsibility. Ellen has always been singularly conscientious about this matter, in so far as her light goes,—which rather puzzles me, as hers is not exactly a magnanimous nature. She is certainly trying to do what she believes to be the right thing. I shall write to her, and you can see her when she returns from Italy."

"I want very much to meet her. She is, I hope, quite recovered in every way," queried MacMaster, hesitatingly.

"No, I can't say that she is. She has remained in much the same condition she sank to before his death. He trampled over pretty much whatever there was in her, I fancy. Women don't recover from wounds of that sort; at least, not women of Ellen's grain. They go on bleeding inwardly."

"You, at any rate, have not grown more reconciled," MacMaster ventured.

"Oh, I give him his dues. He was a colourist, I grant you; but that is a vague and unsatisfactory quality to marry to; Lady Ellen Treffinger found it so."

"But, my dear Lady Mary," expostulated MacMaster, "and just repress me if I'm becoming too personal—but it must, in the first place, have been a marriage of choice on her part as well as on his."

Lady Mary poised her glasses on her large forefinger and assumed an attitude suggestive of the clinical lecture room as she replied. "Ellen, my dear boy, is an essentially romantic person. She is quiet about it, but she runs deep. I never knew how deep until I came against her on the issue of that marriage. She was always discontented as a girl; she found things dull and prosaic, and the ardour of his courtship was agreeable to her. He met her during her first season in town. She is handsome, and there were plenty of other men, but I grant you your scowling brigand was the most picturesque of the lot. In his courtship, as in everything else, he was theatrical to the point of being ridiculous, but Ellen's sense of humour is not her strongest quality. He had the charm of celebrity, the air of a man who could storm his way through anything to get what he wanted. That sort of vehemence is particularly effective with women like Ellen, who can be warmed only by reflected heat, and she couldn't at all stand out against it. He convinced her of his necessity; and that done, all's done."

"I can't help thinking that, even on such a basis, the marriage should have turned out better," MacMaster remarked reflectively.

"The marriage," Lady Mary continued with a shrug, "was made on the basis of a mutual misunderstanding. Ellen, in the nature of the case, believed that she was doing something quite out of the ordinary in accepting him, and expected concessions which, apparently, it never occurred to him to make. After his marriage he relapsed into his old habits of incessant work, broken by violent and often brutal relaxations. He insulted her friends and foisted his own upon her—many of them well calculated to arouse aversion in any well-bred girl. He had Ghillini constantly at the house—a homeless vagabond, whose conversation was impossible. I don't say, mind you, that he had not grievances on his side. He had probably over-rated the girl's possibilities, and he let her see that he was disappointed in her. Only a large and generous nature could have borne with him, and Ellen's is not that. She could not at all understand that odious strain of plebeian pride which plumes itself upon not having risen above its sources."

As MacMaster drove back to his hotel, he reflected that Lady Mary Percy had probably had good cause for dissatisfaction with her brother-in-law. Treffinger was, indeed, the last man who should have married into the Percy family. The son of a small tobacconist, he had grown up a sign painter's apprentice; idle, lawless, and practically letterless until he had drifted into the night classes of the Albert League, where Ghillini sometimes lectured. From the moment he came under the eye and influence of that erratic Italian, then a political exile, his life had swerved sharply from its old channel. This man had been at once incentive and guide, friend and master, to his pupil. He had taken the raw clay out of the London streets and moulded it anew. Seemingly he had divined at once where the boy's possibilities lay, and had thrown aside every canon of orthodox instruction in the training of him. Under him Treffinger acquired his superficial, yet facile, knowledge of the classics; had steeped himself in the monkish Latin and mediaeval romances which later gave his work so naive and remote a quality. That was the beginning of the wattle fences, the cobble pave, the brown roof beams, the cunningly wrought fabrics that gave to his pictures such a richness of decorative effect.

As he had told Lady Mary Percy, MacMaster had found the imperative inspiration of his purpose in Treffinger's unfinished picture, the *Marriage of Phaedra*. He had always believed that the key to Treffinger's individuality lay in his singular education; in the *Roman de la Rose*, in Boccaccio, and Amadis, those works which had literally transcribed themselves upon the blank soul of the London street boy, and through which he had been born into the world of spiritual things. Treffinger had been a man who lived after his imagination; and his mind, his ideals and, as MacMaster believed, even his personal ethics, had to the last been coloured by the trend of his early training. There was in him alike the freshness and spontaneity, the frank brutality and the religious mysticism which lay well back of the fifteenth century. In the *Marriage of Phaedra* MacMaster found the ultimate expression of this spirit, the final word as to Treffinger's point of view.

As in all Treffinger's classical subjects, the conception was wholly mediaeval. This Phaedra, just turning from her husband and maidens to greet her husband's son, giving him her first fearsome glance from under her half lifted veil, was no daughter of Minos. The daughter of *heathenesse* and the early church she was; doomed to torturing visions and scourgings, and the wrangling of soul with flesh. The venerable Theseus might have been victorious Charlemagne, and Phaedra's maidens belonged rather in the train of Blanche of Castile than at the Cretan court. In the earlier studies Hippolytus had been done with a more pagan suggestion, but in each successive drawing the glorious figure had been deflowered of something of its serene unconsciousness; until, in the canvas under the sky-light, he appeared a very Christian knight. This male figure, and the face of Phaedra, painted with such magical preservation of tone under the heavy shadow of the veil, were plainly Treffinger's highest achievements of craftsmanship. By what labour he had reached the seemingly inevitable composition of the picture—with its twenty figures, its plenitude of light and air, its restful distances seen through white porticoes—countless studies bore witness.

From James's attitude toward the picture, MacMaster could well conjecture what the painter's had been. This picture was always uppermost in James's mind; its custodianship formed, in his eyes, his occupation. He was manifestly apprehensive when visitors—not many came now-a-days—lingered near it. "It was the *Marriage* as killed 'im," he would often say, "and for the matter 'o that, it did like to 'av been the death of all of us."

By the end of his second week in London, MacMaster had begun the notes for his study of Hugh Treffinger and his work. When his researches led him occasionally to visit the studios of Treffinger's friends and erst-while disciples, he found their Treffinger manner fading as the ring [of] Treffinger's personality died out in them. One by one they were stealing back into the fold of national British art; the hand that had wound them up was still. MacMaster despaired of them and confined himself more and more exclusively to the studio, to such of Treffinger's letters as were available—they were for the most part singularly negative and colourless —and to his interrogation of Treffinger's man.

He could not himself have traced the successive steps by which he was gradually admitted into James's confidence. Certainly most of his adroit strategies to that end failed humiliatingly, and whatever it was that built up an understanding between them must have been instinctive and intuitive on both sides. When at last James became anecdotal, personal, there was that in every word he let fall which put breath and blood into MacMaster's book. James had so long been steeped in that penetrating personality that he fairly exuded it. Many of his very phrases, mannerisms and opinions were impressions that he had taken on like wet plaster in his daily contact with Treffinger. Inwardly he was lined with cast off epithelia, as outwardly he was clad in the painter's discarded coats. If the painter's letters were formal and perfunctory, if his expressions to his friends had been extravagant, contradictory and often apparently in-sincere—still, MacMaster felt himself not entirely without authentic sources. It was James who possessed Treffinger's legend; it was with James that he had laid aside his pose. Only in his studio, alone, and face to face with his work, as it seemed, had the man invariably been himself. James had known him in the one attitude in which he was entirely honest; their relation had fallen well within the painter's only indubitable integrity. James's report of Treffinger was distorted by no hallucination of artistic insight, coloured by no interpretation of his own. He merely held what he had heard and seen; his mind was a sort of camera obscura. His very limitations made him the more literal and minutely accurate.

One morning, when MacMaster was seated before the *Marriage of Phaedra*, James entered on his usual round of dusting.

"I've 'eard from Lydy Elling by the post, sir," he remarked, "an' she's give h'orders to 'ave the 'ouse put in readiness. I doubt she'll be 'ere by Thursday or Friday next."

"She spends most of her time abroad?" queried MacMaster; on the subject of Lady Treffinger James consistently maintained a very delicate reserve.

"Well, you could 'ardly say she does that, sir. She finds the 'ouse a bit dull, I daresay, so durin' the season she stops mostly with Lydy Mary Percy, at Grosvenor Square. Lydy Mary's a h'only sister." After a few moments he continued, speaking in jerks governed by the rigour of his dusting: "Honly this morning I come upon this scarf-pin," exhibiting a very striking instance of that article, "an' I recalled as 'ow Sir 'Ugh give it me when 'e was a-courting of Lydy Elling. Blowed if I ever see a man go in for a 'oman like 'im! 'E was that gone, sir. 'E never went in on any-think so 'ard before nor since, till 'e went in on the *Marriage* there—though 'e mostly went in on things pretty keen; 'ad the measles when 'e was thirty, strong as cholera, an' come close to dyin' of 'em. 'E wasn't strong for Lydy Elling's set; they was a bit too stiff for 'im. A free an' easy gentleman, 'e was; 'e liked 'is dinner with a few friends an' them jolly, but 'e wasn't much on what you might call big affairs. But once 'e went in for Lydy Elling 'e broke 'imself to new paces. He give away 'is rings an' pins, an' the tylor's man an' the 'aberdasher's man was at 'is rooms continual. 'E got 'imself put up for a club in Piccadilly; 'e starved 'imself thin, an' worrited 'imself white, an' ironed 'imself out, an' drawed 'imself tight as a bow string. It was a good job 'e come a winner, or I don't know w'at'd 'a been to pay."

The next week, in consequence of an invitation from Lady Ellen Treffinger, MacMaster went one afternoon to take tea with her. He was shown into the garden that lay between the residence and the studio, where the tea-table was set under a gnarled pear tree. Lady Ellen rose as he approached—he was astonished to note how tall she was—and greeted him graciously, saying that she already knew him through her sister. MacMaster felt a certain satisfaction in her; in her reassuring poise and repose, in the charming modulations of her voice and the indolent reserve of her full, almond eyes. He was even delighted to find her face so inscrutable, though it chilled his own warmth and made the open frankness he had wished to permit himself impossible. It was a long face, narrow at the chin, very delicately featured, yet steeled by an impassive mask of self-control. It was behind just such finely cut, close-sealed faces, MacMaster reflected, that nature sometimes hid astonishing secrets. But in spite of this suggestion of hardness, he felt that the unerring taste that Treffinger had always shown in larger matters had not deserted him when he came to the choosing of a wife, and he admitted that he could not himself have selected a woman who looked more as Treffinger's wife should look.

While he was explaining the purpose of his frequent visits to the studio, she heard him with courteous interest. "I have read, I think, everything that has been published on Sir Hugh Treffinger's work, and it seems to me that there is much left to be said," he concluded.

"I believe they are rather inadequate," she remarked vaguely. She hesitated a moment, absently fingering the ribbons of her gown, then continued, without raising her eyes; "I hope you will not think me too exacting if I ask to see the proofs of such chapters of your work as have to do with Sir Hugh's personal life. I have always asked that privilege."

MacMaster hastily assured her as to this, adding, "I mean to touch on only such facts in his personal life as have to do directly with his work—such as his monkish education under Ghillini."

"I see your meaning, I think," said Lady Ellen, looking at him with wide, uncomprehending eyes.

When MacMaster stopped at the studio on leaving the house, he stood for some time before Treffinger's one portrait of himself; that brigand of a picture, with its full throat and square head; the short upper lip blackened by the close-clipped moustache, the wiry hair tossed down over the forehead, the strong white teeth set hard on a short pipe stem. He could well understand what manifold tortures the mere grain of the man's strong red and brown flesh might have inflicted upon a woman like Lady Ellen. He could conjecture, too, Treffinger's impotent revolt against that very repose which had so dazzled him when it first defied his daring; and how once possessed of it, his first instinct had been to crush it, since he could not melt it.

Toward the close of the season Lady Ellen Treffinger left town. MacMaster's work was progressing rapidly, and he and James wore away the days in their peculiar relation, which by this time had much of friendliness. Excepting for the regular visits of a Jewish picture dealer, there were few intrusions upon their solitude. Occasionally a party of Americans rang at the little door in the garden wall, but usually they departed speedily for the Moorish hall and tinkling fountain of the great show studio of London, not far away.

This Jew, an Austrian by birth, who had a large business in Melbourne, Australia, was a man of considerable discrimination, and at once selected the *Marriage of Phaedra* as the object of his especial interest. When, upon his first visit, Lichtenstein had declared the picture one of the things done for time, MacMaster had rather warmed toward him and had talked to him very freely. Later, however, the man's repulsive personality and innate vulgarity so wore upon him that, the more genuine the Jew's appreciation, the more he resented it and the more base he somehow felt it to be. It annoyed him to see Lichtenstein walking up and down before the picture, shaking his head and blinking his watery eyes over his nose-glasses, ejaculating: "Dot is a chem, a chem! It is wordt to gome den dousant miles for such a bainting, eh? To make Eurobe abbreciate such a work of ardt it is necessary to take it away while she is napping. She has never abbreciated until she has lost, but," knowingly, "she will buy back."

James had, from the first, felt such a distrust of the man that he would never leave him alone in the studio for a moment. When Lichtenstein insisted upon having Lady Ellen Treffinger's address, James rose to the point of insolence. "It ayn't no use to give it, noway. Lydy Treffinger never has nothink to do with dealers." MacMaster quietly repented his rash confidences, fearing that he might indirectly cause Lady Ellen annoyance from this merciless speculator, and he recalled with chagrin that Lichtenstein had extorted from him, little by little, pretty much the entire plan of his book, and especially the place in it which the *Marriage of Phaedra* was to occupy.

By this time the first chapters of MacMaster's book were in the hands of his publisher, and his visits to the studio were necessarily less frequent. The greater part of his time was now employed with the engravers who were to reproduce such of Treffinger's pictures as he intended to use as illustrations.

He returned to his hotel late one evening after a long and vexing day at the engravers, to find James in his room, seated on his steamer trunk by the window, with the outline of a great square draped in sheets resting against his knee.

"Why, James, what's up?" he cried in astonishment, glancing enquiringly at the sheeted object.

"Ayn't you seen the pypers, sir?" jerked out the man.

"No, now I think of it, I haven't even looked at a paper. I've been at the engravers' plant all day. I haven't seen anything."

James drew a copy of the *Times* from his pocket and handed it to him, pointing with a tragic finger to a paragraph in the social column. It was merely the announcement of Lady Ellen Treffinger's engagement to Captain Alexander Gresham.

"Well, what of it, my man? That surely is her privilege."

James took the paper, turned to another page, and silently pointed to a paragraph in the art notes which stated that Lady Treffinger had presented to the X— gallery the entire collection of paintings and sketches now in her late husband's studio, with the exception of his unfinished picture, the *Marriage of Phaedra*, which she had sold for a large sum to an Australian dealer who had come to London purposely to secure some of Treffinger's paintings.

MacMaster pursed up his lips and sat down, his overcoat still on. "Well, James, this is something of a—something of a jolt, eh? It never occurred to me she'd really do it."

"Lord, you don't know 'er, sir," said James bitterly, still staring at the floor in an attitude of abandoned dejection.

MacMaster started up in a flash of enlightenment, "What on earth have you got there, James? It's not—surely it's not——"

"Yes, it is, sir," broke in the man excitedly. "It's the *Marriage* itself. It aynt a-going to H'australia, no'ow!"

"But man, what are you going to do with it? It's Lichtenstein's property now, as it seems."

"It aynt, sir, that it aynt. No, by Gawd, it aynt!" shouted James, breaking into a choking fury. He controlled himself with an effort and added supplicatingly: "Oh, sir, you aynt a-going to see it go to H'australia, w'ere they send convic's?" He unpinned and flung aside the sheets as though to let *Phaedra* plead for herself.

MacMaster sat down again and looked sadly at the doomed master-piece. The notion of James having carried it across London that night rather appealed to his fancy. There was certainly a flavour about such a high-handed proceeding. "However did you get it here?" he queried.

"I got a four-wheeler and come over direct, sir. Good job I 'appened to 'ave the chaynge about me."

"You came up High Street, up Piccadilly, through the Haymarket and Trafalgar Square, and into the Strand?" queried MacMaster with a relish.

"Yes, sir. Of course, sir," assented James with surprise.

MacMaster laughed delightedly. "It was a beautiful idea, James, but I'm afraid we can't carry it any further."

"I was thinkin' as 'ow it would be a rare chance to get you to take the *Marriage* over to Paris for a year or two, sir, until the thing blows over?" suggested James blandly.

"I'm afraid that's out of the question, James. I haven't the right stuff in me for a pirate, or even a vulgar smuggler, I'm afraid." MacMaster found it surprisingly difficult to say this, and he busied himself with the lamp as he said it. He heard James's hand fall heavily on the trunk top, and he discovered that he very much disliked sinking in the man's estimation.

"Well, sir," remarked James in a more formal tone, after a protracted silence; "then there's nothink for it but as 'ow I'll 'ave to make way with it myself."

"And how about your character, James? The evidence would be heavy against you, and even if Lady Treffinger didn't prosecute you'd be done for."

"Blow my character!—your pardon, sir," cried James, starting to his feet. "W'at do I want of a character? I'll chuck the 'ole thing, and damned lively, too. The shop's to be sold out, an' my place is gone any'ow. I'm a-going to enlist, or try the gold-fields. I've lived too long with h'artists; I'd never give satisfaction in livery now. You know 'ow it is yourself, sir; there aynt no life like it, no'ow."

For a moment MacMaster was almost equal to abetting James in his theft. He reflected that pictures had been white-washed, or hidden in the crypts of churches, or under the floors of palaces from meaner motives, and to save them from a fate less ignominious. But presently, with a sigh, he shook his head.

"No, James, it won't do at all. It has been tried over and over again, ever since the world has been a-going and pictures a-making. It was tried in Florence and in Venice, but the pictures were always carried away in the end. You see the difficulty is that, although Treffinger told you what was not to be done with the picture, he did not say definitely what was to be done with it. Do you think Lady Treffinger really understands that he did not want it to be sold?"

"Well, sir, it was like this, sir," said James, resuming his seat on the trunk and again resting the picture against his knee. "My memory is as clear as glass about it. After Sir 'Ugh got up from 'is first stroke, 'e took a fresh start at the *Marriage*. Before that 'e 'ad been working at it only at night for awhile back; the *Legend* was the big picture then, an' was under the north light w'ere 'e worked of a morning. But one day 'e bid me take the *Legend* down an' put the *Marriage* in its place, an' 'e says, dashin' on 'is jacket, 'Jymes, this is a start for the finish, this time.'

"From that [day] on 'e worked at the night picture in the mornin'—a thing contrary to 'is custom. The *Marriage* went wrong, and wrong—an' Sir 'Ugh a-gettin' seedier an' seedier every day. 'E tried models an' models, an' smudged an' pynted out on account of 'er face goin' wrong in the shadow. Sometimes 'e layed it on the colours, an' swore at me an' things [in] general. He got that discouraged about 'imself that on 'is low days 'e used to say to me: 'Jymes, remember one thing; if anythink 'appens to me, the *Marriage* is not to go out of 'ere unfinished. It's worth the lot of 'em, my boy, an' it's not a-going to go shabby for lack of pains.' 'E said things to that effect repeated.

"He was workin' at the picture the last day, before 'e went to 'is club. 'E kept the carriage waitin' near an hour while 'e put on a stroke an' then drawed back for to look at it, an' then put on another, careful like. After 'e 'ad 'is gloves on, 'e come back an' took away the brushes I was startin' to clean, an' put in another touch or two. 'It's a-comin', Jymes,' 'e says, 'by gad if it aynt.' An' with that 'e goes out. It was cruel sudden, w'at come after.

"That night I was lookin' to 'is clothes at the 'ouse when they brought 'im 'ome. He was conscious, but w'en I ran downstairs for to 'elp lift 'im up, I knowed 'e was a finished man. After we got 'im into bed, 'e kept lookin' restless at me and then at Lydy Elling and a-jerkin' of 'is 'and. Finally 'e quite raised it an' shot 'is thumb out towards the wall. 'He wants water; ring Jymes,' says Lydy Elling, placid. But I knowed 'e was pointin' to the shop.

"'Lydy Treffinger,' says I, bold, 'he's pointin' to the studio. He means about the *Marriage*; 'e told me to-day as 'ow 'e never wanted it sold unfinished. Is that it, Sir 'Ugh?'

"He smiled an' nodded slight an' closed 'is eyes. 'Thank you, Jymes,' says Lydy Elling, placid. Then 'e opened 'is eyes an' looked long and 'ard at Lydy Elling.

"'Of course I'll try to do as you'd wish about the pictures, 'Ugh, if that's w'at's troublin' you,' she says quiet. With that 'e closed 'is eyes and 'e never opened 'em. He died unconscious at four that mornin'.

"You see, sir, Lydy Elling was always cruel 'ard on the *Marriage*. From the first it went wrong, an' Sir 'Ugh was out of temper pretty constant. She came into the studio one day and looked at the picture an' asked 'im why 'e didn't throw it up an' quit a-worriting 'imself. He answered sharp, an' with that she said as 'ow she didn't see w'at there was to make such a row about, no'ow. She spoke 'er mind about that picture, free; an' Sir 'Ugh swore 'ot an' let a 'andful of brushes fly at 'is study, an' Lydy Elling picked up 'er skirts careful an' chill, an' drifted out of the studio with 'er eyes calm and 'er chin 'igh. If there was one thing Lydy Elling 'ad no comprehension of, it was the usefulness of swearin'. So the *Marriage* was a sore thing between 'em. She is uncommon calm, but uncommon bitter, is Lydy Elling. She's never come a-near the studio since that day she went out 'oldin' up of 'er skirts. W'en 'er friends goes over she excuses 'erself along o' the strain. Strain—Gawd!" James ground his wrath short in his teeth.

"I'll tell you what I'll do, James, and it's our only hope. I'll see Lady Ellen to-morrow. The *Times* says she returned to-day. You take the picture back to its place, and I'll do what I can for it. If anything is done to save it, it must be done through Lady Ellen Treffinger herself; that much is clear. I can't think that she fully understands the situation. If she did, you know, she really couldn't have any motive—" He stopped suddenly. Somehow, in the dusky lamplight her small, close-sealed face came ominously back to him. He rubbed his forehead and knitted his brows thoughtfully. After a moment he shook his head and went on: "I am positive that nothing can be gained by high-handed methods, James. Captain Gresham is one of the most popular men in London, and his friends would tear up Treffinger's bones if he were annoyed by any scandal of our making—and this scheme you propose would inevitably result in scandal. Lady Ellen has, of course, every legal right to sell the picture. Treffinger made considerable inroads upon her estate, and, as she is about to marry a man without income, she doubtless feels that she has a right to replenish her patrimony."

He found James amenable, though doggedly sceptical. He went down into the street, called a carriage, and saw James and his burden into it. Standing in the doorway, he watched the carriage roll away through the drizzling mist, weave in and out among the wet, black vehicles and darting cab lights, until it was swallowed up in the glare and confusion of the Strand. "It is rather a fine touch of irony," he reflected, "that he, who is so out of it, should be the one to really care. Poor Treffinger," he murmured as, with a rather spiritless smile, he turned back into his hotel. "Poor Treffinger; *sic transit gloria.*"

The next afternoon MacMaster kept his promise. When he arrived at Lady Mary Percy's house he saw preparations for a function of some sort, but he went resolutely up the steps, telling the footman that his business was urgent. Lady Ellen came down alone, excusing her sister. She was dressed for receiving, and MacMaster had never seen her so beautiful. The colour in her cheeks sent a softening glow over her small, delicately cut features.

MacMaster apologized for his intrusion and came unflinchingly to the object of his call. He had come, he said, not only to offer her his warmest congratulations, but to express his regret that a great work of art was to leave England.

Lady Treffinger looked at him in wide-eyed astonishment. Surely, she said, she had been careful to select the best of the pictures for the X— gallery, in accordance with Sir Hugh Treffinger's wishes.

"And did he—pardon me, Lady Treffinger, but in mercy set my mind at rest—did he or did he not express any definite wish concerning this one picture, which to me seems worth all the others, unfinished as it is?"

Lady Treffinger paled perceptibly, but it was not the pallor of confusion. When she spoke there was a sharp tremor in her smooth voice, the edge of a resentment that tore her like pain. "I think his man has some such impression, but I believe it to be utterly unfounded. I cannot find that he ever expressed any wish concerning the disposition of the picture to any of his friends. Unfortunately, Sir Hugh was not always discreet in his remarks to his servants."

"Captain Gresham, Lady Ellingham and Miss Ellingham," announced a servant, appearing at the door.

There was a murmur in the hall, and MacMaster greeted the smiling Captain and his aunt as he bowed himself out.

To all intents and purposes the *Marriage of Phaedra* was already entombed in a vague continent in the Pacific, somewhere on the other side of the world.

First published in *The Troll Garden* (New York: McClure, Phillips & Co., 1905), pp. 155–192.

A Wagner Matinee

✳ ✳ ✳

I received one morning a letter, written in pale ink on glassy, blue-lined note-paper, and bearing the postmark of a little Nebraska village. This communication, worn and rubbed, looking as though it had been carried for some days in a coat pocket that was none too clean, was from my Uncle Howard and informed me that his wife had been left a small legacy by a bachelor relative who had recently died, and that it would be necessary for her to go to Boston to attend to the settling of the estate. He requested me to meet her at the station and render her whatever services might be necessary. On examining the date indicated as that of her arrival, I found it no later than to-morrow. He had characteristically delayed writing until, had I been away from home for a day, I must have missed the good woman altogether.

The name of my Aunt Georgiana called up not alone her own figure, at once pathetic and grotesque, but opened before my feet a gulf of recollection so wide and deep, that, as the letter dropped from my hand, I felt suddenly a stranger to all the present conditions of my existence, wholly ill at ease and out of place amid the familiar surroundings of my study. I became, in short, the gangling farmer-boy my aunt had known, scourged with chilblains and bashfulness, my hands cracked and sore from the corn husking. I felt the knuckles of my thumb tentatively, as though they were raw again. I sat again before her parlour organ, fumbling the scales with my stiff, red hands, while she, beside me, made canvas mittens for the huskers.

The next morning, after preparing my landlady somewhat, I set out for the station. When the train arrived I had some difficulty in finding my aunt. She was the last of the passengers to alight, and it was not until I got her into the carriage that she seemed really to recognize me. She had come all the way in a day coach; her linen duster had become black with soot and her black bonnet grey with dust during the journey. When we arrived at my boarding-house the landlady put her to bed at once and I did not see her again until the next morning.

Whatever shock Mrs. Springer experienced at my aunt's appearance, she considerately concealed. As for myself, I saw my aunt's misshapen figure with that feeling of awe and respect with which we behold explorers who have left their ears and fingers north of Franz-Josef-Land, or their health somewhere along the Upper Congo. My Aunt Georgiana had been a music teacher at the Boston Conservatory, somewhere back in the latter sixties. One summer, while visiting in the little village among the Green Mountains where her ancestors had dwelt for generations, she had kindled the callow fancy of the most idle and shiftless of all the village lads, and had conceived for this Howard Carpenter one of those extravagant passions which a handsome country boy of twenty-one sometimes inspires in an angular, spectacled woman of thirty. When she returned to her duties in Boston, Howard followed her, and the upshot of this inexplicable infatuation was that she eloped with him, eluding the reproaches of her family and the criticisms of her friends by going with him to the Nebraska frontier. Carpenter, who, of course, had no money, had taken a homestead in Red Willow County, fifty miles from the railroad. There they had measured off their quarter section themselves by driving across the prairie in a wagon, to the wheel of which they had tied a red cotton handkerchief, and counting off its revolutions. They built a dugout in the red hillside, one of those cave dwellings whose inmates so often reverted to primitive conditions. Their water they got from the lagoons where the buffalo drank, and their slender stock of provisions was always at the mercy of bands of roving Indians. For thirty years my aunt had not been further than fifty miles from the homestead.

But Mrs. Springer knew nothing of all this, and must have been considerably shocked at what was left of my kinswoman. Beneath the soiled linen duster which, on her arrival, was the most conspicuous feature of her costume, she wore a black stuff dress, whose ornamentation showed that she had surrendered herself unquestioningly into the hands of a country dressmaker. My poor aunt's figure, however, would have presented astonishing difficulties to any dressmaker. Originally stooped, her shoulders were now almost bent together over her sunken chest. She wore no stays, and her gown, which trailed unevenly behind, rose in a sort of peak over her abdomen. She wore ill-fitting false teeth, and her skin was as yellow as a Mongolian's from constant exposure to a pitiless wind and to the alkaline water which hardens the most transparent cuticle into a sort of flexible leather.

I owed to this woman most of the good that ever came my way in my boyhood, and had a reverential affection for her. During the years when

I was riding herd for my uncle, my aunt, after cooking the three meals—
the first of which was ready at six o'clock in the morning—and putting
the six children to bed, would often stand until midnight at her ironing-
board, with me at the kitchen table beside her, hearing me recite Latin
declensions and conjugations, gently shaking me when my drowsy head
sank down over a page of irregular verbs. It was to her, at her ironing or
mending, that I read my first Shakespere, and her old text-book on
mythology was the first that ever came into my empty hands. She taught
me my scales and exercises, too—on the little parlour organ, which her
husband had bought her after fifteen years, during which she had not so
much as seen any instrument, but an accordion that belonged to one of the
Norwegian farmhands. She would sit beside me by the hour, darning and
counting while I struggled with the "Joyous Farmer," but she seldom
talked to me about music, and I understood why. She was a pious woman;
she had the consolations of religion and, to her at least, her martyrdom
was not wholly sordid. Once when I had been doggedly beating out some
easy passages from an old score of *Euryanthe* I had found among her
music books, she came up to me and, putting her hands over my eyes,
gently drew my head back upon her shoulder, saying tremulously, "Don't
love it so well, Clark, or it may be taken from you. Oh! dear boy, pray
that whatever your sacrifice may be, it be not that."

When my aunt appeared on the morning after her arrival, she was
still in a semi-somnambulant state. She seemed not to realize that she was
in the city where she had spent her youth, the place longed for hungrily
half a lifetime. She had been so wretchedly train-sick throughout the
journey that she had no recollection of anything but her discomfort, and,
to all intents and purposes, there were but a few hours of nightmare
between the farm in Red Willow County and my study on Newbury
Street. I had planned a little pleasure for her that afternoon, to repay her
for some of the glorious moments she had given me when we used to
milk together in the straw-thatched cowshed and she, because I was
more than usually tired, or because her husband had spoken sharply to me,
would tell me of the splendid performance of the *Huguenots* she had seen
in Paris, in her youth. At two o'clock the Symphony Orchestra was to
give a Wagner programme, and I intended to take my aunt; though, as
I conversed with her, I grew doubtful about her enjoyment of it. Indeed,
for her own sake, I could only wish her taste for such things quite dead,
and the long struggle mercifully ended at last. I suggested our visiting the
Conservatory and the Common before lunch, but she seemed altogether
too timid to wish to venture out. She questioned me absently about

various changes in the city, but she was chiefly concerned that she had forgotten to leave instructions about feeding half-skimmed milk to a certain weakling calf, "old Maggie's calf, you know, Clark," she explained, evidently having forgotten how long I had been away. She was further troubled because she had neglected to tell her daughter about the freshly-opened kit of mackerel in the cellar, which would spoil if it were not used directly.

I asked her whether she had ever heard any of the Wagnerian operas, and found that she had not, though she was perfectly familiar with their respective situations, and had once possessed the piano score of *The Flying Dutchman*. I began to think it would have been best to get her back to Red Willow County without waking her, and regretted having suggested the concert.

From the time we entered the concert hall, however, she was a trifle less passive and inert, and for the first time seemed to perceive her surroundings. I had felt some trepidation lest she might become aware of the absurdities of her attire, or might experience some painful embarrassment at stepping suddenly into the world to which she had been dead for a quarter of a century. But, again, I found how superficially I had judged her. She sat looking about her with eyes as impersonal, almost as stony, as those with which the granite Rameses in a museum watches the froth and fret that ebbs and flows about his pedestal—separated from it by the lonely stretch of centuries. I have seen this same aloofness in old miners who drift into the Brown hotel at Denver, their pockets full of bullion, their linen soiled, their haggard faces unshaven; standing in the thronged corridors as solitary as though they were still in a frozen camp on the Yukon, conscious that certain experiences have isolated them from their fellows by a gulf no haberdasher could bridge.

We sat at the extreme left of the first balcony, facing the arc of our own and the balcony above us, veritable hanging gardens, brilliant as tulip beds. The matinée audience was made up chiefly of women. One lost the contour of faces and figures, indeed any effect of line whatever, and there was only the colour of bodices past counting, the shimmer of fabrics soft and firm, silky and sheer; red, mauve, pink, blue, lilac, purple, ecru, rose, yellow, cream, and white, all the colours that an impressionist finds in a sunlit landscape, with here and there the dead shadow of a frock coat. My Aunt Georgiana regarded them as though they had been so many daubs of tube-paint on a palette.

When the musicians came out and took their places, she gave a little stir of anticipation and looked with quickening interest down over the rail at that invariable grouping, perhaps the first wholly familiar thing that had greeted her eye since she had left old Maggie and her weakling calf. I could feel how all those details sank into her soul, for I had not forgotten how they had sunk into mine when I came fresh from ploughing forever and forever between green aisles of corn, where, as in a treadmill, one might walk from daybreak to dusk without perceiving a shadow of change. The clean profiles of the musicians, the gloss of their linen, the dull black of their coats, the beloved shapes of the instruments, the patches of yellow light thrown by the green shaded lamps on the smooth, varnished bellies of the 'cellos and the bass viols in the rear, the restless, wind-tossed forest of fiddle necks and bows—I recalled how, in the first orchestra I had ever heard, those long bow strokes seemed to draw the heart out of me, as a conjurer's stick reels out yards of paper ribbon from a hat.

The first number was the *Tannhauser* overture. When the horns drew out the first strain of the Pilgrim's chorus, my Aunt Georgiana clutched my coat sleeve. Then it was I first realized that for her this broke a silence of thirty years; the inconceivable silence of the plains. With the battle between the two motives, with the frenzy of the Venusberg theme and its ripping of strings, there came to me an overwhelming sense of the waste and wear we are so powerless to combat; and I saw again the tall, naked house on the prairie, black and grim as a wooden fortress; the black pond where I had learned to swim, its margin pitted with sun-dried cattle tracks; the rain gullied clay banks about the naked house, the four dwarf ash seedlings where the dish-cloths were always hung to dry before the kitchen door. The world there was the flat world of the ancients; to the east, a cornfield that stretched to daybreak; to the west, a corral that reached to sunset; between, the conquests of peace, dearer bought than those of war.

The overture closed, my aunt released my coat sleeve, but she said nothing. She sat staring at the orchestra through a dullness of thirty years, through the films made little by little by each of the three hundred and sixty-five days in every one of them. What, I wondered, did she get from it? She had been a good pianist in her day I knew, and her musical education had been broader than that of most music teachers of a quarter of a century ago. She had often told me of Mozart's operas and Meyerbeer's, and I could remember hearing her sing, years ago, certain melodies of Verdi's. When I had fallen ill with a fever in her house she used to sit by my cot in the evening—when the cool, night wind blew in through the faded mosquito netting tacked over the window and I lay watching a certain bright star that burned red above the cornfield—and sing "Home to our mountains, O, let us return!" in a way fit to break the heart of a Vermont boy near dead of homesickness already.

I watched her closely through the prelude to *Tristan and Isolde*, trying vainly to conjecture what that seething turmoil of strings and winds might mean to her, but she sat mutely staring at the violin bows that drove obliquely downward, like the pelting streaks of rain in a summer shower. Had this music any message for her? Had she enough left to at all comprehend this power which had kindled the world since she had left it? I was in a fever of curiosity, but Aunt Georgiana sat silent upon her peak in Darien. She preserved this utter immobility throughout the number from *The Flying Dutchman*, though her fingers worked mechanically upon her black dress, as though, of themselves, they were recalling the piano score they had once played. Poor old hands! They had been stretched and twisted into mere tentacles to hold and lift and knead with; the palms unduly swollen, the fingers bent and knotted—on one of them a thin, worn band that had once been a wedding ring. As I pressed and gently quieted one of those groping hands, I remembered with quivering eyelids their services for me in other days.

Soon after the tenor began the "Prize Song," I heard a quick drawn breath and turned to my aunt. Her eyes were closed, but the tears were glistening on her cheeks, and I think, in a moment more, they were in my eyes as well. It never really died, then—the soul that can suffer so excruciatingly and so interminably; it withers to the outward eye only; like that strange moss which can lie on a dusty shelf half a century and yet, if placed in water, grows green again. She wept so throughout the development and elaboration of the melody.

During the intermission before the second half of the concert, I questioned my aunt and found that the "Prize Song" was not new to her. Some years before there had drifted to the farm in Red Willow County a young German, a tramp cow puncher, who had sung the chorus at Bayreuth, when he was a boy, along with the other peasant boys and girls. Of a Sunday morning he used to sit on his gingham-sheeted bed in the hands' bedroom which opened off the kitchen, cleaning the leather of his boots and saddle, singing the "Prize Song," while my aunt went about her work in the kitchen. She had hovered about him until she had prevailed upon him to join the country church, though his sole fitness for this step, in so far as I could gather, lay in his boyish face and his possession of this divine melody. Shortly afterward he had gone to town on the Fourth of July, been drunk for several days, lost his money at a faro table, ridden a saddled Texan steer on a bet, and disappeared with a fractured collar-bone. All this my aunt told me huskily, wanderingly, as though she were talking in the weak lapses of illness.

"Well, we have come to better things than the old *Trovatore* at any rate, Aunt Georgie?" I queried, with a well meant effort at jocularity.

Her lip quivered and she hastily put her handkerchief up to her mouth. From behind it she murmured, "And you have been hearing this ever since you left me, Clark?" Her question was the gentlest and saddest of reproaches.

The second half of the programme consisted of four numbers from the *Ring*, and closed with Siegfried's funeral march. My aunt wept quietly, but almost continuously, as a shallow vessel overflows in a rainstorm. From time to time her dim eyes looked up at the lights which studded the ceiling, burning softly under their dull glass globes; doubtless they were stars in truth to her. I was still perplexed as to what measure of musical comprehension was left to her, she who had heard nothing but the singing of Gospel Hymns at Methodist services in the square frame school-house on Section Thirteen for so many years. I was wholly unable to gauge how much of it had been dissolved in soapsuds, or worked into bread, or milked into the bottom of a pail.

The deluge of sound poured on and on; I never knew what she found in the shining current of it; I never knew how far it bore her, or past what happy islands. From the trembling of her face I could well believe that before the last numbers she had been carried out where the myriad graves are, into the grey, nameless burying grounds of the sea; or into some world of death vaster yet, where, from the beginning of the world, hope has lain down with hope and dream with dream and, renouncing, slept.

The concert was over; the people filed out of the hall chattering and laughing, glad to relax and find the living level again, but my kinswoman made no effort to rise. The harpist slipped its green felt cover over his instrument; the flute-players shook the water from their mouthpieces; the men of the orchestra went out one by one, leaving the stage to the chairs and music stands, empty as a winter cornfield.

I spoke to my aunt. She burst into tears and sobbed pleadingly. "I don't want to go, Clark, I don't want to go!"

I understood. For her, just outside the door of the concert hall, lay the black pond with the cattle-tracked bluffs; the tall, unpainted house, with weather-curled boards; naked as a tower, the crook-backed ash seedlings where the dish-cloths hung to dry; the gaunt, moulting turkeys picking up refuse about the kitchen door.

First published in *Everybody's Magazine*, X (February, 1904), 325–328.

Paul's Case

A Study in Temperament

❊ ❊ ❊

It was Paul's afternoon to appear before the faculty of the Pittsburgh
High School to account for his various misdemeanours. He had been
suspended a week ago, and his father had called at the Principal's office
and confessed his perplexity about his son. Paul entered the faculty room
suave and smiling. His clothes were a trifle outgrown and the tan velvet
on the collar of his open overcoat was frayed and worn; but for all that
there was something of the dandy about him, and he wore an opal pin in
his neatly knotted black four-in-hand, and a red carnation in his buttonhole. This latter adornment the faculty somehow felt was not properly
significant of the contrite spirit befitting a boy under the ban of suspension.

Paul was tall for his age and very thin, with high, cramped shoulders
and a narrow chest. His eyes were remarkable for a certain hysterical
brilliancy and he continually used them in a conscious, theatrical sort of
way, peculiarly offensive in a boy. The pupils were abnormally large, as
though he were addicted to belladonna, but there was a glassy glitter
about them which that drug does not produce.

When questioned by the Principal as to why he was there, Paul
stated, politely enough, that he wanted to come back to school. This was
a lie, but Paul was quite accustomed to lying; found it, indeed, indispensable for overcoming friction. His teachers were asked to state their
respective charges against him, which they did with such a rancour and
aggrievedness as evinced that this was not a usual case. Disorder and
impertinence were among the offences named, yet each of his instructors
felt that it was scarcely possible to put into words the real cause of the
trouble, which lay in a sort of hysterically defiant manner of the boy's;
in the contempt which they all knew he felt for them, and which he
seemingly made not the least effort to conceal. Once, when he had been
making a synopsis of a paragraph at the blackboard, his English teacher

had stepped to his side and attempted to guide his hand. Paul had started back with a shudder and thrust his hands violently behind him. The astonished woman could scarcely have been more hurt and embarrassed had he struck at her. The insult was so involuntary and definitely personal as to be unforgettable. In one way and another, he had made all his teachers, men and women alike, conscious of the same feeling of physical aversion. In one class he habitually sat with his hand shading his eyes; in another he always looked out of the window during the recitation; in another he made a running commentary on the lecture, with humorous intention.

His teachers felt this afternoon that his whole attitude was symbolized by his shrug and his flippantly red carnation flower, and they fell upon him without mercy, his English teacher leading the pack. He stood through it smiling, his pale lips parted over his white teeth. (His lips were continually twitching, and he had a habit of raising his eyebrows that was contemptuous and irritating to the last degree.) Older boys than Paul had broken down and shed tears under that baptism of fire, but his set smile did not once desert him, and his only sign of discomfort was the nervous trembling of the fingers that toyed with the buttons of his overcoat, and an occasional jerking of the other hand that held his hat. Paul was always smiling, always glancing about him, seeming to feel that people might be watching him and trying to detect something. This conscious expression, since it was as far as possible from boyish mirthfulness, was usually attributed to insolence or "smartness."

As the inquisition proceeded, one of his instructors repeated an impertinent remark of the boy's, and the Principal asked him whether he thought that a courteous speech to have made a woman. Paul shrugged his shoulders slightly and his eyebrows twitched.

"I don't know," he replied. "I didn't mean to be polite or impolite, either. I guess it's a sort of way I have of saying things regardless."

The Principal, who was a sympathetic man, asked him whether he didn't think that a way it would be well to get rid of. Paul grinned and said he guessed so. When he was told that he could go, he bowed gracefully and went out. His bow was but a repetition of the scandalous red carnation.

His teachers were in despair, and his drawing master voiced the feeling of them all when he declared there was something about the boy which none of them understood. He added: "I don't really believe that smile of his comes altogether from insolence; there's something sort of haunted about it. The boy is not strong, for one thing. I happen to know that he was born in Colorado, only a few months before his mother died out there of a long illness. There is something wrong about the fellow."

The drawing master had come to realize that, in looking at Paul, one saw only his white teeth and the forced animation of his eyes. One warm afternoon the boy had gone to sleep at his drawing-board, and his master had noted with amazement what a white, blue-veined face it was; drawn and wrinkled like an old man's about the eyes, the lips twitching even in his sleep, and stiff with a nervous tension that drew them back from his teeth.

His teachers left the building dissatisfied and unhappy; humiliated to have felt so vindictive toward a mere boy, to have uttered this feeling in cutting terms, and to have set each other on, as it were, in the grewsome game of intemperate reproach. Some of them remembered having seen a miserable street cat set at bay by a ring of tormentors.

As for Paul, he ran down the hill whistling the Soldiers' Chorus from *Faust* looking wildly behind him now and then to see whether some of his teachers were not there to writhe under his light-heartedness. As it was now late in the afternoon and Paul was on duty that evening as usher at Carnegie Hall, he decided that he would not go home to supper. When he reached the concert hall the doors were not yet open and, as it was chilly outside, he decided to go up into the picture gallery—always deserted at this hour—where there were some of Raffelli's gay studies of Paris streets and an airy blue Venetian scene or two that always exhilarated him. He was delighted to find no one in the gallery but the old guard, who sat in one corner, a newspaper on his knee, a black patch over one eye and the other closed. Paul possessed himself of the place and walked confidently up and down, whistling under his breath. After a while he sat down before a blue Rico and lost himself. When he bethought him to look at his watch, it was after seven o'clock, and he rose with a start and ran downstairs, making a face at Augustus, peering out from the cast-room, and an evil gesture at the Venus of Milo as he passed her on the stairway.

When Paul reached the ushers' dressing-room half-a-dozen boys were there already, and he began excitedly to tumble into his uniform. It was one of the few that at all approached fitting, and Paul thought it very becoming—though he knew that the tight, straight coat accentuated his narrow chest, about which he was exceedingly sensitive. He was always considerably excited while he dressed, twanging all over to the tuning of the strings and the preliminary flourishes of the horns in the music-room; but to-night he seemed quite beside himself, and he teased and plagued the boys until, telling him that he was crazy, they put him down on the floor and sat on him.

Somewhat calmed by his suppression, Paul dashed out to the front of the house to seat the early comers. He was a model usher; gracious and smiling he ran up and down the aisles; nothing was too much trouble for him; he carried messages and brought programmes as though it were his greatest pleasure in life, and all the people in his section thought him a charming boy, feeling that he remembered and admired them. As the house filled, he grew more and more vivacious and animated, and the colour came to his cheeks and lips. It was very much as though this were a great reception and Paul were the host. Just as the musicians came out to take their places, his English teacher arrived with checks for the seats which a prominent manufacturer had taken for the season. She betrayed some embarrassment when she handed Paul the tickets, and a *hauteur* which subsequently made her feel very foolish. Paul was startled for a moment, and had the feeling of wanting to put her out; what business had she here among all these fine people and gay colours? He looked her over and decided that she was not appropriately dressed and must be a fool to sit downstairs in such togs. The tickets had probably been sent her out of kindness, he reflected as he put down a seat for her, and she had about as much right to sit there as he had.

When the symphony began Paul sank into one of the rear seats with a long sigh of relief, and lost himself as he had done before the Rico. It was not that symphonies, as such, meant anything in particular to Paul, but the first sigh of the instruments seemed to free some hilarious and potent spirit within him; something that struggled there like the Genius in the bottle found by the Arab fisherman. He felt a sudden zest of life; the lights danced before his eyes and the concert hall blazed into unimaginable splendour. When the soprano soloist came on, Paul forgot even the nastiness of his teacher's being there and gave himself up to the peculiar stimulus such personages always had for him. The soloist chanced to be a German woman, by no means in her first youth, and the mother of many children; but she wore an elaborate gown and a tiara, and above all she had that indefinable air of achievement, that world-shine upon her, which, in Paul's eyes, made her a veritable queen of Romance.

After a concert was over Paul was always irritable and wretched until he got to sleep, and to-night he was even more than usually restless.

He had the feeling of not being able to let down, of its being impossible to give up this delicious excitement which was the only thing that could be called living at all. During the last number he withdrew and, after hastily changing his clothes in the dressing-room, slipped out to the side door where the soprano's carriage stood. Here he began pacing rapidly up and down the walk, waiting to see her come out.

Over yonder the Schenley, in its vacant stretch, loomed big and square through the fine rain, the windows of its twelve stories glowing like those of a lighted card-board house under a Christmas tree. All the actors and singers of the better class stayed there when they were in the city, and a number of the big manufacturers of the place lived there in the winter. Paul had often hung about the hotel, watching the people go in and out, longing to enter and leave school-masters and dull care behind him forever.

At last the singer came out, accompanied by the conductor, who helped her into her carriage and closed the door with a cordial *auf wieder-sehen* which set Paul to wondering whether she were not an old sweet-heart of his. Paul followed the carriage over to the hotel, walking so rapidly as not to be far from the entrance when the singer alighted and disappeared behind the swinging glass doors that were opened by a negro in a tall hat and a long coat. In the moment that the door was ajar it seemed to Paul that he, too, entered. He seemed to feel himself go after her up the steps, into the warm, lighted building, into an exotic, a tropical world of shiny, glistening surfaces and basking ease. He reflected upon the mysterious dishes that were brought into the dining-room, the green bottles in buckets of ice, as he had seen them in the supper party pictures of the *Sunday World* supplement. A quick gust of wind brought the rain down with sudden vehemence, and Paul was startled to find that he was still outside in the slush of the gravel driveway; that his boots were letting in the water and his scanty overcoat was clinging wet about him; that the lights in front of the concert hall were out, and that the rain was driving in sheets between him and the orange glow of the windows above him. There it was, what he wanted—tangibly before him, like the fairy world of a Christmas pantomime, but mocking spirits stood guard at the doors, and, as the rain beat in his face, Paul wondered whether he were destined always to shiver in the black night outside, looking up at it.

He turned and walked reluctantly toward the car tracks. The end had to come sometime; his father in his night-clothes at the top of the stairs, explanations that did not explain, hastily improvised fictions that were forever tripping him up, his upstairs room and its horrible yellow wall-paper, the creaking bureau with the greasy plush collar-box, and over his painted wooden bed the pictures of George Washington and John Calvin, and the framed motto, "Feed my Lambs," which had been worked in red worsted by his mother.

Half an hour later, Paul alighted from his car and went slowly down one of the side streets off the main thoroughfare. It was a highly respectable street, where all the houses were exactly alike, and where business men of moderate means begot and reared large families of children, all of whom went to Sabbath-school and learned the shorter catechism, and were interested in arithmetic; all of whom were as exactly alike as their homes, and of a piece with the monotony in which they lived. Paul never went up Cordelia Street without a shudder of loathing. His home was next to the house of the Cumberland minister. He approached it to-night with the nerveless sense of defeat, the hopeless feeling of sinking back forever into ugliness and commonness that he had always had when he came home. The moment he turned into Cordelia Street he felt the waters close above his head. After each of these orgies of living, he experienced all the physical depression which follows a debauch; the loathing of respectable beds, of common food, of a house penetrated by kitchen odours; a shuddering repulsion for the flavourless, colourless mass of every-day existence; a morbid desire for cool things and soft lights and fresh flowers.

The nearer he approached the house, the more absolutely unequal Paul felt to the sight of it all; his ugly sleeping chamber; the cold bathroom with the grimy zinc tub, the cracked mirror, the dripping spiggots; his father, at the top of the stairs, his hairy legs sticking out from his night-shirt, his feet thrust into carpet slippers. He was so much later than usual that there would certainly be inquiries and reproaches. Paul stopped short before the door. He felt that he could not be accosted by his father to-night; that he could not toss again on that miserable bed. He would not go in. He would tell his father that he had no car fare, and it was raining so hard he had gone home with one of the boys and stayed all night.

Meanwhile, he was wet and cold. He went around to the back of the house and tried one of the basement windows, found it open, raised it cautiously, and scrambled down the cellar wall to the floor. There he stood, holding his breath, terrified by the noise he had made, but the floor above him was silent, and there was no creak on the stairs. He found a soap-box, and carried it over to the soft ring of light that streamed from

the furnace door, and sat down. He was horribly afraid of rats, so he did
not try to sleep, but sat looking distrustfully at the dark, still terrified lest
he might have awakened his father. In such reactions, after one of the
experiences which made days and nights out of the dreary blanks of the
calendar, when his senses were deadened, Paul's head was always singularly
clear. Suppose his father had heard him getting in at the window and had
come down and shot him for a burglar? Then, again, suppose his father
had come down, pistol in hand, and he had cried out in time to save
himself, and his father had been horrified to think how nearly he had
killed him? Then, again, suppose a day should come when his father would
remember that night, and wish there had been no warning cry to stay his
hand? With this last supposition Paul entertained himself until daybreak.

The following Sunday was fine; the sodden November chill was
broken by the last flash of autumnal summer. In the morning Paul had to
go to church and Sabbath-school, as always. On seasonable Sunday afternoons the burghers of Cordelia Street always sat out on their front
"stoops," and talked to their neighbours on the next stoop, or called to
those across the street in neighbourly fashion. The men usually sat on gay
cushions placed upon the steps that led down to the sidewalk, while the
women, in their Sunday "waists," sat in rockers on the cramped porches,
pretending to be greatly at their ease. The children played in the streets;
there were so many of them that the place resembled the recreation grounds
of a kindergarten. The men on the steps—all in their shirt sleeves, their
vests unbuttoned—sat with their legs well apart, their stomachs comfortably protruding, and talked of the prices of things, or told anecdotes
of the sagacity of their various chiefs and overlords. They occasionally
looked over the multitude of squabbling children, listened affectionately
to their high-pitched, nasal voices, smiling to see their own proclivities
reproduced in their offspring, and interspersed their legends of the iron
kings with remarks about their sons' progress at school, their grades in
arithmetic, and the amounts they had saved in their toy banks.

On this last Sunday of November, Paul sat all the afternoon on the
lowest step of his "stoop," staring into the street, while his sisters, in their
rockers, were talking to the minister's daughters next door about how
many shirt-waists they had made in the last week, and how many waffles
some one had eaten at the last church supper. When the weather was
warm, and his father was in a particularly jovial frame of mind, the girls
made lemonade, which was always brought out in a red-glass pitcher,
ornamented with forget-me-nots in blue enamel. This the girls thought

very fine, and the neighbours always joked about the suspicious colour of the pitcher.

To-day Paul's father sat on the top step, talking to a young man who shifted a restless baby from knee to knee. He happened to be the young man who was daily held up to Paul as a model, and after whom it was his father's dearest hope that he would pattern. This young man was of a ruddy complexion, with a compressed, red mouth, and faded, near-sighted eyes, over which he wore thick spectacles, with gold bows that curved about his ears. He was clerk to one of the magnates of a great steel corporation, and was looked upon in Cordelia Street as a young man with a future. There was a story that, some five years ago—he was now barely twenty-six—he had been a trifle dissipated but in order to curb his appetites and save the loss of time and strength that a sowing of wild oats might have entailed, he had taken his chief's advice, oft reiterated to his employees, and at twenty-one had married the first woman whom he could persuade to share his fortunes. She happened to be an angular school-mistress, much older than he, who also wore thick glasses, and who had now borne him four children, all near-sighted, like herself.

The young man was relating how his chief, now cruising in the Mediterranean, kept in touch with all the details of the business, arranging his office hours on his yacht just as though he were at home, and "knock-ing off work enough to keep two stenographers busy." His father told, in turn, the plan his corporation was considering, of putting in an electric railway plant at Cairo. Paul snapped his teeth; he had an awful appre-hension that they might spoil it all before he got there. Yet he rather liked to hear these legends of the iron kings, that were told and retold on Sundays and holidays; these stories of palaces in Venice, yachts on the Mediterranean, and high play at Monte Carlo appealed to his fancy, and he was interested in the triumphs of these cash boys who had become famous, though he had no mind for the cash-boy stage.

After supper was over, and he had helped to dry the dishes, Paul nervously asked his father whether he could go to George's to get some help in his geometry, and still more nervously asked for car fare. This latter request he had to repeat, as his father, on principle, did not like to hear requests for money, whether much or little. He asked Paul whether he could not go to some boy who lived nearer, and told him that he ought not to leave his school work until Sunday; but he gave him the dime. He was not a poor man, but he had a worthy ambition to come up in the world. His only reason for allowing Paul to usher was, that he thought a boy ought to be earning a little.

Paul bounded upstairs, scrubbed the greasy odour of the dish-water from his hands with the ill-smelling soap he hated, and then shook over his fingers a few drops of violet water from the bottle he kept hidden in his drawer. He left the house with his geometry conspicuously under his arm, and the moment he got out of Cordelia Street and boarded a downtown car, he shook off the lethargy of two deadening days, and began to live again.

The leading juvenile of the permanent stock company which played at one of the downtown theatres was an acquaintance of Paul's, and the boy had been invited to drop in at the Sunday-night rehearsals whenever he could. For more than a year Paul had spent every available moment loitering about Charley Edwards's dressing-room. He had won a place among Edwards's following not only because the young actor, who could not afford to employ a dresser, often found him useful, but because he recognized in Paul something akin to what churchmen term "vocation."

It was at the theatre and at Carnegie Hall that Paul really lived; the rest was but a sleep and a forgetting. This was Paul's fairy tale, and it had for him all the allurement of a secret love. The moment he inhaled the gassy, painty, dusty odour behind the scenes, he breathed like a prisoner set free, and felt within him the possibility of doing or saying splendid, brilliant, poetic things. The moment the cracked orchestra beat out the overture from *Martha*, or jerked at the serenade from *Rigoletto*, all stupid and ugly things slid from him, and his senses were deliciously, yet delicately fired.

Perhaps it was because, in Paul's world, the natural nearly always wore the guise of ugliness, that a certain element of artificiality seemed to him necessary in beauty. Perhaps it was because his experience of life elsewhere was so full of Sabbath-school picnics, petty economies, wholesome advice as to how to succeed in life, and the unescapable odours of cooking, that he found this existence so alluring, these smartly-clad men and women so attractive, that he was so moved by these starry apple orchards that bloomed perennially under the lime-light.

It would be difficult to put it strongly enough how convincingly the stage entrance of that theatre was for Paul the actual portal of Romance. Certainly none of the company ever suspected it, least of all Charley Edwards. It was very like the old stories that used to float about London of fabulously rich Jews, who had subterranean halls there, with palms, and fountains, and soft lamps and richly apparelled women who never saw the disenchanting light of London day. So, in the midst of that smoke-palled city, enamoured of figures and grimy toil, Paul had his secret temple, his wishing carpet, his bit of blue-and-white Mediterranean shore bathed in perpetual sunshine.

Several of Paul's teachers had a theory that his imagination had been perverted by garish fiction, but the truth was that he scarcely ever read at all. The books at home were not such as would either tempt or corrupt a youthful mind, and as for reading the novels that some of his friends urged upon him—well, he got what he wanted much more quickly from music; any sort of music, from an orchestra to a barrel organ. He needed only the spark, the indescribable thrill that made his imagination master of his senses, and he could make plots and pictures enough of his own. It was equally true that he was not stage struck—not, at any rate, in the usual acceptation of that expression. He had no desire to become an actor, any more than he had to become a musician. He felt no necessity to do any of these things; what he wanted was to see, to be in the atmosphere, float on the wave of it, to be carried out, blue league after blue league, away from everything.

After a night behind the scenes, Paul found the school-room more than ever repulsive; the bare floors and naked walls; the prosy men who never wore frock coats, or violets in their buttonholes; the women with their dull gowns, shrill voices, and pitiful seriousness about prepositions that govern the dative. He could not bear to have the other pupils think, for a moment, that he took these people seriously; he must convey to them that he considered it all trivial, and was there only by way of a jest, anyway. He had autographed pictures of all the members of the stock company which he showed his classmates, telling them the most incredible stories of his familiarity with these people, of his acquaintance with the soloists who came to Carnegie Hall, his suppers with them and the flowers he sent them. When these stories lost their effect, and his audience grew listless, he became desperate and would bid all the boys good-bye, announcing that he was going to travel for a while; going to Naples, to Venice, to Egypt. Then, next Monday, he would slip back, conscious and nervously smiling; his sister was ill, and he should have to defer his voyage until spring.

Matters went steadily worse with Paul at school. In the itch to let his instructors know how heartily he despised them and their homilies, and how thoroughly he was appreciated elsewhere, he mentioned once or twice that he had no time to fool with theorems; adding—with a twitch of the eyebrows and a touch of that nervous bravado which so perplexed them—that he was helping the people down at the stock company; they were old friends of his.

The upshot of the matter was that the Principal went to Paul's father, and Paul was taken out of school and put to work. The manager at Carnegie Hall was told to get another usher in his stead; the door-keeper at the theatre was warned not to admit him to the house; and Charley Edwards remorsefully promised the boy's father not to see him again.

The members of the stock company were vastly amused when some of Paul's stories reached them—especially the women. They were hard-working women, most of them supporting indigent husbands or brothers, and they laughed rather bitterly at having stirred the boy to such fervid and florid inventions. They agreed with the faculty and with his father that Paul's was a bad case.

The east-bound train was ploughing through a January snow-storm; the dull dawn was beginning to show grey when the engine whistled a mile out of Newark. Paul started up from the seat where he had lain curled in uneasy slumber, rubbed the breath-misted window glass with his hand, and peered out. The snow was whirling in curling eddies above the white bottom lands, and the drifts lay already deep in the fields and along the fences, while here and there the long dead grass and dried weed stalks protruded black above it. Lights shone from the scattered houses, and a gang of labourers who stood beside the track waved their lanterns.

Paul had slept very little, and he felt grimy and uncomfortable. He had made the all-night journey in a day coach, partly because he was ashamed, dressed as he was, to go into a Pullman, and partly because he was afraid of being seen there by some Pittsburgh business man, who might have noticed him in Denny & Carson's office. When the whistle awoke him, he clutched quickly at his breast pocket, glancing about him with an uncertain smile. But the little, clay-bespattered Italians were still sleeping, the slatternly women across the aisle were in open-mouthed oblivion, and even the crumby, crying babies were for the nonce stilled. Paul settled back to struggle with his impatience as best he could.

When he arrived at the Jersey City station, he hurried through his breakfast, manifestly ill at ease and keeping a sharp eye about him. After he reached the Twenty-third Street station, he consulted a cabman, and had himself driven to a men's furnishing establishment that was just opening for the day. He spent upward of two hours there, buying with endless reconsidering and great care. His new street suit he put on in the fitting-room; the frock coat and dress clothes he had bundled into the cab with his linen. Then he drove to a hatter's and a shoe house. His next errand was at Tiffany's, where he selected his silver and a new scarf-pin. He would not wait to have his silver marked, he said. Lastly, he stopped at a trunk shop on Broadway, and had his purchases packed into various travelling bags.

It was a little after one o'clock when he drove up to the Waldorf, and after settling with the cabman, went into the office. He registered from Washington; said his mother and father had been abroad, and that he had come down to await the arrival of their steamer. He told his story plausibly and had no trouble, since he volunteered to pay for them in advance, in engaging his rooms; a sleeping-room, sitting-room and bath.

Not once, but a hundred times Paul had planned this entry into New York. He had gone over every detail of it with Charley Edwards, and in his scrap book at home there were pages of description about New York hotels, cut from the Sunday papers. When he was shown to his sitting-room on the eighth floor, he saw at a glance that everything was as it should be; there was but one detail in his mental picture that the place did not realize, so he rang for the bell boy and sent him down for flowers. He moved about nervously until the boy returned, putting away his new linen and fingering it delightedly as he did so. When the flowers came, he put them hastily into water, and then tumbled into a hot bath. Presently he came out of his white bath-room, resplendent in his new silk underwear, and playing with the tassels of his red robe. The snow was whirling so fiercely outside his windows that he could scarcely see across the street, but within the air was deliciously soft and fragrant. He put the violets and jonquils on the taboret beside the couch, and threw himself down, with a long sigh, covering himself with a Roman blanket. He was thoroughly tired; he had been in such haste, he had stood up to such a strain, covered so much ground in the last twenty-four hours, that he wanted to think how it had all come about. Lulled by the sound of the wind, the warm air, and the cool fragrance of the flowers, he sank into deep, drowsy retrospection.

It had been wonderfully simple; when they had shut him out of the theatre and concert hall, when they had taken away his bone, the whole thing was virtually determined. The rest was a mere matter of opportunity. The only thing that at all surprised him was his own courage—for he realized well enough that he had always been tormented by fear, a sort of apprehensive dread that, of late years, as the meshes of the lies he had told closed about him, had been pulling the muscles of his body tighter and tighter. Until now, he could not remember the time when he had not been dreading something. Even when he was a little boy, it was always there—behind him, or before, or on either side. There had always been the shadowed corner, the dark place into which he dared not look, but from which something seemed always to be watching him—and Paul had done things that were not pretty to watch, he knew.

But now he had a curious sense of relief, as though he had at last thrown down the gauntlet to the thing in the corner.

Yet it was but a day since he had been sulking in the traces; but yesterday afternoon that he had been sent to the bank with Denny & Carson's deposit, as usual—but this time he was instructed to leave the book to be balanced. There was above two thousand dollars in checks, and nearly a thousand in the bank notes which he had taken from the book and quietly transferred to his pocket. At the bank he had made out a new deposit slip. His nerves had been steady enough to permit of his returning to the office, where he had finished his work and asked for a full day's holiday to-morrow, Saturday, giving a perfectly reasonable pretext. The bank book, he knew, would not be returned before Monday or Tuesday, and his father would be out of town for the next week. From the time he slipped the bank notes into his pocket until he boarded the night train for New York, he had not known a moment's hesitation. It was not the first time Paul had steered through treacherous waters.

How astonishingly easy it had all been; here he was, the thing done; and this time there would be no awakening, no figure at the top of the stairs. He watched the snow flakes whirling by his window until he fell asleep.

When he awoke, it was three o'clock in the afternoon. He bounded up with a start; half of one of his precious days gone already! He spent more than an hour in dressing, watching every stage of his toilet carefully in the mirror. Everything was quite perfect; he was exactly the kind of boy he had always wanted to be.

When he went downstairs, Paul took a carriage and drove up Fifth Avenue toward the Park. The snow had somewhat abated; carriages and tradesmen's wagons were hurrying soundlessly to and fro in the winter twilight; boys in woollen mufflers were shovelling off the doorsteps; the avenue stages made fine spots of colour against the white street. Here and there on the corners were stands, with whole flower gardens blooming under glass cases, against the sides of which the snow flakes stuck and melted; violets, roses, carnations, lilies of the valley—somehow vastly more lovely and alluring that they blossomed thus unnaturally in the snow. The Park itself was a wonderful stage winterpiece.

When he returned, the pause of the twilight had ceased, and the tune of the streets had changed. The snow was falling faster, lights streamed from the hotels that reared their dozen stories fearlessly up into the storm, defying the raging Atlantic winds. A long, black stream of carriages poured down the avenue, intersected here and there by other streams, tending horizontally. There were a score of cabs about the entrance of his hotel, and his driver had to wait. Boys in livery were running in and out of the awning stretched across the sidewalk, up and down the red velvet carpet laid from the door to the street. Above, about, within it all was the rumble and roar, the hurry and toss of thousands of human beings as hot for pleasure as himself, and on every side of him towered the glaring affirmation of the omnipotence of wealth.

The boy set his teeth and drew his shoulders together in a spasm of realization; the plot of all dramas, the text of all romances, the nerve-stuff of all sensations was whirling about him like the snow flakes. He burnt like a faggot in a tempest.

When Paul went down to dinner, the music of the orchestra came floating up the elevator shaft to greet him. His head whirled as he stepped into the thronged corridor, and he sank back into one of the chairs against the wall to get his breath. The lights, the chatter, the perfumes, the bewildering medley of colour—he had, for a moment, the feeling of not being able to stand it. But only for a moment; these were his own people, he told himself. He went slowly about the corridors, through the writing-rooms, smoking-rooms, reception-rooms, as though he were exploring the chambers of an enchanted palace, built and peopled for him alone.

When he reached the dining-room he sat down at a table near a window. The flowers, the white linen, the many-coloured wine glasses, the gay toilettes of the women, the low popping of corks, the undulating repetitions of the *Blue Danube* from the orchestra, all flooded Paul's dream with bewildering radiance. When the roseate tinge of his champagne was added—that cold, precious, bubbling stuff that creamed and foamed in his glass—Paul wondered that there were honest men in the world at all. This was what all the world was fighting for, he reflected; this was what all the struggle was about. He doubted the reality of his past. Had he ever known a place called Cordelia Street, a place where fagged-looking businessmen got on the early car; mere rivets in a machine they seemed to Paul,—sickening men, with combings of children's hair always hanging to their coats, and the smell of cooking in their clothes. Cordelia Street—Ah! that belonged to another time and country; had he not always been thus, had he not sat here night after night, from as far back as he could remember, looking pensively over just such shimmering textures, and slowly twirling the stem of a glass like this one between his thumb and middle finger? He rather thought he had.

He was not in the least abashed or lonely. He had no especial desire to meet or to know any of these people; all he demanded was the right to look on and conjecture, to watch the pageant. The mere stage properties were all he contended for. Nor was he lonely later in the evening, in his loge at the Metropolitan. He was now entirely rid of his nervous misgivings, of his forced aggressiveness, of the imperative desire to show himself different from his surroundings. He felt now that his surroundings explained him. Nobody questioned the purple; he had only to wear it passively. He had only to glance down at his attire to reassure himself that here it would be impossible for anyone to humiliate him.

He found it hard to leave his beautiful sitting-room to go to bed that night, and sat long watching the raging storm from his turret window. When he went to sleep it was with the lights turned on in his bedroom; partly because of his old timidity, and partly so that, if he should wake in the night, there would be no wretched moment of doubt, no horrible suspicion of yellow wall-paper, or of Washington and Calvin above his bed.

Sunday morning the city was practically snow-bound. Paul breakfasted late, and in the afternoon he fell in with a wild San Francisco boy, a freshman at Yale, who said he had run down for a "little flyer" over Sunday. The young man offered to show Paul the night side of the town, and the two boys went out together after dinner, not returning to the hotel until seven o'clock the next morning. They had started out in the confiding warmth of a champagne friendship, but their parting in the elevator was singularly cool. The freshman pulled himself together to make his train, and Paul went to bed. He awoke at two o'clock in the afternoon, very thirsty and dizzy, and rang for ice-water, coffee, and the Pittsburgh papers.

On the part of the hotel management, Paul excited no suspicion. There was this to be said for him, that he wore his spoils with dignity and in no way made himself conspicuous. Even under the glow of his wine he was never boisterous, though he found the stuff like a magician's wand for wonder-building. His chief greediness lay in his ears and eyes, and his excesses were not offensive ones. His dearest pleasures were the grey winter twilights in his sitting-room; his quiet enjoyment of his flowers, his clothes, his wide divan, his cigarette and his sense of power. He could not remember a time when he had felt so at peace with himself. The mere release from the necessity of petty lying, lying every day and every day, restored his self-respect. He had never lied for pleasure, even at school; but to be noticed and admired, to assert his difference from other Cordelia Street boys; and he felt a good deal more manly, more honest, even, now that he had no need for boastful pretensions, now that he could, as his actor friends used to say, "dress the part." It was characteristic that remorse did not occur to him. His golden days went by without a shadow, and he made each as perfect as he could.

On the eighth day after his arrival in New York, he found the whole affair exploited in the Pittsburgh papers, exploited with a wealth of detail which indicated that local news of a sensational nature was at a low ebb. The firm of Denny & Carson announced that the boy's father had refunded the full amount of the theft, and that they had no intention of prosecuting. The Cumberland minister had been interviewed, and expressed his hope of yet reclaiming the motherless lad, and his Sabbath-school teacher declared that she would spare no effort to that end. The rumour had reached Pittsburgh that the boy had been seen in a New York hotel, and his father had gone East to find him and bring him home.

Paul had just come in to dress for dinner; he sank into a chair, weak to the knees, and clasped his head in his hands. It was to be worse than jail, even; the tepid waters of Cordelia Street were to close over him finally and forever. The grey monotony stretched before him in hopeless, unrelieved years; Sabbath-school, Young People's Meeting, the yellow-papered room, the damp dish-towels; it all rushed back upon him with a sickening vividness. He had the old feeling that the orchestra had suddenly stopped, the sinking sensation that the play was over. The sweat broke out on his face, and he sprang to his feet, looked about him with his white, conscious smile, and winked at himself in the mirror. With something of the old childish belief in miracles with which he had so often gone to class, all his lessons unlearned, Paul dressed and dashed whistling down the corridor to the elevator.

He had no sooner entered the dining-room and caught the measure of the music than his remembrance was lightened by his old elastic power of claiming the moment, mounting with it, and finding it all sufficient. The glare and glitter about him, the mere scenic accessories had again, and for the last time, their old potency. He would show himself that he was game, he would finish the thing splendidly. He doubted, more than ever, the existence of Cordelia Street, and for the first time he drank his wine recklessly. Was he not, after all, one of those fortunate beings born to the purple, was he not still himself and in his own place? He drummed a nervous accompaniment to the Pagliacci music and looked about him, telling himself over and over that it had paid.

He reflected drowsily, to the swell of the music and the chill sweetness of his wine, that he might have done it more wisely. He might have caught an outbound steamer and been well out of their clutches before now. But the other side of the world had seemed too far away and too uncertain then; he could not have waited for it; his need had been too sharp. If he had to choose over again, he would do the same thing to-morrow. He looked affectionately about the dining-room, now gilded with a soft mist. Ah, it had paid indeed!

Paul was awakened next morning by a painful throbbing in his head and feet. He had thrown himself across the bed without undressing, and had slept with his shoes on. His limbs and hands were lead heavy, and his tongue and throat were parched and burnt. There came upon him one of those fateful attacks of clear-headedness that never occurred except when he was physically exhausted and his nerves hung loose. He lay still and closed his eyes and let the tide of things wash over him.

His father was in New York; "stopping at some joint or other," he told himself. The memory of successive summers on the front stoop fell upon him like a weight of black water. He had not a hundred dollars left; and he knew now, more than ever, that money was everything, the wall that stood between all he loathed and all he wanted. The thing was winding itself up; he had thought of that on his first glorious day in New York, and had even provided a way to snap the thread. It lay on his dressing-table now; he had got it out last night when he came blindly up from dinner, but the shiny metal hurt his eyes, and he disliked the looks of it.

He rose and moved about with a painful effort, succumbing now and again to attacks of nausea. It was the old depression exaggerated; all the world had become Cordelia Street. Yet somehow he was not afraid of anything, was absolutely calm; perhaps because he had looked into the dark corner at last and knew. It was bad enough, what he saw there, but somehow not so bad as his long fear of it had been. He saw everything clearly now. He had a feeling that he had made the best of it, that he had lived the sort of life he was meant to live, and for half an hour he sat staring at the revolver. But he told himself that was not the way, so he went downstairs and took a cab to the ferry.

When Paul arrived at Newark, he got off the train and took another cab, directing the driver to follow the Pennsylvania tracks out of the town. The snow lay heavy on the roadways and had drifted deep in the open fields. Only here and there the dead grass or dried weed stalks projected, singularly black, above it. Once well into the country, Paul dismissed the carriage and walked, floundering along the tracks, his mind a medley of irrelevant things. He seemed to hold in his brain an actual picture of everything he had seen that morning. He remembered every feature of both his drivers, of the toothless old woman from whom he had bought the red flowers in his coat, the agent from whom he had got his ticket, and all of his fellow-passengers on the ferry. His mind, unable to cope with vital matters near at hand, worked feverishly and deftly at sorting and grouping these images. They made for him a part of the ugliness of the world, of the ache in his head, and the bitter burning on his tongue. He stooped and put a handful of snow into his mouth as he walked, but that, too, seemed hot. When he reached a little hillside, where the tracks ran through a cut some twenty feet below him, he stopped and sat down.

The carnations in his coat were drooping with the cold, he noticed; their red glory all over. It occurred to him that all the flowers he had seen in the glass cases that first night must have gone the same way, long before this. It was only one splendid breath they had, in spite of their brave mockery at the winter outside the glass; and it was a losing game in the end, it seemed, this revolt against the homilies by which the world is run. Paul took one of the blossoms carefully from his coat and scooped a little hole in the snow, where he covered it up. Then he dozed a while, from his weak condition, seemingly insensible to the cold.

The sound of an approaching train awoke him, and he started to his feet, remembering only his resolution, and afraid lest he should be too late. He stood watching the approaching locomotive, his teeth chattering, his lips drawn away from them in a frightened smile; once or twice he glanced nervously sidewise, as though he were being watched. When the right moment came, he jumped. As he fell, the folly of his haste occurred to him with merciless clearness, the vastness of what he had left undone. There flashed through his brain, clearer than ever before, the blue of Adriatic water, the yellow of Algerian sands.

He felt something strike his chest, and that his body was being thrown swiftly through the air, on and on, immeasurably far and fast, while his limbs were gently relaxed. Then, because the picture making mechanism was crushed, the disturbing visions flashed into black, and Paul dropped back into the immense design of things.

First published in *The Troll Garden* (New York: McClure, Phillips & Co., 1905), pp. 211–253. First magazine publication in *McClure's*, XXV (May, 1905), 74–83.

Volume III

ON
THE
DIVIDE

✤ ✤ ✤

During the first decade of her professional writing career—from November, 1893, when she began to contribute Sunday columns and play reviews to the Nebraska State Journal, until the fall of 1902, when she wrote the first of the Troll Garden stories—Willa Cather's output was prodigious. Because many of her pieces were unsigned or signed with a pseudonym it may never be possible to determine exactly how much she did write, but it is safe to say that in these years she turned out more than five hundred columns, articles, reviews, and feature stories in addition to poems (the best collected in April Twilights, published in 1903), an unpublished volume of drama criticism, "The Player Letters," and twenty-odd short stories.

Seventeen of the signed stories belonging to this period appeared after June of 1896, when Willa Cather went to Pittsburgh as an editor of the Home Monthly.* She resigned the following summer, and in September, 1897, joined the staff of the Pittsburgh Daily Leader, remaining with this paper until the spring of 1900. During the next year Willa Cather lived mostly in Washington, D.C., supporting herself largely by freelancing for various newspapers and periodicals; then in February or March of 1901 she obtained a teaching post in Pittsburgh's Central High School. For a time she continued to contribute sporadically to Pittsburgh and Lincoln newspapers, but after her return from her first trip abroad in the fall of 1902 her days as a freelance journalist to all intents and purposes were at an end.

The four stories which open Volume III came out between the spring of 1901, when Willa Cather met Isabelle McClung and went to live in the McClung household, and the fall of 1902. Three were published in the New England Magazine; one, "Jack-a-Boy," in the Saturday Evening Post. The next group of four all appeared in an ephemeral Pittsburgh magazine, The Library, in the spring and summer of 1900. Of the following nine, written when Willa Cather was working on the Leader and the Home Monthly, "Eric Hermannson's Soul" was first published in Cosmopolitan, "The Westbound Train" and "Nanette: An Aside" in the Lincoln Courier, and the others in the Home Monthly. Six of the seventeen stories have never previously been collected, and four—"The Professor's Commencement," "El Dorado: A Kansas Recessional," "The Way of the World," and "The Westbound Train"—are reprinted here for the first time.

---

* A note on eight earlier stories appears on page 481; three pseudonymous stories and one unsigned story are included in the Appendix.

The Treasure of Far Island

❋ ❋ ❋

Dark brown is the river,
  Golden is the sand;
It flows along forever,
  With trees on either hand.
    —*Robert Louis Stevenson.*

I

Far Island is an oval sand bar, half a mile in length and perhaps a hundred yards wide, which lies about two miles up from Empire City in a turbid little Nebraska river. The island is known chiefly to the children who dwell in that region, and generation after generation of them have claimed it; fished there, and pitched their tents under the great arched tree, and built camp fires on its level, sandy outskirts. In the middle of the island, which is always above water except in flood time, grow thousands of yellow-green creek willows and cottonwood seedlings, brilliantly green, even when the hottest winds blow, by reason of the surrounding moisture. In the summer months, when the capricious stream is low, the children's empire is extended by many rods, and a long irregular beach of white sand is exposed along the east coast of the island, never out of the water long enough to acquire any vegetation, but dazzling white, ripple marked, and full of possibilities for the imagination. The island is No-Man's-Land; every summer a new chief claims it and it has been called by many names; but it seemed particularly to belong to the two children who christened it Far Island, partially because they were the original discoverers and claimants, but more especially because they were of that favored race whom a New England sage called the true land-lords and sea-lords of the world.

One afternoon, early in June, the Silvery Beaches of Far Island were glistening in the sun like pounded glass, and the same slanting yellow rays that scorched the sand beat upon the windows of the passenger train from the East as it swung into the Republican Valley from the uplands. Then a young man dressed in a suit of gray tweed changed his seat in order to be on the side of the car next the river. When he crossed the car several women looked up and smiled, for it was with a movement of boyish abandon and an audible chuckle of delight that he threw himself into the seat to watch for the shining curves of the river as they unwound through the trees. He was sufficiently distinguished in appearance to interest even tired women at the end of a long, sultry day's travel. As the train rumbled over a trestle built above a hollow grown up with sunflowers and ironweed, he sniffed with delight the rank odor, familiar to the prairie bred man, that is exhaled by such places as evening approaches. "Ha," he murmured under his breath, "there's the white chalk cliff where the Indians used to run the buffalo over Bison Leap—we kids called it—the remote sea wall of the boy world. I'm getting home sure enough. And heavens! there's the island, Far Island, the Ultima Thule; and the arched tree, and Spy Glass Hill, and the Silvery Beaches; my heart's going like a boy's. 'Once on a day he sailed away, over the sea to Skye.'"

He sat bolt upright with his lips tightly closed and his chest swelling, for he was none other than the original discoverer of the island, Douglass Burnham, the playwright—our only playwright, certain critics contend— and, for the first time since he left it a boy, he was coming home. It was only twelve years ago that he had gone away, when Pagie and Temp and Birkner and Shorty Thompson had stood on the station siding and waved him goodbye, while he shut his teeth to keep the tears back; and now the train bore him up the old river valley, through the meadows where he used to hunt for cattails, along the streams where he had paddled his canvas boat, and past the willow-grown island where he had buried the pirate's treasure—a man with a man's work done and the world well in hand. Success had never tasted quite so sweet as it tasted then. The whistle sounded, the brakeman called Empire City, and Douglass crossed to the other side of the car and looked out toward the town, which lay half a mile up from the station on a low range of hills, half hidden by the tall cottonwood trees that still shaded its streets. Down the curve of the track he could see the old railroad "eating house," painted the red Burlington color; on the hill above the town the standpipe towered up from the tree-tops. Douglass felt the years dropping away from him. The train stopped. Waiting on the platform stood his father and a tall spare man, with a straggling colorless beard, whose dejected stoop and shapeless hat and ill-fitting clothes were in themselves both introduction and biography.

The narrow chest, long arms, and skinny neck were not to be mistaken. It was Rhinehold Birkner, old Rhine who had not been energetic enough to keep up his father's undertaking business, and who now sold sewing machines and parlor organs in a feeble attempt to support an invalid wife and ten children, all colorless and narrow chested like himself. Douglass sprang from the platform and grasped his father's hand.

"Hello, father, hello, Rhine, where are the other fellows? Why, that's so, you must be the only one left. Heavens! how we *have* scattered. What a lot of talking we two have got before us."

Probably no event had transpired since Rhine's first baby was born that had meant so much to him as Douglass's return, but he only chuckled, putting his limp, rough hand into the young man's smooth, warm one, and ventured,

"Jest the same old coon, Doug."

"How's mother, father?" Douglass asked as he hunted for his checks.

"She's well, son, but she thought she couldn't leave supper to come down to meet you. She has been cooking pretty much all day and worrying for fear the train would be late and your supper would spoil."

"Of course she has. When I am elected to the Academy mother will worry about my supper." Douglass felt a trifle nervous and made a dash for the shabby little street car which ever since he could remember had been drawn by mules that wore jingling bells on their collars.

A silence settled down over the occupants of the car as the mules trotted off. Douglass felt that his father stood somewhat in awe of him, or at least in awe of that dread Providence which ordered such dark things as that a hard-headed, money-saving real-estate man should be the father of a white-fingered playwright who spent more on his fads in a year than his father had saved by the thrift of a lifetime. All the hundred things Douglass had had to say seemed congested upon his tongue, and though he had a good measure of that cheerful assurance common to young people whom the world has made much of, he felt a strange embarrassment in the presence of this angular gray-whiskered man who used to warm his jacket for him in the hayloft.

His mother was waiting for him under the bittersweet vines on the porch, just where she had always stood to greet him when he came home for his college vacations, and, as Douglass had lived in a world where the emotions are cultivated and not despised, he was not ashamed of the lump that rose in his throat when he took her in his arms. She hurried him out of the dark into the parlor lamplight and looked him over from head to foot to assure herself that he was still the handsomest of men, and then she told him to go into her bedroom to wash his face for supper. She followed him, unable to take her eyes from this splendid creature whom all the world claimed but who was only hers after all. She watched him take off his coat and collar, rejoicing in the freshness of his linen and the whiteness of his skin; even the color of his silk suspenders seemed a matter of importance to her.

"Douglass," she said impressively, "Mrs. Governor gives a reception for you tomorrow night, and I have promised her that you will read some selections from your plays."

This was a matter which was very near Mrs. Burnham's heart. Those dazzling first nights and receptions and author's dinners which happened out in the great world were merely hearsay, but it was a proud day when her son was held in honor by the women of her own town, of her own church; women she had shopped and marketed and gone to sewing circle with, women whose cakes and watermelon pickles won premiums over hers at the county fair.

"Read?" ejaculated Douglass, looking out over the towel and pausing in his brisk rubbing, "why, mother, dear, I can't read, not any more than a John rabbit. Besides, plays aren't meant to be read. Let me give them one of my old stunts; 'The Polish Boy' or 'Regulus to the Carthaginians.'"

"But you must do it, my son; it won't do to disappoint Mrs. Governor. Margie was over this morning to see about it. She has grown into a very pretty girl." When his mother spoke in that tone Douglass acquiesced, just as naturally as he helped himself to her violet water, the same kind, he noticed, that he used to covertly sprinkle on his handkerchief when he was primping for Sunday school after she had gone to church.

"Mrs. Governor still leads the pack, then? What a civilizing influence she has been in this community. Taught most of us all the manners we ever knew. Little Margie has grown up pretty, you say? Well, I should never have thought it. How many boys have I slugged for yelling 'Reddy, go dye your hair green' at her. She was not an indifferent slugger herself and never exactly stood in need of masculine protection. What a wild Indian she was! Game, clear through, though! I never found such a mind in a girl. But *is* she a girl? I somehow always fancied she would grow up a man—and a ripping fine one. Oh, I see you are looking at me hard! No, mother, the girls don't trouble me much." His eyes met hers laughingly in the glass as he parted his hair. "You spoiled me so outrageously that women tell me frankly I'm a selfish cad and they will have none of me."

His mother handed him his coat with a troubled glance. "I was afraid, my son, that some of those actresses—"

The young man laughed outright. "Oh, never worry about them, mother. Wait till you've seen them at rehearsals in soiled shirtwaists wearing out their antiques and doing what they call 'resting' their hair. Poor things! They have to work too hard to bother about being attractive."

He went out into the dining room where the table was set for him just as it had always been when he came home on that same eight o'clock train from college. There were all his favorite viands and the old family silver spread on the white cloth with the maidenhair fern pattern, under the soft lamplight. It had been years since he had eaten by the mild light of a kerosene lamp. By his plate stood his own glass that his grandmother had given him with "For a Good Boy" ground on the surface which was dewy from the ice within. The other glasses were unclouded and held only fresh water from the pump, for his mother was very economical about ice and held the most exaggerated views as to the pernicious effects of ice water on the human stomach. Douglass only got it because he was the first dramatist of the country and a great man. When he decided that he would like a cocktail and asked for whiskey, his mother dealt him out a niggardly tablespoonful, saying, "That's as much as you ought to have at your age, Douglass." When he went out into the kitchen to greet the old servant and get some ice for his drink, his mother hurried after him crying with solicitude,

"I'll get the ice for you, Douglass. Don't you go into the refrigerator; you always leave the ice uncovered and it wastes."

Douglass threw up his hands, "Mother, whatever I may do in the world I shall never be clever enough to be trusted with that refrigerator. 'Into all the chambers of the palace mayest thou go, save into this thou shalt not go.'" And now he knew he was at home, indeed, for his father stood chuckling in the doorway, washing his hands from the milking, and the old servant threw her apron over her head to stifle her laughter at this strange reception of a celebrity. The memory of his luxurious rooms in New York, where he lived when he was an artist, faded dim; he was but a boy again in his father's house and must not keep supper waiting.

The next evening Douglass with resignation accompanied his father and mother to the reception given in his honor. The town had advanced somewhat since his day; and he was amused to see his father appear in an apology for a frock coat and a black tie, such as Kentucky politicians wear. Although people wore frock coats nowadays they still walked to receptions, and as Douglass climbed the hill the whole situation struck him as farcical. He dropped his mother's arm and ran up to the porch with his hat in his hand, laughing. "Margie!" he called, intending to dash through the house until he found her. But in the vestibule he bumped up against something large and splendid, then stopped and caught his breath. A woman stood in the dark by the hall lamp with a lighted match in her hand. She was in white and very tall. The match burned but a moment; a moment the light played on her hair, red as Etruscan gold and piled high above the curve of the neck and head; a moment upon the oval chin, the lips curving upward and red as a crimson cactus flower; the deep, gray, fearless eyes; the white shoulders framed about with darkness. Then the match went out, leaving Douglass to wonder whether, like Anchises, he had seen the vision that should forever blind him to the beauty of mortal women.

"I beg your pardon," he stammered, backing toward the door, "I was looking for Miss Van Dyck. Is she—" Perhaps it was a mere breath of stifled laughter, perhaps it was a recognition by some sense more trustworthy than sight and subtler than mind; but there seemed a certain familiarity in the darkness about him, a certain sense of the security and peace which one experiences among dear and intimate things, and with widening eyes he said softly,

"Tell me, is this Margie?"

There was just a murmur of laughter from the tall, white figure. "I was going to be presented to you in the most proper form, and now you've spoiled it all. How are you, Douglass, and did you get a whipping this time? You've played hooky longer than usual. Ten years, isn't it?" She put out her hand in the dark and he took it and drew it through his arm.

"No, I didn't get a whipping, but I may get worse. I wish I'd come back five years ago. I would if I had known," he said promptly.

The reading was just as stupid as he had said it would be, but his audience enjoyed it and he enjoyed his audience. There was the old deacon who had once caught him in his watermelon patch and set the dog on him; the president of the W.C.T.U., with her memorable black lace shawl and cane, who still continued to send him temperance tracts, mindful of the hundredth sheep in the parable; his old Sunday school teacher, a good man of limited information who never read anything but his Bible and *Teachers' Quarterly*, and who had once hung a cheap edition of *Camille* on the church Christmas tree for Douglass, with an inscription on the inside to the effect that the fear of the Lord is the beginning of Wisdom. There was the village criminal lawyer, one of those brilliant wrecks sometimes found in small towns, who, when he was so drunk he could not walk, used to lie back in his office chair and read Shakespeare by the hour to a little barefoot boy. Next him sat the rich banker who used to offer the boys a quarter to hitch up his horse for him, and then drive off, forgetting all about the quarter. Then there were fathers and mothers of Douglass's old clansmen and vassals who were scattered all over the world now. After the reading Douglass spent half an hour chatting with nice tiresome old ladies who reminded him of how much he used to like their teacakes and cookies, and answering labored compliments with genuine feeling. Then he went with a clear conscience and light heart whither his eyes had been wandering ever since he had entered the house.

"Margie, I needn't apologize for not recognizing you, since it was such an involuntary compliment. However did you manage to grow up like this? Was it boarding school that did it? I might have recognized you with your hair down, and oh, I'd know you anywhere when you smile! The teeth are just the same. Do you still crack nuts with them?"

"I haven't tried it for a long time. How remarkably little the years change you, Douglass. I haven't seen you since the night you brought out *The Clover Leaf*, and I heard your curtain speech. Oh, I was very proud of our Pirate Chief!"

Douglass sat down on the piano stool and looked searchingly into her eyes, which met his with laughing frankness.

"What! you were in New York then and didn't let me know? There was a day when you wouldn't have treated me so badly. Didn't you want to see me just a little bit—out of curiosity?"

"Oh, I was visiting some school friends who said it would be atrocious to bother you, and the newspapers were full of interesting details about your being so busy that you ate and got shaved at the theatre. Then one's time isn't one's own when one is visiting, you know." She saw the hurt expression on his face and repented, adding gayly, "But I may as well confess that I kept a sharp lookout for you on the street, and when I did meet you you didn't know me."

"And you didn't stop me? That's worse yet. How in Heaven's name was I to know you? Accost a goddess and say, 'Oh yes, you used to be a Pirate Chief and wear a butcher knife in your belt.' But I hadn't grown into an Apollo, save the mark! and you knew me well enough. I couldn't have passed you like that in a strange land."

"No, you do your duty by your countrymen, Douglass. You haven't grown haughty. One by one our old townspeople go out to see the world and bring us back tales of your glory. What unpromising specimens have you not dined and wined in New York! Why even old Skin Jackson, when he went to New York to have his eyes treated, you took to the Waldorf and to the Players' Club, where he drank with the Immortals. How do you have the courage to do it? *Did* he wear those dreadful gold nugget shirt studs that he dug up in Colorado when we were young?"

"Even the same, Margie, and he scored a hit with them. But you are dodging the point. When and where did you see me in New York?"

"Oh, it was one evening when you were crossing Madison Square. You were probably going to the theatre for Flashingham and Miss Grew were with you and you seemed in a hurry." Margie wished now that she had not mentioned the incident. "I remember that was the time I so deeply offended your mother on my return by telling her that Miss Grew had announced her engagement to you. How did it come out? She certainly did announce it."

"Doubtless, but it was entirely a misunderstanding on the lady's part. We never were anything of the sort," said Douglass impatiently. "That is a disgusting habit of Edith's; she announces a new engagement every fortnight as mechanically as the butler announces dinner. About once a month she calls the dear Twelfth Night girls together to a solemn high tea and gently breaks the news of a new engagement, and they kiss and cry over her and say the things they have said a dozen times before and go away tittering. Why she has been engaged to every society chap in New York and to the whole Milton family, with the possible exception of Sir Henry, and her papa has cabled his blessing all over the known world to her. But it is a waste of time to talk about such nonsense; don't let's," he urged.

"I think it is very interesting; I don't indulge in weekly engagements myself. But there is one thing I do want to know, Douglass; I want to know how you did it."

"Did what?"

Margie threw out her hands with an impetuous gesture. "Oh, all of it, all the wonderful things you have done. You remember that night when we lay on the sand bar—"

"The Uttermost Desert," interrupted Douglass softly.

"Yes, the Uttermost Desert, and in the light of the driftwood fire we planned the conquest of the world? Well, other people plan, too, and fight and suffer and fail the world over, and a very few succeed at the bitter end when they are old and it is no longer worth while. But you have done it as they used to do it in the fairy tales, without soiling your golden armor, and I can't find one line in your face to tell me that you have suffered or found life bitter to your tongue. How have you cheated fate?'

Douglass looked about him and saw that the guests had thronged about the punchbowl, and his mother, beaming in her new black satin, was relating touching incidents of his infancy to a group of old ladies. He leaned forward, clasped his hands between his knees, and launched into an animated description of how his first play, written at college, had taken the fancy of an old school friend of his father's who had turned manager. The second, a political farce, had put him fairly on his feet. Then followed his historical drama, *Lord Fairfax*, in which he had at first failed completely. He told her of those desperate days in New York when he would draw his blinds and work by lamplight until he was utterly exhausted, of how he fell ill and lost the thread of his play and used to wander about the streets trying to beat it out of the paving stones when the very policemen who jostled him on the crossings knew more about *Lord Fairfax* than he.

As he talked he felt the old sense of power, lost for many years; the power of conveying himself wholly to her in speech, of awakening in her mind every tint and shadow and vague association that was in his at the moment. He quite forgot the beauty of the woman beside him in the exultant realization of comradeship, the egoistic satisfaction of being wholly understood. Suddenly he stopped short.

"Come, Margie, you're not playing fair, you're telling me nothing about yourself. What plays have you been playing? Pirate or enchanted princess or sleeping beauty or Helen of Troy, to the disaster of men?"

Margie sighed as she awoke out of the fairyland. Doug's tales were as wonderful as ever.

"Oh, I stopped playing long ago. I have grown up and you have not. Some one has said that is wherein geniuses are different; they go on playing and never grow up. So you see you're only a case of arrested development, after all."

"I don't believe it, you play still, I can see it in your eyes. And don't say genius to me. People say that to me only when they want to be disagreeable or tell me how they would have written my plays. The word is my bogie. But tell me, are the cattails ripe in the Salt Marshes, and will your mother let you wade if the sun is warm, and do the winds still smell sharp with salt when they blow through the mists at night?"

"Why, Douglass, did the wind always smell salty to you there too? It does to me yet, and you know there isn't a particle of salt there. Why did we ever name them the Salt Marshes?"

"Because they *were* the Salt Marshes and couldn't have had any other name any more than the Far Island could. I went down to those pestiferous Maremma marshes in Italy to see whether they would be as real as our marshes, but they were not real at all; only miles and miles of bog. And do the nightingales still sing in the grove?"

"Yes. Other people call them ring doves—but they still sing there."

"And you still call them nightingales to yourself and laugh at the density of big people?"

"Yes, sometimes."

Later in the evening Douglass found another opportunity, and this time he was fortunate enough to encounter Margie alone as she was crossing the veranda.

"Do you know why I have come home in June, instead of July as I had intended, Margie? Well, sit down and let me tell you. They don't need you in there just now. About a month ago I changed my apartment in New York, and as I was sorting over my traps I came across a box of childish souvenirs. Among them was a faded bit of paper on which a map was drawn with elaborate care. It was the map of an island with curly blue lines all around it to represent water, such as we used always to draw around the continents in our geography class. On the west coast of the island a red sword was sticking upright in the earth. Beneath this scientific drawing was an inscription to the effect that '*whoso should dig twelve paces west of the huge fallen tree, in direct line with the path made by the setting sun on the water on the tenth day of June, should find the great treasure and his heart's desire!*'"

Margie laughed and applauded gently with her hands. "And so you have come to dig for it; come two thousand miles almost. There's a dramatic situation for you. I have my map still, and I've often contemplated going down to Far Island and digging, but it wouldn't have been fair, for the treasure was really yours, after all."

"Well, you are going now, and on the tenth day of June, that's next Friday, for that's what I came home for, and I had to spoil the plans and temper of a manager and all his company to do it."

"Nonsense, there are too many mosquitoes on Far Island and I mind them more than I used to. Besides there are no good boats like the *Jolly Roger* nowadays."

"We'll go if I have to build another *Jolly Roger*. You can't make me believe you are afraid of mosquitoes. I know too well the mettle of your pasture. Please do, Margie, please." He used his old insidious coaxing tone.

"Douglass, you have made me do dreadful things enough by using that tone of voice to me. I believe you used to hypnotize me. Will you never, never grow up?"

"Never so long as there are pirate's treasures to dig for and you will play with me, Margie. Oh, I wish I had some of the cake that Alice ate in Wonderland and could make you a little girl again."

That night, after the household was asleep, Douglass went out for a walk about the old town, treading the ways he had trod when he was a founder of cities and a leader of hosts. But he saw few of the old landmarks, for the blaze of Etruscan gold was in his eyes, and he felt as a man might feel who in some sleepy humdrum Italian village had unearthed a new marble goddess, as beautiful as she of Milo; and he felt as a boy might feel who had lost all his favorite marbles and his best pea shooter and the dog that slept with him, and had found them all again. He tried to follow, step by step, the wonderful friendship of his childhood.

A child's normal attitude toward the world is that of the artist, pure and simple. The rest of us have to do with the solids of this world, whereas only their form and color exist for the painter. So, in every wood and street and building there are things, not seen of older people at all, which make up their whole desirableness or objectionableness to children. There are maps and pictures formed by cracks in the walls of bare and unsightly sleeping chambers which make them beautiful; smooth places on the lawn where the grass is greener than anywhere else and which are good to sit upon; trees which are valuable by reason of the peculiar way in which the branches grow, and certain spots under the scrub willows along the creek which are in a manner sacred, like the sacrificial groves of the Druids, so that a boy is almost afraid to walk there. Then there are certain carpets which are more beautiful than others, because with a very little help from the imagination they become the rose garden of the Thousand and One Nights; and certain couches which are peculiarly adapted for playing Sindbad in his days of ease, after the toilsome voyages were over. A child's standard of value is so entirely his own, and his peculiar part and possessions in the material objects around him are so different from those of his elders, that it may be said his rights are granted by a different lease. To these two children the entire external world, like the people who dwelt in it, had been valued solely for what they suggested to the imagination, and people and places alike were merely stage properties, contributing more or less to the intensity of their inner life.

II

> "Green leaves a-floating
> Castles of the foam,
> Boats of mine a-boating
> When will all come home?"

sang Douglass as they pulled from the mill wharf out into the rapid current of the river, which that morning seemed the most beautiful and noble of rivers, an enchanted river flowing peacefully out of Arcady with the Happy Isles somewhere in the distance. The ripples were touched with silver and the sky was as blue as though it had just been made today; the cow bells sounded faintly from the meadows along the shore like the bells of fairy cities ringing on the day the prince errant brought home his bride; the meadows that sloped to the water's edge were the greenest in all the world because they were the meadows of the long ago; and the flowers that grew there were the freshest and sweetest of growing things because once, long ago in the golden age, two children had gathered other flowers like them, and the beauties of vanished summers were everywhere. Douglass sat in the end of the boat, his back to the sun and his straw hat tilted back on his head, pulling slowly and feeling that the day was fine rather than seeing it; for his eyes were fixed upon his helmsman in the other end of the boat, who sat with her hat in her lap, shading her face with a white parasol, and her wonderful hair piled high on her head like a helmet of gleaming bronze.

Of all the possessions of their childhood's Wonderland, Far Island had been dearest; it was graven on their hearts as Calais was upon Mary Tudor's. Long before they had set foot upon it the island was the goal of their loftiest ambitions and most delightful imaginings. They had wondered what trees grew there and what delightful spots were hidden away under the matted grapevines. They had even decided that a race of kindly dwarfs must inhabit it and had built up a civilization and historic annals for these imaginary inhabitants, surrounding the sand bar with all the mystery and enchantment which was attributed to certain islands of the sea by the mariners of Greece. Douglass and Margie had sometimes found it expedient to admit other children into their world, but for the most part these were but hewers of wood and drawers of water, who helped to shift the scenery and construct the balcony and place the king's throne, and were no more in the atmosphere of the play than were the supers who watched Mr. Keane's famous duel with Richmond. Indeed Douglass frequently selected the younger and more passive boys for his vassals on the principle that they did as they were bid and made no trouble. But there is something of the explorer in the least imaginative of boys, and when Douglass came to the building of his famous boat, the *Jolly Roger*, he found willing hands to help him. Indeed the sawing and hammering, the shavings and cut fingers and blood blisters fell chiefly to the lot of dazzled lads who claimed no part in the craft, and who gladly trotted and sweated for their board and keep in this fascinating play world which was so much more exhilarating than any they could make for themselves.

"Think of it, Margie, we are really going back to the island after so many years, just you and I, the captain and his mate. Where are the other gallant lads that sailed with us then?"

"Where are the snows of yester' year?" sighed Margie softly. "It is very sad to grow up."

"Sad for them, yes. But we have never grown up, you know, we have only grown more considerate of our complexions," nodding at the parasol. "What a little mass of freckles you used to be, but I liked you freckled, too. Let me see: old Temp is commanding a regiment in the Philippines, and Bake has a cattle ranch in Wyoming, Mac is a government clerk in Washington, Jim keeps his father's hardware store, poor Ned and Shorty went down in a catboat on the Hudson while they were at college (I went out to hunt for the bodies, you know), and old Rhine is selling sewing machines; he never did get away at all, did he?"

"No, not for any length of time. You know it used to frighten Rhine to go to the next town to see a circus. He went to Arizona once for his lungs, but his family never could tell where he was for he headed all his letters 'Empire City, Nebraska,' from habit."

"Oh, that's delightful, Margie, you must let me use that. Rhine would carry Empire City through Europe with him and never know he was out of it. Have I told you about Pagie? Well, you know Pagie is travelling for a New York tailoring house and I let his people make some clothes for me that I had to give to Flashingham's valet. When he first came to town he tried to be gay, with his fond mother's prayers still about him, a visible nimbus, and the Sunday school boy written all over his open countenance and downy lip and large, white butter teeth. But I know, at heart, he still detested naughty words and whiskey made him sick. One day I was standing at the Hoffman House bar with some fellows, when a slender youth, who looked like a nice girl masquerading as a rake, stepped up and ordered a claret and seltzer. The whine was unmistakable. I turned and said, even before I had looked at him squarely, 'Oh, Pagie! if your mother saw you here!'"

"Poor Pagie! I'll warrant he would rather have had bread and sugar. Do you remember how, at the Sunday school concerts on Children's Day, you and Pagie and Shorty and Temp used to stand in a row behind the flower-wreathed pulpit rail, all in your new round-about suits with large silk bows tied under your collars, your hands behind you, and assure us with sonorous voices that you would come rejoicing bringing in the sheaves? Somehow, even then, I never doubted that you would do it."

The keel grated on the sand and Douglass sprang ashore and gave her his hand.

"Descend, O Miranda, upon your island! Do you know, Margie, it makes me seem fifteen again to feel this sand crunching under my feet. I wonder if I ever again shall feel such a thrill of triumph as I felt when I first leaped upon this sand bar? None of my first nights have given me anything like it. Do you remember *really*, and did you feel the same?"

"Of course I remember, and I knew that you were playing a double rôle that day, and that you were really the trail-breaker and world-finder inside of the pirate all the while. Here are the same ripple marks on the Silvery Beaches, and here is the great arched tree, let's run for it." She started fleetly across the glittering sand and Douglass fell behind to watch with immoderate joy that splendid, generous body that governed itself so well in the open air. There was a wholesomeness of the sun and soil in her that was utterly lacking in the women among whom he had lived for so long. She had preserved that strength of arm and freedom of limb that had made her so fine a playfellow, and which modern modes of life have well-nigh robbed the world of altogether. Surely, he thought, it was like that that Diana's women sped after the stag down the slopes of Ida, with shouting and bright spear. She caught an overhanging branch and swung herself upon the embankment and, leaning against the trunk of a tree, awaited him flushed and panting, her bosom rising and falling with her quick drawn breaths.

"Why did you close the tree behind you, Margie? I have always wanted to see just how Dryads keep house," he exclaimed, brushing away a dried leaf that had fallen on her shoulder.

"Don't strain your inventive powers to make compliments, Douglass; this is your vacation and you are to rest your imagination. See, the willows have scarcely grown at all. I'm sure we shall hear Pagie whimpering over there on the Uttermost Desert where we marooned him, or singing hymns to keep up his courage. Now for the Huge Fallen Tree. Do you suppose the floods have moved it?"

They struck through the dense willow thicket, matted with fragrant wild grapevines which Douglass beat down with his spade, and came upon the great white log, the bleached skeleton of a tree, and found the cross hacked upon it, the rough gashes of the hatchet now worn smooth by the wind and rain and the seething of spring freshets. Near the cross were cut the initials of the entire pirate crew; some of them were cut on gravestones now. The scrub willows had grown over the spot where they had decided the treasure must lie, and together they set to work to break them away. Douglass paused more than once to watch the strong young creature beside him, outlined against the tender green foliage, reaching high and low and snapping the withes where they were weakest. He was still wondering whether it was not all a dream picture, and was half afraid that his man would call him to tell him that some piqued and faded woman was awaiting him at the theatre to quarrel about her part.

"Still averse to manual labor, Douglass?" she laughed as she turned to bend a tall sapling. "The most remarkable thing about your enthusiasm was that you had only to sing of the glories of toil to make other people do all the work for you."

"No, Margie, I was thinking very hard indeed—about the Thracian women when they broke the boughs wherewith they flayed unhappy Orpheus."

"Now, Douglass, you'll spoil the play. A sentimental pirate is impossible. Pagie was a sentimental pirate and that was what spoiled him. A little more of this and I will maroon you upon the Uttermost Desert."

Douglass laughed and settled himself back among the green boughs and gazed at her with the abandoned admiration of an artist contemplating a masterpiece.

When they came to the digging of the treasure a little exertion was enough to unearth what had seemed hidden so fabulously deep in olden time. The chest was rotten and fell apart as the spade struck it, but the glass jar was intact, covered with sand and slime. Douglass spread his handkerchief upon the sand and weighted the corners down with pebbles and upon it poured the treasure of Far Island. There was the manuscript written in blood, a confession of fantastic crimes, and the Spaniard's heart in a bottle of alcohol, and Temp's Confederate bank notes, damp and grewsome to the touch, and Pagie's rare tobacco tags, their brilliant colors faded entirely away, and poor Shorty's bars of tinfoil, dull and eaten with rust.

"And, Douglass," cried Margie, "there is your father's silver ring that was made from a nugget; he whipped you for burying it. You remember it was given to a Christian knight by an English queen, and when he was slain before Jerusalem a Saracen took it and we killed the Saracen in the desert and cut off his finger to get the ring. It is strange how those wild imaginings of ours seem, in retrospect, realities, things that I actually lived through. I suppose that in cold fact my life was a good deal like that of other little girls who grow up in a village; but whenever I look back on it, it is all exultation and romance—sea fights and splendid galleys and Roman triumphs and brilliant caravans winding through the desert."

"To people who live by imagination at all, that is the only life that goes deep enough to leave memories. We were artists in those days, creating for the day only; making epics sung once and then forgotten, building empires that set with the sun. Nobody worked for money then, and nobody worked for fame, but only for the joy of the doing. Keats said the same thing more elegantly in his May Day Ode, and we were not so unlike those Hellenic poets who were content to sing to the shepherds and forget and be forgotten, 'rich in the simple worship of a day.'"

"Why, Douglass," she cried as she bent her face down to the little glass jar, "it was really our childhood that we buried here, never guessing what a precious thing we were putting under the ground. That was the real treasure of Far Island, and we might dig up the whole island for it but all the king's horses and all the king's men could not bring it back to us. That voyage we made to bury our trinkets, just before you went away to school, seems like unconscious symbolism, and somehow it stands out from all the other good times we knew then as the happiest of all." She looked off where the setting sun hung low above the water.

"Shall I tell you why, Margie? That was the end of our childhood, and there the golden days died in a blaze of glory, passed in music out of sight. That night, after our boat had drifted away from us, when we had to wade down the river hand in hand, we two, and the noises and the coldness of the water frightened us, and there were quicksands and sharp rocks and deep holes to shun, and terrible things lurking in the woods on the shore, you cried in a different way from the way you sometimes cried when you hurt yourself, and I found that I loved you afraid better than I had ever loved you fearless, and in that moment we grew up, and shut the gates of Eden behind us, and our empire was at an end."

"And now we are only kings in exile," sighed Margie, softly, "who wander back to look down from the mountain tops upon the happy land we used to rule."

Douglass took her hand gently; "If there is to be any Eden on earth again for us, dear, we must make it with our two hearts."

There was a sudden brightness of tears in her eyes, and she drew away from him. "Ah, Douglass, you are determined to spoil it all. It is you who have grown up and taken on the ways of the world. The play is at an end for me." She tried to rise, but he held her firmly.

"From the moment I looked into your eyes in the vestibule that night we have been parts of the same dream again. Why, Margie, we have more romance behind us than most men and women ever live."

Margie's face grew whiter, but she pushed his hand away and the look in her eyes grew harder. "This is only a new play, Douglass, and you will weary of it tomorrow. I am not so good at playing as I used to be. I am no longer content with the simple worship of a day."

In her touch, in her white face, he divined the greatness of what she had to give. He bit his lip and answered, "I think you owe me more confidence than that, if only for the sake of those days when we trusted each other entirely."

She turned with a quick flash of remorseful tenderness, as she used to do when she hurt him at play. "I only want to keep you from hurting us both, Douglass. We neither of us could go on feeling like this. It's only the dregs of the old enchantment. Things have always come easily to you, I know, for at your birth nature and fortune joined to make you great. But they do not come so to me; I should wake and weep."

"Then weep, my princess, for I will wake you now!"

The fire and fancy that had so bewitched her girlhood that no other man had been able to dim the memory of it came furiously back upon her, with arms that were new and strange and strong, and with tenderness stranger still in this wild fellow of dreams and jests; and all her vows never to grace another of his Roman triumphs were forgotten.

"You are right, Margie; the pirate play is ended and the time has come to divide the prizes, and I choose what I chose fifteen years ago. Out of the spoils of a lifetime of crime and bloodshed I claimed only the captive princess, and I claim her still. I have sought the world over for her, only to find her at last in the land of lost content."

Margie lifted her face from his shoulder, and, after the manner of women of her kind, she played her last card rhapsodically. "And she, O Douglass! the years she has waited have been longer than the waiting of Penelope, and she has woven a thousand webs of dreams by night and torn them asunder by day, and looked out across the Salt Marshes for the night train, and still you did not come. I was only your pensioner like Shorty and Temp and the rest, and I could not play anything alone. You took my world with you when you went and left me only a village of mud huts and my loneliness."

As her eyes and then her lips met his in the dying light, he knew that she had caught the spirit of the play, and that she would ford the river by night with him again and never be afraid.

The locust chirped in the thicket; the setting sun threw a track of flame across the water; the willows burned with fire and were not consumed; a glory was upon the sand and the river and upon the Silvery Beaches; and these two looked about over God's world and saw that it was good. In the western sky the palaces of crystal and gold were quenched in night, like the cities of old empires; and out of the east rose the same moon that has glorified all the romances of the world—that lighted Paris over the blue Ægean and the feet of young Montague to the Capulets' orchard. The dinner hour in Empire City was long past, but the two upon the island wist naught of these things, for they had become as the gods, who dwell in their golden houses, recking little of the woes and labors of mortals, neither heeding any fall of rain or snow.

First published in *New England Magazine*, XXVII (October, 1902), 234–249.

The Professor's
Commencement

❋ ❋ ❋

The professor sat at his library table at six o'clock in the morning. He had risen with the sun, which is up betimes in June. An uncut volume of *Huxley's Life and Letters* lay open on the table before him, but he tapped the pages absently with his paper knife and his eyes were fixed unseeingly on the St. Gaudens medallion of Stevenson on the opposite wall. The professor's library testified to the superior quality of his taste in art as well as to his wide and varied scholarship. Only by a miracle of taste could so unpretentious a room have been made so attractive; it was as dainty as a boudoir and as original in color scheme as a painter's studio. The walls were hung with photographs of the works of the best modern painters— Burne-Jones, Rossetti, Corot, and a dozen others. Above the mantel were delicate reproductions in color of some of Fra Angelico's most beautiful paintings. The rugs were exquisite in pattern and color, pieces of weaving that the Professor had picked up himself in his wanderings in the Orient. On close inspection, however, the contents of the bookshelves formed the most remarkable feature of the library. The shelves were almost equally apportioned to the accommodation of works on literature and science, suggesting a form of bigamy rarely encountered in society. The collection of works of pure literature was wide enough to include nearly all the major languages of modern Europe, besides the Greek and Roman classics.

To an interpretive observer nearly everything that was to be found in the Professor's library was represented in his personality. Occasionally, when he read Hawthorne's "Great Stone Face" with his classes, some clear-sighted student wondered whether the man ever realized how completely he illustrated the allegory in himself. The Professor was truly a part of all that he had met, and he had managed to meet most of the good things that the mind of man had desired. In his face there was much of the laborious precision of the scientist and not a little of Fra Angelico and of the lyric poets whose influence had prolonged his youth well into the fifties. His pupils always remembered the Professor's face long after they had forgotten the things he had endeavored to teach them. He had the bold, prominent nose and chin of the oldest and most beloved of American actors, and the high, broad forehead which Nature loves to build about her finely adjusted minds. The grave, large outlines of his face were softened by an infinite kindness of mouth and eye. His mouth, indeed, was as sensitive and mobile as that of a young man, and, given certain passages from *Tristram and Isolde* or certain lines from Heine, his eyes would flash out at you like wet cornflowers after a spring shower. His hair was very thick, straight, and silver white. This, with his clear skin, gave him a somewhat actor-like appearance. He was slight of build and exceedingly frail, with delicate, sensitive hands curving back at the finger-ends, with dark purple veins showing prominently on the back. They were exceedingly small, white as a girl's, and well kept as a pianist's.

As the Professor sat caressing his Huxley, a lady entered.

"It is half past six, Emerson, and breakfast will be served at seven." Anyone would have recognized her as the Professor's older sister, for she was a sort of simplified and expurgated edition of himself, the more alert and masculine character of the two, and the scholar's protecting angel. She wore a white lace cap on her head and a knitted shawl about her shoulders. Though she had been a widow for twenty-five years and more, she was always called Miss Agatha Graves. She scanned her brother critically and having satisfied herself that his linen was immaculate and his white tie a fresh one, she remarked, "You were up early this morning, even for you."

"The roses never have the fragrance that they have in the first sun, they give out their best then," said her brother nodding toward the window where the garden roses thrust their pink heads close to the screen as though they would not be kept outside. "And I have something on my mind, Agatha," he continued, nervously fingering the sandalwood paper-cutter, "I feel distraught and weary. You know how I shrink from changes of any sort, and this—why this is the most alarming thing that has ever confronted me. It is absolutely cutting my life off at the stalk, and who knows whether it will bud again?"

Miss Agatha turned sharply about from the window where she had been standing, and gravely studied her brother's drooping shoulders and dejected figure.

"There you go at your old tricks, Em," she remonstrated. "I have heard many kinds of ability attributed to you, but to my mind no one has ever put his finger on the right spot. Your real gift is for getting all the possible pain out of life, and extracting needless annoyance from commonplace and trivial things. Here you have buried yourself for the best part of your life in that high school, for motives Quixotic to an absurdity. If you had chosen a university I should not complain, but in that place all your best tools have rusted. Granted that you have done your work a little better than the people about you, it's no great place in which to excel—a city high school where failures in every trade drift to teach the business they cannot make a living by. Now it is time that you do something to justify the faith your friends have always had in you. You owe something to them and to your own name."

"I have builded myself a monument more lasting than brass," quoted the Professor softly, balancing the tips of his slender fingers together.

"Nonsense, Emerson!" said Miss Agatha impatiently. "You are a sentimentalist and your vanity is that of a child. As for those slovenly persons with offensive manners whom you call your colleagues, do you fancy they appreciate you? They are as envious as green gourds and their mouths pucker when they pay you compliments. I hope you are not so unsophisticated as to believe all the sentimental twaddle of your old students. When they want recommendations to some school board, or run for a city office and want your vote, they come here and say that you have been the inspiration of their lives, and I believe in my heart that you are goose enough to accept it all."

"As for my confrères," said the Professor smiling, "I have no doubt that each one receives in the bosom of his family exactly the same advice that you are giving me. If there dwell an appreciated man on earth I have never met him. As for the students, I believe I have, to some at least, in a measure supplied a vital element that their environment failed to give them. Whether they realize this or not is of slight importance; it is in the very nature of youth to forget its sources, physical and mental alike. If one labors at all in the garden of youth, it must be free from the passion of seeing things grow, from an innate love of watching the strange processes of the brain under varying influences and limitations. He gets no more thanks than the novelist gets from the character he creates, nor does he deserve them. He has the whole human comedy before him in embryo, the beginning of all passions and all achievements. As I have often told you, this city is a disputed strategic point. It controls a vast manufacturing region given over to sordid and materialistic ideals. Any work that has been done here for æsthetics cannot be lost. I suppose we shall win in the end, but the reign of Mammon has been long and oppressive. You remember when I was a boy working in the fields how we used to read Bunyan's *Holy War* at night? Well, I have always felt very much as though I were keeping the Ear Gate of the town of Mansoul, and I know not whether the Captains who succeed me be trusty or no."

Miss Agatha was visibly moved, but she shook her head. "Well, I wish you had gone into the church, Emerson. I respect your motives, but there are more tares than wheat in your crop, I suspect."

"My dear girl," said the Professor, his eye brightening, "that is the very reason for the sowing. There is a picture by Vedder of the Enemy Sowing Tares at the foot of the cross, and his seeds are golden coins. That is the call to arms; the other side never sleeps; in the theatres, in the newspapers, in the mills and offices and coal fields, by day and by night the enemy sows tares."

As the Professor slowly climbed the hill to the high school that morning, he indulged in his favorite fancy, that the old grey stone building was a fortress set upon the dominant acclivity of that great manufacturing city, a stronghold of knowledge in the heart of Mammon's kingdom, a Pharos to all those drifting, storm-driven lives in the valley below, where mills and factories thronged, blackening the winding shores of the river, which was dotted with coal barges and frantic, puffing little tugs. The high school commanded the heart of the city, which was like that of any other manufacturing town—a scene of bleakness and naked ugliness and of that remorseless desolation which follows upon the fiercest lust of man. The beautiful valley, where long ago two limpid rivers met at the foot of wooded heights, had become a scorched and blackened waste. The river banks were lined with bellowing mills which broke the silence of the night with periodic crashes of sound, filled the valley with heavy carboniferous smoke, and sent the chilled products of their red forges to all parts of the known world—to fashion railways in Siberia, bridges in Australia, and to tear the virgin soil of Africa. To the west, across the river, rose the steep bluffs, faintly etched through the brown smoke, rising five hundred feet, almost as sheer as a precipice, traversed by cranes and inclines and checkered by winding yellow paths like sheep trails which led to the wretched habitations clinging to the face of the cliff, the lairs of the vicious and the poor, miserable rodents of civilization. In the middle of the stream, among the tugs and barges, were the dredging boats, hoisting muck and filth from the clogged channel. It was difficult to believe that this was the shining river which tumbles down the steep hills of the lumbering district, odorous of wet spruce logs and echoing the ring of axes and the song of the raftsmen, come to this black ugliness at last, with not one throb of its woodland passion and bright vehemence left.

For thirty years the Professor's classroom had overlooked this scene which caused him unceasing admiration and regret. For thirty years he had cried out against the image set up there as the Hebrew prophets cried out against the pride and blind prosperity of Tyre. Nominally he was a professor of English Literature, but his real work had been to try to secure for youth the rights of youth; the right to be generous, to dream, to enjoy; to feel a little the seduction of the old Romance, and to yield a little. His students were boys and girls from the factories and offices, destined to return thither, and hypnotized by the glitter of yellow metal. They were practical, provident, unimaginative, and mercenary at sixteen. Often, when some lad was reading aloud in the classroom, the puffing of the engines in the switch yard at the foot of the hill would drown the verse and the young voice entirely, and the Professor would murmur sadly to himself: "Not even this respite is left to us; even here the voice of youth is drowned by the voice of the taskmaster that waits for them all impatiently enough."

Never had his duty seemed to call him so urgently as on this morning when he was to lay down his arms. As he entered the building he met the boys carrying palms up into the chapel for class-day exercises, and it occurred to him for the first time that this was his last commencement, a commencement without congratulations and without flowers. When he went into the chapel to drill the seniors on their commencement orations, he was unable to fix his mind upon his work. For thirty years he had heard youth say exactly the same thing in the same place; had heard young men swear fealty to the truth, pay honor to the pursuit of noble pleasures, and pledge themselves "to follow knowledge like a sinking star beyond the utmost bound of human thought." How many, he asked himself, had kept their vows? He could remember the occasion of his own commencement in that same chapel; the story that every senior class still told the juniors, of the Professor's humiliation and disgrace when, in attempting to recite "Horatius at the Bridge," he had been unable to recall one word of the poem following

> Then out spake bold Horatius
> The Captain of the gate;

and after some moments of agonizing silence he had shame-facedly left the platform. Even the least receptive of the Professor's students realized that he had risen to a much higher plane of scholarship than any of his colleagues, and they delighted to tell this story of the frail, exquisite, little man whom generations of students had called "the bold Horatius."

All the morning the Professor was busy putting his desk and book-cases in order, impeded by the painful consciousness that he was doing it for the last time. He made many trips to the window and often lapsed into periods of idleness. The room had been connected in one way and another with most of his intellectual passions, and was as full of sentimental associations for him as the haunts of his courtship days are to a lover. At two o'clock he met his last class, which was just finishing *Sohrab and Rustum*, and he was forced to ask one of the boys to read and interpret the majestic closing lines on the "shorn and parceled Oxus." What the boy's comment was the Professor never knew, he felt so close a kinship to that wearied river that he sat stupefied, with his hand shading his eyes and his fingers twitching. When the bell rang announcing the end of the hour he felt a sudden pain clutch his heart; he had a vague hope that the students would gather around his desk to discuss some point that youth loves to discuss, as they often did, but their work was over and they hurried out, eager for their freedom, while the professor sat helplessly watching them.

That evening a banquet was given to the retiring professor in the chapel, but Miss Agatha had to exert all her native power of command to induce him to go. He had come home so melancholy and unnerved that after laying out his dress clothes she literally had to put them on him. When he was in his shirt sleeves and Miss Agatha had carefully brushed his beautiful white hair and arranged his tie, she wheeled him sharply about and retreated to a chair.

"Now, Emerson, say your piece," she commanded.

Plucking up his shirt sleeves and making sure of his cuffs, the Professor began valiantly:

> "Lars Porsena of Clusium,
> By the Nine Gods he swore . . . ."

It was all Miss Agatha's idea. After the invitations to the banquet were out and she discovered that half-a-dozen of the Professor's own classmates and many of his old students were to be present, she divined that it would be a tearful and depressing occasion. Emerson, she knew, was an indifferent speaker when his heart was touched, so she had decided that after a silence of thirty-five years Horatius should be heard from. The idea of correcting his youthful failure in his old age had rather pleased the

Professor on the whole, and he had set to work to memorize Lord Macaulay's lay, rehearsing in private to Miss Agatha, who had drilled him for that fatal exploit of his commencement night.

After this dress rehearsal the Professor's spirits rose, and during the carriage ride he even made several feeble efforts to joke with his sister. But later in the evening when he sat down at the end of the long table in the dusky chapel, green with palms for commencement week, he fell into deep depression. The guests chattered and boasted and gossiped, but the guest of honor sat silent, staring at the candles. Beside him sat old Fairbrother, of the Greek department, who had come into the faculty in the fifth year of Graves's professorship, and had married a pretty senior girl who had rejected Graves's timid suit. She had been dead this many a year; since his bereavement lonely old Fairbrother had clung to Graves, and now the Professor felt a singular sense of support in his presence.

The Professor tried to tell himself that now his holiday time had come, and that he had earned it; that now he could take up the work he had looked forward to and prepared for for years, his History of Modern Painting, the Italian section of which was already practically complete. But his heart told him that he had no longer the strength to take up independent work. Now that the current of young life had cut away from him and into a new channel, he felt like a ruin of some extinct civilization, like a harbor from which the sea has receded. He realized that he had been living by external stimulation from the warm young blood about him, and now that it had left him, all his decrepitude was horribly exposed. All those hundreds of thirsty young lives had drunk him dry. He compared himself to one of those granite colossi of antique lands, from which each traveller has chipped a bit of stone until only a mutilated torso is left.

He looked reflectively down the long table, picking out the faces of his colleagues here and there, souls that had toiled and wrought and thought with him, that simple, unworldly sect of people he loved. They were still discussing the difficulties of the third conjugation, as they had done there for twenty years. They were cases of arrested development, most of them. Always in contact with immature minds, they had kept the simplicity and many of the callow enthusiasms of youth. Those facts and formulae which interest the rest of the world for but a few years at most, were still the vital facts of life for them. They believed quite sincerely in the supreme importance of quadratic equations, and the rule for the special verbs that govern the dative was a part of their decalogue. And he himself—what had he done with the youth, the strength, the enthusiasm and splendid equipment he had brought there from Harvard thirty years ago? He had come to stay but a little while—five years at the most, until he could save money enough to defray the expense of a course in some German university. But then the battle had claimed him; the desire had come upon him to bring some message of repose and peace to the youth of this work-driven, joyless people, to cry the name of beauty so loud that the roar of the mills could not drown it. Then the reward of his first labors had come in the person of his one and only genius; his restless, incorrigible pupil with the gentle eyes and manner of a girl, at once timid and utterly reckless, who had seen even as Graves saw; who had suffered a little, sung a little, struck the true lyric note, and died wretchedly at three-and-twenty in his master's arms, the victim of a tragedy as old as the world and as grim as Samson, the Israelite's.

He looked about at his comrades and wondered what they had done with their lives. Doubtless they had deceived themselves as he had done. With youth always about them, they had believed themselves of it. Like the monk in the legend they had wandered a little way into the wood to hear the bird's song—the magical song of youth so engrossing and so treacherous, and they had come back to their cloister to find themselves old men—spent warriors who could only chatter on the wall, like grass-hoppers, and sigh at the beauty of Helen as she passed.

The toasts were nearly over, but the Professor had heard none of the appreciative and enthusiastic things that his students and colleagues had said of him. He read a deeper meaning into this parting than they had done and his thoughts stopped his ears. He heard Miss Agatha clear her throat and caught her meaning glance. Realizing that everyone was waiting for him, he, blinked his eyes like a man heavy with sleep and arose.

"How handsome he looks," murmured the woman looking at his fine old face and silver hair. The Professor's remarks were as vague as they were brief. After expressing his thanks for the honor done him, he stated that he had still some work to finish among them, which had been too long incomplete. Then with as much of his schoolboy attitude as he could remember, and a smile on his gentle lips, he began his

"Lars Porsena of Clusium,
By the Nine Gods he swore
That the noble house of Tarquin
Should suffer wrong no more."

A murmur of laughter ran up and down the long table, and Dr. Maitland, the great theologian, who had vainly tried to prompt his stage-struck fellow graduate thirty-five years ago, laughed until his nose glasses fell off and dangled across his black waistcoat. Miss Agatha was highly elated over the success of her idea, but the Professor had no heart in what he was doing, and the merriment rather hurt him. Surely this was a time for silence and reflection, if ever such time was. Memories crowded upon him faster than the lines he spoke, and the warm eyes turned upon him, full of pride and affection for their scholar and their "great man," moved him almost beyond endurance.

"—the Consul's brow was sad
And the Consul's speech was low,"

he read, and suited the action marvellously to the word. His eyes wandered to the chapel rostrum. Thirty-five years ago he had stood there repeating those same lines, a young man, resolute and gifted, with the strength of Ulysses and the courage of Hector, with the kingdoms of the earth and the treasures of the ages at his feet, and the singing rose in his heart; a spasm of emotion contracted the old man's vocal cords.

"Outspake the bold Horatius,
The Captain of the gate,"

he faltered;——his white hand nervously sought his collar, then the hook on his breast where his glasses usually hung, and at last tremulously for his handkerchief; then with a gesture of utter defeat, the Professor sat down. There was a tearful silence; white handkerchiefs fluttered down the table as from a magician's wand, and Miss Agatha was sobbing. Dr. Maitland arose to his feet, his face distorted between laughter and tears. "I ask you all," he cried, "whether Horatius has any need to speak, for has he not kept the bridge these thirty years? God bless him!"

"It's all right, so don't worry about it, Emerson," said Miss Agatha as they got into the carriage. "At least they were appreciative, which is more than I would have believed."

"Ah, Agatha," said the Professor, wiping his face wearily with his crumpled handkerchief, "I am a hopeless dunce, and you ought to have known better. If you could make nothing of me at twenty, you showed poor judgment to undertake it at fifty-five. I was not made to shine, for they put a woman's heart in me."

First published in *New England Magazine*, XXVI (June, 1902), 481–488.

El Dorado :
A Kansas Recessional

❖ ❖ ❖

I

People who have been so unfortunate as to have traveled in western Kansas will remember the Solomon Valley for its unique and peculiar desolation. The river is a turbid, muddy little stream, that crawls along between naked bluffs, choked and split by sand bars, and with nothing whatever of that fabled haste to reach the sea. Though there can be little doubt that the Solomon is heartily disgusted with the country through which it flows, it makes no haste to quit it. Indeed, it is one of the most futile little streams under the sun, and never gets anywhere. Its sluggish current splits among the sand bars and buries itself in the mud until it literally dries up from weariness and ennui, without ever reaching anything. The hot winds and the river have been contending for the empire of the valley for years, and the river has had decidedly the worst of it. Never having been a notably ambitious stream, in time it grew tired of giving its strength to moisten barren fields and corn that never matured. Beyond the river with its belt of amber woodland rose the bluffs, ragged, broken, covered with shaggy red grass and bare of trees, save for the few stunted oaks that grew upon their steep sides. They were pathetic little trees, that sent their roots down through thirty feet of hard clay bluff to the river level. They were as old as the first settler could remember, and yet no one could assert that they had ever grown an inch. They seldom, if ever, bore acorns; it took all the nourishment that soil could give just to exist. There was a sort of mysterious kinship between those trees and the men who lived, or tried to live, there. They were alike in more ways than one.

Across the river stretched the level land like the top of an oven. It was a country flat and featureless, without tones or shadows, without

[293]

accent or emphasis of any kind to break its vast monotony. It was a scene done entirely in high lights, without relief, without a single commanding eminence to rest the eye upon. The flat plains rolled to the unbroken horizon vacant and void, forever reaching in empty yearning toward something they never attained. The tilled fields were even more discouraging to look upon than the unbroken land. Although it was late in the autumn, the corn was not three feet high. The leaves were seared and yellow, and as for tassels, there were none. Nature always dispenses with superfluous appendages; and what use had Solomon Valley corn for tassels? Ears were only a tradition there, fabulous fruits like the golden apples of the Hesperides; and many a brawny Hercules had died in his own sweat trying to obtain them. Sometimes, in the dusk of night, when the winds were not quite so hot as usual and only the stars could hear, the dry little corn leaves whispered to each other that once, long ago, real yellow ears grew in the Solomon Valley.

Near the river was a solitary frame building, low and wide, with a high sham front, like most stores in Kansas villages. Over the door was painted in faded letters, "Josiah Bywaters, Dry Goods, Groceries and Notions." In front of the store ran a straight strip of ground, grass grown and weedy, which looked as if it might once have been a road. Here and there, on either side of this deserted way of traffic, were half demolished buildings and excavations where the weeds grew high, which might once have been the sites of houses. For this was once El Dorado, the Queen City of the Plains, the Metropolis of Western Kansas, the coming Commercial Center of the West.

Whatever may have been there once, now there were only those empty, windowless buildings, that one little store, and the lonely old man whose name was painted over the door. Inside the store, on a chair tilted back against the counter, with his pipe in his mouth and a big gray cat on his knee, sat the proprietor. His appearance was not that of the average citizen of western Kansas, and a very little of his conversation told you that he had come from civilization somewhere. He was tall and straight, with an almost military bearing, and an iron jaw. He was thin, but perhaps that was due to his diet. His cat was thin, too, and that was surely owing to its diet, which consisted solely of crackers and water, except when now and then it could catch a gopher; and Solomon Valley gophers are so thin that they never tempt the ambition of any discerning cat. If Colonel Bywaters's manner of living had anything to do with his attenuation, it was the solitude rather than any other hardship that was responsible. He was a sort of "Last Man." The tide of emigration had gone out and had left him high and dry, stranded on a Kansas bluff. He was living where the rattlesnakes and sunflowers found it difficult to exist.

The Colonel was a man of determination; he had sunk his money in this wilderness and he had determined to wait until he had got it out. His capital had represented the industry of a lifetime. He had made it all down in Virginia, where fortunes are not made in a day. He had often told himself that he had been a fool to quit a country of honest men for a desert like this. But he had come West, worse than that, he had come to western Kansas, even to the Solomon Valley, and he must abide the consequences. Even after the whole delusion was dispelled, and the fraud exposed, when the other buildings had been torn down or moved away, when the Eastern brokers had foreclosed their mortgages and held the land empty for miles around, Colonel Bywaters had stubbornly refused to realize that the game was up. Every one had told him that the best thing he could do was to get out of the country; but he refused to listen to advice. Perhaps he had an unreasoning conviction that money could not absolutely vanish, and that, if he stayed there long enough, his must some time come back to him. Perhaps, even had he wished to go, he actually lacked the means wherewith to get away. At any rate, there he remained, becoming almost a part of that vast solitude, trying to live the life of an upright Christian gentleman in this desert, with a heart heavy and homesick for his kind, always living over again in memory the details of that old, peaceful life in the valley of Virginia. He rose at six, as he had always done, ate his meagre breakfast and swept out his store, arranged his faded calicoes and flyspecked fruit cans in the window, and then sat down to wait. Generally he waited until bedtime. In three years he had not sold fifty dollars' worth. Men were almost unknown beings in that region, and men with money were utterly so. When the town broke up, a few of the inhabitants had tried to farm a little—tried until they had no grain to sow and no horses to plough and no money to get away with. They were dead, most of them. The only human faces the Colonel ever saw were the starved, bronzed countenances of the poor fellows who sometimes passed in wagons, plodding along with their wives and children and cookstoves and feather beds, trying to get back to "God's country." They never bought anything; they only stopped to water their horses and swear a little, and then drove slowly eastward. Once a little girl had cried so bitterly for the red stick candy in the window that her father had taken the last nickel out of his worn, flat pocketbook. But the Colonel was too kind a man to take his money, so he gave the child the money and the candy, too; and he also gave her a little pair of red mittens that the moths had got into, which last she accepted gratefully, though it was August.

The first day of the week brought the exceptions in the monotonous routine of the Colonel's life. He never rose till nine o'clock on Sunday. Then, in honor of the day, he shaved his chin and brushed out his mustache, and dressed himself in his black suit that had been made for him down in Winchester four years ago. This suit of clothes was an object of great care with the Colonel, and every Sunday night he brushed it out and folded it away in camphor gum. Generally he fished on Sunday. Not that there are any fish in the Solomon; indeed, the mud turtles, having exhausted all the nutriment in the mud, have pretty much died out. But the Colonel was fond of fishing, and fish he would. So in season, every Sunday morning, he would catch a bottle of flies for bait and take his pole and, after locking his store against impossible intruders, he would go gravely down the street. He really went through the weed patch, but to himself and his cat he always spoke of it as the street.

II

On this particular afternoon, as the Colonel sat watching the autumn sunlight play upon the floor, he was feeling more bitterly discouraged than usual. It was exactly four years ago that day that Major Penelton had brought into his store on Water Street a tall, broad-shouldered young man, with the frankest blue eyes and a good-natured smile, whom he introduced as Mr. Apollo Gump of Kansas. After a little general conversation, the young man had asked him if he wished to invest in Western lands. No, the Colonel did not want to put out any money in the West. He had no faith in any of the new states. Very well; Apollo did not wish to persuade him. But some way he saw a good deal of the young man, who was a clever, openhanded sort of a chap, who drank good whiskey and told a good story so that it lost nothing in the telling. So many were the hints he threw out of the fortunes made every day in Western real estate, that in spite of himself the Colonel began to think about it. Soon letters began pouring in upon him, letters from doctors, merchants, bankers, all with a large map on the envelope, representing a town with all the railroads of the West running into it. Above this spidery object was printed the name, El Dorado. These communications all assured him of the beauty of the location, the marvellous fertility of the surrounding country, the commercial and educational advantages of the town. Apollo seemed to take a wonderful liking to him; he often had him to dine with him at the little hotel, and took him down to Washington to hear Patti, assuring him all the time that the theatres of Kansas City were much better than anything in the East, and that one heard much better music there. The end of the matter was that when Apollo went back to Kansas the Colonel sold out his business and went with him. They were accompanied by half a dozen men from Baltimore, Washington and the smaller towns about, whom Apollo had induced to invest in the fertile tracts of land about El Dorado and in stock in the Gump banking house.

The Colonel was not a little surprised to find that El Dorado, the metropolis of western Kansas, was a mere cluster of frame houses beside a muddy stream, that there was not a railroad within twenty-five miles, and that the much boasted waterworks consisted of a number of lead pipes running from the big windmill tank on the hill; but Apollo assured him that high buildings were dangerous in that windy country, that the railroads were anxious and eager to come as soon as the town voted bonds, and that the waterworks—pipes, pumps, filters and all, a complete "Holly" system—were ordered and would be put in in the spring. The Colonel did not quite understand how an academy of arts and science could be conducted in the three-room sod shack on the hill; but Aristotle Gump showed him the plan of a stately building with an imposing bell tower that hung over the desk in his office, assuring him that it would go up in May, and that the workmen from Topeka were already engaged for the job. He was surprised, too, to find so few people in a town of two thousand inhabitants; but he was told that most of the business men had gone East to settle up their affairs, and would be back in the spring with their new goods. Indeed, in Ezekiel Gump's office, the Colonel saw hundreds of letters, long glowing letters, from these absent citizens, telling of their great business schemes and their unshaken faith in the golden future of El Dorado. There were few houses, indeed, but there were acres and acres of foundations; there were few businesses in operation, but there were hundreds of promises; and Apollo laughingly said that Western towns were built on promises.

But what most puzzled the Colonel was the vast number and importance of the Gumps. The Gumps seemed to be at the head of everything. The eldest brother was Isaiah Gump, the minister, a red-faced, clean-shaven man, with a bald pate and dark, wrinkled little hands. Then

[297]

there were De Witt Gump, the physician and druggist; Chesterfield Gump, the general dry goods merchant; Aristotle Gump, architect and builder, and professor of mathematics in the Gump Academy; Hezekiah Gump, the hardware merchant and president of the El Dorado Board of Trade; Ezekiel Gump, real estate agent, superintendent of waterworks, professor of natural sciences, etc. These were the Gumps. But stay—were there not also Almira Gump, who taught history and Italian in the academy, and Venus Gump, who conducted a dressmaking and millinery establishment? The Colonel learned from Apollo that the Gump brothers had bought the land and founded the town, that it was, in short, a monument of Gump enterprise, it having been their long cherished ambition to become municipal promoters.

The Sunday after the Colonel's arrival, Isaiah preached a sermon on the rebuilding of Jerusalem, and told how the Jews built each man before his own door, with a trowel in one hand and a sword in the other. This was preliminary to urging the citizens of El Dorado to build sidewalks before their respective residences. He gave a long and eloquent discourse upon the builders of great cities from Menes, Nimrod and Romulus down, and among these celebrated personages, the Gumps were by no means forgotten.

After the sermon, the Colonel went to dine with Apollo at the little hotel. As they sat over their claret and cigars, Apollo said, "Colonel, if you can work any kind of a deal with Zeke, I would advise you to buy up your land before the railroad comes, for land is sure to go up then. It's a good plan out here to buy before a road comes and sell as soon as possible afterwards."

"About how much would you advise me to invest in land, Mr. Gump?" inquired the Colonel.

"Well, if I were you, I would about halve my pile. Half I would put into real estate and half into bank stock. Then you've got both realty and personal security and you are pretty safe."

"I think I will get back into business. I may as well open a little shop and give your brother Chesterfield a little competition. I find I have been in the harness so long that I scarcely know what to do with myself out of it. I am too old to learn to be a gentleman of leisure."

"That's a good idea; but whatever you do, do it before the road comes. That's where the mistake is made in Western towns; men buy at high tide of the boom instead of having foresight enough to buy before. A boom makes the man it finds; but woe to the man it leaves in its track."

A year later the Colonel found that Apollo had spoken a great truth.

"I think I rather like that land your brother showed me yesterday. Right next to the 'eighty' Mr. Thompson just bought. I would a little rather get tilled land, though."

"Now, Colonel, you are buying this land to sell; and wild land will sell just as well as any. You don't want to bother with crops; that's for the fellows that come in later. Let them do the digging. As soon as you have made up your mind, I want to spring a little scheme on you. I want to run you for city mayor next spring; and as soon as you have invested, we can begin to talk it up."

That suggestion pleased the Colonel and it rather soothed his conscience. He had his own scruples about land speculation; it seemed to him a good deal like gambling. But if he could really make an effort to further the interests of the town, he felt he would have a better right to make his fortune there.

After dinner they went out to look at Apollo's blooded horses, and then to Apollo's rooms over the bank to smoke. Apollo's rooms were very interesting apartments. They were decorated with boxing gloves, ball bats, fishing rods, an old pair of foils and pictures of innumerable theatrical people, mostly vaudeville celebrities and ladies of the ballet. As the Colonel showed some interest in these, Apollo began rattling off their names and various accomplishments, professional and otherwise, with a familiarity that astonished the old gentleman. One, he declared, could do the best double dislocation act on the horizontal bars to be seen in Europe or America, and his talents had been highly applauded by the Prince of Wales. Another was the best burnt cork artist of his time; and another a languishing blond lady, whose generous outlines were accentuated by the nature of her attire, he declared was "the neatest thing in tights that ever struck Kansas City." From Apollo that was a sweeping statement; for Kansas City was the unit of measure which he applied to the universe. At one end of his sleeping room there was a large, full length painting of a handsome, smiling woman, in short skirts and spangles. She stood on the toe of her left foot, her right foot raised, her arms lifted, her body thrown back in a pose of easy abandon. She was just beginning to dance, and there was something of lassitude in the movement of the picture. Behind her hung a dark red curtain, creating a daring effect of color through the sheer whiteness of her skirts, and the footlights threw a strong glare up into her triumphant face. It was broadly and boldly painted, something after the manner of Degas, but handled less cruelly than his subjects. The name at the bottom of the picture was that of a young American painter, then better known in Paris than in his own country. There were several photographs of the same person ranged about on Apollo's dressing case, and, as he thought her extremely beautiful, and as Apollo had not mentioned her, the Colonel politely inquired who she was.

"She was called Therese Barittini," replied Apollo, not looking at the picture.

"I never heard of her," remarked the Colonel, wondering at Apollo's strange manner.

"Probably not; she is dead," said Apollo shortly; and as the Colonel saw that he did not wish to discuss the subject, he let it drop. But he could never refrain from looking at that picture when he was in Apollo's room; and he had conjectures of his own. Incidentally he learned that Apollo had grown up about the theatres of Kansas City, ushering as a boy, and later working up to the box office. Had he known more of the theatres of that river metropolis, the Colonel would have realized that they are bad places for a boy. As it was, he attributed Apollo's exaggerated manner and many of his bad habits to his early environment.

It chanced that the next day was the day for voting on railroad bonds, and of course bonds were voted. There was great rejoicing among the builders of the city. The Gump band was out, and Apollo fired a fine display of fireworks which he had ordered from Kansas City in anticipation of the happy event. Those fireworks must have cost Apollo a nice little sum, for there were a great many of them. Why, there were actually some of the blackened rocket sticks lying around the streets next spring when every one knew that the railroad companies had never heard of such a place as El Dorado.

None of the Gumps had their families with them; they were to come out in the spring. They spoke often and affectionately of their families— all but Apollo, who never mentioned having any. The Colonel had supposed that he had never been married, until one day when he and Apollo were dining with Isaiah. Isaiah, after droning away in his prosy fashion about his wife and little ones and commenting upon the beauty of family ties, began moralizing upon Apollo's unfortunate marriage. Apollo, who had been growing whiter and whiter, rose, set down his glass and, reaching across the table, struck the Reverend Isaiah in the mouth. This was the first that the Colonel saw of the bitter altercations which sometimes arose among the Gump brothers.

By the close of the winter the Colonel had put out his money and opened his store. Everything went on at a lively enough pace in El Dorado.

Men took large risks because their neighbors did, as blind to the chances against them as the frequenters of the bucket shops on Wall Street. Hope was in the atmosphere, and each man was immersed in his own particular dream of fortune. One thinking man might have saved the community; but many communities have gone to ruin through the lack of that rare man. Afterwards, when the news of the great Gump swindle spread abroad over the land, and its unique details commanded a column's space in one of the New York papers, financiers laughed and said that a child could have grasped the situation. The inhabitants of El Dorado were chiefly men who had made a little capital working for corporations in large cities, and were incompetent to manage an independent business. They had been mere machines in a great system, consulted by no one, subject to complete control. Here they were "prominent citizens," men of affairs, and their vanity and self-confidence expanded unduly. The rest were farming people who came to make homes and paid little attention to what went on in the town. And the farmer is always swindled, no matter by whom offences come. The crash may start in Wall Street, but it ends in the hillside farms and on the prairie. No matter where the lightning strikes, it blackens the soil at last.

As the winter wore away, Apollo Gump drank harder than ever, drank alone in his rooms now, indulging in the solitary form of the vice, which is its worse form. No one saw much of him after business hours. He was gloomy and abstracted and seemed to dread even the necessary intercourse with men which his position in the bank entailed. The Gump brothers commissioned the Colonel to remonstrate with him upon the error of his ways, which he did without much effect. Still, there were many likable things about Apollo. He was different from the rest; his face was finer and franker, in spite of its heavy marks of dissipation, and his heart was kinder. His dogs were better treated than many men's children. His brothers were very clever fellows, some of them, all of them freehanded enough, except old Isaiah, who was the greatest bore and the sorriest rascal of them all. But the Colonel liked Apollo best. The great end of his life was to serve Mammon, but on the side he served other and better gods. Dante's lowest hell was a frozen one; and wherever Apollo's tortured soul writhes, it is not there; that is reserved for colder and perhaps cleaner men than he.

At last spring came, that fabled spring, when all the business men were to return to El Dorado, when the Gump Academy was to be built, when the waterworks were to be put in, when the Gumps were to welcome their wives and children. Chesterfield, Hezekiah and Aristotle had gone East to see to bringing out their families, and the Colonel was impatiently awaiting their return, as the real estate business seemed to be at a standstill and he could get no satisfaction from Apollo about the condition of affairs. One night there came a telegram from New York, brought posthaste across the country from the nearest station, announcing that the father of the Gumps was dying, and summoning the other brothers to his bedside. There was great excitement in El Dorado at these tidings, and the sympathy of its inhabitants was so genuine that they scarcely stopped to think what the departure of the Gumps might mean.

De Witt and Ezekiel left the next day accompanied by Miss Venus and Miss Almira. Apollo and Isaiah remained to look after the bank. The Colonel began to feel anxious, realizing that the Gumps had things pretty much in their own hands and that if the death of their father should make any material difference in their projects and they should decide to leave Kansas for good, the town and his interests would be wofully undone. Still, he said very little, not thinking it a time to bring up business considerations; for even Apollo looked worried and harassed and was entirely sober for days together.

The Gumps left on Monday. On the following Sunday Isaiah delivered a particularly powerful discourse on the mutability of riches. He compared temporal wealth to stock in the great bank of God, which paid such rich dividends of grace daily, hourly. He earnestly exhorted his hearers to choose the good part and lay up for themselves treasures in heaven, where moths cannot corrupt nor thieves break through and steal. Apollo was not at church that morning. The next morning the man who took care of Apollo's blooded horses found that two of them were missing. When he went to report this to Apollo he got no response to his knock, and, not succeeding in finding Isaiah, he went to consult the Colonel. Together they went back to Apollo's room and broke in the door. They found the room in wretched disorder, with clothing strewn about over the furniture; but nothing was missing save Apollo's grip and revolver, the picture of the theatrical-looking person that had hung in his sleeping room, and Apollo himself. Then the truth dawned upon the Colonel. The Gumps had gone, taking with them the Gump banking funds, land funds, city improvement funds, academy funds, and all funds, both public and private.

As soon as the news of the hegira of the Gumps got abroad, carriages and horses came from all the towns in the country, bringing to the citizens of El Dorado their attentive creditors. All the townsmen had paid fabulous prices for their land, borrowed money on it, put the money into the

Gump bank, and done their business principally on credit obtained on the Gump indorsement. Now that their money was gone, they discovered that the land was worth nothing, was a desert which the fertile imagination of the Gumps had made to blossom as the rose. The loan companies also discovered the worthlessness of the land, and used every possible means to induce the tenants to remain on it; but the entire country was panic-stricken and would hear no argument. Their one desire was to get away from this desolate spot, where they had been duped. The infuriated creditors tore down the houses and carried even the foundation stones away. Scarcely a house in the town had been paid for; the money had been paid to Aristotle Gump, contractor and builder, who had done his business in the East almost entirely on credit. The loan agents and various other creditors literally put the town into wagons and carried it off. Meanwhile, the popular indignation was turned against the Colonel as having been immediately associated with the Gumps and implicated in their dishonesty. In vain did he protest his innocence. When men are hurt they must have something to turn upon, like children who kick the door that pinches their fingers. So the poor old Colonel, who was utterly ruined and one of the heaviest losers, was accused of having untold wealth hidden away somewhere in the bluffs; and all the tempest of wrath and hatred which the Gumps had raised broke over his head. He was glad, indeed, when the town was utterly deserted, and he could live without the continual fear of those reproachful and suspicious glances. Often as he sat watching those barren bluffs, he wondered whether some day the whole grand delusion would not pass away, and this great West, with its cities built on borrowed capital, its business done on credit, its temporary homes, its drifting, restless population, become panic-stricken and disappear, vanish utterly and completely, as a bubble that bursts, as a dream that is done. He hated western Kansas; and yet in a way he pitied this poor brown country, which seemed as lonely as himself and as unhappy. No one cared for it, for its soil or its rivers. Every one wanted to speculate in it. It seemed as if God himself had only made it for purposes of speculation and was tired of the deal and doing his best to get it off his hands and deed it over to the Other Party.

III

On this particular morning, the fourth anniversary of the fatal advent of Apollo Gump into his store at Winchester, as the Colonel sat smoking in his chair, a covered wagon came toiling slowly up from the south. The horses were thin and fagged, and it was all that they could do to drag the creaking wagon. The harness was old and patched with rope. Over the hames and along the back strap hung pieces of sunflower brush to serve as fly nets. The wagon stopped at the well and two little boys clambered out and came trotting up the path toward the store. As they came the Colonel heard them chattering together in a broad Southern dialect; and the sound of his own tongue was sweet to his ears.

"What is it, boys?" he asked, coming to the door.

"Say, boss, kin we git some watah at yo' well?"

"Of course you can, boys. Git all you want."

"Thank yo', sir"; and the lads trotted back to the wagon.

The Colonel took up his stick and followed them. He had not seen such good natured, towheaded little chaps for a long while; and he was fond of children. A little girl, dressed in that particularly ugly shade of red in which farming people seem to delight, clambered out of the wagon and went up to the well with a tin cup, picking her way carefully with her bare feet to avoid the sand burrs. A fretful voice called from the wagon.

"Law me, boys, haint you most got that watah yit?"

A wan woman's face appeared at the front of the wagon, and she sat down and coughed heavily, holding her hand over her chest as if it hurt her. The little girl filled the tin cup and ran toward the wagon.

"Howdy do, sir?" said the woman, turning to the Colonel as soon as she had finished drinking.

"Right smart, ma'am, thank 'ee."

"Mercy, air yo' from the South? Virginy? Laws! I am from Miz-zoura myself an' I wisht I was back there. I 'low we'd be well enough off if we could git back to Pap."

She looked wistfully off toward the southwest and put her hand to her side again. There was something in the look of her big, hollow eyes that touched the Colonel. He told her she had better stay there a few days and rest the horses—she did not look well enough to go on.

"No, thank yo', sir, we must git on. I'll be better in the mornin', maybe. I was feelin' right smart yesterday. It's my lungs, the slow consumption. I think I'll last till I git back to Pap. There has been a good deal of the consumption in our family, an' they most all last." She talked nervously on, breathing heavily between her words. "Haint there a town Eldorader somewheres about here?"

The Colonel flushed painfully. "Yes, this is El Dorado."

"Law me, purty lookin' town!" said the woman, laughing dismally. "Superb's better'n this." She pronounced Superb as though it had but one syllable. "They got a black-smith shop an' a hardware store there, anyways. I am from nigh Superb, yo' see. We moved there ten years ago, when the country was lookin' mighty green and purty. It's all done burnt up long ago. It's that dry we couldn't raise any garden stuff there these three years. Everything's gone now, exceptin' these horses Pap give me when I was married. No, my man haint with me; he died just afore we come away. A bull gored him through an' through, an' he crawled outsiden the bob-wire fence and died. It was mighty hard. He didn't want to die there; he craved to die in Mizzoura. We shot the bull and brought t'other cattle with us; but they all died on the way."

She closed her eyes and leaned back against the side of the wagon. Suddenly she roused herself and said:

"Law me, boys, this must be the sto' that man told us on. Yo' see our meat and stuff give out most a week ago, an' we been a livin' on pancakes ever since. We was all gittin' sick, fur we turned agin' 'em, when we met a feller on horseback down the valley, a mighty nice lookin' feller, an' he give us five dollars an' told us we'd find a store someers up here an' could git some groceries."

"It must have been one of them loan company fellows," said the Colonel meditatively. "They still come sneakin' about once in a while, though I don't know what they're after. They haven't left us much but the dirt, an' I reckon that wouldn't do 'em much good if they could carry it off."

"That I can't tell yo'. I never seen him befo'—but he was a mighty kind sort of a feller. He give us the money, and he give me some brandy."

The Colonel helped her out of the wagon, and they went up to the store, while the boys watered the horses. Their purchases were soon made; but the Colonel refused to take their money.

"No, ma'am, I can't do that. You'll need your money before you get to Missouri. It's all in the family, between blood kin like. We're both from the South; and I reckon it would have been enough better for us if we'd never left it."

"Thank yo' mighty kindly, sir. Yo' sholey can't be doin' much business heah; better git in an' go with us. Good day to yo', an' thank you kindly, sir."

The Colonel stood wistfully watching the wagon until it rolled slowly out of sight, and then went back to his store, and with a sigh sat down—sat down to wait until water came from the rock and verdure from the desert, a sort of Sphinx of the Solomon who sat waiting for the end of time. This was a day when his mind dwelt even more than usual upon his misfortunes, and homesickness was heavy upon him, and he yearned for his own people and the faces of his kindred; for the long Virginia twilights in which he and Major Denney used to sit under the great trees in the courthouse yard, living the siege of Richmond over again; for the old comrades who took a drink with him at the Taylor House bar; for the little children who rolled their hoops before his door every morning, and went nutting with him in the fall; for the Great North Mountains, where the frosts would soon be kindling the maples and hickories into flame; for the soft purple of the Blue Ridge lying off to the eastward; and for that sound which every Virginian hears forever and forever in his dreams, that rhythmic song of deathless devotion, deep and solemn as the cadence of epic verse, which the Potomac and Shenandoah sing to the Virginia shore as they meet at Harper's Ferry. To every exile from the Valley of Virginia that sound is as the voice of his mother, bidding him keep his honor clean, and forever calling him to come home. The Colonel had stopped his horse there on the moonlight night in '62 when he rode away to the wars, and listened long to that sound; and looking up at the towering grandeur of Maryland heights above him, he had lifted his hand and sworn the oath that every young Virginian swore and that every young Virginian kept. For if the blood shed for those noble rivers could have been poured into their flood, they would have run crimson to the sea; and it is of that that they sing always as they meet, chanting the story over and over in the moonlight and the sunlight, through time and change unable to forget all that wasted glory of youth, all that heroic love. Before now, when the old man had heard them calling to him in the lonely winter nights, he had bowed his head in his hands and wept in an almost physical passion of homesickness.

Toward evening the clouds banked up in the western sky, and with the night a violent storm set in, one of those drenching rains that always come too late in that country, after a barren summer has waned into a fruitless autumn. For some reason he felt indisposed to go to bed. He sat watching the lightning from the window and listening to the swollen Solomon, that tore between its muddy banks with a sullen roar, as though it resented this intrusion upon its accustomed calm and indolence. Once he thought he saw a light flash from one of the bluffs across the river, but on going to the door all was dark. At last he regretfully put out his lamp and went to bed.

IV

That night, a few hours before, when the storm was at its worst, a horseman had come galloping along the bank of the Solomon. He drew rein at the foot of a steep, naked bluff and sat in his saddle looking about him. It was a sorry night for a man to be out. The blackness of the sky seemed to bear down upon him, save when now and then it was ripped from end to end by a jagged thrust of lightning, which rent it like the veil of the temple. At each flash he could see the muddy water of the swollen river whirling along wraiths of white foam over the little shivering willows. Save for that one lonely light across the river, there was no sign of man. He dismounted from his horse and, tying it to a sapling, he took a spade, strapped to the saddle, and began to climb the bluff. The water from the uplands was running down the hill wearing channels in the soft stone and made the grass so slippery that he could scarcely stand. When he reached the top he took a dark lantern from his pocket and lit it, sheltering it under the cape of his mackintosh; then he set it behind a clump of bunch grass. Starting from a lone oak, he carefully paced a distance and began to dig. His clothing was wet through, and even his mackintosh was wet enough to impede his arms. He impatiently threw off everything but his shirt and trousers and fell to work again. His shirt was wet and his necktie hung like a rag under his collar. His black hair hung wet over his white forehead, his brows were drawn together and his teeth were set. His eyes were fixed on the ground, and he worked with the desperation of a man who works to forget. He drove the spade in to the top at every thrust and threw the soggy earth far down the hillside, blistering his white hands with the rigor of his toil. The rain beat ceaselessly in his face and dripped from his hair and mustache; but he never paused save when now and then he heard some strange sound from the river. Then he started, shut off the light from his dark lantern and waited until all was quiet.

When he had been digging for some time, he knelt down and thrust his arm into the hole to feel its depth. Close beside him he heard a shrill, whirring, metallic sound which a man who hears it once remembers to his dying day. He felt a sharp pain in the big vein of his right arm and sprang to his feet with an oath; and then the rattlesnake, having been the avenger of many, slid quietly off through the wet grass.

V

Next morning the sun rose radiantly over the valley of the Solomon. The sky was blue and warm as the skies of the South, the hard, straight line of the horizon was softened by a little smokelike haze, and the yellow leaves of the cottonwoods, still wet from the drenching rain, gleamed in the sunshine, and through the scant foliage the white bark glittered like polished silver. All the land was washed fresh and clean from the dust of the desert summer. It was a day of opal lights, a day set in a heaven of gold and turquoise and bathed in sapphirine airs; one of those rare and perfect days that happen only in desert countries, where Nature seems sometimes to repent of her own pitilessness and by the glory of her skies seems trying to compensate for the desolation of the lands that stretch beneath them. But when the Colonel came out to view the ravages of the storm the exultant beauty of the morning moved him little. He knew how false it was and how fleeting. He knew how soon Nature forgets. Across the river he heard a horse whinnying in the bushes. Surprised and curious, he went over to see what it might mean. The horse stood, saddled and bridled, among the sumac bushes, and at the back of the saddle carried a long waterproof roll. He seemed uneasy and stood pawing the wet ground and chewing at the withered leaves. Looking about the Colonel could see no rider and he went up the bluff to look for him. And there he found him. About five paces from the oak tree was a newly dug hole, with the spade still sticking upright in the earth. The grass around it was cut and crushed as though it had been beaten by a strong man in his rage. Beside the hole was the body of a man. His shirt was torn open to the waist and was wet and spattered with mud; his left hand was wound in the long grass beside him; his right, swollen and black, was thrown over his head; the eyes were wide open, and the teeth were set hard upon the lower lip. The face was the handsome, dissolute face of Apollo Gump.

The Colonel lifted him up and laid him under the little tree. A glance at his arm told how he died. There was a brandy flask beside him, and the wound had been enlarged with his knife, but the snake had struck a vein and the poison had been too swift. Taking up the spade, the Colonel set to work to finish what the dead man had begun. At a depth of about four feet he found a wooden box, cased in tin. He whistled softly to himself as he loosened the earth about it. So the Gumps had not been so clever, after all; they had brought down more game than they could bag, and at the last moment they had been compelled to bury part of their spoil. For what else on earth or in heaven would Apollo Gump have risked his rascally neck in the Solomon Valley?

But no, there was no money, only the picture of the handsome, theatrical looking woman he had seen in Apollo's room, a few spangled stage dresses, a lot of woman's clothing, dainty garments that looked like a trousseau and some tiny gowns made for a little, little baby, that had never been worn. That was all. The Colonel drew a long breath of astonishment, and stood looking at the picture. There, at the back of the saddle, was the waterproof roll which was to have carried it away. This then was Apollo Gump's weakness, and this was the supreme irony that life had held in store for him, that when he had done evil without penalty and all his sins had left him scathless, his one poor virtue should bring him to his death! As the Colonel glanced at that poor distorted body, lying there in the sunlight amid the glistening grasses, he felt for a moment a throb of that old affection he had once known for him. Already the spiders had woven a rainbow web over that set, white face, a gossamer film of protection against man's vengeance; and it seemed as though Nature had already begun her magnificent and complete work of pardon, as though the ground cried out for him, to take him into her forgiving breast and make him again a part of the clean and fruitful earth.

When he searched the dead man's body he found a leather belt and pouch strapped about his waist next his skin. In this were ten thousand dollars in bank notes and a ticket to San Francisco. The Colonel quietly counted the money and put it into his own pocket.

"There, sir, I've waited a long time to square my account with you. You owe me six thousand still, but they say a dead man's debts are cancelled and I'll take your horse and call it square. If there is a recording angel that keeps the run of these things, you can tell him you are square with me and take that much off your poor soul; you'll have enough to answer for without that, God knows."

That afternoon the Colonel dragged up the bluff a long rough box made from weather boards torn from his store. He brought over his best suit of clothes from its odorous camphor chest and with much difficulty succeeded in forcing it on to the stiffened limbs of the dead man.

"Apollo, I liked you mighty well. It cut me to the heart when you turned rascal—and you were a damned rascal. But I'll give you a decent burial, because you loved somebody once. I always knew you were too good a fellow for your trade and that you'd trip up in it somewhere. This would never have happened to those precious brothers of yours. I guess I won't say any prayers over you. The Lord knows you better than I do; there have been worse men who have lived and died Christians. If I thought any words of mine could help you out, I'd say 'em free. But the Lord has been forgiving sin from the beginning of the world, till it must have kept him pretty busy before now. He knows his business by this time. But I hope it will go a bit easy with you, Apollo, that I do."

He sunk the box in the hole and made a pillow of the light spangled dresses and laid the dead man in upon them. Over him he laid the picture of the handsome, smiling woman, who was smiling still. And so he buried them.

Next day, having got his money out of the place, the Colonel set fire to his old store and urged his horse eastward, never once casting back a look at the last smoking ruin of El Dorado.

In the spring the sunflowers grew tall and fair over every street and house site; and they grew just as fair over the mound beside the oak tree on the bluff. For if Nature forgets, she also forgives. She at least holds no grudge, up in her high place, where she watches the poles of the heavens. The tree itself has stopped growing altogether. It has concluded that it is not worth the effort. The river creeps lazily through the mud; it knows that the sea would be only a great, dirty, salty pond if it should reach it. Year by year it buries itself deeper in the black mud, and burrows among the rotting roots of the dead willows, wondering why a river should ever have been put there at all.

First published in *New England Magazine*, XXIV (June, 1901), 357–369.

Jack-a-Boy

✳ ✳ ✳

I am quite unable to say just why we were all so fond of him, or how he came to mean so much in our lives. He was just a little boy of six, a trifle girlish in his ways, and, as a rule, I do not like effeminate boys. Moreover, he was precocious, and precocious children are almost invariably disagreeable.

Certainly he was handsome, and he carried himself with a spritelike grace and his little suit of "soldier clothes" fitted him like a sheath. But his chiefest charm lay in his eyes, big, tender, gray eyes, that used to make me think of that old song, "Thine Eyes so Blue and Tender": they were soft as the color on a dove's breast, and they looked down into your soul's secrets and made you remember things you had not thought of for years. Yet I do not see why we should have loved him for that: there were things in my own life I had no desire to remember, and there must have been many things in the life of the Woman Nobody Called On that she preferred to forget. And as for the Professor—oh, well! he didn't care to remember anything at all but Sanskrit roots and the metres of difficult Greek choruses, and he grudged the space that anything else took up in his brain. I fancy, generally speaking, that none of the folk who lived in Windsor Terrace were fond of memories. People who live in terraces are not usually those who have made the most brilliant success in life.

We were not prepared to give Jack-a-Boy a very cordial welcome when his parents moved into Number 324. It put us all in an ugly humor when we saw a hobbyhorse lifted out of the moving van. Of course there would be children, we said; we might have known that. Other people's children are one of the most objectionable features attendant upon living in terraces—and such children! We had more than enough of them already, and we resented a single addition. When he came we all eyed him sourly enough, and if looks could kill, the florist would have been sending white roses up to Number 324.

The day after Jack-a-Boy's arrival I went up to the Professor's room to borrow a book and found him in a great state of nervous agitation.

"More children!" he cried, throwing down his pen; "and these partitions are so thin I can hear him laughing. I suppose he will have all the other children in the street in there, romping all day long; and I am just in the middle of a chapter on Vowels of Variable Quantity. Decidedly, I shall have to move!"

My friend, the Professor, was writing a work on Greek prosody, which he believed would be invaluable to English scholars. He had been writing it ever since I had first met him, and I don't care to say just how long ago that was. He was a thin, frail man, angular and much bent, who seemed to have put all his blood into his grammars, and to have only thousands of tiny Greek accent marks and smooth and rough breathings where the red corpuscles should be. His nerves were none of the best, and he worked through two pairs of powerful spectacles, and the strain of his labor was so heavy that I was sorry that he should be subjected to the annoyance of having a boisterous child next door.

The next day the Professor had another visitor, no less a person than the *enfant terrible* himself. The good man was seated at his desk, scratching away furiously, his door slightly ajar. When he got up to go to the case for a book, he saw a little boy dressed in a gray cadet suit standing outside his door, cap in hand. He ground his teeth and sat down and began writing again. Presently he looked up and saw that little gray figure still at his door.

"Well, what is it?" he asked sharply.

"Oh, I was just waiting until you were through. I came to call for a minute. I've been calling on almost everyone in the Terrace, but I saw you were busy, so I thought I'd wait."

"Well, as my occupation is likely to last for some years yet, you may as well come in," said the Professor, rather gruffly. It was impossible to answer that clear little treble voice very savagely.

Jack-a-Boy was accustomed to taking people at their word, so in he went.

"My, what a lot of books you have!" he gasped, looking about. "Are there any with pictures in?"

"Pictures? Um-m, let me see." The Professor got up and turned the revolving bookcase and took out a big book that looked like a portfolio, and smiled grimly as he gave it to the boy.

"Now, you go on with your work, and I'll just sit here and look at these, and I won't bother you. I never bother Papa when he writes."

Jack-a-Boy curled himself up on the soft, woolly hearth rug, his chin propped on his hands and the book open before him, and the Professor went back to his desk and forgot Jack-a-Boy's existence.

I can think of no place where a child's presence—that is, an ordinary child's presence—could be more incongruous than in the Professor's room. It is a very large room, or would be for an ordinary tenant who furnished it in an ordinary manner. But under the Professor's occupancy it looked as though an effort had been made to crowd into it the entire contents of the British Museum. There were detail maps of every dead and forgotten city in which antiquarians had ever burrowed; dusty plaster casts of all the Grecian philosophers marshaled in rows above the book-shelves; bronzes of several of the later Roman emperors; terra-cotta models of the Acropolis and Parthenon and several other edifices whose very names I have forgotten, if I ever knew them; even an Egyptian mummy was wedged in between the lavatory and chiffonier. As for the books, they had overflowed all the cases long ago, and there was not a niche left for another shelf. The Professor's shoe box had been removed to make room for the last bookcase, and he kept his shoes under his bed. So the tomes were packed in under his desk, piled in the corners and on the chairs, on his table and on his bed. They were particularly in evidence on his little iron bed, and almost crowded him out entirely. The house-maid often told me that when she went to make his bed in the morning she found dozens of books piled up on the side next the wall, and a narrow indentation at the outer edge was the only indication that the Professor had gone to bed at all. I believe at one time he had another room in which to sleep, but he caught so many colds trapesing into his study in his pajamas at all hours of the night when some grammatical perplexity awoke him, that he had decided to abolish the last slight barrier between his books and himself and lived with them in good earnest. His room was on the third floor, where the doings of his landlady could not disturb him and where his windows commanded a magnificent view of the harbor, lying far away across the housetops. Not that the Professor spent much time looking out of his windows; when he first moved into the Terrace he had thought he would, but on his way to the window he always caught sight of some book or other and would pick it up and go back to his desk with it. All his life his excursions from his desk had ended just so. Very often, as he was starting out for his dinner, he would stop, hat in hand, for a look into Autenrieth or the Griechische Formenlehre, and the dinner hour would steal by and he would light his pipe and console himself with the thought that he worked more when he ate little, and on the whole was very glad that he had gained an hour.

As I say, the Professor had quite forgotten that he had a visitor when he heard a clear little voice asking politely:

"Would you please tell me what these pictures are about? They are not like the ones in my picture books. I think these must be knights, 'cause they have helmets on!'"

The Professor started, and looked at him over his spectacles. The book he had given the child was a volume of Flaxman's immortal illustrations to Homer. Going over to the hearth rug, he sat down by the boy, and before he knew what he was about he had launched into an abbreviated and expurgated version of the Trojan War. For the Professor's heart was not really dead after all, you see, only buried beneath an accumulation of Sanskrit forms and Greek idioms.

After that, Jack-a-Boy went often to see the Professor. One evening, when I went in to borrow a book from my learned friend, I found a scarlet and gold Harlequin all hung with silver bells perched on a volume of Friedrich Nietzsche. I took no pains to conceal my amusement, and the Professor looked up very sheepishly, muttering: "That rascal left the thing here this afternoon."

He made friends with everyone in the Terrace in just the same way, and seemed personally interested in all our miserable little doings. Even the crabbed old spinster in Number 326, whose lodgers stood in absolute fear of her, was soon known to be one of his conquests. She made him a little toy dog that was stiff and hard and gray like herself. It was solidly stuffed with sawdust, and had four corncob legs of uneven lengths, and it was an awkward and uncomfortable thing to hold in your arms. But Jack-a-Boy carried it about with him religiously for days, "For I wouldn't like to hurt her feelings," he said. He did not care much for toys, but he was very proud of anything that was given to him. I believe if anyone had given Jack-a-Boy the most unsightly of love tokens, he, who was so fond of pretty things, would have received it joyfully and treasured it.

Soon after he came he asked if he might sit in my music room while I was giving lessons, and when the piano was not in use he used to sit down and pick out the most charming little airs for himself, simple minor melodies, indefinitely sad, like the verses of young poets, but so graceful and individual that they made those hours sweet to remember. Music came as easily and naturally to him as speech, and the sense of harmonies was strangely developed in him, though he was such a nervous child we never dared let him practice much. I fell into a habit of playing to him in the twilight, after the long, dull days were over, and when he was not with the Professor, hearing about Grecian heroes, he was usually with me at that hour. I used to fancy that Jack-a-Boy would make music of his own some day, perhaps quite as beautiful as any that I played for him, and I used to wonder what form of expression the beautiful little soul of his would choose.

He did not play much with the other boys of the street. "They are such rough boys," he whispered confidentially to me. The gentle ways of the girls suited him better, and deep down in my heart I was afraid that, in spite of his soldier clothes and his love for the Grecian heroes, Jack-a-Boy was a coward. But one morning as I was sitting on the piazza, watching Jack-a-Boy play with one of the little girls of the Terrace, I saw another boy come up and maliciously stick a pin in the little girl's balloon. Jack-a-Boy flew at him like a wildcat, fists, teeth, feet and all the rest of him. I never saw such anger in a child. It was the frenzied, impotent revolt of a high and delicate nature against brutality and coarseness and baseness, like those outbursts of Stevenson's youth. The boy's comrades flew to his rescue, and in a moment our boy was down under four of them. I ran screaming to the edge of the porch, but an angular form darted past me. It was the Professor, hatless and coatless, with both pairs of spectacles on his nose. In a moment he came back carrying what was left of Jack-a-Boy, with the little girl wailing at his heels.

"Take good care of that little chap, madam," said the Professor as he gave him to his mother; "he carries the heart of more than one of us buttoned under his soldier clothes."

Of all Jack-a-Boy's friends, the Woman Nobody Called On was certainly the strangest. She lived in Number 328 and no one ever went to see her. We knew very little of her, except that she was very handsome, with that large, blond, opulent sort of beauty that is seldom seen off the stage and that one somehow distrusts on sight. Her beauty was a little faded on close inspection, too. She lived well, for her alimony was said to be generous. Some people used to wonder that Jack-a-Boy's mother allowed him to go to see her, but I think she was proud of her little son's elasticity and charm and his power of bringing gladness into people's lives. At any rate, Jack-a-Boy went often to see the woman in Number 328, and, as I passed, I used to see her watching for him at the window. Of all the people she had waited for in days gone by, I doubt if there was one for whom she had ever waited with such eagerness as she did for Jack-a-Boy. She always kept a supply of his favorite bonbons and was very careful to see that he did not eat too many. She knew so well what comes of having too much of what one likes, that Woman Nobody Called On.

One chilly April day, as Jack-a-Boy stretched himself out on the big Persian rug before her fire, he remarked:

"My! What pretty rooms you have; they are the nicest in the Terrace, I think. It's a pity you haven't got any little boys; they'd have such a good time here."

The Woman Nobody Called On looked at him queerly.

"Should you like me for a mother, Jack-a-Boy?"

"Why, yes, of course I would, you are so beautiful. After my own mother, I think I would rather have you than any lady I know. I believe I would like to have a great many mothers, kind of second-best ones, you know. Sometimes on the street cars I see ladies I would like to have for mothers, and then there are others I wouldn't. There is Miss Mellon now, who gave me the dog; she is a very nice lady, but I wouldn't like to have her for a mother!" Jack-a-Boy wondered why the woman laughed and hugged him so.

Jack-a-Boy's great fête that year was his May-basket hanging. I think it meant even more to him than Christmas, because it was his nature to enjoy giving. He began to prepare for it about the middle of April. He got a large supply of tissue paper of many colors, and the old maid in Number 326 gave him a number of wooden baskets in which she bought her butter, and the Woman Nobody Called On gave him bonbon boxes of all shapes and sizes. I think there was no one in the Terrace who was not consulted about the construction of those baskets, but he made them all alone in his nursery, and never weakened into showing any one of us the basket intended for our neighbor. He used to come out from his work with an eager face and sticky fingers, and he confided to me that his mother was making him some paper flowers because the real ones were so expensive, and asked me if I didn't think paper flowers would do pretty well with real leaves to make them look "realer." On the afternoon of the first of May, Jack-a-Boy and I went for a walk, and we got a few dandelions, and I persuaded him to let me add some violets to his collection. I knew that at heart he loathed the paper flowers. The Professor had been selected for the honor of hanging the baskets with him, and when I saw the old gentleman slipping out that night at dusk with a big market basket covered with rustling tissue paper on his arm, and that joyous, shapely little figure skipping beside him, I did not try to conceal my jealousy. I felt rather lonely and ill-used, and I opened my window and sat down beside it in the darkness. There was just a pallid ghost of a new moon in the sky, a faint silver crescent curve, like Artemis' bow, with a shred of gauzy cloud caught on its horn. The violet heavens were nebulous with the spring mistiness. Below, in the dusky street, I heard every little while the ring of a doorbell and the hurry of swift little feet down the steps and up the pavement, and sometimes a clear, silvery little peal of laughter, suddenly muffled. Once, on the other side of the street, I saw Jack-a-Boy scudding down the pavement like a gleeful young elf, with the Professor in the role of a decrepit Old Man of the Mountain shuffling after him.

When the Professor came in he stopped at my door.

"Miss Harris, I must beg your assistance in a little matter tonight," he said.

"Why, certainly, Professor, but surely you have forgotten that I am neither a lexicon nor an authority on Greek metres," I said.

He smiled quaintly. "I am not working at prosody tonight," he replied.

I followed him to his room, and there, on a relief map of the Peloponnesus, was a creation of blue paper and ribbons and flowers.

"I have made it at night, after that chap is in bed, for I am never safe in the daytime," explained the Professor proudly, "but I got the flowers only this afternoon and I doubt if they are very well arranged."

They certainly were not, but they were very pretty ones; yellow jonquils and big English violets.

"How did you happen to select these in particular?" I asked.

The Professor looked off at the bust of Aristotle above his desk and smiled absently over his glasses:

"Oh, they seemed to suit him. The yellow ones are gay, like him, and—and I think the violets are rather like his eyes." This last was said rather timidly. I suppose the Professor had never said that of a woman's eyes, so the comparison was quite fresh and unhackneyed to him.

"Now," I said encouragingly, massing the jonquils together to disguise their stiffness, "that is really a very pretty basket."

"Oh, it must be, if it is for him," chuckled the Professor. "He has taste, the rascal! Ugly things hurt him. He knows the Narcissus story, too. Did you ever notice what a singularly fine head that boy has? And that delicate face with its big violet eyes and arching brows? I tell you, it's a poet's face. There is a boy picture of Keats that looks like that. He has the mind that goes with it, too; all gossamer and phantasy and melody. I want to live to see him grow up."

The summer that year was a cruel one, and Jack-a-Boy's parents were not able to take him out of town. Matters must have gone ill with them just then, for Jack-a-Boy's young, blond papa looked worried and walked slowly with his shoulders bent, and wore his gray business suit on Sundays. I even fancied that Jack-a-Boy's white duck suits were not so many or so resplendent as in the summer when he first came to Windsor Terrace. We all took turns taking him to the park and off for little boat rides on the bay. But the heat was merciless; it withered the foliage in the parks and scorched the little grass plots before our doors, which were barely kept alive by continual spraying. The sultry nights took the fibre out of us all, and left us little courage to begin another day. Jack-a-Boy grew paler and his eyes grew larger and darker under their long black lashes, until we looked at one another over his head with questioning fear.

One burning dusty day in early September I was returning to town after a week's stay in the country, when the Professor met me in front of the Terrace to tell me that Jack-a-Boy had the scarlet fever, that he was very ill and had been asking for me. I hurried off my travel-stained garments and went over to help Jack-a-Boy's mother in whatever way I could. The Woman Nobody Called On was there, and I helped her sponge off his little burning body. Then I knew that the Professor had been the wisest of us, and that this was not a human child, but one of the immortal children of Greek fable made flesh for a little while. Such little bodies have I seen among the marble children of the Borghese Gallery, never otherwhere. He was delirious at moments, but he knew me and said he was glad to see me, and asked if I had brought the cattails and acorns I had promised him. He had seen only pictures of them, and I had promised to bring him some real ones, and had forgotten. I have been forgetting things all my useless life, but I would have given anything in the world, anything, for a few acorns and rushes just then. It was so little that he ever wanted, and it was always such a pleasure to gratify those strange, fanciful, delicate desires of his. But where in the heart of the city could one go for acorns and cattails? As well start upon the quest of the Culprit Fay at once.

"Oh, never mind," he said when he saw that I was troubled. "Maybe it wouldn't be much fun unless I saw them grow. I'm so glad you're back. I like to have all my friends home at night."

His fever ran very high at dusk, and he was much excited and half-delirious and wanted the Professor to come and tell him stories. "I want to know," he said quite distinctly, "about the white horses of Rhesus; I have forgotten who stole them."

The Professor was not far to seek. He sat down in the shadow; the screen was before the droplight to shield Jack-a-Boy's fever-blind eyes, and holding that hot little hand in his, the man of learning told that old, old story of Achilles' wrath. Ordinarily the Professor's voice is hard and didactic, like that of all men who have lectured in classrooms all their lives. But he spoke so softly that night, I thought a certain musical quality crept into it. I could never have believed him capable of the sweetness and directness with which he told that wonderful story, his phrases taking on a certain metrical cadence of their own.

"And now about Achilles shouting at the wall," urged the boy.

But before the Professor had finished with Patroclus' death and his friend's sorrow Jack-a-Boy was wandering again, and talking about what he wanted for Christmas, and the reindeer of Santa Claus and the white horses of Rhesus. He tossed painfully in his little brass bed, and complained that it was hard and that the sheets were burning him. The Woman Nobody Called On took him up in her fine, strong arms and he seemed to rest comfortably there. Presently he looked up and said:

"Are you very tired holding me?"

"No, dear; would you rather lie down?"

"Oh, no! Not unless you're tired. I like to have you hold me, 'cause I can just feel you love me out of your arms," he murmured drowsily.

She held him so all night, while his mother got a little rest, until the dull, gray light of the dawn blanched the lamplight in the room, that hour so common for the passage of souls, when "the glowworm shows the matin to be near."

Then I felt a sense of relief, and there came a change in the oppressive air of the room; it became cooler, and just a faint breeze came in at the open windows, and I seemed to detect above the odors of medicine a fresh, wet smell of violets and of autumn woods and green, mossy places by the mountain streams, and I remembered that it was the time when the spirits of the dead, that have been wandering up and down the world through the night, hurry back to spirit land. I think, as they flitted by our windows, Jack-a-Boy must have recognized some joyous spirit with

[319]

whom he had played long ago in Arcady, for he left us. Perhaps some wood nymph, tall and fair, came in and laid her cool fingers on his brow and bore him off with the happy children of Pan.

The long, bad dream of the flowers and the casket and the dismal hymns, so cruelly inappropriate for such a glad and beautiful little life, and the little white hearse, and the abandoned grief of us all, is merely a blur to me now. I try to forget all that, and to remember only that Jack-a-Boy heard the pipes of Pan as the old wood gods trooped by in the gray morning, and that he could not stay.

The night after it was all over I went to the Professor's room. He was sitting alone in the darkness, before his desk, with his head resting on his hand. The student lamp, that had burned every night for so many years and had lit the scholar's way through so many miles of patient research, was dark. He lay so heavily back in his old reading chair that for the first time I realized that he was an old man, was growing older, and was not just old by nature, like the casts and leatherbound folios about him. I bade him good evening, but he did not lift his head.

"I knew from the first it would be fatal," he said; "I always knew we could not keep him long. Sometimes I fancied he would tarry long enough to sing a little like Keats, or to draw like Beardsley, or to make music like Schubert, and confound the wiseacres and pedants of the world, like those other immortal boys from Parnassus, who were sent to us by mistake. But he had too little to hold him back; less, even, than Keats. The meshes of the clay were too coarse to hold him. He rose from them, beautiful and still a child, like Cupid out of Psyche's arms. They could not spare him up yonder. There are not many such, even on Parnassus."

"I don't care about what he could have done or been," I answered rebelliously. "I don't think it matters so much about children's souls. If only we had his dear little body with us, it would be enough. It was the little human boy that I loved."

"No," said the Professor, shaking his head, "no, it was the soul. Why have we never loved any of the other children who have lived in this terrace? There have been enough of them. They were little animals of our common clay. But sometimes the old divinities reveal themselves in children. In this case it was inexplicable, as it always is. His people are common enough. Why should he have liked Flaxman's drawings better than his picture books? Why should he have liked the story of Theseus' boyhood in the Centaur's cave better than Jack the Giant Killer? Why should he tell me that the two stars that peeped down into his crib between the white curtains were like the eyes of the Golden Helen? That counter-jumper of a father of his never heard of the Golden Helen. No, he simply had that divinity in him, that holiness of beauty which the hardest and basest of us must love when we see it. He was of that antique world, and he would have lived in it always, like Keats. In my Homer over there there is a little, sticky thumbmark on the margin of the picture of the parting of Hector and Andromache. He liked that picture best of all, because, he said, 'it was so kind of Hector to take off his gleaming helmet not to frighten his little boy.' He always said 'gleaming helmet'; he loved the sound of the words. Sometimes I used to fancy that if I should speak the Greek words he would recognize them. At any rate, the Greek spirit was his. I have taught Homer all my life, and I know. He used to lie here on the rug by the hour with that book open before him, and I would have to speak to him again and again to get his attention. Perhaps he was remembering more about it all than the rest of us will ever know."

The Professor got up and wandered aimlessly over to the revolving bookcase by the window, and took up his Homer, turned a few pages, though it was too dark to see anything, then threw it down resentfully.

"Do you know, I had set my heart on teaching him the fine old tongue some day—that boy in knickerbockers?" he said.

Then I told him of the strange fancy I had of the wood gods coming on the night that Jack-a-Boy died. "Perhaps," murmured the old gentleman, "perhaps. We believe things less probable every day."

In the course of time the Professor settled down to Greek prosody again, and I to the giving of music lessons. We saw less of each other and our neighbors than formerly, for the bond which had drawn us all together was broken. Jack-a-Boy's people moved away and left the city, and we did not speak of him any more. For his own sake I almost hoped that the Professor had forgotten. Christmas time came, when everyone was buying presents for the little children they loved, but we bought no presents in Windsor Terrace, and we did not even know whether they kept Christmas in Jack-a-Boy's country. I saw the Professor's light burning far into the night on Christmas Eve, and the next day we avoided each other. But on the night of the first of May the Professor came to my room with a box of flowers in his hand and asked me to go with him to hang a May basket for Jack-a-Boy. When we reached the quiet little spot under the lilac bushes in the cemetery we saw a woman's figure alone by the white stone, and her flowers lay on the green turf. It was the Woman Nobody Called On, and she explained that since Jack-a-Boy's people were so far away she had feared he would not be remembered, and she had come out to him alone. We returned to the city together, talking of him in low tones, as though we had always known each other. When we left her at her door I resolved then and there that I would call. When we reached our own number we sat down a moment on the porch, in the faint May starlight, and the moon was as it had been the year before— pale and wan, and curved like Artemis' bow. The air of the spring night was alluringly soft and warm, and it seemed to revive the withered senti- ments in one, and to replenish the wellheads long gone dry. The mocking- bird owned by the old maid in Number 324 must have dreamed a Southern dream; a dream full of cypress swamps and live-oak boughs and sultry August nights on the bayou, for it broke out into a melody fit only for a tropical forest, a florid, coloratura number, full of brilliant cadenzas and trills and highly colored passages, entirely out of atmosphere in the grim, gray parlors of Number 324.

"We are three very different people, you, and that lonely woman down there, and I," the Professor was saying, "yet we seemed rather alike tonight. Perhaps Pater was right, and it is the revelation of beauty which is to be our redemption, after all. Whenever it comes, as many as see it, choose it, just as you and she and I chose him."

But I was thinking how the revelation of the greatest Revealer drew men together. How the fishermen left their nets, without questioning, to follow Him; and how Nicodemus, who thought himself learned, came to Him secretly by night, and Mary, of Magdala, at the public feast, wiped his feet with her hair.

First published in *Saturday Evening Post*, CLXXIII (March 30, 1901), 4–5, 25.

The Conversion of Sum Loo

✳ ✳ ✳

For who may know how the battle goes,
  Beyond the rim of the world?
And who shall say what gods survive,
  And which in the Pit are hurled?
How if a man should burn sweet smoke
  And offer his prayers and tears
At the shrine of a god who had lost the fight
  And been slain for a thousand years?

The purport of this story is to tell how the joy at the Mission of the Heavenly Rest for the most hopeful conversion of Sum Chin and Sum Loo, his wife, was turned to weeping, and of how little Sister Hannah learned that the soul of the Oriental is a slippery thing, and hard to hold, to hold in the meshes of any creed.

Sum Chin was in those days one of the largest importers of Chinese bronzes and bric-à-brac in San Francisco and a power among his own people, a convert worth a hundred of the coolie people. When he first came to the city he had gone to the Mission Sunday School for a while for the purpose of learning the tongue and picking up something of American manners. But occidental formalities are very simple to one who has mastered the complicated etiquette of southern Asia, and he soon picked up enough English for business purposes and so had fallen away from the Mission. It was not until his wife came to him, and until his little son was born that Sum Chin had regarded the mission people seriously, deeming it wise to invoke the good offices of any and all gods in the boy's behalf.

Of his conversion, or rather his concession, the people of the Heavenly Rest made great show, for besides being respected by the bankers and insurance writers, who are liberal in the matter of creed, he was well known to all the literary and artistic people of the city, both professionals and devout amateurs. Norman Girrard, the "charcoal preacher" as he

[323]

was called, because he always carried a bit of crayon and sketched opportunely and inopportunely, declared that Sum Chin had the critical faculty, and that his shop was the most splendid interior in San Francisco. Girrard was a pale-eyed theological student who helped the devout deaconesses at the Mission of the Heavenly Rest in their good work, and who had vacillated between art and the Church until his whole demeanor was restless, uncertain, and indicative of a deep-seated discontent.

By some strange attraction of opposites he had got into Sum Chin's confidence as far as it is ever possible to penetrate the silent, inscrutable inner self of the Oriental. This fateful, nervous little man found a sedative influence in the big, clean-limbed Chinaman, so smooth and calm and yellow, so content with all things finite and infinite, who could sit any number of hours in the same position without fatigue, and who once, when he saw Girrard playing tennis, had asked him how much he was paid for such terrible exertion. He liked the glowing primitive colors of Sum Chin's shop, they salved his feelings after the ugly things he saw in his mission work. On hot summer days, when the sea breeze slept, and the streets were ablaze with heat and light, he spent much time in the rear of Sum Chin's shop, where it was cool and dusky, and where the air smelt of spices and sandalwood, and the freshly opened boxes exhaled the aroma of another clime which was like an actual physical substance, and food for dreams. Those odors flashed before his eyes whole Orient landscapes, as though the ghosts of Old World cities had been sealed up in the boxes, like the djinn in the Arabian bottle.

There he would sit at the side of a formidable bronze dragon with four wings, near the imported lacquered coffin which Sum Chin kept ready for the final emergency, watching the immaculate Chinaman, as he sat at an American office desk attending to his business correspondence. In his office Sum Chin wore dark purple trousers and white shoes worked with gold, and an overdress of a lighter shade of purple. He wrote with a brush which required very delicate manipulation, scraping his ink from the cake and moistening it with water, tracing the characters with remarkable neatness on the rice paper. Years afterward, when Girrard had gone over to art body and soul, and become an absinthe-drinking, lady-killing, and needlessly profane painter of Oriental subjects and marines on the other side of the water, malicious persons said that in the tortures of his early indecision he had made the acquaintance of Sum Chin's opium pipe and had weakened the underpinning of his orthodoxy, but that is exceedingly improbable.

During these long seances Girrard learned a good deal of Sum Chin's history. Sum Chin was a man of literary tastes and had begun life as a scholar. At an early age he had taken the Eminent Degree of the Flowering Talent, and was preparing for the higher Degree of the Promoted Men, when his father had committed some offense against the Imperial Government, and Sum Chin had taken his guilt upon his own head and had been forced to flee the Empire, being smuggled out of the port at Hong Kong as the body servant of a young Englishman whom he had been tutoring in the Chinese Classics. As a boy he had dwelt in Nanking, the oldest city of the oldest Empire, where the great schools are, and where the tallest pagoda in the world rears its height of shining porcelain. After he had taken the Eminent Degree of the Flowering Talent and been accorded an ovation by the magistrates of his town, he had grown tired of the place; tired of the rice paper books, and the masters in their black gowns, and the interminable prospect of the Seven Thousand Classics; of the distant blue mountains and the shadow of the great tower that grew longer and longer upon the yellow clay all afternoon. Then he had gone south, down the great canal on a barge with big red sails like dragons' wings. He came to Soutcheofou, that is built upon the waterways of the hills of Lake Taihoo. There the air smelt always of flowers, and the bamboo thickets were green, and the canals were bright as quicksilver, and between them the waving rice fields shimmered in the sun like green watered silk. There the actors and jugglers gathered all the year round. And there the mandarins come to find concubines. For once a god loved a maiden of Soutcheofou and gave her the charms of heaven and since then the women of that city have been the most beautiful in the Middle Kingdom and have lived but to love and be loved. There Sum Chin had tarried, preparing for his second degree, when his trouble came upon him and the sacred duty of filial piety made him a fugitive.

Up to the time of his flight Sum Chin had delayed the holy duty of matrimony because the cares of paternity conflict with the meditations of the scholar, and because wives are expensive and scholars are poor. In San Francisco he had married a foreign-born Chinese girl out of Berkeley Place, but she had been sickly from the first and had borne him no children. She had lived a long time, and though she was both shrewish and indolent, it was said that her husband treated her kindly. She had been dead but a few months when the news of his father's death in Nanking, roused Sum Chin to his duty of begetting offspring who should secure repose for his own soul and his dead father's.

He was then fifty, and his choice must be made quickly. Then he bethought him of the daughter of his friend and purchasing agent, Te Wing, in Canton, whom he had visited on his last trip to China, eight years before. She was but a child then, and had lain all day on a mat with her feet swathed in tight bandages, but even then he had liked the little girl because her eyes were the color of jade and very bright, and her mouth was red as a flower. He used to take her costly Chinese sweetmeats and tell her stories of the five Sea Dragon Kings who wear yellow armor, and of their yearly visit to the Middle Heaven, when the other gods are frightened away, and of the unicorn which walks abroad only when sages are born, and of the Phoenix which lays cubical eggs among the mountains, and at whose flute-like voice the tigers flee. So Sum Chin wrote to Te Wing, the Cantonese merchant, and Girrard arranged the girl's admission through the ports with the Rescue Society, and the matter was accomplished.

Now a change of dwelling place, even from one village to another, is regarded as a calamity among Chinese women, and they pray to be delivered from the curse of childlessness and from long journeys. Little Te Loo must have remembered very kindly the elegant stranger who had drunk tea in her father's home and had given her sweetmeats, that she consented to cross the ocean to wed him. Yet she did this willingly, and she kept a sharp lookout for the five Sea Dragon Kings on the way, for she was quite sure that they must be friends of her husband's. She arrived in San Francisco with her many wedding gifts and her trousseau done up in yellow bales bound with bamboo withes, a very silly, giggly maid, with her jade-like eyes and her flower-like mouth, and her feet like the tiny pink shells that one picks up along the seashore.

From the day of her marriage Sum Loo began devout ceremonies before the shrine of the goddess who bestows children, and in a little while she had a joyful announcement to make to her husband. Then Sum Chin ceased from his desultory reading at the Seven Thousand Classics, the last remnant in him of the disappointed scholar, and began to prepare himself for weightier matters. The proper reception of a son into the world, when there are no near relatives at hand, and no maternal grandmother to assist in the august and important functions, is no small responsibility, especially when the child is to have wealth and rank. In many trivial things, such as the wearing of undershirts in winter and straw hats in summer, Sum Chin had conformed to American ways, but the birth of a man's son is the most important event in his life, and he could take no chances. All ceremonials must be observed, and all must transpire as it had among his people since the years when European civilization was not even a name. Sum Loo was cheerful enough in those days, eating greedily, and admiring her trousseau, and always coaxing for new bangles and stories about the five Sea Dragon Kings. But Sum Chin was grave and preoccupied. Suppose, after all his preparations, it should be a girl, whose feet he would have to bind and for whom he would have to find a suitor, and what would it all amount to in the end? He might be too old to have other children, and a girl would not answer his purpose. Even if it were a boy he might not live to see him grow up, and his son might forget the faith of his fathers and neglect the necessary devotions. He began to fear that he had delayed this responsibility too long.

But the child, when it came, was a boy and strong, and he heaved out his chest mightily and cried when they washed his mouth with a picture of the sun dipped in wine, the symbol of a keen intelligence. This little yellow, waxen thing was welcomed into the house of Sum Chin as a divinity, and, indeed, he looked not unlike the yellow clay gods in the temples frequented by expectant mothers. He was smooth and dark as old ivory, and his eyes were like little beads of black opium, and his nose was so diminutive that his father laughed every time he looked at it. He was called Sum Wing, and he was kept wrapped in a gorgeous piece of silk, and he lay all day long quite still, with his thumb in his mouth and his black eyes never blinking; and Girrard said he looked like an ivory image in his father's shop. Sum Wing had marked prejudices against all the important ceremonials which must be performed over all male infants. He spat out the ceremonial rice and kicked over the wine.

"Him Melican babee, I leckon," said his father in explanation of his son's disregard of the important rites. When the child kicked his mother's side so that she scolded him, Sum Chin smiled and bought her a new bracelet. When the child's cry reached him as he sat in his shop, he smiled. Often, at night, when the tiny Sum Wing slept on his mother's arm, Sum Chin would lean over in the dark to hear his son's breathing.

When the child was a month old, on a day that the priest at the joss house declared was indicated as lucky by many omens, Sum Wing's head was shaven for the first time, and that was the most important thing which had yet occurred to him. Many of his father's society—which was the Society Fi, or the Guardianship of Nocturnal Vigils, a band which tried to abolish midnight "hold-ups" in Chinatown—came and brought gifts. Nine little tufts of hair were left on the back of the child's head, to indicate the number of trunks his bride would need to pack her trousseau, and nine times his father rubbed two eggs with red shells over his little pate, which eggs the members of the Society for the Guardianship of Nocturnal Vigils gravely ate, thereby pledging themselves to protect the boy, seek him if lost, and mourn for him if dead. Then a nurse was provided for Sum Wing, and his father asked Girrard to have the mission folk pray to the Jesus god for his son, and he drew a large check on his bankers for the support of the Mission. Sum Chin held that when all a man's goods are stored in one ship, he should insure it with all reputable underwriters. So, surely, when a man has but one son he should secure for him the good offices of all gods of any standing. For, as he would often say to Girrard, in the language of an old Taoist proverb, "Have you seen your god, brother, or have I seen mine? Then why should there be any controversy between us, seeing that we are both unfortunates?"

Sum Wing was a year and a half old, and could already say wise Chinese words and play with his father's queue most intelligently, when fervent little Sister Hannah began to go to Sum Chin's house, first to see his queer little yellow baby and afterwards to save his wife's soul. Sum Loo could speak a little English by this time, and she liked to have her baby admired, and when there was lack of other amusement, she was not averse to talking about her soul. She thought the pictures of the baby Jesus god were cunning, though not so cunning as her Sum Wing, and she learned an English prayer and a hymn or two. Little Sister Hannah made great progress with Sum Loo, though she never cared to discuss theology with Sum Chin. Chinese metaphysics frightened her, and under all Sum Chin's respect for all rites and ceremonials there was a sort of passive, resigned agnosticism, a doubt older than the very beginnings of Sister Hannah's faith, and she felt incompetent to answer it. It is such an ancient doubt, that of China, and it has gradually stolen the odor from the roses and the tenderness from the breasts of the women.

The good little Sister, who should have had children of her own to bother about, became most deeply attached to Sum Wing, who loved to crumple her white headdress and pinch her plump, pink cheeks. Above all things she desired to have the child baptized, and Sum Loo was quite in the notion of it. It would be very nice to dress the child in his best clothes and take him to the Mission chapel and hold him before the preacher with many American women looking on, if only they would promise not to put enough water on him to make him sick. She coaxed Sum Chin, who could see no valid objection, since the boy would be properly instructed in the ceremonials of his own religion by the Taoist priest, and since many of his patrons were among the founders of the Mission, and it was well to be in the good books of all gods, for one never knew how things were going with the Imperial Dynasties of the other world.

So little Sum Wing was prayed, and sung, and wept over by the mission women, and a week later he fell sick and died, and the priest in the joss house chuckled maliciously. He was buried in his father's costly coffin which had come from China, and at the funeral there were many carriages and mourners and roast pigs and rice and gin in bowls of real china, as for a grown man, for he was his father's only son.

Sum Chin, he went about with his queue unbraided and his face haggard and unshaven so that he looked like a wreck from some underground opium den, and he rent many costly garments and counted not the cost of them, for of what use is wealth to an old man who has no son? Who now would pray for the peace of his own soul or for that of his father? The voice of his old father cried out from the grave in bitterness against him, upbraiding him with his neglect to provide offspring to secure rest for his spirit. For of all unfilial crimes, childlessness is the darkest.

It was all clear enough to Sum Chin. There had been omens and omens, and he had disregarded them. And now the Jesus people had thrown cold water in his baby's face and with evil incantations had killed his only son. Had not his heart stood still when the child was seized with madness and screamed when the cold water touched its face, as though demons were tearing it with red-hot pincers?—And the gods of his own people were offended and had not helped him, and the Taoist priest mocked him and grinned from the joss house across the street.

When the days of mourning were over he regained his outward composure, was scrupulous as to his dress and careful to let his nails grow long. But he avoided even the men of his own society, for these men had sons, and he hated them because the gods had prospered them. When Girrard came to his shop, Sum Chin sat writing busily with his camel's hair-brush, making neat characters on the rice paper, but he spoke no word. He maintained all his former courtesy toward the mission people, but sometimes, after they had left his shop, he would creep upstairs with ashen lips, and catching his wife's shoulder, would shake her rudely, crying between his teeth, "Jesus people, Jesus people, killee ma babee!"

As for poor Sum Loo, her life was desolated by her husband's grief. He no longer was gentle and kind. He no longer told her stories or bought her bracelets and sweetmeats. He let her go nowhere except to the joss house, he let her see no one, and roughly told her to cleanse herself from the impurities of the Foreign Devils. Still, he was a broken old man, who called upon the gods in his sleep, and she pitied him. Surely he would never have any more children, and what would her father say when he heard that she had given him no grandchildren? A poor return she made her parents for all their kindness in caring for her in her infancy when she was but a girl baby and might have been quietly slipped out of the world; in binding her beautiful feet when she was foolish enough to cry about it, and in giving her a good husband and a trousseau that filled many bales. Surely, too, the spirit of her husband's father would sit heavy on her stomach that she had allowed the Jesus people to kill her son. She was often very lonely without her little baby, who used to count his toes and call her by a funny name when he wanted his dinner. Then she would cry and wipe her eyes on the gorgeous raiment in which Sum Wing had been baptized.

The mission people were much concerned about Sum Loo. Since her child's death none of them had been able to gain access to the rooms above her husband's store, where she lived. Sister Hannah had again and again made valiant resolutions and set out with determination imprinted on her plump, rosy countenance, but she had never been able to get past the suave, smiling Asiatic who told her that his wife was visiting a neighbor, or had a headache, or was giving a teaparty. It is impossible to contradict the polite and patent fictions of the Chinese, and Sister Hannah always went away nonplussed and berated herself for lack of courage.

One day, however, she was fortunate enough to catch sight of Sum Loo just as she was stepping into the joss house across the street, and Sister Hannah followed her into that dim, dusky place, where the air was heavy with incense. At first she could see no one at all, and she quite lost her way wandering about among the glittering tinselled gods with their offerings of meat, and rice, and wine before them. They were terrible creatures, with hoofs, and horns, and scowling faces, and the little Sister was afraid of the darkness and the heavy air of the place. Suddenly she heard a droning singsong sound, as of a chant, and, moving cautiously, she came upon Sum Loo and stood watching her in terrified amazement. Sum Loo had the copy of the New Testament in Chinese which Sister Hannah had given her husband, open before her. She sat crouching at the shrine of the goddess who bestows children and tore out the pages of the book one by one, and, carefully folding them into narrow strips, she burned them in the candles before the goddess, chanting, as she did so, one name over and over incessantly.

Sister Hannah fled weeping back to the Mission of the Heavenly Rest, and that night she wrote to withdraw the application she had sent in to the Board of Foreign Missions.

First published in *The Library*, I (August 11, 1900), 4–6.

A Singer's Romance

❊ ❊ ❊

The rain fell in torrents and the great stream of people which poured out of the Metropolitan Opera House stagnated about the doors and seemed effectually checked by the black line of bobbing umbrellas on the sidewalk. The entrance was fairly blockaded, and the people who were waiting for carriages formed a solid phalanx, which the more unfortunate opera goers, who had to depend on street cars no matter what the condition of the weather, tried to break through in vain. There was much shouting of numbers and hurrying of drivers, from whose oilcloth-covered hats the water trickled in tiny streams, quite as though the brims had been curved just to accommodate it. The wind made the management of the hundreds of umbrellas difficult, and they rose and fell and swayed about like toy balloons tugging at their moorings. At the stage entrance there was less congestion, but the confusion was not proportionally small, and Frau Selma Schumann was in no very amiable mood when she was at last told that her carriage awaited her. As she stepped out of the door, the wind caught the black lace mantilla wound about her head and lifted it high in the air in such a ludicrous fashion that the substantial soprano cut a figure much like a malicious Beardsley poster. In her frantic endeavor to replace her sportive headgear, she dropped the little velvet bag in which she carried her jewel case. A young man stationed by the door darted forward and snatched it up from the sidewalk, uncovered his head and returned the bag to her with a low bow. He was a tall man, slender and graceful, and he looked as dark as a Spaniard in the bright light that fell upon him from the doorway. His curling black hair would have been rather long even for a tenor, and he wore a dark mustache. His face had that oval contour, slightly effeminate, which belongs to the Latin races. He wore a long black ulster and held in his hand a wide-brimmed, black felt hat. In his buttonhole was a single red carnation. Frau Schumann took the bag with a radiant smile, quite forgetting her ill humor. "I thank you,

sir," she said graciously. But the young man remained standing with
bared head, never raising his eyes. "Merci, Monsieur," she ventured
again, rather timidly, but his only recognition was to bow even lower
than before, and Madame hastened to her carriage to hide her confusion
from her maid, who followed close behind. Once in the carriage, Madame
permitted herself to smile and to sigh a little in the darkness, and
to wonder whether the disagreeable American prima donna, who
manufactured gossip about every member of the company, had
seen the little episode of the jewel bag. She almost hoped she
had.

This Signorino's reserve puzzled her more than his persistence. This
was the third time she had given him an opportunity to speak, to make
himself known, and the third time her timid advance had been met by
silence and downcast eyes. She was unable to comprehend it. She had been
singing in New York now eight weeks, and since the first week this dark
man, clad in black, had followed her like a shadow. When she and Annette
walked in the park, they always encountered him on one of the benches.
When she went shopping, he sauntered after them on the other side of the
street. She continually encountered him in the corridors of her hotel;
when she entered the theatre he was always stationed near the stage door,
and when she came out again, he was still at his post. One evening, just
to assure herself, she had gone to the Opera House when she was not in
the cast, and, as she had hoped, the dark Signor was absent. He had grown
so familiar to her that she knew the outline of his head and shoulders a
square away, and in the densest crowd her eyes instantly singled him out.
She looked for him so constantly that she knew she would miss him if he
should not appear. Yet he made no attempt whatever to address her.
Once, when he was standing near her in the hotel corridor, she made
pointless and incoherent inquiries about directions from the bell boy, in
the hope that the young man would volunteer information, which he did
not. On another occasion, when she found him smoking a cigarette at the
door of the Holland as she went out into a drizzling rain, she had feigned
impossible difficulties in raising her umbrella. He did, indeed, raise it for
her, and bowing passed quickly down the street. Madame had begun to
feel like a very bold and forward woman, and to blush guiltily under the
surveillance of her maid. By every doorstep, at every corner, wherever
she turned, whenever she looked out of a window, she encountered always
the dark Signorino, with his picturesque face and Spanish eyes, his

broad-brimmed black felt hat set at an angle on his glistening black curls, and the inevitable red carnation in his buttonhole.

When they arrived at the hotel Antoinette went to the office to ask for Madame's mail, and returned to Madame's rooms with a letter which bore the familiar post mark of Monte Carlo. This threw Madame into an honest German rage, refreshing to witness, and she threw herself into a chair and wept audibly. The letter was from her husband, who spent most of his time and her money at the Casino, and who continually sent urgent letters for re-enforcement.

"It is too much, 'Toinette, too much," she sobbed. "He says he must have money to pay his doctor. Why I have sent him money enough to pay the doctor bills of the royal family. Here am I singing three and four nights a week—no, I will not do it."

But she ended by sitting down at her desk and writing out a check, with which she enclosed very pointed advice, and directed it to the suave old gentleman at Monte Carlo.

Then she permitted 'Toinette to shake out her hair, and became lost in the contemplation of her own image in the mirror. She had to admit that she had grown a trifle stout, that there were many fine lines about her mouth and eyes, and little wrinkles on her forehead that had defied the arts of massage. Her blonde hair had lost its luster and was somewhat deadened by the heat of the curling iron. She had to hold her chin very high indeed in order not to have two, and there were little puffy places under her eyes that told of her love for pastry and champagne. Above her own face in the glass she saw the reflection of her maid's. Pretty, slender 'Toinette, with her satin-smooth skin and rosy cheeks and little pink ears, her arched brows and long black lashes and her coil of shining black hair. 'Toinette's youth and freshness irritated her tonight: She could not help wondering—but then this man was probably a man of intelligence, quite proof against the charm of mere prettiness. He was probably, she reflected, an artist like herself, a man who revered her art, and art, certainly, does not come at sixteen. Secretly, she wondered what 'Toinette thought of this dark Signorino whom she must have noticed by this time. She had great respect for 'Toinette's opinion. 'Toinette was by no means an ordinary ladies' maid, and Madame had grown to regard her as a companion and confidante. She was the child of a French opera singer who had been one of Madame's earliest professional friends and who had come to an evil end and died in a hospital, leaving her young daughter wholly without protection. As the girl had no vocal possibilities, Madame Schumann had generously rescued her from the awful fate of the chorus by taking her into her service.

"You have been contented here, 'Toinette? You like America, you will be a little sorry to leave?" asked Madame as she said good night.

"Oh, yes, Madame, I should be sorry," returned 'Toinette.

"And so shall I," said Madame softly, smiling to herself.

'Toinette lingered a moment at the door; "Madame will have nothing to eat, no refreshment of any kind?"

"No, nothing tonight, 'Toinette."

"Not even the very smallest glass of champagne?"

"No, no, nothing," said Madame impatiently.

'Toinette turned out the light and left her in bed, where she lay awake for a long time, indulging in luxurious dreams.

In the morning she awoke long before it was time for 'Toinette to bring her coffee, and lay still, with her eyes closed, while the early rumble of the city was audible through the open window.

Selma Schumann was a singer without a romance. No one felt the incongruity of this more than she did, yet she had lived to the age of two-and-forty without ever having known an *affaire de coeur*. After her debut in grand opera she had married her former singing teacher, who at once decided that he had already done quite enough for his wife and the world in the placing and training of that wonderful voice, and lived in cheerful idleness, gambling her earnings with the utmost complacency, and when her reproaches grew too cutting, he would respectfully remind her that he had enlarged her upper register four tones, and in so doing had fulfilled the whole duty of man. Madame had always been industrious and an indefatigable student. She could sing a large repertoire at the shortest notice, and her good nature made her invaluable to managers. She lacked certainly, that poignant individuality which alone secures great eminence in the world of art, and no one ever went to the opera solely because her name was on the bill. She was known as a thoroughly "competent" artist, and as all singers know, that means a thankless life of underpaid drudgery. Her father had been a professor of etymology in a German university and she had inherited something of his taste for grubbing and had been measurably happy in her work. She practiced incessantly and skimped herself and saved money and dutifully supported her husband,

and surely such virtue should bring its own reward. Yet when she saw other women in the company appear in a new tiara of diamonds, or saw them snatch notes from the hands of messenger boys, or take a carriage full of flowers back to the hotel with them, she had felt ill used, and had wondered what that other side of life was like. In short, from the wastes of this humdrum existence which seems so gay to the uninitiated, she had wished for a romance. Under all her laborious habits and thrift and economy there was left enough of the unsatisfied spirit of youth for that.

Since the shadow of the dark Signorino had fallen across her path, the routine of her life hitherto as fixed as that of the planets or of a German housewife, had become less rigid and more variable. She had decided that she owed it to her health to walk frequently in the park, and to sleep later in the morning. She had spent entire afternoons in dreamful idleness, whereas she should have been struggling with the new roles she was to sing in London. She had begun to pay the most scrupulous attention to her toilettes, which she had begun to neglect in the merciless routine of her work. She was visited by many *massageurs*, for she discovered that her figure and skin had been allowed to take care of themselves and had done it ill. She thought with bitter regret that a little less economy and a little more care might have prevented a wrinkle. One great sacrifice she made. She stopped drinking champagne. The sole one of the luxuries of life she had permitted herself was that of the table. She had all her country-women's love for good living, and she had indulged herself freely. She had known for a long time that champagne and sweets were bad for her complexion, and that they made her stout, but she had told herself that it was little enough pleasure she had at best.

But since the appearance of the dark Signorino, all this had been changed, and it was by no means an easy sacrifice.

Madame waited a long time for her coffee, but 'Toinette did not appear. Then she rose and went into her reception room, but no one was there. In the little music room next door she heard a low murmur of voices. She parted the curtains a little, and saw 'Toinette with both her hands clasped in the hands of the dark Signorino.

"But Madame," 'Toinette was saying, "she is so lonely, I cannot find the heart to tell her that I must leave her."

"Ah," murmured the Signorino, and his voice was as caressing as Madame had imagined it in her dreams, "she has been like a mother to you, the Madame, she will be glad of your happiness."

When Selma Schumann reached her own room again she threw herself on her bed and wept furiously. Then she dried her eyes and railed at Fortune in deep German polysyllables, gesturing like an enraged Valkyrie.

Then she ordered her breakfast—and a quart of champagne.

First published in *The Library*, I (July 28, 1900), 15–16.

The Affair at Grover Station

❋ ❋ ❋

I heard this story sitting on the rear platform of an accommodation freight that crawled along through the brown, sun-dried wilderness between Grover Station and Cheyenne. The narrator was "Terrapin" Rodgers, who had been a classmate of mine at Princeton, and who was then cashier in the B—— railroad office at Cheyenne. Rodgers was an Albany boy, but after his father failed in business, his uncle got "Terrapin" a position on a western railroad, and he left college and disappeared completely from our little world, and it was not until I was sent West, by the University with a party of geologists who were digging for fossils in the region about Sterling, Colorado, that I saw him again. On this particular occasion Rodgers had been down at Sterling to spend Sunday with me, and I accompanied him when he returned to Cheyenne.

When the train pulled out of Grover Station, we were sitting smoking on the rear platform, watching the pale yellow disk of the moon that was just rising and that drenched the naked, gray plains in a soft lemon-colored light. The telegraph poles scored the sky like a musical staff as they flashed by, and the stars, seen between the wires, looked like the notes of some erratic symphony. The stillness of the night and the loneliness and barrenness of the plains were conducive to an uncanny train of thought. We had just left Grover Station behind us, and the murder of the station agent at Grover, which had occurred the previous winter, was still the subject of much conjecturing and theorizing all along that line of railroad. Rodgers had been an intimate friend of the murdered agent, and it was said that he knew more about the affair than any other living man, but with that peculiar reticence which at college had won him the sobriquet "Terrapin," he had kept what he knew to himself, and even the most accomplished reporter on the New York Journal, who had traveled halfway across the continent for the express purpose of pumping Rodgers, had given him up as impossible. But I had known Rodgers a long time, and since I had been grubbing in the chalk about Sterling, we had fallen into a habit of exchanging confidences, for it is good to see an old face in a strange land. So, as the little red station house at Grover faded into the distance, I asked him point blank what he knew about the murder of Lawrence O'Toole. Rodgers took a long pull at his black briar pipe as he answered me.

"Well, yes, I could tell you something about it, but the question is how much you'd believe, and whether you could restrain yourself from reporting it to the Society for Psychical Research. I never told the story but once, and then it was to the Division Superintendent, and when I finished the old gentleman asked if I were a drinking man, and remarking that a fertile imagination was not a desirable quality in a railroad employee, said it would be just as well if the story went no further. You see it's a grewsome tale, and someway we don't like to be reminded that there are more things in heaven and earth than our systems of philosophy can grapple with. However, I should rather like to tell the story to a man who would look at it objectively and leave it in the domain of pure incident where it belongs. It would unburden my mind, and I'd like to get a scientific man's opinion on the yarn. But I suppose I'd better begin at the beginning, with the dance which preceded the tragedy, just as such things follow each other in a play. I notice that Destiny, who is a good deal of an artist in her way, frequently falls back upon that elementary principle of contrast to make things interesting for us.

"It was the thirty-first of December, the morning of the incoming Governor's inaugural ball, and I got down to the office early, for I had a heavy day's work ahead of me, and I was going to the dance and wanted to close up by six o'clock. I had scarcely unlocked the door when I heard someone calling Cheyenne on the wire, and hurried over to the instrument to see what was wanted. It was Lawrence O'Toole, at Grover, and he said he was coming up for the ball on the extra, due in Cheyenne at nine o'clock that night. He wanted me to go up to see Miss Masterson and ask her if she could go with him. He had had some trouble in getting leave of absence, as the last regular train for Cheyenne then left Grover at 5:45 in the afternoon, and as there was an eastbound going through Grover at 7:30. The dispatcher didn't want him away, in case there should be orders for the 7:30 train. So Larry had made no arrangement with Miss Masterson, as he was uncertain about getting up until he was notified about the extra.

"I telephoned Miss Masterson and delivered Larry's message. She replied that she had made an arrangement to go to the dance with Mr.

Freymark, but added laughingly that no other arrangement held when Larry could come.

"About noon Freymark dropped in at the office, and I suspected he'd got his time from Miss Masterson. While he was hanging around, Larry called me up to tell me that Helen's flowers would be up from Denver on the Union Pacific passenger at five, and he asked me to have them sent up to her promptly and to call for her that evening in case the extra should be late. Freymark, of course, listened to the message, and when the sounder stopped, he smiled in a slow, disagreeable way, and saying, 'Thank you. That's all I wanted to know,' left the office.

"Lawrence O'Toole had been my predecessor in the cashier's office at Cheyenne, and he needs a little explanation now that he is under ground, though when he was in the world of living men, he explained himself better than any man I have ever met, East or West. I've knocked about a good deal since I cut loose from Princeton, and I've found that there are a great many good fellows in the world, but I've not found many better than Larry. I think I can say, without stretching a point, that he was the most popular man on the Division. He had a faculty of making everyone like him that amounted to a sort of genius. When he first went to working on the road, he was the agent's assistant down at Sterling, a mere kid fresh from Ireland, without a dollar in his pocket, and no sort of backing in the world but his quick wit and handsome face. It was a face that served him as a sight draft, good in all banks.

"Freymark was cashier at the Cheyenne office then, but he had been up to some dirty work with the company, and when it fell in the line of Larry's duty to expose him, he did so without hesitating. Eventually Freymark was discharged, and Larry was made cashier in his place. There was, after that, naturally, little love lost between them, and to make matters worse, Helen Masterson took a fancy to Larry, and Freymark had begun to consider himself pretty solid in that direction. I doubt whether Miss Masterson ever really liked the blackguard, but he was a queer fish, and she was a queer girl and she found him interesting.

"Old John J. Masterson, her father, had been United States Senator from Wyoming, and Helen had been educated at Wellesley and had lived in Washington a good deal. She found Cheyenne dull and had got into the Washington way of tolerating anything but stupidity, and Freymark certainly was not stupid. He passed as an Alsatian Jew, but he had lived a good deal in Paris and had been pretty much all over the world, and spoke the more general European languages fluently. He was a wiry, sallow, unwholesome looking man, slight and meagerly built, and he looked as though he had been dried through and through by the blistering heat of the tropics. His movements were as lithe and agile as those of a cat, and invested with a certain unusual, stealthy grace. His eyes were small and black as bright jet beads; his hair very thick and coarse and straight, black with a sort of purple luster to it, and he always wore it correctly parted in the middle and brushed smoothly about his ears. He had a pair of the most impudent red lips that closed over white, regular teeth. His hands, of which he took the greatest care, were the yellow, wrinkled hands of an old man, and shrivelled at the finger-tips, though I don't think he could have been much over thirty. The long and short of it is that the fellow was uncanny. You somehow felt that there was that in his present, or in his past, or in his destiny which isolated him from other men. He dressed in excellent taste, was always accommodating, with the most polished manners and an address extravagantly deferential. He went into cattle after he lost his job with the company, and had an interest in a ranch ten miles out, though he spent most of his time in Cheyenne at the Capitol card rooms. He had an insatiable passion for gambling, and he was one of the few men who make it pay.

"About a week before the dance, Larry's cousin, Harry Burns, who was a reporter on the London Times, stopped in Cheyenne on his way to 'Frisco, and Larry came up to meet him. We took Burns up to the club, and I noticed that he acted rather queerly when Freymark came in. Burns went down to Grover to spend a day with Larry, and on Saturday Larry wired me to come down and spend Sunday with him, as he had important news for me.

"I went, and the gist of his information was that Freymark, then going by another name, had figured in a particularly ugly London scandal that happened to be in Burns's beat, and his record had been exposed. He was, indeed, from Paris, but there was not a drop of Jewish blood in his veins, and he dated from farther back than Israel. His father was a French soldier who, during his service in the East, had bought a Chinese slave girl, had become attached to her, and married her, and after her death had brought her child back to Europe with him. He had entered the civil service and held several subordinate offices in the capital, where his son was educated. The boy, socially ambitious and extremely sensitive about his Asiatic blood, after having been blackballed at a club, had left and lived by an exceedingly questionable traffic in London, assuming a Jewish patronymic to account for his oriental complexion and traits of feature. That explained everything. That explained why Freymark's

hands were those of a centenarian. In his veins crept the sluggish am-
phibious blood of a race that was already old when Jacob tended the flocks
of Laban upon the hills of Padan-Aram, a race that was in its mort cloth
before Europe's swaddling clothes were made.

"Of course, the question at once came up as to what ought to be
done with Burns's information. Cheyenne clubs are not exclusive, but a
Chinaman who had been engaged in Freymark's peculiarly unsavory
traffic would be disbarred in almost any region outside of Whitechapel.
One thing was sure: Miss Masterson must be informed of the matter at once.

"'On second thought,' said Larry, 'I guess I'd better tell her myself.
It will have to be done easy like, not to hurt her self-respect too much.
Like as not I'll go off my head the first time I see him and call him rat-
eater to his face.'

"Well, to get back to the day of the dance, I was wondering whether
Larry would stay over to tell Miss Masterson about it the next day, for of
course he couldn't spring such a thing on a girl at a party.

"That evening I dressed early and went down to the station at nine
to meet Larry. The extra came in, but no Larry. I saw Connelly, the
conductor, and asked him if he had seen anything of O'Toole, but he said
he hadn't, that the station at Grover was open when he came through,
but that he found no train orders and couldn't raise anyone, so supposed
O'Toole had come up on 153. I went back to the office and called Grover,
but got no answer. Then I sat down at the instrument and called for
fifteen minutes straight. I wanted to go then and hunt up the conductor
on 153, the passenger that went through Grover at 5:30 in the afternoon,
and ask him what he knew about Larry, but it was then 9:45 and I knew
Miss Masterson would be waiting, so I jumped into the carriage and told
the driver to make up time. On my way to the Mastersons' I did some
tall thinking. I could find no explanation for O'Toole's nonappearance,
but the business of the moment was to invent one for Miss Masterson that
would neither alarm nor offend her. I couldn't exactly tell her he wasn't
coming, for he might show up yet, so I decided to say the extra was late,
and I didn't know when it would be in.

"Miss Masterson had been an exceptionally beautiful girl to begin
with, and life had done a great deal for her. Fond as I was of Larry, I used
to wonder whether a girl who had led such a full and independent
existence would ever find the courage to face life with a railroad man who
was so near the bottom of a ladder that is so long and steep.

"She came down the stairs in one of her Paris gowns that are as meat
and drink to Cheyenne society reporters, with her arms full of American

Beauty roses and her eyes and cheeks glowing. I noticed the roses then, though I didn't know that they were the boy's last message to the woman he loved. She paused halfway down the stairs and looked at me, and then over my head into the drawing room, and then her eyes questioned mine. I bungled at my explanation and she thanked me for coming, but she couldn't hide her disappointment, and scarcely glanced at herself in the mirror as I put her wrap about her shoulders.

"It was not a cheerful ride down to the Capitol. Miss Masterson did her duty by me bravely, but I found it difficult to be even decently attentive to what she was saying. Once arrived at Representative Hall, where the dance was held, the strain was relieved, for the fellows all pounced down on her for dances, and there were friends of hers there from Helena and Laramie, and my responsibility was practically at an end. Don't expect me to tell you what a Wyoming inaugural ball is like. I'm not good at that sort of thing, and this dance is merely incidental to my story. Dance followed dance, and still no Larry. The dances I had with Miss Masterson were torture. She began to question and cross-question me, and when I got tangled up in my lies, she became indignant. Freymark was late in arriving. It must have been after midnight when he appeared, correct and smiling, having driven in from his ranch. He was effusively gay and insisted upon shaking hands with me, though I never willingly touched those clammy hands of his. He was constantly dangling about Miss Masterson, who made rather a point of being gracious to him. I couldn't much blame her under the circumstances, but it irritated me, and I'm not ashamed to say that I rather spied on them. When they were on the balcony I heard him say:

"'You see I've forgiven this morning entirely.'

"She answered him rather coolly:

"'Ah, but you are constitutionally forgiving. However, I'll be fair and forgive too. It's more comfortable.'

"Then he said in a slow, insinuating tone, and I could fairly see him thrust out those impudent red lips of his as he said it: 'If I can teach you to forgive, I wonder whether I could not also teach you to forget? I almost think I could. At any rate I shall make you remember this night.

Rappelles-toi lorsque les destinées
M'auront de toi pour jamais séparé.'

"As they came in, I saw him slip one of Larry's red roses into his pocket.

"It was not until near the end of the dance that the clock of destiny sounded the first stroke of the tragedy. I remember how gay the scene was, so gay that I had almost forgotten my anxiety in the music, flowers and laughter. The orchestra was playing a waltz, drawing the strains out long and sweet like the notes of a flute, and Freymark was dancing with Helen. I was not dancing myself then, and suddenly I noticed some confusion among the waiters who stood watching by one of the doors, and Larry's black dog, Duke, all foam at the mouth, shot in the side and bleeding, dashed in through the door and eluding the caterer's men, ran half the length of the hall and threw himself at Freymark's feet, uttering a howl piteous enough to herald any sort of calamity. Freymark, who had not seen him before, turned with an exclamation of rage and a face absolutely livid and kicked the wounded brute halfway across the slippery floor. There was something fiendishly brutal and horrible in the episode, it was the breaking out of the barbarian blood through his mask of European civilization, a jet of black mud that spurted up from some nameless pest hole of filthy heathen cities. The music stopped, people began moving about in a confused mass, and I saw Helen's eyes seeking mine appealingly. I hurried to her, and by the time I reached her Freymark had disappeared.

"'Get the carriage and take care of Duke,' she said, and her voice trembled like that of one shivering with cold.

"When we were in the carriage she spread one of the robes on her knee, and I lifted the dog up to her, and she took him in her arms, comforting him.

"'Where is Larry, and what does all this mean?' she asked. 'You can't put me off any longer, for I danced with a man who came up on the extra.'

"Then I made a clean breast of it, and told her what I knew, which was little enough.

"'Do you think he is ill?' she asked.

"I replied, 'I don't know what to think. I'm all at sea.' For since the appearance of the dog, I was genuinely alarmed.

"She was silent for a long time, but when the rays of the electric street lights flashed at intervals into the carriage, I could see that she was leaning back with her eyes closed and the dog's nose against her throat. At last she said with a note of entreaty in her voice, 'Can't you think of anything?' I saw that she was thoroughly frightened and told her that it would probably all end in a joke, and that I would telephone her as soon as I heard from Larry, and would more than likely have something amusing to tell her.

"It was snowing hard when we reached the Senator's, and when we got out of the carriage she gave Duke tenderly over to me and I remember how she dragged on my arm and how played out and exhausted she seemed.

"'You really must not worry at all,' I said. 'You know how uncertain railroad men are. It's sure to be better at the next inaugural ball; we'll all be dancing together then.'

"'The next inaugural ball,' she said as we went up the steps, putting out her hand to catch the snow-flakes. 'That seems a long way off.'

"I got down to the office late next morning, and before I had time to try Grover, the dispatcher at Holyoke called me up to ask whether Larry were still in Cheyenne. He couldn't raise Grover, he said, and he wanted to give Larry train orders for 151, the eastbound passenger. When he heard what I had to say, he told me I had better go down to Grover on 151 myself, as the storm threatened to tie up all the trains and we might look for trouble.

"I had the veterinary surgeon fix up Duke's side, and I put him in the express car, and boarded 151 with a mighty cold, uncomfortable sensation in the region of my diaphragm.

"It had snowed all night long, and the storm had developed into a blizzard, and the passenger had difficulty in making any headway at all.

"When we got into Grover I thought it was the most desolate spot I had ever looked on, and as the train pulled out, leaving me there, I felt like sending a message of farewell to the world. You know what Grover is, a red box of a station, section house barricaded by coal sheds and a little group of dwellings at the end of everything, with the desert running out on every side to the sky line. The houses and station were covered with a coating of snow that clung to them like wet plaster, and the siding was one deep snow drift, banked against the station door. The plain was a wide, white ocean of swirling, drifting snow, that beat and broke like the thrash of the waves in the merciless wind that swept, with nothing to break it, from the Rockies to the Missouri.

"When I opened the station door, the snow fell in upon the floor, and Duke sat down by the empty, fireless stove and began to howl and whine in a heartbreaking fashion. Larry's sleeping room upstairs was empty. Downstairs, everything was in order, and all the station work had been done up. Apparently the last thing Larry had done was to bill out a car of wool from the Oasis sheep ranch for Dewey, Gould & Co., Boston. The car had gone out on 153, the eastbound that left Grover at seven o'clock the night before, so he must have been there at that time. I copied the bill in the copy book, and went over to the section house to make inquiries.

"The section boss was getting ready to go out to look after his track. He said he had seen O'Toole at 5:30, when the westbound passenger went through, and, not having seen him since, supposed he was still in Cheyenne. I went over to Larry's boarding house, and the woman said he must be in Cheyenne, as he had eaten his supper at five o'clock the night before, so that he would have time to get his station work done and dress. The little girl, she said, had gone over at five to tell him that supper was ready. I questioned the child carefully. She said there was another man, a stranger, in the station with Larry when she went in and that though she didn't hear anything they said, and Larry was sitting with his chair tilted back and his feet on the stove, she somehow had thought they were quarreling. The stranger, she said, was standing; he had a fur coat on and his eyes snapped like he was mad, and she was afraid of him. I asked her if she could recall anything else about him, and she said, 'Yes, he had very red lips.' When I heard that, my heart grew cold as a snow lump, and when I went out the wind seemed to go clear through me. It was evident enough that Freymark had gone down there to make trouble, had quarreled with Larry and had boarded either the 5:30 passenger or the extra, and got the conductor to let him off at his ranch, and accounted for his late appearance at the dance.

"It was five o'clock then, but the 5:30 train was two hours late, so there was nothing to do but sit down and wait for the conductor, who had gone out on the seven o'clock eastbound the night before, and who must have seen Larry when he picked up the car of wool. It was growing dark by that time. The sky was a dull lead color, and the snow had drifted about the little town until it was almost buried, and was still coming down so fast that you could scarcely see your hand before you.

"I was never so glad to hear anything as that whistle, when old 153 came lumbering and groaning in through the snow. I ran out on the platform to meet her, and her headlight looked like the face of an old friend. I caught the conductor's arm the minute he stepped off the train, but he wouldn't talk until he got in by the fire. He said he hadn't seen O'Toole at all the night before, but he had found the bill for the wool car on the table, with a note from Larry asking him to take the car out on the

Q.T., and he had concluded that Larry had gone up to Cheyenne on the 5:30. I wired the Cheyenne office and managed to catch the express clerk who had gone through on the extra the night before. He wired me saying that he had not seen Larry board the extra, but that his dog had crept into his usual place in the express car, and he had supposed Larry was in the coach. He had seen Freymark get on at Grover, and the train had slowed up a trifle at his ranch to let him off, for Freymark stood in with some of the boys and sent his cattle shipments our way.

"When the night fairly closed down on me, I began to wonder how a gay, expensive fellow like O'Toole had ever stood six months at Grover. The snow had let up by that time, and the stars were beginning to glitter cold and bright through the hurrying clouds. I put on my ulster and went outside. I began a minute tour of inspection, I went through empty freight cars run down by the siding, searched the coal houses and primitive cellar, examining them carefully, and calling O'Toole's name. Duke at my heels dragged himself painfully about, but seemed as much at sea as I, and betrayed the nervous suspense and alertness of a bird dog that has lost his game.

'I want back to the office and took the big station lamp upstairs to make a more careful examination of Larry's sleeping room. The suit of clothes that he usually wore at his work was hanging on the wall. His shaving things were lying about, and I recognized the silver-backed military hair brushes that Miss Masterson had given him at Christmas time, lying on his chiffonier. The upper drawer was open and a pair of white kid gloves was lying on the corner. A white string tie hung across his pipe rack, it was crumpled and had evidently proved unsatisfactory when he tied it. On the chiffonier lay several clean handkerchiefs with holes in them, where he had unfolded them and thrown them by in a hasty search for a whole one. A black silk muffler hung on the chair back, and a top hat was set awry on the head of a plaster cast of Parnell, Larry's hero. His dress suit was missing, so there was no doubt that he had dressed for the party. His overcoat lay on his trunk and his dancing shoes were on the floor, at the foot of the bed beside his everyday ones. I knew that his pumps were a little tight, he had joked about them when I was down the Sunday before the dance, but he had only one pair, and he couldn't have got another in Grover if he had tried himself. That set me to thinking. He was a dainty fellow about his shoes and I knew his collection pretty well. I went to his closet and found them all there. Even granting him a prejudice against overcoats, I couldn't conceive of his going out in that stinging weather without shoes. I noticed that a surgeon's case, such as are carried on passenger trains, and which Larry had once appropriated in Cheyenne, was open, and that the roll of medicated cotton had been pulled out and recently used. Each discovery I made served only to add to my perplexity. Granted that Freymark had been there, and granted that he had played the boy an ugly trick, he could not have spirited him away without the knowledge of the train crew.

"'Duke, old doggy,' I said to the poor spaniel who was sniffing and whining about the bed, 'you haven't done your duty. You must have seen what went on between your master and that clam-blooded Asiatic, and you ought to be able to give me a tip of some sort.'

"I decided to go to bed and make a fresh start on the ugly business in the morning. The bed looked as though someone had been lying on it, so I started to beat it up a little before I got in. I took off the pillow and as I pulled up the mattress, on the edge of the ticking at the head of the bed, I saw a dark red stain about the size of my hand. I felt the cold sweat come out on me, and my hands were dangerously unsteady, as I carried the lamp over and set it down on the chair by the bed. But Duke was too quick for me, he had seen that stain and leaping on the bed began sniffling it, and whining like a dog that is being whipped to death. I bent down and felt it with my fingers. It was dry but the color and stiffness were unmistakably those of coagulated blood. I caught up my coat and vest and ran downstairs with Duke yelping at my heels. My first impulse was to go and call someone, but from the platform not a single light was visible, and I knew the section men had been in bed for hours. I remembered then, that Larry was often annoyed by hemorrhages at the nose in that high altitude, but even that did not altogether quiet my nerves, and I realized that sleeping in that bed was quite out of the question.

"Larry always kept a supply of brandy and soda on hand, so I made myself a stiff drink and filled the stove and locked the door, turned down the lamp and lay down on the operator's table. I had often slept there when I was night operator. At first it was impossible to sleep, for Duke kept starting up and limping to the door and scratching at it, yelping nervously. He kept this up until I was thoroughly unstrung, and though I'm ordinarily cool enough, there wasn't money enough in Wyoming to have bribed me to open that door. I felt cold all over every time I went near it, and I even drew the big rusty bolt that was never used, and it seemed to me that it groaned heavily as I drew it, or perhaps it was the wind outside that groaned. As for Duke, I threatened to put him out, and boxed his ears until I hurt his feelings, and he lay down in front of the door with his muzzle between his paws and his eyes shining like live coals and riveted on the crack under the door. The situation was grewsome enough, but the liquor had made me drowsy and at last I fell asleep.

"It must have been about three o'clock in the morning that I was awakened by the crying of the dog, a whimper low, continuous and pitiful, and indescribably human. While I was blinking my eyes in an effort to get thoroughly awake, I heard another sound, the grating sound of chalk on a wooden blackboard, or of a soft pencil on a slate. I turned my head to the right, and saw a man standing with his back to me, chalking something on the bulletin board. At a glance I recognized the broad, high shoulders and the handsome head of my friend. Yet there was that about the figure which kept me from calling his name or from moving a muscle where I lay. He finished his writing and dropped the chalk, and I distinctly heard its click as it fell. He made a gesture as though he were dusting his fingers, and then turned facing me, holding his left hand in front of his mouth. I saw him clearly in the soft light of the station lamp. He wore his dress clothes, and began moving toward the door silently as a shadow in his black stocking feet. There was about his movements an indescribable stiffness, as though his limbs had been frozen. His face was chalky white, his hair seemed damp and was plastered down close about his temples. His eyes were colorless jellies, dull as lead, and staring straight before him. When he reached the door, he lowered the hand he held before his mouth to lift the latch. His face was turned squarely toward me, and the lower jaw had fallen and was set rigidly upon his collar, the mouth was wide open and was *stuffed full of white cotton*! Then I knew it was a dead man's face I looked upon.

"The door opened, and that stiff black figure in stockings walked as noiselessly as a cat out into the night. I think I went quite mad then. I dimly remember that I rushed out upon the siding and ran up and down screaming, 'Larry, Larry!' until the wind seemed to echo my call. The stars were out in myriads, and the snow glistened in their light, but I could see nothing but the wide, white plain, not even a dark shadow anywhere. When at last I found myself back in the station, I saw Duke lying before the door and dropped on my knees beside him, calling him by name. But Duke was past calling back. Master and dog had gone together, and I dragged him into the corner and covered his face, for his eyes were colorless and soft, like the eyes of that horrible face, once so beloved.

"The blackboard? O, I didn't forget that. I had chalked the time of the accommodation on it the night before, from sheer force of habit, for it isn't customary to mark the time of trains in unimportant stations like Grover. My writing had been rubbed out by a moist hand, for I could see the finger marks clearly, and in place of it was written in blue chalk simply,

C. B. & Q. 26387.

"I sat there drinking brandy and muttering to myself before that blackboard until those blue letters danced up and down, like magic lantern pictures when you jiggle the slides. I drank until the sweat poured off me like rain and my teeth chattered, and I turned sick at the stomach. At last an idea flashed upon me. I snatched the waybill off the hook. The car of wool that had left Grover for Boston the night before was numbered 26387.

"I must have got through the rest of the night somehow, for when the sun came up red and angry over the white plains, the section boss found me sitting by the stove, the lamp burning full blaze, the brandy bottle empty beside me, and with but one idea in my head, that box car 26387 must be stopped and opened as soon as possible, and that somehow it would explain.

"I figured that we could easily catch it in Omaha, and wired the freight agent there to go through it carefully and report anything unusual. That night I got a wire from the agent stating that the body of a man had been found under a woolsack at one end of the car with a fan and an invitation to the inaugural ball at Cheyenne in the pocket of his dress coat. I wired him not to disturb the body until I arrived, and started for Omaha. Before I left Grover the Cheyenne office wired me that Freymark had left the town, going west over the Union Pacific. The company detectives never found him.

"The matter was clear enough then. Being a railroad man, he had hidden the body and sealed up the car and billed it out, leaving a note for the conductor. Since he was of a race without conscience or sensibilities, and since his past was more infamous than his birth, he had boarded the extra and had gone to the ball and danced with Miss Masterson with blood undried upon his hands.

"When I saw Larry O'Toole again, he was lying stiff and stark in the undertakers' rooms in Omaha. He was clad in his dress clothes, with black stockings on his feet, as I had seen him forty-eight hours before. Helen Masterson's fan was in his pocket. His mouth was wide open and stuffed full of white cotton.

"He had been shot in the mouth, the bullet lodging between the third and fourth vertebrae. The hemorrhage had been very slight and had been checked by the cotton. The quarrel had taken place about five in the afternoon. After supper Larry had dressed, all but his shoes, and had lain down to snatch a wink of sleep, trusting to the whistle of the extra to waken him. Freymark had gone back and shot him while he was asleep, afterward placing his body in the wool car, which, but for my telegram, would not have been opened for weeks.

"That's the whole story. There is nothing more to tell except one detail that I did not mention to the superintendent. When I said goodbye to the boy before the undertaker and coroner took charge of the body, I lifted his right hand to take off a ring that Miss Masterson had given him and the ends of the fingers were covered with blue chalk."

First published in *The Library*, I (June 16, 23, 1900), 3–4; 14–15.

The Sentimentality of William Tavener

❉ ❉ ❉

It takes a strong woman to make any sort of success of living in the West, and Hester undoubtedly was that. When people spoke of William Tavener as the most prosperous farmer in McPherson County, they usually added that his wife was a "good manager." She was an executive woman, quick of tongue and something of an imperatrix. The only reason her husband did not consult her about his business was that she did not wait to be consulted.

It would have been quite impossible for one man, within the limited sphere of human action, to follow all Hester's advice, but in the end William usually acted upon some of her suggestions. When she incessantly denounced the "shiftlessness" of letting a new threshing machine stand unprotected in the open, he eventually built a shed for it. When she sniffed contemptuously at his notion of fencing a hog corral with sod walls, he made a spiritless beginning on the structure—merely to "show his temper," as she put it—but in the end he went off quietly to town and bought enough barbed wire to complete the fence. When the first heavy rains came on, and the pigs rooted down the sod wall and made little paths all over it to facilitate their ascent, he heard his wife relate with relish the story of the little pig that built a mud house, to the minister at the dinner table, and William's gravity never relaxed for an instant. Silence, indeed, was William's refuge and his strength.

William set his boys a wholesome example to respect their mother. People who knew him very well suspected that he even admired her. He was a hard man towards his neighbors, and even towards his sons: grasping, determined and ambitious.

There was an occasional blue day about the house when William went over the store bills, but he never objected to items relating to his

[353]

wife's gowns or bonnets. So it came about that many of the foolish, unnecessary little things that Hester bought for boys, she had charged to her
personal account.

One spring night Hester sat in a rocking chair by the sitting room
window, darning socks. She rocked violently and sent her long needle
vigorously back and forth over her gourd, and it took only a very casual
glance to see that she was wrought up over something. William sat on the
other side of the table reading his farm paper. If he had noticed his wife's
agitation, his calm, clean-shaven face betrayed no sign of concern. He
must have noticed the sarcastic turn of her remarks at the supper table,
and he must have noticed the moody silence of the older boys as they ate.
When supper was but half over little Billy, the youngest, had suddenly
pushed back his plate and slipped away from the table, manfully trying to
swallow a sob. But William Tavener never heeded ominous forecasts in
the domestic horizon, and he never looked for a storm until it broke.

After supper the boys had gone to the pond under the willows in the
big cattle corral, to get rid of the dust of plowing. Hester could hear an
occasional spash and a laugh ringing clear through the stillness of the night,
as she sat by the open window. She sat silent for almost an hour reviewing
in her mind many plans of attack. But she was too vigorous a woman to
be much of a strategist, and she usually came to her point with directness.
At last she cut her thread and suddenly put her darning down, saying
emphatically:

"William, I don't think it would hurt you to let the boys go to that
circus in town tomorrow."

William continued to read his farm paper, but it was not Hester's
custom to wait for an answer. She usually divined his arguments and
assailed them one by one before he uttered them.

"You've been short of hands all summer, and you've worked the
boys hard, and a man ought use his own flesh and blood as well as he does
his hired hands. We're plenty able to afford it, and it's little enough our
boys ever spend. I don't see how you can expect 'em to be steady and
hard workin', unless you encourage 'em a little. I never could see much
harm in circuses, and our boys have never been to one. Oh, I know Jim
Howley's boys get drunk an' carry on when they go, but our boys ain't
that sort, an' you know it, William. The animals are real instructive, an'
our boys don't get to see much out here on the prairie. It was different
where we were raised, but the boys have got no advantages here, an' if
you don't take care, they'll grow up to be greenhorns."

Hester paused a moment, and William folded up his paper, but vouchsafed no remark. His sisters in Virginia had often said that only a quiet man like William could ever have lived with Hester Perkins. Secretly, William was rather proud of his wife's "gift of speech," and of the fact that she could talk in prayer meeting as fluently as a man. He confined his own efforts in that line to a brief prayer at Covenant meetings.

Hester shook out another sock and went on.

"Nobody was ever hurt by goin' to a circus. Why, law me! I remember I went to one myself once, when I was little. I had most forgot about it. It was over at Pewtown, an' I remember how I had set my heart on going. I don't think I'd ever forgiven my father if he hadn't taken me, though that red clay road was in a frightful way after the rain. I mind they had an elephant and six poll parrots, an' a Rocky Mountain lion, an' a cage of monkeys, an' two camels. My! but they were a sight to me then!"

Hester dropped the black sock and shook her head and smiled at the recollection. She was not expecting anything from William yet, and she was fairly startled when he said gravely, in much the same tone in which he announced the hymns in prayer meeting:

"No, there was only one camel. The other was a dromedary."

She peered around the lamp and looked at him keenly.

"Why, William, how come you to know?"

William folded his paper and answered with some hesitation, "I was there, too."

Hester's interest flashed up. "Well, I never, William! To think of my finding it out after all these years! Why, you couldn't have been much bigger'n our Billy then. It seems queer I never saw you when you was little, to remember about you. But then you Back Creek folks never have anything to do with us Gap people. But how come you to go? Your father was stricter with you than you are with your boys."

"I reckon I shouldn't 'a gone," he said slowly, "but boys will do foolish things. I had done a good deal of fox hunting the winter before, and father let me keep the bounty money. I hired Tom Smith's Tap to weed the corn for me, an' I slipped off unbeknownst to father an' went to the show."

Hester spoke up warmly: "Nonsense, William! It didn't do you no harm, I guess. You was always worked hard enough. It must have been a big sight for a little fellow. That clown must have just tickled you to death."

William crossed his knees and leaned back in his chair.

"I reckon I could tell all that fool's jokes now. Sometimes I can't help thinkin' about 'em in meetin' when the sermon's long. I mind I had on a pair of new boots that hurt me like the mischief, but I forgot all about 'em when that fellow rode the donkey. I recall I had to take them boots off as soon as I got out of sight o' town, and walked home in the mud barefoot."

"O poor little fellow!" Hester ejaculated, drawing her chair nearer and leaning her elbows on the table. "What cruel shoes they did use to make for children. I remember I went up to Back Creek to see the circus wagons go by. They came down from Romney, you know. The circus men stopped at the creek to water the animals, an' the elephant got stubborn an' broke a big limb off the yellow willow tree that grew there by the toll house porch, an' the Scribners were 'fraid as death he'd pull the house down. But this much I saw him do; he waded in the creek an' filled his trunk with water and squirted it in at the window and nearly ruined Ellen Scribner's pink lawn dress that she had just ironed an' laid out on the bed ready to wear to the circus."

"I reckon that must have been a trial to Ellen," chuckled William, "for she was mighty prim in them days."

Hester drew her chair still nearer William's. Since the children had begun growing up, her conversation with her husband had been almost wholly confined to questions of economy and expense. Their relationship had become purely a business one, like that between landlord and tenant. In her desire to indulge her boys she had unconsciously assumed a defensive and almost hostile attitude towards her husband. No debtor ever haggled with his usurer more doggedly than did Hester with her husband in behalf of her sons. The strategic contest had gone on so long that it had almost crowded out the memory of a closer relationship. This exchange of confidences tonight, when common recollections took them unawares and opened their hearts, had all the miracle of romance. They talked on and on; of old neighbors, of old familiar faces in the valley where they had grown up, of long forgotten incidents of their youth—weddings, picnics, sleighing parties and baptizings. For years they had talked of nothing else but butter and eggs and the prices of things, and now they had as much to say to each other as people who meet after a long separation.

When the clock struck ten, William rose and went over to his walnut secretary and unlocked it. From his red leather wallet he took out a ten dollar bill and laid it on the table beside Hester.

"Tell the boys not to stay late, an' not to drive the horses hard," he said quietly, and went off to bed.

Hester blew out the lamp and sat still in the dark a long time. She left the bill lying on the table where William had placed it. She had a painful sense of having missed something, or lost something; she felt that somehow the years had cheated her.

The little locust trees that grew by the fence were white with blossoms. Their heavy odor floated in to her on the night wind and recalled a night long ago, when the first whippoorwill of the Spring was heard, and the rough, buxom girls of Hawkins Gap had held her laughing and struggling under the locust trees, and searched in her bosom for a lock of her sweetheart's hair, which is supposed to be on every girl's breast when the first whippoorwill sings. Two of those same girls had been her bridesmaids. Hester had been a very happy bride. She rose and went softly into the room where William lay. He was sleeping heavily, but occasionally moved his hand before his face to ward off the flies. Hester went into the parlor and took the piece of mosquito net from the basket of wax apples and pears that her sister had made before she died. One of the boys had brought it all the way from Virginia, packed in a tin pail, since Hester would not risk shipping so precious an ornament by freight. She went back to the bedroom and spread the net over William's head. Then she sat down by the bed and listened to his deep, regular breathing until she heard the boys returning. She went out to meet them and warn them not to waken their father.

"I'll be up early to get your breakfast, boys. Your father says you can go to the show." As she handed the money to the eldest, she felt a sudden throb of allegiance to her husband and said sharply, "And you be careful of that, an' don't waste it. Your father works hard for his money."

The boys looked at each other in astonishment and felt that they had lost a powerful ally.

First published in *The Library*, I (May 12, 1900), 13–14.

Eric Hermannson's Soul

❋ ❋ ❋

It was a great night at the Lone Star schoolhouse—a night when the Spirit was present with power and when God was very near to man. So it seemed to Asa Skinner, servant of God and Free Gospeller. The schoolhouse was crowded with the saved and sanctified, robust men and women, trembling and quailing before the power of some mysterious psychic force. Here and there among this cowering, sweating multitude crouched some poor wretch who had felt the pangs of an awakened conscience, but had not yet experienced that complete divestment of reason, that frenzy born of a convulsion of the mind, which, in the parlance of the Free Gospellers, is termed "the Light." On the floor before the mourners' bench lay the unconscious figure of a man in whom outraged nature had sought her last resort. This "trance" state is the highest evidence of grace among the Free Gospellers, and indicates a close walking with God.

Before the desk stood Asa Skinner, shouting of the mercy and vengeance of God, and in his eyes shone a terrible earnestness, an almost prophetic flame. Asa was a converted train gambler who used to run between Omaha and Denver. He was a man made for the extremes of life; from the most debauched of men he had become the most ascetic. His was a bestial face, a face that bore the stamp of Nature's eternal injustice. The forehead was low, projecting over the eyes, and the sandy hair was plastered down over it and then brushed back at an abrupt right angle. The chin was heavy, the nostrils were low and wide, and the lower lip hung loosely except in his moments of spasmodic earnestness, when it shut like a steel trap. Yet about those coarse features there were deep, rugged furrows, the scars of many a hand-to-hand struggle with the weakness of the flesh, and about that drooping lip were sharp, strenuous lines that had conquered it and taught it to pray. Over those seamed cheeks there was a certain pallor, a grayness caught from many a vigil. It was as though, after Nature had done her worst with that face, some fine chisel had gone over it, chastening and almost transfiguring it. Tonight, as his muscles twitched with emotion, and the perspiration dropped from his hair and chin, there was a certain convincing power in the man. For Asa Skinner was a man possessed of a belief, of that sentiment of the sublime before which all inequalities are leveled, that transport of conviction which seems superior to all laws of condition, under which debauchees have become martyrs; which made a tinker an artist and a camel-driver the founder of an empire. This was with Asa Skinner tonight, as he stood proclaiming the vengeance of God.

It might have occurred to an impartial observer that Asa Skinner's God was indeed a vengeful God if he could reserve vengeance for those of his creatures who were packed into the Lone Star schoolhouse that night. Poor exiles of all nations; men from the south and the north, peasants from almost every country of Europe, most of them from the mountainous, night-bound coast of Norway. Honest men for the most part, but men with whom the world had dealt hardly; the failures of all countries, men sobered by toil and saddened by exile, who had been driven to fight for the dominion of an untoward soil, to sow where others should gather, the advance guard of a mighty civilization to be.

Never had Asa Skinner spoken more earnestly than now. He felt that the Lord had this night a special work for him to do. Tonight Eric Hermannson, the wildest lad on all the Divide, sat in his audience with a fiddle on his knee, just as he had dropped in on his way to play for some dance. The violin is an object of particular abhorrence to the Free Gospellers. Their antagonism to the church organ is bitter enough, but the fiddle they regard as a very incarnation of evil desires, singing forever of worldly pleasures and inseparably associated with all forbidden things.

Eric Hermannson had long been the object of the prayers of the revivalists. His mother had felt the power of the Spirit weeks ago, and special prayer-meetings had been held at her house for her son. But Eric had only gone his ways laughing, the ways of youth, which are short enough at best, and none too flowery on the Divide. He slipped away from the prayer-meetings to meet the Campbell boys in Genereau's saloon, or hug the plump little French girls at Chevalier's dances, and sometimes, of a summer night, he even went across the dewy cornfields and through the wild-plum thicket to play the fiddle for Lena Hanson, whose name was a reproach through all the Divide country, where the women are usually too plain and too busy and too tired to depart from the ways of virtue. On such occasions Lena, attired in a pink wrapper and silk stockings and tiny pink slippers, would sing to him, accompanying herself on a battered guitar. It gave him a delicious sense of freedom and experience to be with a woman who, no matter how, had lived in big cities and knew the ways of town folk, who had never worked in the fields and had kept her hands white and soft, her throat fair and tender, who had heard great singers in Denver and Salt Lake, and who knew the strange language of flattery and idleness and mirth.

Yet, careless as he seemed, the frantic prayers of his mother were not altogether without their effect upon Eric. For days he had been fleeing before them as a criminal from his pursuers, and over his pleasures had fallen the shadow of something dark and terrible that dogged his steps. The harder he danced, the louder he sang, the more was he conscious that this phantom was gaining upon him, that in time it would track him down. One Sunday afternoon, late in the fall, when he had been drinking beer with Lena Hanson and listening to a song which made his cheeks burn, a rattlesnake had crawled out of the side of the sod house and thrust its ugly head in under the screen door. He was not afraid of snakes, but he knew enough of Gospellism to feel the significance of the reptile lying coiled there upon her doorstep. His lips were cold when he kissed Lena goodbye, and he went there no more.

The final barrier between Eric and his mother's faith was his violin, and to that he clung as a man sometimes will cling to his dearest sin, to the weakness more precious to him than all his strength. In the great world beauty comes to men in many guises, and art in a hundred forms, but for Eric there was only his violin. It stood, to him, for all the manifestations of art; it was his only bridge into the kingdom of the soul.

It was to Eric Hermannson that the evangelist directed his impassioned pleading that night.

"*Saul, Saul, why persecutest thou me?* Is there a Saul here tonight who has stopped his ears to that gentle pleading, who has thrust a spear into that bleeding side? Think of it, my brother; you are offered this wonderful love and you prefer the worm that dieth not and the fire which will not be quenched. What right have you to lose one of God's precious souls? *Saul, Saul, why persecutest thou me?*"

A great joy dawned in Asa Skinner's pale face, for he saw that Eric Hermannson was swaying to and fro in his seat. The minister fell upon his knees and threw his long arms up over his head.

"O my brothers! I feel it coming, the blessing we have prayed for. I tell you the Spirit is coming! Just a little more prayer, brothers, a little more zeal, and he will be here. I can feel his cooling wing upon my brow. Glory be to God forever and ever, amen!"

The whole congregation groaned under the pressure of this spiritual panic. Shouts and hallelujahs went up from every lip. Another figure fell prostrate upon the floor. From the mourners' bench rose a chant of terror and rapture:

"Eating honey and drinking wine,
   Glory to the bleeding Lamb!
I am my Lord's and he is mine,
   Glory to the bleeding Lamb!"

The hymn was sung in a dozen dialects and voiced all the vague yearning of these hungry lives, of these people who had starved all the passions so long, only to fall victims to the basest of them all, fear.

A groan of ultimate anguish rose from Eric Hermannson's bowed head, and the sound was like the groan of a great tree when it falls in the forest.

The minister rose suddenly to his feet and threw back his head, crying in a loud voice:

"*Lazarus, come forth!* Eric Hermannson, you are lost, going down at sea. In the name of God, and Jesus Christ his Son, I throw you the life line. Take hold! Almighty God, my soul for his!" The minister threw his arms out and lifted his quivering face.

Eric Hermannson rose to his feet; his lips were set and the lightning was in his eyes. He took his violin by the neck and crushed it to splinters across his knee, and to Asa Skinner the sound was like the shackles of sin broken audibly asunder.

II

For more than two years Eric Hermannson kept the austere faith to which he had sworn himself, kept it until a girl from the East came to spend a week on the Nebraska Divide. She was a girl of other manners and conditions, and there were greater distances between her life and Eric's than all the miles which separated Rattlesnake Creek from New York City. Indeed, she had no business to be in the West at all; but ah! across what leagues of land and sea, by what improbable chances, do the unrelenting gods bring to us our fate!

It was in a year of financial depression that Wyllis Elliot came to Nebraska to buy cheap land and revisit the country where he had spent a year of his youth. When he had graduated from Harvard it was still customary for moneyed gentlemen to send their scapegrace sons to rough it on ranches in the wilds of Nebraska or Dakota, or to consign them to a living death in the sagebrush of the Black Hills. These young men did not always return to the ways of civilized life. But Wyllis Elliot had not married a half-breed, nor been shot in a cowpunchers' brawl, nor wrecked by bad whisky, nor appropriated by a smirched adventuress. He had been saved from these things by a girl, his sister, who had been very near to his life ever since the days when they read fairy tales together and dreamed the dreams that never come true. On this, his first visit to his father's ranch since he left it six years before, he brought her with him. She had been laid up half the winter from a sprain received while skating, and had had too much time for reflection during those months. She was restless and filled with a desire to see something of the wild country of which her brother had told her so much. She was to be married the next winter, and Wyllis understood her when she begged him to take her with him on this long, aimless jaunt across the continent, to taste the last of their freedom together. It comes to all women of her type—that desire to taste the unknown which allures and terrifies, to run one's whole soul's length out to the wind—just once.

It had been an eventful journey. Wyllis somehow understood that strain of gypsy blood in his sister, and he knew where to take her. They had slept in sod houses on the Platte River, made the acquaintance of the personnel of a third-rate opera company on the train to Deadwood, dined in a camp of railroad constructors at the world's end beyond New Castle, gone through the Black Hills on horseback, fished for trout in Dome Lake, watched a dance at Cripple Creek, where the lost souls who hide in the hills gathered for their besotted revelry. And now, last of all, before the return to thraldom, there was this little shack, anchored on the windy crest of the Divide, a little black dot against the flaming sunsets, a scented sea of cornland bathed in opalescent air and blinding sunlight.

Margaret Elliot was one of those women of whom there are so many in this day, when old order, passing, giveth place to new; beautiful, talented, critical, unsatisfied, tired of the world at twenty-four. For the moment the life and people of the Divide interested her. She was there but a week; perhaps had she stayed longer, that inexorable ennui which travels faster even than the Vestibule Limited would have overtaken her. The week she tarried there was the week that Eric Hermannson was helping Jerry Lockhart thresh; a week earlier or a week later, and there would have been no story to write.

It was on Thursday and they were to leave on Saturday. Wyllis and his sister were sitting on the wide piazza of the ranchhouse, staring out into the afternoon sunlight and protesting against the gusts of hot wind that blew up from the sandy riverbottom twenty miles to the southward.

The young man pulled his cap lower over his eyes and remarked:

"This wind is the real thing; you don't strike it anywhere else. You remember we had a touch of it in Algiers and I told you it came from Kansas. It's the keynote of this country."

Wyllis touched her hand that lay on the hammock and continued gently:

"I hope it's paid you, Sis. Roughing it's dangerous business; it takes the taste out of things."

She shut her fingers firmly over the brown hand that was so like her own.

"Paid? Why, Wyllis, I haven't been so happy since we were children and were going to discover the ruins of Troy together some day. Do you know, I believe I could just stay on here forever and let the world go on its own gait. It seems as though the tension and strain we used to talk of last winter were gone for good, as though one could never give one's strength out to such petty things any more."

Wyllis brushed the ashes of his pipe away from the silk handkerchief that was knotted about his neck and stared moodily off at the skyline.

"No, you're mistaken. This would bore you after a while. You can't shake the fever of the other life. I've tried it. There was a time when the gay fellows of Rome could trot down into the Thebaid and burrow into the sandhills and get rid of it. But it's all too complex now. You see we've made our dissipations so dainty and respectable that they've gone further in than the flesh, and taken hold of the ego proper. You couldn't rest, even here. The war cry would follow you."

"You don't waste words, Wyllis, but you never miss fire. I talk more than you do, without saying half so much. You must have learned the art of silence from these taciturn Norwegians. I think I like silent men."

"Naturally," said Wyllis, "since you have decided to marry the most brilliant talker you know."

Both were silent for a time, listening to the sighing of the hot wind through the parched morning-glory vines. Margaret spoke first.

"Tell me, Wyllis, were many of the Norwegians you used to know as interesting as Eric Hermannson?"

"Who, Siegfried? Well, no. He used to be the flower of the Norwegian youth in my day, and he's rather an exception, even now. He has retrograded, though. The bonds of the soil have tightened on him, I fancy."

"Siegfried? Come, that's rather good, Wyllis. He looks like a dragon-slayer. What is it that makes him so different from the others? I can talk to him; he seems quite like a human being."

"Well," said Wyllis, meditatively, "I don't read Bourget as much as my cultured sister, and I'm not so well up in analysis, but I fancy it's because one keeps cherishing a perfectly unwarranted suspicion that under that big, hulking anatomy of his, he may conceal a soul somewhere. *Nicht wahr?*"

"Something like that," said Margaret, thoughtfully, "except that it's more than a suspicion, and it isn't groundless. He has one, and he makes it known, somehow, without speaking."

"I always have my doubts about loquacious souls," Wyllis remarked, with the unbelieving smile that had grown habitual with him.

Margaret went on, not heeding the interruption. "I knew it from the first, when he told me about the suicide of his cousin, the Bernstein boy. That kind of blunt pathos can't be summoned at will in anybody. The earlier novelists rose to it, sometimes, unconsciously. But last night when I sang for him I was doubly sure. Oh, I haven't told you about that yet! Better light your pipe again. You see, he stumbled in on me in the dark when I was pumping away at that old parlor organ to please Mrs. Lockhart. It's her household fetish and I've forgotten how many pounds of butter she made and sold to buy it. Well, Eric stumbled in, and in some inarticulate manner made me understand that he wanted me to sing for him. I sang just the old things, of course. It's queer to sing familiar things here at the world's end. It makes one think how the hearts of men have carried them around the world, into the wastes of Iceland and the jungles of Africa and the islands of the Pacific. I think if one lived here long enough one would quite forget how to be trivial, and would read only the great books that we never get time to read in the world, and would remember only the great music, and the things that are really worth while would stand out clearly against that horizon over there. And of course I played the intermezzo from *Cavalleria Rusticana* for him; it goes rather better on an organ than most things do. He shuffled his feet and twisted his big hands up into knots and blurted out that he didn't know there was any music like that in the world. Why, there were tears in his voice, Wyllis! Yes, like Rossetti, I *heard* his tears. Then it dawned upon me that it was probably the first good music he had ever heard in all his life. Think of it, to care for music as he does and never to hear it, never to know that it exists on earth! To long for it as we long for other perfect experiences that never come. I can't tell you what music means to that man. I never saw any one so susceptible to it. It gave him speech, he became alive. When I had finished the intermezzo, he began telling me about a little crippled brother who died and whom he loved and used to carry everywhere in his arms. He did not wait for encouragement. He took up the story and told it slowly, as if to himself, just sort of rose up and told his own woe to answer Mascagni's. It overcame me."

"Poor devil," said Wyllis, looking at her with mysterious eyes, "and so you've given him a new woe. Now he'll go on wanting Grieg and Schubert the rest of his days and never getting them. That's a girl's philanthropy for you!"

Jerry Lockhart came out of the house screwing his chin over the unusual luxury of a stiff white collar, which his wife insisted upon as a necessary article of toilet while Miss Elliot was at the house. Jerry sat down on the step and smiled his broad, red smile at Margaret.

"Well, I've got the music for your dance, Miss Elliot. Olaf Oleson will bring his accordion and Mollie will play the organ, when she isn't lookin' after the grub, and a little chap from Frenchtown will bring his fiddle—though the French don't mix with the Norwegians much."

"Delightful! Mr. Lockhart, that dance will be the feature of our trip, and it's so nice of you to get it up for us. We'll see the Norwegians in character at last," cried Margaret, cordially.

"See here, Lockhart, I'll settle with you for backing her in this scheme," said Wyllis, sitting up and knocking the ashes out of his pipe. "She's done crazy things enough on this trip, but to talk of dancing all night with a gang of half-mad Norwegians and taking the carriage at four to catch the six o'clock train out of Riverton—well, it's tommy-rot, that's what it is!"

"Wyllis, I leave it to your sovereign power of reason to decide whether it isn't easier to stay up all night than to get up at three in the morning. To get up at three, think what that means! No, sir, I prefer to keep my vigil and then get into a sleeper."

"But what do you want with the Norwegians? I thought you were tired of dancing."

"So I am, with some people. But I want to see a Norwegian dance, and I intend to. Come, Wyllis, you know how seldom it is that one really wants to do anything nowadays. I wonder when I have really wanted to go to a party before. It will be something to remember next month at Newport, when we have to and don't want to. Remember your own theory that contrast is about the only thing that makes life endurable. This is my party and Mr. Lockhart's; your whole duty tomorrow night will consist in being nice to the Norwegian girls. I'll warrant you were adept enough at it once. And you'd better be very nice indeed, for if there are many such young Valkyries as Eric's sister among them, they would simply tie you up in a knot if they suspected you were guying them."

Wyllis groaned and sank back into the hammock to consider his fate, while his sister went on.

"And the guests, Mr. Lockhart, did they accept?"

Lockhart took out his knife and began sharpening it on the sole of his plowshoe.

"Well, I guess we'll have a couple dozen. You see it's pretty hard to get a crowd together here any more. Most of 'em have gone over to the Free Gospellers, and they'd rather put their feet in the fire than shake 'em to a fiddle."

Margaret made a gesture of impatience. "Those Free Gospellers have just cast an evil spell over this country, haven't they?"

"Well," said Lockhart, cautiously, "I don't just like to pass judgment on any Christian sect, but if you're to know the chosen by their works, the Gospellers can't make a very proud showin', an' that's a fact. They're responsible for a few suicides, and they've sent a good-sized delegation to the state insane asylum, an' I don't see as they've made the rest of us much better than we were before. I had a little herdboy last spring, as square a little Dane as I want to work for me, but after the Gospellers got hold of him and sanctified him, the little beggar used to get down on his knees out on the prairie and pray by the hour and let the cattle get into the corn, an' I had to fire him. That's about the way it goes. Now there's Eric; that chap used to be a hustler and the spryest dancer in all this section— called all the dances. Now he's got no ambition and he's glum as a preacher. I don't suppose we can even get him to come in tomorrow night."

"Eric? Why, he must dance, we can't let him off," said Margaret, quickly. "Why, I intend to dance with him myself!"

"I'm afraid he won't dance. I asked him this morning if he'd help us out and he said, 'I don't dance now, any more,'" said Lockhart, imitating the labored English of the Norwegian.

"'The Miller of Hofbau, the Miller of Hofbau, O my Princess!'" chirped Wyllis, cheerfully, from his hammock.

The red on his sister's cheek deepened a little, and she laughed mischievously. "We'll see about that, sir. I'll not admit that I am beaten until I have asked him myself."

Every night Eric rode over to St. Anne, a little village in the heart of the French settlement, for the mail. As the road lay through the most attractive part of the Divide country, on several occasions Margaret Elliot and her brother had accompanied him. Tonight Wyllis had business with Lockhart, and Margaret rode with Eric, mounted on a frisky little mustang that Mrs. Lockhart had broken to the sidesaddle. Margaret regarded her escort very much as she did the servant who always accompanied her on long rides at home, and the ride to the village was a silent one. She was occupied with thoughts of another world, and Eric was wrestling with more thoughts than had ever been crowded into his head before. He rode with his eyes riveted on that slight figure before him, as though he wished to absorb it through the optic nerves and hold it in his brain forever. He understood the situation perfectly. His brain worked slowly, but he had a keen sense of the values of things. This girl represented an entirely new species of humanity to him, but he knew where to place her. The prophets of old, when an angel first appeared unto them, never doubted its high origin.

Eric was patient under the adverse conditions of his life, but he was not servile. The Norse blood in him had not entirely lost its self-reliance. He came of a proud fisher line, men who were not afraid of anything but the ice and the devil, and he had prospects before him when his father went down off the North Cape in the long Arctic night, and his mother, seized by a violent horror of seafaring life, had followed her brother to America. Eric was eighteen then, handsome as young Siegfried, a giant in stature, with a skin singularly pure and delicate, like a Swede's; hair as yellow as the locks of Tennyson's amorous Prince, and eyes of a fierce, burning blue, whose flash was most dangerous to women. He had in those days a certain pride of bearing, a certain confidence of approach, that usually accompanies physical perfection. It was even said of him then that he was in love with life, and inclined to levity, a vice most unusual on the Divide. But the sad history of those Norwegian exiles, transplanted in an arid soil and under a scorching sun, had repeated itself in his case. Toil and isolation had sobered him, and he grew more and more like the clods among which he labored. It was as though some red-hot instrument had touched for a moment those delicate fibers of the brain which respond to acute pain or pleasure, in which lies the power of exquisite sensation, and had seared them quite away. It is a painful thing to watch the light die out of the eyes of those Norsemen, leaving an expression of impenetrable sadness, quite passive, quite hopeless, a shadow that is never lifted. With some this change comes almost at once, in the first bitterness of homesickness, with others it comes more slowly, according to the time it takes each man's heart to die.

Oh, those poor Northmen of the Divide! They are dead many a year before they are put to rest in the little graveyard on the windy hill where exiles of all nations grow akin.

The peculiar species of hypochondria to which the exiles of his people sooner or later succumb had not developed in Eric until that night at the Lone Star schoolhouse, when he had broken his violin across his knee. After that, the gloom of his people settled down upon him, and the gospel of maceration began its work. "*If thine eye offend thee, pluck it out,*" et cetera. The pagan smile that once hovered about his lips was gone, and he was one with sorrow. Religion heals a hundred hearts for one that it embitters, but when it destroys, its work is quick and deadly, and where the agony of the cross has been, joy will not come again. This man understood things literally: one must live without pleasure to die without fear; to save the soul it was necessary to starve the soul.

The sun hung low above the cornfields when Margaret and her cavalier left St. Anne. South of the town there is a stretch of road that runs for some three miles through the French settlement, where the prairie is as level as the surface of a lake. There the fields of flax and wheat and rye are bordered by precise rows of slender, tapering Lombard poplars. It was a yellow world that Margaret Elliot saw under the wide light of the setting sun.

The girl gathered up her reins and called back to Eric, "It will be safe to run the horses here, won't it?"

"Yes, I think so, now," he answered, touching his spur to his pony's flank. They were off like the wind. It is an old saying in the West that newcomers always ride a horse or two to death before they get broken in to the country. They are tempted by the great open spaces and try to outride the horizon, to get to the end of something. Margaret galloped over the level road, and Eric, from behind, saw her long veil fluttering in the wind. It had fluttered just so in his dreams last night and the night before. With a sudden inspiration of courage he overtook her and rode beside her, looking intently at her half-averted face. Before, he had only stolen occasional glances at it, seen it in blinding flashes, always with more or less embarrassment, but now he determined to let every line of it sink into his memory. Men of the world would have said that it was an unusual face, nervous, finely cut, with clear, elegant lines that betokened ancestry. Men of letters would have called it a historic face, and would have conjectured at what old passions, long asleep, what old sorrows forgotten time out of mind, doing battle together in ages gone, had curved those delicate nostrils, left their unconscious memory in those eyes. But Eric read no meaning in these details. To him this beauty was something more than color and line; it was as a flash of white light, in which one cannot distinguish color because all colors are there. To him it was a complete revelation, an embodiment of those dreams of impossible loveliness that linger by a young man's pillow on midsummer nights; yet, because it held something more than the attraction of health and youth and shapeliness, it troubled him, and in its presence he felt as the Goths before the white marbles in the Roman Capitol, not knowing whether they were men or gods. At times he felt like uncovering his head before it, again the fury seized him to break and despoil, to find the clay in this spirit-thing and stamp upon it. Away from her, he longed to strike out with his arms, and take and hold; it maddened him that this woman whom he could break in his hands should be so much stronger than he. But near her, he never questioned this strength; he admitted its potentiality as he admitted the miracles of the Bible; it enervated and conquered him. Tonight, when he rode so close to her that he could have touched her, he knew that he might as well reach out his hand to take a star.

Margaret stirred uneasily under his gaze and turned questioningly in her saddle.

"This wind puts me a little out of breath when we ride fast," she said. Eric turned his eyes away.

"I want to ask you if I go to New York to work, if I maybe hear music like you sang last night? I been a purty good hand to work," he asked, timidly.

Margaret looked at him with surprise, and then, as she studied the outline of his face, pityingly.

"Well, you might—but you'd lose a good deal else. I shouldn't like you to go to New York—and be poor, you'd be out of atmosphere, some way," she said, slowly. Inwardly she was thinking: *There he would be altogether sordid, impossible—a machine who would carry one's trunks upstairs, perhaps. Here he is every inch a man, rather picturesque; why is it?* "No," she added aloud, "I shouldn't like that."

"Then I not go," said Eric, decidedly.

Margaret turned her face to hide a smile. She was a trifle amused and a trifle annoyed. Suddenly she spoke again.

"But I'll tell you what I do want you to do, Eric. I want you to dance with us tomorrow night and teach me some of the Norwegian dances; they say you know them all. Won't you?"

Eric straightened himself in his saddle and his eyes flashed as they had done in the Lone Star schoolhouse when he broke his violin across his knee.

"Yes, I will," he said, quietly, and he believed that he delivered his soul to hell as he said it.

They had reached the rougher country now, where the road wound through a narrow cut in one of the bluffs along the creek, when a beat of hoofs ahead and the sharp neighing of horses made the ponies start and Eric rose in his stirrups. Then down the gulch in front of them and over the steep clay banks thundered a herd of wild ponies, nimble as monkeys and wild as rabbits, such as horse-traders drive east from the plains of Montana to sell in the farming country. Margaret's pony made a shrill sound, a neigh that was almost a scream, and started up the clay bank to meet them, all the wild blood of the range breaking out in an instant. Margaret called to Eric just as he threw himself out of the saddle and caught her pony's bit. But the wiry little animal had gone mad and was kicking and biting like a devil. Her wild brothers of the range were all about her, neighing, and pawing the earth, and striking her with their forefeet and snapping at her flanks. It was the old liberty of the range that the little beast fought for.

"Drop the reins and hold tight, tight!" Eric called, throwing all his weight upon the bit, struggling under those frantic forefeet that now beat at his breast, and now kicked at the wild mustangs that surged and tossed about him. He succeeded in wrenching the pony's head toward him and crowding her withers against the clay bank, so that she could not roll.

"Hold tight, tight!" he shouted again, launching a kick at a snorting animal that reared back against Margaret's saddle. If she should lose her courage and fall now, under those hoofs—He struck out again and again, kicking right and left with all his might. Already the negligent drivers had galloped into the cut, and their long quirts were whistling over the heads of the herd. As suddenly as it had come, the struggling, frantic wave of wild life swept up out of the gulch and on across the open prairie, and with a long despairing whinny of farewell the pony dropped her head and stood trembling in her sweat, shaking the foam and blood from her bit.

Eric stepped close to Margaret's side and laid his hand on her saddle. "You are not hurt?" he asked, hoarsely. As he raised his face in the soft starlight she saw that it was white and drawn and that his lips were working nervously.

"No, no, not at all. But you, you are suffering; they struck you!" she cried in sharp alarm.

He stepped back and drew his hand across his brow.

"No, it is not that," he spoke rapidly now, with his hands clenched at his side. "But if they had hurt you, I would beat their brains out with my hands, I would kill them all. I was never afraid before. You are the only beautiful thing that has ever come close to me. You came like an angel out of the sky. You are like the music you sing, you are like the stars and the snow on the mountains where I played when I was a little boy. You are like all that I wanted once and never had, you are all that they have killed in me. I die for you tonight, tomorrow, for all eternity. I am not a coward; I was afraid because I love you more than Christ who died for me, more than I am afraid of hell, or hope for heaven. I was never afraid before. If you had fallen—oh, my God!" he threw his arms out blindly and dropped his head upon the pony's mane, leaning limply against the animal like a man struck by some sickness. His shoulders rose and fell perceptibly with his labored breathing. The horse stood cowed with exhaustion and fear. Presently Margaret laid her hand on Eric's head and said gently:

"You are better now, shall we go on? Can you get your horse?"

"No, he has gone with the herd. I will lead yours, she is not safe. I will not frighten you again." His voice was still husky, but it was steady now. He took hold of the bit and tramped home in silence.

When they reached the house, Eric stood stolidly by the pony's head until Wyllis came to lift his sister from the saddle.

"The horses were badly frightened, Wyllis. I think I was pretty thoroughly scared myself," she said as she took her brother's arm and went slowly up the hill toward the house. "No, I'm not hurt, thanks to Eric. You must thank him for taking such good care of me. He's a mighty fine fellow. I'll tell you all about it in the morning, dear. I was pretty well shaken up and I'm going right to bed now. Good night."

When she reached the low room in which she slept, she sank upon the bed in her riding dress face downward.

"Oh, I pity him! I pity him!" she murmured, with a long sigh of exhaustion. She must have slept a little. When she rose again, she took from her dress a letter that had been waiting for her at the village post office. It was closely written in a long, angular hand, covering a dozen pages of foreign note paper, and began:

My Dearest Margaret: If I should attempt to say *how like a winter hath thine absence been,* I should incur the risk of being tedious. Really, it takes the sparkle out of everything. Having nothing better to do, and not caring to go anywhere in particular without you, I remained in the city until Jack Courtwell noted my general despondency and brought me down here to his place on the sound to manage some open-air theatricals he is getting up. *As You Like It* is of course the piece selected. Miss Harrison plays Rosalind. I wish you had been here to take the part. Miss Harrison reads her lines well, but she is either a maiden-all-forlorn or a tomboy; insists on reading into the part all sorts of deeper meanings and highly colored suggestions wholly out of harmony with the pastoral setting. Like most of the professionals, she exaggerates the emotional element and quite fails to do justice to Rosalind's facile wit and really brilliant mental qualities. Gerard will do Orlando, but rumor says he is *épris* of your sometime friend, Miss Meredith, and his memory is treacherous and his interest fitful.

My new pictures arrived last week on the *Gascogne.* The Puvis de Chavannes is even more beautiful than I thought it in Paris. A pale dream-maiden sits by a pale dream-cow and a stream of anemic water flows at her feet. The Constant, you will remember, I got because you admired it. It is here in all its florid splendor, the whole dominated by a glowing sensuosity. The drapery of the female figure is as wonderful as you said; the fabric all barbaric pearl and gold, painted with an easy, effortless voluptuousness, and that white, gleaming line of African coast in the background recalls memories of you very precious to me. But it is useless to deny that Constant irritates me. Though I cannot prove the charge against him, his brilliancy always makes me suspect him of cheapness.

Here Margaret stopped and glanced at the remaining pages of this strange love-letter. They seemed to be filled chiefly with discussions of pictures and books, and with a slow smile she laid them by.

She rose and began undressing. Before she lay down she went to open the window. With her hand on the sill, she hesitated, feeling suddenly as though some danger were lurking outside, some inordinate desire waiting to spring upon her in the darkness. She stood there for a long time, gazing at the infinite sweep of the sky.

"Oh, it is all so little, so little there," she murmured. "When everything else is so dwarfed, why should one expect love to be great? Why should one try to read highly colored suggestions into a life like that? If only I could find one thing in it all that mattered greatly, one thing that would warm me when I am alone! Will life never give me that one great moment?"

As she raised the window, she heard a sound in the plum bushes outside. It was only the house-dog roused from his sleep, but Margaret started violently and trembled so that she caught the foot of the bed for support. Again she felt herself pursued by some overwhelming longing, some desperate necessity for herself, like the outstretching of helpless, unseen arms in the darkness, and the air seemed heavy with sighs of yearning. She fled to her bed with the words, "I love you more than Christ, who died for me!" ringing in her ears.

III

About midnight the dance at Lockhart's was at its height. Even the old men who had come to "look on" caught the spirit of revelry and stamped the floor with the vigor of old Silenus. Eric took the violin from the Frenchman, and Minna Oleson sat at the organ, and the music grew more and more characteristic—rude, half mournful music, made up of the folksongs of the North, that the villagers sing through the long night in hamlets by the sea, when they are thinking of the sun, and the spring, and the fishermen so long away. To Margaret some of it sounded like Grieg's *Peer Gynt* music. She found something irresistibly infectious in the mirth of these people who were so seldom merry, and she felt almost one of them. Something seemed struggling for freedom in them tonight, something of the joyous childhood of the nations which exile had not killed. The girls were all boisterous with delight. Pleasure came to them but rarely, and when it came, they caught at it wildly and crushed its fluttering wings in their strong brown fingers. They had a hard life enough, most of them. Torrid summers and freezing winters, labor and drudgery and ignorance, were the portion of their girlhood; a short wooing, a hasty, loveless marriage, unlimited maternity, thankless sons, premature age and ugliness, were the dower of their womanhood. But what matter? Tonight there was hot liquor in the glass and hot blood in the heart; tonight they danced.

Tonight Eric Hermannson had renewed his youth. He was no longer the big, silent Norwegian who had sat at Margaret's feet and looked hopelessly into her eyes. Tonight he was a man, with a man's rights and a man's power. Tonight he was Siegfried indeed. His hair was yellow as the heavy wheat in the ripe of summer, and his eyes flashed like the blue water between the ice packs in the North Seas. He was not afraid of Margaret tonight, and when he danced with her he held her firmly. She was tired and dragged on his arm a little, but the strength of the man was like an all-pervading fluid, stealing through her veins, awakening under her heart some nameless, unsuspected existence that had slumbered there all these years and that went out through her throbbing finger-tips to his that answered. She wondered if the hoydenish blood of some lawless ancestor, long asleep, were calling out in her tonight, some drop of a hotter fluid that the centuries had failed to cool, and why, if this curse were in her, it had not spoken before. But was it a curse, this awakening, this wealth before undiscovered, this music set free? For the first time in her life her heart held something stronger than herself, was not this worth while? Then she ceased to wonder. She lost sight of the lights and the faces, and the music was drowned by the beating of her own arteries. She saw only the blue eyes that flashed above her, felt only the warmth of that throbbing hand which held hers and which the blood of his heart fed. Dimly, as in a dream, she saw the drooping shoulders, high white forehead and tight, cynical mouth of the man she was to marry in December. For an hour she had been crowding back the memory of that face with all her strength.

"Let us stop, this is enough," she whispered. His only answer was to tighten the arm behind her. She sighed and let that masterful strength bear her where it would. She forgot that this man was little more than a savage, that they would part at dawn. The blood has no memories, no reflections, no regrets for the past, no consideration of the future.

"Let us go out where it is cooler," she said when the music stopped; thinking, *I am growing faint here, I shall be all right in the open air.* They stepped out into the cool, blue air of the night.

Since the older folk had begun dancing, the young Norwegians had been slipping out in couples to climb the windmill tower into the cooler atmosphere, as is their custom.

"You like to go up?" asked Eric, close to her ear.

She turned and looked at him with suppressed amusement. "How high is it?"

"Forty feet, about. I not let you fall." There was a note of irresistible pleading in his voice, and she felt that he tremendously wished her to go. Well, why not? This was a night of the unusual, when she was not herself at all, but was living an unreality. Tomorrow, yes, in a few hours, there would be the Vestibule Limited and the world.

"Well, if you'll take good care of me. I used to be able to climb, when I was a little girl."

Once at the top and seated on the platform, they were silent. Margaret wondered if she would not hunger for that scene all her life, through all the routine of the days to come. Above them stretched the great Western sky, serenely blue, even in the night, with its big, burning stars, never so cold and dead and far away as in denser atmospheres. The moon would not be up for twenty minutes yet, and all about the horizon, that wide horizon, which seemed to reach around the world, lingered a pale, white light, as of a universal dawn. The weary wind brought up to them the heavy odors of the cornfields. The music of the dance sounded faintly from below. Eric leaned on his elbow beside her, his legs swinging down on the ladder. His great shoulders looked more than ever like those of the stone Doryphorus, who stands in his perfect, reposeful strength in the Louvre, and had often made her wonder if such men died forever with the youth of Greece.

"How sweet the corn smells at night," said Margaret nervously.

"Yes, like the flowers that grow in paradise, I think."

She was somewhat startled by this reply, and more startled when this taciturn man spoke again.

"You go away tomorrow?"

"Yes, we have stayed longer than we thought to now."

"You not come back any more?"

"No, I expect not. You see, it is a long trip halfway across the continent."

"You soon forget about this country, I guess." It seemed to him now a little thing to lose his soul for this woman, but that she should utterly forget this night into which he threw all his life and all his eternity, that was a bitter thought.

"No, Eric, I will not forget. You have all been too kind to me for that. And you won't be sorry you danced this one night, will you?"

"I never be sorry. I have not been so happy before. I not be so happy again, ever. You will be happy many nights yet, I only this one. I will dream sometimes, maybe."

The mighty resignation of his tone alarmed and touched her. It was as when some great animal composes itself for death, as when a great ship goes down at sea.

She sighed, but did not answer him. He drew a little closer and looked into her eyes.

"You are not always happy, too?" he asked.

"No, not always, Eric; not very often, I think."

"You have a trouble?"

"Yes, but I cannot put it into words. Perhaps if I could do that, I could cure it."

He clasped his hands together over his heart, as children do when they pray, and said falteringly, "If I own all the world, I give him you."

Margaret felt a sudden moisture in her eyes, and laid her hand on his.

"Thank you, Eric; I believe you would. But perhaps even then I should not be happy. Perhaps I have too much of it already."

She did not take her hand away from him; she did not dare. She sat still and waited for the traditions in which she had always believed to speak and save her. But they were dumb. She belonged to an ultra-refined civilization which tries to cheat nature with elegant sophistries. Cheat nature? Bah! One generation may do it, perhaps two, but the third—Can we ever rise above nature or sink below her? Did she not turn on Jerusalem as upon Sodom, upon St. Anthony in his desert as upon Nero in his seraglio? Does she not always cry in brutal triumph: "I am here still, at the bottom of things, warming the roots of life; you cannot starve me nor tame me nor thwart me; I made the world, I rule it, and I am its destiny."

This woman, on a windmill tower at the world's end with a giant barbarian, heard that cry tonight, and she was afraid! Ah! the terror and the delight of that moment when first we fear ourselves! Until then we have not lived.

"Come, Eric, let us go down; the moon is up and the music has begun again," she said.

He rose silently and stepped down upon the ladder, putting his arm about her to help her. That arm could have thrown Thor's hammer out in the cornfields yonder, yet it scarcely touched her, and his hand trembled as it had done in the dance. His face was level with hers now and the moonlight fell sharply upon it. All her life she had searched the faces of men for the look that lay in his eyes. She knew that that look had never shone for her before, would never shine for her on earth again, that such love comes to one only in dreams or in impossible places like this, unattainable always. This was Love's self, in a moment it would die. Stung by the agonized appeal that emanated from the man's whole being, she leaned forward and laid her lips on his. Once, twice and again she heard the deep respirations rattle in his throat while she held them there, and the riotous force under her heart became an engulfing weakness. He drew her up to him until he felt all the resistance go out of her body, until every nerve relaxed and yielded. When she drew her face back from his, it was white with fear.

"Let us go down, oh, my God! let us go down!" she muttered. And the drunken stars up yonder seemed reeling to some appointed doom as she clung to the rounds of the ladder. All that she was to know of love she had left upon his lips.

"The devil is loose again," whispered Olaf Oleson, as he saw Eric dancing a moment later, his eyes blazing.

But Eric was thinking with an almost savage exultation of the time when he should pay for this. Ah, there would be no quailing then! If ever a soul went fearlessly, proudly down to the gates infernal, his should go. For a moment he fancied he was there already, treading down the tempest of flame, hugging the fiery hurricane to his breast. He wondered whether in ages gone, all the countless years of sinning in which men had sold and lost and flung their souls away, any man had ever so cheated Satan, had ever bartered his soul for so great a price.

It seemed but a little while till dawn.

The carriage was brought to the door and Wyllis Elliot and his sister said goodbye. She could not meet Eric's eyes as she gave him her hand, but as he stood by the horse's head, just as the carriage moved off, she gave him one swift glance that said, "I will not forget." In a moment the carriage was gone.

Eric changed his coat and plunged his head into the water tank and went to the barn to hook up his team. As he led his horses to the door, a shadow fell across his path, and he saw Skinner rising in his stirrups. His rugged face was pale and worn with looking after his wayward flock, with dragging men into the way of salvation.

"Good morning, Eric. There was a dance here last night?" he asked, sternly.

"A dance? Oh, yes, a dance," replied Eric, cheerfully.

"Certainly you did not dance, Eric?"

"Yes, I danced. I danced all the time."

The minister's shoulders drooped, and an expression of profound discouragement settled over his haggard face. There was almost anguish in the yearning he felt for this soul.

"Eric, I didn't look for this from you. I thought God had set his mark on you if he ever had on any man. And it is for things like this that you set your soul back a thousand years from God. O foolish and perverse generation!"

Eric drew himself up to his full height and looked off to where the new day was gilding the corn-tassels and flooding the uplands with light. As his nostrils drew in the breath of the dew and the morning, something from the only poetry he had ever read flashed across his mind, and he murmured, half to himself, with dreamy exultation:

"'And a day shall be as a thousand years, and a thousand years as a day.'"

First published in *Cosmopolitan*, XXVIII (April, 1900), 633–644.

The Westbound Train

A Thirty Minute Sketch for Two People

❆ ❆ ❆

PERSONS CONCERNED

Reginald Johnston, *a railroad official*
Sybil Johnston, *his wife*
Station Agent
Messenger Boy, *Western Union*

Scene. *The waiting room of the Union Pacific depot at Cheyenne, with clock, mirror, maps, and excursion circulars on the walls. The window communicating with the agent's office is shut.*

Mrs. Sybil Johnston enters attired in a traveling dress. She is followed by a messenger boy who carries a large valise and a small dog with a chain attached to its collar.

SYBIL: There boy, put it down. [*She pays him.*] That's all you can do for me, so run along. [*Boy scuffles toward the door.*] O boy, where will I find the station agent? In there? [*Boy nods and disappears.*] There, now he's gone, and how am I to find the agent! How uncivil the employees on these western lines are! Very different from those on my husband's road. [*Looks at the station clock.*] It is almost twelve and I don't remember at what time my train goes. Well, I'm certainly not equal to reading over those papers of instructions that Reginald sent me again. Why do all men cling to the tradition that women can't travel alone? I must find the agent. [*She raps on the window communicating with the agent's office, but gets no response. She sits down again, rises and begins pacing up and down the waiting room, stopping occasionally to examine the maps and excursion posters.*] What gloomy places these way stations are. I wish Reginald had gotten me through transportation from Chicago. I'll be a wreck by the time I reach San Francisco. I almost hope he can't get to the station to meet me, so that

[381]

I will have an opportunity to get to his hotel and recover my composure and complexion before he sees me. Railway travel always utterly destroys my temper and leaves me a fright, and I never can get my hair to curl on a Pullman. [*She raps again on the window, gets no response and resumes her aimless promenade up and down the waiting room.*] I wonder if he thinks I have gone off much? There are a great many handsome women in San Francisco, and I may look different to him after a four months' separation. [*She approaches the mirror on the wall.*] I can't afford to go off yet awhile. If I hadn't been more than passably good looking, I should never have dared to marry him, should I, Bijou? [*She picks up the dog.*] It takes courage, sir, to marry a man whom dozens of stunning women have flattered and spoiled and begged pretty to and played dead for before you ever got a chance at him. It is a grave matter to assume the responsibility of a man with a naughty past like that. Yet I can't blame him, I am not sure that I am not a little bit proud of it, in a disgusting sort of way. Besides, I rather like to think he is irresistible. Besides it is human nature, and he had only to look at a woman to make them fetch and carry and do tricks for him. Women *are* such fools, but I'll know when I see him whether any powdery object has crossed his path. He ought to lie to me, but he could not deceive me. I know him too well; much, *much* better than he knows himself. Then he has been so busy. Business is a good thing for men. If it were not for business, women would never dare marry at all. That was why I didn't take Jack Van Dynne; he had nothing to do but get into mischief. But Reginald is a man of affairs, he means something to the world. Let me see, it is still twenty-eight hours to San Francisco, and I have not seen the dear boy for four months. He certainly means a great deal to me, at all events. It's simply disgraceful the way women do get fond of men. And I thought I was in love with him *before* I married him. What a mercy that I didn't even know what it meant, or I should have been as abject as the other creatures, and then he never *would* have wanted me. O dear! that agent! [*She raps at the window again but gets no response. She takes out a letter from her pocketbook, and reads aloud:*] "This will land you at Cheyenne. There go to the Union Pacific Station, where the agent will hand you passes over the U.P. to 'Frisco." [*She shrugs her shoulders.*] O, I know all that by heart. [*Turns the page and reads on hurriedly, her voice gradually dying into an unintelligible murmur.*] "There is no engine on the road that will get you here fast enough. My very desire for you seems strong enough to draw you over the plains and across the Rockies and the Sierras to me here, without the aid of such a slow contrivance as steam. I am checking off the days and hours until——." [*She moves her lips noiselessly, smiles and crushes up the letter in her hand.*] O my boy, you can't possibly long for it as I do, you can't! Don't I know what waiting is? Shall I ever forget that night at Calais before we were engaged, when I cabled you that you might come? And I sat out on the upper balcony of that horrid hotel in the storm, a pitiable object, with the rain drenching me, watching the lights of the incoming steamers and crying from loneliness and homesickness for you. Ah! then I knew how much I wanted you, and I felt as though all my life I had just been living in hotels and watching the lights of other people's ships out at sea. But mine came in at last; you came to me in the morning with the sun; such a sun never rose before. What a meeting that was! And this will be almost another such. [*Whistle of a train sounds.*] Heavens! that may be my train, yes it must be my train! It is twelve o'clock and Reginald wrote that some train came or went at twelve o'clock. O that agent! [*She pounds furiously on the window with her umbrella. The window opens and the station agent appears at the window. The agent is suave, well-dressed and talkative, somewhat patronizing.*]

AGENT: Well madam?

SYBIL: Is that the westbound train that just whistled?

AGENT: The through passenger, you mean?

SYBIL: Yes, the through passenger for San Francisco, that's what I want, and now I shall certainly miss it! I have been rapping here for half an hour! [*She dashes for her valise.*]

AGENT: Don't excite yourself, madam, the westbound passenger doesn't leave until two o'clock.

SYBIL: Then it comes in at twelve?

AGENT: Not until twelve forty-five.

SYBIL: Then what train is there at twelve?

AGENT: None here, either way, that I know of.

SYBIL: I am sure my husband wrote me that something happened at twelve.

AGENT: Nothing happens at twelve here but dinner.

SYBIL: [*Stiffly*] My husband, sir, is vice-president of the C.R. & S., and he instructed me to call for some passes. He doubtless will regret that I have taken so much of your valuable time.

AGENT: My time is valuable only when I can serve you, madam, and I would be just as glad to be of service to your husband's wife if he were a brakeman. But there is no train out of Cheyenne over the U.P. at twelve o'clock.

SYBIL: But my husband wrote me most explicit instructions.

AGENT: Do you happen to have them with you?

SYBIL: [*She produces the letter from her pocketbook, reads, blushes, and relaxes.*] I beg your pardon, sir, I am very stupid, it *is* dinner! [*They both laugh.*]

AGENT: Excuse me a minute. [*He steps back and puts on his coat. Sybil wanders absently to the mirror and after a quick glance back over her shoulder gives a few touches to her hair. Agent reappears at the window.*]

SYBIL: You see I have never traveled alone before, and my husband felt nervous about it, and he wrote me pages and pages of instructions, so that I would know what to do with every hour. I am afraid I got them mixed.

AGENT: Most natural thing in the world on a long journey with lots of changes. You have come direct from New York, I take it?

SYBIL: Straight through. Mercy! That reminds me, I haven't got my passes yet! Have you the transportation here from Cheyenne to San Francisco for Mrs. S. Johnston?

[*Agent looks grave, goes back and fumbles at the papers on his desk, returns to the window with a slip of paper in his hand.*]

AGENT: We had transportation here made out for such a person, but it was called for several hours ago.

SYBIL: Called for? Why I am Mrs. Johnston!

[*Agent looks interested and shakes his head.*]

AGENT: Well, so was the other lady, or she claimed to be. Here is her receipt.

SYBIL: I don't care about her receipt. She is an impostor. I am Mrs. Johnston, and you have given my passes to the wrong person.

AGENT: I don't see how that could be; she had a letter from the Central Office apologizing for the delay in sending her passes.

SYBIL: [*Contemptuously*] A forgery, of course. It doesn't take a very long head to see that. Do you mean to tell me that you gave them up to her without further question?

AGENT: Well, she wasn't exactly a lady one would question. She seemed very much like the real thing, you know. I beg your pardon! But I was glad enough to give them to her. She has been in town waiting for them several days, and she called here after every mail and a few times between mails. That is why you had such trouble in raising me; I thought she had come back from force of habit, or because the passes were written out in violet ink and didn't match her clothes. My wife didn't like it, so I kept my window shut. A man has to protect himself in some way.

SYBIL: Of course, she wanted to get them before I got here. Any one could have seen that. And now what am I to do?

AGENT: Well, the lady is still in town; she can't get away before the two o'clock train. You might see her. She is just across the street, at the Inter-Ocean hotel.

SYBIL: See her? Why should I? No indeed! That is your business, sir. You made the mistake and you must rectify it.

AGENT: But how am I to convince her that I have made any mistake? She has an autograph letter from the Central Office and ample identification, while you have shown me none as yet.

SYBIL: [Icily] Here is my card, sir. You must pardon the oversight as I am not accustomed to having my word questioned.

AGENT: She said exactly the same thing, and in the same tone. Now don't misunderstand me, Mrs. Johnston. I believe your claim is all right, but my opinion doesn't go with the road. I must have tangible proof to start to looking the matter up on. And I am afraid your card won't do. Have you checks for your baggage? [She produces them.] Thank you. Excuse me a moment. [He disappears and Sybil paces the floor distractedly.]

SYBIL: What am I to do? If I telegraph Reginald, he may be in Los Angeles, and besides I couldn't get an answer before the train goes. What a blockhead this agent is! And at first I thought him rather nice. The idea of giving my passes to the first impostor that comes along, and then coolly proposing that I trot after her. What western men lack in manners they make up in assurance. This would never have happened on an eastern road. Reggie must have this fellow called down.

[Agent returns and throws checks on window shelf.]

AGENT: These checks claim three trunks, all marked Sybil Ingrahame.

SYBIL: Certainly, my maiden name. They are my old traveling trunks. O dear, how unfortunate! I suppose you think me the adventuress! Perhaps you contemplate having me arrested!

AGENT: Madam, I have far more serious matters to contemplate. I have implicit faith in you, but I can't do much for you on faith; and I certainly can't accost that imposing personage at the Inter-Ocean House without some sort of evidence. I really want to help you if I can, so let's see what can be done. I will be busy with the eastbound passenger pretty soon. You said you had a letter from your husband, didn't you?

SYBIL: [Eagerly] To be sure! Here it is, he is very definite. [She reads.] This will land you at Cheyenne; there go to the Union Pacific Station where the agent will hand you—look there, read for yourself. [Agent examines letter and hands it back, shaking his head.]

AGENT: Yes, I understand, but this letter is addressed to sweetheart and is signed "Your boy, Reggie." I am afraid no road would honor that signature.

SYBIL: [*Indignantly*] I didn't suppose you would feel at liberty to read the whole letter, and your jokes are in very bad taste, sir. My husband will report your conduct to headquarters and have this matter looked into.

AGENT: Then I wish he would go about it now, for I don't know how to. I'll wire the Omaha office and see if they had orders to issue passes for two Mrs. Johnstons. In the meantime I would advise you to see the other woman, or you might send a note to her.

SYBIL: Well, if you will kindly call a boy I suppose I can do that. [*Agent puts stationery on the window shelf. He goes to the telegraph instrument and begins to send a message.*]

SYBIL: Will you let me see that receipt a moment? I want to see whether the creature claims to have a first name. [*He hands it to her.*] Why this is signed Mrs. S. Johnson, J-O-H-N-S-O-N, without the T. Well, she is stupid! So long as she is appropriating other people's passes and names she needn't quibble at a single letter. She might just as well have taken the T along with the rest of it, and I shall not hesitate to tell her so. [*She writes furiously. Messenger boy comes in. Sybil gives him the letter.*] There, get that over to the Inter-Ocean House, and bring me an answer at once.

BOY: Yes'm. [*He goes out.*]

[*Agent comes to the window again. He speaks:*]

AGENT: And while you are waiting, Mrs. Johnston, can't I send out and get some lunch for you?

SYBIL: [*Stiffly*] Thank you, I don't care for anything. But my little dog Bijou has had nothing since morning. I think I must go out and try and find some milk for him.

AGENT: Oh you never mind that! One of my boys will get Bijou's milk for him. At least let me get you a comfortable chair. [*He opens a door and brings out one from his office.*]

SYBIL: [*Seating herself*] Thank you.

AGENT: I am awfully sorry that this trouble has occurred, Mrs. Johnston, and that it puts me in such an ungracious light.

SYBIL: O, I perfectly understand, sir, that you must do your duty. [*The agent disappears with a shrug. He returns carrying a soup plate.*]

AGENT: Here is Bijou's lunch. He's a husky little dog, and by the way, the other Mrs. Johnson, or rather the lady who got your passes, had a dog as like him as two peas. She is a regular high stepper, and pretty trim looking. She didn't seem like a fraud.

SYBIL: [*Freezing harder*] I don't question the lady's charms, and I shall have nothing to say about your apparent susceptibility, if it were not responsible for the loss of my passes.

AGENT: [*Dodging back into his office*] Here's the boy now.

[*Boy comes in and hands Sybil a note.*]

SYBIL: [*Reading*] "Dear Madam: I think there can be no mistake about my passes. They were sent me by Mr. Reginald Johnston, vice-president of the C.R. & S., my old and tried friend. I have a letter of apology from the forwarding clerk of the Union Pacific office in Omaha, apologizing for his delay in overlooking Mr. Johnston's request, and keeping me for four days in this disagreeable place. Moreover, I this morning received a telegram from Mr. Johnston stating that he would meet me here and travel west with me. Regarding the spelling of my name, I must say that I feel the need of nothing from Mrs. Johnston alphabetically. My name is spelt without the T, and the passes were made out in the correct form. My acquaintance is of such long standing, that I can scarcely believe he has forgotten how to spell my name. Sincerely, Sally Johnson." Good heavens! This Volapuk. My husband to meet her and travel west with her? Is the woman insane? Why if he could possibly have left California, he would come east for me. What can she mean and who is she? Sally Johnson, without the T, what a name! Just as common as she is, a cakewalk sort of a name. Where pray did Reginald ever know such a person? Certainly I have met all his friends. Why this woman must know him well if she takes the liberty to ask him for passes over the western roads. She must have some claim—— [*She pauses a moment in deep thought, as a possible solution dawns upon her. She crushes the letter up in her hands.*] O! how horrible! how disgusting! She must have been one of them! Have been? She *is*, and that is why she is hurrying to him. And he is coming to meet her! He could not even wait until she arrived. And that is why he told me that he might be out of town when I got there. He didn't even know whether he could get away from her to meet me. Her passes were delayed, should have been here four days ago, and she would have reached him four days before I would. O! [*She rushes wildly to the window which is closed again, and raps.*] Agent, agent!

[*Window opens and the agent appears.*]

AGENT: Ah! It is you, Mrs. Johnston?

SYBIL: I am sorry to trouble you again, but what did you say this person looks like?

AGENT: The other Mrs. Johnson? O she is a regular fine one. Big, stately woman, good figure and lots of style. Blue eyes, very blue, skin of the sort we never see out here, creamy you know with roses in her cheeks. Blonde hair and lots of it—

SYBIL: [*Contemptuously*] Alkaline probably, such women always have.

AGENT: I can't say as to that, I am not an expert in such matters.

SYBIL: Did she impress you as a person of breeding, a lady, in short?

AGENT: A lady, why bless you, yes, a regular high stepper.

SYBIL: Ah, thank you. [*She turns away from the window.*] How horrible, how horrible and how disgusting. Just the usual sordid, mercenary wrecker of homes, common woman who has to beat her way in the world, and wants to do it easy. [*She sinks wearily into the chair.*] Somehow, whenever I have thought of his past life, I have never thought of it as being cheap and common. I thought he had more imagination. I suppose, though, there is only one way to be bad, and that is the common way. Ah! common enough, God knows. But to think of his sending for her now, when I was hurrying to him with a heart so full of love— Ah, Reggie, you will never know how full! No, you will never know that now. This feature of it is something that no woman could bear without debasing her womanhood. How all those dreadful things the girls used to tell me about him come back to me now. And I used to think it was all envy, because they wanted him and couldn't get him. Why, I used to pity them! They'll be pitying me now. No, I can't endure that. I will not be pitied! Margaret Villers used to tell me about his horrid scrapes at college, and about his keeping an uptown flat with a Skye terrier and things for some person, and a coupé with dark blue upholstering to set off the creature's blonde loveliness. Why this creature is a blonde! [*She rises and begins pacing the floor.*] She may be the same; of course she is. No man, not even the most rapacious, ever wanted two alkaline blondes in succession. Perhaps he has never dropped her at all; perhaps it was on her account that he cut our wedding trip short and hurried back to New York. O horrible! My life is all going to pieces under me; there is nothing left. She even has a terrier like mine, the agent said so. I suppose he has even given her the same jewels, bought duplicates probably. And that is why he works so hard;

the expense of two establishments, and so forth. Perhaps she knows all about me, and they discuss our household affairs together, as people do in Balzac's novels. She may even have read all the letters I wrote him—no, I can't believe that of him, he couldn't be so base. I shall have to get used to thinking of him in this way, I can't do it all at once. Why only yesterday—ah, how happy I was yesterday! I used to tell myself that I was too happy and that I would have to pay for it some day. I even told him so once, and he said, "Of course you will, by seeing your husband more bewitched with you every minute. That is your everlasting punishment." What nice manful things he did say! He was never maudlin or patronizing; somehow he always seemed to respect one's intelligence. Ah! I know he did love me, for a little while any way. Why I even used to wish that I could suffer a little for him in some way, and I used to be so selfish before I loved him. Ah, Reginald, it is not only yourself that you take away from me; you take my conscience and my better self, and the brightness out of the sun and the blueness out of the sky! O Reggie, Reggie! [*She weeps.*]

AGENT: [*From the window*] I've got an answer to my inquiry, Mrs. Johnston. The Central Office wires that they had instructions from Mr. Reginald Johnston to issue but one pass to San Francisco, and they know nothing about any transportation for a second Mrs. Johnston.

SYBIL: [*Absently*] Thank you, but it doesn't matter now. How soon does the eastbound passenger leave?

AGENT: In fifteen minutes. And now I want to go out and get some lunch. If you want anything just call the boy.

SYBIL: Thank you. You have been very kind. [*Agent closes the window.*] Now I must begin to think. What am I to do? Going west is out of the question now. He is coming for her, and he can have her. I will not be one of a *ménage à trois*. There is nothing left for me but to go home, back to that big, dark, gloomy house on Fifth Avenue, where his ghost will walk forever to keep me company. [*Opens her pocketbook.*] I have money enough with me to get to Chicago, and there I will telegraph father. I'll never touch Reginald's money again. Possibly he thinks I married him because he owns a railroad. Men who buy love never believe in any other kind. Yes, I will go home. And *then* what? That's the question. I shall not even have the consolation of telling my woes to my friends and receiving calls of condolence, as Alberta Frick did, since I am not that kind of a person. She made a regular vocation of it. And I shall *never* marry again. Dear me, how long life is, after all. How many days and nights there are to be lived through somehow. And yesterday it seemed so short. How does that song go:

> When the land was white with winter
> And dead love was laid away,
> I was so glad life could not last
> Forever and a day.

It all simmers down to that in the end. There, I might sing. Cicely Fanshawe went on the stage and made a name for herself and sang her husband back to her feet and left him to grovel there until he literally went to the bad for the love of a woman he had neglected shamefully when he had her. And why cannot I, Sybil Ingrahame Johnston, have my voice trained by Marchesi and do the same. I used to think of the stage in the old empty days before I met Reggie. Well, the days to come will be emptier. At school they always said that my voice had great dramatic possibilities. Yes, I will go to Marchesi. That is what they all do. There was a time when disappointed, heartbroken women crept into convents and had their hair cut off; now they blondine it and go to Marchesi. O I can be that sort of a blonde, since he prefers them! [*She looks at clock.*] That train will soon be here. Why I have not been in this place an hour, and it seems years. I am sure the wrinkles are beginning to come; I can feel them. Well, an hour has been long enough to bring my life down about my ears. [*She hears train whistle and an engine bell ringing.*] That must be my train now. Boy, boy! O where is that boy! [*Picks up the dog and heavy satchel and staggers to the door, rushing into the arms of Mr. Reginald Johnston, who has just arrived on the eastbound train.*] Reginald!

REGINALD: O my sweetheart, but this is good! I couldn't wait, you see what a mollycoddle you have made of me! Couldn't let you cross the Sierras for the first time without me to save my life! Come, put down all that lumber and kiss me, there is nobody here. Why, I'll even kiss Bijou, I am so happy. [*She struggles from his embrace and attempts to get out of the door.*] Where are you going? That's the eastbound train that I came in on; ours goes an hour later, and we'll have plenty of time. What's the matter, aren't you glad to see me?

SYBIL: [*Hysterically*] O I have no doubt that the other will be gladder! I'm surprised that you didn't go to her first—or perhaps you didn't know that she was here. Well, she is, the other Mrs. Johnson, without the T; she is waiting across the street for you, and you can take her back with you. I am going home to New York. [*She weeps.*]

REGINALD: Other Mrs. Johnston? Waiting for me with tea, across the street? What in the name of the state lunatic asylum are you talking about? Here, put down that grip, and tell me what's the matter?

SYBIL: O, you might have got her passes on time, since you must have her. You need not have brought us together and given her a chance to insult me. She is here, I tell you, in this very town, and has written me a most shameful letter, the other woman without the T.

REGINALD: Where? What do you mean? Who wants tea? Sybil, dear, do calm yourself, and tell me what you mean. I don't understand one word you are saying. It is all tuttihash.

SYBIL: I tell you that other woman has my passes.

REGINALD: Well, let her have 'em, whoever she is. I can take care of you. I pass, so do you, until hearts are trumps again, see? [*He embraces her, Sybil drawing away from him.*]

SYBIL: Don't touch me until you have explained to whom you gave my passes, and why I found none here.

REGINALD: Why, because I never ordered any. After I wrote you, I decided to come on here and meet you, and give you an all round surprise, and it wasn't until this morning that I discovered that the Burlington passenger had changed time Sunday and that your train would get into Cheyenne before mine did. Then I wired at once; didn't you get my telegram?

SYBIL: No, I did not. I think you are getting mixed and would better stop right there. Your telegram went to the other Mrs. Johnson, without the T.

REGINALD: [*Exasperated*] Am I never to be done hearing about this woman and her tea? Who in heaven's name is she, and what has she got to do with me?

SYBIL: [*Pointedly*] That's just exactly what I wish to know. I arrived here to find this person had taken my passes and expected you to travel west with her.

REGINALD: Travel west with this tea toper, or is she a tea agent? Not if I know myself! Have you encountered a lunatic? Sybil, dear, you have been ill; what doctor did you have? Where's the agent? O somebody's been drinking!

SYBIL: He has gone off to dinner, and I will thank you not to make me any more ridiculous in his eyes than you have done already. He came very near arresting me for an impostor.

REGINALD: Arresting you? [*Sinks into a chair.*] O my God, this is a mix-up! Will somebody explain!

SYBIL: It is from you that explanations are due, if you can think of any you are not ashamed of. Who is this other woman?

REGINALD: [*Dejectedly*] I wish to God I knew. Can't you be a little plainer, Sybil? What are the facts?

SYBIL: The facts are plain enough to me. I arrived here this morning and asked whether passes had been sent the agent for Mrs. S. Johnston. I was told that such passes had been sent, but that they had been claimed a few hours previous by a blonde creature who had credentials from the Central Office and who wrote me a most insulting letter, saying that you were to meet her and accompany her west, and that you were her old and tried friend, and signed Sally Johnson, J-O-H-N-S-O-N, without the T. Now who and what is Sally Johnson?

REGINALD: O Sally *Johnson*, *Sally* Johnson! That explains the matter.

SYBIL: I fail to see it. I am still waiting.

REGINALD: Come now, Sybil, you must recall her. She was sister Mollie's bridesmaid, used to be Sally Toppinger. Her husband was killed in an excursion boat disaster, and she has been a bit touched ever since, not quite right, shy a few marbles, you know. I was glad to help the poor old girl out, but her passes should have been here a week ago. Why I had quite forgotten that she married a T-less Johnson. And how did she ever get the idea that I was going to travel with her? She must be in a really pitiable condition, shy most of her marbles. Hold on, I've got it! You say you didn't get my telegram, then it got here before you did and was sent over to her regardless of the T. O I'll fix that agent's face for him! Now it's all perfectly clear, isn't it? And now will you tell me why you and Bijou were making for that eastbound train and talking about New York and all sorts of crazy things?

SYBIL: [*Slowly*] Yes, I think I understand; I want to believe it anyhow. O Reginald, I've been thinking all sorts of bad things about you! [*Reginald taking her hands and looking very gravely into her eyes.*]

REGINALD: Now look here, sweetheart, you must never do that. It's because you always think good things that I can't do very bad ones. Why, if I had known you all my life I should have grown up in the condition of Adam before the fall, and they would have blackballed me at the clubs. I should have gone about exhaling sanctity—as you do violets—! [*Kisses her.*]

SYBIL: O Reggie, I've been such an idiot, and I made myself so miserable, and now that you have come I am so happy— [*She weeps on his shoulder.*]

REGINALD: Of course you are and always shall be. That is what the C.R. & S. is operated for, just to make you happy, and every engine wiper on the line is working for just that. But before I leave this town I intend to fresco these walls with bleeding fragments of that agent's anatomy. Now I'm hungry as a Rocky Mountain lion so come, let's go and get this poor, daffy, tealess widow and wine and dine with her and make it all up. It will be like a wedding breakfast. And then we'll all get on the westbound train and we'll westward ho! together. She's had a tough time, and it'll do her good just to see a little happiness. You must remember her, you met her at Mollie's wedding; rather handsome but her eyes are a trifle crossed. [*He gathers up the baggage and puts Bijou in his ulster pocket, throwing the chain about his neck.*]

SYBIL: [*Delightedly*] O *are* they? I had forgotten. Come on, dear, and let's be gay, furiously happy, life is so awfully short. I was just thinking about that today. And I am so glad her eyes are just a trifle, trifle crossed.

First published in Lincoln *Courier*, XIV (September 30, 1899), 3–5.

The Way of the World

✻ ✻ ✻

O! the world was full of the summer time,
    And the year was always June,
When we two played together
    In the days that were done too soon.

O! every hand was an honest hand,
    And every heart was true.
When you were the king of the cornlands
    And I was a queen with you.

When I could believe in the fairies still,
    And our elf in the cottonwood tree,
And the pot of gold at the rainbow's end
    And you could believe in me.

Speckle Burnham sat on Mary Eliza's front porch waiting until she finished her practicing. Apparently he was not in a hurry for her to do so. He shuffled his bare feet uneasily over the splintery boards when the dragging, hopeless thumping within quickened in tempo to a rapid, hurried volley of sounds, telling that Mary Eliza's "hour" was nearly over and that she was prodding the lagging moments with fiery impatience.

Indeed, cares of state were weighing heavily upon Speckle, and he had some excuse for gravity, for Speckle was a prince in his own right and a ruler of men.

In Speckle Burnham's back yard were half-a-dozen store boxes of large dimensions, placed evenly in a row against the side of the barn, and there was Speckle's empire. It had long been a cherished project of the boys on Speckle's street to collect their scattered lemonade stands and sidewalk booths and organize a community; but without Speckle's wonderful executive ability the thing would never have been possible.

In the first place, Speckle had the most disreputable back yard in the community. It would have been quite out of the question to have littered up any other yard on the street with half-a-dozen store boxes and the assorted chattels of their respective occupants. But Speckle's folks had been farming people, and regarded their back yard as the natural repository for such encumbrances as were in the way in the house; and Speckle was among them. Speckle had offered his yard as a possible site for a flourishing town, and the other boys brought their store boxes and called the town Speckleville in honor of the founder.

Now it must not be thought that Speckleville was a transient town, such as boys often found in the morning and destroy in the evening. Speckle's especial point was organization. No boy was allowed to change his business or his place of business without due permission from the assembled council of Speckleville. Jimmy Templeton kept a grocery stocked with cinnamon barks, soda crackers, ginger snaps and "Texas Mixed"—a species of cheap candy which came in big wooden buckets; these he pilfered from his father's store. Tommy Sanders was proprietor of a hardware store, stocked with bows and arrows, slingshots, pea shooters and ammunition for the same. "Shorty" Thompson kept a pool room with a table covered with one of his mother's comforters. Dick Hutchinson ran the dime museum where he fearlessly handled live bull snakes for the sum of a few pins and exhibited snapping turtles, pocket gophers, bullets from Chattanooga, rusty firearms, and a piece of the rope with which a horse thief had been lynched. Reinholt Birkner was the son of the village undertaker and was a youth of a dolorous turn of mind and insisted upon keeping a marble shop, where he made little tombstones and neat caskets for the boys' deceased woodpeckers and prairie dogs, and for such of the museum specimens as sought early and honored graves.

Speckle, by reason of inventive genius and real estate monopoly, held all the important offices in the town. He was mayor and postmaster, and he conducted a bank, wherein he compelled the citizens to deposit their pins, charging them heavily for that privilege and lending out their own funds to them at a ruinous usury, taking mortgages on the stock and business houses of such unfortunates as failed to meet their obligations promptly. His father was a chattel broker in the days when money changed hands quickly in the country beyond the Missouri, and from his tenderest years Speckle had been initiated into the nefarious arts of the business. But although his threats many a time caused poor delinquents to tremble, I never heard of him actually foreclosing on any one, and I can assert on good authority that when Dick Hutchinson's father failed in business, causing great consternation throughout the village, Speckle went to Dick privately and offered to lend him a few hundred pins gratis to tide him over any present difficulties.

But certainly Speckle had a right to be autocratic, for it was Speckle's fecund fancy more than his back yard that was the real site of that town, and his imagination was the coin current of the realm, and made those store boxes seem temples of trade to more eyes than his own. A really creative imagination was Speckle's—one that could invent occupations for half-a-dozen boys, metamorphize an express wagon into a street-car line, a rubber hose into city water works, devise feast days and circuses and public rejoicings, railway accidents and universal disasters, even invent a Fourth of July in the middle of June and cause the hearts of his fellow townsmen to beat high with patriotism. For Speckle, by a species of innocent hypnotism, colored the mental visions of his fellow townsmen until his fancies seemed weighty realities to them, just as a clever play actor makes you tremble and catch your breath when he draws his harmless rapier. And, like the play actors, Speckle was the willing victim of his own conceit. What matter if he had to peddle milk to the neighbor women at night? What matter even if he were chastised because he had lost the hatchet or forgotten to dig around the trees on his father's lots? Tomorrow he was the founder of a city and a king of men!

So the inhabitants of Speckleville had dwelt together in all peace and concord until Mary Eliza Jenkins had peered at them through the morning-glory vines on her back porch and had envied these six male beings their happiness; for although Mary Eliza was the tomboy of the street, the instincts of her sex were strong in her, and that six male beings should dwell together in ease and happiness seemed to her an unnatural and a monstrous thing. Furthermore, she and Speckle had played together ever since the days when he had been father to all her dolls and had rocked them to sleep, and until the founding of Speckleville he had openly preferred her to any boy on the street, and she bitterly resented his desertion.

Once, in a moment of rashness, the boys invited her over to a circus in Speckle's barn, and after that Speckle knew no peace of his life. Night and day Mary Eliza importuned him for admittance to his town. She hung around his back porch as soon as she was through practicing in the morning; she nudged him and whispered to him as she sat next to him at Sunday school; she waylaid him while he was taking his cow out to pasture and sprang upon him from ambush when he was taking his milk in the evening, even offering to accompany him and carry one of the tin pails. Taking his milk was the prime curse of Speckle's life and he weakly accepted her company, especially to the house of the old woman who kept the big dog. When Speckle went there alone he usually played he was a burglar.

Now Speckle himself had really no objection to granting Mary Eliza naturalization papers and full rights of citizenship, but the other boys would not hear of it.

"She'll try to boss us all just like she bosses you," objected Tommy Sanders.

"Anyhow, she's a girl and this ain't a girl's play. I suppose she'd keep a dressmaking shop and dress our dolls for us," snorted Dick Hutchinson contemptuously.

"Put it any way you like, she'll spoil the town," said Jimmy Templeton.

"You began it all yourself, Temp. You asked her to the circus, you know you did," retorted Speckle.

Poor Speckle! He had never heard of that old mud-walled town in Latium that was also founded by a boy, and where so many good fellows dwelt together in jovial comradeship until they invited some ladies from the Sabine hills to a party, with such disastrous results.

On this particular morning Speckle had come over to, if possible, persuade Mary Eliza to desist from her appeals, and he sat in the sunshine gloomily awaiting the interview. Presently a triumphant "one, two, three, FOUR," and a triumphant bang announced that her hour of penal servitude was over for the day, and she dashed out on the porch.

"Well, have you made them?" she demanded.

Speckle braced himself and came directly to the point.

"I can't make them, Mary 'Liza, and they say you'd get tired and spoil the town."

"O stuff! What makes them say that?"

"Well, it's 'cause you're a girl, I guess," said Speckle reflectively, wrinkling the big yellow freckle on his nose that was accountable for his nickname.

"Girl nothin'! I'd play I was a man, and that's all you do. M. E. Jenkins—that's what I'll have over my store. I've got the signs already made. 'Delmonico Resteraunt, M. E. Jenkins, Prop.' Come, Speckle, you know I can skin a cat as well as you can and I can beat Hutch running, can't I now?"

"Course you can. I'd like to have you in, Mary 'Liza," remonstrated Speckle.

"O well, I don't care so much about getting in your old town anyhow, only my father keeps the bakery and I could have cookies and cream puffs and candy to sell in my store, chocolates and things, none of your old Texas Mixed, and I thought I could be a good deal of use in your town."

"Say, Mary 'Liza, do you mean that? I guess I'd better tell them. I guess I'll tell them tonight," said Speckle, with a new interest.

"O do, Speckle, and do get me in!" cried Mary Eliza, as she hopped gleefully about on one foot. "You know you can if you want to, 'cause it's in your yard. And we can have Strawberry for a ring horse when we have circuses. His tail isn't all rubbed off like your Billy's and he can be a pony in the side show, too."

Speckle did not reply at once. He was wondering whether Mary Eliza could meet the large demands on the imagination requisite to citizenship in Speckleville. He was not wholly certain as to the enduring qualities of feminine imagination, but he did not know exactly how to express his doubts, so he remained silent.

"What are you thinking about now?" demanded Mary Eliza.

"O nothing. I'll see them about it tonight."

"And if they don't let me in I'll know it's all your fault," called Mary Eliza threateningly, as she dashed into the house.

That evening after Speckle had taken his milk he hung the empty pails on the fence and went around to interview each of the boys privately. He suspected that by seeing them separately he could best appeal to their individual weaknesses. He bribed Dick Hutchinson with a dozen of his rarest tin tobacco tags, all with euphuistic names such as "Rose Leaf" and "Lily of the Valley," which his uncle had sent him from Florida. He won Reinholt Birkner with promises of many a solemn funeral cortege for Mary Eliza's deceased pets, and charmed "Shorty" Thompson's ears with stories of the cream puffs from old Jenkins' bakery. Over Jimmy Templeton he had no hold, Jimmy being of that peculiarly odious species of humanity that is thoroughly upright and without secret weakness. So he merely told him of the consent of the other boys and used his personal influence for all it was worth.

"All right, if you fellows say so," Temp replied gravely. He was soaking cattails in the kerosene can preparatory to a torchlight procession of the Speckleville Republican Club. "I won't be the man to kick, but you mark my word, Speckle, she'll spoil the town. Girls always spoil everything a boy's got if you give 'em a chance."

That night after Speckle's mother had anointed his sunburned face with cold cream and he had climbed into bed and was reposing peacefully on his stomach, enjoying the only real comfort he had had that day, he heard a violent "tic-tac" at the window at the head of his bed.

"Hello, Temp, is that you?" he called.

"No, Speckle, it's me. Did you make them?" whispered Mary Eliza.

"Yes, I made them," replied Speckle, rather wearily.

"O, Speckle, you are a dandy! I just love you, Speckle!" and Mary Eliza pounded and scratched joyfully at the screen as she departed.

The next day Speckle vacated his piano box, the largest and most commodious structure in his town, and fitted it up for Mary Eliza with a lavishness which astonished his comrades. In the afternoon Mary Eliza made her triumphant entry into Speckleville with an old-fashioned carpet sack in one hand and a Japanese umbrella in the other.

She was all smiles and sweetmeats and showed neither resentment nor embarrassment at her chilling reception. She set forth her cream puffs and chocolates and in half an hour the Delmonico Restaurant was the center of interest and commercial activity.

I shall not attempt to rehearse all the arts and wiles by which Mary Eliza deposed Speckle and made herself sole imperatrix of Speckleville. She made it her business to appeal to every masculine instinct in the boys, beginning with their stomachs. When first a woman tempted a man she said unto him, "Eat." The cream puffs alone would have assured her victory, but she did not stop there. She possessed cunning of hand and could make wonderful neckties of colored tissue paper, and stiff hats of pasteboard covered with black paper and polished with white of egg, which she disposed of for a number of pins. She became the star of the circus ring, and it was considered a great sight to behold Mary Eliza attired in blue cambric tights with an abundance of blonde locks, made by unraveling a few feet of new heavy rope, flowing about her shoulders, executing feats of marvelous dexterity upon the flying trapeze.

Indeed, Mary Eliza possessed certain talents which peculiarly fitted her to dwell and rule in a boys' town. Otherwise she could never have brought disaster and ruin upon the town of Speckleville. For all boys will admit that there are some girls who would make the best boys in the world—if they were not girls.

It soon befell that Mary Eliza's word, her lightest wish, was law in Speckleville. Half the letters that went through Speckle's post office were for her, and even the phlegmatic Reinholt Birkner made her a beautiful little tombstone with a rose carved on it as an ornament for her center table.

Meanwhile Speckle—poor, deposed Speckle—sat by without demur and without more than an occasional pang of jealousy and watched the success of his protégée, learning, as many another monarch had done before him, how pleasant it sometimes is to serve.

Now, alas! it is time to introduce the tragic motif in this simple chronicle of Speckleville, to bring about the advent of the heavy villain into the comedy. He came in the form of a boy from Chicago, to spend the summer with his aunt just across the street from Speckle's home. From the first he found small favor in the eyes of the Speckleville boys. To begin with, he invariably wore shoes and stockings, a habit disgustingly effeminate to any true and loyal Specklevillian. To this he added the grievance of a stiff hat, and on Sundays even sunk to the infamy of kid gloves. He also smoked many cubeb cigarettes—corn-silks were considered the only manly smoke in Speckleville—and ate some odorous confection to conceal his guilt from his mamma. The good citizens of Speckleville all looked with horror upon these gilded vices—all, save one, perhaps.

The first time the New Boy visited the town he bought a cream puff of Mary Eliza, and on being told that the price of the same was ten pins, he laughed scornfully, saying that he did not carry a pincushion and had not brought his workbox with him. He then threw down a nickel upon the counter. Now to offer money to a citizen of Speckleville was an insult, like offering a bribe, and the boys were painfully surprised when Mary Eliza accepted that shameful coin, bestowing upon the purchaser a smile more desirable than many cream puffs.

After that the New Boy came often, usually confining his trade to the Delmonico Restaurant, where he hung about telling of his trip on Lake Michigan and his outings in Lincoln Park, while the proprietor listened with greedy ears. He persisted in paying for his purchases in coppers and nickels, and Mary Eliza persisted in accepting the despised currency, while the Speckleville boys went about with a secret shame in their hearts, feeling that somehow she had disgraced herself and them. They began to wonder as to just what a girl's notion of the square thing was, a question that has sometimes vexed older heads.

As for Mary Eliza, although she sometimes joined with the boys in a laugh at his expense, she by no means shared the general dislike of the New Boy. She thought his city clothes and superior manners very impressive, and felt more grown up and important when in his company. Even his letters, which were always written on real note paper with a monogram at the top and signed SEMPER IDEM seemed vastly more dignified than the rude scrawls of the other boys.

She had tact enough to know that this fine young gentleman would never wear tissue paper neckties, so she made him a red paper rose, which he wore, daily perfuming it with Florida water. Speckle had noted the growing discontent in his town, and sought to conceal Mary Eliza's disgraceful conduct and shield her from open contempt by asking her to make him a paper rose. But she laughed heartlessly with a wink at the New Boy and said she had no more paper. I doubt if any of the rebuffs his gallantry may have received in after years ever cut Speckle as that wink did.

Matters hastened from bad to worse in the town. The days came and went as days will, but over Mary Eliza's throne there was the shadow of the New Boy. The crisis came at last when in a meeting of the city council Mary Eliza boldly proposed admitting the New Boy to the town. Her motion was greeted by indignant howls and hisses and Speckle blushed to the roots of his red hair.

"Very well," said Mary Eliza, "if you won't have him in then I won't be in either. Him and me'll start another town over in his yard."

"You can just go and do it, then! We won't have that Chicago dude hanging around here any longer!" howled councilman Sanders, knocking over his chair.

To this all the rest echoed a wrathful assent. It was the utterance of an old grievance.

Mary Eliza arose with great dignity and began to pack her wares into her carpetbag. She made no display of ill humor, and talked cheerfully of her new town as she wrapped up her candies in tissue paper; the boys stood by and watched her, they did not believe she would go. But Mary Eliza departed even as she had come, with her carpetbag in her hand and her Japanese parasol tilted gaily over her head, while Speckle held the gate open for her, feeling that his illusions were vanishing fast.

"I'll send over for my box in the morning, Speckle, and you must all come over to our town and buy things, and we'll come over and buy things at yours," she called after him.

The treachery, the infamy of her deception never seemed to have occurred to her. It was as though Coriolanus, when he deserted Rome for the camp of the Volscians, had asked the Conscript Fathers to call on him and bring their families!

"She'll be back tomorrow all right enough," said Speckle.

But on the morrow the New Boy came for the piano box, and by noon Mary Eliza was fairly installed across the street, making paper neckties for the New Boy and canvassing the neighborhood for the New Boy's town. There could be no doubt that she had transferred her allegiance.

The Speckleville boys went resolutely to their stores and bought and sold and made a great show, but they had little heart in it all. They missed the cream puffs and the paper ties, and they missed something else more than these—something they could not name. If Speckle had chanced to confide in his young uncle, who was in the rapturous tortures of his first love affair, he would have been told that it was the "eternal feminine" they missed, and he would have been as much in the dark as before.

Mary Eliza had put herself at the head of everything, and now nothing went on without her. After the manner of her kind, she had come where she was not wanted, made herself indispensable, and gone again, taking with her, oh, so much more than her parasol and chocolate creams!

Everything went wrong in Speckleville that afternoon, and after the day was over the citizens of that passing village were quarreling violently, not, as in former times, because every one wanted to do something in a different way, but because no one wanted to do anything at all.

"It's all your fault, Speckle. We ought never to have [had] her in, and we wouldn't if it hadn't been for you."

"Well, now she's gone," protested Speckle, "so why can't we go on like we did before?"

No one attempted to answer. It was scarcely a wise question to ask.

"I always told you she'd spoil the town, Speckle, and now she's done it," said Jimmy Templeton.

"Well, you fellows seemed mighty glad to get her after she came, anyway, and you needn't put your lip in, Temp; you loafed around her store like a ninny," retorted Speckle, who felt that his persecution was more than he could bear.

Jimmy was not in a mood to endure a jibe at his weakness and by way of an answer he biffed Speckle one on the side of his nose, and it required the united strength of their fellow citizens to part them.

"I'm not going to stay in your old town any longer. I can have more fun in my own yard, and I'm going to take my things home," announced Dick Hutchinson, as he began pocketing the properties of his museum.

"I'll be darned if I do!" cried Jimmy Templeton. "And I'll thank you to give me my pins out of your old tin box, Mr. Speckle."

Speckle had woes enough without a run on his bank, but when Providence helps a man to trouble it is usually generous and dishes out all manner of calamities, regardless of what he may already have on his plate. Speckle sat there until he had paid out the last pin from his spice box. The boys all fell to packing their belongings as though fleeing from a doomed city, and they ceased not from making unkind remarks as they did so. Even Reinholt Birkner gathered up his chisels and monuments, all save one big block of granite that was too heavy for him, and that stood by his store box like a white tombstone. Under Speckle's very eyes his town vanished as many another western town has done since then.

"It's all your fault, Speckle!" bawled Jimmy Templeton, as he vaulted over the back fence, and Speckle, after having said all the swear words he knew, went off to the barn to smoke innumerable corn-silk cigarettes and to wonder at the queer way things are run down here.

After he had taken his milk that night he heard Mary Eliza laughing as she played tag with the New Boy under the electric light, and he sat down with his empty pails in his deserted town, as Caius Marius once sat among the ruins of Carthage.

First published in *Home Monthly*, VI (April, 1898), 10–11.

Nanette: An Aside

❋ ❋ ❋

Of course you do not know Nanette. You go to hear Tradutorri, go every night she is in the cast perhaps, and rave for days afterward over her voice, her beauty, her power, and when all is said the thing you most admire is a something which has no name, the indescribable quality which is Tradutorri herself. But of Nanette, the preserver of Madame's beauty, the mistress of Madame's finances, the executrix of Madame's affairs, the power behind the scenes, of course you know nothing.

It was after twelve o'clock when Nanette entered Madame's sleeping apartments at the Savoy and threw up the blinds, for Tradutorri always slept late after a performance. Last night it was *Cavalleria Rusticana*, and Santuzza is a trying role when it is enacted not merely with the emotions but with the soul, and it is this peculiar soul-note that has made Tradutorri great and unique among the artists of her generation.

"Madame has slept well, I hope?" inquired Nanette respectfully, as she presented herself at the foot of the bed.

"As well as usual, I believe," said Tradutorri rather wearily. "You have brought my breakfast? Well, you may put it here and put the ribbons in my gown while I eat. I will get up afterward."

Nanette took a chair by the bed and busied herself with a mass of white tulle.

"We leave America next week, Madame?"

"Yes, Friday; on the *Paris*," said Madame, absently glancing up from her strawberries. "Why, Nanette, you are crying! One would think you had sung 'Voi lo sapete' yourself last night. What is the matter, my child?"

"O, it is nothing worthy of Madame's notice. One is always sorry to say good bye, that is all."

"To one's own country, perhaps, but this is different. You have no friends here; pray, why should you be sorry to go?"

"Madame is mistaken when she says I have no friends here."

"Friends! Why, I thought you saw no one. Who, for example?"

"Well, there is a gentleman—"

"Bah! Must there always be a 'gentleman,' even with you? But who is this fellow? Go on!"

"Surely Madame has noticed?"

"Not I; I have noticed nothing. I have been very absentminded, rather ill, and abominably busy. Who is it?"

"Surely Madame must have noticed Signor Luongo, the head waiter?"

"The tall one, you mean, with the fine head like poor Sandro Salvini's? Yes, certainly I have noticed him; he is a very impressive piece of furniture. Well, what of him?"

"Nothing, Madame, but that he is very desirous that I should marry him."

"Indeed! And you?"

"I could wish for no greater happiness on earth, Madame."

Tradutorri laid a strawberry stem carefully upon her plate.

"Um-m-m, let me see; we have been here just two months and this affair has all come about. You have profited by your stage training, Nanette."

"O, Madame! Have you forgotten last season? We stopped here for six weeks then."

"The same 'gentleman' for two successive seasons? You are very disappointing, Nanette. You have not profited by your opportunities after all."

"Madame is pleased to jest, but I assure her that it is a very serious affair to me."

"O, yes, they all are. *Affaires très sérieux*. That is scarcely an original remark, Nanette. I think I remember having made it once myself."

The look of bitter unbelief that Nanette feared came over Madame's face. Presently, as Nanette said nothing, Tradutorri spoke again.

"So you expect me to believe that this is really a serious matter?"

"No, Madame," said Nanette quietly. "He believes it and I believe. It is not necessary that any one else should."

Madame glanced curiously at the girl's face, and when she spoke again it was in a different tone.

"Very well: I do not see any objection. I need a man. It is not a bad thing to have your own porter in London, and after our London engagement is over we will go directly to Paris. He can take charge of my house there, my present steward is not entirely satisfactory, you know. You can spend the summer together there and doubtless by next season you can endure to be separated from him for a few months. So stop crying and send this statuesque signor to me tomorrow, and I will arrange matters. I want you to be happy, my girl—at least to try."

"Madame is good—too good, as always. I know your great heart. Out of your very compassion you would burden yourself with this man because I fancy him, as you once burdened yourself with me. But that is impossible, Madame. He would never leave New York. He will have his wife to himself or not at all. Very many professional people stay here, not all like Madame, and he has his prejudices. He would never allow me to travel, not even with Madame. He is very firm in these matters."

"O, ho! So he has prejudices against our profession, this *garçon*? Certainly you have contrived to do the usual thing in a very usual manner. You have fallen in with a man who objects to your work."

Tradutorri pushed the tray away from her and lay down laughing a little as she threw her arms over her head.

"You see, Madame, that is where all the trouble comes. For of course I could not leave you."

Tradutorri looked up sharply, almost pleadingly, into Nanette's face.

"Leave me? Good Heavens, no! Of course you can not leave me. Why who could ever learn all the needs of my life as you know them? What I may eat and what I may not, when I may see people and when they will tire me, what costumes I can wear and at what temperature I can have my baths. You know I am as helpless as a child in these matters. Leave me? The possibility has never occurred to me. Why, girl, I have grown fond of you! You have come entirely into my life. You have been my confidante and friend, the only creature I have trusted these last ten years. Leave me? I think it would break my heart. Come, brush out my hair, I will get up. The thing is impossible!"

"So I told him, Madame," said Nanette tragically. "I said to him: 'Had it pleased Heaven to give me a voice I should have given myself wholly to my art, without one reservation, without one regret, as Madame has done. As it is, I am devoted to Madame and her art as long as she has need of me.' Yes, that is what I said."

Tradutorri looked gravely at Nanette's face in the glass. "I am not at all sure that either I or my art are worth it, Nanette."

II

Tradutorri had just returned from her last performance in New York. It had been one of those eventful nights when the audience catches fire and drives a singer to her best, drives her beyond herself until she is greater than she knows or means to be. Now that it was over she was utterly exhausted and the life-force in her was low.

I have said she is the only woman of our generation who sings with the soul rather than the senses, the only one indeed since Malibran, who died of that prodigal expense of spirit. Other singers there are who feel and vent their suffering. Their methods are simple and transparent: they pour out their self-inflicted anguish and when it is over they are merely tired as children are after excitement. But Tradutorri holds back her suffering within herself; she suffers as the flesh and blood women of her century suffer. She is intense without being emotional. She takes this great anguish of hers and lays it in a tomb and rolls a stone before the door and walls it up. You wonder that one woman's heart can hold a grief so great. It is this stifled pain that wrings your heart when you hear her, that gives you the impression of horrible reality. It is this too, of which she is slowly dying now.

See, in all great impersonation there are two stages. One in which the object is the generation of emotional power; to produce from one's own brain a whirlwind that will sweep the commonplaces of the world away from the naked souls of men and women and leave them defenseless and strange to each other. The other is the conservation of all this emotional energy; to bind the whirlwind down within one's straining heart, to feel the tears of many burning in one's eyes and yet not to weep, to hold all these chaotic faces still and silent within one's self until out of this tempest of pain and passion there speaks the still, small voice unto the soul of man. This is the theory of "repression." This is classical art, art exalted, art deified. And of all the mighty artists of her time Tradutorri is the only woman who has given us art like this. And now she is dying of it, they say.

Nanette was undoing Madame's shoes. She had put the mail silently on the writing desk. She had not given it to her before the performance as there was one of those blue letters from Madame's husband, written in an unsteady hand with the postmark of Monte Carlo, which always made Madame weep and were always answered by large drafts. There was also another from Madame's little crippled daughter hidden away in a convent in Italy.

"I will see to my letters presently, Nanette. With me news is generally bad news. I wish to speak with you tonight. We leave New York in two days, and the glances of this signor statuesque of yours is more than I can endure. I feel a veritable *mère Capulet*."

"Has he dared to look impertinently at Madame? I will see that this is stopped."

"You think that you could be really happy with this man, Nanette?"

Nanette was sitting upon the floor with the flowers from Madame's corsage in her lap. She rested her sharp little chin on her hand.

"Is any one really happy, Madame? But this I know, that I could endure to be very unhappy always to be with him." Her saucy little French face grew grave and her lips trembled.

Madame Tradutorri took her hand tenderly.

"Then if you feel like that I have nothing to say. How strange that this should come to you, Nanette; it never has to me. Listen: Your mother and I were friends once when we both sang in the chorus in a miserable little theatre in Naples. She sang quite as well as I then, and she was a handsome girl and her future looked brighter than mine. But somehow in the strange lottery of art I rose and she went under with the wheel. She had youth, beauty, vigor, but was one of the countless thousands who fail. When I found her years afterward, dying in a charity hospital in Paris, I took you from her. You were scarcely ten years old then. If you had sung I should have given you the best instruction; as it was I was only able to save you from that most horrible of fates, the chorus. You have been with me so long. Through all my troubles you were the one person who did not change toward me. You have become indispensable to me, but I am no longer so to you. I have inquired as to the reputation of this signor of yours from the proprietors of the house and I find it excellent. Ah, Nanette, did you really think I could stand between you and happiness? You have been a good girl, Nanette. You have stayed with me when we did not stop at hotels like this one, and when your wages were not paid you for weeks together."

"Madame, it is you who have been good! Always giving and giving to a poor girl like me with no voice at all. You know that I would not leave you for anything in the world but this."

"Are you sure you can be happy so? Think what it means! No more music, no more great personages, no more plunges from winter to summer in a single night, no more Russia, no more Paris, no more Italy. Just a little house somewhere in a strange country with a man who may have faults of his own, and perhaps little children growing up about you to be cared for always. You have been used to changes and money and excitement, and those habits of life are hard to change, my girl."

"Madame, you know how it is. One sees much and stops at the best hotels, and goes to the best milliners—and yet one is not happy, but a stranger always. That is, I mean—"

"Yes, I know too well what you mean. Don't spoil it now you have said it. And yet one is not happy! You will not be lonely, you think, all alone in this big strange city, so far from our world?"

"Alone! Why, Madame, Arturo is here!"

Tradutorri looked wistfully at her shining face.

"How strange that this should come to you, Nanette. Be very happy in it, dear. Let nothing come between you and it; no desire, no ambition. It is not given to every one. There are women who wear crowns who would give them for an hour of it."

"O, Madame, if I could but see you happy before I leave you!"

"Hush, we will not speak of that. When the flowers thrown me in my youth shall live again, or when the dead crater of my own mountain shall be red once more—then, perhaps. Now go and tell your lover that the dragon has renounced her prey."

"Madame, I rebel against this loveless life of yours! You should be happy. Surely with so much else you should at least have that."

Tradutorri pulled up from her dressing case the score of the last great opera written in Europe which had been sent her to originate the title role.

"You see this, Nanette? When I began life, between me and this lay everything dear in life—every love, every human hope. I have had to bury what lay between. It is the same thing florists do when they cut away all the buds that one flower may blossom with the strength of all. God is a very merciless artist, and when he works out his purposes in the flesh his chisel does not falter. But no more of this, my child. Go find your lover. I shall undress alone tonight. I must get used to it. Good night, my dear. You are the last of them all, the last of all who have brought warmth into my life. You must let me kiss you tonight. No, not that way—on the lips. Such a happy face tonight, Nanette! May it be so always!"

After Nanette was gone Madame put her head down on her dressing case and wept, those lonely tears of utter wretchedness that a homesick girl sheds at school. And yet upon her brow shone the coronet that the nations had given her when they called her queen.

First published in Lincoln *Courier*, XII (July 31, 1897), 11–12.

The Prodigies

✳ ✳ ✳

"I am ready at last, Nelson. Have I kept you very long?" asked Mrs Nelson Mackenzie as she came hurriedly down the stairs. "I'm sorry, but I just had one misfortune after another in dressing."

"You don't look it," replied her husband, as he glanced up at her admiringly.

"Do you like it? O, thank you! I am never quite sure about this shade of green, it's so treacherous. I have had such a time. The children would not stay in the nursery and poor Elsie has lost her 'Alice in Wonderland' and wails without ceasing because nurse cannot repeat 'The Walrus and the Carpenter' off hand."

"I should think every one about this house could do that. I know the whole fool book like the catechism," said Mackenzie as he drew on his coat.

"Is the carriage there?"

Mackenzie didn't answer. He knew that Harriet knew perfectly well that the carriage had been waiting for half an hour.

"I hope we shan't be late," remarked Harriet as they drove away. "But it's just like Kate to select the most difficult hour in the day and recognize no obstacles to our appearing. She admits of no obstacles either for herself or other people. You've never met her except formally, have you? We saw a great deal of each other years ago. I took a few vocal lessons from her father and was for a time the object of her superabundant enthusiasm. If there is anything in the world that has not at some time been its object I don't know it. One must always take her with a grain of allowance. But even her characteristic impracticability does not excuse her for inviting busy people at four o'clock in the afternoon."

"I suppose it's the only hour at which the prodigies exhibit."

"Now don't speak disrespectfully, Nelson. They really are very wonderful children. I fancy Kate is working them to death, that's her way. But I don't think I ever heard two young voices of such promise. They

sang at Christ Church that Sunday you didn't go, and I was quite overcome with astonishment. They have had the best instruction. It's wonderful to think of mere children having such method. As a rule juvenile
exhibitions merely appeal to the maternal element in one, but when I
heard them I quite forgot that they were children. I assure you they quite
deserve to be taken seriously."

"All the same I shouldn't like to be exhibiting my children about like
freaks."

"Poor Nelson! there's not much danger of your ever being tempted.
It's extremely unlikely that poor Billy or Elsie will ever startle the world.
Really, do you know when I heard those Massey children and thought
of all they have done, of all they may do, I envied them myself? To youth
everything is possible—when anything at all is possible."

Harriet sighed and Mackenzie fancied he detected a note of disappointment in her voice. He had suspected before that Harriet was
disappointed in her children. They suited him well enough, but Harriet
was different.

If Harriet Norton had taken up missionary work in the Cannibal
Islands her friends could not have been more surprised than when she
married Nelson Mackenzie. They had slated her for a very different
career. As a girl she had possessed unusual talent. After taking sundry
honors at the New England Conservatory, she had studied music abroad.
It had been rumored that Leschetizky was about to launch her on a
concert tour as a piano virtuoso, when she had suddenly returned to
America and married the one among all her admirers who seemed particularly unsuited to her. Mackenzie was a young physician, a thoroughly
practical, methodical Scotchman, rather stout, with a tendency to bald-
ness, and with a propensity for playing the cornet. This latter fact alone
was certainly enough to disqualify him for becoming the husband of a
pianiste. When it reached Leschetizky's ears that Miss Norton had married
a cornet-playing doctor, he "recorded one lost soul more," and her name
never passed his lips again. Even her former rivals felt that they could
now afford to be generous, and with one accord sent their congratulations
to herself and husband "whom they had heard was also a musician."

Harriet received these neat sarcasms with great amusement. She had
known when she married him that Mackenzie played the cornet, that he
even played "Promise Me"; but she considered it one of the most
innocent diversions in which a married man could indulge. But Harriet

had not married him to inaugurate a romance or to develop one. She had seen romances enough abroad and knew by heart that fatal fifth act of marriages between artists. She was sometimes glad that there was not a romantic fiber in Mackenzie's substantial frame. She had married him because for some inexplicable reason she had always been fond of him, and since her marriage she had never been disappointed or disillusioned in him. He was not a brilliant man, and his chief merits were those of character—virtues not always fascinating, but they wear well in a husband and are generally about the safest things to be married to.

So, in Mackenzie's phraseology, they had "pulled well enough together." Of course Mrs. Mackenzie had her moments of rebellion against the monotony of the domestic routine, and felt occasional stirrings of the old restlessness for achievement and the old thirst of the spirit. But knowing to what unspiritual things this soul-thirst had led women aforetime, she resolved to live the common life at least commonly well.

But her married life had held one very bitter disappointment, her children. Someway she had never doubted that her children would be like her. She had settled upon innumerable artistic careers for them. Of course they would both have her talent for music, probably talent of a much finer sort than her own, and the boy would do all the great things that she had not done. She knew well enough that if the cruelly exacting life of art is not wholly denied a woman, it is offered to her at a terrible price. She had not chosen to pay it. But with the boy it would be different. He should realize all the dreams that once stirred in the breast on which he slept.

She had awaited impatiently the time when his little fingers were strong enough to strike the keys. But although he had heard music from the time he could hear at all, the child displayed neither interest nor aptitude for it. In vain his papa tooted familiar airs to him on the cornet; sometimes he recognized them and sometimes he did not. It was just the same with the little girl. The poor child could never sing the simplest nursery air correctly. They were both healthy, lively children, unusually truthful and well conducted, but thoroughly commonplace. Harriet could not resign herself to this, she could not understand it. There was always a note of envy in her voice when she spoke of the wonderful Massey children, whose names were on every one's lips. It seemed just as though Kate Massey had got what she should have had herself.

When the Mackenzies arrived at the Masseys' door Mrs. Massey rushed past the servant and met them herself.

"I'm so glad you've come, Harriet, dear. We were just about to begin and I didn't want you to miss Adrienne's first number. It's the waltz song from *Romeo et Juliette*; she had special drill on that from Madame Marchesi you know, and in London they considered it one of her best. I know this is a difficult hour, but they have to sing again after dinner and I don't want to tax them too much. Poor dears! there are so many demands on their time and strength that I sometimes feel like fleeing to the North Pole with them. To the left, upstairs, Mr. Mackenzie. Harriet, you know the way." And their animated hostess dashed off in search of more worlds to conquer. Mrs. Massey's manner was always that of a conqueror fresh from the fray. She demanded of every one absolute capitulation and absolute surrender to the object of her particular enthusiasm, whatever that happened to be at the moment. Usually it was her wonderful children.

When the Mackenzies descended, Kate met them with a warning gesture and ushered them into the music room where the other guests were seated silently and expectantly. When they were seated she herself sank into a chair with an air of rapt and breathless anticipation.

The accompanist took her seat and a very pale, languid little girl came forward and stood beside the piano. She looked to be about fourteen but was unusually small for her age. She was a singularly frail child with apparently almost no physical reserve power, and stood with a slight natural stoop which she quickly corrected as she caught her mother's eye. Her great dark eyes seemed even larger than they were by reason of the dark circles under them. She clasped her little hands and waited until the brief prelude was over. She seemed not at all nervous, but very weary. Even the spirited measures of that most vivacious of arias could not wholly dispel the listlessness from those eyes that were so sad for a child's face. As to the merit or even the "wonder" of her singing, there was no doubt. Even the unmusical Mackenzie, who could not have described her voice in technical language, knew that this voice was marvellous from the throat of a child. The volume of a mature singer was of course not there, but her tones were pure and limpid and wonderfully correct. The thing that most surprised him was what his wife had called the "method" of the child's singing. Gounod's waltz aria is not an easy one, and the child must have been perfectly taught. It seemed to him, though, that the little dash of gaiety she threw into it had been taught her, too, and that this child herself had never known what it was to be gay.

"O Kate, how I envy you!" sighed Harriet in a burst of admiration too sincere to be concealed.

Her hostess smiled triumphantly; she expected every one to envy her, took that for granted. As Mackenzie saw the little figure glide between the portieres, he was not quite so sure that he envied Massey.

Massey was a practical man of business like himself, who seemed rather overcome by the surprising talent of his children. He always stood a little apart from the musical circle which surrounded them, even in his own house, and when his wife took them abroad for instruction he stayed at home and supplied the funds. His natural reserve grew more marked as the years went by, and he seemed so obliterated even at his own fireside that Mackenzie sometimes fancied he regretted having given prodigies to the world.

Mrs. Massey turned to Harriet in an excited whisper: "Hermann will only sing the 'Serenade.' He selected that because it saves his voice. The duet they will sing after dinner is very trying, it's the parting scene from *Juliette*, the one they will sing in concert next week."

The boy was the elder of the two; and not so thin as his sister perhaps, but still pitifully fragile, with an unusually large head, all forehead, and those same dark, tired eyes. He sang the German words of that matchless serenade of Schubert's, so familiar, yet so perennially new and strange; so old, yet so immortally young. It was a voice like those one sometimes hears in the boy choirs of the great cathedrals of the Old World, a voice that, untrained, would have been alto rather than tenor; clear, sweet, and vibrant, with an indefinable echo of melancholy. He was less limited by his physique than his sister, and it seemed impossible that such strong, sustained tones could come from that fragile body. Although he sang so feelingly there was no fervor, rather a yearning, joyless and hopeless. It was a serenade to which no lattice would open, which expected no answer. It was as though this boy of fifteen were tired of the very name of love, and sang of a lost dream, inexpressibly sweet. He, at least, had not been taught that strange unboyish sadness, thought Mackenzie.

When the last vibrant note had died away the boy bowed, and, coughing slightly, crossed the room and stood by his father.

Every one rose and crowded about the hostess, whose enthusiasm burst forth afresh. By her side stood her father, a placid old gentleman who was thoroughly satisfied with himself, his daughter and his grandchildren. He had once been a vocal teacher himself, and it was he who accompanied his daughter and her prodigies on their trips abroad. The father and boy stood apart.

"Yes," Kate was replying to the comments of her friends, "Yes, it has always been so. When I would sing them to sleep when they were little things, just learning to talk, Hermann would take up the contralto with me and little Adrienne would form the soprano for herself. Of course it comes from my side of the house. Papa might have been a great baritone had he not devoted himself to teaching. They have never heard anything but good music. They had a nurse who used to sing Sunday school songs and street airs, and when Hermann was a little fellow of five he came to me one day and said: 'Mamma, I don't like to ask you to send Annie away, but please ask her not to sing to us, she sings such dreadful things!' We took them to Dr. Harrison's church one day and the soloist sang an aria from the Messiah. After that I had no rest; all day long it was, 'Mamma, sing Man a' Sorrows'—it was before they could talk plainly. They would do anything for me if I would only sing 'In questa tomba' for them." Here she turned to her father, who was slightly deaf, and raising her voice said, "I was telling them about 'In questa tomba,' father."

The old gentleman smiled serenely and nodded.

Mackenzie heard his wife say, "But Kate, it seems almost impossible that they should have cared for such music so young."

Mrs. Massey caught up the conversation with renewed energy.

"That's just what I once said to Madame Marchesi in Paris, my dear. I said, 'These children seem impossible to me, I cannot think they are my own.' 'Madame,' she replied, 'genius is just that: the impossible.' Of course, Harriet, that's Madame Marchesi; I don't claim genius for them, I'm afraid of the very word. It means such responsibility. You must not think I am too vain. Of course I speak quite freely today because only my intimate friends are present."

Mackenzie glanced apprehensively at the boy who must be hearing all this. But he did not seem to hear; he still stood holding his father's hand and looking out of the window. By this time Mackenzie had edged his way until he stood quite near the hostess, and he was thinking of something nice to say. He could say nice things sometimes, but he always had to think for them. He knew that on this occasion his speech must be sufficiently appreciative. He took his hostess' hand warmly and said in a low tone for her ear alone:

"I should think you would feel blessed among women, Mrs. Massey."

Kate beamed upon him and then turned to her father and shouted, "He says he should think I'd feel blessed among women, father."

The old gentleman smiled serenely his superior smile, his daughter's smile. Poor Mackenzie blushed violently at hearing his bit of soulful rhetoric shouted to the world and retreated. His wife smiled slyly at him. She knew Kate better than he. Kate was always beside herself; she could never be unemotional for an instant. She dined, dressed, talked, shopped, called, all at high pressure. Harriet could never imagine her passive even in sleep. She was always at white heat. Her enthusiasm was a Niagara and its supply seemed exhaustless. She threw herself and her whole self into everything, at everything, as an exhibition modeller throws his clay at his easel.

"I should think with the two of them your responsibility would be a grave one," ventured one robust old gentleman whose knowledge of music was limited, and who confined his remarks to safe generalities.

"That's just it, there are two of them! You would think that one would be care and responsibility enough. But there are two, think of it! Madame Marchesi used to say, 'A little Patti and Campanini': And I would reply, 'And only one poor commonplace mortal mother to look after them.' As I say, when I hear them sing I don't feel as if they belong to me at all. I can't comprehend why I should be selected from among all other women for such a unique position."

Mackenzie cast a look of amazed inquiry at his wife. She laughed and whispered, "O, Kate's always like this when she's excited, and she's generally excited."

The little girl had slipped quietly in and now the guests were shaking hands with the children and making them compliments. They received them with quiet indifference, only smiling when courtesy seemed to require it.

"Now Adrienne, get the handkerchief case the Princess of Wales made for you herself and show it to the ladies."

"I think they are all there on the mantel, mamma," replied the child quietly.

"So they are. And here, Mr. Mackenzie, is Jean de Reszke's photograph that he gave Adrienne with the inscription, 'To the Juliette of the future from an old Romeo.' Prettily worded, isn't it? And here is the jewelled miniature of Malibran that the Duke of Orleans gave her, and the opera glasses from Madame Marchesi. And there is the portrait of her husband that Frau Cosima Wagner gave Hermann. Of course he doesn't sing Wagnerian music yet, but ça ira, ça ira, as Madame used to say."

After examining trinkets enough to stock a small museum, Mackenzie said quietly:

"Aren't you just a little afraid of all this notoriety for them at their age? It seems as if there will be nothing left for them later."

He saw at once that he had touched a delicate subject and she threw herself on the defensive. "No, Mr. Mackenzie, I am afraid of nothing that will spur them to their work or make them feel the importance and weight of their art. Remember the age at which Patti began."

Mackenzie glanced at the two frail figures and ventured further. "That's just it, the weight of it. Their shoulders are young to bear it all, I'm thinking. Aren't you sometimes afraid it will exhaust them physically?"

"O, they are never ill, and," with her superior smile, "in their art one cannot begin too soon. It is the work of a lifetime, you know, a life-long consecration. I do not feel that I have any right to curb them or to stop the flight of Pegasus. You see they are beyond me; I can only follow and help them as I may."

Mackenzie turned wearily away. He was thinking of the mother in a certain novel of Daudet's who refused to risk her son's life for a throne. Mrs. Massey shot across the room to show the rotund gentleman those trophies which were perhaps given so lightly, but were in her eyes precious beyond price.

Mackenzie saw the children slip through the portieres into the library and determined to follow them and discover whether these strange little beings were fay or human. They were standing by the big window watching a group of children who were playing in the snow outside.

"Say, Ad," said the boy, "do you suppose mamma would let us go out there and snowball for a while? Suppose you ask her."

"It would be no use to ask, Hermann. We should both be in wretched voice this evening. Besides, you know mamma considers those Hamilton children very common. They do have awfully good times though. Perhaps that's why they are so common. Most people seem to be who have a good time."

"I suppose so. We never get to do anything nice. John Hamilton has a new pair of skates and goes down on the ice in the park every day. I think I might learn to skate, anyhow."

"But you'd never get time to skate if you did learn. We haven't time to keep up our Italian, even. I'm forgetting mine."

"O bother our Italian! Ad, I'm just sick of it all. Sometimes I think I'll run away. But I'd practice forever if she'd just let us go tomorrow night. Do you suppose she would?"

"I'm awfully afraid not. You know at the beginning of the season she said we must hear that opera. I'll tell you; I'll go to the opera if she'll let you go to see them."

"No you won't either! You want to see them just as much as I do. I think we might go! We never get to do anything we want to." He struck the window casing impatiently with his clenched hand.

"What's the matter, children?" said Mackenzie, feeling that he was overhearing too much.

"O we're talking secrets, sir. We didn't know there was any one in here."

"Well, I'm not any one much, but just an old fellow who likes little folks. Come over here on the divan and talk to me."

They followed him passively, like children who were accustomed to doing what they were told. He sat down and took the little girl on his knee and put his arm around the boy. He felt so sorry for them, these poor little prodigies who seemed so tired out with life.

"Now I want you to come over and visit my little folks some day and see Billy's goats."

"Are your children musical?" asked the girl.

Mackenzie felt rather abashed. "No, they're not. But they are very nice children, at least I think so."

"Then what could we talk about?"

"O, about lots of things! What do young folks usually talk about? They have a great many books. Do you like to read?"

"Yes, pretty well, but we don't often have time. What do your children read?"

"Well, they like rather old-fashioned books: *Robinson Crusoe* and *The Swiss Family Robinson* and *Pilgrim's Progress*. Do you like *Pilgrim's Progress*?"

"We never read it, did we Hermann?"

The boy shook his head.

"Never read it? then you must before you are a year older. It's a great old book; full of fights and adventures, you know."

"We have read the legends of the Holy Grail and Frau Cosima Wagner gave us a book of the legends of the Nibelung Trilogy. We liked that. It was full of fights and things. I suppose I will have to sing all that music some day; there is a great deal of it, you know," said the boy apprehensively.

"You work very hard, don't you?"

"O yes, very hard. You see there is so much to do," he replied feverishly.

"Plenty of time, my lad, plenty of time. Of course you play and take plenty of exercise to make you strong?"

"We have a gymnasium and exercise there. I fence half an hour every morning. I will need to know how some day, when I sing *Faust* and parts like that."

"And what do you do, Miss? Do you take good care of your dolls?"

"I haven't any now. I used to have a dear one, but one day when we were driving in from Fontainebleau I left her in the carriage. We advertised for her, but we never found her and I never wanted another."

"Ad cared so much for that one, you see," explained the boy. "Next day when we were taking our lesson she felt so badly about it she cried, and Madame asked what was the matter and said, 'Never mind, *ma chère*, wait a little and you will have dolls enough. Girls who sing like you never lack for toys in this world. I taught the beautiful Sybil,* and behold what toys she has!' I have often wondered what she meant. But it was often very difficult to tell just what Madame meant. Sometimes I used to think she was making fun of us."

Mackenzie looked at the boy sharply and veered into safer waters.

"Aren't you glad to be home again?"

"Yes, but of course we are better abroad. There's no artistic atmosphere over here. I think we go back to Paris in the spring, or London, maybe."

"You go to the opera often, don't you?"

"Yes," replied the little girl, "we are going to the *Damnation of Faust* tomorrow night—that is if we don't go somewhere else."

"Now Ad, don't you tell secrets," said her brother sternly.

"Well, I thought we might just tell him. Perhaps he'd coax her for us."

"You'll not laugh at us and you'll not tell?"

"On my honor," said Mackenzie.

"You see," explained Hermann, "we want to see the dog show tomorrow night. We've never been to one and I think we might. The Hamilton children go every night and they say there are just hundreds of dogs."

"And why can't you, pray?"

"Well, you see it's the only time they will sing Berlioz's *Damnation of Faust* here this season, and we ought to hear it. Then mamma don't like us to go to such things."

Mackenzie set his teeth. "Now I'll just tell you; my children are going to the dog show and you shall go with them. I'll fix it up with your

* Sybil Sanderson (1864–1903), American-born opera star.

mother. And what's more I'll send you over one of our Skye terrier pups. Even singers are permitted to have dogs, aren't they? At least they are always losing them. You go and ask your mother if you may keep the pup, my son."

As the boy shot off the little girl nestled closer to him. "I'm so awfully glad! Hermann has just been wild to go. And perhaps we'll see the Hamilton children. You see mamma doesn't like the Hamilton children very well. They wear lots of jewels and are not always careful about their grammar, but they do have good times. Sometimes Hermann and I play we are the Hamilton children; and he pretends he has been off skating and tells me what he saw, and I pretend I've been to school and making fancy work like Mollie Hamilton. That's a very secret play and we only play it when we're alone."

So these poor little prodigies loved to play that they were just the common children of the "new rich" next door! Mackenzie took the little hand that a single ruby made look so bloodless and his eyes were very tender.

"Why, my child, how hot your hands are, and your cheeks are all flushed. Your pulse is going like a triphammer. Are you ill?"

"O no, I'm just tired. We've been working very hard for our big concert next week. That's a very important concert, you know. But there, they are all going out to dinner, and you are to take mamma out, I think. Goodbye."

"But aren't you coming too?"

"O no! We sing later, so of course we can't dine now."

"O no, of course you can't dine!" said Mackenzie.

After dinner the more formal guests arrived and the party again assembled in the music room.

"They are going to sing the parting scene from *Juliette*, those babies! Why will Kate select such music for them? The effect will be little short of grotesque. But then it's just like Kate, she never admits of distinctions or conditions," whispered Mrs. Mackenzie to her husband. "Here they come. O Nelson, that boy Romeo and his baby Juliet, it's sacrilege!"

They quietly took their places, "the boy Romeo and his baby Juliet," looking earnestly at each other, and began that frenzied song of pain and parting: "*Tu die partir ohime!*" Poor little children! What could they know of the immeasurable anguish of that farewell—or of the immeasurable joy which alone can make such sorrow possible? What could they know of the fearful potency of the words they uttered—words that have governed nations and wrecked empires! They sang bravely enough, but the effect was that of trying to force the tones of a 'cello from a violin.

Suddenly a quick paleness came over the face of the little Juliet. Still struggling with the score she threw out her hand and caught her Romeo's shoulder, swaying like a flower before the breath of a hurricane.

"Ad, Ad!" shrieked the boy as he sank upon one knee with his sister in his arms.

There was wild confusion among the guests; the men threw open the doors and struggled with the windows. Mackenzie sprang to the child's side but her mother was there before him, whiter than the little Juliet herself.

"Doctor, what does it mean? She has never done like this before, she is never ill."

As she bent over the child her husband thrust her back, lifting the little girl in his arms.

"Let me take her now—you have done enough!" he said sternly, with an ominous flash in his eyes. It was the only time he was ever heard to issue a command in his own household.

"O Nelson, it is terrible!" said Mrs. Mackenzie as they drove home that night. "Kate Massey must be mad. Poor little girl! And the boy— why I wouldn't have that haunted look in Billy's eyes for the world!"

"Not even to make a tenor of him?" asked Mackenzie.

A month later Mackenzie stood again in the Masseys' music room with Kate beside him. The woman was so pale and broken that he could almost find it in his heart to be sorry for her.

"I don't think I need come again now, Mrs. Massey, unless there is a relapse."

"And you still think, Doctor, that there is no hope at all? For her voice, I mean?"

"The best specialists in New York agree with me in that. Your foreign teachers have not been content with duping you out of your money, they have simply drained your child's life out of her veins," said Mackenzie brutally.

There was a ghost of the old superior smile. "Doctor, you forget yourself. Whatever you American physicians may say, I know that the child was properly taught. This has broken my heart, but it has not convinced me that I am in error. I have said I could make any sacrifice for their art, but God knows I never thought it would be this!"

The little boy entered the room with a roll of music under his arm. His mother caught him to her impulsively.

"Ah, my boy, you must travel your way alone now. I suppose the day must have come when one of you must have suffered for the other. Two of the same blood can never achieve equally. Perhaps it is best that it should come now. But remember, my son, you carry not one destiny in your throat, but two. You must be great enough for both!"

The boy kissed her and said gently, "Don't cry, mother. I will try."

His mother hid her face on his shoulder and he turned to the Doctor, who was drawing on his gloves, and shrugging his frail shoulders smiled. It was the smile which might have touched the face of some Roman youth on the bloody sand, when the reversed thumb of the Empress pointed deathward.

First published in *Home Monthly*, VI (July, 1897), 9-11.

A Resurrection

❋   ❋   ❋

"I contend that you ought to have set them house plants different, Margie, closer around the pulpit rail." Mrs. Skimmons retreated to the back of the church to take in the full effect of the decorations and give further directions to Margie. Mrs. Skimmons had a way of confining her services as chairman of the decorative committee to giving directions, and the benefit of her artistic eye.

Miss Margie good naturedly readjusted the "house plants" and asked, "How is that?"

"Well, it's some better," admitted Mrs. Skimmons, critically, "but I contend we ought to have had some evergreens, even if they do look like Christmas. And now that you've used them hy'cinths for the lamp brackets, what are you goin' to put on the little stand before the pulpit?"

"Martin Dempster promised to bring some Easter lilies up from Kansas City. I thought we'd put them there. He ought to be here pretty soon. I heard the train whistle in a bit ago."

"That's three times he's been to Kansas City this month. I don't see how he can afford it. Everybody knows the old ferry boat can't pay him very well, and he wasn't never much of a business man. It beats me how some people can fly high on nothing. There's his railroad fare and his expenses while he is there. I can't make out what he's doin' down there so much. More'n likely it's some girl or other he's goin' down the river after agin. Now that you and your mother have brought up his baby for him, it would be just like Mart Dempster to go trapesin' off and marry some giddy thing and maybe fetch her up here for you to bring up, too. I can't never think he's acted right by you, Margie."

"So long as I'm satisfied, I can't see why it should trouble other people, Mrs. Skimmons."

"O, certainly not, if you are goin' to take offense. I meant well."

Margie turned her face away to avoid Mrs. Skimmons' scrutinizing gaze, and went on quietly with the decorations.

Miss Margie was no longer a girl. Most of the girls of her set who had frolicked and gone to school with her had married and moved away. Yet, though she had passed that dread meridian of thirty, and was the village schoolmistress to boot, she was not openly spoken of as an old maid. When a woman retains much of her beauty and youthful vigor the world, even the petty provincial world, feels a delicacy about applying to her that condemning title that when once adopted is so irrevocable. Then Miss Marjorie Pierson had belonged to one of the best families in the old days, before Brownville was shorn of its glory and importance by the railroad maneuvers that had left everybody poor. She had not always taught towheaded urchins for a living, but had once lived in a big house on the hill and gone to boarding school and driven her own phaeton, and entertained company from Omaha. These facts protected her somewhat.

She was a tall woman, finely, almost powerfully built and admirably developed. She carried herself with an erect pride that ill accorded with the humble position as the village schoolmistress. Her features were regular and well cut, but her face was comely chiefly because of her vivid coloring and her deeply set gray eyes, that were serious and frank like a man's. She was one of those women one sometimes sees, designed by nature in her more artistic moments, especially fashioned for all the fullness of life; for large experiences and the great world where a commanding personality is felt and valued, but condemned by circumstances to poverty, obscurity and all manner of pettiness. There are plenty of such women, who were made to ride in carriages and wear jewels and grace first nights at the opera, who, through some unaccountable blunder of stage management in this little *comédie humaine*, have the wrong parts assigned them, and cook for farm hands, or teach a country school like this one, or make gowns for ugly women and pad them into some semblance of shapeliness, while they themselves, who need no such artificial treatment, wear cast-offs; women who were made to rule, but who are doomed to serve. There are plenty of living masterpieces that are as completely lost to the world as the lost nine books of Sappho, or as the Grecian marbles that were broken under the barbarians' battle axes. The world is full of waste of this sort.

While Margie was arranging the "house plants" about the pulpit platform, and the other member of the committee was giving her the benefit of her advice, a man strode lazily into the church carrying a small traveling bag and a large pasteboard box.

"There you are, Miss Margie," he cried, throwing the box on the platform; and sitting down in the front pew he proceeded to fan himself with his soft felt hat.

"O, Martin, they are beautiful! They are the first things that have made me feel a bit like Easter."

"One of 'em is for you, Miss Margie, to wear tomorrow," said Martin bashfully. Then he hastened to add, "I feel more like it's Fourth of July than Easter. I'm right afraid of this weather, Mrs. Skimmons. It'll coax all the buds out on the fruit trees and then turn cold and nip 'em. And the buds'll just be silly enough to come out when they are asked. You've done well with your decorations, Mrs. Skimmons."

Mrs. Skimmons looked quizzically at Martin, puzzled by this unusual loquaciousness.

"Well, yes," she admitted, in a satisfied tone, "I think we've done right well considerin' this tryin' weather. I'm about prostrated with the heat myself. How are things goin' down in Kansas City? You must know a good deal about everything there, seein' you go down so much lately."

"'Bout the same," replied Martin, in an uncommunicative tone which evidently offended Mrs. Skimmons.

"Well," remarked that lady briskly, "I guess I can't help you no more now, Margie. I've got to run home and see to them boys of mine. Mr. Dempster can probably help you finish." With this contemptuous use of his surname as a final thrust, Mrs. Skimmons departed.

Martin leaned back in the pew and watched Margie arranging the lilies. He was a big broad-chested fellow, who wore his broad shoulders carelessly and whose full muscular throat betrayed unusual physical strength. His face was simple and honest, bronzed by the weather, and with deep lines about the mild eyes that told that his simple life had not been altogether negative, and that he had not sojourned in this world for forty years without leaving a good deal of himself by the wayside.

"I didn't thank you for the lilies, Martin. It was very kind of you," said Margie, breaking the silence.

"O, that's all right. I just thought you'd like 'em," and he again relapsed into silence, his eyes following the sunny path of the first venturesome flies of the season that buzzed in and out of the open windows. Then his gaze strayed back to where the sunlight fell on Miss Margie and her lilies.

"The fact is, Miss Margie, I've got something to tell you. You know for a long time I've thought I'd like to quit the ferry and get somewhere where I'd have a chance to get ahead. There's no use trying to get ahead in Brownville, for there's nothing to get ahead of. Of late years I wanted to get a job on the lower Mississippi again, on a boat, you know. I've been going down to Kansas City lately to see some gentlemen who own boats down the river, and I've got a place at last, a first rate one that will pay well, and it looks like I could hold it as long as I want it."

Miss Margie looked up from the lilies she was holding and asked sharply, "Then you are going away, Martin?"

"Yes, and I'm going away this time so you won't never have to be ashamed of me for it."

"I ought to be glad on your account. You're right, there's nothing here for you, nor anybody else. But we'll miss you very much, Martin. There are so few of the old crowd left. Will you sell the ferry?"

"I don't just know about that. I'd kind of hate to sell the old ferry. You see I haven't got things planned out very clear yet. After all it's just the going away that matters most."

"Yes, it's just the going away that matters most," repeated Miss Margie slowly, while she watched something out of the window. "But of course you'll have to come back often to see Bobbie."

"Well, you see I was counting on taking Bobbie with me. He's about old enough now, and I don't think I could bear to be apart from him."

"You are not going to take Bobbie away from us, Martin?" cried Miss Margie in a tone of alarm.

"Why yes, Miss Margie. Of course I'll take him, and if you say so—"

"But I don't say so," cried Miss Margie in a tone of tremulous excitement. "He is not old enough, it would be cruel to take a bit of a child knocking around the world like that."

"I can't go without Bobbie. But, Miss Margie—"

"Martin," cried Miss Margie—she had risen to her feet now and stood facing him, her eyes full of gathering anger and her breast rising and falling perceptibly with her quick-drawn breathing—"Martin, you shall not take Bobbie away from me. He's more my child than yours, anyway. I've been through everything for him. When he was sick I walked the floor with him all night many a time and went with a headache to my work next morning. I've lived and worked and hoped just for him. And I've done it in the face of everything. Not a day passes but some old woman throws it in my face that I'm staying here drivelling my life out to take care of the child of the man who jilted me. I've borne all this because I loved him, because he is all my niggardly life has given me to love. My God! a woman must have something. Every woman's got to have. And I've given him everything, all that I'd starved and beat down and crucified in me. You brought him to me when he was a little wee baby, the only thing of your life you've ever given to mine. From the first time I felt his little cheek on mine I knew that a new life had come into me, and through another woman's weakness and selfishness I had at least one of the things which was mine by right. He was a helpless little baby, dependent on me for everything, and I loved him for just that. He needed my youth and strength and blood, and the very warmth of my body, and he was the only creature on earth who did. In spite of yourself you've given me half my womanhood and you shall not take it from me now. You shall not take it from me now!"

Martin heard her going, he heard the sob that broke as she reached the door but he did not stir from his seat or lift his bowed head. He sat staring at the sunlit spot in front of the pulpit where she had stood with the lilies in her hand, looking to him, somehow, despite her anger, like the pictures of the Holy woman who is always painted with lilies.

When the twilight began to fall and the shadows in the church grew dim he got up and went slowly down to the river toward the ferry boat. Back over the horseshoe-shaped gulch in which the town is built the sky was glorious with red splotches of sunset cloud just above the horizon. The big trees on the bluffs were tossing their arms restlessly in the breeze that blew up the river, and across on the level plains of the Missouri side the lights of the farm houses began to glow through the soft humid atmosphere of the April night. The smell of burning grass was everywhere, and the very air tasted of spring.

The boat hands had all gone to supper, and Martin sat down on the empty deck and lit his pipe. When he was perplexed or troubled he always went to the river. For the river means everything to Brownville folk; it has been at once their making and their undoing.

Brownville was not always the sleepy, deserted town that it is today, full of empty buildings and idle men and of boys growing up without aim or purpose. No, the town has had a history, a brief, sad little history which recalls the scathing epigram that Herr Heine once applied to M. Alfred de Musset; it is a young town with a brilliant past. It was the first town built on the Nebraska side of the river, and there, sheltered by the rugged bluffs and washed by the restless Missouri, a new state struggled into existence and proclaimed its right to be. Martin Dempster was the first child born on the Nebraska side, and he had seen the earth broken for the first grave. There, in Senator Tipton's big house on the hillside, when he was a very little boy, he had heard the first telegraph wire ever stretched across the Missouri click its first message that made the blood leap in all his boyish veins, "Westward the course of Empire takes it way."★

In the days of his boyhood Brownville was the head of river navigation and the old steamboat trade. He had seen the time when a dozen river steamers used to tie up at the wharves at one time, and unload supplies for the wagon trains that went overland to Pikes Peak and Cherry Creek, that is Denver now. He had sat on the upper veranda of the old Marsh House and listened to the strange talk of the foreign potentates that the *Montana* and *Silver Heels* used to bring up the river and who stopped there on their way into the big game country. He had listened with them to the distant throbbing of the engines that once stirred the lonely sand-split waters of the old river, and watched the steamers swing around the bend at night, glittering with lights, with bands of music playing on their decks and the sparks from the smokestacks blowing back into the darkness. He had sat under the gigantic oak before the Lone Tree saloon and heard the teamsters of the wagon trains and the boat hands exchange stories of the mountains and alkali deserts for stories of the busy world and its doings, filling up the pauses in conversation with old frontier songs and the strumming of banjos. And he could remember only too well when the old *Hannibal* brought up the steel rails for the Union Pacific Railroad, the road that was to kill Brownville.

Brownville had happened because of the steamboat trade, and when the channel of the river had become so uncertain and capricious that navigation was impossible, Brownville became impossible too, and all the prosperity that the river had given it took back in its muddy arms again and swept away. And ever since, overcome by shame and remorse, it had been trying to commit suicide by burying itself in the sand. Every year the channel grows narrower and more treacherous and its waters more turbid. Perhaps it does not even remember any more how it used to hurry along into the great aorta of the continent, or the throb of the wheels of commerce that used to beat up the white foam on its dark waters, or how a certain old Indian chief desired to be buried sitting bolt upright upon the bluff that he might always watch the steamers go up and down the river.

So it was that the tide went out at Brownville, and the village became a little Pompeii buried in bonded indebtedness. The sturdy pioneers moved away and the "river rats" drifted in, a nondescript people who came up

---

★ Thomas W. Tipton was one of the first two United States Senators from Nebraska. Brownville is a real town, not a fictional one, and its history is substantially as given here. The names of the steamboats also are real, not invented.

the river from nowhere, and bought up the big houses for a song, cut down the tall oaks and cedars in the yards for firewood, and plowed up the terraces for potato patches, and were content after the manner of their kind. The river gypsies are a peculiar people; like the Egyptians of old their lives are for and of the river. They each have their skiff and burn driftwood and subsist on catfish and play their banjos, and forget that the world moves—if they ever knew it. The river is the school and religion of these people.

And Martin Dempster was one of them. When most of the better people of the town moved away Martin remained loyal to the river. The feeling of near kinship with the river had always been in him, he was born with it. When he was a little boy he had continually run away from school, and when his father hunted for him he always found him about the river. River boys never take kindly to education; they are always hankering for the water. In summer its muddy coolness is irresistibly alluring, and in winter its frozen surface is equally so. The continual danger which attends its treacherous currents only adds to its enticing charm. They know the river in all its changes and fluctuations as a stock broker knows the markets.

When Martin was a boy his father owned a great deal of Brownville real estate and was considered a wealthy man. Town property was a marketable article in those days, though now no real estate ever sells in Brownville—except cemetery lots. But Martin never cared for business. The first ambition he was ever guilty of was that vague yearning which stirs in the breasts of all river boys, to go down the river sometime, clear down, as far as the river goes. Then, a little later, when he heard an old stump speaker who used to end all his oratorical flights with a figure about "rearing here in the Missouri Valley a monument as high as the thought of man," he had determined to be a great navigator and to bring glory and honor to the town of Brownville. And here he was, running the old ferry boat that was the last and meanest of all the flock of mighty river crafts. So it goes. When we are very little we all dream of driving a street car or wearing a policeman's star or keeping a peanut stand; and generally, after catching at the clouds a few times, we live to accomplish our juvenile ambitions more nearly than we ever realize.

When he was sixteen Martin had run away as cabin boy on the *Silver Heels*. Gradually he had risen to the pilot house on the same boat. People wondered why Marjorie Pierson should care for a fellow of that stamp, but the fact that she did care was no secret. Perhaps it was just because he was simple and unworldly and lived for what he liked best that she cared.

Martin's downfall dated back to the death of the steamboat trade at Brownville. His fate was curiously linked with that of his river. When the channel became so choked with sand that the steamers quit going up to Brownville, Martin went lower down the river, making his headquarters at St. Louis. And there the misfortune of his life befell him. There was a girl of French extraction, an Aimée de Mar, who lived down in the shipping district. She lived by her wits principally. She was just a wee mite of a thing, with brown hair that fluffed about her face and eyes that were large and soft like those of Guido's penitent Magdalen, and which utterly belied her. You would wonder how so small a person could make so much harm and trouble in the world. Not that she was naturally malignant or evil at all. She simply wanted the nice things of this world and was determined to have them, no matter who paid for them, and she enjoyed life with a frank sort of hedonism, quite regardless of what her pleasure might cost others. Martin was a young man who stood high in favor with the captains and boat owners and who seemed destined to rise. So Aimée concentrated all her energies to one end, and her project was not difficult of accomplishment under the circumstances. A wiser or worse man would have met her on her own ground and managed her easily enough. But Martin was slow at life as he had been at books, heady and loyal and foolish, the kind of man who pays for his follies right here in this world and who keeps his word if he walks alive into hell for it. The upshot of it was that, after writing to Margie the hardest letter he ever wrote in his life, he married Aimée de Mar.

Then followed those three years that had left deep lines in Martin's face and gray hairs over his temples. Once married Aimée did not sing "*Toujours j'aimais!*" any more. She attired herself gorgeously in satins and laces and perfumed herself heavily with *violettes de Parme* and spent her days visiting her old friends of the milliners' and hairdressers' shops and impressing them with her elegance. The evenings she would pass in a box at some second rate theatre, ordering ices brought to her between the acts. When Martin was in town he was dragged willy-nilly through all these absurdly vulgar performances, and when he was away matters went even worse. This would continue until Martin's salary was exhausted, after which Aimée would languish at home in bitter resentment against the way the world is run, and consoling herself with innumerable *cigarettes de Caporale* until pay day. Then she would blossom forth in a new outfit and the same program would be repeated. After running him heavily into debt, by some foolish attempt at a flirtation with a man on board his own boat, she drove Martin into a quarrel which resulted in a fierce hand-to-hand scrimmage on board ship and was the cause of his immediate discharge. In December, while he was hunting work, living from hand to mouth and hiding from his creditors, his baby was born. "As if," Aimée remarked, "the weather were not disagreeable enough without that!"

In the spring, at Mardi-Gras time, Martin happened to be out of town. Aimée was thoroughly weary of domesticity and poverty and of being shut up in the house. She strained her credit for all it was worth for one last time, and on the first night of the fête, though it was bitterly cold, she donned an airy domino and ran away from her baby, and went down the river in a steam launch, hung with colored lights and manned by some gentlemen who were neither sober nor good boatmen. The launch was overturned a mile below the Point, and three of the party went to the bottom. Two days later poor little Aimée was picked up in the river, the yellow and black velvet of her butterfly dress covered with mud and slime, and her gay gauze wings frozen fast to her pretty shoulders.

So Martin spoke the truth when he said that everything that had ever affected his life one way or the other was of the river. To him the river stood for Providence, for fate.

Some of the saddest fables of ancient myth are of the fates of the devotees of the River Gods. And the worship of the River Gods is by no means dead. Martin had been a constant worshipper and a most faithful one, and here he was at forty, not so well off as when he began the world for himself at sixteen. But let no one dream that because the wages of the River God cannot be counted in coin or numbered in herds of cattle, that they are never paid. Its real wages are of the soul alone, and not visible to any man. To all who follow it faithfully, and not for gain but from inclination, the river gives a certain simpleness of life and freshness of feeling and receptiveness of mind not to be found among the money changers of the market place. It feeds his imagination and trains his eye, and gives him strength and courage. And it gives him something better than these, if aught can be better. It gives him, no matter how unlettered he may be, something of that intimate sympathy with inanimate nature that is the base of all poetry, something of that which the high-faced rocks of the gleaming Sicilian shore gave Theocritus.

Martin had come back to Brownville to live down the memory of his disgrace. He might have found a much easier task without going so far. Every day for six years he had met the reproachful eyes of his neighbors unflinchingly, and he knew that his mistake was neither condoned nor forgotten. Brownville people have nothing to do but to keep such memories perennially green. If he had been a coward he would have run away from this perpetual condemnation. But he had the quiet courage of all men who have wrestled hand to hand with the elements, and who have found out how big and terrible nature is. So he stayed.

Miss Margie left the church with a stinging sense of shame at what she had said, and wondered if she were losing her mind. For the women who are cast in that tragic mould are always trying to be like their milder sisters, and are always flattering themselves that they have succeeded. And when some fine day the fire flames out they are more astonished and confounded than anyone else can be. Miss Margie walked rapidly through the dusty road, called by courtesy a street, and crossed the vacant building lots unmindful that her skirts were switching among the stalks of last year's golden rods and sunflowers. As she reached the door a little boy in much abbreviated trousers ran around the house from the back yard and threw his arms about her. She kissed him passionately and felt better. The child seemed to justify her in her own eyes. Then she led him in and began to get supper.

"Don't make my tea as strong as you did last night, Margie. It seems like you ought to know how to make it by this time," said the querulous invalid from the corner.

"All right, mother. Why mother, you worked my buttonholes in black silk instead of blue!"

"How was I to tell, with my eyes so bad? You ought to have laid it out for me. But there is always something wrong about everything I do," complained the old lady in an injured tone.

"No, there isn't, it was all my fault. You can work a better button-hole than I can, any day."

"Well, in my time they used to say so," said Mrs. Pierson somewhat mollified.

Margie was practically burdened with the care of two children. Her mother was crippled with rheumatism, and only at rare intervals could "help about the house." She insisted on doing a little sewing for her daughter, but usually it had to come out and be done over again after she went to bed. With the housework and the monotonous grind of her work at school, Miss Margie had little time to think about her misfortunes, and so perhaps did not feel them as keenly as she would otherwise have done. It was a perplexing matter, too, to meet even the modest expenses of their small household with the salary paid a country teacher. She had never touched a penny of the money Martin paid for the child's board, but put it regularly in the bank for the boy's own use when he should need it.

After supper she put her mother to bed and then put on the red wrapper that she always wore in the evening hour that she had alone with Bobbie. The woman in one dies hard, and after she had ceased to dress for men the old persistent instinct made her wish to be attractive to the boy. She heard him say his "piece" that he was to recite at the Easter service tomorrow, and then sat down in the big rocking chair before the fire and Bobbie climbed up into her lap.

"Bobbie, I want to tell you a secret that we mustn't tell grandma yet. Your father is talking about taking you away."

"Away on the ferry boat?" his eyes glistened with excitement.

"No dear, away down the river; away from grandma and me for good."

"But I won't go away from you and grandma, Miss Margie. Don't you remember how I cried all night the time you were away?"

"Yes, Bobbie, I know, but you must always do what your father says. But you wouldn't like to go, would you?"

"Of course I wouldn't. There wouldn't be anybody to pick up chips, or go to the store, or take care of you and grandma, 'cause I'm the only boy you've got."

"Yes, Bobbie, that's just it, dear heart, you're the only boy I've got!" And Miss Margie gathered him up in her arms and laid her hot cheek on his and fell to sobbing, holding him closer and closer.

Bobbie lay very still, not even complaining about the tears that wetted his face. But he wondered very much why any one should cry who had not cut a finger or been stung by a wasp or trodden on a sand-burr. Poor little Bobbie, he had so much to learn! And while he was wondering he fell asleep, and Miss Margie undressed him and put him to bed.

During the five years since that night when Marjorie Pierson and her mother, in the very face of the village gossips, had gone to the train to meet Martin Dempster when he came back to Brownville, worn and weak with fever, and had taken his wailing little baby from his arms, giving it the first touch of womanly tenderness it had ever known, the two lonely women had grown to love it better than anything else in the world, better even than they loved each other. Marjorie had felt every ambition of her girlhood die out before the strength of the vital instinct which this child awakened and satisfied within her. She had told Martin in the church that afternoon that "a woman must have something." Of women of her kind this is certainly true. You can find them everywhere slaving for and loving other women's children. In this sorry haphazard world such women are often cut off from the natural outlet of what is within them; but they always make one. Sometimes it is an aged relative, sometimes an invalid sister, sometimes a waif from the streets no one else wants, sometimes it is only a dog. But there is something, always.

When the child was in his bed Miss Margie took up a bunch of examination papers and began looking through them. As she worked she heard a slow rapping at the door, a rap she knew well indeed, that had sent the blood to her cheeks one day. Now it only left them white.

She started and hesitated, but as the rap was repeated she rose and went to the door, setting her lips firmly.

"Good evening, Martin, come in," she said quietly. "Bobbie is in bed. I'm sorry."

Martin stood by the door and shook his head at the proffered chair. "I didn't come to see Bobbie, Margie. I came to finish what I began to say this afternoon when you cut me off. I know I'm slow spoken. It's always been like it was at school, when the teacher asked a question I knew as well as I knew my own name, but some other fellow'd get the answer out before me. I started to say this afternoon that if I took Bobbie to St. Louis I couldn't take him alone. There is somebody else I couldn't bear to be apart from, and I guess you've known who that is this many a year."

A painful blush overspread Miss Margie's face and she turned away and rested her arm on the mantel. "It is not like you to take advantage of what I said this afternoon when I was angry. I wouldn't have believed it of you. You have given me pain enough in years gone by without this— this that makes me sick and ashamed."

"Sick and ashamed? Why Margie, you must have known what I've been waiting in Brownville for all these years. Don't tell me I've waited too long. I've done my best to live it down. I haven't bothered you nor pestered you so folks could talk. I've just stayed and stuck it out till I could feel I was worthy. Not that I think I'm worthy now, Margie, but the time has come for me to go and I can't go alone."

He paused, but there was no answer. He took a step nearer. "Why Margie, you don't mean that you haven't known I've been loving you all the time till my heart's near burst in me? Many a night down on the old ferry I've told it over and over again to the river till even it seemed to understand. Why Margie, I've"—the note of fear caught in his throat and his voice broke and he stood looking helplessly at his boots.

Miss Margie still stood leaning on her elbow, her face from him. "You'd better have been telling it to me, Martin," she said bitterly.

"Why Margie, I couldn't till I got my place. I couldn't have married you here and had folks always throwing that other woman in your face."

"But if you had loved me you would have told me, Martin, you couldn't have helped that."

He caught her hand and bent over it, lifting it tenderly to his lips. "O Margie, I was ashamed, bitter ashamed! I couldn't forget that letter I had to write you once. And you might have had a hundred better men than me. I never was good enough for you to think of one minute. I wasn't clever nor ready spoken like you, just a tramp of a river rat who could somehow believe better in God because of you."

Margie felt herself going and made one last desperate stand. "Perhaps you've forgotten all you said in that letter, perhaps you've forgotten the shame it would bring to any woman. Would you like to see it? I have always kept it."

He dropped her hand.

"No, I don't want to see it and I've not forgot. I only know I'd rather have signed my soul away than written it. Maybe you're right and there are things a man can't live down—not in this world. Of course you can keep the boy. As you say he is more yours than mine, a thousand times more. I've never had anything I could call my own. It's always been like this and I ought to be used to it by this time. Some men are made that way. Good night, dear."

"O Martin, don't talk like that, you could have had me any day for the asking. But why didn't you speak before? I'm too old now!" Margie leaned closer to the mantel and the sobs shook her.

He looked at her for a moment in wonder, and, just as she turned to look for him, caught her in his arms. "I've always been slow spoken, Margie—I was ashamed—you were too good for me," he muttered between his kisses.

"Don't Martin, don't! That's all asleep in me and it must not come, it shan't come back! Let me go!" cried Margie breathlessly.

"O I'm not near through yet! I'm just just showing you how young you are—it's the quickest way," came Martin's answer muffled by the trimmings of her gown.

"O Martin, you may be slow spoken, but you're quick enough at some things," laughed Margie as she retreated to the window, struggling hard against the throb of reckless elation that arose in her. She felt as though some great force had been unlocked within her, great and terrible enough to rend her asunder, as when a brake snaps or a band slips and some ponderous machine grinds itself in pieces. It is not an easy thing, after a woman has shut the great natural hope out of her life, to open the flood gates and let the riotous, aching current come throbbing again through the shrunken channels, waking a thousand undreamed-of possibilities of pleasure and pain.

Martin followed her to the window and they stood together leaning against the deep casing while the spring wind blew in their faces, bearing with it the yearning groans of the river.

"We can kind of say goodbye to the old place tonight. We'll be going in a week or two now," he said nervously.

"I've wanted to get away from Brownville all my life, but now I'm someway afraid to think of going."

"How did that piece end we used to read at school, 'My chains and I—' Go on, you always remember such things."

"My very chains and I grew friends,
    So much a long communion tends
      To make us what we are. Even I
        Regained my freedom with a sigh,"

quoted Margie softly.

"Yes, that's it. I'm counting on you taking some singing lessons again when we get down to St. Louis."

"Why I'm too old to take singing lessons now. I'm too old for everything. O Martin, I don't believe we've done right. I'm afraid of all this! It hurts me."

He put his arm about her tenderly and whispered: "Of course it does, darling. Don't you suppose it hurts the old river down there tonight when the spring floods are stirring up the old bottom and tearing a new channel through the sand? Don't you suppose it hurts the trees tonight when the sap is climbing up and up till it breaks through the bark and runs down their sides like blood? Of course it hurts."

"Oh Martin, when you talk like that it don't hurt any more," whispered Margie.

Truly the service of the river has its wages and its recompense, though they are not seen of men. Just then the door opened and Bobby came stumbling sleepily across the floor, trailing his little night gown after him.

"It was so dark in there, and I'm scared of the river when it sounds so loud," he said, hiding his face in Margie's skirts.

Martin lifted him gently in his arms and said, "The water won't hurt you, my lad. My boy must never be afraid of the river."

And as he stood there listening to the angry grumble of the swollen waters, Martin asked their benediction on his happiness. For he knew that a river man may be happy only as the river wills.

First published in *Home Monthly*, VI (April, 1897), 4–8.

The Strategy of the
Were-Wolf Dog

❊ ❊ ❊

This is a tale of the bleak, bitter Northland, where the frost is eternal and
the snows never melt, where the wide white plains stretch for miles and
miles without a tree or shrub, where the Heavens at night are made
terribly beautiful by the trembling flashes of the northern lights, and the
green icebergs float in stately grandeur down the dark currents of the
hungry polar sea. It is a desolate region, where there is no spring, and even
in the short summers only a few stunted willows blossom and grow green
along the rocky channels through which the melting snow water runs
clear and cold. The only cheerful thing about all this country is that far
up within the Arctic circle, just on the edge of the boundless snow plains,
there is a big house of gray stone, where the lights shine all the year round
from the windows, and the wide halls are warmed by blazing fires. For
this is the house of his beloved Saintship, Nicholas, whom the children
the world over call Santa Claus.

Now every child knows this house is beautiful, and beautiful it is,
for it is one of the most home-like places in the world. Just inside the front
door is the big hall, where every evening after his work is done Santa
Claus sits by the roaring fire and chats with his wife, Mamma Santa, and
the White Bear. Then there is the dining room, and the room where
Papa and Mamma Santa sleep, and to the rear are the workshops, where
all the wonderful toys are made, and last of all the White Bear's sleeping
room, for the White Bear has to sleep in a bed of clean white snow every
night, and so his room is away from the heated part of the house.

But most boys and girls do not know much about the White Bear,
for though he is really a very important personage, he has been strangely
neglected by the biographers of Santa Claus. But that is often the way of
the historians: they concentrate themselves upon a single important figure

of a place or time, and forget to mention at all other factors quite as important. Then after a while some one takes up the people whom the historians have left in the dark, and tries to do them long-delayed justice. Now I would consider it quite a sufficient purpose in life and a very considerable accomplishment if I could set the White Bear right with history, and convince the world of his importance. He is not at all like the bears who carry off naughty children, and does not even belong to the same family as the bears who ate up the forty children who mocked at the Prophet's bald head. On the contrary, this bear is a most gentle and kindly fellow, and fonder of boys and girls than any one else in the world, except Santa Claus himself. He has lived with Papa Santa from time immemorial, helping him in his workshop, painting rocking horses, and stretching drum heads, and gluing yellow wigs on doll babies. But his principal duty is to care for the reindeer, those swift, strong, nervous little beasts, without whom the hobby horses and dolls and red drums would never reach the little children in the world.

One evening, on the twenty-third of December—the rest of the date does not matter—Papa Santa sat by the fire in the great hall, blowing the smoke from his nostrils, until his ruddy round face shone through it like a full moon through the mist. He was in a happier mood even than usual, for his long year's work in his shop was done, the last nail had been driven and the last coat of paint had dried. All the vast array of toys stood ready to go into the sealskin bags and be piled into the sleigh.

Opposite him sat Mamma Santa, putting the last dainty stitches on a doll dress for a little sick girl somewhere down in the world. Mamma Santa never kept track of where the different children lived; Papa Santa and the White Bear attended to the address book. It was enough for her to know that they were children and good children, she didn't care to know any more. By her chair sat the White Bear, eating his dog sausage. The White Bear was always hungry between meals, and Mamma Santa always kept a plate of his favorite sausage ready for him in the pantry, which, as there was no fire there, was a refrigerator as well.

As Papa Santa bent to light his pipe again, he spoke to the White Bear:

"The reindeer are all in good shape, are they? You've seen them tonight?"

"I gave them their feed and rubbed them down an hour ago, and I never saw them friskier. They ought to skim like birds tomorrow night. As I came away, though, I thought I saw the Were-Wolf Dog hanging around, so I locked up the stable."

"That was right," said Papa Santa, approvingly. "He was there for no good, depend on that. Last year he tampered with the harness and cut it so that four traces broke before I reached Norway."

Mamma Santa sent her needle through the fine cambric she was stitching with an indignant thrust, and spoke so emphatically that the little white curls under her cap bobbed about her face. "I cannot understand the perverse wickedness of that animal, nor what he has against you, that he should be forever troubling you, or against those World-Children, poor little innocents, that he should be forever trying to defraud them of their Christmas presents. He is certainly the meanest animal from here to the Pole."

"That he is," said Papa Santa, "and there is no reason for it at all. But he hates everything that is not as mean as himself."

"I am sure, Papa, that he will never be at rest until he has brought about some serious accident. Hadn't the Bear better look about the stables again?"

"I'll sleep there tonight and watch, if you say so," said the White Bear, rapping the floor with his shaggy tail.

"O, there is no need of that, we must all get our sleep tonight, for we have hard work and a long journey before us tomorrow. I can trust the reindeer pretty well to look after themselves. Come, Mamma, come, we must get to bed." Papa Santa shook the ashes out of his pipe and blew out the lights, and the White Bear went to stretch himself in his clean white snow.

When all was quiet about the house, there stole from out the shadow of the wall a great dog, shaggy and monstrous to look upon. His hair was red, and his eyes were bright, like ominous fires. His teeth were long and projected from his mouth like tusks, and there was always a little foam about his lips as though he were raging with some inward fury. He carried his tail between his legs, for he was as cowardly as he was vicious. This was the wicked Were-Wolf Dog who hated everything; the beasts and the birds and Santa Claus and the White Bear, and most of all the little children of the world. Nothing made him so angry as to think that there really are good children in the world, little children who love each other, and are simple and gentle and fond of everything that lives, whether it breathes or blooms. For years he had been trying in one way and another to delay Santa Claus' journey so that the children would get no beautiful gifts from him at Christmas time. For the Were-Wolf Dog hated Christmas too, incomprehensible as that may seem. He was thoroughly wicked and evil, and Christmas time is the birthday of Goodness, and every year on Christmas Eve the rage in his dark heart burned anew.

He stole softly to the window of the stable, and peered in where the swift, tiny reindeer stood each in his warm little stall, pawing the ground impatiently. For on glorious moonlight nights like that the reindeer never slept, they were always so homesick for their freedom and their wide white snow plains.

"Little reindeer," called the Were-Wolf Dog, softly, and all the little reindeer pricked up their ears. "Little reindeer, it is a lovely night," and all the little reindeer sighed softly. They knew, ah, how well they knew!

"Little reindeer, the moon is shining as brightly as the sun does in the summer, the North wind is blowing fresh and cold, driving the little clouds across the sky like white sea birds. The snow is just hard enough to bear without breaking, and your brothers are running like wild things over its white crust. And the stars, ah, the stars, little brothers, they gleam like a million jewels, and glitter like icicles all over the face of the sky."

The reindeer stamped impatiently in their little stalls. It was very hard.

"Come, little reindeer, let me tell you why all your brothers run toward the Polar Sea tonight. It is because tonight the northern lights will flash as they never did before, and the great streaks of red and purple and violet will shoot across the sky until all the people of the world shall see them, who never saw before. Listen, little reindeer, it is just the night for a run, a long free run, with no traces to tangle your feet and no sledge to drag. Come, let us go, you will be back again by dawn and no one will ever know."

Dunder stamped in his stall, it made him long to be gone, to hear what the Were-Wolf Dog said. "No, no, we cannot, for tomorrow we must start with the toys for the little children of the world."

"But you will be back tomorrow. Just when the dim light is touching the tops of the icebergs and making the fresh snow red, you will be speeding home. Ah, it will be a glorious run, and you will see the lights as they never shone before. Do you not pant to feel the wind about you, little reindeer?"

Then Cupid and Blitzen could withstand his enticing words no longer, and begged, "Come, Dunder, let us go tonight. It has been so long since we have seen the lights, and we will be back tomorrow."

Now the reindeer knew well enough they ought not to go, but reindeer are not like people, and sometimes the things they want most awfully to do are the very things that they ought not to do. The thought of the fresh winds and their dear lights of the North and the moonlit snow drove them wild, for the reindeer love their freedom more than any other animal, and swift motion, and the free winds.

So the dog pried open the door, with the help of the reindeer forcing it from within, and they all dashed out into the clear moonlight and scurried away toward the North like gleeful rabbits. "We will be back by morning," said Cupid. "We will be back," said Dunder. And, poor little reindeer, they loved the snow so well that it scarcely seemed wrong to go.

O, how fine it was to feel that wind in their fur again! They tossed their antlers in the fresh wind, and their tiny hoofs rang on the hard snow as they ran. They ran for miles and miles without growing tired, or losing their first pleasure in it. Their nostrils were distended and their eyes were bright.

"Slower, slower, little reindeer, for I must lead the way. You will not find the place where all the beasts are assembled," called the Were-Wolf Dog.

The little reindeer could no more go slowly than a boy can when the fire engines dash by. So they got the Were-Wolf Dog in the center of the pack and fairly bore him on with them. On they ran over those vast plains of snow that sparkled as brightly as the sky did above, and Dasher and Prancer bellowed aloud with glee. At last there lay before them the boundless stretch of the Polar Sea. Dark and silent it was, as mysterious as the strange secret of the Pole which it guards forever. Here and there where the ice floes had parted showed a crevice of black water, and the great walls of ice glittered like flame when the northern lights flung their red banners across the sky, and tipped the icebergs with fire. There the reindeer paused a moment for very joy, and the Were-Wolf Dog fell behind.

"Is the ice safe, old Dog?" asked Vixen.

"To the right it is, off and away, little reindeer. It is growing late," said the Were-Wolf Dog, shouting hoarsely.

And the heedless little reindeer dashed on, never noticing that the wicked Were-Wolf Dog stayed behind on the shore. Now when they were out a good way upon the sea they heard a frightful cracking, grinding sound, such as the ice makes when it breaks up.

"To the shore, little brothers, to the shore!" cried Dunder, but it was too late. The wicked Were-Wolf Dog where he stood on the land saw the treacherous ice break and part, and the head of every little reindeer go down under the black water. Then he turned and fled over the snow, with his tail tighter between his legs than ever, for he was too cowardly to look upon his own evil work.

As for the reindeer, the black current caught them and whirled them down under the ice, all but Dunder and Dasher and Prancer, who at last rose to the surface and lifted their heads above the water.

"Swim, little brothers, we may yet make the shore," cried Dunder. So among the cakes of broken ice that cut them at every stroke, the three brave little beasts began to struggle toward the shore that seemed so far away. A great chunk of ice struck Prancer in the breast, and he groaned and sank. Then Dasher began to breathe heavily and fell behind, and when Dunder stayed to help him he said, "No, no, little brother, I cannot make it. You must not try to help me, or we will both go down. Go tell it all to the White Bear. Goodbye, little brother, we will skim the white snow fields no more together." And with that he, too, sank down into the black water, and Dunder struggled on alone.

When at last he dragged himself wearily upon the shore he was exhausted and cruelly cut and bleeding. But there was no time to be lost. Spent and suffering as he was, he set out across the plains.

Late in the night the White Bear heard some one tapping against his window and saw poor Dunder standing there all covered with ice and blood.

"Come out, brother," he gasped, "the others are all dead and drowned, only I am left. For this night the treacherous Were-Wolf Dog came to us and with enticing words lured us to go with him toward the Pole, promising to show us the northern lights brighter than we had ever seen them before. But black Death he showed us, and the bottom of the Polar Sea."

Then the White Bear hastened out in his nightcap, and Dunder told him all about the cruel treachery of the Were-Wolf Dog.

"Alas," cried the White Bear, "and who shall tell Santa of this, and who will drag his sleigh tomorrow to carry the gifts to the little children of the world? Empty will their stockings hang on Christmas morning, and Santa's heart will be broken."

Then poor Dunder sank down in the snow and wept.

"Do not despair, Dunder. We must go tonight to the ice hummock where the beasts meet to begin their Christmas revels. Can you run a little longer, poor reindeer?"

"I will run until I die," said Dunder, bravely. "Get on my back and we will go."

So reluctantly the White Bear got on Dunder's back, for bears cannot run themselves, and they sped away to the great ice hummock where the animals of the North all gather to keep their Christmas.

The ice hummock is a great pile of ice and snow right under the North Star, and all the animals were there drinking punches and wishing each other a Merry Christmas. There were seals, and fur otters, and white ermines, and whales, and bears, and many strange birds, and the tawny Lapland dogs that are as strong as horses. But the Were-Wolf Dog was not there. The White Bear paid no heed to any of them, but climbed up to the very top of the huge ice hummock. Then he stood up and cried out:

"Animals of the North, listen to me!" and all the animals ceased from their merrymaking and looked up to the ice hummock where the White Bear stood, looking very strange up there, all alone in the starlight, with his nightcap still on.

"Listen to me," thundered the White Bear, "and I will tell you such a tale of wickedness and treachery as never came up among us before. This night the wicked Were-Wolf Dog, who is ever raging in his black heart against the innocent World-Children, came to the reindeer of Santa Claus and with enticing words lured them northward, promising to show them the great lights as they never shone before. But black Death he showed them, and the bottom of the Polar Sea." Then he showed them poor bleeding Dunder, and told how all the tiny reindeer had been drowned and all the treachery of the Were-Wolf Dog. And all the animals were very indignant and ashamed that one of their number should be guilty of such a thing. And the big whale flapped his tail, and all the bears growled.

"Now, O animals," the White Bear went on, "who among you will go back with me and draw the sleigh full of presents down to the little World-Children, for a shame would it be to all of us if they should awaken and find themselves forgotten and their stockings empty."

But none of the animals replied, for though they felt sorry enough for what had been done, they all loved their freedom and to race over the star-lit snow, and were loath to give it up even for the snug, warm stables of Santa Claus.

"What," cried the White Bear. "Is there not one of you who will take this reproach from us and go back with me to the stables of Santa Claus and take the place of our brothers who are dead? A warm stable shall each of you have, and your fill of clean dry moss-feed, and snow water to drink."

But the animals all thought of the wide plains and the stinging North wind and their scampers of old, and hung their heads and were silent. Poor Dunder groaned aloud, and even the White Bear had begun to despair, when there spoke up a poor old seal with but one fin, for he had fallen into the seal fishers' hands and been maimed. He had been drinking too much punch, and he spoke thickly, but he had a good heart, that old crippled seal. "It wrings my heart, brothers, that you should be silent to such a call as this, when for the first time since Christmas began it seems that the little children of the world will not get their presents. I am only an old seal who have been twice wounded by the hunters, and am a cripple, but lo, I myself will go with the White Bear, and though I can travel but a mile a day at best, yet will I hobble on my tail and my one fin until I have dragged the sleigh full of presents to the World-Children."

Then the animals were all ashamed of themselves, and the reindeer all sprang forward and cried, "We will go, take us!"

So the next day, a little later than usual, Santa Claus wrapped himself in his fur lap robes, and seven new reindeer, headed by Dunder, flew like the winged wind toward the coast of Norway. And if any of you remember getting your presents a little late that year, it was because the new reindeer were not used to their work yet, though they tried hard enough.

First published in *Home Monthly*, VI (December, 1896), 13–14, 24.

The Count of Crow's Nest

✳ ✳ ✳

Crow's Nest was an overcrowded boarding house on West Side, over-crowded because there one could obtain shelter and sustenance of a respectable nature cheaper than anywhere else in ante-Columbian Chicago.★ Of course the real name of the place was not Crow's Nest; it had, indeed, a very euphuistic name; but a boarder once called it Crow's Nest, and the rest felt the fitness of the title, so after that the name clung to it. The cost of existing had been reduced to its minimum there, and it was for that reason that Harold Buchanan found the Count de Koch among the guests of the house. Buchanan himself was there from the same cause, a cause responsible for most of the disagreeable things in this world. For Buchanan was just out of college, an honor man of whom great things were expected, and was waiting about Chicago to find a drive wheel to which to apply his undisputed genius. He found this waiting to see what one is good for one of the most trying tasks allotted to the sons of men. He hung about studios, publishing houses and concert halls hunting a medium, an opportunity. He knew that he was gifted in more ways than one, but he knew equally well that he was painfully immature, and that between him and success of any kind lay an indefinable, intangible some-thing which only time could dispose of. Once it had been a question of which of several professions he should concentrate his energies upon; now the problem was to find any one in which he could gain the slightest foothold. When he had begun his search it was a quest of the marvelous, of the pot of fairy gold at the rainbow's end; but now it was a quest for gold of another sort, just the ordinary prosaic gold of the work-a-day world that will buy a man his dinner and a coat to his back.

In the meantime, among the tragic disillusionments of his first hazard of fortune, Buchanan had to live, and this he did at Crow's Nest because existence was much simplified there, almost reduced to first principles, and one could dine in a sack coat and still hold up his head with

★ The Chicago World's Fair of 1893 was officially known as the World's Columbian Exposition.

assurance among his fellow men. So there he had his study, where he began pictures and tragedies that were never completed, and wrote comic operas that were never produced, and hated humanity as only a nervous sensitive man in a crowded boarding house can hate it. The rooms above his were occupied by a prima donna who practiced incessantly, a thin, pale, unhappy-looking woman with dark rings under her eyes, whose strength and salary were spent in endeavoring to force her voice up to a note which forever eluded her. On his left lived a discontented man, bearded like a lion, who had intended to be a novelist and had ended by becoming a very ordinary reviewer, putting the reproach of his failure entirely upon a dull and unappreciative public.

The occupants of the house were mostly people of this sort, who had come short of their own expectations and thought that the world had treated them badly and that the time was out of joint. The atmosphere of failure and that peculiar rancor which it begets seemed to have settled down over the place. It seemed to have entered into the very walls; it was in the close reception room with its gloomy hangings, clammy wall paper, hard sofas and bad pictures. It was in the old grand piano, with the worn yellow keys that clicked like castanets as they gave out their wavering, tinny treble notes in an ineffectual staccato. It was in the long, dark dining room, where the gas was burning all day, in the reluctant chairs that were always dismembering themselves under one, in the inevitable wan chromo of the sad-eyed Cenci who is daily martyred anew at the hands of relentless copyists, in the very clock above the sideboard whose despairing, hopeless hands never reached the hour at the proper time, and which always struck plaintively, long after all the other clocks were through.

The prima donna sneered at the chilly style of the great Australian soprano* who was singing for a thousand dollars a night down at the Auditorium, the reviewer declared that literature had stopped with Thackeray, the art student railed day and night against all pictures but his own.

Buchanan sometimes wondered if this were a dark prophecy of his own future. Perhaps he, too, would some day be old and poor and disappointed, would have touched that wall which marks the limitations of men's lives, and would hate the name of a successful man as the dwarfs of the underworld hated the giants in the golden groves of Asgard. He felt it would be better to contrive to get capsized in the lake some night. Could

* Nellie Melba (1861–1931), Australian opera star.

there be any greater degradation than to learn to hate an art and its exponents merely because one had failed in it himself? He fervently hoped that some happy accident would carry him off before he reached that stage.

Day after day he sat down in that dining room that was so conducive to pessimistic reflection, with the same distasteful people: The blonde stenographer who giggled so that she often had to leave the table, the cadaverous art student who talked of originating a new school of landscape painting, and who meantime taught clay modeling in a design school to defray his modest expenses at the Nest, the reviewer, the prima donna, the languid old widow who wore lilacs in her false front and coquetted with the fat man with the ear trumpet. She had, in days gone by, made coy overtures to Buchanan and the surly reviewer, but as they were more than unresponsive and would have none of her, she now devoted herself exclusively to the deaf man, though undoubtedly ear trumpets are an impediment to coquetry. But as the deaf man could not hear her at all, he stood it very well. He might also be short sighted, Buchanan reflected.

In all that vista of faces, there were some twenty in all, there was but one which was not unpleasant; that of the courtly old gentleman who ate alone at a small table at the end of the dining room. He was only there at dinner, his breakfast and luncheon were always sent to his room. He had no acquaintances in the house and spoke to no one, yet every one knew that he was Paul, Count de Koch, and during breakfast and luncheon hours he and his possible history had furnished the *pièce de résistance* of conversation for some months. In that absorbing theme even the decadence of French art and English letters and the execution of the Australian soprano were forgotten. The stenographer called attention to the fact that his coat was of a prehistoric cut, though she acknowledged its fit was above criticism. The widow had learned from the landlady that he shaved himself and blacked his own boots. She was certain he had been a desperately wicked man and lost all his money at Monte Carlo, for unless Counts were very reprehensible indeed they were always rich. This scrutinizing gossip about a courteous and defenseless old gentleman was the most harassing of all Buchanan's table trials, and it savored altogether too much of the treatment of Père Goriot in Madame Vanquar's "Pension Bourgeoise."

He was always glad at dinner when the Count's presence put a stop at least to audible queries, and his calm patrician face again made its strange contrast with the sordid unhappy ones about him. His clear gray eyes, his slight erect figure, and white, tapering hands seemed quite as anomalous there as his name. That gentlemanly figure made life at Crow's Nest possible to Buchanan; it was like seeing a Vandyke portrait in the gallery of daubs. The Count's whole conduct, like his person, was simple, dignified and artistic. It was a cause for much indignation among the boarders, particularly so in the case of the widow and prima donna, that he met no one. Yet his manner was never one of superiority, simply of amiable and dignified reserve. He might at all times have stood the scrutiny of a court drawing room, yet he was perfectly unostentatious and unconscious. There was something regal about his gestures. When he held back the swinging door for the hurried maid with her groaning tray of dishes, you half expected to see the Empress Eugenie and her train sweep through, or gay old Ludwig with his padded calves and painted cheeks and enormous wig, his troupe of poets and dancers behind him. He drank his pale California claret as if it were Madeira of one of those priceless vintages of the last century.

In his college days Buchanan had been a good deal among well-bred people, but he had never seen any one so quietly and faultlessly correct. Sometimes he met him walking by the Lake Shore, and he thought he would have noticed his carriage and walk among a thousand. In watching him that phrase of Lang's, "A gentleman among *canaille*," constantly occurred to him.

One of the saddest defects of that ponderous machinery which we call society is the impenetrable wall which is built up between personalities; one of the saddest of our finite weaknesses is our incapacity to recognize and know and claim the people who are made for us. Every day we pass men who want us and whom we bitterly need, unknowing, unthinking, as friends pass each other at a masked ball: pursuing the tinkle of the harlequin's bells, not knowing that under the friar's hood is the *camaraderie* they seek. Following persistently the fluttering hem of the priestly gown, never dreaming that the heart of gold is under the spangled corsage of Folly there, sitting tired out on the stairway. It seems as if there ought to be a floor manager to arrange these things for us. However, given a close proximity and continue it long enough, and the right people will find each other out as certainly as the satellites know their proper suns. It was impossible that, in such a place as Crow's Nest, Buchanan's relations to the Count should continue the same as those of the other boarders. It was impossible that the Count should not notice that one respectful glance that was neither curious nor vulgar, only frankly interested and appreciative.

One evening as Buchanan sat in the reception room reading a volume of Gautier's romances while waiting for the dinner that was always late, he glanced up and detected the Count looking over his shoulder.

"I must ask your pardon for my seeming discourtesy, but one so seldom sees those delightful romances read in this country, that for the moment I quite forgot myself. And as I caught the title 'La Morte Amoureuse,' an old favorite of mine, I could scarcely refrain from glancing a second time."

Buchanan decided that since chance had thrown this opportunity in his way, he had a right to make the most of it. He closed the book and turned, smiling.

"I am only too glad to meet some one who is familiar with it. I have met the idea before, it has been imitated in English, I think."

"Ah, yes, doubtless. Many of those things have been imitated in English, but—"

He shrugged his shoulders expressively. "Yes, I understand your hiatus. These things are quite impossible in English, especially the one we are speaking of. Some way we haven't the feeling for absolute and specific beauty of diction. We have no sense for the aroma of words as they have. We are never content with the effect of material beauty alone, we are always looking for something else. Of course we lose by it, it is like always thinking about one's dinner when one is invited out."

The Count nodded. "Yes, you look for the definite, whereas the domain of pure art is always the indefinite. You want the fact under the illusion, whereas the illusion is in itself the most wonderful of facts. It is a mistake not to be content with perfection and not find its sermon sufficient. As opposed to chaos, harmony was the original good, the first created virtue. And of course a great production of art must be the perfection of harmony. Even in the grotesque the harmony of the whole must be there. To be impervious to this indicates a certain bluntness toward the finer spiritual laws."

"And yet," said Buchanan, "we have been accustomed to look at all this as quite the opposite of spiritual. Our standpoint is certainly rather inconsistent, but I believe it is honest enough."

The Count smiled. "Certainly. It is a question of whether you want your sermon in a flower or in a Greek word, in poetry or in prose, whether you want the formula of goodness or goodness itself. So many of your authors write formulae. There was, however, one of your *littérateurs* who knew the distinction, even if he was something of a charlatan in using it.

Poe surpassed even Gautier in using some effects of that character," pointing to the book in Buchanan's hand. "Perhaps under happier circumstances he might have done so in all. You had there a true stylist, who knew the value of an effect; a master of single and graceful conceptions, who was content to leave them as such, unexplained and without apology."

"Perhaps that is the reason we say he was crazy," said Buchanan, sadly.

"Perhaps," said the Count as he lighted his cigar. "I hope to have the pleasure of discussing this again with you. You have read 'Fortunio'? No? When you have read 'Fortunio' I will wish to see you." He smiled and went out for his wintery walk on the Lake Shore.

After that Buchanan met the Count frequently, in the hallway, on the veranda, on his walks. They always had some conversation during these encounters, but their remarks were generally of a very casual nature. Buchanan felt some hesitancy about pushing the acquaintance lest he should exhaust it too soon. His tendency had always lain that way. In his intemperate youth he had plunged hotheaded and rapacious into friendship after friendship, giving more than any one cared to receive and exacting more than any one had leisure to give, only to reach that almost inevitable point where, independent of any volition of his own, the impetus slackened and stopped, the wells of sweet water were dry and the cisterns were broken. These promising oases that flourish among monotonous humanity dry up so quickly, most of them. They are verdant to us but a night. There are so few minds that are fitted to race side by side, to wrestle and rejoice together, even unto the paean. And after all that is the base of affinities, that mental brotherhood. The glamour of every other passion and enthusiasm fades like the brilliance of an afterglow, leaving shadow and chill and a nameless ennui.

One evening Buchanan stopped the Count in the hall.

"May I trouble you for a moment, sir? A friend of mine who is something of a bibliomaniac has sent me from Munich a copy of Rabelais stamped with the Bavarian arms. There is an autograph on the fly leaf, indeed, two of them, and he suspects that one of them may be Ludwig's."

The Count adjusted his eye glasses and looked thoughtfully at the faded writing: "Lola M.," and further down the page, "Ludwig."*

* Lola Montez, mistress of King Ludwig I of Bavaria, controlled the Bavarian government in 1847. She was ousted by Austrian and Jesuit influences in 1848, and King Ludwig abdicated in favor of his son the same year.

"You have certainly every reason for such a supposition. Ludwig was one of the few monarchs who really cared enough for books to put his name in one, and Lola Montez' name, too, for that matter. However, in these autographs one can never tell. If you will step upstairs with me we can soon assure ourselves."

"O, I did not mean to trouble you; you were just going out, were you not?"

"It was nothing of importance, nothing that I would not gladly abandon for the prospect of your company."

Buchanan followed him up the stuffy stairway and down the narrow hall. He was conscious of a subdued thrill of quickened curiosity upon entering the Count's apartments. But as his host lit the gas one covert glance about him told him that he need not exercise rigid surveillance over his eyes. Beyond a number of books and pictures, portraits, most of them, there was little to distinguish the room from the ordinary furnished apartment. There was the usual faded moquette carpet, the same cheap rugs and the inevitable shiny oak furniture. The silver fittings of the writing table, engraved with a crest and monogram, were the only suggestions of the rank of the occupant.

"Be seated there, on the divan, and I will find a signature I know to be authentic. We will compare them." As he spoke he tugged at the unwilling drawers of a chiffonier in the corner.

"This furniture," he remarked apologetically, "partakes somewhat of the sullen nature of the house. There, we have it at last."

He lifted from the drawer a small steel chest and placed it upon the table. After opening it with a key attached to his watchguard, he drew out a pile of papers and began sorting them. Buchanan watched curiously the various documents as they passed through his hands. Some of them were on parchment and suggested venerable histories, some of them were encased in modern envelopes, and some were on tinted note paper with heavily embossed monograms, suggesting histories equally alluring if less venerable. If those notes could speak the import of their contents, what a roar of guttural bassos, soaring sopranos, and impassioned contraltos and tenors there would be! And would the dominant note of the chorus be of Ares or Eros, he wondered?

He was aroused from his speculations by the Count's slight exclamation when he found the paper he was hunting for. He unfolded a stiff sheet of note paper, and then folding it back so that only the signature was visible, sat down beside his guest. The signature, "Ludwig W.," stood out clearly from the paper he held.

"Not Ludwig's, evidently," said the Count, "now we will look as to the other. I am sorry to say we have that, too."

He opened the other paper he held, and folded it as he had done the first. The signature in this case was simply "Lola."

"They seem to be identical. I fancied as much. It was Madame Montez' custom to take whatever she wanted from the royal library, and she seldom troubled herself to return it. The second name is only another evidence of her inordinate vanity, and they are too numerous to be of any especial interest. I must apologize for showing you the signatures in this singularly unsatisfactory manner, but the contents of these communications were strictly personal, and, of course, were not addressed to me. I remember very little of the reign of the first Ludwig myself. There are a number of names among those papers that might interest you, if you care to see them and will omit the body of the documents. They are, many of them, papers that should never have been written at all. Such things are inevitable in very old families, though I could never understand their motive for preserving them. There is only one way to handle such things, and that is with absolute and unvarying care. To show them even to an appreciative friend is a form of blackmail. I dislike the responsibility of knowing their contents myself. I have not read any of them for years."

"And yet you, too, keep them?"

"Certainly, inbred tradition, I suppose. I have often intended to destroy them, but I have always deferred the actual doing of it. Since they have enabled me to be of some service to you, I am glad I have delayed the holocaust."

The conventional ring of the last remark seemed to politely close all further serious discussion of the subject. Buchanan checked the question he had already mentally uttered, and taking a chair by the table, looked at the signatures his host selected. They were names that consumed him with an overwhelming curiosity and made his ears tingle and his cheeks burn; single names, most of them, those single names that Balzac said made the observer dream. As the Count took another package of documents from the box his fingers caught a small gold chain attached to some metallic object that rang sharply against the sides of the box as he lifted his hand.

"The iron cross!" cried Buchanan involuntarily, with a quick inward breath.

"Yes, it is one that I won on the field of Gravelotte years ago. It is my only contribution to this box. I have been a very ordinary man, Mr. Buchanan. In families like ours there must be some men who neither make nor break, but try to keep things together. That my efforts in that direction were somewhat futile was not entirely my fault. I had two brothers who bore the title before me; they were both talented men, and when my turn came there was very little left to save."

"I fancied you had been more of a student than a man of affairs."

"Student is too grave a word. I have always read; at one time I thought that of itself gave one a sufficient purpose, but like other things it fails one at last, at least the living interest of it. At present I am only a survivor. Here, where every one plays for some stake, I realize how nearly extinct is the class to which I belong, and that I am a sort of survival of the unfit, with no duty but to keep an escutcheon that is only a name and a sword that the world no longer needs. An old pagan back in Julian's time who still clung to a despoiled Olympus and a vain philosophy, dead as its own abstruse syllogisms, might have felt as I do when the new faith, throbbing with potentialities, was coming in. The life of my own father seems to be as far away as the lives of the ancient emperors. It is not a pleasant thing to be the last of one's kind. The *tedium vitae* descends heavily upon one."

As the Count was speaking, they heard a ripple of loud laughter on the stairs and a rustle of draperies in the hall, and a tall blonde woman, dressed in a tight-fitting tailor-made gown, with a pair of long lavender gloves lying jauntily over her shoulder, entered and bowed graciously to the Count.

"*Bon soir, mon père*, I was not aware you had company." There was in her voice that peculiarly hard throat tone that stage people so often use in conversation.

"Mr. Buchanan, my daughter, Helena."

Buchanan bowed and muttered a greeting, uncertain by just what title he should address her.

"No Countess, if you please, Mr. Buchanan. Just plain Helena de Koch. Titles are out of date, and more than absurd in our case. I come from a rehearsal of a concert where I sing for money, attired in a ready-made gown, botched over by a tailor, to visit my respected parent in a fourth-rate lodging house, and you call me Countess! Could anything be more innately funny? Titles only go in comic opera now. I have often tried to persuade my father to content himself with Paul de Koch."

The Count smiled. "My name was not mine to make, Helena, and I am not at all ashamed of it."

The young lady's keen but rather indifferent eyes had dwelt on Buchanan but a moment, but he felt as though he had been inspected by a drill sergeant, and that no detail of his person or attire had escaped her.

She glanced at the table and then at the Count. "So you have decided to become practical at last?"

A shade of extreme annoyance swept quickly over the Count's face. He replied stiffly.

"I have merely been showing Mr. Buchanan an autograph he wished to see."

"O, so that is all! I might have known it. People do not recover from a mania in a day." She laughed rather unpleasantly and turned graciously to Buchanan. "Have you persuaded him to show you any of them? The contents are much more interesting than the autographs, rather side lights on history, you know." Her eyelid drooped a little with an insinuating glance, just enough to suggest a wink that did not come to pass, but he felt strangely repelled by even the suggestion. It must have been the connection that made it so objectionable, he reflected. She seemed to cheapen the Count and all his surroundings.

"No, my interest goes no further than the autographs."

"A polite prevarication, I imagine. You will have to get more in the shadow if you hide the curiosity in your eyes. I don't blame you, he found me reading them once, and all the old Koch temper came out. I never knew he had it until then. Our tempers and our title are the only remnants of our former glory. The one is quite as ridiculous as the other, since we have no one to get angry at but each other. Poverty has no right to indignation at all. I speak respectfully even to a cabman. Papa shows his superiority by having no cabman at all."

"I think neither of you need do anything at all to show that," said Buchanan, politely.

"O, come, you are all like impressarios, you Americans, and the further West one goes the worse it is. I never saw a manager who could resist a title; I only use mine on such occasions."

Buchanan saw that his host looked ill at ease, so he endeavored to change the subject.

"You sing, I believe?"

"O, yes, in oratorio and concert. *Cher papa* will not hear of the opera. Oratorio seems to be the special retreat of decayed gentility. I don't believe in those distinctions myself; I have found that a title dating from the foundation of the Empire does not buy one a spring bonnet, and that one of the oldest names in Europe will not keep one in gloves. One of your clever Frenchmen said there is nothing in the world but money, the gallows excepted. But His Excellency here never quotes that. Papa is an aristocrat, while I am bourgeoise to the tips of my fingers." She waved her highly polished nails toward Buchanan.

He thought that she could not have summarized herself better. The instinctive dislike he had always felt for her had been steadily growing into an aversion since she entered the room. It was by no means the first time he had seen her, she was almost a familiar figure about the boarding house, and often came to dine with the Count. Her florid coloring and elaborately waved blonde hair might have been said to be a general expression of her style. Under that yellow bang was a low straight forehead, and straight brows from behind which looked out a pair of blue eyes, large and full but utterly without depth, and cold as icicles, which seemed to be continually estimating the pecuniary value of the world. The cheeks were full and the chin decided in spite of its dimple. The upper lip was full and short and the nostril spare. They were scarcely the features one would expect to find in the descendant of an ancient house, seeming more accidental than formed by any perpetuated tendencies of blood. Her hands were broad and plump like her wrists.

Mademoiselle was on almost familiar terms with the landlady of Crow's Nest, and Buchanan fancied that she was responsible for the bits of gossip concerning the Count that floated about the house and were daily rehearsed by the languid widow. The widow had gone so far as to darkly express her doubts as to this effulgent blonde being the Count's daughter at all, and Buchanan had been guilty of rather hoping that she was right. It would be rather less of a reflection on the Count, he thought. But tonight's conversation left him no room for doubt, and in watching the contrast between her full, florid countenance and the chastened face across the table, he wondered if the materialists of this world were always hale and full-fed, while the idealists were pale and gray as the shadows that kept them company. But one did not find time to muse much about anything in Mademoiselle de Koch's presence.

"By the way, *cher papa*, you are coming tomorrow night to hear me sing that waltz song of Arditti's?"

"Certainly, if you wish, but I am not fond of that style of music."

"O, certainly not, that's not to be expected or hoped for, nothing but mossbacks. But, seriously, one cannot sing Mendelssohn or Haydn forever, and all the modern classics are so abominably difficult," said Mademoiselle, beginning to draw on her gloves, which Buchanan noticed were several sizes too small and required a great deal of coaxing. Indeed everything that Mademoiselle wore fit her closely. She was of that peculiar type of blonde loveliness which impresses one as being always on the verge of *embonpoint*, and its possessor seems always to be in a state of nervous apprehension lest she should cross the dead line and openly and fearlessly be called stout.

At this juncture a gentle knock was heard at the door, and Mademoiselle remarked carelessly, "That's only Tony. Come in!"

A gentleman entered and bowed humbly to Mademoiselle. He was a little tenor whom Buchanan remembered having seen before, and whose mild dark eyes and swarthy skin had given him a pretext to adopt an Italian stage name. He was a slight, narrow chested man and [had] a receding chin and a generally "professional" and foreign air which was unmistakably cultivated.

"A charming evening, Count. Chicago weather is so seldom genial in the winter."

After presenting him to Buchanan the Count answered him, "I have not been out, but it seems so here."

"Doubtless, in Mademoiselle's society. But you are busy?"

He glanced inquiringly at Mademoiselle. Buchanan fancied that the question was addressed to her rather than to the Count, and thought he intercepted an answering glance.

"Not at all, we were merely amusing ourselves. Must you leave us already?"

"I think Mademoiselle has another rehearsal. You know what it means to presume to keep pace with an art, eternal vigilance. There is no rest for the weary in our profession—not, at least, in this world." This was said with a weighty sincerity that almost provoked a smile from Buchanan. There are two words which no Chicago singer can talk ten minutes without using: "art" and "Chicago," and this gentleman had already indulged in both.

"O, yes, we must be gone to practice the despised Arditti. Come tomorrow night if you can. Tony here will give you tickets. And if Mr. Buchanan should have nothing better to do, pray bring him with you."

Buchanan assured her that he could have nothing more agreeable at any rate, and would be delighted to go. She took possession of the tenor and departed.

II

Harold Buchanan accompanied the Count next evening, and his impressions of Mademoiselle Helena de Koch were only intensified. She sang floridly and with that peculiar confidence which always seems to attend uncertain execution. She had a peculiar trick of just seeming to catch a note by the skirts and then falling back from it, just touching it, as it were, but totally unable to sustain it. More than that, her very unconsciousness of this showed that she had absolutely no musical sense. Buchanan was inclined to think that, next to her coarse disappreciation of her father, her singing was rather the worst feature about her. To sing badly and not to have perception enough to know it was such a bad index of one's mental and aesthetic constitution.

After the concert they went up on the stage to see her, and she came forward to meet them, accompanied by the tenor, and greeted them graciously, bearing her blushing honors quite as thick upon her as if she had sung well.

"It was nice of you to come. Did you catch my eye?"

"I am still glowing with the pleasure of thinking I did so, but I was afraid perhaps it was only a delusion. One so often goes about puffed up over favors that were meant for the fellow back of him."

"O, I hoped mine were more intelligible than that. But now you shall be rewarded for your patience. Tony and I are going to have a little supper down at Kingsley's, and you must come, just us, you know. Papa may come to chaperone us, if it is not too late for him."

The Count hastily excused himself, and indeed he must have been very dense to have accepted such a hostile invitation, even from his own daughter. But Buchanan had already bowed his acceptance, and felt that it was too late to retreat. Reluctantly he accompanied Mademoiselle and the silent tenor, and saw the Count depart alone. And yet, he reflected, this merciful intervention would relieve him from the awkward necessity of discussing the concert with his friend.

When they were seated at Kingsley's and had given their orders, it struck him that Mademoiselle had some purpose in bringing him, for it soon became obvious that the tenor's charms were of that nature which one usually prefers to enjoy alone. What this might be, however, did not at once appear. She discussed current music and light opera in quite an amiable and disinterested manner, and for a time contented herself with this.

"You are a journalist, I believe, Mr. Buchanan?"

"Scarcely, yet. That is one of the many things I would like to be."

"You are a Chicago man, at any rate?" inquired the tenor.

"Well, one of the queer things about Chicago is that no one is really a native. I have lived here a good deal, off and on. My father used to be in business here before I went East to school. Just at present I want to get into something, and I think that lightning is about as likely to strike one here as any where."

"More likely! Chicago is the place for young talent. I have found it so. They want new blood and new ideas. Success comes sooner and more directly here than elsewhere in your profession as in my own. I would rather sing to a Chicago audience than any other, and I think I have been before most of the best ones in this country." When the taciturn gentleman spoke at all it was of one all-important theme. Indeed, do tenors ever talk of anything else? *Art et moi; L'art, c'est moi!*

"O, Tony here takes things too seriously. 'Life is a plaything, life is a toy!' You have sung that often enough to believe it a little by this time. By the way, Mr. Buchanan, have you been down to hear the threadbare Robin Hood? O, no, I never go; there are no light operas worth hearing except those of the Viennese. Think of that odious waltz song, ta, ta, ta-ta-te, ta; ta-ta-te, ta, ta, ta!"

Buchanan looked apprehensively about at the other supper parties in the room, and wished she would not sing so loud. But she went merrily on.

"I can endure everything American except American music, and the less said of it the better. By the way, don't you think I have taken to your language rather kindly? Of course I learned English when I was a child, but I had to learn American after arriving, and I assure you that is quite another language."

"I was just thinking that you were quite wonderful in that respect. I should never know you were not one of us; you have all the *sermo familiaris* even to our local touches."

"O yes, I went at your slang as conscientiously as if it were grammar. That is the characteristic part of a language, anyway."

When their order arrived, the drift of the talk changed.

"You see a good deal of papa, Mr. Buchanan?"

"Not half so much as I want to."

"I am glad you like him; he is very lonely and has those antiquated class notions about mixing up with people."

"I have always felt that and have been a little bit backward. I don't want to seem to intrude."

"O, you need never be afraid of that; he likes you immensely. We've heard lots about you, haven't we, Tony?"

"Most enthusiastic and flattering accounts," responded that gentleman, looking up a moment from his lobster.

"We have thought about suggesting something, Mr. Buchanan, that might be immensely to your advantage. You are a young literary man, waiting to make a hit like all the rest of us. Now let me tell you something; if you can work papa, your fame is ready made for you."

"Well, if I could find any fame of that variety, I would be willing to pay pretty dearly for it. I had about decided that the virgin article was not lying about in very extensive deposits."

"Well, it is, just in chunks, inside of that box you saw the other night. He has hundreds of papers there that would turn the court history of Europe for the last century upside down. I know whereof I speak. His friends have urged him to publish them for the last twenty years, and I— but, of course, men never listen to their daughters. Of course he wouldn't care to edit them himself, his everlasting name, you know. But you are a practical literary man and know what *fin de siècle* taste demands, and if you could sort of combine forces, I have an idea it would be a great thing for both of you."

"But," protested Buchanan, "your father assured me those documents were of a wholly private nature."

"Of course they are. That's the sort of history that goes now-a-days. It's the sort of thing that sells and that people read, 'something spicy,' they call it. You could edit them with historical notes to give tone to the thing, you know. Of course you would have to overcome innumerable scruples on papa's part. Go at it in the name of art and history and all that. He is unyielding in his notions about such things, but if there is any living man who can do it, you are the man!" She had quite forgotten now the calm indifference of her first method of attack; her lips were set and her eyes biting keen. Buchanan could not help noticing how she leaned forward and how tightly she held her fork. Evidently this plan was not a new one. There was a purpose in those hard eyes that could not be new. He shifted his position slightly.

"I would rather you would leave me and my interests out of the question, Miss de Koch, though don't think I don't appreciate your kindness in thinking of me. If there is anything in the papers themselves to justify their publication, why does your father object to it?"

"O, he considers people's feelings—much they've ever considered ours! Of course it would make big scandals all over Europe, and no end of a fuss. There would be answers, denials, refutations; the national museums would be ransacked for counter-proofs. That one book would bring out a dozen. Just think of it, a grand wholesale *exposé* of all the courts of Europe, hailing from image-breaking Chicago! It's your chance for fame, young man, and as for money, we'd all be throwing it at the birdies in six months."

She had dropped the pass word of the conspiracy. Buchanan began to feel less at sea.

"Of course there would be grave considerations attending the publication of such matter."

"Not a bit of it. This is an age of disillusionment. William Tell was a myth, Josephine only a Creole coquette, and Shakespeare wasn't Shakespeare at all. This generation wants to get at the bottom of things. Now it's not the man who can invent a romance, but the man who can explode one who holds the winning card," she touched him lightly on the shoulder.

"It's a good deal as you say, undoubtedly. But I doubt the dignity, or even the decency of it."

She put her glass down impatiently. "That all may be, but when we are in Rome we must be either Romans or provincials. You must give the people what they want. Really, now, don't you like to get a tip on those old figurehead guys yourself, just to get even with them by shaking them off their pedestals a little? They were all very common clay like the rest of us."

Buchanan leaned back in his chair and decided to gain time and measure, if he could, the depth of the conspiracy sprung upon him. Mademoiselle was aglow with excitement, and even her gentleman-in-waiting had forgotten his supper, and his mild eyes were flashing with the first animation he had displayed.

"Well," he said, amused in spite of himself, "I have often thought I should like to get behind the scenes in history and see how all the great effects were really produced. How the tragic buskin is worn to make men look taller than they are, by what wires the angels are carried up to their apotheosis, and where the unfortunates go when they disappear through the trap. It would be a satisfaction to know just how often simpletons are cast for heroic parts, and great men for trivial ones, how often Hamlet and the grave digger ought to change places. I have even thought I would like to go into the dressing-room, and see just how the conventional historic puppets were made up; see the real head under the powdered wig and the real cheek under the rouge. And yet I am not anxious to be wholly disillusioned. If Caesar without his toga would not be Caesar, I would rather stay down in the orchestra chairs. I don't care to read a history of Napoleon written by his valet."

"Come, you know all this is moonshine. Nobody believes those things now-a-days. The more you take the halo from those fellows, the more popular you make them. A new scandal about Napoleon gives him a new lease of life. It revives the interest. Who would ever know anything about Rousseau, if it wasn't for his 'Confessions'? That keeps him popular; even my hairdresser reads it."

"Of course it is something to have immortality among hairdressers."

"It's very much better than having none at all, and being on the shelf all around. You are a young man with your mark to make, and you've got to meet the world on its own ground and give it what it wants, or it'll have none of you. If you take the people's money, you ought to cater to their tastes, that's fair enough. You cannot afford to be an old fogy, you have too much future. You see where it has put papa. Do you want to be stranded in Crow's Nest all your life, say fifty years of it? Chances to take the world by the horns do not occur every day; if you let them go by, you have a good long time for reflection, a lifetime, generally. One chance for one man, you know."

"I know that only too well, but I can't see that this is in any sense my chance. It's wholly your father's affair."

"Make it yours. Let's get to something definite; don't let him put you off with high sounding words; they aren't in the modern vocabulary and don't mean anything. Now you'll take up this matter? There is only one man in a thousand I would speak to openly in this way, but I have every faith in your ability. When things become definite, if papa is elusive about the business features of it, you and I can arrange that together."

Buchanan crumpled his napkin and threw it on the table.

"I am sorry, but I am afraid that you have misplaced your confidence; that is, you have expected too much of me. I am not an enterprising man, or a very practical one; if I were I would already have some legitimate occupation. I seem to be rather another case of the round block versus the square hole, and decidedly I can't fit into this. I could never propose such a thing to your father. If he ever speaks to me on the subject I will be frank enough, I promise you, but further than that I cannot pledge myself. Moreover, I doubt my own ability to either gauge the popular taste or fill its demands."

Mademoiselle's amiability at once disappeared, and she took no pains to conceal the fact that she considered him both ungracious and ungrateful, though she vented her displeasure principally upon her dusky minion, the tenor, who was struggling with her rubbers. From the dogged look on his face, Buchanan imagined that that silent gentleman would one day avenge the tyrannies of his apprenticeship. Feeling very much as though he had obtained a supper under false pretenses, he said good night.

As he lit his cigar in the street, and faced the cold wet wind that blew in from the lake, he muttered to himself, "Of all mercenary creatures! it's loathsome enough in a man, but in a woman—bah, it's positively reptilian! I don't believe she has a drop of the old man's blood in her body."

III

Some way his very aversion to the daughter drew Buchanan's sympathies more than ever to the Count. He found himself in the evening instinctively pausing at the Count's door, and when he went out to hear music or to see a play he felt more at ease when the Count was with him. He was of that temperament which quickly learns to depend on others. During their talks and rambles about the theatres he learned a good deal of the Count's history. Not directly, as the old gentleman seldom talked about himself, but in scrappy fragments that he mentally sorted and expanded into a biography. He learned how Paul had been born in the Winter Palace at St. Petersburg, where his father had superintended the education of the Czar Nicholas' sons. He had been considered rather dull socially in his youth, and had been kept in the background in a military school at Leipsic, while his two elder brothers spent his substance and amassed colossal debts in a manner that demonstrated their social talents to the world. After a good deal of reckless living, William had been killed in a duel about some vague diplomatic matter, and Nicholas by some accident at the races. When Paul at last came in to his shorn and parceled patrimony, he did something that established all the charges of imbecility that had been made against him; he sold the Koch estates and paid the Koch debts, the first time they had been paid in three centuries. By such an unheard of proceeding he at once lost caste in the diplomatic circles of the continent. To part with his family estates, to sell the home of the Counts de Koch to pay tradespeople and laborers, it was really more than well conducted society could be expected to condone. So Paul drifted to America, not until after the death of his wife, though of his wife he never spoke except formally. When he considered the daughter, Buchanan could not wonder at his reticence.

The man's quiet charm, his distinctive fineness of life and thought meant a great deal to a young man like Buchanan. They helped him to keep his standards and his tastes clean at a despondent age when that is sometimes difficult to do. It was certainly a strange thing to find this instinctive autocrat, this type of an effete nobility in that city of all cities, in Chicago, where the Present and the Practical are apotheosized and paid divine honors. But, then, what can one not find in Chicago? He never stepped, without feeling the contrast, from the hurried world of barter and trade into the quiet of that little room where memories and souvenirs of other times and another world were kept hidden, as, in the days of their far captivity in the city of Baal, the Jews kept the sacred vessels of their pillaged temple.

One night, as he was indulging in his reprehensible habit of reading in bed, Buchanan heard a hurried knock at his door. At his bidding the Count entered. He was still in street dress, hat in hand, pale and in evident excitement. His hair was disordered and his forehead shone with moisture. He would not sit down, but went straight up to the bed and grasped Buchanan's hand. Buchanan felt that his was trembling and cold.

"My friend," he spoke thickly, "I need you tonight, the letters . . . the box . . . it is gone."

"The box? O, yes, the steel chest, but how, where, what do you mean?"

"When I came to my rooms tonight, I opened the drawer of the chiffonier. It was a most unusual thing, it must have been instinct, those letters are the only things left to watch. They should have been in a vault, I know, but I kept delaying. When I opened the drawer they were gone."

"This is serious. What can you do?"

"I must go out at once. You have retired and I would not disturb you for any trivial matter, but this—this is the honor of my family! Great God! The descendants of those people are living in Europe today, living honorably and bearing great names. You hear me? Those letters must not get abroad. They would shake men's faith in God and make them curse their mothers."

Buchanan was already dressing. Suddenly he stopped short and dropped his shoe on the floor.

"Who knew where you kept them? Do you suspect any one who was interested?"

The Count's voice was almost inaudible as he answered, "I think,

Mr. Buchanan, we must first go to my daughter's rooms. It is with regret and shame that I drag you into this; it is terrible enough for me." He stood with his eyes downcast, like one in bitter shame. Buchanan had never noticed that he was so old a man before.

He felt that nothing could be said that would not be more than superfluous. When he finished dressing, the Count remarked, "Put on your ulster, it is cold."

They went softly downstairs and hailed a cab. During the drive the Count said nothing. Buchanan could see by the flash of the street lights as they passed them that his head was sunk on his breast. Only once he broke the silence by a sort of despairing groan. Buchanan guessed that some memory which bore immediately upon the grief of the moment had suddenly arisen before him. Perhaps it was one of those casual actions which we scatter so recklessly in our youth, and which, grown monstrous like the creature of Frankenstein, rise up to shame us in our age and spread desolation which we are powerless to check.

When they reached the house, Buchanan saw that the windows of the third floor were lighted, while the rest of the house was in darkness. It was easy to guess on which floor Mademoiselle de Koch resided. After repeated ringing, a sleepy servant maid opened the door. The Count asked no questions, but simply gave his name and passed upstairs, while the maid gathered her disheveled robes about her and stumbled down the hallway. The knock at Mademoiselle de Koch's door was greeted by a cheerful "Entrez!"

The open door revealed Mademoiselle attired in a traveling dress with a pile of letters on the desk before her, and a pen in her hand. A half packed valise lay open on the bed, and her trunks were strapped as though for sudden departure.

On seeing her visitors she gave a start of surprise, followed by a knowing glance, and then was quite at her ease. She would make a good defence, Buchanan suspected.

"Ah, it is you, *cher papa*, and you have brought company. Well, it is not exactly a conventional hour, but you are always welcome. I am delighted, Mr. Buchanan. Papa's chaperonage is certainly sufficient, even at three in the morning, so be seated."

The Count closed the door and met her. "Helena, you know why I have come and what you must do. There is no need of expletives."

"Not for you, perhaps, but I insist upon an explanation. What do you mean? I am at your service, as always, but I do not understand."

"This scene is disgraceful enough. I will allow you to spare yourself any explanations. I want the letters you took from my room. I will have them, so make no ado about it."

"You speak to me, sir, as though I were a chambermaid; you accuse me of taking your letters. What letters? I did not know you had correspondence so delicate now. Fie, papa! D'Albert said you were in your dotage ten years ago, but I have done you the honor to think him mistaken. Please do not altogether destroy my faith in you, I have so few illusions left at best." The sneer in that last sentence made Buchanan shiver as with a chill.

"I have not come to bandy words with you, Helena, nor to sermonize. You have never known what honor means. That is a distinction which cannot be taught. Don't try to act with me. I will take what I have come for, and leave you to your own felicitous philosophy of life, which I thank God is not mine. Give me the key of your trunk."

"Really, Your Excellency, this is quite too much. I shall do nothing of the sort. Come back tomorrow and I will do anything within reason. At present you are simply insane with anger, after the charming manner of your house."

"Then in just three minutes Mr. Buchanan will call an officer."

She started visibly, "You would not dare, pride—if nothing else—"

"I have no pride but the honor of my house. Quick, there is a law which can touch even you. Law was made for such as you."

The man of pale reflection was no more. This was the man of the iron cross who had led the charge on the field of Gravelotte.

Slowly, sullenly, she reached for her purse, and biting her lips handed him the key.

"Now, Mr. Buchanan, if you will assist me." He went quickly and deftly to the bottom of the trunk, almost without disturbing the clothing, and drew out the box, wrapped in numberless undergarments. After opening it and assuring himself as to the contents, he closed the trunk and Buchanan strapped it up.

Mademoiselle, who had returned to her seat and was making a pretense of writing, dropped her pen with a fierce exclamation.

"What is this honor you are always ranting about? Is it to leave your daughter to pick up her living as she may, to whine about beasts of managers, and go begging for fourth-rate engagements, when you might have supported her by the sale of a few scandalous letters? A fine sort of code to make all this racket about! Fine words will not conceal ugly facts."

The Count straightened himself as under a blow, "Stop! since you will drag out this whole ugly matter; you know that if you would have lived as I have had to live there would have been enough. As long as there was a picture, a vase, a jewel left, you know where they went. You took until there was no more to take. I simply have nothing but the pension. Even now my home is open to you, but I cannot keep you in yours. Will you never understand, I simply have no money! You know why I came here and why I must die here. When there was money what use did you make of it? Why is it that neither of us will ever dare to show our faces on the Continent again, that we tremble at the name of a continental newspaper? You remember that heading in *Figaro*? It will stare me in my grave! 'Adventuress!' Great God, it was true!"

His voice broke, and his white head sank on his breast in an attitude of abject shame and anguish. Buchanan put his hand before his eyes to shut out the sight of it. But again that rasping pitiless woman's voice broke on his ear.

"And who began it all, by selling my inheritance over my head? Was it yours to sell?"

The Count spoke quietly now and his voice was steady.

"For the moment you brought back the old shame, and I almost pitied you and myself again. Generally I simply forget it; you have exhausted my power to suffer. I never feel. Helena, there is nothing I can say to you, for we have no language in common. Words do not mean the same to us. Good night."

She sprang from her seat and stood with clenched hands. "Those papers do not belong to you. They are ancient history, and they belong to the world!"

"They are the follies of men, and they belong to God," said the Count as he closed the door. As they reached the cab he spoke heavily, "It was ungenerous of me to drag you into this, but I did not feel equal to it alone."

"I think that good friends need not explain why they need each other, even if they know themselves," said Buchanan gently.

When they were in the cab he felt as though he ought to speak of something. He was afraid that perhaps the Count had not noticed it. "Miss de Koch's trunks were packed. Is she going away?"

The Count sighed wearily and leaned back in his seat, speaking so low that Buchanan had to lean forward to catch his words above the rumble of the cab.

"Yes, I saw. It is probably an elopement—the tenor. But I am helpless. I have no money. What she said was true enough; I am no more successful as a father than I was as a nobleman. And I have been mad enough to wish that I had sons! It is a terrible thing, this degeneration of great families. You are very happy to see nothing of it here. The rot begins inside and is hidden for a time, but it demonstrates itself even physically at last. My ancestors had the frames of giants, field marshals and generals, all of them. We were all dwarfs, exhausted physically from the first, frayed ends of the strands of a great skein. Even my father was a slight man, always ill. My brothers were men of no principle, but they at least preserved the traditions. Nicholas was killed at the races, like a common jockey. In me it showed itself in my marriage. Before that the men of our house had at least chosen gentlewomen as their wives; they acknowledged the obligation. But this, even I never thought it would come to this. My mother would have starved with my father, begged in the streets, even lived at Crow's Nest, but she would never have thought of this. The possibility would never have occurred to her. I am the last of them. Helena will hardly choose a domestic career. Our little comedy is over, it is time the lights were out; the fifth act has dragged out too long. I am in haste to give back to the earth this blood I carry and free the world from it. In it is inherent failure, germinal weakness, madness, and chaos. When all sense of honor dies utterly out of an old stock, there is nothing left but annihilation. It should be buried deep, deep as they bury victims of a plague, blotted out like the forgotten dynasties of history."

First published in *Home Monthly*, VI (September, October, 1896), 9–11; 12–13, 22–23.

Tommy, the Unsentimental

❅ ❅ ❅

"Your father says he has no business tact at all, and of course that's dreadfully unfortunate."

"Business," replied Tommy, "he's a baby in business; he's good for nothing on earth but to keep his hair parted straight and wear that white carnation in his buttonhole. He has 'em sent down from Hastings twice a week as regularly as the mail comes, but the drafts he cashes lie in his safe until they are lost, or somebody finds them. I go up occasionally and send a package away for him myself. He'll answer your notes promptly enough, but his business letters—I believe he destroys them unopened to shake the responsibility of answering them."

"I am at a loss to see how you can have such patience with him, Tommy, in so many ways he is thoroughly reprehensible."

"Well, a man's likeableness don't depend at all on his virtues or acquirements, nor a woman's either, unfortunately. You like them or you don't like them, and that's all there is to it. For the why of it you must appeal to a higher oracle than I. Jay is a likeable fellow, and that's his only and sole acquirement, but after all it's a rather happy one."

"Yes, he certainly is that," replied Miss Jessica, as she deliberately turned off the gas jet and proceeded to arrange her toilet articles. Tommy watched her closely and then turned away with a baffled expression.

Needless to say, Tommy was not a boy, although her keen gray eyes and wide forehead were scarcely girlish, and she had the lank figure of an active half grown lad. Her real name was Theodosia, but during Thomas Shirley's frequent absences from the bank she had attended to his business and correspondence signing herself "T. Shirley," until everyone in Southdown called her "Tommy." That blunt sort of familiarity is not unfrequent in the West, and is meant well enough. People rather expect some business ability in a girl there, and they respect it immensely. That, Tommy undoubtedly had, and if she had not, things would have gone at sixes and sevens in the Southdown National. For Thomas Shirley had big land interests in Wyoming that called him constantly away from home, and his cashier, little Jay Ellington Harper, was, in the local phrase, a weak brother in the bank. He was the son of a friend of old Shirley's, whose papa had sent him West, because he had made a sad mess of his college career, and had spent too much money and gone at too giddy a pace down East. Conditions changed the young gentleman's life, for it was simply impossible to live either prodigally or rapidly in Southdown, but they could not materially affect his mental habits or inclinations. He was made cashier of Shirley's bank because his father bought in half the stock, but Tommy did his work for him.

The relation between these two young people was peculiar; Harper was, in his way, very grateful to her for keeping him out of disgrace with her father, and showed it by a hundred little attentions which were new to her and much more agreeable than the work she did for him was irksome. Tommy knew that she was immensely fond of him, and she knew at the same time that she was thoroughly foolish for being so. As she expressed it, she was not of his sort, and never would be. She did not often take pains to think, but when she did she saw matters pretty clearly, and she was of a peculiarly unfeminine mind that could not escape meeting and acknowledging a logical conclusion. But she went on liking Jay Ellington Harper, just the same. Now Harper was the only foolish man of Tommy's acquaintance. She knew plenty of active young business men and sturdy ranchers, such as one meets about live western towns, and took no particular interest in them, probably just because they were practical and sensible and thoroughly of her own kind. She knew almost no women, because in those days there were few women in Southdown who were in any sense interesting, or interested in anything but babies and salads. Her best friends were her father's old business friends, elderly men who had seen a good deal of the world, and who were very proud and fond of Tommy. They recognized a sort of squareness and honesty of spirit in the girl that Jay Ellington Harper never discovered, or, if he did, knew too little of its rareness to value highly. Those old speculators and men of business had always felt a sort of responsibility for Tom Shirley's little girl, and had rather taken her mother's place, and been her advisers on many points upon which men seldom feel at liberty to address a girl.

She was just one of them; she played whist and billiards with them, and made their cocktails for them, not scorning to take one herself occasionally. Indeed, Tommy's cocktails were things of fame in Southdown, and the professional compounders of drinks always bowed respectfully to her as though acknowledging a powerful rival.

Now all these things displeased and puzzled Jay Ellington Harper, and Tommy knew it full well, but clung to her old manner of living with a stubborn pertinacity, feeling somehow that to change would be both foolish and disloyal to the Old Boys. And as things went on, the seven Old Boys made greater demands upon her time than ever, for they were shrewd men, most of them, and had not lived fifty years in this world without learning a few things and unlearning many more. And while Tommy lived on in the blissful delusion that her role of indifference was perfectly played and without a flaw, they suspected how things were going and were perplexed as to the outcome. Still, their confidence was by no means shaken, and as Joe Elsworth said to Joe Sawyer one evening at billiards, "I think we can pretty nearly depend on Tommy's good sense."

They were too wise to say anything to Tommy, but they said just a word or two to Thomas Shirley, Sr., and combined to make things very unpleasant for Mr. Jay Ellington Harper.

At length their relations with Harper became so strained that the young man felt it would be better for him to leave town, so his father started him in a little bank of his own up in Red Willow. Red Willow, however, was scarcely a safe distance, being only some twenty-five miles north, upon the Divide, and Tommy occasionally found excuse to run up on her wheel to straighten out the young man's business for him. So when she suddenly decided to go East to school for a year, Thomas, Sr., drew a sigh of great relief. But the seven Old Boys shook their heads; they did not like to see her gravitating toward the East; it was a sign of weakening, they said, and showed an inclination to experiment with another kind of life, Jay Ellington Harper's kind.

But to school Tommy went, and from all reports conducted herself in a most seemly manner; made no more cocktails, played no more billiards. She took rather her own way with the curriculum, but she distinguished herself in athletics, which in Southdown counted for vastly more than erudition.

Her evident joy on getting back to Southdown was appreciated by everyone. She went about shaking hands with everybody, her shrewd face, that was so like a clever wholesome boy's, held high with happiness. As she said to old Joe Elsworth one morning, when they were driving behind his stud through a little thicket of cottonwood scattered along the sun-parched bluffs, "It's all very fine down East there, and the hills are great, but one gets mighty homesick for this sky, the old intense blue of it, you know. Down there the skies are all pale and smoky. And this wind, this hateful, dear, old everlasting wind that comes down like the sweep of cavalry and is never tamed or broken, O Joe, I used to get hungry for this wind! I couldn't sleep in that lifeless stillness down there."

"How about the people, Tom?"

"O, they are fine enough folk, but we're not their sort, Joe, and never can be."

"You realize that, do you, fully?"

"Quite fully enough, thank you, Joe." She laughed rather dismally, and Joe cut his horse with the whip.

The only unsatisfactory thing about Tommy's return was that she brought with her a girl she had grown fond of at school, a dainty, white, languid bit of a thing, who used violet perfumes and carried a sunshade. The Old Boys said it was a bad sign when a rebellious girl like Tommy took to being sweet and gentle to one of her own sex, the worst sign in the world.

The new girl was no sooner in town than a new complication came about. There was no doubt of the impression she made on Jay Ellington Harper. She indisputably had all those little evidences of good breeding that were about the only things which could touch the timid, harassed young man who was so much out of his element. It was a very plain case on his part, and the souls of the seven were troubled within them. Said Joe Elsworth to the other Joe, "The heart of the cad is gone out to the little muff, as is right and proper and in accordance with the eternal fitness of things. But there's the other girl who has the blindness that may not be cured, and she gets all the rub of it. It's no use, I can't help her, and I am going to run down to Kansas City for awhile. I can't stay here and see the abominable suffering of it." He didn't go, however.

There was just one other person who understood the hopelessness of the situation quite as well as Joe, and that was Tommy. That is, she understood Harper's attitude. As to Miss Jessica's she was not quite so certain, for Miss Jessica, though pale and languid and addicted to sunshades, was a maiden most discreet. Conversations on the subject usually ended without any further information as to Miss Jessica's feelings, and Tommy sometimes wondered if she were capable of having any at all.

At last the calamity which Tommy had long foretold descended upon Jay Ellington Harper. One morning she received a telegram from him begging her to intercede with her father; there was a run on his bank and he must have help before noon. It was then ten thirty, and the one sleepy little train that ran up to Red Willow daily had crawled out of the station an hour before. Thomas Shirley, Sr., was not at home.

"And it's a good thing for Jay Ellington he's not, he might be more stony hearted than I," remarked Tommy, as she closed the ledger and turned to the terrified Miss Jessica. "Of course we're his only chance, no one else would turn their hand over to help him. The train went an hour ago and he says it must be there by noon. It's the only bank in the town, so nothing can be done by telegraph. There is nothing left but to wheel for it. I may make it, and I may not. Jess, you scamper up to the house and get my wheel out, the tire may need a little attention. I will be along in a minute."

"O, Theodosia, can't I go with you? I must go!"

"You go! O, yes, of course, if you want to. You know what you are getting into, though. It's twenty-five miles uppish grade and hilly, and only an hour and a quarter to do it in."

"O, Theodosia, I can do anything now!" cried Miss Jessica, as she put up her sunshade and fled precipitately. Tommy smiled as she began cramming bank notes into a canvas bag. "May be you can, my dear, and may be you can't."

The road from Southdown to Red Willow is not by any means a favorite bicycle road; it is rough, hilly and climbs from the river bottoms up to the big Divide by a steady up grade, running white and hot through the scorched corn fields and grazing lands where the long-horned Texan cattle browse about in the old buffalo wallows. Miss Jessica soon found that with the pedaling that had to be done there was little time left for emotion of any sort, or little sensibility for anything but the throbbing, dazzling heat that had to be endured. Down there in the valley the distant bluffs were vibrating and dancing with the heat, the cattle, completely overcome by it, had hidden under the shelving banks of the "draws" and the prairie dogs had fled to the bottom of their holes that are said to reach to water. The whirr of the seventeen-year locust was the only thing that spoke of animation, and that ground on as if only animated and enlivened by the sickening, destroying heat. The sun was like hot brass, and the wind that blew up from the south was hotter still. But Tommy knew that wind was their only chance. Miss Jessica began to feel that unless she could stop and get some water she was not much longer for this vale of tears. She suggested this possibility to Tommy, but Tommy only shook her head, "Take too much time," and bent over her handle bars, never lifting her eyes from the road in front of her. It flashed upon Miss Jessica that Tommy was not only very unkind, but that she sat very badly on her wheel and looked aggressively masculine and professional when she bent her shoulders and pumped like that. But just then Miss Jessica found it harder than ever to breathe, and the bluffs across the river began doing serpentines and skirt dances, and more important and personal considerations occupied the young lady.

When they were fairly over the first half of the road, Tommy took out her watch. "Have to hurry up, Jess, I can't wait for you."

"O, Tommy, I can't," panted Miss Jessica, dismounting and sitting down in a little heap by the roadside. "You go on, Tommy, and tell him—tell him I hope it won't fail, and I'd do anything to save him."

By this time the discreet Miss Jessica was reduced to tears, and Tommy nodded as she disappeared over the hill laughing to herself. "Poor Jess, anything but the one thing he needs. Well, your kind have the best of it generally, but in little affairs of this sort my kind come out rather strongly. We're rather better at them than at dancing. It's only fair, one side shouldn't have all."

Just at twelve o'clock, when Jay Ellington Harper, his collar crushed and wet about his throat, his eyeglass dimmed with perspiration, his hair hanging damp over his forehead, and even the ends of his moustache dripping with moisture, was attempting to reason with a score of angry Bohemians, Tommy came quietly through the door, grip in hand. She went straight behind the grating, and standing screened by the book-keeper's desk, handed the bag to Harper and turned to the spokesman of the Bohemians.

"What's all this business mean, Anton? Do you all come to bank at once nowadays?"

"We want 'a money, want 'a our money, he no got it, no give it," bawled the big beery Bohemian.

"O, don't chaff 'em any longer, give 'em their money and get rid of 'em, I want to see you," said Tommy carelessly, as she went into the consulting room.

When Harper entered half an hour later, after the rush was over, all that was left of his usual immaculate appearance was his eyeglass and the white flower in his buttonhole.

"This has been terrible!" he gasped. "Miss Theodosia, I can never thank you."

"No," interrupted Tommy. "You never can, and I don't want any thanks. It was rather a tight place, though, wasn't it? You looked like a ghost when I came in. What started them?"

"How should I know? They just came down like the wolf on the fold. It sounded like the approach of a ghost dance."★

"And of course you had no reserve? O, I always told you this would come, it was inevitable with your charming methods. By the way, Jess sends her regrets and says she would do anything to save you. She started out with me, but she has fallen by the wayside. O, don't be alarmed, she is not hurt, just winded. I left her all bunched up by the road like a little white rabbit. I think the lack of romance in the escapade did her up about as much as anything; she is essentially romantic. If we had been on fiery steeds bespattered with foam I think she would have made it, but a wheel hurt her dignity. I'll tend bank; you'd better get your wheel and go and look her up and comfort her. And as soon as it is convenient, Jay, I wish you'd marry her and be done with it, I want to get this thing off my mind."

Jay Ellington Harper dropped into a chair and turned a shade whiter.

"Theodosia, what do you mean? Don't you remember what I said to you last fall, the night before you went to school? Don't you remember what I wrote you—"

Tommy sat down on the table beside him and looked seriously and frankly into his eyes.

"Now, see here, Jay Ellington, we have been playing a nice little game, and now it's time to quit. One must grow up sometime. You are horribly wrought up over Jess, and why deny it? She's your kind, and clean daft about you, so there is only one thing to do. That's all."

Jay Ellington wiped his brow, and felt unequal to the situation. Perhaps he really came nearer to being moved down to his stolid little depths than he ever had before. His voice shook a good deal and was very low as he answered her.

"You have been very good to me, I didn't believe any woman could be at once so kind and clever. You almost made a man of even me."

"Well, I certainly didn't succeed. As to being good to you, that's rather a break, you know; I am amiable, but I am only flesh and blood

★ The ghost dance, a ritualistic worship of Wovoka, a self-appointed Indian Messiah, was associated with the so-called Sioux Uprising of 1890, which culminated in the battle of Wounded Knee, in South Dakota near the Nebraska border, on December 29, 1890.

after all. Since I have known you I have not been at all good, in any sense of the word, and I suspect I have been anything but clever. Now, take mercy upon Jess—and me—and go. Go on, that ride is beginning to tell on me. Such things strain one's nerve. . . . Thank Heaven he's gone at last and had sense enough not to say anything more. It was growing rather critical. As I told him I am not at all superhuman."

After Jay Ellington Harper had bowed himself out, when Tommy sat alone in the darkened office, watching the flapping blinds, with the bank books before her, she noticed a white flower on the floor. It was the one Jay Ellington Harper had worn in his coat and had dropped in his nervous agitation. She picked it up and stood holding it a moment, biting her lip. Then she dropped it into the grate and turned away, shrugging her thin shoulders.

"They are awful idiots, half of them, and never think of anything beyond their dinner. But O, how we do like 'em!"

First published in *Home Monthly*, VI (August, 1896), 6–7.

"*A Night at Greenway Court*" *and* "*On the Divide*," *the opening stories in the following group of eight, were first published in 1896, when Willa Cather was dividing her time between Lincoln and Red Cloud after her graduation from the University of Nebraska. Curiously enough, these two stories—the last she wrote before leaving the Midwest to take an editorial position on the Pittsburgh* Home Monthly—*forecast the two main fictional paths she was to follow in her artistic maturity. In* "*A Night at Greenway Court*," *a story of Virginia in colonial days, Willa Cather is looking back to America's historic past as she was to do in* Death Comes for the Archbishop *and* Shadows on the Rock, *while the locale of* "*On the Divide*" *is that of* O Pioneers!, My Ántonia, The Song of the Lark, "*Neighbor Rosicky*," "*The Best Years*," *and the other Nebraska novels and stories.*

The six remaining stories, written while she was an undergraduate, all appeared in student publications. "*The Fear That Walks by Noonday*" (*1894*) *was suggested to the author by Dorothy Canfield Fisher, and is interesting chiefly for that reason. It was first published in the student annual, the* Sombrero; *in 1931—to Miss Cather's great distress—it was reprinted in a select edition of thirty copies. Two 1893 stories,* "*A Son of the Celestial*" *and* "*The Clemency of the Court*," *first came out in a campus literary magazine,* The Hesperian. "*A Son of the Celestial*" *was subsequently reworked and published in* The Library (*August 11, 1900*) *as* "*The Conversion of Sum Loo*" (*see page 323*). "*A Tale of the White Pyramid*," "*Lou, the Prophet*," *and* "*Peter*" *all appeared in* The Hesperian *in the fall and winter of 1892.* "*Peter*," *Willa Cather's first published story, had appeared earlier that year in a Boston literary weekly,* The Mahogany Tree. *Slightly revised for* The Hesperian, *it was revised again and published in* The Library (*July 21, 1900*) *under the title* "*Peter Sadelack, Father of Anton*." *The version reprinted here is the earliest—that which appeared in* The Mahogany Tree, *May 21, 1892.*

A Night at Greenway Court

✻ ✻ ✻

I, Richard Morgan, of the town of Winchester, county of Frederick, of the Commonwealth of Virginia, having been asked by my friend Josiah Goodrich, who purports making a history of this valley, to set down all I know concerning the death of M. Philip Marie Maurepas, a gentleman, it seems, of considerable importance in his own country, will proceed to do so briefly and with what little skill I am master of.

The incident which I am about to relate occurred in my early youth, but so deeply did it fix itself upon my memory that the details are as clear as though it had happened but yesterday. Indeed, of all the stirring events that have happened in my time, those nights spent at Greenway Court in my youth stand out most boldly in my memory. It was, I think, one evening late in October, in the year 1752, that my Lord Fairfax sent his man over to my father's house at Winchester to say that on the morrow his master desired my company at the Court. My father, a prosperous tobacco merchant, greatly regretted that I should be brought up in a new country, so far from the world of polite letters and social accomplishments, and contrived that I should pass much of my leisure in the company of one of the most gracious gentlemen and foremost scholars of his time, Thomas, Lord Fairfax. Accordingly, I was not surprised at my lord's summons. Late in the afternoon of the following day I rode over to the Court, and was first shown into my lord's private office, where for some time we discussed my lord's suit, then pending with the sons of Joist Hite, concerning certain lands beyond the Blue Ridge, then held by them, which my lord claimed through the extension of his grant from the crown. Our business being dispatched, he said:

"Come, Richard, in the hall I will present you to some gentlemen who will entertain you until supper time. There is a Frenchman stopping here, M. Maurepas, a gentleman of most engaging conversation. The Viscount Chillingham you will not meet until later, as he has gone out with the hounds."

We crossed the yard and entered the hall where the table was already laid with my lord's silver platters and thin glass goblets, which never ceased to delight me when I dined with him, and though since, in London, I have drunk wine at a king's table, I have seen none finer. At the end of the room, by the fire place, sat two men over their cards. One was a clergyman, whom I had met before, the other a tall spare gentleman whom my lord introduced as M. Philip Marie Maurepas. As I sat down, the gentleman addressed me in excellent English. The bright firelight gave me an excellent opportunity for observing this man, which I did, for with us strangers were too few not to be of especial interest, and in a way their very appearance spoke to us of an older world beyond the seas for which the hearts of all of us still hungered.

He was, as I have said, a tall man, narrow chested and with unusually long arms. His forehead was high and his chin sharp, his skin was dark, tanned, as I later learned, by his long service in the Indes. He had a pair of restless black eyes and thin lips shaded by a dark mustache. His hair was coal black and grew long upon his shoulders; later I noticed that it was slightly touched with gray. His dress had once been fine, but had seen considerable service and was somewhat the worse for the weather. He wore breeches of dark blue velvet and leather leggins. His shirt and vest were of dark red and had once been worked with gold.

In his belt he wore a long knife with a slender blade and a handle of gold curiously worked in the form of a serpent, with eyes of pure red stones which sparkled mightily in the firelight. I must confess that in the very appearance of this man there was something that both interested and attracted me, and I fell to wondering what strange sights those keen eyes of his had looked upon.

"M. Maurepas intends spending the winter in our wilderness, Richard, and I fear he will find that our woods offer a cold welcome to a stranger."

"Well, my lord, all the more to my taste. Having seen how hot the world can be, I am willing to see how cold."

"To see that, sir," said I, "you should go to Quebec where I have been with trappers. There I have thrown a cup full of water in the air and seen it descend solid ice."

"I fear it will be cold enough here for my present attire," said he laughing, "yet it may be that I will taste the air of Quebec before quitting this wilderness of yours."

My lord then excused himself and withdrew, leaving me alone with the gentlemen.

"Come join me in a game of hazard, Master Morgan; it is yet half an hour until supper time," said the clergyman, who had little thought for anything but his cards and his dinner.

"And I will look at the portraits; you have fleeced me quite enough for one day, good brother of the Church. I have nothing left but my diamond that I cut from the hand of a dead Rajpoot, finger and all, and it is a lucky stone, and I have no mind to lose it."

"With your permission, M. Maurepas, I will look at the portraits with you, as I have no mind to play tonight; besides I think this is the hour for Mr. Courtney's devotions," said I, for I had no liking for the fat churchman. He, like so many of my lord's guests, was in a sense a refugee from justice; having fallen into disgrace with the heads of the English church, he had fled to our country and sought out Lord Fairfax, whose door was closed against no man. He had been there then three months, dwelling in shameful idleness, one of that band of renegades who continually ate at my lord's table and hunted with his dogs and devoured his substance, waiting for some turn of fortune, like the suitors in the halls of Penelope. So we left the clergyman counting his gains and repaired to the other end of the hall, where, above the mahogany bookcases, the portraits hung. Of these there were a considerable number, and I told the Frenchman the names of as many as I knew. There was my lord's father and mother, and his younger brother, to whom he had given his English estate. There was his late majesty George I, and old Fernando Fairfax. Hanging under the dark picture of the king he had deposed and yet loved was Fernando's son, fighting Thomas Fairfax, third Lord and Baron of Cameron, the great leader of the commoners with Cromwell, who rode after Charles at Heyworth Moor and thrust the people's petition in the indignant monarch's saddle bow; who defeated the king's forces at Naseby, and after Charles was delivered over to the commissioners of Parliament, met him at Nottingham and kissed his fallen sovereign's hand, refusing to sit in judgment over God's anointed.

Among these pictures there was one upon which I had often gazed in wonderment. It was the portrait of a lady, holding in her hand a white lily. Some heavy instrument had been thrust through the canvas, marring the face beyond all recognition, but the masses of powdered hair, and throat and arms were enough to testify to the beauty of the original. The hands especially were of surpassing loveliness, and the thumb was ornamented with a single emerald, as though to call attention to its singular perfection. The costume was the court dress of the then present reign, and with the eagerness of youthful imagination I had often fancied that could that picture speak it might tell something of that upon which all men wondered; why, in the prime of his manhood and success at court, Lord Fairfax had left home and country, friends, and all that men hold dear, renounced the gay society in which he had shone and his favorite pursuit of letters, and buried himself in the North American wilderness. Upon this canvas the Frenchman's eye was soon fixed.

"And this?" he asked.

"I do not know, sir; of that my lord has never told me."

"Well, let me see; what is a man's memory good for, if not for such things? I must have seen those hands before, and that coronet."

He looked at it closely and then stood back and looked at it from a distance. Suddenly an exclamation broke from him, and a sharp light flashed over his features.

"Ah, I thought so! So your lord has never told you of this, *parbleau, il a beaucoup de cause*! Look you, my boy, that emerald is the only beautiful thing that ever came out of Herrenhausen—that, and she who wears it. Perhaps you will see that emerald, too, some day; how many and how various they will yet be, God alone knows. How long, O Lord, how long? as your countrymen say."

So bitter was his manner that I was half afraid, yet had a mind to question him, when my lord returned. He brought with him a young man of an appearance by no means distinguished, yet kindly and affable, whom he introduced as the Viscount Chillingham.

"You've a good country here, Master Norton, and better sport than we, for all our game laws. Hang laws, I say, they're naught but a trouble to them that make 'em and them that break 'em, and it's little good they do any of us. My lord, you must sell me your deer hound, Fanny, I want to take her home with me, and show 'em what your dogs are made of over here."

"You are right welcome to her, or any of the pack."

At this juncture my lord's housekeeper, Mistress Crawford, brought in the silver candlesticks, and the servants smoking dishes of bear's meat and venison, and many another delicacy for which my lord's table was famous, besides French wines and preserved cherries from his old estates in England.

The viscount flung himself into his chair, still flushed from his chase after the hounds, and stretched his long limbs.

"This is a man's life you have here, my lord. I tell you, you do well to be away from London now; it's as dull there as Mr. Courtney's church without its spiritual pastor."

The clergyman lifted his eyes from his venison long enough to remark slyly, "Or as Hampton Court without its cleverest gamester," at which the young man reddened under his fresh coat of tan, for he had been forced to leave England because of some gaming scandal which cast grave doubts upon his personal honor.

The talk drifted to the death of the queen of Denmark, the king's last visit to Hanover, and various matters of court gossip. Of these the gentlemen spoke freely, more freely, perhaps, than they would have dared do at home. As I have said, my lord's guests were too often gentlemen who had left dark histories behind them, and had fled into the wilds where law was scarce more than a name and man had to contend only with the savage condition of nature, and a strong arm stood in better stead than a tender conscience. I have met many a strange man at Greenway Court, men who had cheated at play, men who had failed in great political plots, men who fled from a debtor's prison, and men charged with treason, and with a price upon their heads. For in some respects Lord Fairfax was a strangely conservative man, slow to judge and slow to anger, having seen much of the world, and thinking its conditions hard and its temptations heavy, deeming, I believe, all humanity more sinned against than sinning. And yet I have seldom known his confidence to be misplaced or his trust to be ill repaid. Whatever of information I may have acquired in my youth, I owe to the conversation of these men, for about my lord's board exiles and outlaws of all nations gathered, and unfolded in the friendly solitude of the wilderness plots and intrigues then scarce known in Europe.

On all the matters that were discussed the Frenchman seemed the best versed man present, even touching the most minute details of the English court. At last the viscount, who was visibly surprised, turned upon him sharply.

"Have you been presented at court, monsieur?"

"Not in England, count, but I have seen something of your king in Hanover; there, I think, on the banks of the stupid Leine, is his proper court, and 'tis there he sends the riches of your English. But in exchange I hear that he has brought you his treasure of Herrenhausen in her private carriage with a hundred postilions to herald her advent."

His eyes were fixed keenly on my lord's face, but Fairfax only asked coldly:

"And where, monsieur, have you gained so perfect a mastery of the English tongue?"

"At Madras, your lordship, under Bourdonnais, where I fought your gallant countrymen, high and low, for the empire of the Indes. They taught me the sound of English speech well enough, and the music of English swords."

"Faith," broke in the viscount, "then they taught you better than they know themselves, though it's their mother tongue. You've seen hot service there, I warrant?"

"Well, what with English guns sweeping our decks by sea, and the Indian sun broiling our skin by land, and the cholera tearing our entrails, we saw hot service indeed."

"Were you in the Indian service after the return of Governor Bourdonnais to France, M. Maurepas?"

"After his return to the Bastille, you mean, my lord. Yes, I was less fortunate than my commander. There are worse prisons on earth than the Bastille, and Madras is one of them. When France sends a man to the Indes she has no intention he shall return alive. How I did so is another matter. Yes, I served afterward under Dupleix, who seized Bourdonnais' troops as well as his treasure. I was with him in the Deccan when he joined his troops with Murzapha Jung against the Nabob of the Carnatic, and white men were set to fight side by side with heathen. And I say to you, gentlemen, that the bravest man in all that mêlée was the old Nabob himself. He was a hundred and seven years old, and he had been a soldier from his mother's knee. He was mounted on the finest elephant in the Indian army, and he led his soldiers right up into the thick of the fight in full sweep of the French bullets, ordering his body-guard back and attended only by his driver. And when he saw his old enemy, Tecunda Sahib, in the very midst of the French guards, he ordered his driver to up and at him, and he prodded the beast forward with his own hand. When the beast came crashing through our lines a bullet struck the old man in the breast, but still he urged him on. And when the elephant was stopped the driver was gone and the old Nabob was stone dead, sitting bolt upright in his curtained cage with a naked scimitar in his hand, ready for his vengeance. And I tell ye now, gentlemen, that I for one was right sorry that the bullet went home, for I am not the man who would see a brave soldier balked of his revenge."

It is quite impossible with the pen to give any adequate idea of the dramatic manner in which he related this. I think it stirred the blood of more than one of us. The viscount struck the table with his hand and cried:

"That's talking, sir; you see the best of life, you French. As for us, we are so ridden by kingcraft and statecraft we are as good as dead men. Between Walpole and the little German we have forgot the looks of a sword, and we never hear a gun these times but at the christening of some brat or other."

The clergyman looked up reproachfully from his preserved cherries, and Lord Fairfax, who seldom suffered any talk that savored of disloyalty, rose to his feet and lifted his glass.

"Gentlemen, the king's health."

"The king's health," echoed we all rising. But M. Maurepas sat stiff in his chair, and his glass stood full beside him. The viscount turned upon him fiercely.

"Monsieur, you do not drink the king's health?"

"No, sir; your king, nor my king, nor no man's king. I have no king. May the devil take them one and all! and that's my health to them."

"Monsieur," cried my lord sternly, "I am surprised to hear a soldier of the king of France speak in this fashion."

"Yes, my lord, I have been a soldier of the king, and I know the wages of kings. What were they for Bourdonnais, the bravest general who ever drew a sword? The Bastille! What were they for all my gallant comrades? Cholera, massacre, death in the rotting marshes of Pondicherry. *Le Diable!* I know them well; prison, the sword, the stake, the recompense of kings." He laughed terribly and struck his forehead with his hand.

"Monsieur," said my lord, "It may be that you have suffered much, and for that reason only do I excuse much that you say. Human justice is often at fault, and kings are but human. Nevertheless, they are ordained of heaven, and so long as there is breath in our bodies we owe them loyal service."

The Frenchman rose and stood, his dark eyes flashing like coals of fire and his hands trembling as he waved them in the air. And methought the prophets of Israel must have looked so when they cried out unto the people, though his words were as dark blasphemy as ever fell from human lips.

"I tell you, sir, that the day will come and is now at hand when there will be no more kings. When a king's blood will be cheaper than pot-house wine and flow as plentifully. When crowned heads will pray for a peasant's cap, and princes will hide their royal lineage as lepers hide their sores. Ordained of God! Look you, sir, there is a wise man of France, so wise indeed that he dares not dwell in France, but hides among the Prussians, who says that there is no God! No Jehovah with his frying pan of lost souls! That it is all a tale made up by kings to terrify their slaves; that instead of God making kings, the kings made God."

We were all struck with horror and the viscount rose to his feet again and threw himself into an attitude of attack, while Mr. Courtney, whose place it was to speak, cowered in his seat and continued to look wistfully at the cherries.

"Stop, sir," bawled the viscount, "we have not much faith left in England, thanks to such as Mr. Courtney here, but we've enough still to fight for. Little George may have his faults, but he's a brave man and a soldier. Let us see whether you can be as much."

But the Frenchman did not so much as look at him. He was well sped with wine, and in his eyes there was a fierce light as of some ancient hatred woke anew. Staggering down the hall he pointed to the canvas which had so interested him in the afternoon.

"My lord, I wonder at you, that you should dare to keep that picture here, though three thousand miles of perilous sea, and savagery, and forests, and mountains impassable lie between you and Hampton Court. If you are a man, I think you have no cause to love the name of king. Yet, is not your heart as good as any man's, and will not your money buy as many trinkets? I tell you, this wilderness is not dark enough to hide that woman's face! And she carries a lily in her hand, the lilies of Herren-hausen! *Justice de Dieu*—" but he got no further, for my lord's hand had struck him in the mouth.

It all came about so quickly that even then it was but a blur of sudden action to me. We sprang between them, but Fairfax had no intention of striking twice.

"We can settle this in the morning, sir," he said quietly. As he turned away M. Maurepas drew himself together with the litheness of a cat, and before I could catch his arm he had seized the long knife from his belt and thrown it after his host. It whizzed past my lord and stuck quivering in the oak wainscoting, while the man who threw it sank upon the floor a pitiable heap of intoxication. My lord turned to his man, who still stood behind his chair. "Henry, call me at five; at six I shall kill a scoundrel."

With that he left us to watch over the drunken slumbers of the Frenchman.

In the morning they met on the level stretch before the court. At my lord's request I stood as second to M. Maurepas. My principal was much shaken by his debauch of last night, and I thought when my lord looked upon him he was already dead. For in Lord Fairfax's face was a purpose which it seemed no human will could thwart. Never have I seen him look the noble, Christian gentleman as he looked it then. Just as the autumn mists were rising from the hills, their weapons crossed, and the rising sun shot my lord's blade with fire until it looked the sword of righteousness indeed. It lasted but a moment. M. Maurepas, so renowned in war and gallantry, who had been the shame of two courts and the rival of two kings, fell, unknown and friendless, in the wilderness.

Two years later, after I had been presented and, through my father, stood in favor at court, I once had the honor to dine with his majesty at Hampton Court. At his right sat a woman known to history only too well; still brilliant, still beautiful, as she was unto the end. By her side I was seated. When the dishes were removed, as we sat over our wine, the king bade me tell him some of the adventures that had befallen in my own land.

"I can tell you, your majesty, how Lord Fairfax fought and killed M. Maurepas about a woman's picture."

"That sounds well, tell on," said the monarch in his heavy accent.

Then upon my hand under the table I felt a clasp, cold and trembling. I glanced down and saw there a white hand of wondrous beauty, the thumb ornamented with a single emerald. I sat still in amazement, for the lady's face was smiling and gave no sign.

The king clinked his glass impatiently with his nail.

"Well, go on with your story. Are we to wait on you all day?"

Again I felt that trembling pressure in mute entreaty on my hand.

"I think there is no story to tell, your majesty."

"And I think you are a very stupid young man," said his majesty testily, as he rose from the table.

"Perhaps he is abashed," laughed my lady, but her bosom heaved with a deep sigh of relief.

So my day of royal favor was a short one, nor was I sorry, for I had kept my friend's secret and shielded a fair lady's honor, which are the two first duties of a Virginian.

First published in *Nebraska Literary Magazine*, I (June, 1896), 215–224.

On the Divide

❋　❋　❋

Near Rattlesnake Creek, on the side of a little draw, stood Canute's shanty. North, east, south, stretched the level Nebraska plain of long rust-red grass that undulated constantly in the wind. To the west the ground was broken and rough, and a narrow strip of timber wound along the turbid, muddy little stream that had scarcely ambition enough to crawl over its black bottom. If it had not been for the few stunted cottonwoods and elms that grew along its banks, Canute would have shot himself years ago. The Norwegians are a timber-loving people, and if there is even a turtle pond with a few plum bushes around it they seem irresistibly drawn toward it.

As to the shanty itself, Canute had built it without aid of any kind, for when he first squatted along the banks of Rattlesnake Creek there was not a human being within twenty miles. It was built of logs split in halves, the chinks stopped with mud and plaster. The roof was covered with earth and was supported by one gigantic beam curved in the shape of a round arch. It was almost impossible that any tree had ever grown in that shape. The Norwegians used to say that Canute had taken the log across his knee and bent it into the shape he wished. There were two rooms, or rather there was one room with a partition made of ash saplings interwoven and bound together like big straw basket work. In one corner there was a cook stove, rusted and broken. In the other a bed made of unplaned planks and poles. It was fully eight feet long, and upon it was a heap of dark bed clothing. There was a chair and a bench of colossal proportions. There was an ordinary kitchen cupboard with a few cracked dirty dishes in it, and beside it on a tall box a tin washbasin. Under the bed was a pile of pint flasks, some broken, some whole, all empty. On the wood box lay a pair of shoes of almost incredible dimensions. On the wall hung a saddle, a gun, and some ragged clothing, conspicuous among which was a suit of dark cloth, apparently new, with a paper collar carefully wrapped in a red silk handkerchief and pinned to the sleeve. Over the door hung a wolf and a badger skin, and on the door itself a brace of thirty or forty snake skins whose noisy tails rattled ominously every time it opened. The strangest things in the shanty were the wide window sills. At first glance they looked as though they had been ruthlessly hacked and mutilated with a hatchet, but on closer inspection all the notches and holes in the wood took form and shape. There seemed to be a series of pictures. They were, in a rough way, artistic, but the figures were heavy and labored, as though they had been cut very slowly and with very awkward instruments. There were men plowing with little horned imps sitting on their shoulders and on their horses' heads. There were men praying with a skull hanging over their heads and little demons behind them mocking their attitudes. There were men fighting with big serpents, and skeletons dancing together. All about these pictures were blooming vines and foliage such as never grew in this world, and coiled among the branches of the vines there was always the scaly body of a serpent, and behind every flower there was a serpent's head. It was a veritable Dance of Death by one who had felt its sting. In the wood box lay some boards, and every inch of them was cut up in the same manner. Sometimes the work was very rude and careless, and looked as though the hand of the workman had trembled. It would sometimes have been hard to distinguish the men from their evil geniuses but for one fact, the men were always grave and were either toiling or praying, while the devils were always smiling and dancing. Several of these boards had been split for kindling and it was evident that the artist did not value his work highly.

It was the first day of winter on the Divide. Canute stumbled into his shanty carrying a basket of cobs, and after filling the stove, sat down on a stool and crouched his seven foot frame over the fire, staring drearily out of the window at the wide gray sky. He knew by heart every individual clump of bunch grass in the miles of red shaggy prairie that stretched before his cabin. He knew it in all the deceitful loveliness of its early summer, in all the bitter barrenness of its autumn. He had seen it smitten by all the plagues of Egypt. He had seen it parched by drought, and sogged by rain, beaten by hail, and swept by fire, and in the grasshopper years he had seen it eaten as bare and clean as bones that the vultures have left. After the great fires he had seen it stretch for miles and miles, black and smoking as the floor of hell.

He rose slowly and crossed the room, dragging his big feet heavily as though they were burdens to him. He looked out of the window into the hog corral and saw the pigs burying themselves in the straw before the shed. The leaden gray clouds were beginning to spill themselves, and the snow-flakes were settling down over the white leprous patches of frozen earth where the hogs had gnawed even the sod away. He shuddered and began to walk, trampling heavily with his ungainly feet. He was the wreck of ten winters on the Divide and he knew what they meant. Men fear the winters of the Divide as a child fears night or as men in the North Seas fear the still dark cold of the polar twilight.

His eyes fell upon his gun, and he took it down from the wall and looked it over. He sat down on the edge of his bed and held the barrel towards his face, letting his forehead rest upon it, and laid his finger on the trigger. He was perfectly calm, there was neither passion nor despair in his face, but the thoughtful look of a man who is considering. Presently he laid down the gun, and reaching into the cupboard, drew out a pint bottle of raw white alcohol. Lifting it to his lips, he drank greedily. He washed his face in the tin basin and combed his rough hair and shaggy blond beard. Then he stood in uncertainty before the suit of dark clothes that hung on the wall. For the fiftieth time he took them in his hands and tried to summon courage to put them on. He took the paper collar that was pinned to the sleeve of the coat and cautiously slipped it under his rough beard, looking with timid expectancy into the cracked, splashed glass that hung over the bench. With a short laugh he threw it down on the bed, and pulling on his old black hat, he went out, striking off across the level.

It was a physical necessity for him to get away from his cabin once in a while. He had been there for ten years, digging and plowing and sowing, and reaping what little the hail and the hot winds and the frosts left him to reap. Insanity and suicide are very common things on the Divide. They come on like an epidemic in the hot wind season. Those scorching dusty winds that blow up over the bluffs from Kansas seem to dry up the blood in men's veins as they do the sap in the corn leaves. Whenever the yellow scorch creeps down over the tender inside leaves about the ear, then the coroners prepare for active duty; for the oil of the country is burned out and it does not take long for the flame to eat up the wick. It causes no great sensation there when a Dane is found swinging to his own windmill tower, and most of the Poles after they have become too careless and discouraged to shave themselves keep their razors to cut their throats with.

It may be that the next generation on the Divide will be very happy, but the present one came too late in life. It is useless for men that have cut hemlocks among the mountains of Sweden for forty years to try to be happy in a country as flat and gray and as naked as the sea. It is not easy for men that have spent their youths fishing in the Northern seas to be content with following a plow, and men that have served in the Austrian army hate hard work and coarse clothing and the loneliness of the plains, and long for marches and excitement and tavern company and pretty barmaids. After a man has passed his fortieth birthday it is not easy for him to change the habits and conditions of his life. Most men bring with them to the Divide only the dregs of the lives that they have squandered in other lands and among other peoples.

Canute Canuteson was as mad as any of them, but his madness did not take the form of suicide or religion but of alcohol. He had always taken liquor when he wanted it, as all Norwegians do, but after his first year of solitary life he settled down to it steadily. He exhausted whisky after a while, and went to alcohol, because its effects were speedier and surer. He was a big man with a terrible amount of resistant force, and it took a great deal of alcohol even to move him. After nine years of drinking, the quantities he could take would seem fabulous to an ordinary drinking man. He never let it interfere with his work, he generally drank at night and on Sundays. Every night, as soon as his chores were done, he began to drink. While he was able to sit up he would play on his mouth harp or hack away at his window sills with his jackknife. When the liquor went to his head he would lie down on his bed and stare out of the window until he went to sleep. He drank alone and in solitude not for pleasure or good cheer, but to forget the awful loneliness and level of the Divide. Milton made a sad blunder when he put mountains in hell. Mountains postulate faith and aspiration. All mountain peoples are religious. It was the cities of the plains that, because of their utter lack of spirituality and the mad caprice of their vice, were cursed of God.

Alcohol is perfectly consistent in its effects upon man. Drunkenness is merely an exaggeration. A foolish man drunk becomes maudlin; a bloody man, vicious; a coarse man, vulgar. Canute was none of these, but he was morose and gloomy, and liquor took him through all the hells of Dante. As he lay on his giant's bed all the horrors of this world and every other were laid bare to his chilled senses. He was a man who knew no joy, a man who toiled in silence and bitterness. The skull and the serpent were always before him, the symbols of eternal futileness and of eternal hate.

When the first Norwegians near enough to be called neighbors came, Canute rejoiced, and planned to escape from his bosom vice. But he was not a social man by nature and had not the power of drawing out the social side of other people. His new neighbors rather feared him because of his great strength and size, his silence and his lowering brows. Perhaps, too, they knew that he was mad, mad from the eternal treachery of the plains, which every spring stretch green and rustle with the promises of Eden, showing long grassy lagoons full of clear water and cattle whose hoofs are stained with wild roses. Before autumn the lagoons are dried up, and the ground is burnt dry and hard until it blisters and cracks open.

So instead of becoming a friend and neighbor to the men that settled about him, Canute became a mystery and a terror. They told awful stories of his size and strength and of the alcohol he drank. They said that one night, when he went out to see to his horses just before he went to bed, his steps were unsteady and the rotten planks of the floor gave way and threw him behind the feet of a fiery young stallion. His foot was caught fast in the floor, and the nervous horse began kicking frantically. When Canute felt the blood trickling down into his eyes from a scalp wound in his head, he roused himself from his kingly indifference, and with the quiet stoical courage of a drunken man leaned forward and wound his arms about the horse's hind legs and held them against his breast with crushing embrace. All through the darkness and cold of the night he lay there, matching strength against strength. When little Jim Peterson went over the next morning at four o'clock to go with him to the Blue to cut wood, he found him so, and the horse was on its foreknees, trembling and whinnying with fear. This is the story the Norwegians tell of him, and if it is true it is no wonder that they feared and hated this Holder of the Heels of Horses.

One spring there moved to the next "eighty" a family that made a great change in Canute's life. Ole Yensen was too drunk most of the time to be afraid of any one, and his wife Mary was too garrulous to be afraid of any one who listened to her talk, and Lena, their pretty daughter, was not afraid of man nor devil. So it came about that Canute went over to take his alcohol with Ole oftener than he took it alone. After a while the report spread that he was going to marry Yensen's daughter, and the Norwegian girls began to tease Lena about the great bear she was going to keep house for. No one could quite see how the affair had come about, for Canute's tactics of courtship were somewhat peculiar. He apparently never spoke to her at all: he would sit for hours with Mary chattering on one side of him and Ole drinking on the other and watch Lena at her work. She teased him, and threw flour in his face and put vinegar in his coffee, but he took her rough jokes with silent wonder, never even smiling. He took her to church occasionally, but the most watchful and curious people never saw him speak to her. He would sit staring at her while she giggled and flirted with the other men.

Next spring Mary Lee went to town to work in a steam laundry. She came home every Sunday, and always ran across to Yensens to startle Lena with stories of ten cent theatres, firemen's dances, and all the other esthetic delights of metropolitan life. In a few weeks Lena's head was completely turned, and she gave her father no rest until he let her go to town to seek her fortune at the ironing board. From the time she came home on her first visit she began to treat Canute with contempt. She had bought a plush cloak and kid gloves, had her clothes made by the dressmaker, and assumed airs and graces that made the other women of the neighborhood cordially detest her. She generally brought with her a young man from town who waxed his mustache and wore a red necktie, and she did not even introduce him to Canute.

The neighbors teased Canute a good deal until he knocked one of them down. He gave no sign of suffering from her neglect except that he drank more and avoided the other Norwegians more carefully than ever. He lay around in his den and no one knew what he felt or thought, but little Jim Peterson, who had seen him glowering at Lena in church one Sunday when she was there with the town man, said that he would not give an acre of his wheat for Lena's life or the town chap's either; and Jim's wheat was so wondrously worthless that the statement was an exceedingly strong one.

Canute had bought a new suit of clothes that looked as nearly like the town man's as possible. They had cost him half a millet crop; for tailors are not accustomed to fitting giants and they charge for it. He had hung those clothes in his shanty two months ago and had never put them on, partly from fear of ridicule, partly from discouragement, and partly because there was something in his own soul that revolted at the littleness of the device.

Lena was at home just at this time. Work was slack in the laundry and Mary had not been well, so Lena stayed at home, glad enough to get an opportunity to torment Canute once more.

She was washing in the side kitchen, singing loudly as she worked. Mary was on her knees, blacking the stove and scolding violently about the young man who was coming out from town that night. The young man had committed the fatal error of laughing at Mary's ceaseless babble and had never been forgiven.

"He is no good, and you will come to a bad end by running with him! I do not see why a daughter of mine should act so. I do not see why the Lord should visit such a punishment upon me as to give me such a daughter. There are plenty of good men you can marry."

Lena tossed her head and answered curtly, "I don't happen to want to marry any man right away, and so long as Dick dresses nice and has plenty of money to spend, there is no harm in my going with him."

"Money to spend? Yes, and that is all he does with it I'll be bound. You think it very fine now, but you will change your tune when you have been married five years and see your children running naked and your cupboard empty. Did Anne Hermanson come to any good end by marrying a town man?"

"I don't know anything about Anne Hermanson, but I know any of the laundry girls would have Dick quick enough if they could get him."

"Yes, and a nice lot of store clothes huzzies you are too. Now there is Canuteson who has an 'eighty' proved up and fifty head of cattle and—"

"And hair that ain't been cut since he was a baby, and a big dirty beard, and he wears overalls on Sundays, and drinks like a pig. Besides he will keep. I can have all the fun I want, and when I am old and ugly like you he can have me and take care of me. The Lord knows there ain't nobody else going to marry him."

Canute drew his hand back from the latch as though it were red hot. He was not the kind of man to make a good eavesdropper, and he wished he had knocked sooner. He pulled himself together and struck the door like a battering ram. Mary jumped and opened it with a screech.

"God! Canute, how you scared us! I thought it was crazy Lou—he has been tearing around the neighborhood trying to convert folks. I am afraid as death of him. He ought to be sent off, I think. He is just as liable as not to kill us all, or burn the barn, or poison the dogs. He has been worrying even the poor minister to death, and he laid up with the rheumatism, too! Did you notice that he was too sick to preach last Sunday? But don't stand there in the cold—come in. Yensen isn't here, but he just went over to Sorenson's for the mail; he won't be gone long. Walk right in the other room and sit down."

Canute followed her, looking steadily in front of him and not noticing Lena as he passed her. But Lena's vanity would not allow him to pass unmolested. She took the wet sheet she was wringing out and cracked him across the face with it, and ran giggling to the other side of the room. The blow stung his cheeks and the soapy water flew in his eyes, and he involuntarily began rubbing them with his hands. Lena giggled with delight at his discomfiture, and the wrath in Canute's face grew blacker than ever. A big man humiliated is vastly more undignified than a little one. He forgot the sting of his face in the bitter consciousness that he had made a fool of himself. He stumbled blindly into the living room, knocking his head against the door jamb because he forgot to stoop. He dropped into a chair behind the stove, thrusting his big feet back helplessly on either side of him.

Ole was a long time in coming, and Canute sat there, still and silent, with his hands clenched on his knees, and the skin of his face seemed to have shriveled up into little wrinkles that trembled when he lowered his brows. His life had been one long lethargy of solitude and alcohol, but now he was awakening, and it was as when the dumb stagnant heat of summer breaks out into thunder.

When Ole came staggering in, heavy with liquor, Canute rose at once.

"Yensen," he said quietly, "I have come to see if you will let me marry your daughter today."

"Today!" gasped Ole.

"Yes, I will not wait until tomorrow. I am tired of living alone."

Ole braced his staggering knees against the bedstead, and stammered eloquently: "Do you think I will marry my daughter to a drunkard? a man who drinks raw alcohol? a man who sleeps with rattlesnakes? Get out of my house or I will kick you out for your impudence." And Ole began looking anxiously for his feet.

Canute answered not a word, but he put on his hat and went out into the kitchen. He went up to Lena and said without looking at her, "Get your things on and come with me!"

The tone of his voice startled her, and she said angrily, dropping the soap, "Are you drunk?"

"If you do not come with me, I will take you—you had better come," said Canute quietly.

She lifted a sheet to strike him, but he caught her arm roughly and wrenched the sheet from her. He turned to the wall and took down a hood and shawl that hung there, and began wrapping her up. Lena scratched and fought like a wild thing. Ole stood in the door, cursing, and Mary howled and screeched at the top of her voice. As for Canute, he lifted the girl in his arms and went out of the house. She kicked and struggled, but the helpless wailing of Mary and Ole soon died away in the distance, and her face was held down tightly on Canute's shoulder so that she could not see whither he was taking her. She was conscious only of the north wind whistling in her ears, and of rapid steady motion and of a great breast that heaved beneath her in quick, irregular breaths. The harder she struggled the tighter those iron arms that had held the heels of horses crushed about her, until she felt as if they would crush the breath from her, and lay still with fear. Canute was striding across the level fields at a pace at which man never went before, drawing the stinging north wind into his lungs in great gulps. He walked with his eyes half closed and looking straight in front of him, only lowering them when he bent his head to blow away the snow-flakes that settled on her hair. So it was that Canute took her to his home, even as his bearded barbarian ancestors took the fair frivolous women of the South in their hairy arms and bore them down to their war ships. For ever and anon the soul becomes weary of the conventions that are not of it, and with a single stroke shatters the civilized lies with which it is unable to cope, and the strong arm reaches out and takes by force what it cannot win by cunning.

When Canute reached his shanty he placed the girl upon a chair, where she sat sobbing. He stayed only a few minutes. He filled the stove with wood and lit the lamp, drank a huge swallow of alcohol and put the bottle in his pocket. He paused a moment, staring heavily at the weeping girl, then he went off and locked the door and disappeared in the gathering gloom of the night.

Wrapped in flannels and soaked with turpentine, the little Norwegian preacher sat reading his Bible, when he heard a thundering knock at his door, and Canute entered, covered with snow and with his beard frozen fast to his coat.

"Come in, Canute, you must be frozen," said the little man, shoving a chair towards his visitor.

Canute remained standing with his hat on and said quietly, "I want you to come over to my house tonight to marry me to Lena Yensen."

"Have you got a license, Canute?"

"No, I don't want a license. I want to be married."

"But I can't marry you without a license, man. It would not be legal."

A dangerous light came in the big Norwegian's eye. "I want you to come over to my house to marry me to Lena Yensen."

"No, I can't, it would kill an ox to go out in a storm like this, and my rheumatism is bad tonight."

"Then if you will not go I must take you," said Canute with a sigh.

He took down the preacher's bearskin coat and bade him put it on while he hitched up his buggy. He went out and closed the door softly after him. Presently he returned and found the frightened minister crouching before the fire with his coat lying beside him. Canute helped him put it on and gently wrapped his head in his big muffler. Then he picked him up and carried him out and placed him in his buggy. As he tucked the buffalo robes around him he said: "Your horse is old, he might flounder or lose his way in this storm. I will lead him."

The minister took the reins feebly in his hands and sat shivering with the cold. Sometimes when there was a lull in the wind, he could see the horse struggling through the snow with the man plodding steadily beside him. Again the blowing snow would hide them from him altogether. He had no idea where they were or what direction they were going. He felt as though he were being whirled away in the heart of the storm, and he said all the prayers he knew. But at last the long four miles were over, and Canute set him down in the snow while he unlocked the door. He saw the bride sitting by the fire with her eyes red and swollen as though she had been weeping. Canute placed a huge chair for him, and said roughly,

"Warm yourself."

Lena began to cry and moan afresh, begging the minister to take her home. He looked helplessly at Canute. Canute said simply,

"If you are warm now, you can marry us."

"My daughter, do you take this step of your own free will?" asked the minister in a trembling voice.

"No sir, I don't, and it is disgraceful he should force me into it! I won't marry him."

"Then, Canute, I cannot marry you," said the minister, standing as straight as his rheumatic limbs would let him.

"Are you ready to marry us now, sir?" said Canute, laying one iron hand on his stooped shoulder. The little preacher was a good man, but like most men of weak body he was a coward and had a horror of physical suffering, although he had known so much of it. So with many qualms of conscience he began to repeat the marriage service. Lena sat sullenly in her chair, staring at the fire. Canute stood beside her, listening with his head bent reverently and his hands folded on his breast. When the little man had prayed and said amen, Canute began bundling him up again.

"I will take you home, now," he said as he carried him out and placed him in his buggy, and started off with him through the fury of the storm, floundering among the snow drifts that brought even the giant himself to his knees.

After she was left alone, Lena soon ceased weeping. She was not of a particularly sensitive temperament, and had little pride beyond that of vanity. After the first bitter anger wore itself out, she felt nothing more than a healthy sense of humiliation and defeat. She had no inclination to run away, for she was married now, and in her eyes that was final and all rebellion was useless. She knew nothing about a license, but she knew that a preacher married folks. She consoled herself by thinking that she had always intended to marry Canute someday, anyway.

She grew tired of crying and looking into the fire, so she got up and began to look about her. She had heard queer tales about the inside of Canute's shanty, and her curiosity soon got the better of her rage. One of the first things she noticed was the new black suit of clothes hanging on the wall. She was dull, but it did not take a vain woman long to interpret anything so decidedly flattering, and she was pleased in spite of herself. As she looked through the cupboard, the general air of neglect and discomfort made her pity the man who lived there.

"Poor fellow, no wonder he wants to get married to get somebody to wash up his dishes. Batchin's pretty hard on a man."

It is easy to pity when once one's vanity has been tickled. She looked at the window sill and gave a little shudder and wondered if the man were crazy. Then she sat down again and sat a long time wondering what her Dick and Ole would do.

"It is queer Dick didn't come right over after me. He surely came, for he would have left town before the storm began and he might just as well come right on as go back. If he'd hurried he would have gotten here before the preacher came. I suppose he was afraid to come, for he knew Canuteson could pound him to jelly, the coward!" Her eyes flashed angrily.

The weary hours wore on and Lena began to grow horribly lonesome. It was an uncanny night and this was an uncanny place to be in. She could hear the coyotes howling hungrily a little way from the cabin, and more terrible still were all the unknown noises of the storm. She remembered the tales they told of the big log overhead and she was afraid of those snaky things on the window sills. She remembered the man who had been killed in the draw, and she wondered what she would do if she saw crazy Lou's white face glaring into the window. The rattling of the door became unbearable, she thought the latch must be loose and took the lamp to look at it. Then for the first time she saw the ugly brown snake skins whose death rattle sounded every time the wind jarred the door.

"Canute, Canute!" she screamed in terror.

Outside the door she heard a heavy sound as of a big dog getting up and shaking himself. The door opened and Canute stood before her, white as a snow drift.

"What is it?" he asked kindly.

"I am cold," she faltered.

He went out and got an armful of wood and a basket of cobs and filled the stove. Then he went out and lay in the snow before the door. Presently he heard her calling again.

"What is it?" he said, sitting up.

"I'm so lonesome, I'm afraid to stay in here all alone."

"I will go over and get your mother." And he got up.

"She won't come."

"I'll bring her," said Canute grimly.

"No, no. I don't want her, she will scold all the time."

"Well, I will bring your father."

She spoke again and it seemed as though her mouth was close up to the key hole. She spoke lower than he had ever heard her speak before, so low that he had to put his ear up to the lock to hear her.

"I don't want him either, Canute—I'd rather have you."

For a moment she heard no noise at all, then something like a groan. With a cry of fear she opened the door, and saw Canute stretched in the snow at her feet, his face in his hands, sobbing on the door step.

First published in *Overland Monthly*, XXVII (January, 1896), 65–74.

"The Fear that Walks
by Noonday"

❋ ❋ ❋

"Where is my shin guard? Horton, you lazy dog, get your duds off, won't you? Why didn't you dress at the hotel with the rest of us? There's got to be a stop to your blamed eccentricities some day," fumed Reggie, hunting wildly about in a pile of overcoats.

Horton began pulling off his coat with that air of disinterested deliberation he always assumed to hide any particular nervousness. He was to play two positions that day, both half and full, and he knew it meant stiff work.

"What do you think of the man who plays in Morrison's place, Strike?" he asked as he took off his shoes.

"I can tell you better in about half an hour; I suppose the 'Injuns' knew what they were about when they put him there."

"They probably put him there because they hadn't another man who could even look like a fullback. He played quarter badly enough, if I remember him."

"I don't see where they get the face to play us at all. They would never have scored last month if it hadn't been for Morrison's punting. That fellow played a great game, but the rest of them are light men, and their coach is an idiot. That man would have made his mark if he'd lived. He could play different positions just as easily as Chum-Chum plays different roles—pardon the liberty, Fred—and then there was that awful stone wall strength of his to back it; he was a mighty man."

"If you are palpitating to know why the 'Injuns' insist on playing us, I'll tell you; it's for blood. Exhibition game be damned! It's to break our bones they're playing. We were surprised when they didn't let down on us harder as soon as the fellow died, but they have been cherishing their wrath, they haven't lost an ounce of it, and they are going into us today for vengeance."

"Well, their sentiments are worthy, but they haven't got the players."

"Let up on Morrison there, Horton," shouted Reggie, "we sent flowers and sympathies at the time, but we are not going to lose this game out of respect to his memory: shut up and get your shin guard on. I say, Nelson, if you don't get out of here with that cigarette I'll kick you out. I'll get so hungry I'll break training rules. Besides, the coach will be in here in a minute going around smelling our breaths like our mammas used to do, if he catches a scent of it. I'm humming glad it's the last week of training; I couldn't stand another day of it. I brought a whole pocket full of cigars, and I'll have one well under way before the cheering is over. Won't we see the town tonight, Freddy?"

Horton nodded and laughed one of his wicked laughs. "Training has gone a shade too far this season. It's all nonsense to say that nobody but hermits and anchorites can play football. A Methodist parson don't have to practice half such rigid abstinence as a man on the eleven." And he kicked viciously at the straw on the floor as he remembered the supper parties he had renounced, the invitations he had declined, and the pretty faces he had avoided in the last three months.

"Five minutes to three!" said the coach, as he entered, pounding on the door with his cane. Strike began to hunt frantically for the inflater, one of the tackles went striding around the room seeking his nose protector with lamentations and profanity, and the rest of the men got on their knees and began burrowing in the pile of coats for things they had forgotten to take out of their pockets. Reggie began to hurry his men and make the usual encouraging remarks to the effect that the universe was not created to the especial end that they should win that football game, that the game was going to the men who kept the coolest heads and played the hardest ball. The coach rapped impatiently again, and Horton and Reggie stepped out together, the rest following them. As soon as Horton heard the shouts which greeted their appearance, his eyes flashed, and he threw his head back like a cavalry horse that hears the bugle sound a charge. He jumped over the ropes and ran swiftly across the field, leaving Reggie to saunter along at his leisure, bowing to the ladies in the grandstand and on the tallyhos as he passed.

When he reached the lower part of the field he found a hundred Marathon college men around the team yelling and shouting their encouragement. Reggie promptly directed the policemen to clear the field, and, taking his favorite attitude, his feet wide apart and his body very straight, he carelessly tossed the quarter into the air.

"Line 'em up, Reggie, line 'em up. Let us into it while the divine afflatus lasts," whispered Horton.

The men sprang to their places, and Reggie forgot the ladies on the tallyhos; the color came to his face, and he drew himself up and threw every sinew of his little body on a tension. The crowd outside began to cheer again, as the wedge started off for [the] north goal. The western men were poor on defensive work, and the Marathon wedge gained ground on the first play. The first impetus of success was broken by Horton fumbling and losing the ball. The eleven looked rather dazed at this, and Horton was the most dazed looking man of them all, for he did not indulge in that kind of thing often. Reggie could scarcely believe his senses, and stood staring at Horton in unspeakable amazement, but Horton only spread out his hands and stared at them as though to see if they were still there. There was little time for reflection or conjecture. The western men gave their Indian yell and prepared to play; their captain sang out his signals, and the rushing began. In spite of the desperate resistance on the part of Reggie's men, the ball went steadily south, and in twelve minutes the "Injuns" had scored. No one quite knew how they did it, least of all their bewildered opponents. They did some bad fumbling on the five-yard line, but though Reggie's men fell all over the ball, they did not seem to be able to take hold of it.

"Call in a doctor," shouted Reggie; "they're paralyzed in the arms, every one of 'em."

Time was given to bandage a hurt, and half a dozen men jumped over the ropes and shot past the policemen and rushed up to Reggie, pitifully asking what the matter was.

"Matter! I don't know! They're all asleep or drunk. Go kick them, pound them, anything to get them awake." And the little captain threw his sweater over his shoulder and swore long and loud at all mankind in general and Frederick Horton in particular. Horton turned away without looking at him. He was a younger man than Reggie, and, although he had had more experiences, they were not of the kind that counted much with the men of the eleven. He was very proud of being the captain's right-hand man, and it cut him hard to fail him.

"I believe I've been drugged, Black," he said, turning to the right tackle. "I am as cold as ice all over and I can't use my arms at all; I've a notion to ask Reggie to call in a sub."

"Don't, for heaven's sake, Horton; he is almost frantic now; [I] believe it would completely demoralize the team; you have never laid off since you were on the eleven, and if you should now when you have no visible hurt it would frighten them to death."

"I feel awful, I am so horribly cold."

"So am I, so are all the fellows; see how the 'Injuns' are shivering over there, will you? There must be a cold wave; see how Strike's hair is blowing down in his eyes."

"The cold wave seems to be confined to our locality," remarked Horton in a matter-of-fact way; but in somewhat strained tones. "The girls out there are all in their summer dresses without wraps, and the wind which is cutting our faces all up don't even stir the ribbon on their hats."

"Y-a-s, horribly draughty place, this," said Black blankly.

"Horribly draughty as all out doors," said Horton with a grim laugh.

"Bur-r-r!" said Strike, as he handed his sweater over to a substitute and took his last pull at a lemon, "this wind is awful; I never felt anything so cold; it's a raw, wet cold that goes clear into the marrow of a fellow's bones. I don't see where it comes from; there is no wind outside the ropes apparently."

"The winds blow in such strange directions here," said Horton, picking up a straw and dropping it. "It goes straight down with force enough to break several camels' backs."

"Ugh! it's as though the firmament had sprung a leak and the winds were sucking in from the other side."

"Shut your mouths, both of you," said Reggie, with an emphatic oath. "You will have them all scared to death; there's a panic now, that's what's the matter, one of those quiet, stupid panics that are the worst to manage. Laugh, Freddie, laugh hard; get up some enthusiasm; come, you, shut up, if you can't do any better than that. Start the yell, Strike, perhaps that will fetch them."

A weak yell that sounded like an echo rose from the field and the Marathon men outside the ropes caught it up and cheered till the air rang. This seemed to rouse the men on the field, and they got to their places with considerable energy. Reggie gave an exultant cry, as the western men soon lost the ball, and his men started it north and kept steadily gaining. They were within ten yards of the goal, when suddenly the ball rose serenely out a mass of struggling humanity and flew back twenty, forty, sixty, eighty yards toward the southern goal! But the half was versed in his occupation; he ran across and stood under the ball, waiting for it with outstretched arms. It seemed to Horton that the ball was all day in falling; it was right over him and yet it seemed to hang back from him, like Chum-Chum when she was playing with him. With an impatient oath he ground his teeth together and bowed his body forward to hold it with his breast, and even his knees if need be, waiting with strength and eagerness enough in his arm to burst the ball to shreds. The crowd shouted with delight, but suddenly caught its breath; the ball fell into his arms, between them, through them, and rolled on the ground at his feet. Still he stood there with his face raised and his arms stretched upward in an attitude ridiculously suggestive of prayer. The men rushed fiercely around him shouting and reviling; his arms dropped like lead to his side, and he stood without moving a muscle, and in his face there was a look that a man might have who had seen what he loved best go down to death through his very arms and had not been able to close them and save. Reggie came up with his longest oaths on his lip, but when he saw Horton's face he checked himself and said with that sweetness of temper that always came to him when he saw the black bottom of despair,

"Keep quiet, fellows, Horton's all right, only he is a bit nervous." Horton moved for the first time and turned on the little captain, "You can say anything else you like, Reggie, but if you say I am scared I'll knock you down."

"No, Fred, I don't mean that; we must hang together, man, every one of us, there are powers enough against us," said Reggie, sadly. The men looked at each other with startled faces. So long as Reggie swore there was hope, but when he became gentle all was lost.

In another part of the field another captain fell on his fullback's neck and cried, "Thomas, my son, how did you do it? Morrison in his palmiest days never made a better lift than that."

"I—I didn't do it, I guess; some of the other fellows did; Towmen, I think."

"Not much I didn't," said Towmen, "you were so excited you didn't know what you were doing. You did it, though; I saw it go right up from your foot."

"Well, it may be," growled the "Injun" half, "but when I make plays like that I'd really like to be conscious of them. I must be getting to be a darned excitable individual if I can punt eighty yards and never know it."

"Heavens! how cold it is. This is a great game, though; I don't believe they'll score."

"I don't; they act like dead men; I would say their man Horton was sick or drunk if all the others didn't act just like him."

The "Injuns" lost the ball again, but when Reggie's men were working it north the same old punting scheme was worked somewhere by someone in the "Injuns'" ranks. This time Amack, the right half, ran bravely for it; but when he was almost beneath it he fell violently to the ground, for no visible reason, and lay there struggling like a man in a fit. As they were taking him off the field, time was called for the first half. Reggie's friends and several of his professors broke through the gang of policemen and rushed up to him. Reggie stepped in front of his men and spoke to the first man who came up, "If you say one word or ask one question I'll quit the field. Keep away from me and from my men. Let us alone." The paleness that showed through the dirt on Reggie's face alarmed the visitors, and they went away as quickly as they had come. Reggie and his men lay down and covered themselves with their overcoats, and lay there shuddering under that icy wind that sucked down upon them. The men were perfectly quiet and each one crept off by himself. Even the substitutes who brought them lemons and water did not talk much; they had neither disparagement nor encouragement to offer; they sat around and shivered like the rest. Horton hid his face on his arm and lay like one stunned. He muttered the score, 18 to 0, but he did not feel the words his lips spoke, nor comprehend them. Like most dreamy, imaginative men, Horton was not very much at home in college. Sometimes in his loneliness he tried to draw near to the average man, and be on a level with him, and in so doing made a consummate fool of himself, as dreamers always do when they try to get themselves awake. He was awkward and shy among women, silent and morose among men. He was tolerated in the societies because he could write good poetry, and in the clubs because he could play football. He was very proud of his accomplishments as a halfback, for they made him seem like other men. However ornamental and useful a large imagination and sensitive temperament may be to a man of mature years, to a young man they are often very like a deformity which he longs to hide. He wondered what the captain would think of him and groaned. He feared Reggie as much as he adored him. Reggie was one of those men who, by the very practicality of their intellects, astonish the world. He was a glorious man for a college. He was brilliant, adaptable, and successful; yet all his brains he managed to cover up by a pate of tow hair, parted very carefully in the middle, and his iron strength was generally very successfully disguised by a very dudish exterior. In short, he possessed the one thing which is greater than genius, the faculty of clothing genius in such boundless good nature that it is offensive to nobody. Horton felt to a painful degree his inferiority to him in most things, and it was not pleasant to him to lose ground in the one thing in which he felt they could meet on an equal footing.

Horton turned over and looked up at the leaden sky, feeling the wind sweep into his eyes and nostrils. He looked about him and saw the other men all lying down with their heads covered, as though they were trying to get away from the awful cold and the sense of Reggie's reproach. He wondered what was the matter with them; whether they had been drugged or mesmerized. He tried to remember something in all the books he had read that would fit the case, but his memory seemed as cold and dazed as the rest of him; he only remembered some hazy Greek, which read to the effect that the gods sometimes bring madness upon those they wish to destroy. And here was another proof that the world was going wrong— it was not a normal thing for him to remember any Greek.

He was glad when at last he heard Reggie's voice calling the men together; he went slowly up to him and said rather feebly, "I say, a little brandy wouldn't hurt us, would it? I am so awfully cold I don't know what the devil is the matter with me, Reggie, my arms are so stiff I can't use 'em at all."

Reggie handed him a bottle from his grip, saying briefly, "It can't make things any worse."

In the second half the Marathon men went about as though they were walking in their sleep. They seldom said anything, and the captain was beyond coaxing or swearing; he only gave his signals in a voice as hollow as if it came from an empty church. His men got the ball a dozen times, but they always lost it as soon as they got it, or, when they had worked it down to one goal the "Injuns" would punt it back to the other. The very spectators sat still and silent, feeling that they were seeing something strange and unnatural. Every now and then some "Injun" would make a run, and a Marathon man would dash up and run beside him for a long distance without ever catching him, but with his hands hanging at his side. People asked the physicians in the audience what was the matter; but they shook their heads.

It was at this juncture that Freddie Horton awoke and bestirred himself. Horton was a peculiar player; he was either passive or brilliant. He could not do good line work; he could not help other men play. If he did anything he must take matters into his own hands, and he generally did; no one in the northwest had ever made such nervy, dashing plays as he; he seemed to have the faculty of making sensational and romantic situations in football just as he did in poetry. He played with his imagination. The second half was half over, and as yet he had done nothing but blunder. His honor and the honor of the team had been trampled on. As he thought of it the big veins stood out in his forehead and he set his teeth hard together. At last his opportunity came, or rather he made it. In a general scramble for the ball he caught it in his arms and ran. He held the ball tight against his breast until he could feel his heart knocking against the hard skin; he was conscious of nothing but the wind whistling in his ears and the ground flying under his feet, and the fact that he had ninety yards to run. Both teams followed him as fast as they could, but Horton was running for his honor, and his feet scarcely touched the earth. The spectators, who had waited all afternoon for a chance to shout, now rose to their feet and all the lungs full of pent-up enthusiasm burst forth. But the gods are not to be frustrated for a man's honor or his dishonor, and when Freddie Horton was within ten yards of the goal he threw his arms over his head and leaped into the air and fell. When the crowd reached him they found no marks of injury except the blood and foam at his mouth where his teeth had bitten into his lip. But when they looked at him the men of both teams turned away shuddering. His knees were drawn up to his chin; his hands were dug into the ground on either side of him; his face was the livid, bruised blue of a man who dies with apoplexy; his eyes were wide open and full of unspeakable horror and fear, glassy as ice, and still as though they had been frozen fast in their sockets.

It was an hour before they brought him to, and then he lay perfectly silent and would answer no questions. When he was stretched obliquely across the seats of a carriage going home he spoke for the first time.

"Give me your hand, Reggie; for God's sake let me feel something warm and human. I am awful sorry, Reggie; I tried for all my life was worth to make that goal, but—" he drew the captain's head down to his lips and whispered something that made Reggie's face turn white and the sweat break out on his forehead. He drew big Horton's head upon his breast and stroked it as tenderly as a woman.

PART II

There was silence in the dining room of the Exeter House that night when the waiters brought in the last course. The evening had not been a lively one. The defeated men were tired with that heavy weariness which follows defeat, and the victors seemed strained and uneasy in their manners. They all avoided speaking of the game and forced themselves to speak of things they could not fix their minds upon. Reggie sat at the head of the table correct and faultless. Reggie was always correct, but tonight there was very little of festal cheer about him. He was cleanly shaved, his hair was parted with the usual mathematical accuracy. A little strip of black court plaster covered the only external wound defeat had left. But his face was as white as the spotless expanse of his shirt bosom, and his eyes had big black circles under them like those of a man coming down with the fever. All evening he had been nervous and excited; he had not eaten anything and was evidently keeping something under. Every one wondered what it was, and yet feared to hear it. When asked about Horton he simply shuddered, mumbled something, and had his wine glass filled again.

Laughter or fear are contagious, and by the time the last course was on the table every one was as nervous as Reggie. The talk started up fitfully now and then but it soon died down, and the weakly attempts at wit were received in silence.

Suddenly every one became conscious of the awful cold and inexplicable downward draught that they had felt that afternoon. Every one was determined not to show it. No one pretended to even notice the flicker of the gas jets, and the fact that their breath curled upward from their mouths in little wreaths of vapor. Every one turned his attention to his plate and his glass stood full beside him. Black made some remarks about politics, but his teeth chattered so he gave it up. Reggie's face was working nervously, and he suddenly rose to his feet and said in a harsh, strained voice,

"Gentlemen, you had one man on your side this afternoon who came a long journey to beat us. I mean the man who did that wonderful punting and who stood before the goal when Mr. Horton made his run. I propose the first toast of the evening to the twelfth man, who won the game. Need I name him?"

The silence was as heavy as before. Reggie extended his glass to the captain beside him, but suddenly his arm changed direction; he held the glass out over the table and tipped it in empty air as though touching glasses with some one. The sweat broke out on Reggie's face; he put his glass to his lips and tried to drink, but only succeeded in biting out a big piece of the rim of his wine glass. He spat the glass out quickly upon his plate and began to laugh, with the wine oozing out between his white lips. Then everyone laughed; leaning upon each other's shoulders, they gave way to volleys and shrieks of laughter, waving their glasses in hands that could scarcely hold them. The Negro waiter, who had been leaning against the wall asleep, came forward rubbing his eyes to see what was the matter. As he approached the end of the table he felt that chilling wind, with its damp, wet smell like the air from a vault, and the unnatural cold that drove to the heart's center like a knife blade.

"My Gawd!" he shrieked, dropping his tray, and with an inarticulate gurgling cry he fled out of the door and down the stairway with the banqueters after him, all but Reggie, who fell to the floor, cursing and struggling and grappling with the powers of darkness. When the men reached the lower hall they stood without speaking, holding tightly to each other's hands like frightened children. At last Reggie came down the stairs, steadying himself against the banister. His dress coat was torn, his hair was rumpled down over his forehead, his shirt front was stained with wine, and the ends of his tie were hanging to his waist. He stood looking at the men and they looked at him, and no one spoke.

Presently a man rushed into the hall from the office and shouted "McKinley has carried Ohio by eighty-one thousand majority!" and Regiland Ashton, the product of centuries of democratic faith and tradition, leaped down the six remaining stairs and shouted, "Hurrah for Bill McKinley."*

In a few minutes the men were looking for a carriage to take Regiland Ashton home.

* The reference is not to McKinley's victory in the presidential campaign of November, 1895, but to his re-election as Governor of Ohio in 1893.

First published in *Sombrero*, III (1894), 224–231.

The Clemency of the Court

❊ ❊ ❊

"Damn you! What do you mean by giving me hooping like that?"

Serge Povolitchky folded his big workworn hands and was silent. That helpless, doglike silence of his always had a bad effect on the guard's temper, and he turned on him afresh.

"What do you mean by it, I say? Maybe you think you are some better than the rest of us; maybe you think you are too good to work. We'll see about that."

Serge still stared at the ground, muttering in a low, husky voice, "I could make some broom, I think. I would try much."

"O, you would, would you? So you don't try now? We will see about that. We will send you to a school where you can learn to hoop barrels. We have a school here, a little, dark school, a night school, you know, where we teach men a great many things."

Serge looked up appealingly into the man's face and his eyelids quivered with terror, but he said nothing, so the guard continued:

"Now I'll sit down here and watch you hoop them barrels, and if you don't do a mighty good job, I'll report you to the warden and have you strung up as high as a rope can twist."

Serge turned to his work again. He did wish the guard would not watch him; it seemed to him that he could hoop all right if he did not feel the guard's eye on him all the time. His hands had never done anything but dig and plow and they were so clumsy he could not make them do right. The guard began to swear and Serge trembled so he could scarcely hold his hammer. He was very much afraid of the dark cell. His cell was next to it and often at night he had heard the men groaning and shrieking when the pain got bad, and begging the guards for water. He heard one poor fellow get delirious when the rope cut and strangled him, and talk to his mother all night long, begging her not to hug him so hard, for she hurt him.

The guard went out and Serge worked on, never even stopping to wipe the sweat from his face. It was strange he could not hoop as well as

[515]

the other men, for he was as strong and stalwart as they, but he was so clumsy at it. He thought he could work in the broom room if they would only let him. He had handled straw all his life, and it would seem good to work at the broom corn that had the scent of outdoors about it. But they said the broom room was full. He felt weak and sick all over, someway. He could not work in the house, he had never been indoors a whole day in his life until he came here.

Serge was born in the western part of the State, where he did not see many people. His mother was a handsome Russian girl, one of a Russian colony that a railroad had brought West to build grades. His father was supposed to be a railroad contractor, no one knew surely. At any rate by no will of his own or wish of his own, Serge existed. When he was a few months old, his mother had drowned herself in a pond so small that no one ever quite saw how she managed to do it.

Baba Skaldi, an old Russian woman of the colony, took Serge and brought him up among her own children. A hard enough life he had of it with her. She fed him what her children would not eat, and clothed him in what her children would not wear. She used to boast to *baba* Konach that she got a man's work out of the young rat. There was one pleasure in Serge's life with her. Often at night after she had beaten him and he lay sobbing on the floor in the corner, she would tell her children stories of Russia. They were beautiful stories, Serge thought. In spite of all her cruelty he never quite disliked *baba* Skaldi because she could tell such fine stories. The story told oftenest was óne about her own brother. He had done something wrong, Serge could never make out just what, and had been sent to Siberia. His wife had gone with him. The *baba* told all about the journey to Siberia as she had heard it from returned convicts; all about the awful marches in the mud and ice, and how on the boundary line the men would weep and fall down and kiss the soil of Russia. When her brother reached the prison, he and his wife used to work in the mines. His wife was too good a woman to get on well in the prison, the *baba* said, and one day she had been knouted to death at the command of an officer. After that her husband tried in many ways to kill himself, but they always caught him at it. At last, one night, he bit deep into his arm and tore open the veins with his teeth and bled to death. The officials found him dead with his teeth still set in his lacerated arm.

When she finished the little boys used to cry out at the awfulness of it, but their mother would soothe them and tell them that such things could not possibly happen here, because in this country the State took care of people. In Russia there was no State, only the great Tzar. Ah, yes, the State would take care of the children! The *baba* had heard a Fourth-of-July speech once, and she had great ideas about the State.

Serge used to listen till his eyes grew big, and play that he was that brother of the *baba*'s and that he had been knouted by the officials and that was why his little legs smarted so. Sometimes he would steal out in the snow in his bare feet and take a sunflower stalk and play he was hunting bears in Russia, or would walk about on the little frozen pond where his mother had died and think it was the Volga. Before his birth his mother used to go off alone and sit in the snow for hours to cool the fever in her head and weep and think about her own country. The feeling for the snow and the love for it seemed to go into the boy's blood, somehow. He was never so happy as when he saw the white flakes whirling.

When he was twelve years old a farmer took him to work for his board and clothes. Then a change came into Serge's life. That first morning [as] he stood, awkward and embarrassed, in the Davis kitchen, holding his hands under his hat and shuffling his bare feet over the floor, a little yellow cur came up to him and began to rub its nose against his leg. He held out his hand and the dog licked it. Serge bent over him, stroking him and calling him Russian pet names. For the first time in his lonely, loveless life, he felt that something liked him.

The Davises gave him enough to eat and enough to wear and they did not beat him. He could not read or talk English, so they treated him very much as they did the horses. He stayed there seven years because he did not have sense enough to know that he was utterly miserable and could go somewhere else, and because the Slavonic instinct was in him to labor and keep silent. The dog was the only thing that made life endurable. He called the dog Matushka, which was the name by which he always thought of his mother. He used to go to town sometimes, but he did not enjoy it, people frightened him so. When the town girls used to pass him dressed in their pretty dresses with their clean, white hands, he thought of his bare feet and his rough, tawny hair and his ragged overalls, and he would slink away behind his team with Matushka. On the coldest winter nights he always slept in the barn with the dog for a bedfellow. As he and the dog cuddled up to each other in the hay, he used to think about things, most often about Russia and the State. Russia must be a fine country but he was glad he did not live there, because the State was much better. The State was so very good to people. Once a man came there to get Davis to vote for him, and he asked Serge who his father was. Serge said he had none. The man only smiled and said, "Well, never mind, the State will be a father to you, my lad, and a mother."

Serge had a vague idea that the State must be an abstract thing of some kind, but he always thought of her as a woman with kind eyes, dressed in white with a yellow light about her head, and a little child in her arms, like the picture of the virgin in the church. He always took off his hat when he passed the court house in town, because he had an idea that it had something to do with the State someway. He thought he owed the State a great deal for something, he did not know what; that the State would do something great for him some day, because he had no one else. After his chores he used to go and sit down in the corral with his back against the wire fence and his chin on his knees and look at the sunset. He never got much pleasure out of it, it was always like watching something die. It made him feel desolate and lonesome to see so much sky, yet he always sat there, irresistibly fascinated. It was not much wonder that his eyes grew dull and his brain heavy, sitting there evening after evening with his dog, staring across the brown, windswept prairies that never lead anywhere, but always stretch on and on in a great yearning for something they never reach. He liked the plains because he thought they must be like the Russian steppes, and because they seemed like himself, always lonely and empty-handed.

One day when he was helping Davis top a haystack, Davis got angry at the dog for some reason and kicked at it. Serge threw out his arm and caught the blow himself. Davis, angrier than before, caught the hatchet and laid the dog's head open. He threw down the bloody hatchet and, telling Serge to go clean it, he bent over his work. Serge stood motionless, as dazed and helpless as if he had been struck himself. The dog's tail quivered and its legs moved weakly, its breath came through its throat in faint, wheezing groans and from its bleeding head its two dark eyes, clouded with pain, still looked lovingly up at him. He dropped on his knees beside it and lifted its poor head against his heart. It was only for a moment. It laid its paw upon his arm and then was still. Serge laid the dog gently down and rose. He took the bloody hatchet and went up behind his master. He did not hurry and he did not falter. He raised the weapon and struck down, clove through the man's skull from crown to chin, even as the man had struck the dog. Then he went to the barn to get a shovel to bury the dog. As he passed the house, the woman called out to him to tell her husband to come to dinner. He answered simply, "He will not come to dinner today. I killed him behind the haystack."

She rushed from the house with a shriek and when she caught sight of what lay behind the haystack, she started for the nearest farm house. Serge went to the barn for the shovel. He had no consciousness of having done wrong. He did not even think about the dead man. His heart seemed to cling to the side of his chest, the only thing he had ever loved was dead. He went to the haymow where he and Matushka slept every night and took a box from under the hay from which he drew a red silk handkerchief, the only "pretty thing," and indeed, the only handkerchief he had ever possessed. He went back to the haystack and never once glancing at the man, took the dog in his arms.

There was one spot on the farm that Serge liked. He and Matushka used often to go there on Sundays. It was a little, marshy pool, grown up in cattails and reeds with a few scraggy willows on the banks. The grass used to be quite green there, not red and gray like the buffalo grass. There he carried Matushka. He laid him down and began to dig a grave under the willows. The worst of it was that the world went on just as usual. The winds were laughing away among the rushes, sending the water slapping against the banks. The meadow larks sang in the corn field and the sun shone just as it did yesterday and all the while Matushka was dead and his own heart was breaking in his breast. When the hole was deep enough, he took the handkerchief from his pocket and tied it neatly about poor Matushka's mangled head. Then he pulled a few wild roses and laid them on its breast and fell sobbing across the body of the little yellow cur. Presently he saw the neighbors coming over the hill with Mrs. Davis, and he laid the dog in the grave and covered him up.

About his trial Serge remembered very little, except that they had taken him to the court house and he had not found the State. He remembered that the room was full of people, and some of them talked a great deal, and that the young lawyer who defended him cried when his sentence was read. That lawyer seemed to understand it all, about Matushka and the State, and everything. Serge thought he was the handsomest and most learned man in the world. He had fought day and night for Serge, without sleeping and almost without eating. Serge could always see him as he looked when he paced up and down the platform, shaking the hair back from his brow and trying to get it through the heads of the jurymen that love was love, even if it was for a dog. The people told Serge that his sentence had been commuted from death to imprisonment for life by the clemency of the court, but he knew well enough that it was by the talk of that lawyer. He had not deserted Serge after the trial even, he had come with him to the prison and had seen him put on his convict clothing.

"It's the State's badge of knighthood, Serge," he said, bitterly, touching one of the stripes. "The old emblem of the royal garter, to show that your blood is royal."

Just as the six o'clock whistle was blowing, the guard returned.

"You are to go to your cell tonight, and if you don't do no better in the morning, you are to be strung up in the dark cell, come along."

Serge laid down his hammer and followed him to his cell. Some of the men made little bookshelves for their cells and pasted pictures on the walls. Serge had neither books nor pictures, and he did not know how to ask for any, so his cell was bare. The cells were only six by four, just a little larger than a grave.

As a rule, the prisoners suffered from no particular cruelty, only from the elimination of all those little delicacies that make men men. The aim of the prison authorities seemed to be to make everything unnecessarily ugly and repulsive. The little things in which fine feeling is most truly manifest received no respect at all. Serge's bringing up had been none of the best, but it took him some time to get used to eating without knife or fork the indifferent food thrust in square tin bowls under the door of his cell. Most of the men read at night, but he could not read, so he lay tossing on his iron bunk, wondering how the fields were looking. His greatest deprivation was that he could not see the fields. The love of the plains was strong in him. It had always been so, ever since he was a little fellow, when the brown grass was up to his shoulders and the straw stacks were the golden mountains of fairyland. Men from the cities on the hills never understand this love, but the men from the plain country know what I mean. When he had tired himself out with longing, he turned over and fell asleep. He was never impatient, for he believed that the State would come some day and explain, and take him to herself. He watched for her coming every day, hoped for it every night.

In the morning the work went no better. They watched him all the time and he could do nothing. At noon they took him into the dark cell and strung him up. They put his arms behind him and tied them together, then passed the rope about his neck, drawing [his] arms up as high as they could be stretched, so that if he let them "sag" he would strangle, and so they left him. The cell was perfectly bare and was not long enough for a man to lie at full length in. The prisoners were told to stand up, so Serge stood. At night his arms were let down long enough for him to eat his bread and water, then he was roped up again. All night long he stood there. By the end of the next day the pain in his arms was almost unendurable. They were paralyzed from the shoulder down so that the guard had to feed him like a baby. The next day and the next night and the next day he lay upon the floor of the cell, suffering as though every muscle were being individually wrenched from his arms. He had not been out of the bare cell for four days. All the ventilation came through some little auger holes in the door and the heat and odor were becoming unbearable. He had thought on the first night that the pain would kill him before morning, but he had endured over eighty-four hours of it and when the guard came in with his bread and water he found him lying with his eyes closed and his teeth set on his lip. He roused him with a kick and held the bread and water out to him, but Serge took only the water.

"Rope too tight?" growled the guard. Serge said nothing. He was almost dead now and he wanted to finish for he could not hoop barrels.

"Gittin so stuck up you can't speak, are you? Well, we'll just stretch you up a bit tighter." And he gave the stick in the rope another vicious twist that almost tore the arms from their sockets and sent a thrill of agony through the man's whole frame. Then Serge was left alone. The fever raged in his veins and about midnight his thirst was intolerable. He lay with his mouth open and his tongue hanging out. The pain in his arms made his whole body tremble like a man with a chill. He could no longer keep his arms up and the ropes were beginning to strangle him. He did not call for help. He had heard poor devils shriek for help all night long and get no relief. He suffered, as the people of his mother's nation, in hopeless silence. The blood of the serf was in him, blood that has cowered beneath the knout for centuries and uttered no complaint. Then the State would surely come soon, she would not let them kill him. His mother, the State!

He fell into a half stupor. He dreamed about what the *baba* used to tell about the bargemen in their bearskin coats coming down the Volga in the spring when the ice had broken up and gone out; about how the wolves used to howl and follow the sledges across the snow in the starlight. That cold, white snow, that lay in ridges and banks! He thought he felt it in his mouth and he awoke and found himself licking the stone floor. He thought how lovely the plains would look in the morning when the sun was up; how the sunflowers would shake themselves in the wind, how the corn leaves would shine and how the cobwebs would sparkle all over the grass and the air would be clear and blue, the birds would begin to sing, the colts would run and jump in the pasture and the black bull would begin to bellow for his corn.

The rope grew tighter and tighter. The State must come soon now. He thought he felt the dog's cold nose against his throat. He tried to call its name, but the sound only came in an inarticulate gurgle. He drew his knees up to his chin and died.

And so it was that this great mother, the State, took this wilful, restless child of hers and put him to sleep in her bosom.

First published in *The Hesperian*, XXII (October 26, 1893), 3–7.

A Son of the Celestial

A Character

✳ ✳ ✳

Ah lie me dead in the sunrise land,
Where the sky is blue and the hills are gray,
Where the camels doze in the desert sun,
And the sea gulls scream o'er the big blue bay.

Where the Hwang-Ho glides through the golden sand,
And the herons play in the rushes tall,
Where pagodas rise upon every hill
And the peach trees bloom by the Chinese wall.

Where the great grim gods sit still in the dark,
And lamps burn dim at their carven feet,
And their eyes like the eyes of the serpent king
Flash green through the dusk of the incense sweet.

Though deep under ground I shall see the sun,
And shall feel the stretch of the blue overhead,
And the gems that gleam on the breast of the god.
And shall smell the scent of the peach—though dead.

Most of the world knew him only as Yung Le Ho, one of the few white-haired Chinamen who were to be seen about the streets of San Francisco. His cue was as long as that of any other John, and with the exception of wearing spectacles, he adhered strictly to his national costume. He sat all day long in an open bazaar where he worked in silk and ivory and sandal-wood. Americans who had lived there long said he must be worth a vast deal of money, for Yung was the best workman in the city. All the ladies who were enthusiastic over Chinese art bought his painted silken birds, and beautiful lacquered boxes, his bronze vases, his little ivory gods and his carved sandalwood, and paid him whatsoever he demanded for them. Had he possessed a dozen hands he might have sold the work of all of them; as it was, he was very skillful with two. Yung was like Michel Angelo, he allowed no one to touch his work but himself; he did it all, rough work and delicate. When the ship brought him strange black boxes with a sweet spicy odor about them, he opened them with his own hands and took out the yellow ivory tusks, and the bales of silk, and the blocks of shining ebony. And no hands but his touched them until they were fashioned into the beautiful things with which the ladies of San Francisco loved to adorn their drawing rooms.

Day after day he sat in his stall, cross-legged and silent like the gods of his country, carving his ivory into strange images and his sandalwood into shapes of foliage and birds. Sometimes he cut it into the shapes of foliage of his own land; the mulberry and apricot and chestnut and juniper that grew about the sacred mountain; the bamboo and camphor tree, and the rich Indian bean, and the odorous camellias and japonicas that grew far to the south on the low banks of the Yang-Tse-Kiang. Sometimes he cut shapes and leaves that were not of earth, but were things he had seen in his dreams when the Smoke was on him.

There were some people beside the artistic public who knew Yung; they were the linguistic scholars of the city—there are a few of these, even so far west as San Francisco. The two or three men who knew a little Sanskrit and attacked an extract from the Vedas now and then, used often to go to Yung to get help. For the little white-haired Chinaman knew Sanskrit as thoroughly as his own tongue. The professors had a good deal of respect for Yung, though they never told anyone of it, and kept him completely obscured in the background as professors and doctors of philosophy always do persons whom they consider "doubtful" acquaintances. Yung never pushed himself forward, nor courted the learned gentlemen. He always gave them what they wanted, then shut up like a clam and no more could be gotten out of him. Perhaps Yung did not have quite as much respect for the gentlemen as they had for him. He had seen a good many countries and a good many people, and he knew knowledge from pedantry. He found American schoolmen distasteful. "Too muchee good to know muchee," he once sarcastically remarked. Of course Yung was only a heathen Chinee who bowed down to wood and stone, his judgment in this and other matters does not count for much.

There was one American whom Yung took to his heart and loved, if a Chinaman can love, and that was old Ponter. Ponter was one of the most learned men who ever drifted into 'Frisco, but his best days were over before he came. He had held the chair of Sanskrit in a western university for years, but he could drink too much beer and was too good a shot at billiards to keep that place forever, so the college had requested his resignation. He went from place to place until at last he drifted into San Francisco, where he stayed. He went clear down to the mud sills there. How he lived no one knew. He did some copying for the lawyers, and he waited on the table in a third-rate boarding house, and he smoked a great deal of opium. Yung, too, loved the Smoke; perhaps it was that as much as Sanskrit that drew the two men together. At any rate, as soon as Yung's bazaar was closed, they went together down to his dark little den in the Chinese quarters, and there they talked Buddha and Confucius and Lau-tsz [Lao-tse] till midnight. Then they went across the hall to the Seven Portals of Paradise. There they each took a mat and each his own sweet pipe with bowls of jade and mouthpieces of amber—Yung had given Ponter one— and pulled a few steady puffs and were in bliss till morning.

To Ponter, Yung told a good deal of his history. Not in regular narrative form, for he never talked about himself long, but he let it out bit by bit. When he was a boy he lived in Nanking, the oldest city of the oldest empire, where the great schools are and the tallest pagoda in the world rears its height of shining porcelain. There he had been educated, and had learned all the wisdom of the Chinese. He became tired of all that after awhile; tired of the rice paper books and of the masters in their black gowns, of the blue mountains and of the shadows of the great tower that fell sharp upon the yellow pavement in the glare of the sun. He went south; down the great canal in a red barge with big sails like dragon's wings. He came to Soutcheofou that is built upon the waterways among the hills of Lake Taihoo. There the air smelt always of flowers, and the bamboo woods were green, and the rice fields shook in the wind. There the actors and jugglers gather the year around, and the Mandarins come to find brides for their harems. For once a god had loved a woman of that city, and he gave to her the charms of heaven, and since then the maidens of Soutcheofou have been the most beautiful in the Middle Kingdom, and have lived but to love and be loved. There Yung dwelt until he tired of pleasure. Then he went on foot across the barren plains of Thibet and the snow-capped Himalayas into India. He spent ten years in a temple there among the Brahamin priests, learning the sacred books. Then he fell in with some high caste Indian magicians and went with them. Of the next five years of his life Yung never spoke. Once, when Ponter questioned him about them, he laughed an ugly laugh which showed his broken yellow teeth and said:

"I not know what I did then. The devil he know, he and the fiends."

At last Yung came to California. There he took to carving and the Smoke.

Yung was rich; he might have dwelt in a fine house, but he preferred to live among his own people in a little room across from the Seven Portals. He celebrated all the feasts and festivals with the other Chinamen, and bowed down to the gods in the joss house. He explained this to Ponter one day by saying:

"It is to keep us together, keep us Chinamen."

Wise Yung! It was not because of the cheapness of Chinese labor that the Chinese bill was enacted.* It was because church and state feared this people who went about unproselyting and unproselyted. Who had printed centuries before Gutenberg was born, who had used anesthetics before chloroform was ever dreamed of. Who, in the new west, settled down and ate and drank and dressed as men had done in the days of the flood. Their terrible antiquity weighed upon us like a dead hand upon a living heart.

Yung did not know much about English literature. He liked the Bible, and he had picked up a copy of *Hiawatha* and was very fond of it. I suppose the artificialness of the poem appealed to his natural instinct and his training. Ponter was much disgusted with his taste, and one night be read the whole of *Hamlet* aloud to him, translating the archaic phrases into doggerel Chinese as he read. When he finished, Yung stared at him with a troubled look and said in Chinese:

"Yes, it is a great book, but I do not understand. If I were a young man I might try, but it is different. We cut our trees into shape, we bind our women into shape, we make our books into shape by rule. Your trees and women and books just grow, and yet they have shape. I do not understand. Come, let us smoke, the Smoke is good."

Ponter threw the book on the floor and arose and paced the floor shouting angrily:

"O yes, d—n you! You are a terrible people! I have come as near losing all human feeling and all human kinship as ever a white man did,

---

* The Chinese Treaty of 1880 gave the United States the right to "regulate, limit or suspend" but not absolutely to prohibit entry to Chinese laborers. On May 6, 1882, the Exclusion Act restricted such immigration for a ten-year period.

but you make me shudder, every one of you. You live right under the sun's face, but you cannot feel his fire. The breast of God heaves just over you, but you never know it. You ought to be a feeling, passionate people, but you are as heartless and devilish as your accursed stone gods that leer at you in your pagodas. Your sages learn rites, rites, rites, like so many parrots. They have forgotten how to think so long ago that they have forgotten they ever forgot. Your drama has outlived pathos, your science has outlived investigation, your poetry has outlived passion. Your very roses do not smell, they have forgotten how to give odor ages and ages ago. Your devilish gods have cursed you with immortality and you have outlived your souls. You are so old that you are born yellow and wrinkled and blind. You ought to have been buried centuries before Europe was civilized. You ought to have been wrapped in your mort cloth ages before our swaddling clothes were made. You are dead things that move!"

Yung answered never a word, but smiled his hideous smile and went across to the Portals of Paradise, and lay down upon his mat, and drew long whiffs from his mouthpiece, slowly, solemnly, as though he were doing sacrifice to some god. He dreams of his own country, dreams of the sea and the mountains and forests and the slopes of sunny land. When he awakes there is not much of his dream left, only masses and masses of color that haunt him all day.

"Ponter," said Yung one day as he sat cutting a little three-faced Vishnu in ivory, "when I die do not even bury me here. Let them go through the rites and then send me home. I must lie there while the flesh is yet on my bones. Let the funeral be grand. Let there be many mourners, and roast pigs, and rice and gin. Let the gin bowls be of real China, and let the coffin be a costly one like the coffins of Liauchau, there is money enough. Let my pipe stay in my hand, and put me on the first ship that sails."

Not long after that, Ponter arose from his mat one morning, and went over to waken Yung. But Yung would not waken any more. He had tasted his last ounce of the Smoke, and he lay with the mouthpiece in his mouth, and his fingers clutched about the bowl. Ponter sat down by him and said slowly:

"A white man has got pretty low down, Yung, when he takes to the Smoke and runs with a heathen. But I liked you, Yung, as much as a man can like a stone thing. You weren't a bad fellow, sir. You knew more Sanskrit than Muller dreamed of knowing, and more ethics than Plato, a long sight, and more black art than the devil himself. You knew more than any man I ever saw, more good and more evil. You could do a neater job with a knife and a piece of bone than any man in civilization, and you got away with more Smoke than any yaller man I ever saw. You were not a bad fellow, Yung, but your heart has been dead these last six thousand years, and it was better for your carcass to follow suit."

He went out and got the finest lacquered coffin in 'Frisco and he put old Yung inside with a pound of rice and his pipe and a pound of the best opium in the market. Then he nailed him up singing: "*Ibimus, Ibimus, Utcumque praecedes, supernum, Carpere iter comites parati,*"* softly as he hammered away.

He took the body to the graveyard where the Chinamen went through the rites. Then they loaded Yung on an outbound steamer. Next day Ponter stood on the docks and watched her plowing her way toward the Celestial shore.

* Ponter is quoting Horace: "We shall go however you lead the way, prepared to make the final journey as companions" (*Odes*, Book II, Ode 17, lines 10–12).

First published in *The Hesperian*, XXII (January 15, 1893), 7–10.

A Tale of the White Pyramid

❄ ❄ ❄

(I, Kakau, son of Ramenka, high priest of Phtahah [Ptah] in the great temple at Memphis, write this, which is an account of what I, Kakau, saw on the first day of my arrival at Memphis, and the first day of my sojourn in the home of Rui, my uncle, who was a priest of Phtahah before me.)

As I drew near the city the sun hung hot over the valley which wound like a green thread toward the south. On either side the river lay the fields of grain, and beyond was the desert of yellow sand which stretched away to where the low line of Libyan hills rose against the sky. The heat was very great, and the breeze scarce stirred the reeds which grew in the black mud down where the Nile, like a great tawny serpent, crept lazily away through the desert. Memphis stood as silent as the judgment hall of Osiris. The shops and even the temples were deserted, and no man stirred in the streets save the watchmen of the city. Early in the morning the people had arisen and washed the ashes from their faces, shaved their bodies, taken off the robes of mourning, and had gone out into the plain, for the seventy-two days of mourning were now over.

Senefrau the first, Lord of the Light and Ruler of the Upper and Lower Kingdoms, was dead and gathered unto his fathers. His body had passed into the hands of the embalmers, and lain for the allotted seventy days in niter, and had been wrapped in gums and spices and white linen and placed in a golden mummy case, and today it was to be placed in the stone sarcophagus in the white pyramid, where it was to await its soul.

Early in the morning, when I came unto the house of my uncle, he took me in his chariot and drove out of the city into the great plain which is north of the city, where the pyramid stood. The great plain was covered with a multitude of men. There all the men of the city were gathered together, and men from all over the land of Khem. Here and there were tethered many horses and camels of those who had come from afar. The army was there, and the priesthood, and men of all ranks; slaves, and swineherds, and the princes of the people. At the head of the army stood a tall dark man in a chariot of ivory and gold, speaking with a youth who stood beside the chariot.

"It is Kufu, the king," said Rui, "men say that before the Nile rises again he will begin to build a pyramid, and that it will be such a one as men have never seen before, nor shall we afterwards."

"Who is he that stands near unto the king, and with whom the king speaks?" I asked. Then there came a cloud upon the face of Rui, the brother of my father, and he answered and said unto me:

"He is a youth of the Shepherd people of the north, he is a builder and has worked upon the tomb. He is cunning of hand and wise of heart, and Kufu has shown him great favor, but the people like him not, for he is of the blood of strangers."

I spoke no more of the youth, for I saw that Rui liked him not, but my eyes were upon him continually, for I had seen no other man like unto him for beauty of face or of form.

After a time it came to pass that the great tumult ceased throughout the plain, and the words of men died upon their lips. Up from the shore of the sacred lake wound the funeral procession toward the tomb, and by the Lord of Truth I then thought the glory of Isis could be no grander. There were boys clad in white and wreathed with lotus flowers, and thousands of slaves clad in the skins of leopards, bearing bread and wine and oil, and carrying the images of the gods. There were maidens, bands of harpers and of musicians, and the captives which the king had taken in war leading tigers and lions of the desert. There was the sacred ark drawn by twenty white oxen, and there were many priests, and the guards of the king, and the sacred body of Senefrau, borne by carriers. After the body of the king came all the women of his household, beating their hearts, and weeping bitterly. As the train approached men fell upon their faces and prayed to Phtahah, the Great South Wall, and Kufu bowed his head. At the foot of the pyramid the train halted, and the youths clothed in white, and the priests, and those who bore the body began to ascend the pyramid, singing as they went:

> *Enter into thy rest, oh Pharaoh!*
> *Enter into thy kingdom.*
> *For the crown of the two lands was heavy,*
> *And thy head was old,*

And thou hast laid it aside forever.
Thy two arms were weak,
And the scepter was a great weight,
And thou hast put it from thee.
Enter thou into thy new reign,
Longer than the eternities.
Darkness shall be thy realm, O King,
And sleep thy minion.
The chariots of Ethiopia shall surround thee no more,
Nor the multitudes of the mighty encompass thee in battle,
For thou, being dead, art become as a god;
Good thou knowest, oh king;
And evil has been nigh unto thee,
Yet neither approach thee now,
For thou art dead, and like unto the gods.

They bore him down into the pyramid, and left him to sleep, and to wait. Then I saw a multitude of men gather about a great white stone that lay at the base of the tomb, and I questioned Rui concerning it, and he answered me:

"This pyramid as thou seest opens not at the side, but from the top down. That great slab of stone is to cover the top of the tomb. See, even now the workmen spread mortar upon the top of the tomb, and fasten ropes about the great stone to lift it into place. Neith grant that they harm not the stone, for it has taken a thousand men ten years to cut and polish it and to bring it thither."

I saw slaves bending over the great stone, fastening about it ropes which hung from the great pulleys built upon the shafts which rose from the upper stage of the pyramid. While they did this, companies of slaves began to ascend the sides of the tomb, each company with its master. The men were all fashioned like the men of the north, and their strength was like ribbed steel, for these were the mightiest men in Egypt. After a time there was silence in the plain. The slaves took hold of the ropes that swung from the pulleys, and every voice was hushed. It was as still without the pyramid as it was within. At last the sound of the Sistrum broke the stillness, the master builders waved their lashes, and the two thousand slaves who were upon the pyramid set their feet firmly upon the polished stone and threw the weight of their bodies upon the ropes. Slowly, slowly, amid the creaking and groaning of the ropes, the great stone left the earth. The musicians played and the people shouted, for never before in all Egypt had so great a stone been raised. But suddenly the shouting ceased, and the music was hushed, and a stillness like the sleep of Nut fell over the plain. All the people gazed upward, and the heart of Khem grew sick as they looked. The great stone had risen halfway, the lifting ropes were firm as the pillars of heaven, but one of the ropes which held the stone in place gave way and stretched, and the great stone which was the pride of the land, was settling at one end and slipping from its fastenings. The slaves crouched upon the pyramid, the builders spoke no word, and the people turned their eyes from the stone, that they might not see it fall. As I looked up, I saw a man running rapidly along the tier of the pyramid opposite the rocking stone. I knew his face to be the face of the stranger whom I saw speaking with the king. He threw off his garments as he ran, and at the edge of the stone tier he paused for a moment, he crouched low, gathering all his strength, then suddenly straightening his body he threw back his head and shot straight forward, like an arrow shot from the bow, over eighteen cubits, and fell lightly upon his feet on the uppermost end of the stone. He stood with both hands clenched at his side, his right foot a little before his left, erect and fair as the statue of Houris [Horus], watching the farther end of the stone. For a little the stone stood still, then swung back and lay evenly as when all was well, and then the end upon which the youth stood, sank. He thrust his right foot further forward, his toes clinging to the polished stone, and clasping his hands about his waist above the hips, slowly bowed his great frame forward. The stone slab felt its master and swung slowly back, and again the end on which the youth stood was uppermost. So he stood, his dusky limbs showing clear against the white stone, his every muscle quivering, the sweat pouring from his body, swaying the great stone. The great white desert seemed to rock and sway, the sun grew hotter and stood still in heaven, the sky and the sea of faces seemed to whirl and reel, then blend into one awful face, grinning horribly. The slaves, not daring to breathe, crouched upon the tomb, the multitude stood still and gazed upward, and earth and heaven and men were as dumb as if the gods had smitten them mad with thunder. Then a great cry rang out:

"In the name of Phtahah and of your fathers' souls, pull!"

It was the voice of Kufu. Slowly, like men awakened from a dream, the slaves drew up that swinging stone, and he stood upon it. Below the king stood, his hands clutching the front of his chariot, and his eyes strained upon the stone. When the slab reached the top of the shaft on which the pulley hung, it was swung back over the pyramid, and the descent began. The slaves, sick with fear, lost control of it, and the great stone plunged down faster and faster. I wondered if the mortar spread upon the top was thick enough to break its fall. Just as it struck the top in safety, he who stood upon it, gathering all his strength leaped high into the air to break the shock and fell motionless upon the stone. Then such a cry as went up, never before roused old Nilus from his dreams, or made the walls of the city to tremble. They bore him down from the tomb and placed him in the chariot of the king. Then the king's trumpeter sounded, and then Kufu spake:

"We have this day seen a deed the like of which we have never seen before, neither have our fathers told us of such a thing. Know, men of Egypt that he, the Shepherd stranger, who has risen upon the swinging stone, shall build the great pyramid, for he is worthy in my sight. The king has said."

Then the people cheered, but their faces were dark. And the charioteer of the king lashed his horses across the plain toward the city.

Of the great pyramid and of the mystery thereof, and of the strange builder, and of the sin of the king, I may not speak, for my lips are sealed.

First published in *The Hesperian*, XXII (December 22, 1892), 8–11.

Lou, the Prophet

✳ ✳ ✳

It had been a very trying summer to every one, and most of all to Lou. He had been in the West for seven years, but he had never quite gotten over his homesickness for Denmark. Among the northern people who emigrate to the great west, only the children and the old people ever long much for the lands they have left over the water. The men only know that in this new land their plow runs across the field tearing up the fresh, warm earth, with never a stone to stay its course. That if they dig and delve the land long enough, and if they are not compelled to mortgage it to keep body and soul together, some day it will be theirs, their very own. They are not like the southern people; they lose their love for their fatherland quicker and have less of sentiment about them. They have to think too much about how they shall get bread to care much what soil gives it to them. But among even the most blunted, mechanical people, the youths and the aged always have a touch of romance in them.

Lou was only twenty-two; he had been but a boy when his family left Denmark, and had never ceased to remember it. He was a rather simple fellow, and was always considered less promising than his brothers; but last year he had taken up a claim of his own and made a rough dugout upon it and he lived there all alone. His life was that of many another young man in our country. He rose early in the morning, in the summer just before daybreak; in the winter, long before. First he fed his stock, then himself, which was a much less important matter. He ate the same food at dinner that he ate at breakfast, and the same at supper that he ate at dinner. His bill of fare never changed the year round; bread, coffee, beans and sorghum molasses, sometimes a little salt pork. After breakfast he worked until dinner time, ate, and then worked again. He always went to bed soon after the sunset, for he was always tired, and it saved oil. Sometimes, on Sundays, he would go over home after he had done his washing and house cleaning, and sometimes he hunted. His life was as sane and as uneventful as the life of his plow horses, and it was as hard and thankless. He was thrifty for a simple, thickheaded fellow, and in the spring he was to have married Nelse Sorenson's daughter, but he had lost all his cattle during the winter, and was not so prosperous as he had hoped to be; so, instead she married her cousin, who had an "eighty" of his own. That hurt Lou more than anyone ever dreamed.

A few weeks later his mother died. He had always loved his mother. She had been kind to him and used to come over to see him sometimes, and shake up his hard bed for him, and sweep, and make his bread. She had a strong affection for the boy, he was her youngest, and she always felt sorry for him; she had danced a great deal before his birth, and an old woman in Denmark had told her that was the cause of the boy's weak head.

Perhaps the greatest calamity of all was the threatened loss of his corn crop. He had bought a new corn planter on time that spring, and had intended that his corn should pay for it. Now, it looked as though he would not have corn enough to feed his horses. Unless rain fell within the next two weeks, his entire crop would be ruined; it was half gone now. All these things together were too much for poor Lou, and one morning he felt a strange loathing for the bread and sorghum which he usually ate as mechanically as he slept. He kept thinking about the strawberries he used to gather on the mountains after the snows were gone, and the cold water in the mountain streams. He felt hot someway, and wanted cold water. He had no well, and he hauled his water from a neighbor's well every Sunday, and it got warm in the barrels those hot summer days. He worked at his haying all day; at night, when he was through feeding, he stood a long time by the pig stye with a basket on his arm. When the moon came up, he sighed restlessly and tore the buffalo pea flowers with his bare toes. After a while, he put his basket away, and went into his hot, close, little dugout. He did not sleep well, and he dreamed a horrible dream. He thought he saw the Devil and all his angels in the air holding back the rain clouds, and they loosed all the damned in Hell, and they came, poor tortured things, and drank up whole clouds of rain. Then he thought a strange light shone from the south, just over the river bluffs, and the clouds parted, and Christ and all his angels were descending. They were coming, coming, myriads and myriads of them, in a great blaze of glory. Then he felt something give way in his poor, weak head, and with a cry of pain he awoke. He lay shuddering a long time in the dark, then got up and lit his lantern and took from the shelf his mother's Bible. It opened of itself at Revelation, and Lou began to read, slowly indeed, for it was hard work for him. Page by page, he read those burning, blinding, blasting words, and they seemed to shrivel up his poor brain altogether. At last the book slipped from his hands and he sank down upon his knees in prayer, and stayed so until the dull gray dawn stole over the land and he heard the pigs clamoring for their feed.

He worked about the place until noon, and then prayed and read again. So he went on several days, praying and reading and fasting, until he grew thin and haggard. Nature did not comfort him any, he knew nothing about nature, he had never seen her; he had only stared into a black plow furrow all his life. Before, he had only seen in the wide, green lands and the open blue the possibilities of earning his bread; now, he only saw in them a great world ready for the judgment, a funeral pyre ready for the torch.

One morning, he went over to the big prairie dog town, where several little Danish boys herded their fathers' cattle. The boys were very fond of Lou; he never teased them as the other men did, but used to help them with their cattle, and let them come over to his dugout to make sorghum taffy. When they saw him coming, they ran to meet him and asked him where he had been all these days. He did not answer their questions, but said: "Come into the cave, I want to see you."

Some six or eight boys herded near the dog town every summer, and by their combined efforts they had dug a cave in the side of a high bank. It was large enough to hold them all comfortably, and high enough to stand in. There the boys used to go when it rained or when it was cold in the fall. They followed Lou silently and sat down on the floor. Lou stood up and looked tenderly down into the little faces before him. They were old-faced little fellows, though they were not over twelve or thirteen years old, hard work matures boys quickly.

"Boys," he said earnestly, "I have found out why it don't rain, it's because of the sins of the world. You don't know how wicked the world is, it's all bad, all, even Denmark. People have been sinning a long time, but they won't much longer. God has been watching and watching for thousands of years, and filling up the phials of wrath, and now he is going to pour out his vengeance and let Hell loose upon the world. He is burning up our corn now, and worse things will happen; for the sun shall be as sackcloth, and the moon shall be like blood, and the stars of heaven shall fall, and the heavens shall part like a scroll, and the mountains shall be moved out of their places, and the great day of his wrath shall come, against which none may stand. Oh, boys! the floods and the flames shall come down upon us together and the whole world shall perish." Lou paused for breath, and the little boys gazed at him in wonder. The sweat was running down his haggard face, and his eyes were staring wildly. Presently, he resumed in a softer tone, "Boys, if you want rain, there is only one way to get it, by prayer. The people of the world won't pray, perhaps if they did God would not hear them, for they are so wicked; but he will hear you, for you are little children and are likened unto the kingdom of heaven, and he loved ye."

Lou's haggard, unshaven face bent toward them and his blue eyes gazed at them with terrible earnestness.

"Show us how, Lou," said one little fellow in an awed whisper. Lou knelt down in the cave, his long, shaggy hair hung down over his face, and his voice trembled as he spoke:

"Oh God, they call thee many long names in thy book, thy prophets; but we are only simple folk, the boys are all little and I am weak headed ever since I was born, therefore, let us call thee Father, for thy other names are hard to remember. O Father, we are so thirsty, all the world is thirsty; the creeks are all dried up, and the river is so low that the fishes die and rot in it; the corn is almost gone; the hay is light; and even the little flowers are no more beautiful. O God! our corn may yet be saved. O, give us rain! Our corn means so much to us, if it fails, all our pigs and cattle will die, and we ourselves come very near it; but if you do not send rain, O Father, and if the end is indeed come, be merciful to thy great, wicked world. They do many wrong things, but I think they forget thy word, for it is a long book to remember, and some are little and some are born weak headed, like me, and some are born very strong headed, which is near as bad. Oh, forgive them their abominations in all the world, both in Denmark and here, for the fire hurts so, O God! Amen."

The little boys knelt and each said a few blundering words. Outside, the sun shone brightly and the cattle nibbled at the short, dry grass, and the hot wind blew through the shriveled corn; within the cave, they knelt as many another had knelt before them, some in temples, some in prison cells, some in the caves of earth, and One, indeed, in the garden, praying for the sin of the world.

The next day, Lou went to town, and prayed in the streets. When the people saw his emaciated frame and wild eyes, and heard his wild words, they told the sheriff to do his duty, the man must be mad. Then Lou ran away; he ran for miles, then walked and limped and stumbled on, until he reached the cave; there the boys found him in the morning. The officials hunted him for days, but he hid in the cave, and the little Danes kept his secret well. They shared their dinners with him, and prayed with him all day long. They had always liked him, but now they would have gone straight through fire for him, any one of them, they almost worshipped him. He had about him that mysticism which always appeals so quickly to children. I have always thought that bear story which the Hebrews used to tell their children very improbable. If it was true, then I have my doubts about the prophet; no one in the world will hoot at insincere and affected piety sooner than a child, but no one feels the true prophetic flame quicker, no one is more readily touched by simple goodness. A very young child can tell a sincere man better than any phrenologist.

One morning, he told the boys that he had had another "true dream." He was not going to die like other men, but God was going to take him to himself as he was. The end of the world was close at hand, too very close. He prayed more than usual that day, and when they sat eating their dinner in the sunshine, he suddenly sprang to his feet and stared wildly south, crying, "See, see, it is the great light! the end comes!! and they do not know it; they will keep on sinning, I must tell them, I must!"

"No, no, Lou, they will catch you; they are looking for you, you must not go!"

"I must go, my boys; but first let me speak once more to you. Men would not heed me, or believe me, because my head is weak, but you have always believed in me, that God has revealed his word to me, and I will pray God to take you to himself quickly, for ye are worthy. Watch and pray always, boys, watch the light over the bluffs, it is breaking, breaking, and shall grow brighter. Goodbye, my boys, I must leave ye in the world yet awhile." He kissed them all tenderly and blessed them, and started south. He walked at first, then he ran, faster and faster he went, all the while shouting at the top of his voice, "The sword of the Lord and of Gideon!"

The police officers heard of it, and set out to find him. They hunted the country over and even dragged the river, but they never found him again, living or dead. It is thought that he was drowned and the quick-sands of the river sucked his body under. But the little Dane boys in our country firmly believe that he was translated like Enoch of old. On stormy nights, when the great winds sweep down from the north they huddle together in their beds and fancy that in the wind they still hear that wild cry, "The sword of the Lord and of Gideon."

First published in *The Hesperian*, XXII (October 15, 1892), 7–10.

Peter

❖ ❖ ❖

"No, Antone, I have told thee many times, no, thou shalt not sell it until I am gone."

"But I need money; what good is that old fiddle to thee? The very crows laugh at thee when thou art trying to play. Thy hand trembles so thou canst scarce hold the bow. Thou shalt go with me to the Blue to cut wood tomorrow. See to it thou art up early."

"What, on the Sabbath, Antone, when it is so cold? I get so very cold, my son, let us not go tomorrow."

"Yes, tomorrow, thou lazy old man. Do not I cut wood upon the Sabbath? Care I how cold it is? Wood thou shalt cut, and haul it too, and as for the fiddle, I tell thee I will sell it yet." Antone pulled his ragged cap down over his low heavy brow, and went out. The old man drew his stool up nearer the fire, and sat stroking his violin with trembling fingers and muttering, "Not while I live, not while I live."

Five years ago they had come here, Peter Sadelack, and his wife, and oldest son Antone, and countless smaller Sadelacks, here to the dreariest part of southwestern Nebraska, and had taken up a homestead. Antone was the acknowledged master of the premises, and people said he was a likely youth, and would do well. That he was mean and untrustworthy every one knew, but that made little difference. His corn was better tended than any in the county, and his wheat always yielded more than other men's.

Of Peter no one knew much, nor had any one a good word to say for him. He drank whenever he could get out of Antone's sight long enough to pawn his hat or coat for whisky. Indeed there were but two things he would not pawn, his pipe and his violin. He was a lazy, absent-minded old fellow, who liked to fiddle better than to plow, though Antone surely got work enough out of them all, for that matter. In the house of which Antone was master there was no one, from the little boy three years old, to the old man of sixty, who did not earn his bread. Still people said that Peter was worthless, and was a great drag on Antone, his son, who never drank, and was a much better man than his father had ever been. Peter did not care what people said. He did not like the country, nor the people, least of all he liked the plowing. He was very homesick for Bohemia. Long ago, only eight years ago by the calendar, but it seemed eight centuries to Peter, he had been a second violinist in the great theatre at Prague. He had gone into the theatre very young, and had been there all his life, until he had a stroke of paralysis, which made his arm so weak that his bowing was uncertain. Then they told him he could go. Those were great days at the theatre. He had plenty to drink then, and wore a dress coat every evening, and there were always parties after the play. He could play in those days, ay, that he could! He could never read the notes well, so he did not play first; but his touch, he had a touch indeed, so Herr Mikilsdoff, who led the orchestra, had said. Sometimes now Peter thought he could plow better if he could only bow as he used to. He had seen all the lovely women in the world there, all the great singers and the great players. He was in the orchestra when Rachel played, and he heard Liszt play when the Countess d'Agoult sat in the stage box and threw the master white lilies. Once, a French woman came and played for weeks, he did not remember her name now.★ He did not remember her face very well either, for it changed so, it was never twice the same. But the beauty of it, and the great hunger men felt at the sight of it, that he remembered. Most of all he remembered her voice. He did not know French, and could not understand a word she said, but it seemed to him that she must be talking the music of Chopin. And her voice, he thought he should know that in the other world. The last night she played a play in which a man touched her arm, and she stabbed him. As Peter sat among the smoking gas jets down below the footlights with his fiddle on his knee, and looked up at her, he thought he would like to die too, if he could touch her arm once, and have her stab him so. Peter went home to his wife very drunk that night. Even in those days he was a foolish fellow, who cared for nothing but music and pretty faces.

It was all different now. He had nothing to drink and little to eat, and here, there was nothing but sun, and grass, and sky. He had forgotten almost everything, but some things he remembered well enough. He loved his violin and the holy Mary, and above all else he feared the Evil One, and his son Antone.

★ The "French woman" is Sarah Bernhardt; the play described is Sardou's *Tosca*.

The fire was low, and it grew cold. Still Peter sat by the fire remembering. He dared not throw more cobs on the fire; Antone would be angry. He did not want to cut wood tomorrow, it would be Sunday, and he wanted to go to mass. Antone might let him do that. He held his violin under his wrinkled chin, his white hair fell over it, and he began to play "Ave Maria." His hand shook more than ever before, and at last refused to work the bow at all. He sat stupefied for a while, then arose, and taking his violin with him, stole out into the old sod stable. He took Antone's shotgun down from its peg, and loaded it by the moonlight which streamed in through the door. He sat down on the dirt floor, and leaned back against the dirt wall. He heard the wolves howling in the distance, and the night wind screaming as it swept over the snow. Near him he heard the regular breathing of the horses in the dark. He put his crucifix above his heart, and folding his hands said brokenly all the Latin he had ever known, "*Pater noster, qui in coelum est.*" Then he raised his head and sighed, "Not one kreutzer will Antone pay them to pray for my soul, not one kreutzer, he is so careful of his money, is Antone, he does not waste it in drink, he is a better man than I, but hard sometimes. He works the girls too hard, women were not made to work so. But he shall not sell thee, my fiddle, I can play thee no more, but they shall not part us. We have seen it all together, and we will forget it together, the French woman and all." He held his fiddle under his chin a moment, where it had lain so often, then put it across his knee and broke it through the middle. He pulled off his old boot, held the gun between his knees with the muzzle against his forehead, and pressed the trigger with his toe.

In the morning Antone found him stiff, frozen fast in a pool of blood. They could not straighten him out enough to fit a coffin, so they buried him in a pine box. Before the funeral Antone carried to town the fiddle-bow which Peter had forgotten to break. Antone was very thrifty, and a better man than his father had been.

First published in *The Mahogany Tree* (May 21, 1892), pp. 323–324.

Appendix

PSEUDONYMOUS STORIES

An important and fascinating area of recent and continuing research in the study of Willa Cather is concerned with her use of pseudonyms. Proving a pseudonym presents no difficulties in cases where a work which appeared in one outlet under a pen name was published elsewhere under her own name. For example, "When I Knew Stephen Crane," which appeared in The Library, June 23, 1900, under the name "Henry Nicklemann," was reprinted in the Lincoln Courier, July 14, 1900, signed Willa Sibert Cather. In other cases, a pseudonymous work may incorporate passages used in a signed or proved piece: for example, "The Hottest Day I Ever Spent" (The Library, July 7, 1900), signed "George Overing"—the name of a Red Cloud neighbor—repeated material from a signed article, "An Old River Metropolis" (Nebraska State Journal, August 12, 1894). Among other proved pseudonyms dating from the Pittsburgh years are "Helen Delay" (used frequently in the Home Monthly), "John Esten" (Willa Cather's youngest brother was named John Esten Cather), "Elizabeth L. Seymour" (borrowed from a cousin who lived with the Cather family in Red Cloud), and "Charles Douglass" (combining the first names of her father and one of her brothers). "Sibert," the middle name she adopted in 1896, was the byline on many of her Leader drama reviews.

The first of the following four stories, "The Dance at Chevalier's," appeared in The Library and was signed "Henry Nicklemann." The setting is the same as that of "On the Divide" and "Eric Hermannson's Soul," and some of the same people figure in it. "The Burglar's Christmas," signed "Elizabeth L. Seymour," and "The Princess Baladina—Her Adventure," signed "Charles Douglass," came out in the Home Monthly during the first months of Willa Cather's editorship, when she was writing virtually the whole magazine. The fourth story, added to the revised edition of this volume, appeared in The Hesperian when Willa Cather was literary editor; perhaps for this reason it was unsigned. The story was identified by Bernice Slote, who has noted that it "contains nothing less than a capsule description and recreation of Willa Cather's Virginia home, paralleled in almost every detail by passages in Sapphira and the Slave Girl"—her last novel.*

* For a discussion of the story's identification, see The Kingdom of Art: Willa Cather's First Principles and Critical Statements, 1893–1896, selected and edited with a commentary and two essays by Bernice Slote (Lincoln: University of Nebraska Press, 1967), pp. 104–106. For a discussion of Willa Cather's alterations of her own name, see Mildred R. Bennett, The World of Willa Cather (Lincoln: University of Nebraska Press, 1961), pp. 234–235.

The Dance at Chevalier's

✳ ✳ ✳

It was a dance that was a dance, that dance at Chevalier's, and it will be long remembered in our country.

But first as to what happened in the afternoon. Denis and Signor had put the cattle in the corral and come in early to rest before the dance. The Signor was a little Mexican who had strayed up into the cattle country. What his real name was, heaven only knows, but we called him "The Signor," as if he had been Italian instead of Mexican. After they had put the horses away, they went into the feed room, which was a sort of stable salon, where old Chevalier received his friends and where his hands amused themselves on Sundays. The Signor suggested a game of cards, and placed a board across the top of a millet barrel for a table. Denis lit his pipe and began to mix the cards.

Little Harry Burns sat on the tool box sketching. Burns was an eastern newspaper man, who had come to live in Oklahoma because of his lungs. He found a good deal that was interesting besides the air. As the game went on, he kept busily filling in his picture, which was really a picture of Denis, the Mexican being merely indicated by a few careless strokes. Burns had a decided weakness for Denis. It was his business to be interested in people, and practice had made his eye quick to pick out a man from whom unusual things might be expected. Then he admired Denis for his great physical proportions. Indeed, even with his pipe in his mouth and the fresh soil of the spring ploughing on his boots, Denis made a striking figure. He was a remarkably attractive man, that Denis, as all the girls in the neighborhood knew to their sorrow. For Denis was a ladies' man and had heady impulses that were hard to resist. What we call sentiment in cultured men is called by a coarser name in the pure animal products of nature and is a dangerous force to encounter. Burns used to say to himself that this big choleric Irishman was an erotic poet undeveloped and untamed by the processes of thought; a pure creature of emotional impulses who went about seeking rhymes and harmonies in the flesh, the original Adam. Burns wondered if he would not revel in the fervid verses of his great countryman Tom Moore—if he should ever see them. But Denis never read anything but the Sunday New York papers—a week old, always, when he got them—and he was totally untrammelled by anything of a reflective nature. So he remained merely a smiling giant, who had the knack of saying pretty things to girls. After all, he was just as happy that way, and very much more irresistible, and Harry Burns knew it, for all his theories.

Just as he was finishing his picture, Burns was startled by a loud exclamation.

"Stop pulling cards out of your sleeve, you confounded Mexican cheat!"

"You lie! You lie!" shouted the Signor, throwing a card on the table and attempting to rise. But Denis was too quick for him. He caught the back of the Mexican's greasy hand with the point of his belt knife and, regardless of the blood that trickled through his fingers, proceeded to search his sleeve.

"There, Signor, chuck a whole deck up, why don't you? Now the next time you try that game on me I'll run my knife clean through your dirty paw, and leave a mark that men will know."

"I'll kill you for this, you dog of an Irishman! Wait and see how I will kill you," snarled the Mexican, livid with rage and pain, as he shot out of the door. Denis laughed and lay down on a pile of corn.

"Better look out for that man, Denis," said little Burns, as he lit a cigarette.

"Oh, if I was looking for a man to be afraid of I wouldn't pick the Signor."

"Look out for him, all the same. They are a nasty lot, these Greasers. I've known them down in Old Mexico. They'll knife you in the dark, any one of them. It's the only country I could never feel comfortable in. Everything is dangerous—the climate, the sun, the men, and most of all the women. The very flowers are poisonous. Why does old Chevalier keep this fellow?"

"Oh, he's a good hand enough, and a first-rate man with the cattle. I don't like Greasers myself, they're all sneaks. Not many of 'em ever come up in this country, and they've always got into some sort of trouble and had to light out. The Signor has kept pretty straight around the place, though, and as long as he behaves himself he can hold his job."

"You don't think Chevalier's daughter has anything to do with his staying?"

"If I did I'd trample him like a snake!"

When the Signor left the barn he shook the blood from his wounded hand and went up to the house and straight into the sitting room, where Severine Chevalier was shaving a tallow candle on the floor for the dance. The Signor's scowl vanished, and he approached her with an exaggerated smile.

"Come, Severine. I've cut my hand; tie it up for me, like the sweet one that you are."

"How came you to cut your hand on the day of the dance? And how on the back, too? I believe you did it on purpose."

"And so I did, to have you tie it up for me. I would cut myself all over for that." And as Severine bent over to twist the bandage he kissed her on the cheek.

"Begone, you sneak; you can tie up your own cuts, if that's the way you treat me."

"*Dios mio!* that is treating you very well, my sweet. If that is not good what is there in this world that is? I saw that hulking Irishman kiss you last night, and you seemed to like it well enough."

"That depends on the person, Monsieur Signor," said Severine, tartly, as she slid over the tallow shavings. But she blushed hotly, all the same.

"See here, Severine, you have played with both of us long enough. If you kiss him again I will kill you. I like to kill the things I love, do you understand?"

"*Merci, monsieur!* I compliment you. You have great tact. You know how to coax a sweetheart. You know all about love-making."

"You baby! women have gone mad after me before now. You see how I love you, and it does not move you. That is because you are a baby and do not know how to love. A girl who doesn't know how to love is stupid, tasteless, like—like so much water. Baby!"

The girl's eyes were hot with anger as she drew herself up and faced him.

"You fool! you think you know all about love, and yet you cannot see that I am in love all the time, that I burn up with love, that I am tortured by it, that my pillows are hot with it all night, and my hands are wet with it in the day. You fool! But it is not with you, Monsieur Signor, *grace à Dieu*, it is not with you."

The swarthy little Signor looked at her admiringly a moment, and then spoke in a low voice that whistled in the air like a knife—

"Is it the Irishman? It is the Irishman!"

"Yes, stupid beast, it is. But that is my own affair."

Frightened at her own rashness, she fell to shaving the candle with trembling hands, while the Mexican watched her with a smile that showed all his white teeth. Severine had time to repent her rashness, and a sickening fear of the consequences arose within her.

"You'll keep that to yourself, Signor? You won't tell father?"

"That is my affair, Mademoiselle."

She dropped the wax and touched his arm.

"Play fair, Signor, and keep it, please."

"It is I who make terms now, Mademoiselle. Well, yes, I will keep it, and I will ask a very little price for my silence. You must come out and kiss me tonight when I ask you."

"Yes, yes, I will if you will only keep your word."

He caught her in his slender, sinewy arms.

"You said once!" she cried, in angry protest, as she broke away from him.

"This was only to show you how, my sweet," he laughed.

As he left the room he looked back over his shoulder and saw that she was still rubbing her lips with her hand, and all the way up stairs to his own room he laughed, and when he packed his belongings away in his canvas saddlebags he was still smiling. When he had finished and strapped his bags he stood looking about him. He heard a snatch of an old French song through the window and saw Severine working out in her flower bed.

He hesitated a moment, then shook his head and patted his bandaged hand. "Ah, love is sweet, but sweeter is revenge. It is the saying of my people."

And now for the dance at Chevalier's, which was a dance, indeed. It was the last before the hot season came on and everybody was there— all the French for miles around. Some came in road wagons, some in buggies, some on horseback, and not a few on foot. Girls with pretty faces and rough hands, and men in creaking boots, with broad throats tanned by the sun, reeking with violent perfumes and the odors of the soil.

At nine o'clock the dance began, the dance that was to have lasted all night. Harry Burns played an old bass viol, and Alplosen de Mar played the organ, but the chief musician was the old Bohemian, Peter Sadelack, who played the violin. Peter had seen better days, and had played in a theatre in Prague until he had paralysis and was discharged because his bowing was uncertain. Then in some way, God knows how, he and his slatternly wife and countless progeny had crossed the ocean and drifted out into the cattle country. The three of them made right merry music, though the two violinists were considerably the more skilful, and poor Alplosen quite lost her breath in keeping up with them. Waltzes, quadrilles and polkas they played until the perspiration streamed down their faces, and for the square dances little Burns "called off." Occasionally he got down and took a waltz himself, giving some young Frenchman his instrument. All those Frenchmen could play a fiddle from the time they were old enough to hold one. But dancing was bad for his lungs, and with the exception of Severine and Marie Generaux there were very few girls he cared to dance with. It was more amusing to saw away on the squeaky old bass viol and watch those gleeful young Frenchmen seize a girl and whirl her away with a dexterity and grace really quite remarkable, considering the crowd and the roughness of the floor, and the affectionate positions in which they insisted upon holding their partners. They were not of pure French blood, of course; most of them had been crossed and recrossed with Canadians and Indians, and they spoke a vile patois which no Christian man could understand. Almost the only traces they retained of their original nationality were their names, and their old French songs, and their grace in the dance. Deep down in the heart of every one of them, uncrushed by labor, undulled by enforced abstinence, there was a mad, insatiable love of pleasure that continually warred with the blood of dull submission they drew from their red squaw ancestors. Tonight it broke out like a devouring flame, it flashed in dark eyes and glowed in red cheeks. Ah that old hot, imperious blood of the Latins! It is never quite lost. These women had long since forgotten the wit of their motherland, they were dull of mind and slow of tongue; but in the eyes, on the lips, in the temperament was the old, ineffaceable stamp. The Latin blood was there.

The most animated and by far the most beautiful among them was Severine Chevalier. At those dances little attempt was made at evening dress, but Severine was in white, with her gown cut low, showing the curves of her neck and shoulders. For she was different from the other French girls, she had more taste and more ambition, and more money. She had been sent two years to a convent school in Toronto, and when she came back the other girls could never quite get used to her ways, though they admired and envied her from afar. She could speak the French of France, could Severine, and sometimes when it was dull and too rainy to gallop across the prairies after the cattle, or to town for the mail, and when there was nothing better to do, she used to read books. She talked with little Burns about books sometimes. But, on the whole, she preferred her pony, and the wild flowers, and the wind and the sun, and romping with her boys. She was a very human young woman, and not wise enough to disguise or to affect anything. She knew what the good things of life were, and was quite frank about them. Tonight she seemed glowing with some unspoken joy, and many a French lad felt his heart thump faster as he clutched her hand with an iron grasp and guided her over the rough floor and among the swaying couples; many a lad cast timid glances at old Jean Chevalier as he sat complacently by his brandy bottle, proudly watching his daughter. For old Chevalier was a king in the cattle country, and they knew that none might aspire to his daughter's hand who had not wider acres and more cattle than any of them possessed.

And for every glance that Severine drew from the men, Denis drew a sigh from the women. Though he was only Jean Chevalier's herdman, and an Irishman at that, Denis was the lion of the French dances. He danced hard, and drank hard, and made love hardest of all. But tonight he was chary of his favors, and when he could not dance with Severine he was careless of his other partners. After a long waltz he took Severine out to the windmill in the grove. It was refreshingly cool out there, the moonlight was clear and pale, and the tall lombard poplars were rustling their cool leaves. The moon was just up and was still reflected in the long lagoon on the eastern horizon. Denis put his arms about the girl and drew her up to him. The Signor saw them so, as he slipped down to the barn to saddle his horse, and he whispered to himself, "It is high time." But what the great Irishman whispered in her ear, the Signor never knew.

As Denis led her back to the house, he felt a dizzy sensation of tenderness and awe come over him, such as he had sometimes felt when he was riding alone across the moonlit lagoons under the eyes of countless stars, or when he was driving his cattle out in the purple lights of springtide dawns.

As they entered the house, the Mexican slipped in behind them and tried to edge his way through the crowd unseen. But Marie Generaux caught him by the arm.

"This is our dance, Signor, come along."

"Make it the next, my girl," he whispered, and escaped upstairs into his own room.

His saddlebags were already on his horse, but in his chest there lay one article which belonged to him, a pint whisky flask. He took it out and unscrewed the top, and smelt it, and held it up to the light, shaking it gently and gazing on it with real affection in his narrow, snaky eyes. For it was not ordinary liquor. An old, withered Negro from the gold coast of Guinea had told him how to make it, down in Mexico. He himself had gathered rank, noxious plants and poured their distilled juices into that whisky, and had killed the little lizards that sun themselves on the crumbling stones of the old ruined missions, and dried their bodies and boiled them in the contents of that flask. For five years that bright liquor had lain sparkling in his chest, waiting for such a time as this.

When the Signor went downstairs a quadrille was just over, and the room was echoing with loud laughter. He beckoned Severine into a corner, and whispered with a meaning glance:

"Send your Irishman upstairs to me. I must see him. And save the next dance for me. There he is. Hurry."

Reluctantly she approached Denis, blushing furiously as she accosted him.

"Go upstairs and see the Signor, please, Denis."

"What can he want with me?"

"I don't know. I wish you'd go, though."

"Well, Signor, what is it?" he asked as he reached the top of the stairs.

"I must tell you something. Take a drink to brace you, and then I'll talk. It will not be pleasant news."

Denis laughed and drank, never noticing how the hand that held out the glass to him was shaking.

"I can't say much for your whisky," he remarked, as he set down the empty glass.

The Mexican came up to him, his eyes glittering with suppressed excitement.

"I want to tell you that we have both been fools. That French girl has played with us both. We have let her cuff us about like schoolboys, and coax us with sugar like children. Today she promised to marry me, tonight she promises to marry you. We are decidedly fools, my friend."

"You liar! You say that again—"

"Tut, tut, my friend, not so fast. You are a big man, and I am a little one. I cannot fight you. I try to do you a service, and you abuse me. That is not unusual. But you wait here by the window through the next dance and watch the windmill, and if I don't prove what I say, then you may kill me at your pleasure. Is not that fair enough?"

"Prove it, prove it!" said Denis from a dry throat.

In a moment he was alone, and stood watching out of the window, scarcely knowing why he was there. "It's all a lie; I felt the truth in her," he kept saying to himself while he waited. The music struck up downstairs, the squeak of the cracked organ and the screech of the violins, and with it the sound of the heavy feet. His first impulse was to go down and join them, but he waited. In a few minutes, perhaps two, perhaps three, before the waltz was half over, he saw the Signor stroll down towards the windmill. Beside him was Severine. They went straight to that moonlit bit of ground under the poplars, the spot where twenty minutes before he had been seized and mastered and borne away by that floodtide of tenderness which we can know but once in our lives, and then seek, hunger for all the rest of our sunless days. There, in that spot, which even to his careless mind was holy ground, he saw Severine stop and lift her little flower-like face to another man's. Long, long he held her. God knows how long it must have seemed to the man who watched and held his breath until his veins seemed bursting. Then they were gone, and only the quivering poplar leaves cast their shadows over that moonlit spot.

He felt a deadly sickness come over him. He caught the flask on the table and drank again. Presently the door opened, and the Signor entered. He should have been gone indeed, but he could not resist one more long look at the man who sat limply on the bed, with his face buried in his hands.

"I am glad you take it patiently; it is better," he remarked, soothingly.

Then over the big Irishman, who sat with his head bowed and his eyes darkened and the hand of death already heavy upon him, there came a flood of remembrances and of remorse.

"Yes," he groaned. "I can be patient. I can take torture with my mouth shut—women have taught me how." Then suddenly starting to his feet he shouted, "Begone, you Satan, or I'll strangle ye!"

When Denis stumbled downstairs his face was burning, but not with anger. Severine had been hunting for him and came up to him eagerly. "I've been looking for you everywhere. Where have you been so long? Let's dance this; it's the one you like."

He followed her passively. Even his resentment was half dead. He felt an awful sense of weakness and isolation; he wanted to touch something warm and living. In a few minutes something would happen—something. He caught her roughly, half loving her, half loathing her, and weak, trembling, with his head on fire and his breast bursting with pain, he began to dance. Over and over again the fiddles scraped their trite measures, while Severine wondered why the hand that gripped hers grew so cold. He lost the time and then swayed back and forth. A sharp cry of alarm rang from the end of the room, and little Burns bounded from the table, and reached him just as he fell.

"What is it, Denis, my boy, what is it?"

Severine knelt on the other side, still holding one of his hands.

The man's face was drawn in horrible agony, his blue eyes were distended and shot with blood, his hair hung wet over his face, and his lips were dashed with froth. He gasped heavily from his laboring breast.

"Poison—they—she and the Mexican—they have done me.— Damn—damn—women!"

He struck at Severine, but she caught his hand and kissed it.

But all the protestations, all the words of love, imperious as a whirlwind, that she poured out there on her knees fell upon deaf ears. Not even those words, winged with flame, could break the silences for him. If the lips of the living could give warmth to those of the dead, death would be often robbed, and the grave cheated of its victory.

Harry Burns sprang to his feet. "It's that damned Mexican. Where is he?"

But no one answered. The Signor had been in his saddle half an hour, speeding across the plains, on the swiftest horse in the cattle country.

First published in *The Library*, I (April 28, 1900), 12–13.

The Burglar's Christmas

❄ ❄ ❄

Two very shabby looking young men stood at the corner of Prairie Avenue and Eightieth Street, looking despondently at the carriages that whirled by. It was Christmas Eve, and the streets were full of vehicles; florists' wagons, grocers' carts and carriages. The streets were in that half-liquid, half-congealed condition peculiar to the streets of Chicago at that season of the year. The swift wheels that spun by sometimes threw the slush of mud and snow over the two young men who were talking on the corner.

"Well," remarked the elder of the two, "I guess we are at our rope's end, sure enough. How do you feel?"

"Pretty shaky. The wind's sharp tonight. If I had had anything to eat I mightn't mind it so much. There is simply no show. I'm sick of the whole business. Looks like there's nothing for it but the lake."

"O, nonsense, I thought you had more grit. Got anything left you can hock?"

"Nothing but my beard, and I am afraid they wouldn't find it worth a pawn ticket," said the younger man ruefully, rubbing the week's growth of stubble on his face.

"Got any folks anywhere? Now's your time to strike 'em if you have."

"Never mind if I have, they're out of the question."

"Well, you'll be out of it before many hours if you don't make a move of some sort. A man's got to eat. See here, I am going down to Longtin's saloon. I used to play the banjo in there with a couple of coons, and I'll bone him for some of his free-lunch stuff. You'd better come along, perhaps they'll fill an order for two."

"How far down is it?"

"Well, it's clear downtown, of course, 'way down on Michigan avenue."

"Thanks, I guess I'll loaf around here. I don't feel equal to the walk, and the cars—well, the cars are crowded." His features drew themselves into what might have been a smile under happier circumstances.

"No, you never did like street cars, you're too aristocratic. See here, Crawford, I don't like leaving you here. You ain't good company for yourself tonight."

"Crawford? O, yes, that's the last one. There have been so many I forget them."

"Have you got a real name, anyway?"

"O, yes, but it's one of the ones I've forgotten. Don't you worry about me. You go along and get your free lunch. I think I had a row in Longtin's place once. I'd better not show myself there again." As he spoke the young man nodded and turned slowly up the avenue.

He was miserable enough to want to be quite alone. Even the crowd that jostled by him annoyed him. He wanted to think about himself. He had avoided this final reckoning with himself for a year now. He had laughed it off and drunk it off. But now, when all those artificial devices which are employed to turn our thoughts into other channels and shield us from ourselves had failed him, it must come. Hunger is a powerful incentive to introspection.

It is a tragic hour, that hour when we are finally driven to reckon with ourselves, when every avenue of mental distraction has been cut off and our own life and all its ineffaceable failures closes about us like the walls of that old torture chamber of the Inquisition. Tonight, as this man stood stranded in the streets of the city, his hour came. It was not the first time he had been hungry and desperate and alone. But always before there had been some outlook, some chance ahead, some pleasure yet untasted that seemed worth the effort, some face that he fancied was, or would be, dear. But it was not so tonight. The unyielding conviction was upon him that he had failed in everything, had outlived everything. It had been near him for a long time, that Pale Spectre. He had caught its shadow at the bottom of his glass many a time, at the head of his bed when he was sleepless at night, in the twilight shadows when some great sunset broke upon him. It had made life hateful to him when he awoke in the morning before now. But now it settled slowly over him, like night, the endless Northern nights that bid the sun a long farewell. It rose up before him like granite. From this brilliant city with its glad bustle of Yuletide he was shut off as completely as though he were a creature of another species. His days seemed numbered and done, sealed over like the little coral cells at the bottom of the sea. Involuntarily he drew that cold air through his lungs slowly, as though he were tasting it for the last time.

Yet he was but four and twenty, this man—he looked even younger—and he had a father some place down East who had been very proud of him once. Well, he had taken his life into his own hands, and this was what he had made of it. That was all there was to be said. He could remember the hopeful things they used to say about him at college in the old days, before he had cut away and begun to live by his wits, and he found courage to smile at them now. They had read him wrongly. He knew now that he never had the essentials of success, only the superficial agility that is often mistaken for it. He was tow without the tinder, and he had burnt himself out at other people's fires. He had helped other people to make it win, but he himself—he had never touched an enterprise that had not failed eventually. Or, if it survived his connection with it, it left him behind.

His last venture had been with some ten-cent specialty company, a little lower than all the others, that had gone to pieces in Buffalo, and he had worked his way to Chicago by boat. When the boat made up its crew for the outward voyage, he was dispensed with as usual. He was used to that. The reason for it? O, there are so many reasons for failure! His was a very common one.

As he stood there in the wet under the street light he drew up his reckoning with the world and decided that it had treated him as well as he deserved. He had overdrawn his account once too often. There had been a day when he thought otherwise; when he had said he was unjustly handled, that his failure was merely the lack of proper adjustment between himself and other men, that some day he would be recognized and it would all come right. But he knew better than that now, and he was still man enough to bear no grudge against any one—man or woman.

Tonight was his birthday, too. There seemed something particularly amusing in that. He turned up a limp little coat collar to try to keep a little of the wet chill from his throat, and instinctively began to remember all the birthday parties he used to have. He was so cold and empty that his mind seemed unable to grapple with any serious question. He kept thinking about gingerbread and frosted cakes like a child. He could remember the splendid birthday parties his mother used to give him, when all the other little boys in the block came in their Sunday clothes and creaking shoes, with their ears still red from their mother's towel, and the pink and white birthday cake, and the stuffed olives and all the dishes of which he had been particularly fond, and how he would eat and eat and then go to bed and dream of Santa Claus. And in the morning he would awaken and eat again, until by night the family doctor arrived with his castor oil, and poor William used to dolefully say that it was altogether too much to have your birthday and Christmas all at once. He could remember, too, the royal birthday suppers he had given at college, and the stag dinners, and the toasts, and the music, and the good fellows who had wished him happiness and really meant what they said.

And since then there were other birthday suppers that he could not remember so clearly; the memory of them was heavy and flat, like cigarette smoke that has been shut in a room all night, like champagne that has been a day opened, a song that has been too often sung, an acute sensation that has been overstrained. They seemed tawdry and garish, discordant to him now. He rather wished he could forget them altogether.

Whichever way his mind now turned there was one thought that it could not escape, and that was the idea of food. He caught the scent of a cigar suddenly, and felt a sharp pain in the pit of his abdomen and a sudden moisture in his mouth. His cold hands clenched angrily, and for a moment he felt that bitter hatred of wealth, of ease, of everything that is well fed and well housed that is common to starving men. At any rate he had a right to eat! He had demanded great things from the world once: fame and wealth and admiration. Now it was simply bread—and he would have it! He looked about him quickly and felt the blood begin to stir in his veins. In all his straits he had never stolen anything, his tastes were above it. But tonight there would be no tomorrow. He was amused at the way in which the idea excited him. Was it possible there was yet one more experience that would distract him, one thing that had power to excite his jaded interest? Good! he had failed at everything else, now he would see what his chances would be as a common thief. It would be amusing to watch the beautiful consistency of his destiny work itself out even in that role. It would be interesting to add another study to his gallery of futile attempts, and then label them all: "the failure as a journalist," "the failure as a lecturer," "the failure as a business man," "the failure as a thief," and so on, like the titles under the pictures of the Dance of Death. It was time that Childe Roland came to the dark tower.

A girl hastened by him with her arms full of packages. She walked quickly and nervously, keeping well within the shadow, as if she were not accustomed to carrying bundles and did not care to meet any of her friends. As she crossed the muddy street, she made an effort to lift her skirt a little, and as she did so one of the packages slipped unnoticed from beneath her arm. He caught it up and overtook her. "Excuse me, but I think you dropped something."

She started, "O, yes, thank you, I would rather have lost anything than that."

The young man turned angrily upon himself. The package must have contained something of value. Why had he not kept it? Was this the sort of thief he would make? He ground his teeth together. There is nothing more maddening than to have morally consented to crime and then lack the nerve force to carry it out.

A carriage drove up to the house before which he stood. Several richly dressed women alighted and went in. It was a new house, and must have been built since he was in Chicago last. The front door was open and he could see down the hallway and up the staircase. The servant had left the door and gone with the guests. The first floor was brilliantly lighted, but the windows upstairs were dark. It looked very easy, just to slip upstairs to the darkened chambers where the jewels and trinkets of the fashionable occupants were kept.

Still burning with impatience against himself he entered quickly. Instinctively he removed his mud-stained hat as he passed quickly and quietly up the stair case. It struck him as being a rather superfluous courtesy in a burglar, but he had done it before he had thought. His way was clear enough, he met no one on the stairway or in the upper hall. The gas was lit in the upper hall. He passed the first chamber door through sheer cowardice. The second he entered quickly, thinking of something else lest his courage should fail him, and closed the door behind him. The light from the hall shone into the room through the transom. The apartment was furnished richly enough to justify his expectations. He went at once to the dressing case. A number of rings and small trinkets lay in a silver tray. These he put hastily in his pocket. He opened the upper drawer and found, as he expected, several leather cases. In the first he opened was a lady's watch, in the second a pair of old-fashioned bracelets; he seemed to dimly remember having seen bracelets like them before, somewhere. The third case was heavier, the spring was much worn, and it opened easily. It held a cup of some kind. He held it up to the light and then his strained nerves gave way and he uttered a sharp exclamation. It was the silver mug he used to drink from when he was a little boy.

The door opened, and a woman stood in the doorway facing him. She was a tall woman, with white hair, in evening dress. The light from the hall streamed in upon him, but she was not afraid. She stood looking at him a moment, then she threw out her hand and went quickly toward him.

"Willie, Willie! Is it you?"

He struggled to loose her arms from him, to keep her lips from his cheek. "Mother—you must not! You do not understand! O, my God, this is worst of all!" Hunger, weakness, cold, shame, all came back to him, and shook his self-control completely. Physically he was too weak to stand a shock like this. Why could it not have been an ordinary discovery, arrest, the station house and all the rest of it. Anything but this! A hard dry sob broke from him. Again he strove to disengage himself.

"Who is it says I shall not kiss my son? O, my boy, we have waited so long for this! You have been so long in coming, even I almost gave you up."

Her lips upon his cheek burnt him like fire. He put his hand to his throat, and spoke thickly and incoherently: "You do not understand. I did not know you were here. I came here to rob—it is the first time—I swear it—but I am a common thief. My pockets are full of your jewels now. Can't you hear me? I am a common thief!"

"Hush, my boy, those are ugly words. How could you rob your own house? How could you take what is your own? They are all yours, my son, as wholly yours as my great love—and you can't doubt that, Will, do you?"

That soft voice, the warmth and fragrance of her person stole through his chill, empty veins like a gentle stimulant. He felt as though all his strength were leaving him and even consciousness. He held fast to her and bowed his head on her strong shoulder, and groaned aloud.

"O, mother, life is hard, hard!"

She said nothing, but held him closer. And O, the strength of those white arms that held him! O, the assurance of safety in that warm bosom that rose and fell under his cheek! For a moment they stood so, silently. Then they heard a heavy step upon the stair. She led him to a chair and went out and closed the door. At the top of the staircase she met a tall, broad-shouldered man, with iron gray hair, and a face alert and stern. Her eyes were shining and her cheeks on fire, her whole face was one expression of intense determination.

"James, it is William in there, come home. You must keep him at any cost. If he goes this time, I go with him. O, James, be easy with him, he has suffered so." She broke from a command to an entreaty, and laid her hand on his shoulder. He looked questioningly at her a moment, then went in the room and quietly shut the door.

She stood leaning against the wall, clasping her temples with her hands and listening to the low indistinct sound of the voices within. Her own lips moved silently. She waited a long time, scarcely breathing. At last the door opened, and her husband came out. He stopped to say in a shaken voice,

"You go to him now, he will stay. I will go to my room. I will see him again in the morning."

She put her arm about his neck, "O, James, I thank you, I thank you! This is the night he came so long ago, you remember? I gave him to you then, and now you give him back to me!"

"Don't, Helen," he muttered. "He is my son, I have never forgotten that. I failed with him. I don't like to fail, it cuts my pride. Take him and make a man of him." He passed on down the hall.

She flew into the room where the young man sat with his head bowed upon his knee. She dropped upon her knees beside him. Ah, it was so good to him to feel those arms again!

"He is so glad, Willie, so glad! He may not show it, but he is as happy as I. He never was demonstrative with either of us, you know."

"O, my God, he was good enough," groaned the man. "I told him everything, and he was good enough. I don't see how either of you can look at me, speak to me, touch me." He shivered under her clasp again as when she had first touched him, and tried weakly to throw her off.

But she whispered softly,

"This is my right, my son."

Presently, when he was calmer, she rose. "Now, come with me into the library, and I will have your dinner brought there."

As they went downstairs she remarked apologetically, "I will not call Ellen tonight; she has a number of guests to attend to. She is a big girl now, you know, and came out last winter. Besides, I want you all to myself tonight."

When the dinner came, and it came very soon, he fell upon it savagely. As he ate she told him all that had transpired during the years of his absence, and how his father's business had brought them there. "I was glad when we came. I thought you would drift West. I seemed a good deal nearer to you here."

There was a gentle unobtrusive sadness in her tone that was too soft for a reproach.

"Have you everything you want? It is a comfort to see you eat."

He smiled grimly, "It is certainly a comfort to me. I have not indulged in this frivolous habit for some thirty-five hours."

She caught his hand and pressed it sharply, uttering a quick remonstrance.

"Don't say that! I know, but I can't hear you say it—it's too terrible! My boy, food has choked me many a time when I have thought of the possibility of that. Now take the old lounging chair by the fire, and if you are too tired to talk, we will just sit and rest together."

He sank into the depths of the big leather chair with the lions' heads on the arms, where he had sat so often in the days when his feet did not touch the floor and he was half afraid of the grim monsters cut in the polished wood. That chair seemed to speak to him of things long forgotten. It was like the touch of an old familiar friend. He felt a sudden yearning tenderness for the happy little boy who had sat there and dreamed of the big world so long ago. Alas, he had been dead many a summer, that little boy!

He sat looking up at the magnificent woman beside him. He had almost forgotten how handsome she was; how lustrous and sad were the eyes that were set under that serene brow, how impetuous and wayward the mouth even now, how superb the white throat and shoulders! Ah, the wit and grace and fineness of this woman! He remembered how proud he had been of her as a boy when she came to see him at school. Then in the deep red coals of the grate he saw the faces of other women who had come since then into his vexed, disordered life. Laughing faces, with eyes artificially bright, eyes without depth or meaning, features without the stamp of high sensibilities. And he had left this face for such as those!

He sighed restlessly and laid his hand on hers. There seemed refuge and protection in the touch of her, as in the old days when he was afraid of the dark. He had been in the dark so long now, his confidence was so thoroughly shaken, and he was bitterly afraid of the night and of himself.

"Ah, mother, you make other things seem so false. You must feel that I owe you an explanation, but I can't make any, even to myself. Ah, but we make poor exchanges in life. I can't make out the riddle of it all. Yet there are things I ought to tell you before I accept your confidence like this."

"I'd rather you wouldn't, Will. Listen: Between you and me there can be no secrets. We are more alike than other people. Dear boy, I know all about it. I am a woman, and circumstances were different with me, but we are of one blood. I have lived all your life before you. You have never had an impulse that I have not known, you have never touched a brink that my feet have not trod. This is your birthday night. Twenty-four years ago I foresaw all this. I was a young woman then and I had hot battles of my own, and I felt your likeness to me. You were not like other babies. From the hour you were born you were restless and discontented, as I had been before you. You used to brace your strong little limbs against mine and try to throw me off as you did tonight. Tonight you have come back to me, just as you always did after you ran away to swim in the river that was forbidden you, the river you loved because it was forbidden. You are tired and sleepy, just as you used to be then, only a little older and a little paler and a little more foolish. I never asked you where you had been then, nor will I now. You have come back to me, that's all in all to me. I know your every possibility and limitation, as a composer knows his instrument."

He found no answer that was worthy to give to talk like this. He had not found life easy since he had lived by his wits. He had come to know poverty at close quarters. He had known what it was to be gay with an empty pocket, to wear violets in his buttonhole when he had not break-fasted, and all the hateful shams of the poverty of idleness. He had been a reporter on a big metropolitan daily, where men grind out their brains on paper until they have not one idea left—and still grind on. He had worked in a real estate office, where ignorant men were swindled. He had sung in a comic opera chorus and played Harris in an *Uncle Tom's Cabin* company, and edited a socialist weekly. He had been dogged by debt and hunger and grinding poverty, until to sit here by a warm fire without concern as to how it would be paid for seemed unnatural.

He looked up at her questioningly. "I wonder if you know how much you pardon?"

"O, my poor boy, much or little, what does it matter? Have you wandered so far and paid such a bitter price for knowledge and not yet learned that love has nothing to do with pardon or forgiveness, that it only loves, and loves—and loves? They have not taught you well, the women of your world." She leaned over and kissed him, as no woman had kissed him since he left her.

He drew a long sigh of rich content. The old life, with all its bitterness and useless antagonism and flimsy sophistries, its brief delights that were always tinged with fear and distrust and unfaith, that whole miserable, futile, swindled world of Bohemia seemed immeasurably distant and far away, like a dream that is over and done. And as the chimes rang joyfully outside and sleep pressed heavily upon his eyelids, he wondered dimly if the Author of this sad little riddle of ours were not able to solve it after all, and if the Potter would not finally mete out his all comprehensive justice, such as none but he could have, to his Things of Clay, which are made in his own patterns, weak or strong, for his own ends; and if some day we will not awaken and find that all evil is a dream, a mental distortion that will pass when the dawn shall break.

First published in *Home Monthly*, VI (December, 1896), 8–10.

The Princess Baladina—Her Adventure

❈ ❈ ❈

The Princess Baladina sat sullenly gazing out of her nursery window. There was no use in crying any more for there was no one there to see and pity her tears, and who ever cries unless there is some one to pity them? She had kicked at the golden door until it became evident that she was much more discomforted than the door, and then she gave it up and sat sullenly down and did nothing but watch the big bumblebees buzzing about the honeysuckles outside the window. The Princess Baladina had been shut up in her nursery for being naughty. Indeed, she had been unusually naughty that day. In the first place she had scratched and bitten the nurse who had combed her golden hair in the morning. Later, while she was playing about the palace grounds, she had lost in the moat one of the three beautiful golden balls which her father had bought for her of an old Jewish magician from Bagdad who was staying at the court, and who bought up the queen's old dresses and loaned the courtiers money on their diamonds. Then she had been so rude to her fairy godmother who came to luncheon with them that her mother had reprimanded her twice. Finally, when she poured custard in her fairy godmother's ear-trumpet, she was sent up to her nursery. Now she sat locked up there and thinking how cruelly her family had used her. She wondered what she could do to make them repent of their harsh behavior and wish they had been kinder to their little Princess Baladina. Perhaps if she should die they would realize how brutal they had been. O yes, if she were to die, then they would grieve and mourn and put flowers on her grave every day, and cry for their little Baladina who would never gather flowers any more. Baladina wept a little herself at the pathetic picture she had conjured up. But she decided not to die, that was such a very decisive thing to do; besides, then she could not see the remorse of her family, and what good is it to have your family repent if you cannot have the satisfaction of seeing them reduced to sackcloth and ashes? So the Princess cast about for another plan. She might cut off her beautiful golden hair, but then she had no scissors; besides, if a young Prince should happen to come that way it would be awkward not to have any golden hair. Princesses are taught to think of these things early. She began thinking over all the stories she had read about Princesses and their adventures, until suddenly she thought of the story of the Princess Alice, who had been enchanted by a wizard. Yes, that was it, that would be the best revenge of all, she would be enchanted by a wizard, and her family would be in despair; her father would offer [half] his kingdom to the knight who should free her, and some young Prince would come and break the spell and bear her triumphantly off to his own realm, on his saddle bow. Then her unfeeling parents would never see her any more, and her sisters and brothers would have no dear sweet little Princess to wait on.

But the next question was where to find a wizard. The Princess went over all the gentlemen of her acquaintance, but could not think of one who belonged to that somewhat complicated profession. Never mind, she would find one, she had heard of Princesses wandering away from their palaces on strange missions before. She waited through all the hot afternoon, and when the nurse brought her tea she took two of the buns and a piece of raisin cake and did them up carefully in a handkerchief, and said her prayers and let them put her to bed. She lay awake for a time, half hoping that her mother would come up to see her and relieve her from the obvious necessity of running away. But there was a court ball that night and no one came, so listening to the tempting strains of music and feeling more aggrieved and forgotten than ever, the little Princess fell asleep.

As soon as she had breakfasted in the morning, she took the buns tied up in the handkerchief and went down into the yard.

She waited awhile until there was no one looking and then slipped out through one of the rear gates. Once fairly outside, she drew a long breath and looked about her; yes, there was the green meadow and the blue sky, just as they always were in the Princess books. She started off across the meadow, keeping a little under the shadow of the wild crab hedge to better screen herself from the palace windows. She saw some little peasant children down by the pool watching some white things that must be sheep. O yes, they were sheep and the boys were shepherds' sons, thought Baladina. She approached them and greeted them politely.

"Kind shepherds, why keep ye your sheep so near the town?"

"These are not sheep, but geese, Silly," replied the biggest boy surlily.

"That is not the way to speak to a Princess," said Baladina angrily.

"Princess, so that's what you call yourself, Miss Stuck Up?" cried the big boy, and with that he set the geese on her.

The Princess fled in the wildest alarm, with the squawking geese after her, while the little peasant children rolled over and over on the grass, screaming with merriment. The chase did not continue long, for the Princess' long silk gown tripped her and she fell, covering her eyes with her hands and screaming with fright, expecting to feel the sharp beaks of the geese in her face at any moment. But just then a chubby curly-headed boy rode up on a donkey. He chased the geese away with his staff, and sliding down from his beast picked up the little Princess and brushed the dust from her hair.

"Who are you, little girl?" he asked.

"I am the Princess Baladina, and those naughty boys set their geese on me because I corrected them for being rude. They don't believe I'm a Princess; you believe it, don't you?"

"If you say so, of course I do," returned the boy, looking wonderingly at her with his big blue eyes and then doubtfully at his bare feet and rough clothes. "But what are you doing out here?"

"I want to find a wizard; do you know of one?"

"O yes, there's Lean Jack, he lives back of the mill. If you'll get on my donkey I'll walk and lead him and we'll get there in no time."

The Princess accepted this homage as her due and was soon on the donkey, while the boy trotted along beside her.

"What do you want of a wizard anyway, a spell to cure something?" he asked curiously.

"No," said Baladina. "I wish to become enchanted because my family have been unkind to me. And then I want some Prince to come and free me. You are not a Prince in disguise, I suppose?" she added hopefully.

The boy shook his head regretfully. "No, I am only the miller's son."

When they came to Lean Jack's house, they found the old man out in his garden hoeing melon vines. They approached slowly and stood still for some time, Baladina expecting him to at once perceive her and cast his spell. But the old man worked on until the braying of the donkey attracted his attention.

"Well, youngsters, what is it?" he asked, leaning on his spade and wiping his brow.

"I believe you are a wizard, sir?" inquired Baladina politely.

He nodded. "So they say; what can I do for you?"

"I have come," said Baladina, "to allow you to cast a spell upon me, as my family are very unkind to me and if I am enchanted some Prince will come and free me from your power and carry me off to his own country."

The wizard smiled grimly and returned to his hoeing. "Sorry I can't accommodate you, but I can't leave my melons. There is a fat wizard who lives in a little red house over the hill yonder; he may be able to give you what you want."

"Dear me," sighed Baladina as they turned away, "how very rude every one is. Most wizards would be glad enough to get a chance to enchant a Princess."

"I wish you wouldn't be enchanted at all. It must be very uncomfortable, and I shouldn't like to see you changed into an owl or a fox or anything," said the miller's boy as he trotted beside her.

"It must be;" said Baladina firmly, "all Princesses should be enchanted at least once."

When they reached the red house behind the hill they had considerable trouble in finding the wizard, and the miller's boy pounded on the door until his knuckles were quite blue. At last a big, jolly-looking man with a red cap on his head came to the window. The Princess rode her donkey up quite close to the window and told him what she wanted. The fat wizard leaned up against the window sill and laughed until the tears came to his eyes, and the Princess again felt that her dignity was hurt.

"So you want to be enchanted, do you, so a Prince can come and release you? Who sent you here? It was that lean rascal of a Jack, I'll warrant; he's always putting up jokes on me. This is a little the best yet. Has it occurred to you that when your Prince comes he will certainly kill me? That's the way they always do, you know; they slay the cruel enchanter and then bear off the maiden."

The Princess looked puzzled. "Well," she said thoughtfully, "in this case, if you leave me the power of speech, I will request him not to. It's unusual, but I should hate to have him kill you."

"Thank you, my dear, now I call that considerate. But there is another point. Suppose your Prince should not hear of you, and should never come?"

"But they always do come," objected Baladina.

"Not always; I've known them to tarry a good many years. No, I positively cannot enchant you until you find your Prince."

Baladina turned her donkey and went slowly down to the road, leaving the fat wizard still laughing in the window.

"How disobliging these wizards seem to be, but this one seems to mean well. I believe they are afraid to undertake it with a Princess. Do you know where we can find a Prince?"

The miller's boy shook his head. "No, I don't know of any at all."

"Then I suppose we must just hunt for one," said Baladina.

They asked several carters whom they met if they knew where a Prince was to be found, but they all laughed so that Baladina grew quite discouraged. She stopped one boy on horseback and asked if he were a Prince in disguise, but he indignantly denied the charge.

So they went up the road and down a country lane that ran under the willow trees, and when they were both very tired and hungry Baladina opened her handkerchief and gave the miller's boy a bun. He refused the raisin cake, although he looked longingly at it, for he saw there was scarcely enough for two. Baladina sat down and ate it in the shade while he pulled some grass for the donkey. After their lunch they went on again. Just at the top of the hill they met a young man riding a black horse with a pack of hounds running beside him. "I know he is a Prince out hunting. You must stop him," whispered Baladina. So the miller's boy ran on ahead and shouted to the horseman.

"Are you a Prince, sir?" asked Baladina as she approached.

"Yes, miss, I am," he replied curtly.

Nothing daunted, Baladina told her story. The young man laughed and said impatiently, "You foolish child, have you stopped me all this time to tell me a fairy tale? Go home to your parents and let me follow my dogs; I have no time to be playing with silly little girls," and rode away.

"How unkind of him to talk so," said the Princess. "Besides, he is very little older than I."

"If he were here, I'd thrash him!" declared the miller's boy stoutly, clenching his fist.

They went on for a little while in a spiritless sort of way, but the boy hurt his toe on a stone until it bled and the Princess was hot and dusty and ached in every bone of her body. Suddenly she stopped the donkey and began to cry.

"There, there," said the miller's boy kindly, "don't do that. I'll find a Prince for you. You go home and rest and I'll hunt until I find one, if it takes forever."

Baladina dried her tears and spoke with sudden determination.

"You shall be my Prince yourself. I know you are one, really. You must be a changeling left at the mill by some wicked fairy who stole you from your palace."

The boy shook his head stubbornly. "No, I wish I were, but I am only a miller's boy."

"Well, you are the only nice person I have met all day; you have walked till your feet are sore and have let me ride your donkey, and your face is all scratched by the briars and you have had no dinner, and if you are not a Prince, you ought to be one. You are Prince enough for me, anyway. But I am so tired and hungry now, we will go home to the palace tonight and I will be enchanted in the morning. Come, get on the donkey and take me in front of you."

In vain he protested that the donkey could not carry them both; the Princess said that a Prince could not walk.

"I wish you had on shoes and stockings, though," she said. "I think a Prince should always have those."

"I have some for Sunday," said the miller's boy. "If I had only known I would have brought them."

As they turned slowly out of the lane they met a party of horsemen who were hunting for the Princess, and the king himself was among them.

"Ha there, you precious runaway, so here you are, and who is this you have with you?"

"He is my Prince," said the Princess, "and he is to have half the kingdom."

"Oh-h, he is, is he? Who are you, my man?"

"Please, sir, I am only the miller's son, but the Princess was hunting for a Prince and couldn't find one, so she asked me to be one."

"Hear, gentlemen, the Princess is out Prince-hunting early. Come here, you little baggage." He lifted her on the saddle in front of him.

"He must come too, for he is my Prince!" cried the wilful Princess.

But the king only laughed and gave the boy a gold piece, and rode away followed by his gentlemen, who were all laughing too. The miller's boy stood by his donkey, looking wistfully after them, and the Princess Baladina wept bitterly at the dearth of Princes.

First published in *Home Monthly*, VI (August, 1896), 20–21.

The Elopement of Allen Poole

✻ ✻ ✻

I

"Seein' yo' folks ain't willin', sweetheart, I tell yo' there hain't no other way."

"No, I reckon there hain't." She sighed and looked with a troubled expression at the thin spiral of blue smoke that curled up from a house hidden behind the pine trees.

"Besides, I done got the license now, an' told the preacher we was comin'. Yo' ain't goin' back on me now, Nell?"

"No, no, Allen, of course I hain't, only—" her mouth quivered a little and she still looked away from him. The man stood uneasily, his hands hanging helplessly at his side, and watched her. As he saw the color leave her cheeks and her eyes fill up, he began to fear lest he might lose her altogether, and he saw that something must be done. Rousing himself he went up to her, and taking her hand drew himself up to the full height of his six feet.

"See here, Nell, I hain't goin' to make yo' leave yo' folks, I hain't got no right to. Yo' kin come with me, or bide with 'em, jist as yo' choose, only fo' Gawd's sake tell me now, so if yo' won't have me I kin leave yo'."

The girl drew close to him with that appealing gesture of a woman who wants help or strength from some one, and laid her face on his arm.

"I want yo', Allen, yo' know that. I hain't feelin' bad to go, only I do hate to wear that dress mighty bad. Yo' know Pap bought it fo' me to wear to the Bethel camp-meetin'. He got real silk ribbon fo' it, too, jist after he sold the sheep, yo' know. It seems real mean to run away in it."

"Don't wear it then, I kin get yo' plenty o' dresses, wear what yo' got on, yo' surely purty enough fo' me that way."

"No, I must wear it, cause I ain't got nothin' else good enough to marry yo' in. But don't lets talk about it no mo' dear. What time yo' goin' to come tonight?"

"'Bout ten o'clock I reckon. I better not come too early, yo' folks might hear me. I lay I won't go fer away today, them revenue fellers is lookin' fo' me purty sharp."

"I knowed they would be, I knowed it all along. I wish yo' wouldn't still no mo'. I jist am scared to death now all the time fo' fear they'll ketch yo'. Why don't yo' quit stillin' now, Allen?"

"Law me, honey! there hain't no harm in it. I jist makes a little fo' the camp-meetin's."

"I don't keer 'bout the harm, it's yo' I'm feerd fo'."

"Don't yo' worry 'bout me. I kin give 'em the slip. I'll be here tonight at ten o'clock if all the revenue officers in the country are after me. I'll come down here by the big chistnut an' whistle. What shall I whistle, anyhow, so yo' kin know it's me?"

"'Nelly Bly,' course," she whispered, blushing.

"An' yo'll come to me, sho?"

Her only answer was to draw his big, blonde head down to her and hold it against her cheek.

"I must go now, Allen, mammy will be lookin' fo' me soon." And she slipped from his arms and ran swiftly up the steep path toward the house.

Allen watched her disappear among the pines, and then threw himself down beside a laurel bush and clasping his hands under his head began to whistle softly. It takes a man of the South to do nothing perfectly, and Allen was as skilled in that art as were any of the F. F. V.'s who wore broadcloth. It was the kind of a summer morning to encourage idleness. Behind him were the sleepy pine woods, the slatey ground beneath them strewn red with slippery needles. Around him the laurels were just blushing into bloom. Here and there rose tall chestnut trees with the red sumach growing under them. Down in the valley lay the fields of wheat and corn, and among them the creek wound between its willow-grown banks. Across it was the old, black, creaking foot-bridge which had neither props nor piles, but was swung from the arms of a great sycamore tree. The reapers were at work in the wheat fields; the mowers swinging their cradles and the binders following close behind. Along the fences companies of bare-footed children were picking berries. On the bridge a lank youth sat patiently fishing in the stream where no fish had been caught for years. Allen watched them all until a passing cloud made the valley dark, then his eyes wandered to where the Blue Ridge lay against the sky, faint and hazy as the mountains of Beulah Land.

Allen still whistled lazily as he lay there. He was noted for his whistling. He was naturally musical, but on Limber Ridge the mouth organ and jews harp are considered the only thoroughly respectable instruments, and he preferred whistling to either. He could whistle anything from "Champagne Charley" to the opera airs he heard the city folks playing in the summer at the Springs. There was a marvelous sweet and mellow quality about that chirp of his, like the softened fire of the famous apple brandy he made from his little still in the mountains. The mountain folk always said they could tell Allen Poole's whiskey or his whistle wherever they found them. Beyond his music and his brandy and his good heart there was not much to Allen. He was never known to do any work except to pour apples into his still and drink freely of the honied fire which came out of the worm. As he said himself, between his still and the women and the revenue officers he had scarcely time to eat. The officers of the law hated him because they knew him to be an incorrigible "moonshiner," yet never could prove anything against him. The women all loved him because he was so big and blue-eyed and so thoroughly a man. He was happy enough and good natured enough; still it was no wonder that old Sargent did not want his daughter to marry the young man, for making whiskey on one's own hook and one's own authority is not a particularly safe or honorable business. But the girl was willing and Allen was very much so, and they had taken matters into their own hands and meant to elope that night. Allen was not thinking very seriously about it. He never took anything very seriously. He was just thinking that the dim blueness of the mountains over there was like her eyes when they had tears in them, and wondering why it was that when he was near her he always felt such an irresistible impulse to pick her up and carry her. When he began to get hungry he arose and yawned and began to stroll lazily down the mountain side, his heavy boot heels cutting through the green moss and craunching the soft slate rock underneath, whistling "My Bonnie Lies Over the Ocean" as he went.

II

It was about nine o'clock that evening when Allen crossed the old foot-bridge and started down the creek lane toward the mountain. He kept carefully in the shadow of the trees, for he had good cause to fear that night. There was a little frown on his face, for when he got home at noon he found his shanty in confusion; the revenue officer had been there and had knocked the still to pieces and chopped through the copper worm with an ax. Even the winning of his sweetheart could not quite make up for the loss of his still.

The creek lane, hedged on either side by tall maples, ran by a little graveyard. It was one of those little family burying grounds so common in the south, with its white headstones, tall, dark cedars, and masses of rosemary, myrtle and rue. Allen, like all the rest of the Mountain men, was superstitious, and ordinarily he would have hurried past, not anxious to be near a graveyard after night. But now he went up and leaned on the stone fence, and looked over at the headstones which marked the sunken graves. Somehow he felt more pity for them than fear of them that night. That night of all nights he was so rich in hope and love, lord of so much life, that he wished he could give a little of it to those poor, cold, stiff fellows shut up down there in their narrow boxes with prosy scripture text on their coffin plates, give a little of the warm blood that tingled through his own veins, just enough, perhaps, to make them dream of love. He sighed as he went on, leaving them to their sleep and their understanding.

He turned aside into a road that ran between the fields. The red harvest moon was just rising; on one side of the road the tall, green corn stood whispering and rustling in the moonrise, sighing fretfully now and then when the hot south breeze swept over it. On the other side lay the long fields of wheat where the poppies drooped among the stubble and the sheaves gave out that odor of indescribable richness and ripeness which newly cut grain always has. From the wavering line of locust trees the song of the whip-poor-will throbbed through the summer night. Above it all were the dark pine-clad mountains, in the repose and strength of their immortality.

The man's heart went out to the heart of the night, and he broke out into such a passion of music as made the singer in the locusts sick with melody. As he went on, whistling, he suddenly heard the beat of a horse's feet upon the road, and silenced his chirping.

"Like as not it's them government chaps," he muttered.

A cart came around the bend in the road, Allen saw two men in it and turned aside into the corn field, but he was too late, they had already seen him. One of them raised his pistol and shouted, "Halt!"

But Allen knew too well who they were, and did not stop. The officer called again, and then fired. Allen stopped a moment, clutched the air above his head, cried "My Gawd!" and then ran wildly on. The officer was not a bad fellow, only young and a little hot headed, and that agonized cry took all the nerve out of him, and he drove back toward town to get the ringing sound out of his ears.

Allen ran on, plunging and floundering through the corn like some wounded animal, tearing up stalk after stalk as he clutched it in his pain. When he reached the foot of the mountain he started up, dragging himself on by the laurel and sumach bushes. When his legs failed him he used his hands and knees, wrenching the vines and saplings to pieces and tearing the flesh on [his] hands as he pulled himself up. At last he reached the chestnut tree and sank with a groan upon the ground. But he rose again muttering to himself: "She'd be skeered to death if she seen me layin' down."

He braced himself against the tree, all blood and dirt as he was, his wedding clothes torn and soiled, and drawing his white lips up in the old way he whistled for his love:

Nelly Bly shuts her eye when she goes to sleep,
But in the morning when she wakes then they begin to peep.
Hi Nelly! Ho Nelly! listen unto me,
I'll sing for you, I'll play for you a charming melody.

He had not long to wait. She came softly through the black pines, holding her white dress up carefully from the dewy grass, with the moonlight all about her in a halo, like a little Madonna of the hills. She slipped up to him and leaned her cheek upon his breast.

"Allen, my own boy! Why yo' all wet, Oh it's blood! it's blood! have they hurt yo' honey, have they hurt yo'?"

He sank to the ground, saying gently, "I'm afeerd they've done fo' me this time, sweetheart. It's them damned revenue men."

"Let me call Pap, Allen, he'll go fo' the doctor, let me go, Allen, please."

"No, yo' shan't leave me. It ain't fo' many minutes, a doctor won't do no good. Stay with me Nell, stay with me, I'm afeerd to be alone."

She sat down and drew his head on her knee and leaned her face down to his.

"Take keer, darlin', yo' goin' to git yo' dress all bloody, yo' nice new frock what yo' goin' to wear to the Bethel picnic."

"Oh Allen! there ain't no Bethel picnic no more, nor nothin' but yo'. Oh my boy! my boy!" and she rocked herself over him as a mother does over a little baby that is in pain.

"It's mighty hard to lose yo', Nell, but maybe it's best. Maybe if I'd lived an' married yo' I might a' got old an' cross an' used to yo' some day, an' might a' swore at you an' beat yo' like the mountain folks round here does, an' I'd sooner die now, while I love yo' better'n anything else in Gawd's world. Yo' like me, too, don't yo' dear?"

"Oh Allen! more'n I ever knowed, more'n I ever knowed."

"Don't take on so, honey. Yo' will stay with me tonight? Yo' won't leave me even after I'm dead? Yo' know we was to be married an' I was to have yo' tonight. Yo' won't go way an' leave me the first night an' the last, will yo' Nell?"

The girl calmed herself for his sake and answered him steadily: "No, Allen. I will set an' hold yo' till mornin' comes. I won't leave yo'."

"Thank yo'. Never mind, dear, the best thing in livin' is to love hard, and the best thing in dyin' is to die game; an' I've done my best at both. Never mind."

He drew a long sigh, and the rest was silence.

First published in *The Hesperian*, XXII (April 15, 1893), 4–7.

A Note on the Editing

✳ ✳ ✳

The stories in Volumes I and III and in the Appendix of this collection have been lightly copyedited. It has not been our intention to impose absolute consistency or to offer a completely modernized text, although we have regularized conspicuously variant forms (*good-by*, *good-bye*, *goodby*; *theatre*, *theater*) and have altered old-fashioned forms which called attention to themselves (as, for example, the hyphenations in *to-day*, *to-morrow*, *to-night*, *up-stairs*, *down-stairs*). We have usually, but not invariably, treated compound words in accordance with present-day usage (*dugout*, *shotgun*, *haystack* for *dug-out*, *shot-gun*, *hay-stack*; *post office* for *post-office*, *grandstand* for *grand stand*), and we have usually, but not invariably, followed modern style with regard to capitalization. When there seemed a possibility that an editorial emendation might alter the color, pace, inflection, or rhythm of a line, in every case we have allowed the original form to stand. (In dialogue, for example, "Oh, yes," "Oh yes," and "O yes" all appear.) Obvious spelling errors (*doggarel*, *Mandrin*) and typographical errors have been silently corrected; but if a missing word has been supplied it appears enclosed in brackets.

Although in most cases spelling has been regularized, some variant forms have been retained. For example, in "A Son of the Celestial," written in 1893, we find the spelling *cue*; in "The Conversion of Sum Loo," a 1900 reworking of the same story, it has become *queue*. (It is, of course, impossible to say whether the author or the copyeditor was responsible for the change, for we cannot be certain that Willa Cather saw proofs of any of the stories in this book except those collected in *The Troll Garden* and those which appeared in the *Home Monthly* and *McClure's* during her editorial tenure on these periodicals.) In "The Prodigies," p. 421, l. 36, the line cited from the duet in Gounod's *Roméo et Juliette*—"*Tu die* [dis?] *partir ohime!*"—is apparently a misquotation; perhaps "*Il faut partir, hélas*" was what the author had in mind. In "The Count of Crow's Nest," p. 468, l. 37, *explicatives* rather than *expletives* may have been the word intended. In "The Burglar's Christmas," p. 559, l. 12, some words appear to have been dropped out ("other people to make it win"). And in "The Princess Baladina—Her Adventure," p. 569, l. 37, a hoe suddenly becomes a spade. In "Eric Hermannson's Soul," because the original punctuation made it difficult to distinguish between what was thought and what was said, p. 371, ll. 3–5 and p. 375, l. 35, the speaker's thoughts have been put in italic type. In "A Singer's Romance," p. 334, l. 16, Selma Schumann's maid is introduced as Annette, but thereafter she is referred to as Antoinette or 'Toinette. A similar lapse occurs in "A Night at Greenway Court," p. 486, l. 25, where Richard Morgan is addressed as "Master Norton."

The seven *Troll Garden* stories comprising Volume II have not been copyedited. Except for the corrections listed below, they are reprinted exactly as they appeared in the 1905 edition published by McClure, Phillips & Co. We have presented them in their original form primarily to facilitate comparison with the revised versions of the four stories ("The Sculptor's Funeral," "'A Death in the Desert,'" "A Wagner Matinee," and "Paul's Case") which Willa Cather included in *Youth and the Bright Medusa* (New York: Alfred A. Knopf, 1920).

FLAVIA AND HER ARTISTS

P. 153, l. 11: *perseverance* for *perseverence*. P. 156, l. 9: close quotes placed inside semicolon. P. 157, l. 10: *exclusive* for *exculsive*. P. 157, l. 19: *purplish* for *purpleish*. P. 159, l. 4: single instead of double quote marks. P. 159, l. 39: *madam* for *madame*. P. 162, ll. 25–26: *White Rabbit* for *white rabbit*. P. 164, l. 35: *Emile* for *Emil*. P. 165, l. 15: *futilely* for *futily*. P. 168, l. 9: *hate* for *heat*.

THE SCULPTOR'S FUNERAL

P. 179, l. 22: *gallus* for *gallows*. P. 182, ll. 4–5: single quotes added around quoted speech.

THE GARDEN LODGE

P. 189, l. 21: *ebullitions* for *ebulitions*. P. 190, l. 28: *Street* for *street*. P. 195, l. 19: *duet* for *duett*. P. 195, l. 25: *repellent* for *repellant*.

"A DEATH IN THE DESERT"

P. 199, l. 9: *Holdrege* for *Holdridge*. P. 199, l. 25: *Holdrege* for *Holdridge*. P. 202, l. 12: [*more*] inserted.

THE MARRIAGE OF PHAEDRA

P. 221, l. 36: *bus* for *buss*. P. 223, l. 8: *doesn't* for *dosen't*. P. 223, l. 9: period for comma after *blandly*. P. 226, l. 16: [*of*] inserted. P. 227, l. 30: *'aberdasher's* for *'abberdasher's*. P. 229, l. 22: *she* for *She*. P. 232, l. 11: [*day*] inserted. P. 232, l. 16: [*in*] inserted. P. 232, ll. 10 and 20: close quotes deleted. P. 233, l. 3: close quotes deleted.

A WAGNER MATINEE

P. 235, l. 5: *Uncle* for *uncle*. P. 237, l. 32: *tired* for *tried*. P. 238, l. 11: period after *Dutchman*. P. 238, l. 33: comma inserted after *counting*. P. 240, l. 14: italic *The* for roman *the*. P. 240, l. 18: *palms* for *palm*. P. 240, l. 34: *Bayreuth* for *Beyruth*.

PAUL'S CASE

P. 253, l. 3: comma deleted after *was*. P. 257, l. 13: *loge* for *lodge*. P. 258, l. 3: *offensive* for *offencive*. P. 260, l. 33: *lest* for *least*.

Chronology

WILLA CATHER · 1873–1912

❖   ❖   ❖

Since date and place of publication of Willa Cather's stories are listed in the Bibliography, only representative titles are included here. No attempt has been made to show the poems, articles, reviews (of books, plays, operas, concerts, art exhibits, lectures), and other journalistic writing which appeared during the period covered. An idea of the astonishing extent of Willa Cather's published writing (exclusive of fiction) up to 1903 may be gained from the bibliographies in three other collections in this series: *The Kingdom of Art: Willa Cather's First Principles and Critical Statements, 1893–1896*, selected and edited with two essays and a commentary by Bernice Slote (Lincoln: University of Nebraska Press, 1967); *The World and the Parish: Willa Cather's Articles and Reviews, 1893–1902*, selected and edited with a commentary by William M. Curtin (2 vols.; Lincoln: University of Nebraska Press, 1970); and *April Twilights (1903)*, edited with an introduction by Bernice Slote (rev. ed.; Lincoln: University of Nebraska Press, 1968).

1872

December 5   Charles Fectigue Cather marries Mary Virginia Boak.

1873

Summer   Charles Cather's elder brother, George, and his wife Frances (Aunt Franc) move to Webster County, Nebraska.

December 7   Willa Cather born in home of maternal grandmother, Rachel Boak, Back Creek Valley, near Winchester, Virginia.

1874

Fall   The Charles Cather family moves to Willowshade, home of Willa's paternal grandparents, William and Caroline Cather, located between Back Creek Valley and Winchester.

1883

February   Willowshade sold.

April   Charles and Virginia Cather and their children, Willa, Roscoe

(b. 1877), Douglas (b. 1880), and Jessica (b. 1881), move to Catherton Precinct, Webster County, Nebraska. This region, a broad plateau between the Little Blue and Republican rivers, is known as "The Divide."

Fall

Willa attends the New Virginia country school.

1884–1885

The Charles Cather family moves to the county seat, Red Cloud, sometime during this year.

1885–1890

During these years Willa receives her early education, attending grammar school and high school, although at first she was taught at home. Two more children, James (b. 1886) and Elsie (b. 1890), are born. Other members of the household are Mrs. Rachel Boak, a cousin Bess Seymour, and Margie Anderson, the "hired girl." In June, 1890, Willa graduates from high school; in September, she goes to Lincoln, Nebraska, and enrolls in the Latin School (University Prep).

1891

March 1

Willa's essay on Carlyle appears in *Nebraska State Journal*, submitted by her teacher, Ebenezer Hunt, without her knowledge.

September

Willa matriculates at the University of Nebraska.

November

Essay on Hamlet in *State Journal*.

1892

May

Story, "Peter," in *The Mahogany Tree*, submitted by Professor Herbert Bates. First published fiction.

June

Poem, "Shakespeare: A Freshman Theme," in the student newspaper, *The Hesperian*. First published poetry.

Fall

Literary editor of *Hesperian*. Youngest brother, John (Jack) Cather, born.

1893

November

Becomes regular contributor to *State Journal*. Begins to review plays as well as do a Sunday column. She is also managing editor of *The Hesperian*, contributing numerous pieces.

1894–1895

Continues as regular contributor to the *State Journal;* contributions also in University publications. In February, 1895, she meets Stephen Crane. In March, travels to Chicago, sees a week of opera. Graduates from University in June. In the fall is briefly associated with the Lincoln *Courier*.

1896

January–May Mostly living at home in Red Cloud. Tries and fails to get a teaching appointment at the University of Nebraska. Has stories in *Overland Monthly* and *Nebraska Literary Magazine.*

Late June Leaves Red Cloud for Pittsburgh, where she is to edit a family magazine, the *Home Monthly*. By July 13 is settled in a Pittsburgh boarding house, and at work on the August issue. In a letter of that date to Mrs. Charles Gere, mentions that she is using a half-dozen pen names.

October Bicycle trip through Shenandoah Valley.

November By this time is contributing drama criticism to the Pittsburgh *Leader*. Review signed "Willa" on November 24.

1897

January–June Working on the *Home Monthly*. Contributes column ("The Passing Show") to the *State Journal* up through May 30. In June returns to Red Cloud.

July Writes her friend George Seibel, in Pittsburgh, that the *Home Monthly* is sold, but she is planning to come back anyway and hopes to get into newspaper work.

September Offered a job on the Pittsburgh *Leader;* is back in Pittsburgh early in September.

Fall Working on telegraph desk and writing play and book reviews. Begins sending "The Passing Show" to the *Courier*. Continues to write her "Helen Delay" book column for the *Home Monthly*.

1898

February Spends a week in New York, has lunch with Modjeska; may have contributed a review or reviews to the *New York Sun.*

May Visits her cousin, Howard Gore, in Washington, D.C.

July–August Vacationing in Red Cloud; makes a trip to the Black Hills and Wyoming.

October– Mostly in Pittsburgh working on *Leader;* spends some time in
December Columbus, Ohio, with her friends the Canfields, first recuperating from an illness, then for Thanksgiving.

1899

Except for an interval in Red Cloud during the summer, remains in Pittsburgh, working on the *Leader*. Continues to contribute to *Courier*. Last contribution to *Home Monthly* in December. Meets Isabelle McClung during this year.

1900

During the late spring (?) of this year Willa Cather resigned

	from the Pittsburgh *Leader*. Her poems appear in national magazines.
March– August	A number of contributions in *The Library*, a short-lived Pittsburgh periodical.
April	Story, "Eric Hermannson's Soul," in *Cosmopolitan*.
May	Last "Passing Show" in the *Courier* May 12.
Fall	Moves to Washington, D.C. Secures a part-time job there editing translations.
November– December	Article about Nevin in *Ladies' Home Journal*. Writes a Washington column which appears in *Nebraska State Journal* and *Index of Pittsburg Life* until the following March.

1901

March	"Jack-a-Boy" in *Saturday Evening Post*. Back in Pittsburgh; begins teaching Latin and English at Central High School. During the spring begins living at the McClung residence.
June	"El Dorado" in *New England Magazine*.
July–August	Visits in Red Cloud—first time home in two years.
September	Resumes teaching at Central High School.

1902

April	Last contribution to *Courier*.
June– September	Abroad with Isabelle McClung. "The Professor's Commencement" in *New England Magazine*. Weekly columns about her trip in *Nebraska State Journal*. Articles also in Pittsburgh *Gazette*.
Fall	"The Treasure of Far Island" in *New England Magazine;* "Poets of Our Younger Generation" in *Gazette*.

1903

January	"'A Death in the Desert'" in *Scribner's*.
April	Publication of a book of verse, *April Twilights*.
Summer	Vacationing in Nebraska.

1904–1905

Teaching at Allegheny High School and freelancing. Collection of short stories, *The Troll Garden*, published in May, 1905. Visits Edith Lewis in New York in both years.

1906

June	Ends teaching career, and moves to New York. Joins *McClure's* editorial staff during this year.

1907

Working on *McClure's*. Much of the year spent in Boston, working on life of Mary Baker Eddy. Three stories in *McClure's*, one in *Century*.

1908

March	Meets Sarah Orne Jewett and Mrs. Fields.
April–May	Promoted to managing editor of *McClure's*. Trip abroad with Isabelle McClung. Probably returns in July.
December	"On the Gulls' Road" in *McClure's*.

1909

	Working on *McClure's*. "The Enchanted Bluff" in *Harper's*. Trip to London to get material for *McClure's*. Meets many well-known literary figures.
September	Takes an apartment on Washington Place with Edith Lewis.

1910–1911

May	Again to London for *McClure's*. Begins working on first novel, *Alexander's Bridge*.

1911

June	Still doing editorial work at *McClure's*.
Summer	Completes *Alexander's Bridge*.
Fall	On leave of absence from *McClure's*. Rents house in Cherry Valley, New York, with Isabelle McClung. Works on "The Bohemian Girl" and "Alexandra"—latter eventually becomes part of *O Pioneers!*

1912

February	First installment of *Alexander's Bridge* appears in *McClure's* under title *Alexander's Masquerade*.
March	Visits Isabelle McClung in Pittsburgh.
April	*Alexander's Bridge* published.
May	"Behind the Singer Tower" in *Collier's*. Visits brother Douglas in Winslow, Arizona. Apparently still on leave of absence from *McClure's;* resignation some time during the year.
June–July	Visiting in Red Cloud.
August	"The Bohemian Girl" in *McClure's*. Visits Isabelle McClung in Pittsburgh. At work on "The White Mulberry Tree"—an episode of *O Pioneers!*, which is published in June, 1913.
Fall	With Edith Lewis moves into 5 Bank Street, New York, her home for the next fifteen years.

Bibliography

✤ ✤ ✤

The stories are listed chronologically according to date of first publication. Stories published after 1912 are given in the Checklist immediately following. Both the Bibliography and the Checklist are limited to American publications and editions.

The collections made by Willa Cather are: *The Troll Garden* (New York: McClure, Phillips & Co., 1905), out of print; *Youth and the Bright Medusa* (New York: Alfred A. Knopf, Inc., 1920), which includes four of the stories in the present volume and four written after 1912; *Obscure Destinies* (New York: Alfred A. Knopf, Inc., 1932), three stories written in the early 1930's; and *The Novels and Stories of Willa Cather* (13 vols.; Boston: Houghton Mifflin Co., 1937–1941), collecting all the stories in *Obscure Destinies* and *Youth and the Bright Medusa* except "'A Death in the Desert.'" Two posthumous collections have been issued by Willa Cather's publishers: *The Old Beauty and Others* (New York: Alfred A. Knopf, Inc., 1948), three stories written between 1936 and 1947; and *Five Stories* (New York: Vintage Books, 1956), including two of the stories in this volume, one from *Obscure Destinies*, one from *The Old Beauty and Others*, and "Tom Outland's Story" from *The Professor's House*, a novel published in 1925 by Alfred A. Knopf, Inc.

The first collection of the early writings, *Willa Cather's Campus Years*, edited by James R. Shively (Lincoln: University of Nebraska Press, 1950), is out of print. *Early Stories of Willa Cather*, selected and edited by Mildred R. Bennett (New York: Dodd, Mead & Co., 1957) was out of print when this volume appeared, but has since been reissued in a paperbound edition (New York: Apollo Books, 1966). It is not listed in this Bibliography: the pagination is the same as that in the cloth edition and the errors noted here are uncorrected. A paper edition of *The Troll Garden* has been published by the New American Library (New York: Signet Classics, 1961). Although it carries no note on the editing and thus is presumably a reprint, a comparison of the text with that of the original 1905 edition shows approximately seven hundred alterations. Most of these alterations are in respect to spelling and punctuation, but in a few cases words have been omitted or added, or another word substituted.

1892

Peter. Signed Willa Cather.

The Mahogany Tree, May 21, 1892, pp. 323–324.

The Hesperian, XXII (November 24, 1892), 10–12. Unsigned. Sixteen changes from the original version.

The Library, I (July 21, 1900), 5. Additional revisions. Retitled "Peter Sadelack, Father of Anton." Signed Willa Sibert Cather.

Willa Cather's Campus Years, edited by James R. Shively (Lincoln: University of Nebraska Press, 1950), pp. 41–45. *Hesperian* version.

Early Stories, selected by Mildred R. Bennett (New York: Dodd, Mead & Co., 1957), pp. 1–8. *Hesperian* and *Library* versions.

Lou, the Prophet. Signed W. Cather.

The Hesperian, XXII (October 15, 1892), 7–10.

James R. Shively, "Willa Cather's Juvenilia," *Prairie Schooner*, XXII (Spring, 1948), 100–104.

Willa Cather's Campus Years, edited by James R. Shively (Lincoln: University of Nebraska Press, 1950), pp. 46–53.

Early Stories, selected by Mildred R. Bennett (New York: Dodd, Mead & Co., 1957), pp. 9–17.

A Tale of the White Pyramid. Signed W. Cather.

The Hesperian, XXII (December 22, 1892), 8–11.

Willa Cather's Campus Years, edited by James R. Shively (Lincoln: University of Nebraska Press, 1950), pp. 54–60.

Early Stories, selected by Mildred R. Bennett (New York: Dodd, Mead & Co., 1957), pp. 19–24.

1893

A Son of the Celestial. Subtitled A Character. Signed W. Cather.

The Hesperian, XXII (January 15, 1893), 7–10.

Willa Cather's Campus Years, edited by James R. Shively (Lincoln: University of Nebraska Press, 1950), pp. 61–68.

Early Stories, selected by Mildred R. Bennett (New York: Dodd, Mead & Co., 1957), pp. 25–32.

The Elopement of Allen Poole. Unsigned.

The Hesperian, XXII (April 15, 1893), 4–7.

The Kingdom of Art: Willa Cather's First Principles and Critical Statements, 1893–1896, selected and edited with two essays and a commentary by Bernice Slote (Lincoln: University of Nebraska Press, 1967), pp. 437–441.

The Clemency of the Court. Signed W. Cather.
  The Hesperian, XXII (October 26, 1893), 3–7.
  James R. Shively, "Willa Cather's Juvenilia," *Prairie Schooner*, XXII (Spring, 1948), 104–111.
  Willa Cather's Campus Years, edited by James R. Shively (Lincoln: University of Nebraska Press, 1950), pp. 69–79.
  Early Stories, selected by Mildred R. Bennett (New York: Dodd, Mead & Co., 1957), pp. 33–43.

1894

"The Fear That Walks by Noonday." Signed Willa Cather and Dorothy Canfield.
  Sombrero, III (1894), 224–231. The idea for the story was suggested to Willa Cather by Dorothy Canfield. The story was awarded first prize ($10.00) by the *Sombrero*, the University of Nebraska yearbook.
  The Fear That Walks by Noonday (New York: Phoenix Book Shop, 1931). An edition of thirty numbered copies.
  Early Stories, selected by Mildred R. Bennett (New York: Dodd, Mead & Co., 1957), pp. 45–57. The publication date of the story is given erroneously as 1895.

1896

On the Divide. Signed W. Cather.
  Overland Monthly, Ser. 2, XXVII (January, 1896), 65–74.
  Early Stories, selected by Mildred R. Bennett (New York: Dodd, Mead & Co., 1957), pp. 59–75.

A Night at Greenway Court. Signed Willa Cather.
  Nebraska Literary Magazine, I (June, 1896), 215–224.
  The Library, I (April 21, 1900), 5–7. Signed Willa Sibert.Cather. Revised version.
  Willa Cather's Campus Years, edited by James R. Shively (Lincoln: University of Nebraska Press, 1950), pp. 80–92. Original (1896) version.
  Early Stories, selected by Mildred R. Bennett (New York: Dodd, Mead & Co., 1957), pp. 77–91. Both versions.

Tommy, the Unsentimental. Signed Willa Cather.
  Home Monthly, VI (August, 1896), 6–7.
  Early Stories, selected by Mildred R. Bennett (New York: Dodd, Mead & Co., 1957), pp. 103–113.

The Princess Baladina—Her Adventure. Signed Charles Douglass.
  Home Monthly, VI (August, 1896), 20–21.

The Count of Crow's Nest. Signed Willa Cather.
   Home Monthly, VI (September, October, 1896), 9–11; 12–13, 22–23.
   Early Stories, selected by Mildred R. Bennett (New York: Dodd, Mead &
   Co., 1957), pp. 115–145.

The Burglar's Christmas. Signed Elizabeth L. Seymour.
   Home Monthly, VI (December, 1896), 8–10.

The Strategy of the Were-Wolf Dog. Signed Willa Cather.
   Home Monthly, VI (December, 1896), 13–14, 24.

1897

A Resurrection. Signed Willa Cather.
   Home Monthly, VI (April, 1897), 4–8.
   Early Stories, selected by Mildred R. Bennett (New York: Dodd, Mead &
   Co., 1957), pp. 147–167.

The Prodigies. Signed Willa Cather.
   Home Monthly, VI (July, 1897), 9–11.
   Lincoln *Courier*, XII (July 10, 17, 1897), 4–5; 8–9.
   Early Stories, selected by Mildred R. Bennett (New York: Dodd, Mead &
   Co.), pp. 169–185.

Nanette: An Aside. Signed Willa Cather.
   Lincoln *Courier*, XII (July 31, 1897), 11–12.
   Home Monthly, VI (August, 1897), 5–6.
   Early Stories, selected by Mildred R. Bennett (New York: Dodd, Mead &
   Co., 1957), pp. 93–102. The publication date of the story is given erro-
   neously as August, 1896.

1898

The Way of the World. Signed Willa Cather.
   Home Monthly, VI (April, 1898), 10–11.
   Lincoln *Courier*, XIV (August 19, 1899), 9–10.

1899

The Westbound Train. Signed Willa Cather.
   Lincoln *Courier*, XIV (September 30, 1899), 3–5.

1900

Eric Hermannson's Soul. Signed Willa Sibert Cather.
   Cosmopolitan, XXVIII (April, 1900), 633–644.

Early Stories, selected by Mildred R. Bennett (New York: Dodd, Mead & Co., 1957), pp. 187–215. According to Mrs. Bennett: "The story was translated into German by Eugene von Tempsky who labeled it a 'psychological masterpiece.' A request for translation rights was not usual at that time" (215).

The Dance at Chevalier's. Signed Henry Nicklemann.
  The Library, I (April 28, 1900), 12–13.
  Early Stories, selected by Mildred R. Bennett (New York: Dodd, Mead & Co., 1957), pp. 217–229.

The Sentimentality of William Tavener. Signed Willa Sibert Cather.
  The Library, I (May 12, 1900), 13–14.
  Early Stories, selected by Mildred R. Bennett (New York: Dodd, Mead & Co., 1957), pp. 231–237.

The Affair at Grover Station. Signed Willa Sibert Cather.
  The Library, I (June 16, 23, 1900), 3–4; 14–15.
  Lincoln *Courier*, XV (July 7, 1900), 3–5, 8–9.
  Early Stories, selected by Mildred R. Bennett (New York: Dodd, Mead & Co., 1957), pp. 239–256.

A Singer's Romance. Signed Willa Sibert Cather.
  The Library, I (July 28, 1900), 15–16.
  Early Stories, selected by Mildred R. Bennett (New York: Dodd, Mead & Co., 1957), pp. 257–263.

The Conversion of Sum Loo. Signed Willa Sibert Cather.
  The Library, I (August 11, 1900), 4–6.
  Early Stories, selected by Mildred R. Bennett (New York: Dodd, Mead & Co., 1957), pp. 265–275.

1901

Jack-a-Boy. Signed Willa Sibert Cather.
  Saturday Evening Post, CLXXIII (March 30, 1901), 4–5, 25.
  Prairie Schooner, XXXIII (Spring, 1959), 77–87.

El Dorado: A Kansas Recessional. Signed Willa Sibert Cather.
  New England Magazine, n.s., XXIV (June, 1901), 357–369.

1902

The Professor's Commencement. Signed Willa Sibert Cather.
  New England Magazine, n.s., XXVI (June, 1902), 481–488.

The Treasure of Far Island. Signed Willa Sibert Cather.
New England Magazine, n.s., XXVII (October, 1902), 234–249.
Prairie Schooner, XXXVIII (Winter, 1964/65), 323–343.

1903

"A Death in the Desert." Signed Willa Sibert Cather.
Scribner's, XXXIII (January, 1903), 109–121. No quotation marks around the
title in this version.
The Troll Garden (New York: McClure, Phillips & Co., 1905), pp. 111–154.
Ninety-eight substantive changes including twenty-five deep cuts, mostly
descriptive passages. Numerous changes in spelling, capitalization, and
punctuation. The character originally called Windermere Hilgarde is
renamed Everett Hilgarde.
Youth and the Bright Medusa (New York: Alfred A. Knopf, 1920), pp. 273–303.
One hundred and seventy-nine substantive changes from the 1905 version.
The Troll Garden (New York: Signet Classics, 1961), pp. 65–86. The 1905
version, with spelling and punctuation modernized by the publisher. See
note on this edition at the beginning of the Bibliography.

1904

A Wagner Matinee. Signed Willa Sibert Cather.
Everybody's Magazine, X (February, 1904), 325–328.
The Troll Garden (New York: McClure, Phillips & Co., 1905), pp. 193–210.
Revised throughout. Important additions as well as three major cuts and
many minor ones. Alterations in wording, spelling, capitalization, and
punctuation. A total of one hundred and two substantive changes.
Youth and the Bright Medusa (New York: Alfred A. Knopf, 1920), pp. 235–247.
Thirty-five substantive changes, including paragraph cuts, from the 1905
version.
The Novels and Stories of Willa Cather (13 vols.; Boston: Houghton Mifflin
Co., 1937–1941), VI, 247–261. Fourteen substantive changes from the 1920
version.
The Troll Garden (New York: Signet Classics, 1961), pp. 107–115. The 1905
version, with spelling and punctuation modernized by the publisher. See
note on this edition at the beginning of the Bibliography.

1905

The Sculptor's Funeral. Signed Willa Sibert Cather.
McClure's, XXIV (January, 1905), 329–336.

The Troll Garden (New York: McClure, Phillips & Co., 1905), pp. 55–84. Word order altered in one sentence. Numerous changes in spelling, capitalization, punctuation.

Youth and the Bright Medusa (New York: Alfred A. Knopf, 1920), pp. 248–272. Additional revisions by the author.

The Novels and Stories of Willa Cather (13 vols.; Boston: Houghton Mifflin Co., 1937–1941), VI, 263–289. Twenty substantive changes from the 1920 version.

The Troll Garden (New York: Signet Classics, 1961), pp. 35–49. The 1905 version, with spelling and punctuation modernized by the publisher. See note on this edition at the beginning of the Bibliography.

Flavia and Her Artists. Signed Willa Sibert Cather.

The Troll Garden (New York: McClure, Phillips & Co., 1905), pp. 1–54.

The Troll Garden (New York: Signet Classics, 1961), pp. 7–34. Spelling and punctuation modernized by the publisher. See note on this edition at the beginning of the Bibliography.

The Garden Lodge. Signed Willa Sibert Cather.

The Troll Garden (New York: McClure, Phillips & Co., 1905), pp. 85–110.

The Troll Garden (New York: Signet Classics, 1961), pp. 51–63. Spelling and punctuation modernized by the publisher. See note on this edition at the beginning of the Bibliography.

The Marriage of Phaedra. Signed Willa Sibert Cather.

The Troll Garden (New York: McClure, Phillips & Co., 1905), pp. 155–192.

The Troll Garden (New York: Signet Classics, 1961), pp. 87–105. Spelling and punctuation modernized by the publisher. See note on this edition at the beginning of the Bibliography.

Paul's Case. Subtitled A Study in Temperament. Signed Willa Sibert Cather.

The Troll Garden (New York: McClure, Phillips & Co., 1905), pp. 211–253.

McClure's, XXV (May, 1905), 74–83. Numerous changes in spelling and punctuation. Two passages, totaling about 400 words, have been cut; in the first instance, a few words were supplied to maintain the continuity. Since the story was published at almost the same time as the book in which it was collected, it seems certain that the cuts were made to meet the space requirements of the magazine. The passages were restored by the author in subsequent reprintings.

Youth and the Bright Medusa (New York: Alfred A. Knopf, 1920), pp. 199–234. Subtitle omitted. Revision of the 1905 *Troll Garden* version.

The Novels and Stories of Willa Cather (13 vols.; Boston: Houghton Mifflin Co., 1937–1941), VI, 207–245. Eight substantive changes from the 1920 version.

Five Stories (New York: Vintage Books, 1956), pp. 149–174. The 1920 version.
The Troll Garden (New York: Signet Classics, 1961), pp. 117–138. The 1905 version, with spelling and punctuation modernized by the publisher. See note on this edition at the beginning of the Bibliography.

1907

The Namesake. Signed Willa Sibert Cather.
  McClure's, XXVIII (March, 1907), 492–497.

The Profile. Signed Willa Sibert Cather.
  McClure's, XXIX (June, 1907), 135–140.

The Willing Muse. Signed Willa Sibert Cather.
  Century, LXXIV (August, 1907), 550–557.

Eleanor's House. Signed Willa Sibert Cather.
  McClure's, XXIX (October, 1907), 623–630.

1908

On the Gulls' Road. Subtitled The Ambassador's Story. Signed Willa Sibert Cather.
  McClure's, XXXII (December, 1908), 145–152.

1909

The Enchanted Bluff. Signed Willa Sibert Cather.
  Harper's, CXVIII (April, 1909), 774–781.
  Five Stories (New York: Vintage Books, 1956), pp. 3–15.

1911

The Joy of Nelly Deane. Signed Willa Sibert Cather.
  Century, LXXXII (October, 1911), 859–867.

1912

Behind the Singer Tower. Signed Willa Sibert Cather.
  Collier's, XLIX (May, 1912), 16–17, 41.

The Bohemian Girl. Signed Willa Sibert Cather.
  McClure's, XXXIX (August, 1912), 420–443.

Checklist

OF WILLA CATHER'S SHORT FICTION · 1915–1948

❊ ❊ ❊

1915

Consequences. Signed Willa Sibert Cather.
  McClure's, XLVI (November, 1915), 30–32, 63–64.

1916

The Bookkeeper's Wife. Signed Willa Sibert Cather.
  Century, XCII (May, 1916), 51–59.

The Diamond Mine. Signed Willa Sibert Cather.
  McClure's, LXVII (October, 1916), 7–11.
  Youth and the Bright Medusa (New York: Alfred A. Knopf, 1920), pp. 79–139.
  The Novels and Stories of Willa Cather (13 vols.; Boston: Houghton Mifflin
    Co., 1937–1941), VI, 75–140.

1917

A Gold Slipper. Signed Willa Sibert Cather.
  Harper's, CXXXIV (January, 1917), 166–174.
  Youth and the Bright Medusa (New York: Alfred A. Knopf, 1920), pp. 140–168.
  The Novels and Stories of Willa Cather (13 vols.; Boston: Houghton Mifflin
    Co., 1937–1941), VI, 141–172.

1918

Ardessa. Signed Willa Sibert Cather.
  Century, XCVI (May, 1918), 105–116.

1919

Scandal. Signed Willa Sibert Cather.
  Century, XCVIII (August, 1919), 433–445.
  Youth and the Bright Medusa (New York: Alfred A. Knopf, 1920), pp. 169–198.
  The Novels and Stories of Willa Cather (13 vols.; Boston: Houghton Mifflin
    Co., 1937–1941), VI, 173–205.

Her Boss. Signed Willa Sibert Cather.
  Smart Set, XC (October, 1919), 95–108.

1920

Coming, Aphrodite! Signed Willa Cather.
  Youth and the Bright Medusa (New York: Alfred A. Knopf, 1920), pp. 11–78.
  Smart Set, XCII (August, 1920), 3–25. Signed Willa Sibert Cather. Here
    titled "Coming, Eden Bower!," with many significant differences from
    the collected version.

The Novels and Stories of Willa Cather (13 vols.; Boston: Houghton Mifflin Co., 1937–1941), VI, 1–74.

1925

Uncle Valentine. Signed Willa Cather.
Woman's Home Companion, LII (February, March, 1925), 7–9, 86, 89–90; 15–16, 75–76, 79–80.

1929

Double Birthday. Signed Willa Cather.
Forum, LXXXI (February, 1929), 78–82, 124–128. In *Best Short Stories of 1929*, ed. E. J. O'Brien (New York: Dodd, Mead & Co., 1929), pp. 60–85.

1930

Neighbor Rosicky. Signed Willa Cather.
Woman's Home Companion, LVII (April, May, 1930), 7–9, 52, 54, 57; 13–14, 92, 95–96. The spelling *Neighbour* used in collected versions.
Obscure Destinies (New York: Alfred A. Knopf, 1932), pp. 1–71.
The Novels and Stories of Willa Cather (13 vols.; Boston: Houghton Mifflin Co., 1937–1941), XII, 5–62.
Five Stories (New York: Vintage Books, 1956), pp. 72–111.

1932

Two Friends. Signed Willa Cather.
Woman's Home Companion, LIX (July, 1932), 7–9, 54–56.
Obscure Destinies (New York: Alfred A. Knopf, 1932), pp. 191–230.
The Novels and Stories of Willa Cather (13 vols.; Boston: Houghton Mifflin Co., 1937–1941), XII, 159–191.
Old Mrs. Harris. Signed Willa Cather.
Obscure Destinies (New York: Alfred A. Knopf, 1932), pp. 73–190.
Ladies' Home Journal, XLIX (September–November, 1932), 3, 70, 72, 74, 76–77; 18, 85–87; 16, 84–85, 89. Titled "Three Women."
The Novels and Stories of Willa Cather (13 vols.; Boston: Houghton Mifflin Co., 1937–1941), XII, 63–158.

1948

The Old Beauty. Signed Willa Cather. Written in 1936.
The Old Beauty and Others (New York: Alfred A. Knopf, 1948), pp. 3–72.
Before Breakfast. Signed Willa Cather. Completed in 1944.
The Old Beauty and Others (New York: Alfred A. Knopf, 1948), pp. 141–166.
The Best Years. Signed Willa Cather. Completed in 1945.
The Old Beauty and Others (New York: Alfred A. Knopf, 1948), pp. 75–138.
Five Stories (New York: Vintage Books, 1956), pp. 112–148.

Bibliography

OF SELECTED BIOGRAPHICAL
AND CRITICAL WRITINGS

❖ ❖ ❖

The books and articles listed below are particularly helpful in regard to Willa Cather's life and work in the years preceding the publication of *O Pioneers!*.

BENNETT, MILDRED R. *The World of Willa Cather*. Lincoln: University of Nebraska Press, 1961. First published 1951. The revised edition includes notes documenting the textual matter, much of which was derived from Willa Cather's own letters. Primarily concerned with the Nebraska years.

BRADFORD, CURTIS. "Willa Cather's Uncollected Short Stories," *American Literature*, XXVI, 4 (January, 1955), 537–551. The first and one of the most useful discussions of the uncollected stories.

BROWN, E. K., completed by LEON EDEL. *Willa Cather: A Critical Biography*. New York: Alfred A. Knopf, 1953. See especially chapters 3 through 6.

GIANNONE, RICHARD. *Music in Willa Cather's Fiction*. Lincoln: University of Nebraska Press, 1968. See especially Prologue and chapters 1 through 3.

HINZ, JOHN P. "Willa Cather in Pittsburgh," *New Colophon*, III (1950), 198–207. Includes the first extensive discussion of Cather's pseudonymous writing.

LATHROP, JOANNA. *Willa Cather: A Checklist of Her Published Writing*. Lincoln: University of Nebraska Press, 1975. Indispensable to Cather scholars.

LEWIS, EDITH. *Willa Cather Living: A Personal Record*. Lincoln: University of Nebraska Press, 1976. First published 1953. See chapters 3 through 6.

MOORHEAD, ELIZABETH: *These Too Were Here: Louise Homer and Willa Cather*. Pittsburgh: University of Pittsburgh Press, 1950. See pp. 45–62.

SEIBEL, GEORGE. "Miss Willa Cather from Nebraska," *New Colophon*, II, Pt. 7 (1949), 195–208. Extremely informative about Willa Cather's musical and literary tastes and activities during the Pittsburgh years.

SERGEANT, ELIZABETH SHEPLEY: *Willa Cather: A Memoir*. Lincoln: University of Nebraska Press, 1963. First published 1953. The revised edition includes a new foreword and index. See especially chapters 1 through 3.

SLOTE, BERNICE. "Stephen Crane and Willa Cather." *The Serif*, IV, 4 (December, 1969), 3–15. The fullest published account of Willa Cather's first meeting with a major writer and of a significant literary relationship.

———. "Willa Cather" in *Sixteen Modern American Authors: A Survey of Research and Criticism*. Edited by Jackson R. Bryer. Durham, N.C.: Duke University Press, 1973. (Paper ed. New York: W. W. Norton, 1973.) Evaluates all significant critical and biographical work on Cather through 1970.

————. "Willa Cather and Her First Book." Introduction to *April Twilights* (1903). See below. The first study to show the relationship of Cather's poetry to her fiction and to demonstrate the organic character of the Cather canon.

————. "Willa Cather as a Regional Writer." *Kansas Quarterly*, II, 2 (Spring, 1970), 7–15. Includes new biographical information.

————. "Writer in Nebraska" and "The Kingdom of Art." In *The Kingdom of Art*. See below. The first essay incorporates new biographical findings in the most complete picture to date of Cather's university years; the second analyzes her views of art as revealed in her 1893–1896 writings and shows their application to her later work.

SLOTE, BERNICE and VIRGINIA FAULKNER, eds. *The Art of Willa Cather*. Lincoln: University of Nebraska Press, 1974. Proceedings of the Willa Cather International Seminar commemorating the centenary of the author's birth.

STOUCK, DAVID. *Willa Cather's Imagination*. Lincoln: University of Nebraska Press, 1975. See especially chapters 1, 2, 5, and 6.

WOODS, LUCIA and BERNICE SLOTE. *Willa Cather: A Pictorial Memoir*. Lincoln: University of Nebraska Press, 1973. See especially pp. 1–55.

WOODRESS, JAMES. *Willa Cather: Her Life and Art*. Lincoln: University of Nebraska Press, 1975. First published 1970. Making fuller use of Cather's letters than any previous work, this succinct study adds much new material and corrects errors in earlier biographies.

The following volumes, all published by the University of Nebraska Press, have been planned in conjunction with WILLA CATHER'S COLLECTED SHORT FICTION, 1892–1912 to comprise a comprehensive selection of Willa Cather's early writings.

APRIL TWILIGHTS (1903). Revised edition. Edited with an introduction by Bernice Slote.

THE KINGDOM OF ART: *Willa Cather's First Principles and Critical Statements*, 1893–1896. Selected and edited with two essays and a commentary by Bernice Slote.

UNCLE VALENTINE AND OTHER STORIES: *Willa Cather's Uncollected Short Fiction*, 1915–1929. Edited with an introduction by Bernice Slote.

THE WORLD AND THE PARISH: *Willa Cather's Articles and Reviews*, 1893–1902. 2 vols. Selected and edited with a commentary by William M. Curtin.

N.B. Willa Cather's first novel, ALEXANDER'S BRIDGE, with an introduction by Bernice Slote is available in a paper edition only.

Acknowledgments

✻ ✻ ✻

The University of Nebraska Press is deeply grateful to Miss Edith Lewis and to Alfred A. Knopf, Willa Cather's literary trustees, for permission to reprint seven copyrighted stories. Our thanks also go to Mrs. George Seibel for permission to quote from Mr. Seibel's articles, and to *Prairie Schooner* for permission to incorporate in the Introduction portions of "Willa Cather in Pittsburgh" by Mildred R. Bennett, which originally appeared in the Spring 1959 issue in somewhat different form.

We are indebted to Mrs. Bennett for reading proof on this collection, and to Mrs. Bennett and Bernice Slote, professor of English, University of Nebraska, for checking and emending the Chronology, the Bibliography, and the Checklist. The Chronology as it appeared in the first three printings of this volume was based on research independently undertaken by Mrs. Bennett, Professor Slote, William M. Curtin, associate professor of English, University of Connecticut, and John March, New York City. James Woodress, professor of English, University of California, Davis, kindly provided additional information concerning substantive changes in four of *The Troll Garden* stories for the revised edition.

Finally, we wish to thank the Willa Cather Pioneer Memorial and Educational Foundation, Red Cloud, Nebraska, for the loan of primary materials used in establishing the text of the stories; Mrs. Julia Cunningham, Pennsylvania Division, Carnegie Library of Pittsburgh, for assistance in verifying texts; the Research and Humanities Division, the New York Public Library; and the staffs of the Nebraska State Historical Society Library and of the University of Nebraska Libraries for their customary friendly and intelligent cooperation in locating and obtaining research materials.